READER'S DIGEST
CONDENSED BOOKS

www.readersdigest.co.uk

The Reader's Digest Association
Limited 11 Westferry Circus
Canary Wharf London E14 4HE

For information as to ownership of
copyright in the material of this
book, and acknowledgments, see
last page.

Printed in France
ISBN 0 276 42736 X

READER'S DIGEST
CONDENSED BOOKS

*Selected and edited
by Reader's Digest*

CONDENSED BOOKS DIVISION

THE READER'S DIGEST ASSOCIATION LIMITED, LONDON

CONTENTS

When the US vice-president receives an
anonymous death threat, the security services are on red alert. Anxious to make sure
that their wall of protection is unbreachable,
and hungry to know who wants Brook
Armstrong dead, they call on the help of
freelancer Jack Reacher, renowned for his
toughness, integrity and cool nerves. This
topical and relentlessly suspenseful thriller
has been hailed as one of Lee Child's best.

PUBLISHED BY BANTAM PRESS

Newly returned from the Napoleonic Wars,
Captain Rider Sandman has been asked to
investigate a murder. When the accused
declares his innocence, Sandman's only
way to save him from the gallows is to track
down the real killer, pursuing clues that take
him from London's criminal underworld to
the secretive inner circle of a gentlemen's
club. A lively tale of detection, steeped in
the atmosphere of Regency England.

PUBLISHED BY HARPERCOLLINS

HEAD OVER HEELS IN THE DALES

Gervase Phinn

In his latest book, former school inspector Gervase Phinn takes the reader on another memorable journey into the classrooms of the Yorkshire Dales and the corridors of County Hall, where the bureaucrats hold sway. Endearing children, dedicated teachers, alarmingly bossy colleagues and affable local gentry are among the many characters that Phinn brings to life with delightful wit and a sharp eye for human foibles.

PUBLISHED BY MICHAEL JOSEPH

VALHALLA RISING

Clive Cussler

When the revolutionary new luxury cruise liner *Emerald Dolphin* suddenly catches fire and sinks on her maiden voyage, NUMA special projects director Dirk Pitt is called in to investigate. He soon finds himself uncovering a bizarre chain of events that reaches back to the time of Jules Verne and beyond, to startling, long-hidden evidence of Viking settlers. A highly imaginative, action-filled adventure from a hugely popular author.

PUBLISHED BY MICHAEL JOSEPH

LEE CHILD

JACK REACHER WALKS ALONE. NO
FIXED JOB, NO ID, NO LAST KNOWN
ADDRESS. BUT HE NEVER TURNS
DOWN A PLEA FOR HELP. AND NOW
AGENT M. E. FROELICH OF THE US
SECURITY SERVICES HAS COME TO HIM
FOR HELP OVER A MATTER OF THE
HIGHEST NATIONAL SECURITY.

IT'S A CHALLENGE THAT WILL REQUIRE
EVERY OUNCE OF REACHER'S NATIVE
CUNNING, STEELY DETERMINATION AND
SURE SENSE OF JUSTICE. AND IT WILL
PUT HIM RIGHT IN THE LINE OF FIRE.

ONE

They found out about him in July and stayed angry all through August. They tried to kill him in September. It was way too soon. They weren't ready. The attempt was a failure. It could have been a disaster, but it was actually a miracle.

Because nobody noticed.

They used their usual method to get past security and set up 100 feet from where he was speaking. They used a silencer and missed him by an inch. The bullet must have passed right over his head. Maybe even *through his hair*, because he immediately raised his hand and patted it back into place as if a gust of wind had disturbed it. They saw it over and over again, afterwards, on television. He did nothing else. He just kept on with his speech, unaware. The silenced bullet missed everybody standing behind him. It struck no obstacles, hit no buildings. It flew on straight and true until its energy was spent and gravity hauled it to earth in the far distance where there was nothing except empty grassland. There was no response. No reaction.

Nobody noticed.

They didn't fire again. They were too shaken up.

So, a failure, but a miracle. And a lesson. They spent October acting like the professionals they were, starting over, calming down, learning, preparing for their second attempt. It would be a better attempt, carefully planned and properly executed. A worthy attempt. A *creative* attempt. Above all, an attempt that wouldn't fail.

TEAM LEADER M. E. FROELICH came to work on the Monday morning thirteen days after the election, seven days after the word 'assassination' had first been used, and made her decision. She set off in search of her immediate superior and found him in the secretarial pen outside his office. He had a file under his arm. She made it clear that she needed to talk. So he turned and went back inside his office. He let her step in after him and closed the door behind her.

He was a twenty-five-year veteran well into his middle fifties. He was tall, still fairly lean and athletic, but greying fast. His name was Stuyvesant, like the cigarette. His office was small, quiet, sparsely furnished and very clean.

'I need to ask your permission for something I want to try,' Froelich said. She was twenty years younger than Stuyvesant, exactly thirty-five. Maybe only an inch or two over the average height for American women of her generation, but the kind of intelligence and energy and vitality she radiated took the word 'medium' right out of the equation. She was halfway between lithe and muscular, with a bright glow in her skin and her eyes that made her look like an athlete. Her hair was short and fair and casually unkempt.

'What kind of something?' Stuyvesant asked. He placed the file he was carrying on his desk. His desk was large, topped with a slab of polished grey composite. He was famous for always keeping his desktop completely empty. The habit created an air of extreme efficiency.

'I want an outsider to do it,' Froelich said.

Stuyvesant squared the file on the desk corner and ran his fingers along the spine. 'I promoted you four months ago,' he said. 'Four months is a long time. Choosing to bring in an outsider *now* might be seen to betray a certain lack of self-confidence, mightn't it?'

'I can't worry about that.'

'Maybe you should,' he said. 'There were six guys who wanted your job. So if you do this and it leaks, then you've got half a dozen vultures muttering 'told you so' the rest of your career.'

'I'm not happy about it,' Froelich said. 'Believe me. But I think it's got to be done. And that's my judgment call.'

'This could stall your career. No more promotions.'

'The alternative would *finish* my career.'

Stuyvesant picked up his file. 'OK, do it,' he said.

SHE STARTED IMMEDIATELY. All she had was a last name and a sketchy biography that might or might not have been accurate eight years ago. The details had been mentioned late one night, by her lover, part of some drowsy pillow talk. She couldn't even be sure she had been paying full attention. So she decided not to rely on the details. She would rely on the name.

She wrote it in capital letters at the top of a sheet of yellow paper. It brought back a lot of memories. Some bad, most good. She stared at it for a long moment, and then she crossed it out and wrote *UNSUB* instead. That would help her concentration, because it made the thing impersonal. An *unknown subject* was somebody to be identified and located. That was all.

Her main advantage was computer power. She had access to more data bases than the average citizen. *UNSUB* was military, she knew that, so she went to the National Personnel Records Center's data base. It listed every man or woman who had served in a US military uniform. She typed in the last name and the enquiry software came back with just three responses. One she eliminated by given name, another by date of birth. So the third had to be *UNSUB*. She stared at the full name for a second and copied the date of birth and Social Security number onto her yellow paper. Then she hit the icon for DETAILS. The screen came up with an abbreviated career summary.

Bad news. UNSUB wasn't military any more. The career summary dead-ended five years ago with an honourable discharge after thirteen years of service. Final rank was major. There were medals listed, including a Silver Star and a Purple Heart. She read the citations, then drew a line across the yellow paper.

The next logical step was to look at Social Security's Master Death Index. No point trying to chase down somebody who was dead. She entered the number and the enquiry came back blank. *UNSUB* was still alive as far as the government knew.

She clicked her way into the nationwide Department of Motor Vehicles data base. *Bad news again. UNSUB* didn't have a driving licence. *Which was weird. And a pain in the butt.* Because no driving licence meant no current photograph and no current address. She went back into Social Security and asked for contributions records. There weren't any. *UNSUB* hadn't been employed since leaving the military, at least not legally. She tried the IRS for confirmation. Same story. *UNSUB* hadn't paid taxes in five years. Hadn't even filed.

OK, so let's get serious. She quit the government sites and fired up some illicit software that took her straight into the banking industry's private world. If *UNSUB* had even a single bank account anywhere in the fifty states, it would show up.

ONE HUNDRED AND EIGHTY miles away, Jack Reacher shivered. Atlantic City in the middle of November wasn't the warmest spot on earth. Five days ago he had been in Los Angeles, and he was pretty sure he should have stayed there.

He had come east with an old black woman and her brother. He had been hitching out of LA to take a look at the Mojave Desert. The couple had picked him up in an ancient Buick Roadmaster and the old lady told him she was a singer heading for a short residency in Atlantic City. Told him her brother accompanied her on the keyboard and drove the car, but he wasn't much of a talker any more and he wasn't much of a driver any more. It was true. The old guy was silent and they were in mortal danger several times in the first five miles. The old lady started singing to calm herself. She gave it a few bars of Dawn Penn's 'You Don't Love Me' and Reacher decided to go all the way east with her just to hear more. He offered to take over the driving. She kept on singing. She had the kind of sweet, smoky voice that should have made her a blues superstar long ago, except she was probably in the wrong place too many times. Reacher drove eighteen hours a day for three days, and arrived in New Jersey feeling like he'd been on vacation.

The residency was at a fifth-rate lounge eight blocks from the boardwalk, and the manager wasn't the kind of guy you would trust to respect a contract. So Reacher made it his business to count the customers and keep a running total of the cash that should show up in the pay envelope at the end of the week. He made it obvious and watched the manager grow resentful about it. Reacher sat through all three sets two weekend nights running, but then he started to get restless. And cold. So on the Monday morning he was about to get back on the road when the old keyboard player broke his silence.

'I want to ask you to stick around,' he said. 'You don't stick around, that manager's going to stiff us. But we get paid, we got gas money to head up to New York, maybe get us a gig from B. B. King in Times Square. Guy like you could make a big difference. What are you, anyway? Some kind of a boxer?'

'I was a military cop,' Reacher said. 'In the army, thirteen years.'

'You quit?'

'As near as makes no difference.'

'No jobs for you folks afterwards?'

'None that I want,' Reacher said.

'You live in LA?'

'I don't live anywhere,' Reacher said. 'I move around.'

'Road folk should stick together,' the old guy said. 'Help each other.'

'It's very cold here,' Reacher said.

'That's for damn sure,' the old guy said. 'But you could buy a coat.'

So he was on a corner with the sea gale flattening his trousers against his legs, making a decision. *The highway, or a coat?* He ran a fantasy through his head, La Jolla maybe, a cheap room, warm nights, bright stars, cold beer. Then: the old woman at B. B. King's new club in New York, some retro-obsessed young A. & R. man stops by, gives her a contract, she makes a CD, gets a national tour, fame, money, a new house. A new car. He turned his back on the highway, hunched against the wind and walked in search of a clothing store.

ON THAT PARTICULAR MONDAY there were nearly 12,000 licensed banking organisations operating in the United States and between them they carried over a billion separate accounts, but only one was listed against *UNSUB*'s name and Social Security number. It was a current account held at a branch of a regional bank in Arlington, Virginia. M. E. Froelich copied the details onto her yellow paper. Picked up her phone and called a senior colleague on the other side of the organisation and asked him to contact the bank in question for all the details he could get. Especially a home address. She asked him to be as fast as possible, but discreet, too. Then she hung up and waited, frustrated about being temporarily hands-off. Problem was, the other side of the organisation could ask banks discreet questions easily, whereas for Froelich to do so would be regarded as very odd.

REACHER FOUND a discount store three blocks nearer the ocean and ducked inside. There were racks of garments stretching as far as the eye could see. He started in the far back corner and worked forwards. The first two rails had short padded jackets. The third rail had thigh-length canvas coats made bulky by thick flannel linings.

'Can I help you?'

He turned and saw a young woman standing right behind him.

'Are these coats good for the weather up here?' he asked.

'They're perfect,' the woman said.

He ran his hand down the rail and pulled out a dark olive XXL. 'OK, I'll take this one,' he said.

'You don't want to try it on?'

He paused and then shrugged into it. It fitted pretty well. Nearly. Maybe it was a little tight across the shoulders.

'You need the big-and-tall fitting,' the woman said. 'Try the 3XLT.'

The 3XLT she handed him was the same dull colour as the XXL he had picked. It fitted much better.

'You OK for pants?' the woman called. She had ducked away to another rail and was flicking through heavy canvas work trousers. She came out with a pair that matched one of the colours in the flannel lining inside the coat. 'And try these shirts,' she said. She jumped over to another rail and showed him a rainbow of flannel shirts. 'Which colour do you like?'

'Something dull,' he said.

She laid everything out on top of a rail. The coat, the trousers, the shirt. 'OK?' the woman said. He nodded and she led him to the register and bleeped all the tags under the little red light. 'One hundred and eighty-nine dollars even,' she said.

'I thought this was a discount store,' he said.

'That's incredibly reasonable, really,' she said. He shook his head and dug into his pocket and came out with a wad of crumpled bills. Counted out a hundred and ninety. The dollar change she gave him left him with four bucks in his hand.

THE SENIOR COLLEAGUE from the other side of the organisation called Froelich back within twenty-five minutes.

'You get a home address?' she asked him.

'One hundred Washington Boulevard,' the guy said. 'Arlington, Virginia. It's a phoney address. One side of Washington Boulevard is Arlington Cemetery and the other side is the Pentagon. There's no number one hundred. I checked with the Postal Service.'

'Great,' Froelich said. 'I'm back at square one.'

'Maybe not. This is a bizarre set-up, Froelich. Six-figure balance, but it's stuck in a current account, earning nothing. And the customer accesses it via Western Union only. Never comes in. Phones in with a password, the bank wires cash through Western Union, wherever.'

'No ATM card?'

'No cards at all. No cheque book was ever issued, either.'

'Western Union *only*? Are there any records?'

'Geographically, all over the place. Forty states in five years. Occasional deposits and plenty of nickel-and-dime withdrawals, all to Western Union offices in the boonies, in the cities, everywhere.'

'Anything you can do?'

'Done it. They'll call me next time the customer calls them.'

'And then you'll call me?'

'I might.'

'Is there a frequency pattern?'

'It varies,' the guy said. 'Maximum interval recently has been a few weeks. Sometimes it's every few days. Mondays are popular. Banks are closed on the weekend.'

'So I could get lucky today.'

'Sure you could. Question is, am I going to get lucky too?'

'Not that lucky,' Froelich said.

REACHER CHANGED one of his four dollars for quarters at the motel desk and headed for the payphone. Dialled his bank and gave his password and arranged for $500 to be wired to Western Union in Atlantic City by close of business. Then he went to his room, put his new clothes on and threw his summer gear in the trash.

He wasted an hour in his room and then went out to test the insulating properties of his new coat. He headed east towards the ocean, into the wind. Felt rather than saw somebody behind him. He slowed up and used a store window for a mirror. Caught a glimpse of movement fifty yards back. Too far away for details.

He walked on. The coat was pretty good. He reached the boardwalk and walked south. He turned and led his invisible shadows out onto the Central Pier. It was deserted, which was no surprise considering the weather. He walked to the end of the pier. Stood and watched the grey ocean for a spell. Then he turned back and headed for the shore and saw two men walking towards him.

They were useful-sized guys, short but wide, dressed in blue pea jackets and jeans, grey knitted watch caps jammed down over meaty heads. They had their hands in their pockets. Reacher stopped walking.

The two men walked on and stopped eight feet in front of him. The guy on the left took his hands out of his pockets. Either he had bad arthritis or he was holding rolls of quarters in both palms. 'We got a message for you,' he said.

'From that club manager?' Reacher asked.

'From his people, yeah.'

Reacher nodded. 'So let me guess. I'm supposed to get out of town, get lost, never come back, forget I was ever here.'

'You're on the ball today.'

'I can read minds,' Reacher said. 'I used to work a fairground booth. Right next to the bearded lady. Weren't you guys there too? Three booths along? The World's Ugliest Twins?'

The guy on the right took his hands out of his pockets. He had the same pain in his knuckles, or else a couple more rolls of quarters.

15

Reacher smiled. He liked rolls of quarters. Nobody clutches rolls of coins if they've got a gun in their pocket.

'We don't want to hurt you,' the guy on the right said.

'But you got to go,' the guy on the left said. 'We don't need people interfering in this town's economic procedures.'

'So take the easy way out,' the other guy said. 'Let us walk you to the bus depot. Or the old folk could wind up getting hurt, too.'

Reacher moved a little closer to them, tightening the triangle. He raised his hand and smoothed his hair where the wind was disturbing it. 'Better just to walk away now,' he said.

They responded to the challenge by crowding in towards him, imperceptibly, just a fractional muscle movement that eased their body weight forward. *They need to be laid up for a week*, he thought. *Nothing too severe.* He waited until the wind gusted again and raised his right hand and swept his hair back behind his ear. Then kept his hand there, elbow poised high, like a thought had just struck him.

'Can you guys swim?' he asked.

It would have taken superhuman self-control not to glance at the ocean. They weren't superhuman. They turned their heads like robots. He clubbed the right-hand guy in the face with his raised elbow and cocked it again and hit the left-hand guy as his head snapped back towards the sound of his buddy's bones breaking. They went down together and their rolls of quarters split open and coins rolled everywhere. Reacher walked away. Stepped off the pier onto the broadwalk and went in search of Western Union.

THE WESTERN UNION office had a two-year-old Chevy Suburban parked right outside the door. The truck was black with smoked windows, and immaculately clean and shiny. It had three short UHF antennae on the roof. There was a woman in the driver's seat. He glanced at her. She was fair-haired and looked relaxed and alert at the same time. And she was cute. He glanced away and went inside the office and claimed his cash. Came back out and found the woman standing on the sidewalk, looking straight at him, like she was checking off similarities and differences against a mental image. It was a process he recognised. He had been looked at like that before.

'Jack Reacher?' she said.

He double-checked his memory. Short fair hair, great eyes looking right at him, some kind of quiet confidence in the way she held herself. She had qualities he would remember. But he didn't remember them. Therefore he had never seen her before.

'You knew my brother,' he said. She looked surprised and a little gratified. And lost for words. 'I could tell,' he said. 'People look at me like that, they're thinking how we look alike, but also different.'

She said nothing.

'Nice meeting you,' he said, and moved away.

'Wait,' she called. He turned back. 'Can we talk?' she said.

'We could talk in the car. I'm freezing my ass off out here.'

She opened the passenger door. 'Please,' she said. He climbed in and she walked round the hood and climbed in on her side. Started the engine to run the heater, but didn't go anywhere.

'I knew your brother very well,' she said. 'We dated, Joe and I. We were pretty serious for a time.'

'When?' Reacher asked.

'We were together two years. We broke up a year before he died.'

Reacher nodded.

'I'm M. E. Froelich,' she said.

'Emmy?' he said. 'Like the television thing?'

'M. E.,' she said. 'I go by my initials.'

'What are they for?'

'I won't tell you that.'

He paused a beat. 'What did Joe call you?'

'He called me Froelich,' she said.

Reacher nodded. 'Yes, he would.'

'I still miss him,' she said.

'Me too, I guess,' he said. 'So is this about Joe, or something else?'

'I want to hire you for something,' she said. 'On a kind of posthumous recommendation from Joe.'

Reacher nodded. 'Hire me for what?'

'To assassinate the Vice President of the United States.'

TWO

'Good line,' Reacher said. 'Interesting proposition. But no. It's probably the safest response.'

Froelich picked up her purse. 'Let me show you some ID,' she said.

'Don't need it,' he said. 'You're United States Secret Service.'

She looked at him. 'You're pretty quick.'

'It's pretty clear,' he said. 'Joe worked for them. And knowing the way he was he probably worked pretty hard, and he was a little shy, so anybody he dated was probably in the office, otherwise he would never have met them. Plus, who else but the Secret Service could track me through my banking arrangements?'

'You're pretty quick,' she said again.

'Thank you,' he said. 'But Joe didn't have anything to do with Vice Presidents. He was in Financial Crimes.'

She nodded. 'We all start out in Financial Crimes. We pay our dues as anticounterfeiting grunts. And he ran anticounterfeiting. And you're right, we met in the office. But he wouldn't date me then. He said it wasn't appropriate. But I was planning on transferring across to the protection detail as soon as I could anyway, and as soon as I did, we started going out.' She went quiet.

'And?' Reacher said.

'Something he said one night. I was keen and ambitious back then, you know, starting a new job and all, and I was always trying to figure out if we were doing the best we could, and he said the only real way for us to test ourselves would be to hire some outsider to try to get to the target. A security audit, he called it. I asked him, like who? And he said, my little brother would be the one. If anybody could do it, he could.'

Reacher smiled. 'That sounds like Joe. A typical harebrained scheme. For a smart guy, Joe could be very dumb sometimes.'

'Why is it dumb?'

'Because if you hire some outsider, all you need to do is watch for him coming. Makes it way too easy.'

'No, his idea was the person would come in anonymously and unannounced. Like now, nobody knows about you except me.'

'OK, maybe he wasn't so dumb. But why wait so long to try it?'

'Because now I'm in charge. I was promoted head of the Vice President's detail four months ago. And I'm still keen and ambitious, and I still want to know we're doing it right. So I decided to follow Joe's advice, now that it's my call. I decided to try a security audit. And you were recommended, so to speak. All those years ago, by somebody I trusted very much. So I'm here to ask you if you'll do it.'

'You want to get a cup of coffee?' he said. 'Drive me back to my motel and I'll take you to the downstairs lounge. Coffee's OK, and it's a very dark room. Just right for a conversation like this.'

SHE PARKED OUTSIDE the motel and he led her down a half-flight of stairs to the lounge. There was a flask of coffee on the machine behind the bar. He pointed at it, and then at himself and Froelich, and the barman got busy. Then he walked to a corner booth and slid in across the vinyl with his back to the wall and the whole room in sight. *Old habits.* Froelich clearly had the same habits because she did the same thing, so they ended up side by side.

'You're very similar to him,' she said.

'In some ways,' he said. 'Not in others. Like, I'm still alive.'

'You weren't at his funeral.'

'It came at an inopportune time.'

The barman brought the coffee, on a beer-stained cork tray.

'Nobody ever think of doing it, apart from Joe?' Reacher asked. 'Using an outsider for a security audit?'

'Nobody.'

'The Secret Service is a relatively old organisation. You use an outsider for the very first time, got to be because of something more than you're a perfectionist.'

She started to answer, and then stopped. He saw her decide to lie. He could sense it, in the angle of her shoulder.

'I'm under big pressure,' she said. 'You know, professionally. There are a lot of people waiting for me to screw up. I need to be sure. It's still rare for a woman to head up a team. Some of my colleagues are a little Neanderthal.'

'Which vice president?' he asked. 'The new one or the old one?'

'The new one,' she said. 'Brook Armstrong. The Vice President-elect, strictly speaking.'

'What did Joe say about me?' Reacher asked.

'He said you'd relish the challenge. He said you'd find three or four ways of doing it and we'd learn a lot from you.'

'And you said?'

'I said no way would you even get close.'

Reacher said nothing.

'Would you consider doing it?' Froelich asked.

'I don't know a lot about Armstrong. Never heard much about him before.'

She nodded. 'Nobody has. He was a surprise choice. Junior senator from North Dakota, standard-issue family man, wife, grown-up daughter, cares long-distance for his sick old mother, never made any kind of national impact. But he's an OK guy, for a politician.'

Reacher nodded. Said nothing.

'We would pay you, obviously,' Froelich said.

'I'm not very interested in money,' Reacher said. 'But there would be expenses, probably, if a person did this sort of a thing properly.'

'It'll be dangerous,' she said. 'I have to warn you nobody will know you're out there except me. That's a big problem if you're spotted.'

Reacher said nothing.

'It's very important,' she said. 'And urgent.'

'Want to tell me why it's urgent?'

She said nothing.

'I don't think this is theoretical at all,' he said. 'I think you know somebody is out there,' he said. 'An active threat.'

'It's just a security audit,' she said. 'Will you do it for me?'

'On one condition,' he said. He dug in his pocket and slid her a matchbook and pointed to the name and address printed on it. 'There's an old couple working a week in this club and they're worried about getting ripped off for their wages. Musicians. They should be OK, but I need to be sure. I want you to talk to the cops here.'

'When's payday supposed to be?'

'Friday night, after the last set. They need to pick up their money and get their stuff to their car. They'll be heading to New York.'

'I'll ask one of our agents to check in with them every day.'

'When does it need to be done?' he asked.

'As soon as possible,' she said.

He nodded. Slid out of the booth and stood up. 'I'll call you in ten days,' he said. 'To tell you how it went.'

VICE PRESIDENT-ELECT Brook Armstrong spent the third week after the election in Washington working with the transition team. His wife was at home in North Dakota.

He had four agents camping out with him in in his Georgetown terraced house and four Metro cops stationed outside in cars, two in front and two in the alley behind. A Secret Service limo picked him up every morning and drove him to the Senate offices, with a second car following. The gun car, it was called. Then three agents stayed with him throughout the day. His personal detail—three tall men, dark suits, sunglasses even in November—kept him inside a tight, unobtrusive triangle of protection, always unsmiling, eyes always roving. Sometimes he could hear faint sounds from their radio earpieces. They wore microphones on their wrists and automatic weapons under their jackets. It was impressive, but he knew he was in no real danger inside the office building. There were DC cops outside, the Hill's own security inside, metal detectors on all the street doors, and all the people he saw were either elected members or their staffers, who had been security-cleared many times over.

His first reception for mid-level donors to the campaign was held on the Thursday evening, in the ballroom of a big hotel. The building was swept by dogs during the afternoon, and key interior positions were occupied by Metro cops, who would stay put until Armstrong left. Froelich put two Secret Service agents on the door, six in the lobby and eight in the ballroom itself. Another four secured the loading dock, where Armstrong would enter. Discreet video cameras covered the lobby and the ballroom.

The guest list was a thousand people long. November weather meant they couldn't line up on the sidewalk and the tenor of the event meant security had to be pleasantly unobtrusive, so the protocol was to get the guests in off the street and into the lobby immediately through a temporary metal detector. Then they made their way to the ballroom door. Their invitations were checked and they were asked for photo-ID. The invitations were laid face down on a glass sheet for a moment, and then handed back as souvenirs. Under the glass sheet was a video camera so names and faces were tied together in the visual record. Finally, they passed through a second metal detector and into the ballroom.

Armstrong's two-car convoy entered the loading dock a half-hour later. His personal three-man detail brought him in through a rear passageway. His appearance was timed to last two hours, which gave him an average of a little over seven seconds per guest. Some guests were content with a brief handshake but others hung on a little longer, gushing their congratulations. There were some men who put their arm round his shoulders for private photographs. There was one woman in particular who took his hand in a firm grip and held on for ten or twelve seconds, even pulling him nice and close and whispering something in his ear. She was surprisingly strong and nearly pulled him off balance. He didn't really hear what she whispered. Maybe her room number. But she was slim and pretty, with dark hair and a great smile, so he wasn't too upset about it. His Secret Service detail didn't bat an eye.

He worked a complete circle round the room, and made it back out of the rear door after two hours and eleven minutes. His personal detail put him back in his car and drove him home. Eight minutes later his house was locked down for the night and secure.

ON THE FRIDAY MORNING Armstrong's detail drove him to Andrews Air Force Base for a midday flight to New York City. They used an armoured Cadillac with two escort Suburbans flanked by two cop cars and a motorcycle escort. As a courtesy, the defeated incumbents had allowed him the use of Air Force Two. It flew into La Guardia and three cars from the Secret Service's New York field office picked the party up and drove them to Wall Street.

Froelich was already in position inside the Stock Exchange, and was comfortable that the building was secure. Armstrong's investor-reassurance meetings were held in a back office and lasted two hours, so she relaxed until the photo call. The transition team's media handlers wanted news pictures on the sidewalk in front of the building. She had agents video the photographers for the record and check their press credentials and search every camera bag and every pocket. She checked with the local NYPD lieutenant and confirmed that the perimeter was secured to 1,000 feet on the ground and 500 vertically. Then she allowed Armstrong out with the assorted brokers and bankers and they posed for five agonising minutes. Then, mercifully, it was over. Armstrong gave his *I'd-love-to-stay* wave and backed away into the building. Froelich relaxed again.

Next up was a routine road trip back to Air Force Two and a flight to North Dakota. The first of two rallies to ease Armstrong's Senate successor into place was scheduled for the next day.

Air Force Two landed in Bismarck and Armstrong went home to join his wife and spend the night in the family house in the lake country south of the city. It was a big place with an apartment above the garage block that the Secret Service took over. Froelich tasked four agents to stake out the house, two in front, two behind. State troopers made up the numbers, parked in cars on a 300-yard radius. She walked the area herself as a final check then went back to the apartment. It was a quiet night. Very lonely. Cold. No moon, no stars. She hated nights like this.

SATURDAY DAWNED bright and cold in North Dakota, and preparations began immediately after breakfast. The rally was scheduled for one o'clock in the grounds of a church community centre on the south side of the city. The centre's grounds were bordered to the north by the church itself, a traditional white clapboard structure. The other three sides were well fenced, and two of them backed onto established housing subdivisions, with the third fronting onto the street. Froelich banned parking for the day and put two agents and a local cop car on the gate, with twelve more cops on foot just inside the perimeter. She put two cop cars in each of the surrounding streets and had the church searched by the local police canine unit and then closed and locked. She doubled the personal detail to six agents, because Armstrong's wife was accompanying him.

The Armstrongs had an early lunch at home and drove up in convoy. The afternoon turned out to be not much more than a pleasant stroll around a pleasant piece of real estate.

Towards the end of the rally Armstrong's chief of staff fielded a call. The outgoing President and Vice President were formally summoning the President-elect and the Vice President-elect to a one-day transition conference at Camp David. Froelich was delighted, because there is no safer place in the world than that wooded clearing in the Maryland mountains. She decided they should all fly back to Andrews immediately and take Marine helicopters straight out to the compound. If they spent all night and all day there she would be able to relax completely for twenty-four hours.

BUT LATE ON THE SUNDAY morning a navy steward found her at breakfast in the mess hall and plugged a telephone into a socket near her chair.

'Call transferred from your main office, ma'am,' the steward said.

There was empty silence for a second, and then a voice.

'We should get together,' Reacher said.

'Where are you?'

'In a room at the hotel you used for the reception Thursday.'

'You got something urgent for me?'

'A conclusion.'

'Already? It's only been five days. You said ten.'

'Five was enough.'

Froelich cupped the phone. 'What's the conclusion?'

'It's impossible,' Reacher said.

She smiled. 'Told you so.'

'No, your job is impossible. You need to talk to me urgently.'

SHE DROVE BACK to DC in her Suburban and parked outside the hotel. The desk was expecting her and sent her straight up to 1201, twelfth floor. She followed a waiter through the door. He was carrying a tray with a pot of coffee and two upside-down cups on saucers. The room was standard-issue city hotel. Two beds, a table, two chairs, a desk with a phone. Reacher was sitting on the nearer bed. He was wearing a black nylon warm-up jacket with a black T-shirt and black jeans and black shoes. He had an earpiece in his ear and a pretty good fake Secret Service pin in the collar of the jacket. He was clean-shaven and his hair had been cut very short.

The waiter put the tray on the table and backed out of the room. Reacher stood up and stepped across to the table. Righted the cups and picked up the pot and poured the coffee.

'So what have you got to tell me?' she said.

'That you're good,' he said. 'Really good. I don't think anybody could do this better. But you're not good enough. You need to face that whoever it is out there could walk right in and get the job done.'

'I never said there's anybody out there.'

He said nothing.

'Just give me the information, Reacher.'

'Three and a half,' he said.

'Three and a half what? Out of ten?'

'No, Armstrong's dead, three and a half times over. That's how I score it.'

'What do you mean, a half?'

'Three definites and one possible.'

'In five *days*?' she said. 'How? What aren't we doing?'

'Have some coffee,' he said.

She moved towards the table like an automaton. He handed her a cup. She took it and backed away to the bed.

'Two main approaches,' Reacher said. 'Like in the movies, John Malkovich or Edward Fox. You've seen those movies?'

She nodded blankly. 'We have a guy monitoring the movies. In the Office of Protection Research. He analyses all the assassination movies. John Malkovich made *In the Line of Fire* with Clint Eastwood. Edward Fox was in *The Day of the Jackal*, way back.'

Reacher nodded. 'John Malkovich was looking to take out the President of the United States, and Edward Fox was looking to take out the President of France. Two competent assassins, working solo, but a fundamental difference between them. John Malkovich knew he wasn't going to survive the mission. He knew he'd die a second after the President. But Edward Fox aimed to get away with it.'

'He didn't, though.'

'It was a movie, Froelich. Had to end that way. He could have gotten away with it, easy as anything.'

'So?'

'It gives us two strategies to consider. A close-up suicide mission, or a clean long-distance job.'

'We know all that. I told you, we have a person working on it.'

'Learn anything?'

'*The Day of the Jackal* impressed us,' she said. 'Edward Fox got into a nearby building some hours before a public appearance and planned a long-range head shot, using a silencer. But the story was set a long time ago. We enforce far wider perimeters now.'

'And *In the Line of Fire*?' Reacher asked.

'John Malkovich played a renegade CIA operative,' she said. 'He manufactured a plastic pistol in his basement so he could beat the metal detectors and conned his way into a campaign rally and intended to shoot the President from very close range. Whereupon, as you say, we would have taken him down immediately. Implausible, we thought. The idea that you can build a working pistol from hobbyist material is absurd.'

'It was only a movie,' Reacher said. 'But it was illustrative.'

'Of what?'

'Of the idea of getting into a rally and attacking the target from close quarters. '

'Is this all you've got?' Froelich said. 'Ideas? You had me worried.'

'Like the rally here on Thursday night,' Reacher said. 'A thousand guests. Time and place announced in advance. Advertised, even.'

'You found the transition's web site?'

Reacher nodded. 'It was very useful. It told me every place Armstrong's going to be. Like the rally right here, Thursday night. With the thousand guests.'

'What about them?'

'One of them was a dark-haired woman who got hold of Armstrong's hand and pulled him a little off-balance.'

She stared at him. 'You were there?'

He shook his head. 'No, but I heard about it. Did you see it?'

'Only on video,' she said. 'Afterwards.'

'That woman could have killed Armstrong. That was the first opportunity. Up to that point you were doing real well. You were scoring A-plus during the government stuff around the Capitol.'

She smiled, a little dismissively. 'Could have? You're wasting my time, Reacher. That woman was an invited guest. She was a party contributor and she was ID-checked at the door.'

'Suppose she was a martial-arts expert. Military-trained. She could have broken Armstrong's neck like you could break a pencil.'

'Suppose, suppose.'

'Suppose she was armed.'

'She wasn't. She passed through two metal detectors.'

Reacher put his hand in the pocket of his jacket and came out with a slim brown object. 'Ever seen one of these?' he asked.

It looked like a penknife, maybe three and a half inches long. He clicked a button and a brown blade snapped out.

'This is entirely ceramic,' he said. 'Harder than steel, sharper than steel. And it doesn't trigger a metal detector. Made by a German firm called Böker. Expensive, but relatively available. That woman could have been carrying this. She could have cut Armstrong's throat.'

He passed the weapon over. Froelich took it and studied it. 'OK, so you bought a knife. Doesn't prove anything.'

'That knife was in that woman's left hand, in her pocket, with the blade open, all the time she was shaking Armstrong's hand and pulling him close. She got his belly within three inches of it.'

Froelich stared at him. 'Are you serious? Who was she?'

'She was a party supporter called Elizabeth Wright, from New Jersey. She gave the campaign four thousand bucks.'

'So why would she carry a knife?'

'Well, actually, she didn't.'

He stood up and walked to the connecting door. Pulled his half open and knocked hard on the inner half. 'OK, Neagley,' he called.

The inner door opened and a woman walked in from the next room. She was in her late thirties, medium height and slim, dressed in blue jeans and a soft grey sweatshirt. She had dark hair. Dark eyes. A great smile. The tendons in her wrists spoke of serious gym time.

'You're the woman on the video,' Froelich said.

Reacher smiled. 'Frances Neagley, meet M. E. Froelich. M. E. Froelich, meet Frances Neagley.'

Froelich stared at Reacher. 'Who is she?'

'The best master sergeant I ever worked with. Beyond expert-qualified on every kind of close-quarters combat. She got cut loose the same time I did. Works as a security consultant in Chicago.'

'So what happened to Elizabeth Wright from New Jersey?'

'I bought these clothes,' Reacher said. 'And the shoes. Sunglasses, too. My version of Secret Service fatigues. I went to the barber. I wanted to look plausible. Then I wanted a lone woman from New Jersey, so I met a couple of Newark flights at the airport here on Thursday. Watched the crowd and latched onto Ms Wright and told her I was a Secret Service agent and there was a big security snafu going on and she should come with me.'

'How did you know she was headed to the rally?'

'I didn't. I just looked at all the women coming out of baggage claim and tried to judge by how they looked and what they were carrying. Elizabeth Wright was the sixth woman I approached.'

'And she believed you?'

'I had impressive ID. I bought this earpiece from Radio Shack. Little electrical cord disappearing down the back of my neck, see? I had a rented Town Car, black. I looked the part, believe me. She was quite excited about the whole thing, really. I brought her back to this room and guarded her all evening while Neagley took over. I kept listening to my earpiece and talking into my watch.'

'We wanted New Jersey for a reason,' Neagley said. 'Their driving licences are the easiest to forge. I had a laptop and a colour printer with me. I'd just gotten through making Reacher's Secret Service ID. So I made up a Jersey licence with my picture and her name and address on it, printed it out, laminated it with a thing we bought for sixty bucks, scuffed it around a little and shoved it in my bag. Then I dressed up, took Ms Wright's invitation with me and headed downstairs. I got into the ballroom OK. With the knife in my pocket.'

Froelich looked straight at her. 'How would you have done it?'

'I'd have stuck it through his carotid artery. He'd have bled to death inside thirty seconds. Your guys were ten feet away. They'd have plugged me afterwards for sure, but they couldn't have stopped me getting it done. Without the knife would have been harder. But not impossible. Breaking his neck would have been tricky because he's got some muscle up there. So I guess I'd have gone with a blow to his larynx, hard enough to crush it. I'd have been dead before him, probably, but he'd have suffocated right afterwards, unless you've got people who could do an emergency tracheotomy on the ballroom floor within a minute or so, which I guess you don't.'

'No, we don't,' said Froelich. 'What did you whisper to him?'

'I said, I've got a knife. But very quietly. If anybody had challenged me I was going to claim I'd said, Where's your wife? Like I was coming on to him. I imagine that happens, time to time.'

Froelich nodded. 'What else?'

'Well, he's safe in his house,' Neagley said.

'How did you know where he lives?'

'We followed your limos.'

'Good limos,' Reacher said. 'Slick tactics. Friday morning was especially good. But the rest of Friday was pretty bad. Lack of coordination produced a major communications error.'

'Where?'

'Your DC people had video of the ballroom but clearly your New York people never saw it, because as well as being the woman in the party dress Thursday night Neagley was also one of the photographers outside the Stock Exchange.'

'Some North Dakota paper has a web site,' Neagley said. 'With a graphic of their masthead. I downloaded it and modified it into a press pass. Laminated it and put brass eyelets in it and slung it round my neck with a nylon cord. Trawled the secondhand stores in lower Manhattan for battered photo gear. Kept a camera in front of my face the whole time so Armstrong wouldn't recognise me.'

'But the photographers were all searched,' Froelich said.

'I wasn't carrying,' Neagley said. 'But I *could* have been carrying. I could have gotten a bazooka past that kind of a search.'

Reacher stood up and stepped to the desk. Pulled open a drawer and took out a stack of photographs. He held up the first picture. It was a low-angle shot of Armstrong standing outside the Stock Exchange. 'Neagley's,' Reacher said.

He stepped back to the bed and sat down and passed the photograph to Froelich. She took it and stared at it.

'Point is I was four feet away,' Neagley said. 'I could have gotten to him if I'd wanted to.'

Reacher dealt the next print, like a playing card. It was a grainy telephoto picture clearly taken from a great distance, looking down from way above street level. It showed Armstrong outside the Stock Exchange, tiny in the centre of the frame. There was a crude gun-sight drawn round his head with a ballpoint pen.

'This is the half,' Reacher said. 'I was on the sixtieth floor of an office building three hundred yards away. Inside the police perimeter, but higher than they were checking.'

'With a rifle?'

He shook his head. 'With a piece of wood the same size and shape as a rifle. And a camera, obviously. And a big lens. But I played it out for real. I figured people wouldn't like to see a rifle-shaped package, so I got a big square box from a computer monitor and put the wood in diagonally. Then I wheeled it into the elevator on a hand truck. I saw a few cops. I was wearing these clothes. I guess they thought I was a delivery driver. I found a window in an empty conference room. I could have taken a shot, just like I took the picture. And I'd have been Edward Fox. I could have gotten clean away.'

Froelich nodded, reluctantly. 'Why only a half?' she asked.

'I was about nine hundred feet away and six hundred feet up. That's an eleven-hundred-foot shot, give or take. Not a problem for me ordinarily, but the wind currents and the thermals around those towers turn it into a lottery. You can't guarantee a hit. No competent rifleman would try a distance shot in Manhattan.'

Froelich nodded again, a little relieved.

'So,' Reacher said. 'Call it a total score of three, if you want, and forget the half. Don't worry about New York. It was tenuous.'

'But Bismarck wasn't tenuous,' Neagley said. 'We got there about midnight. Commercial flights, through Chicago.'

Reacher dealt the next two photographs. 'Infrared film,' he said.

The first picture showed the back of the Armstrong family house. The colours were distorted, because of the infrared photography. But it was a fairly close shot. Every detail was clearly visible. Froelich could even see one of her agents, standing in the yard.

'Where were you?' she asked.

'On the neighbour's property,' Reacher said. 'Maybe fifty feet away. Simple night manoeuvre, infiltration in the dark.'

Neagley pointed to the second picture. It showed the front of the house. Same detail, same distance. 'I was across the street, at the front,' she said. 'Behind somebody's garage.'

Reacher sat forward on the bed. 'Plan would have been to have an M16 each, with the grenade launcher on it. Plus some other full-auto long guns. We'd have put phosphorus grenades into the building with the M16s, simultaneously front and back, ground floor, and either Armstrong would burn in bed or we'd shoot him as he ran out the door or jumped out the window. We'd have timed it for maybe four in the morning. We could have taken your agents out in the melee, easy as anything. We'd have probably exfiltrated OK too, and then it would have boiled down to a standard manhunt, but we'd probably have made it, with a bit of luck. Edward Fox again.'

Froelich stared at the infrared pictures and said nothing.

'So the ballroom and the family house were definites,' Reacher said. 'But the next day was the real clincher. That rally at the church.'

He passed the last photo across. It was regular daylight film, taken from a high angle. It showed Armstrong walking across the community centre lawns. He was surrounded by people but his head was clearly visible. It had another crude gunsight inked round it.

'I was in the church tower,' Reacher said.

'The church was locked.'

'At eight o'clock in the morning. I'd been in there since five.'

'It was searched.'

'I was up where the bells were. At the top of a wooden ladder, behind a trap door. I put pepper on the ladder. Your dogs lost interest and stayed on the ground floor.'

'John Malkovich or Edward Fox?' she asked.

'I'd have hit Armstrong and then as many other people as I could, three or four seconds. I'd have aimed to wound them, not kill them. People flopping around and bleeding all over the place, it would have created mass panic. Enough to get away, probably. I'd have busted out of the church within ten seconds and gotten away into the surrounding subdivision fast enough. Neagley was standing by in a car. So I'd probably have been Edward Fox.'

Froelich stood up and walked to the window. Put her hands palms down on the sill and stared out. 'This is a disaster,' she said.

Neagley stepped over and perched on the sill next to her. 'Reacher and I were US army criminal investigation specialists,' she said. 'Trained to be inventive, ruthless and self-confident. So we're very unusual. People as specialised as us, there's not more than ten thousand in the whole country.'

'Ten thousand is a lot,' Froelich said.

'Out of two hundred and eighty-one million? It's a statistically irrelevant fraction. So don't sweat it. You're *required* to leave him vulnerable. Because he's a politician. He's got to do all this visible stuff.'

'Thanks,' Froelich said. 'For trying to make me feel better. But I've got some thinking to do, haven't I?'

Neagley peeled off the windowsill and walked across the room to the desk. Took two thin files out of the drawer the photographs had been in. She held up the first. 'A written report,' she said. 'Salient points and recommendations, from a professional perspective.' She held up the second file. 'And our expenses.'

'OK,' Froelich said. She took the files.

'And there's Elizabeth Wright from New Jersey,' Reacher said. 'Don't forget her. I told her to make up for missing the reception you'd probably invite her to the Inauguration Ball.'

'OK,' Froelich said again. 'I'll speak to somebody about it.' She stacked the photographs on the desk and put them in her bag. 'Got to go,' she said. Then she walked out of the room.

Neagley stood up. 'I guess I'll head home,' she said. 'Back to Chicago. But I got to say, it was a pleasure working with you again.'

'Liar.'

'No, really, I mean it.'

'So stick around. A buck gets ten she'll be back inside an hour.'

Neagley smiled. 'What, to ask you out?'

Reacher shook his head. 'No, to tell us what her real problem is.'

THREE

Froelich drove to her office. She parked in the garage and headed upstairs. Presidential protection was a nonstop operation, but Sundays still felt different. People dressed different. Some people spent the day at home. *Like Stuyvesant, for instance*. She closed her office door and sat at her desk and opened a drawer. Took out the things she needed and slipped them into a large brown envelope. Opened Reacher's expenses file and copied the figure on the bottom line onto the top sheet of her yellow pad. Then she switched her shredder on. Fed the whole file into it and followed it with the file of recommendations and the photographs. Then she switched the machine off and picked up the envelope and headed back down to the garage.

REACHER SAW HER CAR from the hotel room window. Two minutes later they heard a knock on the door. He opened up and Froelich walked in and stopped in the middle of the room. Glanced first at Neagley, then at Reacher.

'Can we have a minute in private?' she asked him.

'Don't need one,' he said. 'The answer is yes.'

'You don't know the question yet.'

'You trust me, because you trusted Joe and Joe trusted me. Now you want to know if I trust Neagley, and the answer is yes, I trust her absolutely, therefore you can too.'

'OK,' Froelich said. 'I guess that was the question.'

'So make yourself at home. You want more coffee?'

Froelich laid the envelope on the table. Slipped out of her jacket and dumped it on the bed. 'More coffee would be fine,' she said.

Reacher dialled room service. Asked for a large pot and three cups.

'I only told you half the truth before,' Froelich said.

'I guessed,' Reacher said.

Froelich nodded and picked up the envelope. Opened the flap and pulled out a clear vinyl page protector with something in it.

'This is a copy of something that came in the mail,' she said.

She dropped it on the table and Reacher and Neagley inched their chairs closer to take a look. The thing inside the page protector was a photograph of a single sheet of white paper. Centred left-to-right on it were five words: **You are going to die.** The words were crisp and bold, obviously printed from a computer.

'When did it come?' Reacher asked.

'The Monday after the election,' Froelich said. 'First-class mail.'

'Addressed to Armstrong?'

'At the Senate. But he hasn't seen it yet. We open all public mail addressed to protectees. We pass on whatever is appropriate. We didn't think this was appropriate. What do you think of it?'

'It's true. Everybody's going to die. So it's a statement of fact.'

'Maybe the sender phrased it that way on purpose,' Neagley said. 'To avoid prosecution if you find him. Or her. To be able to say, hey, it wasn't a threat, it was a statement of fact.'

'But why are you worrying about it?' Reacher asked. 'Surely those guys get sackloads of threats in the mail.'

Froelich nodded. 'Several thousand a year, typically. But most of them are sent to the President. It's unusual to get one directed at the Vice President. And most are on old scraps of paper, written in crayon, bad spelling, crossings out. Defective, in some way. This one isn't defective. It stood out from the start. So we looked at it pretty hard.'

'Where was it mailed?'

'Las Vegas,' Froelich said. 'We think the sender travelled there to mail it.'

'Because?' Neagley asked.

'Because of the forensics. They indicate a very cautious guy.'

'Details?'

'We sent this to the FBI. Their facilities are better than ours.'

There was a knock at the door. Reacher walked over and put his eye to the peephole. The room service guy, with the coffee. Reacher opened the door, took the tray and carried it back to the table. Neagley righted the cups and started to pour.

'What did the FBI find?' she asked.

'The envelope was clean,' Froelich said. 'Standard brown nine-by-twelve, gummed flap, metal butterfly closure. The address was printed on a self-adhesive label using a Hewlett-Packard laser printer, in Times New Roman, fourteen point bold, same as the message. The message was inserted unfolded. The flap gum was wetted with faucet water. No saliva, no DNA. No fingerprints on the metal closure. There were five sets of prints on the envelope itself. Three of them were postal workers. Their prints are on file as government workers. The fourth was the Senate mail handler who passed it on to us. And the fifth was our agent, who opened it.'

'No prints on the letter itself, I guess,' Neagley said.

Froelich pointed to a spot an inch below the top edge of the photograph. 'Right here we've got two smudges of talcum dust, one on the back, one on the front.'

'Latex gloves,' Neagley said.

'Exactly. Disposable latex gloves, like a doctor's or dentist's. They come in boxes of fifty or a hundred pairs. Talcum powder inside the gloves, to help them slip on. But there's always some loose talcum in the box, so it transfers from the outside of the glove, too.'

'OK,' Neagley said. 'So no prints.'

Froelich's face changed. 'No, this is where it gets weird.' She pointed to a spot on the photograph an inch below the printed message and a little right of centre. 'What might we expect to find here, if this were a regular letter, for instance?'

'A signature,' Reacher said.

'Exactly,' Froelich said. 'And what we've got here is a thumbprint. A big, clear, definite thumbprint. Obviously deliberate. Bold as anything, exactly vertical, clear as a bell. Way too big to be a woman's.'

'You're tracing the print, obviously,' Neagley said.

'They won't find anything,' Reacher said. 'The guy must be confident his prints aren't on file anywhere.'

'We've come up blank so far,' Froelich said.

Reacher studied the photograph. 'He signs the note with his thumbprint but goes to extraordinary lengths to make sure his prints don't appear anywhere else on the letter or the envelope. Why?'

'Effect?' Neagley said. 'Drama? Neatness?'

'What else?' Reacher said to Froelich. 'Why are you so uptight?'

Froelich sighed and picked up her envelope and slid out a second item. Another plastic page protector, with a photograph inside it. The photograph showed a sheet of white paper. There were eight words printed on it: **Vice-President-elect Armstrong is going to die.**

'It's virtually identical,' Froelich said. 'The forensics are the same, and it's got the same thumbprint for a signature. It showed up on my boss's desk. One morning, it was just *there*. No envelope, no nothing.'

'When did it show up?' Reacher asked.

'Three days after the first one came in the mail,' Froelich said.

'Aimed at you,' Neagley said. 'Rather than Armstrong himself. Why? To make sure you take the first one seriously?'

'We were already taking it seriously,' Froelich said.

'Who's your boss?' Reacher asked.

'Guy called Stuyvesant,' Froelich said. 'Like the cigarette.'

'You tell him about the last five days?'

Froelich shook her head. 'I decided not to.'

'Wise,' Reacher said. 'Exactly what do you want us to do?'

'I really want to talk to somebody. Specifically, I really want to talk to Joe. Because there are complexities here, aren't there? And Joe would find a way through them.'

'You want me to be Joe?' Reacher said.

'Maybe you could be the next best thing.' Then she was quiet for a spell. 'I'm sorry. That didn't come out very well.'

'Tell me about the Neanderthals,' Reacher said. 'In your office.'

She nodded. 'That was my first thought too.'

'It's a definite possibility,' he said. 'Some guy gets all jealous and resentful, lays all this stuff on you and hopes you'll crack up and look stupid. Any likely candidates in particular?'

She shrugged. 'On the surface, none of them. Below the surface, any of them. There are six guys on my old pay grade who got passed over when I got the promotion. Each one of them has got friends and allies and supporters in the grades below.'

'Gut feeling?'

'I can't come up with a favourite. And all their prints are on file. And this period between the election and the inauguration is very busy. We're stretched. Nobody's had time for a weekend in Vegas.'

'Didn't have to be a weekend. Could have been in and out in a single day.'

'I think it's a genuine threat from out there in the world.'

'Me too,' Neagley said. 'But there's *some* insider involvement, right? Like, who else could leave something on your boss's desk?'

Froelich nodded. 'I need you to come see the office,' she said.

THEY RODE the short distance in the government Suburban. Reacher glimpsed the White House railings before Froelich turned a corner and drove into a narrow alley and headed for a garage entrance. There was a steep ramp and a guard in a glass booth. She parked the Suburban. There was a door with a porthole of wired glass. Froelich led them through it and up a staircase into a lobby with a single elevator door.

'You two shouldn't really be here,' Froelich said. 'So say nothing, stick close to me and walk fast, OK?'

They went up three floors to a world of narrow corridors and low ceilings. Offices divided into cubicles with shoulder-high padded fabric panels. Inside the main door was a reception desk with a man in a suit behind it. He had a phone cradled in his shoulder and was writing something on a message log and couldn't manage more than a puzzled glance and a distracted nod of greeting.

'Duty officer,' Froelich said. 'They work a three-shift system round the clock. This desk is always manned.'

'Is this the only way in?' Reacher asked.

'There are fire stairs at the back,' Froelich said. 'But don't get ahead of yourself. See the cameras?' She pointed to the ceiling. Miniature surveillance cameras covered every corridor.

She led them deeper into the complex, until they ended up at the back of the floor. A long, narrow corridor opened out into a window-less square space. Against the side wall of the square was a secretarial station for one person. There was a coat rack in a corner. Behind the secretary's desk was the fire exit. Above the exit was a surveillance camera. Opposite it was a single blank door. It was closed.

'Stuyvesant's office,' Froelich said.

She opened the door and led them inside. Flicked a switch and bright halogen light filled the room. It was a reasonably small office. There was a window, with white blinds closed against the night.

'Does the window open?' Neagley asked.

'No,' Froelich said. 'And it faces Pennsylvania Avenue, anyway. Some burglar climbs up three floors, somebody's going to notice.'

The office was dominated by a huge desk with a grey composite top. It was completely empty.

'Doesn't he use a phone?' Reacher asked.

'Keeps it in the drawer,' Froelich said. 'He likes the desktop clear.'

There were tall cabinets against the wall, two leather chairs. Apart from that, nothing. It was a serene space. It spoke of a tidy mind.

'OK,' Froelich said. 'The week after the election, on the Wednesday evening, Stuyvesant went home about seven thirty. Left his desk clear. His secretary left a half-hour later. Popped her head in the door just before she went, like she always does. She confirms that the desk was clear. And she'd notice, right? If there was a sheet of paper on the desk, it would stand out.'

Reacher nodded. A speck of dust would have stood out.

'Eight o'clock Thursday morning, the secretary comes in again,' Froelich said. 'She walks to her own desk and starts work. Doesn't open Stuyvesant's door at all. Ten after eight, Stuyvesant shows up. He takes off his raincoat and hangs it on the coat rack. He sets his brief-case on his secretary's desk and confers with her about something. Then he opens his door and walks into his office. He's not carrying anything. He's left his briefcase on the secretary's desk. Four or five seconds later he comes back out. Calls his secretary in. They both confirm that at that point the sheet of paper was on the desk.'

'Do the surveillance cameras record to videotape?' Neagley asked.

'All the cameras record to separate tapes,' Froelich said. 'I've looked at this one, and everything happens exactly as they describe it.'

'So unless they're in it together, neither of them put the paper there.'

Froelich nodded. 'That's the way I see it.'

'So who did?' Reacher asked. 'What else does the tape show?'

'The cleaning crew,' Froelich said. She led them to her own office and took three video cassettes out of her desk drawer. Stepped over to a bank of shelves, where a small Sony television with a built-in video nestled between a printer and a fax machine. 'These are copies,' she said. 'The originals are locked away. The recorders work on timers, six hours on each tape. Six in the morning until noon, noon until six, six until midnight, midnight until six, and start again.'

She found the remote in a drawer and switched the TV on. Put the first tape in the mechanism. A dim picture settled on the screen.

'This is the Wednesday evening,' she said. 'Six o'clock onwards.'

The picture showed the whole square area from behind the secretary's head. She was at her desk. She looked old. She had white hair. Stuyvesant's door was on the right of the picture. It was closed. There was a date and time burned into the picture at the bottom left. Froelich hit fast forward and the motion sped up.

'OK, this is where Stuyvesant goes home,' she said.

Reacher saw the time counter race through 7.30, then 7.31. Stuyvesant stepped out of his office, triple speed. He was a tall man, greying at the temples. He was carrying a slim briefcase. The video made him move with absurd energy. He raced across to the coat rack and took down a raincoat. Raced away out of sight. Froelich pressed the fast wind button harder and the speed redoubled again. The time counter blurred. As the seven turned to an eight the secretary jumped up and Froelich slowed the tape back to triple speed in time to catch her opening Stuyvesant's door for a second. She held on to the handle and leaned inside and turned and closed the door. Collected a coat and disappeared into the corridor. Froelich doubled the playback speed once again but the picture remained static.

'When do the cleaners come in?' Reacher asked.

'Just before midnight,' Froelich said.

'And there's nothing else visible before then?'

'Nothing at all.'

'So spool ahead. We get the picture.'

Froelich operated the buttons. At 11.50pm she let the tape run. At 11.52 there was motion at the end of the corridor. A team of three emerged from the gloom: two women and a man, all wearing dark overalls. They looked Hispanic. The man was pushing a cart. It had a black garbage bag in a hoop at the front, and trays stacked with cloths and spray bottles on shelves at the rear. One of the women was carrying a vacuum cleaner. The other was carrying a bucket and mop. All three were wearing rubber gloves. All three looked tired. Like night workers. But they looked neat and clean and professional. They had tidy haircuts and their expressions said: *We know this ain't the world's most exciting job, but we're going to do it properly.*

'Who are they?' Reacher asked.

'Direct government employees,' Froelich said. 'Most office cleaners are contract people, minimum wage, high-turnover nobodies. But we hire our own. We need reliability. We keep two crews at all times. They're properly interviewed and background-checked. We pay them well, give them full health plans, paid vacations, the whole nine yards. They're department members, same as anybody else.'

'And they respond?'

She nodded. 'They're terrific, generally.'

'But you think this crew smuggled the letter in.'

'No other conclusion to come to.'

Reacher pointed at the screen. 'So where is it now?'

'Could be in the garbage bag, in a stiff envelope. Could be in a page protector, taped underneath one of the trays or shelves.'

The cleaners continued into Stuyvesant's office. The door swung shut behind them. The camera stared forward blankly. The time counter ticked on, five minutes, seven, eight. Then the tape ran out.

'Midnight,' Froelich said.

She ejected the cassette and put the second tape in. Pressed play and the date changed to Thursday and the timer restarted at midnight exactly. It crawled onwards, two minutes, four, six.

'They certainly do a thorough job,' Neagley said. 'Our office cleaners would have done the whole building by now.'

'Stuyvesant likes a clean working environment,' Froelich said.

At 12.07am the door opened and the crew filed out.

'So now you figure the letter is there on the desk,' Reacher said.

Froelich nodded. The video showed the cleaners starting work around the secretarial station. Everything was energetically dusted and wiped and polished. Every inch of carpet was vacuumed.

Garbage was emptied into the black bag. It had bellied out to twice its size. The man looked a little dishevelled by his efforts. Sixteen minutes past midnight, they backed away into the gloom.

'That's it,' Froelich said. 'Nothing more for the next five hours and forty-four minutes. Then we change tapes again and find nothing at all from six o'clock until eight, when the secretary comes in, and then it goes down exactly as she and Stuyvesant claimed it did.'

'As one might expect,' said a voice from the door. 'I think our word can be trusted. After all, I've been in government service for twenty-five years, and my secretary even longer than that, I believe.'

FOUR

The guy at the door was Stuyvesant. Reacher recognised him from the tape. Froelich was looking at him, worried. But he in turn was staring straight at Neagley.

'You're the woman on the video,' he said. 'In the ballroom, Thursday night.' He moved his gaze from Neagley to Reacher. 'And you're Joe Reacher's brother,' he said. 'You look just like him.'

Reacher nodded. 'Jack Reacher,' he said, and offered his hand.

Stuyvesant took it. 'I'm sorry for your loss,' he said. 'The Treasury Department still remembers your brother with affection.'

Reacher nodded again. 'This is Frances Neagley,' he said. 'We worked together in the military.'

'Reacher brought her in to help with the audit,' Froelich said.

Stuyvesant smiled a brief smile. 'I gathered that,' he said. 'Smart move. What were the results?'

The office went quiet.

'That bad?' Stuyvesant said to Froelich. 'Well, I knew Joe Reacher. I'm assuming his brother is at least half as smart. Ms Neagley, probably smarter still. In which case they must have found ways through.'

'Three definites,' Froelich said.

'Let's go to the conference room,' Stuyvesant said.

He led them to a relatively spacious room in the heart of the complex. It had a long table in it with ten chairs, five to a side. There was a cabinet against one wall. Stuyvesant sat down and waved to the chairs on the other side of the table.

'Let's talk about baseball,' he said.

They all waited.

'The thing about baseball is that the regular season is one hundred and sixty-two games long,' Stuyvesant said. 'Way longer than any other sport. It's impossible to win every single game all season long. The very best teams lose around a third of their games. Imagine what that feels like. You're a superb athlete, fanatically competitive, but you know you're going to lose repeatedly. You have to make mental adjustments, or you couldn't cope. And presidential protection is the same. We can't win every day. So we get used to it.'

'You only lost once,' Neagley said. 'Back in 1963.'

'No,' Stuyvesant said. 'We lose repeatedly. But not every loss is significant. Just like baseball. Not every defeat they inflict loses you the World Series. And with us, not every mistake kills our guy.'

'So what are you saying?' Neagley asked.

Stuyvesant sat forward. 'I'm saying that despite what your audit revealed you should still have faith in us. Your audit showed up a few holes, and what we have to do now is judge whether it's possible to fill them. I'm going to leave that to Froelich's judgment. It's her show. But what I'm suggesting is that there are always going to be holes. Part of the job. This is a democracy. Get used to it.'

'What about this specific threat?' Reacher asked.

He paused, and then shook his head. His face had changed. The mood in the whole room had changed. 'It was a serious lapse on Froelich's part to reveal the existence of any threat at all,' Stuyvesant said. He stood up and walked over to the cabinet. Opened it and took out two legal pads and two ballpoint pens. Walked back and dropped one of each in front of Reacher and Neagley. 'Write your full names,' he said. 'Any aliases, dates of birth, social security and military ID numbers, current addresses.'

'What for?' Reacher asked.

'Just do it,' Stuyvesant said.

Neagley shrugged and started writing. Reacher followed her example. Stuyvesant scooped the pads off the table. Walked out of the room with them under his arm. The door slammed behind him.

'I'm in trouble,' Froelich said. 'And I've made trouble for you guys.'

'Don't worry about it,' Reacher said. 'He's going to make us sign some kind of confidentiality agreement, is all. He's gone to get them typed up, I guess.'

They waited, five minutes, then ten, then fifteen. Reacher stood up and stretched. Sat down again and turned his chair and tilted it back and put his feet on the next one. Glanced at his watch.

Stuyvesant had been gone twenty minutes.

'Hell is he doing?' he said. 'Typing them himself? We'll give him ten more minutes. Then we'll all go out and get some dinner.'

Stuyvesant came back after five more. He walked into the room and closed the door. 'OK,' he said. 'Where were we? Reacher asked about this specific threat. Well, it's either an inside job or it's an outside job. If it's an outside job, should we necessarily worry? Perhaps not, because that's like baseball, too. If the Yankees come to town saying they're going to beat the Orioles, does that mean it's true? Boasting about it is not the same thing as actually doing it.'

Nobody spoke.

'I'm asking for your input here,' Stuyvesant said.

Reacher shrugged. 'OK. You think it *is* an outside threat?'

'No, I think it's inside intimidation intended to damage Froelich's career. Now ask me what I'm going to do about it.'

Reacher glanced at him. 'You're going to hire me and Neagley for an internal investigation.'

'Am I?'

Reacher nodded. 'If you're worried about inside intimidation then you need an internal investigation. That's clear. You can't use one of your own people, because you might hit on the bad guy by chance. And you don't want to bring the FBI in, because that's not how Washington works. Nobody washes their dirty linen in public. So you need some other outsider. And you've got two of them sitting right in front of you. They're already involved, because Froelich just involved them. So can you use us? Of course you can. Who better than Joe Reacher's little brother? Inside Treasury, Joe Reacher is practically a saint. So your ass is covered. And I was a good investigator in the military. So was Neagley. You know that, because you just checked. My guess is you just spent twenty-five minutes talking to the Pentagon and the National Security Agency. They ran our details through their computers and we came out clean. More than clean, probably, because I'm sure our security clearances are still on file, and I'm sure they're way higher than you actually need them to be.'

'An excellent analysis,' Stuyvesant said. 'You get the job, just as soon as I get hard copies of those clearances. They should be here in an hour or two.'

Silence in the room.

'Will I be a suspect?' Stuyvesant asked.

'No,' Reacher said.

'Maybe I should be. Perhaps I felt forced to promote a woman, but I secretly resent it, so I'm working behind her back to panic and discredit her. Or maybe Froelich's setting this whole thing up in order to deal with it spectacularly and earn some enhanced credibility.'

'Neither of you is a suspect,' Reacher said.

'Why not?' Stuyvesant asked.

'Because Froelich came to me voluntarily, and she knew something about me from my brother. You hired us directly after seeing our military records. Neither of you would have done those things if you had something to hide. Too much risk.'

'Maybe we think we're smarter than you are.'

Reacher shook his head. 'Neither of you is that dumb.'

'Good,' Stuyvesant replied. 'So let's assume it's a jealous rival elsewhere in the department, who conspired with the cleaners.'

'Where are the cleaners now?' Reacher asked.

'Suspended,' Stuyvesant said. 'At home, on full pay. They live together. One of the women is the man's wife and the other woman is his sister-in-law. The other crew is working overtime to make up.'

'What's their story?'

'They know nothing about anything. They didn't bring in any sheet of paper, it wasn't there when they were there.'

'But you don't believe them.'

'All three of them passed a lie-detector test,' Stuyvesant said.

'So you do believe them.'

Stuyvesant shook his head. 'I think somebody they knew inside the building asked them to do it, and explained it away as a routine test procedure, said there was no harm in it, and coached them through what would happen afterwards. I think that might give a person enough composure to pass the polygraph. If they were convinced they weren't in the wrong and there'd be no adverse consequences. If they were convinced they were helping the department somehow.'

'Have you pursued that with them yet?'

Stuyvesant shook his head again. 'That'll be your job,' he said.

He left as suddenly as he had arrived. Just upped and walked out of the room. The door swung shut behind him and left Reacher and Neagley and Froelich sitting together at the table.

'You want to get that dinner?' Froelich asked.

Neagley shook her head. 'No, I'll eat in my room.'

They wound their way back through the corridors to Froelich's office and she called a driver for Neagley. Then she escorted her down to the garage and came back upstairs to Reacher.

'Let's go,' she said. 'Dinner, my place.'

'Your place?'

'Restaurants are impossible here on Sunday night. And I've still got some of Joe's things. Maybe you should have them.'

SHE LIVED in a small terraced house in an unglamorous neighbourhood. There was a wooden front door with a small foyer behind it that led into a living room. Froelich moved to the back of the room where an arch opened into a kitchen. She looked around, a little vague, like she was wondering what all the machines and cabinets were for.

'We could send out for Chinese food,' Reacher called.

'Maybe we should,' she said. She found a takeaway menu in a drawer and dialled a number and called in an order. Hot and sour soup and General Tso's chicken, times two. 'That OK?' she asked.

'Don't tell me,' he said. 'It's what Joe liked.'

'I've still got some of his things. You should come see them.'

She walked ahead of him back to the foyer and up the stairs. There was a guest room at the front of the house. It had a deep closet with a single door. The hanging rail had a long line of suits and shirts still wrapped in dry-cleaner's plastic. 'These are his,' Froelich said. 'I figured he'd come back for them. But he didn't. You should have them. They're your property, anyway. You were his next of kin, I guess.'

'Why did you break up?' Reacher asked.

The doorbell rang downstairs.

'The food,' Froelich said.

They went down and ate together at the kitchen table.

'You can stay here tonight,' she said. 'If you like.'

'I didn't check out of the hotel.'

She nodded. 'So check out tomorrow. Then base yourself here.'

'What about Neagley?'

'If she wants. There's another bedroom on the third floor.'

'OK,' he said.

Froelich's phone rang. She stepped through to the living room to answer it. Talked for a moment and then hung up and came back.

'That was Stuyvesant. He's giving you the formal go-ahead.'

He nodded. 'So call Neagley and tell her to get her ass in gear.'

'Now?'

'Get a problem, solve a problem,' he said. 'That's my way. Tell her to be out front of the hotel in thirty minutes.'

'Where are you going to start?'

'With the video,' he said. 'I want to watch the tapes again. And I want to meet with the guy who runs that part of the operation.'

THIRTY MINUTES LATER they scooped Neagley off the sidewalk in front of the hotel. She had changed into a black suit with a short jacket. The trousers were cut tight. They looked pretty good from the back, in Reacher's opinion. He saw Froelich arrive at the same conclusion. But she said nothing. Just drove, five minutes, and they were back in the Secret Service offices. Froelich headed for her desk and left Reacher and Neagley with the agent who ran the video surveillance. He was a thin, nervous guy who had come in at short notice to meet with them. He led them to a closet-sized equipment room full of recorders. One wall was a floor-to-ceiling shelving unit with hundreds of VHS tapes stacked neatly in black plastic boxes.

'There are four recorders slaved to each camera,' the guy said. 'Six hours to a tape, so we change all the tapes once a day, file them away, keep them three months and then reuse them.'

'Where are the originals from that night?' Reacher asked.

'Right here,' the guy said. He fiddled in his pocket and came out with a bunch of small brass keys on a ring. Squatted down and opened a low cupboard. Took out three boxes. 'These are the three I copied for Froelich.'

'Some place where we can look at them?'

'They're no different than the copies.'

'Copying causes detail loss,' Reacher said.

'OK,' the guy said. 'You can look at them right here, I guess.'

He stood up and angled a small monitor outwards and switched on a stand-alone player. The guy glanced around like he was unhappy about leaving strangers alone in his little domain. 'I guess I'll wait in the foyer,' he said. 'Call me when you're through.'

'What's your name?' Neagley asked.

'Nendick,' the guy said, shyly.

He left the room and Reacher put the third tape in the machine.

'You know what?' Neagley said. 'That guy didn't sneak a peek at my ass.'

'Didn't he?'

'Guys usually do when I'm wearing these pants.'

'Maybe he's gay,' Reacher said.

'He was wearing a wedding band.'

'Then maybe he tries hard to avoid inappropriate feelings. Or maybe he's tired.' He hit fast rewind. The motor whirred.

'Third tape,' he said. 'Thursday morning. We'll do this backwards.'

The player spooled fast. He watched the counter and hit play and the picture came up with an empty office with the timecode burned in over it showing the relevant Thursday's date and the time at 7.55am. He hit forward scan and then froze the picture when the secretary entered the frame at exactly eight o'clock. He settled in his chair and hit play and the secretary walked into the square area and took off her coat and hung it on the rack. She was a woman of maybe sixty. She sat down and didn't move from her chair. Reacher fast-forwarded until Stuyvesant himself swept into view at ten past eight. He was wearing a raincoat and carrying a slim briefcase. He took off his coat and hung it on the rack. Advanced into the square area and set his briefcase on the secretary's desk. Bent to confer with her. Straightened up and stepped to his door and disappeared into his office. The timer ticked off four seconds. Then he was back out in the doorway, calling to his secretary.

'He found it,' Reacher said. He hit reverse scan. The morning's activity unfolded again, backwards. 'Now for the boring part.'

The picture settled to a steady shot of an empty area with the timer rushing backwards. Absolutely nothing happened.

At 6.00am the tape jammed to a stop and Reacher ejected it and fast wound the second tape to the end and started the patient backward search again. Nothing happened.

'Why are we doing this tonight?' Neagley asked.

'Because I'm an impatient guy,' Reacher said.

'Or maybe you're trying to outpoint your brother.'

'Don't need to. I know exactly how we compared.'

'What happened to him?'

'He was killed. In the line of duty. Just after I left the army. Clandestine rendezvous with an informer from a counterfeiting operation. They were ambushed. He was shot in the head, twice.'

'They get the guys who did it?'

'No. I got them instead.'

'Any comeback?'

'I exfiltrated fast. Stayed out of circulation. Missed the funeral.'

The video sped back. Nothing happening.

'The whole thing was a can of worms,' he said. 'It was his own fault, really.'

'That's harsh.'

'Would you get ambushed at a rendezvous?'

'No,' Neagley said. 'I'd do all the usual stuff. You know, arrive three hours early, stake it out, block the approaches.'

'Joe didn't do any of that. He was out of his depth. Thing about Joe, he looked tough. He was six-six, built like a brick outhouse, hands like shovels. We were clones, physically, the two of us. But we had different brains. Deep down, he was a cerebral guy. Kind of *pure*. Naive, even. He never thought dirty. Everything was a game of chess with him. He gets a call, sets up a meet, drives down there. Like he's moving his knight or his bishop. He just didn't expect somebody to come along and blow the whole chessboard away.'

'Could he have reacted? At the scene?'

'They were pretty good, I guess. Semiproficient, by our standards. There must have been some chance. But it would have been a split-second thing, purely instinctive. And Joe's instincts were all buried under the cerebral stuff. He probably stopped to think. He always did. Just enough to make him come out timid.'

'Naive and timid. They don't share that opinion around here.'

'Around here he must have looked like a wild man. Everything's comparative.'

The timer spun back through half past midnight. The office was undisturbed. Then at 12.16 the cleaning crew rushed backwards out of the exit corridor. Reacher watched them at high speed until they reversed into Stuyvesant's office at 12.07. Then he ran the tape forward at normal speed and watched them come out again and clean the secretarial station.

'What do you think?' he asked. 'If they'd just left the letter in there, would they look so composed?'

They weren't hurrying. They weren't furtive or anxious. They weren't glancing back at Stuyvesant's door. They were just cleaning. He reversed the tape again and sped back until it jammed to a stop at midnight. He ejected it and inserted the first tape. Wound to the end and scanned back until they first entered the picture just before 11.52pm. Ran the tape forward and watched them walk into shot and froze the tape when they were all clearly visible.

'Do they look worried?' he asked.

Neagley shrugged. 'Run the tape. See how they move.'

He let them walk on. They headed straight for Stuyvesant's door and disappeared from view inside, 11.52 exactly.

Neagley leaned back and half closed her eyes. 'Their energy level is a little different than when they came out,' she said. 'A little slower. Like they're hesitant.'

'Or like they're dreading having to do something bad in there?'

He ran it again. There was no real overt difference. Maybe they looked a little less wired going in than coming out. Or more tired. But then, they spent fifteen minutes in there. And it was a relatively small office. Already quite clean and neat. Maybe it was their habit to take a ten-minute rest in there, out of sight of the camera.

Reacher hit fast rewind until he found 8.00pm. The secretary got up from her desk, put her head round Stuyvesant's door, and went home. He wound back to 7.31 and watched Stuyvesant himself leave.

'OK,' he said. 'The cleaners did it. On their own initiative?'

'I seriously doubt it.'

'So who told them to?'

THEY STOPPED in the foyer and found Nendick and sent him back to tidy up his equipment room. Then they went in search of Froelich and found her deep in a stack of paperwork at her desk.

'We need to speak with the cleaners,' Reacher said.

'Now?' Froelich said.

'No better time. Late-night interrogation always works best.'

She looked blank. 'OK. I'll drive you, I guess.'

'They're going to feel better talking to us if there's nobody else from the department around.'

'OK, I'll wait outside. But I'm going with you.'

She led them back down to the garage. They climbed into the Suburban and Reacher closed his eyes for twenty minutes as she drove. Then the car came to a stop and he opened his eyes in a mean neighbourhood full of ten-year-old sedans and hurricane fencing.

'This is it,' Froelich said. 'Number 2301. I'll wait right here.'

Reacher and Neagley climbed out of the car. They went up a cracked concrete walk to the door. Reacher pressed the bell. They waited. Heard footsteps on a bare floor, then something metal being hauled out of the way. The door opened and a man stood there. He was the cleaner from the video. His skin and hair were dark and his cheekbones were high and flat.

'Yes?' he said.

'We need to talk about the thing at the office,' Reacher said.

The guy didn't ask for ID. Just glanced at Reacher's face and stepped back over the thing he had moved to get the door open. It was a children's seesaw made out of brightly coloured metal tubes.

'Can't leave it outside at night,' the guy said. 'It would be stolen.'

Neagley and Reacher climbed over it into a narrow hallway. There were more toys neatly packed onto shelves. Bright paintings visible on the front of the refrigerator in the kitchen. The smell of cooking. There was a living room off the hallway with two silent, scared women in it, wearing Sunday dresses.

'We need to know your names,' Neagley said.

'Julio,' the man said.

'Anita,' the first woman said. Reacher assumed she was Julio's wife, by the way she glanced at him before answering.

'Maria,' the second woman said. 'I'm Anita's sister.'

There was a sofa and two armchairs. Anita and Maria squeezed up to let Julio sit with them on the sofa. Reacher took that as an invitation and sat down in one armchair. Neagley took the other.

'We think you guys put the letter in the office,' Neagley said.

There was no reply. No reaction at all. No expression on the three faces. Just some kind of silent blank stoicism.

'Did you?' Neagley asked.

No reply.

'The kids in bed?' Reacher asked.

'They're not here,' Anita said.

'Where are they?'

She paused. 'With cousins.'

'Why?'

'Because we work nights.'

'Not for much longer,' Neagley said. 'You won't be working at all, unless you tell somebody something.'

No response.

'Did somebody ask you to put it there? Somebody in the office?'

'We didn't do anything with any letter.'

'So what *did* you do?' Reacher asked.

'We cleaned. That's what we're there for.'

'You were in there an awful long time.'

Julio looked at his wife, like he was puzzled.

'We saw the tape,' Reacher said. 'Spend that long there every night?'

Julio shrugged. 'I guess so.'

'Same every night?'

'Unless somebody's spilled some coffee or left a lot of trash around or something. That might slow us up some.'

'Was there something like that in Stuyvesant's office that night?'

'No,' Julio said. 'Stuyvesant is a clean guy.'

'You spent some big amount of time in there.'

'No more than usual.'

'OK,' Neagley said. 'The tape shows you going in there. Afterwards, there was a letter on the desk. We think you put it there because somebody asked you to. Maybe they told you it was a joke. Maybe they told you it was OK to do it. And it was OK. No harm done. But we need to know who asked you. Because this is part of the game, too, us trying to find out. And you've got to tell us, otherwise we have to figure you put it there off your own bat. And that's not OK. That's making a threat against the Vice President-elect of the United States. And you can go to prison for that.'

No reaction. Another long silence. Still faces, blank eyes, stoic, miserable expressions.

'Let's go,' Reacher said.

They stood up and stepped through to the hallway. Climbed over the seesaw and let themselves out into the night. Made it back to the Suburban in time to see Froelich snapping her cellphone shut. There was panic in her eyes.

'What?' Reacher asked.

'We got another one,' she said. 'Ten minutes ago. And it's worse.'

FIVE

It was waiting for them in the centre of the long table in the conference room. A small crowd of people had gathered round it. There was a brown nine-by-twelve envelope with a metal closure and a torn flap. And a single sheet of white letter-size paper. On it was printed: **The day upon which Armstrong will die is fast approaching.**

The guy in the suit from the reception desk pushed back through the crowd and spoke to Froelich. 'I handled the envelope,' he said. 'I didn't touch the letter. Just spilled it out.'

'How did it arrive?' she asked.

'The garage guard took a bathroom break. Came back and found it on the ledge inside his booth. He brought it straight up to me. So I guess his prints are on the envelope too.'

'When, exactly?'

'Half-hour ago.'

'How does the garage guard work his breaks?' Reacher asked.

The room went quiet. People turned towards the new voice. The desk guy started in with a fierce *who-the-hell-are-you* look. But then he saw Froelich's face and shrugged and answered obediently.

'He locks the barrier down,' he said. 'That's how. Runs to the bathroom, runs back. Maybe two or three times a shift. He's down there eight hours at a stretch.'

'Is there a camera in the garage?' Reacher asked.

'Yes, there is.'

'So get Nendick to bring us tonight's tape, right now.'

Neagley craned over the table. 'Rather florid wording, don't you think? And "fast" definitely takes the prediction defence away. Turns the whole thing into an overt threat.'

'You got that right,' Froelich said slowly. 'If this is somebody's idea of a game or a joke, it just turned very serious very suddenly.'

She said it loud and clear and Reacher watched the faces in the room. There was absolutely no reaction on any of them.

Reacher and Neagley followed Froelich back to her office. She called an FBI number and asked for a forensics team, urgent.

Nendick knocked and came in, carrying two tapes. 'Two cameras,' he said. 'One inside the booth, high up, looking down and sideways, to ID individual drivers in their cars. The other outside, looking straight up the alley, to pick up approaching vehicles.' He put both cassettes on the desk and went back out.

Froelich picked up the first tape and scooted her chair over to her TV set. Put the tape in and wound back thirty-five minutes. Pressed play. It was the sideways view from inside the booth. The guard was sitting on his stool with the back of his left shoulder in shot. She fast-forwarded until he stood up. He touched a couple of buttons and disappeared. Nothing happened for thirty seconds. Then an arm snaked into view from the right edge of the picture. Just an arm, in a heavy soft sleeve. The hand on the end of it was gloved. There was an envelope in the hand. It was pushed through the half-closed sliding window and dropped onto the ledge. Then the arm disappeared.

'He knew about the camera,' Froelich said.

'But did he know about the other one?' Reacher asked.

Froelich ejected the first tape and inserted the second. Wound back thirty-five minutes. Pressed play. The view was straight up the alley. They watched the timecode counter until it reached a point twenty seconds before the arm had appeared. Then they watched the screen. A figure appeared at the top. Definitely male. He was wearing a tweed overcoat, maybe grey or brown. Dark trousers, heavy shoes, a muffler round his neck. And a dark, wide-brimmed hat, tilted down in front. He walked with his chin tucked down. The video picked up a perfect view of the crown of his hat, all the way down the alley.

'He knew about the second camera,' Reacher said.

The guy walked fast, but not hurrying, not out of control. He had the envelope in his right hand, holding it flat against his body. He disappeared out of the bottom of the shot and reappeared three seconds later. Without the envelope. He walked at the same purposeful pace all the way back up the alley and out of shot.

'He had inside knowledge,' Froelich said. 'He knew about the cameras and the bathroom breaks. So he's one of us.'

'Not necessarily,' Reacher said. 'He could be an outsider who staked you out. The exterior camera must be visible if you're looking for it. And he could assume the interior camera. Most places have them. And a couple of nights' surveillance would teach him the bathroom break procedure.'

'So what do we do?' Froelich asked.

'Concentrate on Armstrong,' Reacher said, 'just in case this whole thing is for real. Keep him wrapped up tight.'

'What's his schedule?' Neagley asked.

'Home tonight, the Hill tomorrow,' Froelich said.

'So you'll be OK. You scored perfect round the Capitol.'

Froelich looked at the ceiling. 'What would Joe do now?'

Reacher paused and smiled. 'He'd work it all out like it was a chess problem. Let's say it *is* an insider doing this. Joe would ask, how does the insider plan to benefit from it?'

'By making me look bad in front of Stuyvesant.'

'And getting you demoted or whatever, because that rewards him in some way. But that would be his *only* aim. Situation like that, there's no serious threat against Armstrong. So Joe would say what you've got to do is proceed *as if* it's an outsider, and proceed calmly. If you're calm, you deny the insider his benefit. If you're successful, you deny the outsider *his* benefit. Just stay calm and tough it out.'

Froelich was still and silent for a spell. Then she nodded. 'OK,' she said. 'I'll get you a driver. Be back here at nine in the morning. There'll be a strategy meeting.'

THE MORNING WAS DAMP and cold, as if nature wanted to be done with fall and start with winter. Neagley and Reacher met at 8.40 at the cab line outside the hotel and found a Secret Service Town Car waiting for them. The driver bulled through the traffic and squealed into the underground garage. Led them through the lobby to the elevator. Up three floors and across to the reception desk. It was manned by a different guy. He pointed down the corridor towards the conference room.

'Started without you,' he said. 'You better hurry.'

The conference room was empty apart from Froelich and

Stuyvesant. On the polished wood between them lay two photographs. One was the official FBI crime scene eight-by-ten of yesterday's message: **The day upon which Armstrong will die is fast approaching.** The other was a Polaroid. Reacher stepped close and bent to look. It showed a sheet of paper, like the first three. It followed the same format, a printed message near the middle of the page: **A demonstration of your vulnerability will be staged today.**

'When did it come?' he asked.

'This morning,' Froelich said. 'In the mail. Addressed to Armstrong at his office. But we're bringing all his mail through here now.'

'Where is it from?'

'Orlando, Florida, postmarked Friday.'

Reacher nodded. 'Forensics on yesterday's?'

'Everything's identical,' Froelich said, 'thumbprint and all. I'm sure this one will be the same. They're working on it now.'

'I had the cleaners arrested,' Stuyvesant said.

Nobody spoke. Reacher looked at the Polaroid again.

'How secure are his movements today?' he asked.

'As good as it gets,' Froelich said. 'He's scheduled to leave home at eleven. I'm using the armoured stretch again. Full motorcade. We're using awnings across the sidewalks at both ends. He won't see open air at any point. We'll tell him it's another rehearsal procedure.'

'He still doesn't know about this yet?'

'No,' Froelich said.

'Standard practice,' Stuyvesant said. 'We don't tell them.'

'Thousands of threats a year,' Neagley said.

Stuyvesant nodded. 'Exactly. Most of them background noise. We wait until we're sure. And even then, we don't always make a big point out of it. They've got better things to do. It's our job to worry.'

'I want Neagley and me on the ground, observing,' Reacher said.

'Think we're going to screw up?' Froelich asked.

'No, but I think you're going to have your hands full. If the guy's in the neighbourhood, you might be too busy to spot him.'

'OK,' Stuyvesant said. 'You and Neagley on the ground, observing.'

FROELICH DROVE THEM to Georgetown in her Suburban. They arrived just before ten o'clock. They got out three blocks short of Armstrong's house and Froelich drove on.

'Deployment?' Neagley asked.

'Circles, on a three-block radius. You go clockwise and I'll go counterclockwise. Then you stay south and I'll stay north.

Meet back at the house after he's gone.'

Neagley nodded and walked away west. Reacher went east into the weak morning sun. There were people on the sidewalks. Some of them looking like they had no particular place to go. He watched them all out of the corner of his eye, but nothing special jumped out at him.

He turned a corner and came out at the top of Armstrong's street. There was a small crowd of onlookers watching the Secret Service team erect an awning between Armstrong's house and the kerb. It was like a long narrow tent. Heavy white canvas, completely opaque. The house end fitted flat against the brick round Armstrong's front door. The kerb end would hug the profile of the limo. The limo's door would open right inside it. Armstrong would pass from his house straight into the armoured car without being visible to an observer.

Reacher walked a circle round the group of curious people. They looked unthreatening. Neighbours mostly, he guessed. Dressed like they weren't going far. He moved back up the street and looked for people loitering. There were plenty of those, sitting in coffee shops, sipping espressos, reading papers, talking on cellphones.

He picked a coffee shop that gave him a good view south down the street and a marginal view east and west. He bought a tall regular, black, and took a table. Sat down to wait and watch. At 10.55 a black Suburban came up the street and parked tight against the kerb just north of the tent. It was followed by a black Cadillac stretch that parked tight against the tent's opening. Behind that was a black Town Car. All three vehicles had reinforced window frames and one-way glass. Four agents spilled out of the lead Suburban and took up station on the sidewalk, two north of the house and two south. Two Metro police cruisers snuffled up the street and the first stopped in the centre of the road, well ahead of the Secret Service convoy, and the second hung back well behind it. They lit up their light bars to hold the traffic. There wasn't much. Reacher looked at the tent and tried to guess when Armstrong was passing through it. Impossible. He was still gazing at the house end when he heard the faint thump of an armoured door closing and the four agents stepped back to their Suburban and the whole convoy took off.

Reacher finished his coffee and walked towards Armstrong's house. He met Neagley coming up from the opposite direction.

'OK?' he asked her.

'Opportunities,' she said. 'Didn't see anybody about to exploit any of them.'

Then there was the hiss of tyres and the sound of a big engine behind them and they turned to see Froelich easing up in her Suburban. She stopped alongside them, gestured them into the vehicle. Neagley got in the front and Reacher sprawled in the back.

'See anybody?' Froelich asked.

'Lots of people,' Reacher said. 'Wouldn't buy a cheap watch from any of them.'

Froelich took her foot off the brake and let the engine's idle speed crawl the car along the road. She kept it tight in the gutter and stopped it again when the nearside rear door was exactly level with the end of the tent. Lifted her hand from the wheel and spoke into the microphone wired to her wrist. 'One, ready,' she said.

Reacher looked to his right down the canvas tunnel and saw the front door open and a man step out. It was Brook Armstrong. He was wearing a raincoat and carrying a briefcase. He walked through the tent. An agent watched him from the door.

'The convoy was a decoy,' Froelich said.

Reacher sat up straight and moved over to make room. Armstrong opened the door and climbed in beside him.

'Morning, M. E.,' he said.

'Morning, sir,' she replied. 'These are associates of mine, Jack Reacher and Frances Neagley.'

Neagley half turned and Armstrong threaded a long arm over the seat to shake her hand.

'I know you,' he said. 'I met you at the party on Thursday evening. You're a contributor, aren't you?'

'She's a security person, actually,' Froelich said. 'We had a little cloak-and-dagger stuff going there. An efficiency analysis.'

'Excellent,' Armstrong said to Neagley. 'Believe me, ma'am, I'm very grateful for the care everybody takes of me.'

He was magnificent, Reacher thought. His voice and his face and his eyes spoke of nothing but boundless fascination with Neagley. And he had one hell of a visual memory, to place one face in a thousand from four days ago. That was clear. A born politician.

He turned and shook Reacher's hand and lit up the car with a smile of genuine pleasure. 'Pleased to meet you, Mr Reacher.'

'Pleasure's all mine,' Reacher said. Then he found himself smiling back. He liked the guy, immediately. He had charm to burn.

'You in security too?' Armstrong asked him.

'Adviser,' Reacher said.

'Well, you guys do a hell of a great job. Glad to have you aboard.'

There was a tiny sound from Froelich's earpiece and she took off down the street. Merged into the traffic stream and headed for the centre of town. She drove past the side of the Capitol, made a left and headed for a white tent leading to a side door in the Senate Offices. There were two Secret Service Town Cars flanking the tent. Four agents on the sidewalks. Froelich drove straight for the tent and eased to a stop tight against the kerb, then rolled forward a foot to put Armstrong's door right inside the canvas shelter. Reacher saw a group of three agents waiting inside the tunnel. One of them stepped forward and opened the Suburban's door.

Armstrong raised his eyebrows, like he was bemused by all the attention. 'Good meeting you both,' he said. 'And thanks, M. E.'

He stepped out into the canvas gloom and the agents surrounded him and walked him down the length of the tent to the building. Uniformed Capitol security people waited inside. Armstrong stepped through the door and it closed solidly behind him.

'OK,' Froelich said. 'He's in there all day for meetings. We'll take him home around seven o'clock. His wife is back in DC. So we'll rent them a video or something. Keep them locked up tight all evening.'

'We need intelligence,' Reacher said. 'We don't know what exact form this demonstration might take. Or where it will be. Could be anything from graffiti upwards. We don't want to let it pass us by without noticing. If it happens at all.'

THEY DROVE BACK to Froelich's office. FBI forensics reports were in on the latest two messages. They were identical to the first two in every respect. Froelich opened a drawer and flipped through a file and pulled a single sheet. Passed it across. It was a life-size fluoroscope photograph of a thumbprint.

'This our guy?' Reacher asked.

Froelich nodded.

It was a very clear print. All the ridges and whorls were exactly delineated. And it was big. Very big. The pad of the thumb measured nearly an inch and a half across. The guy must have hands like bunches of bananas. And rough skin, to print with that degree of clarity.

'Manual worker,' Reacher said. 'Now make some calls. See if anything's happened yet that we need to know about.'

Froelich checked with the DC cops first. There was the usual list of urban crimes and misdemeanours, but it would have been a stretch to categorise any of them as a demonstration of Armstrong's vulnerability. Then she opened up the National Crime Information Center data base and looked at recent entries. They were flooding in faster than one every second. Faster than she could read them.

'Hopeless,' she said. 'We'll have to wait until midnight.'

'Or one o'clock,' Neagley said. 'It might happen on central time, out there in Bismarck. They might shoot up his house.'

So Froelich called the cops in Bismarck and asked for immediate notification of anything that could be even remotely connected to an interest in Armstrong. Then she made the same request to the North Dakota State Police and the FBI nationwide.

'Maybe it won't happen,' she said.

Reacher looked away. *You better hope it does*, he thought.

A round seven o'clock in the evening the office complex began to quieten down. Most of the people visible in the corridors were drifting one way only, towards the front exit.

'Did you check out of the hotel?' Froelich asked.

'Yes,' Reacher said.

'No,' Neagley said. 'I make a terrible house guest.'

Froelich paused, a little taken aback. But Reacher wasn't surprised. Neagley was a solitary person. Kept herself to herself.

'OK,' Froelich said. 'But we should take some time out. Rest up and regroup later. I'll drop you guys off and then go try to get Armstrong home safely.'

They rode together down to the garage and Froelich fired up her Suburban and drove Neagley to the hotel. Reacher walked in with her and reclaimed his Atlantic City clothes. They were packed with his old shoes and his toothbrush and razor, folded up inside a black garbage bag he had taken from a maid's cart. Then he climbed back in alongside Froelich and she drove on to her house.

She double-parked with the motor running and took her door key off its ring. Handed it to him. 'I'll be back in a couple of hours,' she said. 'Make yourself at home.'

He took his bag and got out and watched her drive off. Then he crossed the sidewalk and unlocked her front door. The house was dark. He closed the door behind him and fumbled for a light switch. A lamp on a small chest of drawers came on. He put the key down next to it and dropped his bag and stepped into the living room.

Switched on the light. Looked around.

He stood still for a second with his ritual curiosity nagging at him. It was an ingrained reflex. But was it polite to search your host's house? Of course not. But he couldn't resist.

He looked in all the usual places people hide things and found an M9 Beretta nine-millimetre sidearm in a kitchen drawer, hidden under a stack of place mats. It was old and scratched and stained with dried oil. Last-generation Secret Service issue, without a doubt. It was unloaded. The magazine was missing. He opened the next drawer to the left and put his hand on four spares laid out in a line under an oven glove. They were all loaded. Good news and bad. The layout was smart. Pick up the gun with your right hand, access the magazines with your left. Sound ergonomics. But storing magazines full of bullets was a bad idea. Leave them long enough, the spring in the magazine learns its compressed shape and won't function right.

He closed the kitchen drawers and carried his garbage bag up to the guest room. Hung his Atlantic City clothes in the closet next to Joe's suits. He looked at them and then pulled one off the rail.

He stripped away the plastic wrap. He laid the jacket on the bed and put the trousers next to it. Went back to the closet and took out a shirt. Lifted the plastic off it. It was pure white broadcloth.

He unlaced his shoes. Took off his clothes and folded them over a chair. Went into the bathroom and set the shower running. Stepped into the stall. There was soap and shampoo in there. He washed his hair and body. Leaned out and grabbed his razor and shaved. Got out and found a towel in a cupboard. He dried himself and then stepped back into the bedroom and put Joe's shirt on. Opened the closet door and checked the fit in the mirror. It was perfect, more or less. He caught sight of a shelf behind the rail. There were neckties neatly rolled and placed side by side. Tissue-paper packages from a laundry. He opened one and found a pile of clean white boxers. Opened another and found black socks folded together in pairs.

He dressed in his brother's clothes. Selected a dark maroon tie. He put it on and cracked the shirt collar down over it. Walked back to the mirror. The suit fitted well. It was maybe a fraction long in the arms and legs, because he was a fraction shorter than Joe had been. But overall he looked impressive in it. Like a different person. Older. More authoritative. More serious. More like Joe.

He heard a sound down in the hallway. Somebody out on the step, knocking on the front door. He headed down the stairs. Opened up. It was Froelich.

'I gave you my key,' she said.

He stepped back and she stepped in. Looked up and froze. She fumbled behind her back and pushed the door shut and leaned hard up against it. Just stared at him.

'What?' he said.

'I thought you were Joe,' she said. 'Just for a second.'

Her eyes filled with tears and she laid her head back against the wood of the door. She looked at him again and started crying hard. He stood still for a second and then stepped forward and took her in his arms. She dropped her bag and burrowed into his chest.

'I'm sorry,' he said. 'I tried on his suit. Stupid, I guess.'

She moved her head, but he couldn't tell if she was saying *yes, it was* or *no, it wasn't*. She locked her arms around his body and just held on. He put one hand low on her back and used the other to smooth her hair. He held her like that for minutes.

She fought the tears and then gulped and pulled away. Swiped at her eyes with the back of her hand. 'Not your fault,' she said. 'You looked so real. I bought him that tie.'

'I should have thought,' Reacher said.

She ducked down to her purse and came back with a tissue. Blew her nose and smoothed her hair. 'Oh, God,' she said.

'I'm sorry,' he said again.

'You looked so good, is all,' she said. 'Just standing there.'

She reached out and straightened his tie. Ran her fingers behind the lapels of his jacket. Stepped forward on tiptoe and locked her hands behind his neck and kissed him on the mouth.

'So good,' she said, and kissed him again, hard.

He held still for a second and then kissed her back. Hard. He put one hand low on her side and the other behind her head. He could feel her breasts against his chest. Her hair between his fingers. Her fingers were raking upward into the stubble from his haircut. Then she pulled away. She was breathing heavily.

'We shouldn't do this,' she said.

He looked at her. 'Probably not,' he said.

She opened her eyes. Said nothing.

'So what should we do?' he asked.

She moved sideways and stepped into her living room. 'I don't know,' she said. 'Eat dinner, I guess. Did you wait?'

He followed her into the room. 'Yes,' he said. 'I waited.'

'You're very like him,' she said.

'I know,' he said.

'Do you understand what I mean?'

He nodded. 'What you saw in him you see in me, a little bit.'

'But *are* you like him?'

He knew exactly what she was asking. *Did you see things the same? Did you share tastes? Were you attracted to the same women?*

'Like I told you,' he said. 'There are similarities. And differences.'

She said nothing in reply. Just moved her wrist and checked her watch. It was a strange gesture, so he checked his, too. The second hand hit nine thirty exactly. Her cellphone rang inside her open bag out in the hallway. It was loud in the silence.

'My people checking in,' she said. 'From Armstrong's house.'

She stepped back to the hallway and bent down and answered the call. Hung up without comment.

'All quiet,' she said. 'I told them to call every hour.'

He nodded. She looked anywhere but at him. The moment was gone.

'Chinese again?' she asked.

'Suits me,' he said. 'Same order.'

She called it in from the kitchen phone and disappeared upstairs to take a shower. He waited in the living room and took the food from the delivery guy when he showed up. She came down again and they ate at the kitchen table. Her cellphone rang again at exactly ten thirty. She answered it. Just a short message.

'All quiet,' she said. 'So far so good. We should get back to the office. See if anything's happened anywhere else. You call Neagley while I clear up. Tell her to be ready to roll in twenty minutes.'

THEY WERE BACK in the office before eleven fifteen. The message logs were blank. Nothing of significance from the DC police department. Nothing from North Dakota, nothing from the FBI. Reports were still streaming into the National Crime Information Center's data base. Froelich started combing through them. She found nothing of interest. Her cellphone rang at eleven thirty. All was quiet in Georgetown. Time ticked round to midnight. Monday finished and Tuesday started. Stuyvesant showed up again.

Froelich waited ten minutes and called the DC cops. They had nothing to report. She called the Hoover Building and the FBI told her nothing significant had happened before midnight in the east. She turned back to the computer screen. Called out occasional incoming stories but no one could twist them into a connection with a potential threat to Armstrong. The clock moved on to one in the morning. Midnight, central time. She called the police department in

Bismarck. They had nothing for her. She called the North Dakota State Police. Nothing at all. She tried the FBI again. Nothing from their field offices in the last sixty minutes. She put the phone down.

'Well, that's it,' she said. 'Nothing happened.'

'Excellent,' Stuyvesant said.

'No,' Reacher said. 'It's the worst news we could have gotten.'

STUYVESANT LED THEM straight back to the conference room. He shepherded them in, hit the lights and closed the door. Reacher and Neagley sat on one side of the long table and Stuyvesant sat next to Froelich on the other.

'Explain,' Stuyvesant said.

'This is definitely *not* an inside job,' Neagley said.

Reacher nodded. 'Although we were fooling ourselves by thinking it was entirely one thing or the other. It was always both. The question was where the balance lay. Was it an inside job with trivial help from outside? Or an outside job with trivial help from inside?'

'The trivial help being what?' Stuyvesant asked.

'A potential insider needed a thumbprint that wasn't his. A potential outsider needed to get the second message inside the building.'

'And you've concluded that it's the outsider?'

Reacher nodded again. 'Which is absolutely the worst news we could have gotten. Because whereas an insider messing around is merely a pain in the ass, an outsider is truly dangerous.'

'Explain,' Stuyvesant said again.

'I look for simplicity,' Reacher said.

Stuyvesant nodded. 'So do I. But the simple explanation here is an insider trying to get under Froelich's skin.'

'Not really,' Reacher said. 'The chosen method is too complex for that. They'd be doing all the usual stuff instead. Mysterious communications failures, computer crashes, bogus alarm calls to nonexistent addresses in the bad part of town.'

'That's conjecture,' Stuyvesant said. 'I'm asking how you *know*.'

'I know because nothing happened today,' Reacher said. 'This is a smart opponent. He's bright and he's confident. He's in *command*. But he threatened something and he didn't deliver.'

'So? He failed, is all.'

'No,' Reacher said. 'He didn't even *try*. Because he didn't know his letter arrived today. He expected it to arrive tomorrow. It was mailed on Friday. Friday to Monday is pretty fast for the US mail. It was a fluke. He banked on Friday to Tuesday.'

Nobody spoke.

'He's an outsider,' Reacher said. 'He's got no direct connection to the department and therefore he's unaware his threat showed up a day early, or he'd have delivered today *for sure*. Because he's an arrogant son of a bitch, and he wouldn't have wanted to let himself down. So he's out there somewhere, waiting to deliver on his threat tomorrow, which is when he expected he'd have to all along.'

Stuyvesant was quiet for a beat. 'We have to identify this guy,' he said. 'What do we know about him?'

'Well, we know we're fooling ourselves again,' Reacher said. 'It's not a *him*. It's *them*. It always is. It's two people, working together.'

'You don't really need us any more,' Neagley said. 'This isn't an internal investigation now. This is out there in the world.'

'No,' Stuyvesant said. 'It's still internal as long as there's something to get from the cleaners. They must have met with these people. They must know who they are.'

Froelich shook her head. 'First priority is getting Armstrong to midnight alive.'

'It's only going to be a demonstration.'

'Your interpretation might be wrong,' Froelich said. 'I mean, what better demonstration would there be than actually doing it?'

Neagley nodded. 'And it would be a way of hedging their bets. A failed attempt could be passed off as a demonstration, to save face.'

The meeting came to an end a couple of minutes later. Stuyvesant made Froelich run through Armstrong's schedule for the day. First, intelligence briefings from the CIA at home. Then afternoon transition meetings on the Hill. Then in the evening another contributor reception at the same hotel as Thursday.

WASHINGTON DC is empty in the middle of the night and it took just two minutes to reach Neagley's hotel and only another ten to get back to Froelich's house. They opened the door and stepped inside.

Froelich paused in the doorway. 'Are we OK?' she asked. 'About earlier?'

'We're fine,' he said.

'I had other boyfriends,' she said. 'You know, after. And Joe had other girlfriends. He wasn't all that shy, really.'

'But he left his stuff here. Got to mean something.'

She was quiet for a second. 'I'm going to make tea,' she said. 'You want some?'

Reacher shook his head. 'I'm going to bed.' He walked upstairs.

Closed the guest room door behind him and undressed. Walked into the bathroom wearing only his boxers.

He took his time in there and when he came out Froelich was standing in the guest room doorway. Wearing a nightgown. It was white cotton. Longer than a T-shirt, but not a whole lot longer.

'Joe broke up with me,' she said. 'It was his choice, not mine.'

'Why?'

'He met somebody he preferred. His stuff is still here because I wouldn't let him come back to get it. I wouldn't let him in the door. I was hurt and angry with him.'

'Why are you telling me?'

'So you can start with a blank slate,' she said. 'How you react to me can be about you and me, not about you and me and Joe. He took himself out of the picture. It was his choice. So it's none of his business, even if he was still around.'

'But how blank is your slate?' he asked.

'He was a great guy,' she said. 'I loved him once. But you're not him. You're a separate person. I know that.'

'That's good,' he said. 'Because I'm not like him. Hardly at all. You need to be real clear about that from the start.'

'I'm clear about it,' she said. 'The start of what?'

'The start of whatever,' he said. 'But the end will turn out the same, you know. You need to be real clear about that, too. I'll leave, just like he did. I always do.'

She came closer. They were a yard apart.

'I'll take my chances,' she said. 'Nothing lasts for ever.'

She raised her arms above her head. Her nightgown slipped off very easily. Fell to the floor. They barely made it to the bed.

THEY GOT THREE hours' sleep and woke up at seven when her alarm started ringing in her own room. He was on his back and she was curled under his arm. He felt comfortable in that position and wanted to ignore the noise and stay put. But she struggled free and sat up in bed, dazed and sleepy.

'Good morning,' he said.

She smiled and yawned. 'Good morning to you too,' she said.

The alarm blared on through the wall. He pulled her down on top of him and kissed her.

'Got to get up,' she said. She heaved herself out of bed and ran through to shut the noise off. She came back, naked.

'Come back to bed,' he said.

'Can't,' she said. 'Got to go to work.'

She walked away to her own bathroom. He threw back the covers and stood up and walked to the guest bathroom and went for the full twenty-two-minute ablution sequence. Teeth, shave, hair, shower. He dressed in another of Joe's old suits. He paired it with another fresh shirt. Clean boxers, clean socks. A dark blue tie. Then he ruined the look by putting his new Atlantic City coat over the suit. He figured to be spending some time out in the cold today.

He met Froelich at the bottom of the stairs. She was in a feminine version of his own outfit, a black trouser suit with an open-necked white blouse. But her coat was better. It was grey wool, very formal.

'OK,' she said. Then she took a deep breath. Checked her watch. Reacher did the same thing. It was nearly a quarter to eight.

'Sixteen hours and sixteen minutes to go,' she said. 'Call Neagley and tell her we're on our way.'

He used her mobile as they walked back to her Suburban. The morning was damp and cold. But the Suburban's heater worked fast and the interior was warm and comfortable by the time Neagley climbed on board outside the hotel.

The traffic was bad and it was nearly nine o'clock before they arrived in Armstrong's Georgetown street. Froelich parked near the mouth of the tent. Froelich half turned to face Reacher and Neagley equally. 'Foot patrol?' she said.

'Why I wore my coat,' Reacher said.

'Four eyes are better than two,' Neagley said.

They got out together and left Froelich in the warmth of the car. The street side of the house was quiet and well covered so they walked north and turned right to get a view of the back. There were cop cars top and bottom of the alley. Nothing was happening. They walked on to the next street. There were cop cars there, too.

'Let's get breakfast,' Reacher said. They walked back to the cross street and found a doughnut shop. Bought coffee and crullers and perched on stools in front of a counter built inside the store window.

'So,' Neagley said. 'Ms Froelich collected the set.'

'You could tell?'

'Unmistakable.'

'Free will on my part,' Reacher said. 'You disapprove?'

'Hell no. She's a nice lady. But so am I. And you never come on to *me*. We've never even touched. You've never even shaken my hand.'

'Haven't I?' he said. 'Is that good or bad?'

'It's good,' she said. 'I don't like to be touched. I always figured you could sense it. And I always appreciated that.'

'That's the point. I like my interest to be welcome.' He ate a cruller. Finished his coffee. 'Let's go. Once round the block for form's sake.'

They walked as slowly as they could bear to in the cold. Nothing was happening. Everything was quiet. They turned corners and came up on Armstrong's street from the south. Froelich was out of her car, waving urgently. They hurried up the sidewalk to meet her.

'Change of plan,' she said. 'There was a problem on the Hill. He cut the CIA thing short and headed up there.'

They drove back to the office and waited the rest of the morning and most of the afternoon. Froelich received regular situation reports.

At four o'clock they drove over to Neagley's hotel, which was being used again for the contributor function, scheduled to start at seven.

'Ask for two forms of ID this time,' Neagley said. 'Driving licence and a credit card, maybe.'

'Don't worry,' Froelich said. 'I plan to.'

By 6.40 there were almost 700 guests in the hotel lobby. They formed a long, loose line from the street door to the coat check to the ballroom entrance. Reacher watched it all, leaning on a pillar near the elevators. He could see three agents through the glass on the street. Two were at the street door. Eight were roaming the lobby. Three were at the ballroom door.

Neagley was across the lobby on the second step of the mezzanine staircase. Her gaze moved back and forth across the sea of people. Reacher could see Froelich moving randomly. She looked good, full of authority. Time to time she would talk to one of her agents face to face. Other times she would talk to her wrist.

By seven o'clock most of the guests were in the ballroom. Froelich had sent her agents into the ballroom one by one as the lobby crowd thinned out. They joined the eight already in there. She wanted all sixteen prowling around by the time the action started. Plus the three on the personal detail, and three on the ballroom door, and two on the street door. Plus cops in the kitchen, cops in the loading bay, cops on all seventeen floors, cops on the street.

Neagley came down off the staircase and joined Froelich and Reacher by the pillar. 'Is he here yet?' she asked.

Froelich shook her head. 'He's arriving late and leaving early.' Then she stiffened and listened to her earpiece. She raised her wrist and spoke into the microphone. 'Copy, out,' she said. She was pale.

'What?' Reacher asked.

She ignored him. Spun round and called to the last remaining agent free in the lobby. Told him he was acting on-site team leader for the rest of the night. Spoke into her microphone and repeated that information to all the agents on the local net. Told them to double their vigilance.

'What?' Reacher asked again.

'Back to base,' Froelich said. 'Now. That was Stuyvesant. Seems like we've got a real big problem.'

SEVEN

She used the red strobes behind the Suburban's grille and barged through the traffic like it was life and death. Didn't talk at all. They made it back to the garage inside four minutes. They were in Stuyvesant's office less than two minutes after that. He was sitting motionless behind his immaculate desk. Slumped in his chair.

'What?' Reacher said.

Stuyvesant glanced up at him. 'Now I know. For sure. That this is an outside job. Without any possible doubt.'

'How?'

'You know what the homicide rate is, nationally? Almost twenty thousand every year. That's about fifty-five homicides every day. Want to hear about two of today's?'

'Who?' Froelich asked.

'Small sugar-beet farm in Minnesota,' Stuyvesant said. 'The farmer walks out his back gate this morning and gets shot in the head. For no apparent reason. Then this afternoon there's an accountant's office in a small strip mall outside Boulder, Colorado. The guy walks out of the rear entrance and gets killed with a machine gun in the service yard. Again, no apparent reason.'

'So?'

'The farmer's name was Bruce Armstrong. The accountant's was Brian Armstrong. Both of them were white men about Brook Armstrong's age, similar appearance.'

'Are they family? Are they related?'

'No,' Stuyvesant said. 'Not to each other, not to the VP. So, what are the odds? That two random men whose last name is Armstrong and whose first names both begin with BR are going to get sense-lessly killed the same day we're facing a serious threat against our guy? The answer is about a trillion to one.'

'The demonstration,' Reacher said.

'Yes,' Stuyvesant said. 'That was the demonstration. Cold-blooded murder. So I agree with you. These are not insiders having a joke.'

'How were you notified?' Reacher asked.

'FBI alerted us. They've got software that scans the NCIC reports. Armstrong is one of the names that they flag up.'

'We got any details from the scenes?' Neagley asked.

'Some,' Stuyvesant said. 'The first guy was a single shot to the head. Killed him instantly. The guy's wife didn't hear anything.'

'Where was she?'

'About twenty feet away in the kitchen. Doors and windows shut because of the weather. But you'd expect her to hear something.'

'How big was the hole in his head?' Reacher asked.

'Bigger than a .22. If that's what you're thinking.'

Reacher nodded. The only handgun inaudible from twenty feet would be a silenced .22. Anything bigger, you'd probably hear something, suppressor or no suppressor, windows or no windows.

'So it was a rifle,' he said.

'Trajectory looks like it. Medical examiner figures the bullet was travelling downwards. It went through his head high to low.'

'Hilly country?'

'All around,' Stuyvesant said.

'So it was either a very distant rifle or a silenced rifle. And I don't like either one. Distant rifle means somebody's a great shooter, silenced rifle means somebody owns a bunch of exotic weapons.'

'What about the second guy?' Neagley asked.

'It was less than eight hours later,' Stuyvesant said. 'But more than eight hundred miles away. So most likely the team split up for the day. First impression from the locals is the weapon was some kind of machine gun. But again, nobody heard anything.'

'A silenced machine gun?' Froelich said. 'Hell of a demonstration.'

'But what exactly does it demonstrate?' Reacher asked.

'That these are not very nice people.'

He nodded. 'But not much more than that, does it? It doesn't really demonstrate Armstrong's vulnerability as such, not if they weren't connected to him in any way. Are we *sure* they weren't related? Distant cousins or something?'

Stuyvesant shook his head. 'I double checked. First, the VP isn't from North Dakota originally. He moved in from Oregon. Plus, outside his wife, daughter and mother, he doesn't have any living relatives except an elder sister who lives in California. His wife has got a bunch of cousins but none of them are called Armstrong and most of them are younger. Kids, basically.'

'OK,' Reacher said. *Kids*. He had a flash in his mind of a seesaw, and stuffed toys and lurid paintings stuck to a refrigerator with magnets. *Cousins*. 'We need to rethink a couple of things. Information is stacking up fast and we're not processing it. Like, now we know these guys are outsiders. Now we know this is not a genteel inside game.'

'So?' Neagley asked.

'The cleaners. What do we know about them?'

'That they're scared. That they're not saying anything.'

'Correct,' Reacher said. 'But why? Way back we thought they might be playing some cute game with an insider. But they're not doing that. Because these guys aren't insiders. And they're not cute.'

'So?'

'So they're being coerced in some serious way.'

'OK, how?'

'How do you scare somebody without leaving a mark on them?'

'You threaten something. Serious harm in the future, maybe.'

Reacher nodded. 'To them, or to somebody they care about. Where have you heard the word *cousins* before?'

'The cleaners. Their kids are with cousins. They told us.'

'Maybe their kids *aren't* with cousins. Is there a better way to coerce somebody than taking their kids away as insurance?'

THEY MOVED FAST, but Stuyvesant made sure they moved properly. He called the cleaners' lawyers and told them he needed the name and address of the children's babysitters. The lawyers called back within a quarter of an hour. The name was Gálvez and the address was a house a mile from the cleaners' own.

Froelich got on the radio net and asked for a situation update from the hotel. There were no problems. Armstrong was working the room.

They squeezed into the elevator and rode down to the garage. Climbed into Froelich's Suburban. Froelich raced through traffic to the cheap part of town. They passed the cleaners' house. Threaded another mile through dark streets made narrow by parked cars and came to a stop outside a tall, thin family house.

'So what do we do?' Stuyvesant said.

Reacher looked through the window. 'We go talk with these

people. But we don't want to panic them. They might think the bad guys are back. So Neagley should go first.'

Stuyvesant was about to object but Neagley slid out of the car and headed for the gate. Reacher watched her glance left and right as she walked up the path. Nobody was around. She reached the door. Couldn't find a bell, so rapped on the wood with her knuckles.

There was a one-minute wait and then the door opened and was stopped short by a chain. Warm light flooded out. There was a one-minute conversation. The door eased forward to release the chain. Neagley turned and waved. Froelich and Stuyvesant and Reacher climbed out of the Suburban and walked up the path. A small, dark guy was standing in the doorway, waiting for them, smiling shyly.

'This is Mr Gálvez,' Neagley said. They introduced themselves and Gálvez backed into the hallway and made a *follow-me* gesture. He had a fresh haircut and an open expression. They followed him inside. The house was small and clearly overcrowded, but very clean. There were seven children's coats hung neatly on a row of pegs inside the door. Seven school backpacks and seven pairs of shoes lined up on the floor underneath them. Three women visible in the kitchen. Children peering out from behind their skirts. More easing their heads round the living-room door. They kept moving. Appearing and disappearing in random sequences. They all looked the same. Reacher couldn't get an accurate count.

He lifted one of the little coats off its peg. It had a white patch inside the collar. Somebody had used a laundry marker and written *J. Gálvez* on it in careful script. He put it back and checked the other six. Each was labelled with a surname and a single initial. Total of five *Gálvez* and two *Alvárez*.

Reacher caught Mr Gálvez's eye and nodded him through to the living room. Two children scuttled out as they stepped in.

'You got five kids?' Reacher asked.

Gálvez nodded. 'I'm a lucky man.'

'So who do the two Alvárez coats belong to?'

'My wife's cousin Julio's children.'

'I need to see them,' Reacher said.

'You just saw them. In the kitchen.'

'I need to see which ones they are exactly.'

Gálvez called out in Spanish and two children separated themselves from the group in the kitchen and trotted into the room. They stopped near the doorway, side by side. Two little girls, dark eyes, black hair, serious expressions. Maybe five and seven years old.

'Hey, kids,' Reacher said. 'Show me your coats.'

He followed them out to the hallway and watched as they stood up on tiptoe and touched the two little jackets he knew were marked *Alvárez*. 'OK,' he said. 'Now go get a cookie or something.'

They scuttled back to the kitchen. He stepped back to the living room. Got close to Gálvez and lowered his voice again.

'Anybody else been enquiring about them?' he asked.

Gálvez just shook his head.

'You sure?' Reacher asked. 'Nobody watching them, no strangers?'

Gálvez shook his head again.

'We can fix it,' Reacher said. 'If you're worried about anything, you should go ahead and tell us right now. We'll take care of it.'

Gálvez just looked blank. Reacher watched his eyes. He had spent his career watching eyes, and these two were innocent. A little disconcerted, a little puzzled, but the guy wasn't hiding anything.

'OK,' he said. 'We're sorry to have interrupted your evening.'

He kept very quiet on the drive back to the office.

THEY USED THE CONFERENCE ROOM again. Froelich got on the radio net and heard that Armstrong was about to leave the hotel. She listened to her earpiece and tracked him out of the ballroom, through the kitchens, into the loading bay, into the limo. Then she relaxed. She sat back and glanced at the others, questions in her eyes.

'Makes no sense to me,' Neagley said. 'It implies there's something they're *more* worried about than their children.'

'Which would be what?' Froelich asked.

'Green cards? Are they legal?'

Stuyvesant nodded. 'Of course they are. They're Secret Service employees. Background-checked from here to hell and back.'

Reacher let the talk drift into the background. He rubbed the back of his neck with the palm of his hand. The stubble from his haircut was growing out. It felt softer. He closed his eyes. Thought hard. Ran the surveillance video in his head all over again. Ran it again, forward and back. Concentrated on every frame. Then he opened his eyes. Everybody was staring at him like he had been ignoring their questions. He smiled. A wide, happy grin.

'I liked Mr Gálvez,' he said. 'He had just been to the barber, you notice that?'

'So?'

'And with the greatest possible respect, Neagley, I'm thinking about your ass.'

Froelich stared at him. Neagley blushed.

Reacher glanced across at Stuyvesant. 'Can I see your office again? Right now?'

Stuyvesant looked blank, but he stood up and led the way to his office. The door was closed. He pushed it open and hit the lights.

'Now,' Reacher said, 'is this how your office usually looks?'

Stuyvesant glanced around the room. 'Exactly,' he said.

'OK,' Reacher said. 'Let's go.'

They walked back to the conference room.

'Why did you want to see my office?' Stuyvesant asked.

'We're wrong about the cleaners,' Reacher said.

'In what way?' Neagley asked.

'In every way. What happened when we talked to them?'

'They stonewalled like crazy.'

'That's what I thought too. They went into some kind of a stoic silence. I interpreted that as a response to danger. But you know what? They just didn't have a clue what we were talking about. We were two crazy white people asking them impossible questions, is all. They were too polite to tell us to get lost. They just sat there patiently while we rambled on.'

'So what are you saying?'

'Think about what else we know. There's a weird sequence of facts on the tape. They look a little tired going into Stuyvesant's office, and a little less tired coming out. They look fairly neat going in, and a little dishevelled coming out. They spend fifteen minutes in there, and only nine in the secretarial area.'

'So?' Stuyvesant asked.

Reacher smiled. 'Your office is probably the world's cleanest room. You could do surgery in there. It's tidy to the point of obsession. And yet the cleaners spent fifteen minutes in there. Why?'

'They were unpacking the letter,' Stuyvesant said.

'No, they weren't. Think about the dishevelment,' he said. 'What exactly created that impression for us?'

Everybody shrugged.

Reacher smiled. 'Something else on the tape,' he said. 'Going in, the garbage bag is reasonably empty. Coming out, it's much fuller. So was there a lot of trash in the office?'

'No.' Stuyvesant sounded offended. 'I never leave trash in there.'

Froelich sat forward. 'So what was in the bag?'

'Trash,' Reacher said.

'I don't understand,' Froelich said.

'They worked thoroughly in the secretarial area and had it done in nine minutes,' Reacher said. 'That's a slightly bigger and more cluttered area. Fifteen minutes in the office is excessive. And we asked them, why so long in there? And what did they say?'

'They didn't answer,' Neagley said. 'Just looked puzzled.'

'Then we asked them whether they spent the same amount of time in there every night. And they said yes, they did. OK. We've boiled it down. Now tell me how they spent that time.'

Nobody spoke.

'Two possibilities,' Reacher said. 'Either they didn't, or they spent the time growing their hair.'

'What?' Froelich said.

'That's what makes them look dishevelled. Julio especially. His hair is a little longer coming out than going in.'

'How is that possible?'

'It's possible because we weren't looking at one night's activities. We were looking at two separate nights spliced together. Two halves of two different nights.'

Silence in the room.

'Two tapes,' Reacher said. 'The tape change at midnight is the key. The first tape has to be kosher, because early on it shows Stuyvesant and his secretary going home. That was the real Wednesday. The cleaners show up at 11.52. They look tired, maybe because that's the first night in their shift pattern. But it's been a routine night at work so far. They're on time. The garbage bag is reasonably empty. My guess is they had the office finished in about nine minutes. Which is probably their normal speed. Which is why they were puzzled when we claimed it was slow. My guess is in reality they came out at maybe one minute past midnight and spent another nine minutes on the secretarial station and left the area at ten past midnight. But after midnight we were looking at a different night altogether. Maybe from a couple of weeks ago, before the guy got his latest haircut. A night when they arrived in the area later, and therefore left the area later. Because of some earlier snafu in some other office. Maybe some big pile of trash that filled up their bag. They looked more energetic coming out because they were hurrying to catch up. And maybe it was a night in the middle of their work week and they'd adjusted to their pattern and slept properly. So we saw them go in on Wednesday and come out on a completely different night.'

'But the date was correct,' Froelich said. 'It was Thursday's date.'

Reacher nodded. 'Nendick planned it ahead of time.'

'Nendick?'

'Your tape guy,' Reacher said. 'My guess is for a whole week he had that particular camera's midnight-to-six tape set up to show that particular Thursday's date. Maybe two weeks. Because he needed three options. Either the cleaners would be in and out before midnight, or in before midnight and out after midnight, or in and out *after* midnight. He had to wait to match his options. If they'd been in and out before midnight, he'd have given you a matching tape showing nothing at all between midnight and six. If they'd been in and out after midnight, that's what you'd have seen. But the way it happened, he had to use one that showed them leaving only.'

'Nendick left the letter?' Stuyvesant asked.

Reacher nodded. 'Nendick is the insider. Not the cleaners. What that particular camera *really* recorded that night was the cleaners leaving just after midnight and then sometime before six in the morning Nendick himself stepping in through the fire door with gloves on and the letter in his hand. Probably around five thirty, I would guess, so he wouldn't have to wait long before trashing the real tape and choosing his substitute.'

'How did you spot it?' Stuyvesant asked. 'The hair?'

'Partly. It was Neagley's ass, really. Nendick was so nervous around the tapes he didn't pay attention to Neagley's ass. She noticed. She told me that's very unusual.'

Stuyvesant blushed, like maybe he was able to vouch for that fact personally.

'So we should let the cleaners go,' Reacher said. 'Then we should talk to Nendick. He's the one who's met with these guys.'

STUYVESANT USED his master key and entered the video recording room with the duty officer as a witness. They found that ten consecutive midnight-to-six tapes were missing prior to the Thursday in question. Nendick had entered them in a technical log as faulty recordings. Then they picked a dozen random tapes from the last three months and watched parts of them. They confirmed that the cleaners never spent more than nine minutes in his office. So Stuyvesant made a call and secured their immediate release.

Then there were three options: call Nendick in on a pretext, or send agents out to arrest him, or drive themselves over to his house and get some questioning started before the Sixth Amendment kicked in and began to complicate things.

'We should go right now,' Reacher said. 'Element of surprise.'

Stuyvesant booted up his secretary's computer and found Nendick's home address. It was in a suburb ten miles out in Virginia. It took twenty minutes to get there. The house was dark except for the blue flicker of a television set in one of the windows.

Froelich swung straight onto the driveway and parked in front of the garage. They climbed out and walked to the front door. Stuyvesant put his thumb on the bell. Thirty seconds later a porch light came on over their heads. The door opened and Nendick just stood in his hallway and said nothing. He looked slack with fear. Stuyvesant stepped inside. Froelich followed. Then Reacher. Then Neagley. She closed the door behind her and took up station in front of it like a sentry, feet apart, hands clasped easy in the small of her back.

Stuyvesant put a hand on Nendick's shoulder and turned him round. Pushed him towards the kitchen. He didn't resist. Just stumbled limply towards the back of his house. Stuyvesant followed him and hit a switch and fluorescent tubes sputtered to life.

'Sit,' he said, like he was talking to a dog.

Nendick sat on a stool at his breakfast bar. Said nothing. Just wrapped his arms around himself like a man chilled by fever.

'Names,' Stuyvesant said.

Nendick's hands started shaking, so he tucked them up under his arms to keep them still and began to rock back and forth on the stool. Reacher looked around the kitchen. It was a pretty room. There were yellow check drapes at the window. There were flowers in vases. They were all dead. There were dishes in the sink. A couple of weeks' worth. Some of them were crusted.

Reacher stepped back to the hallway. Into the living room. The television was tuned to a commercial network. There was a remote control on the arm of a chair opposite the screen. There was a low mantel above the fireplace with a row of photographs in brass frames. Nendick and a woman featured in all of them. There were no pictures of children. And this wasn't a house where children lived. There were no toys anywhere. No mess.

The remote on the arm of the chair was labelled VIDEO, not TV. Reacher glanced at the screen and pressed play. The video machine clicked and whirred and a second later the picture went black and was replaced by an amateur video of a wedding. Nendick and his wife smiled into the camera from several years in the past.

Reacher pressed stop and stepped back into the kitchen. Nendick was still shaking and rocking. He still wasn't saying anything.

'We can get her back for you,' Reacher said.

Nendick said nothing.

'Just tell us who, and we'll go get her right now.'

No reply.

'Sooner the better,' Reacher said. 'Thing like this, we don't want to have her wait any longer than she has to, do we?'

Nendick stared at the far wall. Neagley drifted into the half of the kitchen that was set up as a family room. There was a matching set of furniture grouped along one wall, bookcase, credenza, bookcase.

'We can help you,' Reacher said. 'But we need to know where to start.'

Nendick just stared and shook and hugged himself tight.

'Reacher,' Neagley called. Soft voice, with some kind of strain in it. He stepped away from Nendick and joined her at the credenza. She handed him an envelope. There was a Polaroid in it. The photograph showed a woman sitting on a chair. Her face was white and panicked, her eyes wide, her hair dirty. It was Nendick's wife, looking about a hundred years older than the pictures in the living room. She was holding up a copy of *USA Today*. The masthead was under her chin. Neagley passed him another envelope. Another Polaroid in it. Same woman. Same pose. Same paper, but a different day.

'Proofs of life,' Reacher said.

Neagley nodded. She passed him another envelope. A small padded brown mailer. There was a box in it. A tiny cardboard thing such as a jeweller might put a pair of earrings in. There was a pad of cotton wool in it. The cotton wool was browned with old blood, because lying on top of it was a fingertip. It had been clipped off at the first knuckle. There was still paint on the nail.

Reacher walked round and faced Nendick head on across the breakfast bar. Looked straight into his eyes. Gambled.

'Stuyvesant,' he called. 'And Froelich. Go wait in the hallway.'

They stood still for a second, surprised. He glared hard at them. They shuffled obediently out of the room.

'Neagley,' he called. 'Come over here with me.'

She walked round and stood quiet at his side. He leaned down and put his elbows on the counter. Put his face level with Nendick's.

'OK, they're gone,' he said softly. 'It's just us now. And we're not Secret Service. You know that, right? You never saw us before the other day. So you can trust us. We won't screw up like they will. We come from a place where they don't have rules. So we can get her back. We know how to do this. We'll get the bad guys and we'll bring her back. Safe. Without fail, OK? That's a promise. Me to you.'

Nendick leaned his head back and opened his mouth. His lips were flecked with sticky foam. Then he closed his mouth. Tight. Clamped his jaw hard. He brought one shaking hand out from under his arm and drew the thumb and forefinger sideways across his lips, slowly, like he was closing a zipper. He put his hand back under his arm. There was crazy fear in his eyes. He started coughing and choking. His mouth was clamped tight. He was shaking, clutching his sides, gulping desperately. His eyes were wild and staring. Then they rolled up inside his head and he pitched backwards off the stool.

EIGHT

They did what they could at the scene, but it was useless. Nendick just lay on the kitchen floor, not really conscious but not unconscious either. He was responsive to touch and light but nothing else. An hour later he was in a guarded room at the Walter Reed Army Medical Center with a tentative diagnosis of psychosis-induced catatonia.

'Paralysed with fear,' the doctor said. 'It's a genuine medical condition. The heart slows, the large blood vessels in the abdomen take blood away from the brain, most voluntary function shuts down.'

'What kind of threat could do that to a person?' Froelich asked.

'One that the person sincerely believes,' the doctor answered. 'My guess is his wife's kidnappers described to him what they would do to her if he talked. Then your arrival triggered a crisis, because he was afraid he *would* talk.'

'When can we talk to him?' Stuyvesant asked. 'It's very important.'

'Could be days,' the doctor said. 'Could be never.'

They left Nendick there and drove back to the office. Regrouped in the windowless conference room.

'FBI has got to be told,' Neagley said. 'This isn't just about Armstrong now. There's a kidnap victim in serious danger or dead. That's the Bureau's jurisdiction, no question. Plus the interstate homicide. That's their bag too.'

Stuyvesant sighed. 'Yes. They need to know. God knows I don't want to, but I'll hand everything over to them. Meanwhile we'll focus on Armstrong. That's all we can do.'

'Tomorrow is North Dakota again,' Froelich said. 'More open-air fun and games. Same place as before. We leave at ten.'

'And Thursday?'

'Thursday is Thanksgiving Day. He's serving turkey dinners in a homeless shelter here in DC. He'll be very exposed.'

'OK,' Stuyvesant said. 'Be back in here at seven tomorrow morning. I'm sure the Bureau will be delighted to send over a liaison guy.'

'I FEEL HELPLESS,' Froelich said. 'I want to be more proactive. We're not investigative enough.'

They were in her bed, in her room. It was larger than the guest room. Prettier. And quieter, because it was at the back of the house. The bed was warm. A cocoon of warmth in the cold city night.

'So try a few things,' he said.

'Like what?'

'We're back to the original evidence, with Nendick crapping out. So we have to start over. You should concentrate on the thumbprint.'

'It's not on file.'

'Widen the search. And check the thumbprint thing as an MO. Search the data bases to see if anybody ever signed threatening letters with their thumb before.'

SEEMED LIKE about a minute and a half later they were up again and showered and back in the Secret Service conference room eating doughnuts and drinking coffee with an FBI liaison agent named Bannon.

Bannon was a guy of about forty. He was in a tweed sports jacket and grey flannels and looked bluff and Irish and was tall and heavy. He had a red complexion that the winter morning hadn't helped. But he had supplied the doughnuts and the coffee. Two different stores, each chosen for its respective quality. Twenty bucks' worth of food and drink had broken a lot of interagency ice.

'No secrets either way,' he said. 'That's what we're proposing. And no blame anywhere. But no bullshit, either. We're guessing Nendick has met with these guys, and we're assuming they've been to his house, if only to grab his wife. So that's a crime scene, and we're going over it today. Nendick will help us if he ever wakes up. But assuming he won't any time soon, we'll go at it from three different directions. First, the message stuff that went down here in DC. Second, the scene in Minnesota. Third, the scene in Colorado.'

'Are your people in charge out there?' Froelich asked.

'Both places,' Bannon said. 'Our ballistics people figure the Colorado weapon for a Heckler & Koch submachine gun called the

MP5. Probably silenced. They're military and paramilitary weapons. Police and federal SWAT teams use them, people like that.'

'What about Minnesota?' Neagley asked.

'We found the bullet,' Bannon said. 'We swept the farmyard with a metal detector. It was buried in the mud. Consistent with a shot from a small wooded hillside about a hundred and twenty yards away.'

'What was the bullet?' Reacher asked.

'NATO 7.62 millimetre,' Bannon said.

Reacher nodded. 'You test it for burn?'

Bannon nodded. 'Low power, weak charge.'

'Subsonic ammunition,' Reacher said. 'In that calibre it has to be a Vaime Mk2 silenced sniper rifle.'

'Which is also a police and paramilitary weapon,' Bannon said. 'Often supplied to antiterrorist units, people like that.' He looked round the room. 'You know what? Put a list of who buys Heckler & Koch MP5s in America side to side with a list of who buys Vaime Mk2s, and you see only one official purchaser on both lists. The United States Secret Service.'

There was a knock at the door. The duty officer.

'Mail just arrived,' he said. 'Something you need to see.'

THEY LAID IT on the conference room table. It was a familiar brown envelope, gummed flap, metal closure. A computer-printed self-adhesive label addressed to Brook Armstrong at the Senate.

Bannon opened his briefcase and took out a pair of white cotton gloves. Pulled them on. 'Got these from the lab,' he said. 'We don't want to use latex. Don't want to confuse the talcum traces.'

He looked for something to open the envelope with. Reacher took his ceramic knife out of his pocket and snapped it open. Bannon took it, eased the blade under the flap, cut the paper. He handed the knife back, turned the envelope over and tipped something out.

It was a single sheet of letter-size paper. Five words, in the familiar Times New Roman bold typeface: **Did you like the demonstration?**

Bannon checked the postmark on the envelope. 'Vegas again. Saturday. They're confident, aren't they? They're asking if he liked the demonstration three days before they staged it.'

'We have to move out now,' Froelich said. 'Lift-off at ten. I want Reacher and Neagley with me. They know the ground.'

Stuyvesant raised his hand. A vague gesture. Either *OK* or *Whatever* or *Don't bother me*, Reacher couldn't tell.

'I want twice-daily meetings,' Bannon said. 'In here, seven every morning and maybe ten at night?'

'If we're in town,' Froelich said. She headed for the door. Reacher and Neagley followed her out of the room. Reacher caught her and nudged her elbow and steered her left instead of right, down the corridor towards her office.

'Do the data-base search,' he whispered.

She glanced at her watch. 'It's way too slow.'

'So start it now and let it compile all day.'

She turned and headed for the interior of the floor. Lit up her office and turned on her computer. The NCIC data base had a complex search protocol. She entered her password and clicked the cursor into the box and typed 'thumbprint + document + letter + signature'. She clicked on SEARCH and the hard disk chattered and the enquiry box disappeared from the screen. 'Let's go,' she said.

REACHER WENT TO SLEEP on the plane, and woke up on the descent into Bismarck. Froelich was talking to her agents, giving them their instructions. Reacher glanced out of the window and saw brilliant blue sky and no clouds.

'We're leaving the perimeter to the local cops,' Froelich was saying. 'We've got forty of them on duty, maybe more. Plus State troopers in cars. Our job is to stick close together. We'll be in and out quick.'

The plane put down gently and taxied over to a corner of the tarmac where a five-car motorcade waited. There was a State Police cruiser at each end and three identical stretched Town Cars sandwiched between. A small knot of ground crew standing by with a rolling staircase. Armstrong travelled with his detail in the centre limo. The back-up crew took the one behind it. Froelich and Reacher and Neagley took the one in front.

'You'll be freelancing,' Froelich said. 'Wherever you feel you need to be.'

There was a short, fast trip over smooth concrete roads and suddenly Reacher saw the familiar church tower in the distance, and the surrounding huddle of houses. There were cars parked solid along the side of the approach road all the way up to a State Police roadblock 100 yards from the community centre entrance. The motorcade eased past it and headed for the parking lot. There was a crowd already assembled. The church tower loomed over them.

'I hope this time they checked every inch of it,' Froelich said.

The five cars swept onto the gravel and crunched to a stop. The back-up agents were out first. They fanned out in front of Armstrong's car, checking faces in the crowd, waiting until Froelich heard the all-clear from the local police commander on her radio. She got it and instantly relayed it to the back-up leader. He acknowledged immediately and stepped to Armstrong's door and opened it.

Armstrong stepped out of his car, and stretched out his hand to greet his successor at the head of the reception line. His personal detail moved in close. The back-up agents got close, too, manoeuvring themselves so they kept the tallest two of the three between Armstrong and the church.

'That damn church,' Froelich said. 'It's like a shooting gallery.'

'We should go check it again,' Reacher said. 'Ourselves, just to be sure. Have him circulate counterclockwise until we do.'

'That takes him *nearer* the church.'

'He's safer nearer the church. Makes the downward angle too steep. There are wooden louvres up there round the bells. The field of fire starts about forty feet out from the base of the tower. Closer than that, he's in a blind spot.'

Froelich raised her wrist and spoke to her lead agent. Seconds later they saw him ease Armstrong to his right, into a wide counterclockwise loop round the field. The new senator tagged along.

'Now find the guy with the church keys,' Reacher said.

Froelich spoke to the local police captain. Listened to his response.

'The churchwarden will meet us there,' she said. 'Five minutes.'

They got out of the car and walked to the church gate.

Reacher turned to Neagley. 'Check the streets,' he said. 'All the access points we found before.'

Neagley nodded and moved out towards the entrance drive.

'You go,' Reacher said to Froelich. 'I'll check the church.'

She headed back towards the field. Reacher headed on towards the church. Waited at the door. It was a huge thing, carved oak, maybe four inches thick.

A minute later he saw the churchwarden approaching. He was a small man in a black cassock. He had a huge iron key in his hand. He held it out and Reacher took it from him.

'That's the original key,' the warden said. 'From 1870.'

'I'll bring it back to you,' Reacher said. 'Wait for me on the field.'

The guy turned and walked back the way he had come. Reacher stepped to the door and lined up the old key with the hole. Put it in the lock. Turned it hard. Nothing happened. He tried the handle.

The door was not locked.

It swung open six inches with a squeal from the hinges. He pushed it all the way open, then stepped quietly into the gloom inside.

He closed the door and locked it from the inside. Hid the key inside a wooden chest full of hymnals. Crept the length of the aisle and stood still and listened. He could hear nothing. He crept on and checked the three small rooms behind the altar. They were all empty except for piles of old books and church garments.

He crept back. Through the door into the base of the tower. There was a square area with three bell ropes hanging down in the centre. The sides of the square were defined by a steep narrow staircase that wound up into the gloom. He stood at the bottom and listened hard. Heard nothing. Eased himself up. After three consecutive right-angle turns the stairs ended on a ledge. Then there was a wooden ladder bolted to the inside of the tower wall. It ran up twenty feet to a trap door in the ceiling. The ceiling was boarded solid except for three precise nine-inch holes for the bell ropes. If anybody was up there, he could see and hear through the holes. Reacher knew that. He had heard the dogs pattering around below him, five days ago.

He took the ceramic knife out of his coat pocket and shrugged the coat and jacket off and left them piled on the ledge. Stepped onto the ladder. It creaked loudly under his weight. He eased up to the next rung. The ladder creaked again.

He paused. Opened the knife and held it between his teeth. Reached up and grasped the side rails of the ladder as far above his head as he could stretch. Catapulted himself upwards. He made the remaining eighteen feet in three or four seconds. At the top he kept one foot and one hand on the ladder and swung his body out into open space. Stabilised himself with his fingertips spread on the ceiling above. Felt for movement.

There was none. He reached out and poked the trap door up an inch and let it fall closed. Put his fingertips back on the ceiling. No movement up there. No tremor, no vibration. He waited thirty seconds. Still nothing. He swung back onto the ladder and pushed the trap door all the way open and swarmed up into the bell chamber.

He saw the bells, hanging mute in their cradles. Sunlight came through the louvres and threw bars of light across them. The rest of the chamber was empty. There was nothing up there. It looked exactly as he had left it five days ago.

Except it didn't.

The dust was disturbed. There were unexplained marks on the floor. Heels and toes, knees and elbows. They weren't his. He was sure of that. And there was a faint smell in the air, right at the edge of his consciousness. It was the smell of sweat and tension and gun oil and machined steel and new brass cartridge cases.

Sound came through the louvres, as well as sunlight. He could hear people clustered near the base of the tower seventy feet below. He stepped over to the louvres and squinted down. The fringe of the crowd was visible.

He saw movement in the corner of his eye. A hundred yards away across the field cops were running. They were gathering at a point near the back corner of the enclosure. They were glancing down at something and spinning away and hunching into their radio microphones. He saw Froelich forcing her way out through the crowd. She had her index finger pressed onto her earpiece. She was moving fast. Heading towards the cops.

He clambered down through the trap door. Slammed it shut above his head and climbed down the ladder. He picked up his coat and jacket and ran down the narrow winding stairs. Past the ends of the bell ropes and through to the main body of the church.

The oak door was standing wide open.

The lid of the hymnal box was up and the key was in the door lock from the inside. He stepped over and stood a yard inside the building. Waited. Listened. Sprinted out into the cold and stopped again six feet down the path. Spun round. There was nobody there. The area was deserted. He could hear noise far away on the field. He shrugged into his coat and headed towards it. Saw a man running towards him across the gravel, fast and urgent. He was wearing a long brown coat, some kind of heavy twill, halfway between a raincoat and an overcoat. It was flapping open behind him. Tweed jacket and flannel trousers under it. Stout shoes. He had his hand raised like a greeting. A gold badge palmed in the hand. Some kind of a Bismarck detective. Maybe the police captain himself.

'Is the tower secure?' he shouted from twenty feet away.

'It's empty,' Reacher shouted back. 'What's going on?'

The cop stopped where he was and bent over, panting, his hands on his knees. 'Don't know yet,' he called. 'Some big commotion.'

Then he stared beyond Reacher's shoulder at the church. 'Damn it, you should have locked the door,' he called. 'Can't leave the damn thing open.' He raced on towards the church.

Reacher ran the other way, to the field. Met Neagley running in from the entrance road.

'What?' she shouted.

'It's going down,' he shouted back.

They ran on together. Froelich was moving fast towards the cars. They changed direction and cut her off.

'Rifle hidden at the base of the fence,' she said.

'Someone's been in the church,' Reacher said. He was out of breath. 'In the tower. Probably still around someplace.'

Froelich raised her hand and spoke into the microphone on her wrist. 'Stand by to abort,' she said. 'Emergency extraction on my count of three. Stand by all vehicles. Main car and gun car to target on my count of three. One, two, three, abort now.'

There was a roar of engines from the motorcade and it split apart like a starburst. The lead cop car jumped forward and the rear cop car slewed back and the first two stretch limos turned and accelerated across the gravel and onto the field. At the same time the personal detail jumped all over Armstrong and buried him from view, then drove him forward through the crowd, which scattered in panic. The cars skidded to a stop and the personal detail pushed Armstrong straight into the first and the back-up crew piled into the second.

The lead cop had his lights and siren started already and was crawling forward down the exit road. The two loaded limos turned round on the field and headed back to the blacktop. They rolled up straight behind the cop car and then all three vehicles accelerated hard and headed out while the third stretch headed for Froelich.

'We can get these guys,' Reacher said to her. 'They're here.'

She didn't reply. Just grabbed him and Neagley and pulled them into the limo with her. It roared after the lead vehicles. The second cop fell in directly behind it, and just twenty short seconds after the initial abort command the whole motorcade was screaming away from the scene at seventy miles an hour with every siren blaring.

NINE

Froelich stood in the chill and spoke to Armstrong at the foot of the plane's steps. She told him about the discovery of the concealed rifle and told him it was more than enough to justify the extraction. He didn't argue. Didn't ask any awkward questions.

Reacher took a seat next to Froelich and across the aisle from Neagley. 'We should have stayed around,' he said.

'The place is swarming with cops,' Froelich said. 'FBI will join them. That's their job. We focus on Armstrong. And I don't like it any better than you do.'

'What was the rifle? Did you see it?'

She shook her head. 'We'll get a report. They said it was in a bag.'

'Hidden in the grass?'

She nodded. 'Where it's long at the base of the fence.'

'When was the church locked?'

'Last thing Sunday. More than sixty hours ago.'

'So I guess our guys picked the lock. It's a crude old mechanism.'

'You sure you didn't see them?'

Reacher shook his head. 'But they saw me. They were in there with me. They saw where I hid the key. They let themselves out.'

'I don't understand their plan. They were in the church and their rifle was a hundred yards away?'

'Wait until we know what the rifle was. Maybe we'll understand.'

THEY TOUCHED DOWN at Andrews at 6.30 local time. The motorcade drove to Georgetown. Armstrong was shepherded into his house through the white tent. Then the cars headed back to base.

Reacher and Neagley followed Froelich to her desk and she accessed her NCIC search results. There was a small rubric at the top of the screen that claimed the software had come up with 243,791 matches.

'We need to refine the parameters,' Neagley said. She squatted next to Froelich and moved the keyboard closer. Cleared the screen and called up the enquiry box and typed 'thumbprint-as-signature'. Reached for the mouse and clicked on SEARCH. The hard drive chattered and the enquiry box disappeared. The phone rang and Froelich picked it up. Listened for a moment and put it down.

'Stuyvesant's got the preliminary FBI report on the rifle,' she said. 'He wants us in the conference room.'

STUYVESANT WAS AT THE HEAD of the table with sheets of faxed paper spread out in front of him.

'What was the rifle?' Reacher asked.

Stuyvesant squared the paper in front of him. 'Your guess?'

'Something disposable,' Reacher said. 'Something they weren't actually planning on using. In my experience something that gets found that easily is supposed to get found that easily.'

Stuyvesant nodded. 'It was barely a rifle at all. It was an ancient .22 varmint gun.'

'Decoy,' Reacher said.

Stuyvesant nodded again. 'They imagined it would be spotted at the fence, the bulk of the police presence would move somewhat towards it, we would move Armstrong towards the motorcade, whereupon they would have a clear shot at him.'

'Sounds right to me. But I didn't actually see anybody in there.'

'Plenty of places to hide in a country church,' Stuyvesant said. 'Go eat dinner and be back here at ten for the FBI meeting.'

FIRST THEY WENT BACK to Froelich's office to check on Neagley's NCIC search. The rubric at the top of the screen said the search had lasted nine-hundredths of a second and come up with zero matches. Froelich called up the enquiry box again and typed 'thumbprint-on-letter'. Clicked on SEARCH. The screen redrew immediately and came up with no matches in eight-hundredths of a second.

'Getting nowhere even faster now,' she said.

'Let me have a go,' Reacher said. He typed 'a-short-letter-signed-with-a-big-thumbprint'. He clicked the mouse. The screen redrew instantly and reported that within seven-hundredths of a second the software had detected no matches.

'But it was a new speed record,' Reacher said. 'Let's go eat.'

'Wait,' Froelich said. 'Let me try again.' She typed a single word: 'thumb'. Hit SEARCH.

The enquiry box disappeared and the screen paused for a whole second and came back with a single entry.

A single short paragraph. It was a police report from Sacramento, California. An emergency room doctor from a city hospital had notified the local police department five weeks ago that he had treated a man who had severed his thumb in a carpentry accident. But the doctor was convinced by the nature of the wound that it had been deliberate albeit amateur surgery. The cops had followed up and the victim had assured them it had been an accident with a power saw. Case closed.

'Weird stuff in this system,' Froelich said.

'Let's go eat,' Reacher said again.

THEY DROVE OUT to Dupont Circle and ate at an Armenian restaurant. Reacher had lamb and Froelich and Neagley stuck to various chickpea concoctions. They had baklava for dessert and three small cups each of strong muddy coffee. They were about to order a fourth round when Froelich's cellphone rang. It was just after nine o'clock.

Froelich got the phone out and answered the call.

'OK,' she said, and closed the phone. Looked across at Reacher. 'Stuyvesant wants you back in the office, right now, immediately.'

STUYVESANT WAS WAITING for them behind the reception desk just inside the main door. A telephone had been dragged up out of position and was sitting on the counter.

'We got a call,' Stuyvesant said. 'Didn't get a name. Or a number. Caller ID was blocked. Male voice, no particular accent. He called the switchboard and asked to speak with the big guy. Something in the voice made the duty officer take it seriously, so he patched it through, thinking perhaps the big guy was me, you know, the boss. But it wasn't. The caller didn't want to speak with me. He wanted the big guy he's been seeing around recently.'

'Me?' Reacher said.

'You're the only big guy new on the scene.'

'Why would he want to speak with me?'

'We're about to find out. He's calling back at nine thirty.'

Reacher glanced at his watch. Twenty-two minutes past.

'It's them,' Froelich said. 'They saw you in the church.'

'That's my guess,' Stuyvesant said. 'This is our first real contact. We've got a recorder set up. We'll get a voice print. And we've got a trace on the line. You need to talk for as long as you can.'

Reacher nodded. 'Can we get a weather report for Chicago?'

'I could call Andrews,' Froelich said. 'But why?'

'Just do it, OK?'

She stepped away to use another line. The air force meteorological people took five minutes to tell her Chicago was cold but clear.

'Is the Thanksgiving thing on the web site?' Reacher asked.

'Yes,' Froelich said.

'What else is upcoming?' Reacher asked.

'Wall Street again in ten days,' Froelich said. 'That's all.'

The phone rang. Reacher glanced at his watch again. Nine twenty-nine. 'A little early,' he said. 'Somebody's anxious.'

'Talk as long as you can,' Stuyvesant said. 'Keep it going.'

Reacher picked up the phone. 'Hello,' he said.

'You won't get that lucky again,' a voice said.

Reacher ignored it and listened hard to the background sounds.

'Hey,' the voice said. 'I want to talk to you.'

'But I don't want to talk to you, asshole,' Reacher said, and put the phone down.

Stuyvesant and Froelich just stared at him.

'Hell are you doing?' Stuyvesant asked. 'I told you to talk as long as you could.'

'I wasn't feeling very talkative,' Reacher said.

'That was deliberate sabotage. We needed information.'

'Get real,' Reacher said. 'You were never going to get information.'

Stuyvesant was silent.

'I want a cup of coffee,' Reacher said. 'You dragged us out of the restaurant before we were finished.'

'We're staying here,' Stuyvesant said. 'They might call back.'

'They won't,' Reacher said.

They waited five minutes and then gave up and took plastic cups of coffee with them to the conference room. Reacher sat down alone at one end of the table. Neagley occupied neutral territory halfway down one side. Froelich and Stuyvesant sat together at the far end.

'Explain,' Stuyvesant said.

'These guys use faucet water to seal their envelopes,' Reacher said. 'So there's not one chance in a million they're going to make a traceable call to the main office of the United States Secret Service, for God's sake. *They* would have cut the call short. I didn't want to let them have the satisfaction. They need to know that if they're tangling with me then I take the upper hand, not them.'

'You blew it because you think you're in a pissing contest?'

'I didn't blow anything,' Reacher said. 'We got all the information we were ever going to get.'

'We got absolutely nothing.'

'No, you got a voice print. The guy said thirteen words. All the vowel sounds, most of the consonants. You got the sibilant characteristics, and some of the fricatives.'

'We needed to know where they were, you idiot.'

'They were at a payphone with caller ID blocked. Somewhere in the Midwest. Think about it. They were in Bismarck today with heavy weapons. Therefore they're driving. They're on a four-hundred-mile radius by now. They're somewhere in one of about six huge states, in a bar or a country store, using the payphone. And anybody smart enough to use faucet water to seal an envelope knows exactly how short to keep a phone call to make it untraceable.'

'You don't know they're driving.'

'No,' Reacher said. 'You're right. I don't know. There is a possibility that they were frustrated about today's outcome. And they know from the web site that there's another chance tomorrow, right here.

And then nothing much for a spell. So it's possible they ditched their weapons and aimed to fly in tonight. In which case they might be at O'Hare right now, waiting for a connection. It might have been worth while putting some cops in place to see who's using the payphones. But I only had eight minutes. You had a whole half-hour. You could have arranged something easily. In which case I would have talked their damn ears off, to let the cops get a good look around. But you didn't arrange anything. So don't tell me *I'm* the one who blew something here.'

'Why did you want the weather report?' asked Froelich.

'Because if the weather was bad the night before Thanksgiving in Chicago the airport would be so backed up they'd be sitting around there for hours. In which case I would have provoked some kind of call-back later, for after we got some cops in place. But the weather was OK. Therefore no delays, therefore no time.'

The room was quiet for a long moment.

'I apologise,' Stuyvesant said. 'You probably did the right thing.'

'Don't worry about it,' Reacher said. 'Million to one we were ever going to get a location. It was a snap decision, really. A gut thing. If they're puzzled about me, I want to keep them puzzled. Keep them guessing. And I wanted to make them mad at me. To take some focus off Armstrong. Better that they focus on me for a spell.'

'You want these people coming after you personally?'

'Better than have them coming after Armstrong personally.'

'Are you nuts? He's got the Secret Service round him. You haven't.'

Reacher smiled. 'I'm not too worried about them.'

There was a knock at the door. The duty officer put his head into the room. 'Special Agent Bannon is here,' he said. 'Ready for the evening meeting.'

STUYVESANT BRIEFED BANNON privately in his office about the telephone communications. They came back into the conference room together at ten past ten. Bannon was carrying a thin file folder.

'Nendick is still unresponsive,' he said, sitting heavily in the chair opposite Neagley's. He opened his file folder and took out a thin stack of colour photographs. Dealt them like cards around the table. Two each. 'Bruce Armstrong and Brian Armstrong. Late of Minnesota and Colorado, respectively.'

The photographs were inkjet prints on glossy paper. The originals must have been snapshots borrowed from the families, scanned and emailed, then blown up and cropped to a head-and-shoulders format. Neither of them looked much like Brook Armstrong. But they were three American men with fair hair and blue eyes, somewhere in their middle forties. Therefore, they *were* alike.

'What do you think?' Bannon asked.

'Close enough to make the point,' Reacher said.

'You got anything else for us?' Stuyvesant asked.

'We canvassed Nendick's neighbours. They didn't get many visitors. Seems like they socialised as a couple, mostly in a bar about ten miles from their place, out towards Dulles. It's a cop bar. Seems like Nendick trades on his employment status. We're trying to trace anybody he was seen talking to more than the average.'

'What about when the wife got taken away?' Stuyvesant said. 'Must have been some kind of commotion.'

Bannon shook his head. 'Nobody remembers anything. It could have happened at night, of course.'

Stuyvesant paused a second. 'Anything else?' he said.

'We'll talk about it tomorrow morning,' Bannon said. 'We're working on a theory right now.'

FROELICH DROPPED NEAGLEY at the hotel and then drove Reacher home with her. They reached her house. She unlocked the door. They stepped inside. There was a sheet of paper lying on the hallway floor.

It was the familiar letter-size sheet. It was lying precisely aligned with the oak flooring strips. It was in the geometric centre of the hallway, near the bottom of the stairs. It had a simple statement printed neatly on it, in the familiar Times New Roman bold script: **It's going to happen soon.**

Reacher ducked his head back out of the door and checked the street. All the nearby cars were empty. No pedestrians. No loiterers in the dark. He came back inside and closed the door.

'How did they get it in here?' Froelich said.

'Through the door,' Reacher said. 'Probably at the back.'

Froelich pulled her SIG-Sauer from her holster and they walked through the living room and into the kitchen. The door to the back yard was closed, but it was unlocked. Reacher opened it a foot. Scanned the outside surroundings and saw nothing at all. Eased the door back wide so the inside light fell onto the exterior surface. Leaned close and looked at the scratch plate around the keyhole.

'Marks,' he said. 'Very small. They were pretty good.'

'They're here in DC,' she said. 'Right now. They're not in some Midwest bar.' She moved away from the rear door and stopped at the kitchen counter. Snatched open a drawer. 'They took my gun. I had a back-up gun in here.' She opened the drawer next to it. 'The magazines are gone too. I had ammo in here.' Then she stiffened. 'They might still be in the house,' she said, quietly.

'I'll check,' he said.

She handed him her pistol. He turned out the kitchen light so he wouldn't be silhouetted on the basement stairs and walked slowly down. Listened hard past the creaks and sighs of the house, and the hum and trickle of the heating system. Stood still in the dark and let his eyes adjust. There was nobody there. Nobody upstairs, either. Nobody hiding and waiting. The house was empty and undisturbed, apart from the missing Beretta and the message on the hallway floor. He came back to the kitchen and held out the SIG, butt first.

'Secure,' he said.

'I better make some calls,' she said.

SPECIAL AGENT BANNON showed up forty minutes later in a Bureau sedan with three members of his task force. Stuyvesant arrived five minutes after them in a department Suburban.

'How long have you been out?' Bannon asked Froelich.

'All day. We left at six thirty this morning to meet with you.'

'We?'

'Reacher's staying here,' she said.

'Not any more, he's not,' Bannon said. 'Neither of you is staying here. It's too dangerous. We're putting you in a secure location. Besides, we need to work here. This is a crime scene. We'll have to rip it up some. Better that you stay away until we put it back together.'

'This is my house,' Froelich said.

'Don't argue,' Stuyvesant said. 'I want you protected. We'll put you in a motel. Couple of US Marshals outside the door, until this is over.'

'Neagley, too,' Reacher said.

'Don't worry,' Stuyvesant said. 'I've already sent somebody to pick her up.'

REACHER TOOK HIS THINGS from the guest bathroom and his garbage bag of Atlantic City clothes and all of Joe's suits and shirts that were still clean. He stuffed clean socks and underwear into the pockets. Carried the clothes down the stairs and stepped out into the night air. He loaded them into the Suburban's trunk and then climbed into the back seat. Froelich came out of her house carrying a small valise. Stuyvesant stowed it and they climbed into the front together.

They drove to a Georgetown motel about ten blocks shy of Armstrong's street. There was a Town Car parked outside, with a driver in it. The motel itself was hemmed in by embassies with fenced grounds. It was a very protected location. Only one way in, and a marshal in the lobby would take care of that. An extra marshal in the corridor would be icing on the cake.

Stuyvesant had booked three rooms. Neagley had already arrived. They found her in the lobby, talking to one of the US Marshals.

Stuyvesant did the paperwork at the desk and came back with three key cards. Handed them round. Mentioned three room numbers. They were sequential. Then he scrabbled in his pocket and came out with the Suburban's keys. Gave them to Froelich.

'I'll ride back with the guy who brought Neagley over,' he said. 'I'll see you all tomorrow, seven o'clock in the office, with Bannon.'

Then he turned and left. Neagley went looking for her room. Froelich and Reacher followed behind her. There was another marshal at the head of the bedroom corridor, sitting on a chair. Reacher squeezed his untidy luggage past him and stopped at his door. Froelich was already two rooms down, not looking in his direction.

He went inside and found a compact version of what he had seen a thousand times before. One bed, one chair, a table, a telephone, a TV. He stowed his baggage and arranged his bathroom articles on the shelf above the sink. Checked his watch. Past midnight. He took off Joe's jacket and dropped it on the table. Loosened his tie and yawned. There was a knock at the door. He opened up and found Froelich standing there.

'Come in,' he said.

THEY GOT A WAKE-UP CALL from the motel desk at six o'clock in the morning. *Stuyvesant must have arranged it last night*, Reacher thought. *I wish he'd forgotten.* Froelich stirred at his side. Then her eyes snapped open and she sat up, wide awake.

'Happy Thanksgiving,' he said.

She pushed back the covers. 'Dress casual,' she said. 'Suits don't look right on a holiday at a soup kitchen.'

She put her suit back on and left. He padded over to the closet and pulled out the bag full of Atlantic City clothes. He spilled them on the bed and did his best to flatten out the wrinkles. Then he showered without shaving.

He found Neagley in the lobby. She was wearing her jeans and sweatshirt with a battered leather jackett. There was a buffet table with coffee and muffins. The US Marshals had already eaten most of them.

He took a cup and filled it with coffee. Selected a raisin muffin. Then Froelich showed up, newly showered and wearing black denim jeans with a black polo shirt and a black nylon jacket. They ate and drank what the marshals had left and then walked out together to Stuyvesant's Suburban. It was cold, but the air was still and the sky was blue. The roads were empty. It took no time to reach the office. Stuyvesant was waiting for them in the conference room. His interpretation of casual was a pair of pressed grey slacks and a pink sweater under a bright blue golf jacket. Bannon was sitting opposite Stuyvesant. He was in the same tweed and flannel. He looked like a guy without too many options in his closet.

'Let's get to it,' Stuyvesant said. 'We've got a big agenda.'

'First item,' Bannon said. 'The FBI formally advises cancellation today. We know the bad guys are in the city and therefore it's reasonable to assume there may be some kind of imminent hostile attempt.'

'Out of the question,' Stuyvesant said. 'Free turkey at a homeless shelter might sound trivial, but this is a town that runs on symbols. If Armstrong pulled out the political damage would be catastrophic.'

'OK, then we're going to be there on the ground with you,' Bannon said. 'Not to duplicate your role. We'll stay strictly out of your way on all matters that concern Armstrong's personal security. But if something does go down, the closer we are the luckier we'll get.'

'I'm changing the plan,' Froelich said. 'I'm moving the event outdoors.'

'*Out*doors?' Bannon said. 'Isn't that worse?'

'No,' Froelich said. 'On balance, it's better. It's a long, low room. Kitchen at the back. It's going to get very crowded. We've got no realistic chance of using metal detectors on the doors. It's the end of November, and most of these people are going to be wearing five layers and carrying God knows what kind of metal stuff. We can't search them. It would take for ever. So we have to concede there's a fair chance that the bad guys could mingle in and get close, and we have to concede we've got no real way of stopping them.'

'So how does it help to be outdoors?'

'There's a side yard. We'll put the serving tables in a long line at right angles to the wall of the building. Pass stuff out through the kitchen window. Behind the serving table is the wall of the yard. We'll put Armstrong and his wife and four agents in a line behind the serving table, backs to the wall. We'll have the guests approach from the left, single file through a screen of more agents. They'll get their food and walk on inside to sit down and eat it.'

'Upside?' Stuyvesant asked.

'Extensive,' Froelich said. 'Much better crowd security. Nobody can pull a weapon before they get near Armstrong, because they're filtering through an agent screen the whole time until they're right across the table from him. Whereupon if they wait to do it at that point, he's got four agents right alongside him.'

'Downside?'

'Limited. We'll be screened on three sides by walls. But the yard is open at the front. There's a block of five-storey buildings directly across the street. Old warehousing. The windows are boarded, which is a bonus. But we'll need to put an agent on every roof.'

'Is this basically a conventional plan?' Bannon asked. 'Like normal Secret Service thinking?'

Froelich shrugged. 'Why are you asking?'

'Because we've done a lot of thinking,' Bannon said.

'And?' Stuyvesant said.

'We're looking at four specific factors here. First, what's the purpose behind the messages?'

'They're threats,' Froelich said.

'Who are they threatening?'

'Armstrong, of course.'

'Are they? Some were addressed to you, and some were addressed to him. But does he know anything about them?'

'We never tell our protectees. That's policy, always has been.'

'So Armstrong's not sweating, is he? Who's sweating?'

'We are.'

'So are the messages *really* aimed at Armstrong, or are they really aimed at the United States Secret Service?'

Froelich said nothing.

'OK,' Bannon said. 'Now think about Minnesota and Colorado. Hell of a demonstration. Not easy to stage. Whoever you are, shooting people down takes nerve and skill and care and preparation. Not something you undertake lightly. But they undertook it, because they had some kind of point to make. Then what did they do? How did they tip you off? How did they tell you where to look?'

'They didn't.'

'Exactly,' Bannon said. 'They went to all that trouble, took all that risk, and then they just sat back and waited. And sure enough, the NCIC reports were filed by the local police departments, and the FBI computers scanned through NCIC and spotted the word *Armstrong* like they're programmed to do, and we called you with the good news. How many Joe Publics would know all that would happen?'

'So what are you saying? Who are they?'

'What weapons did they use?'

'An H&K MP5 and a Vaime Mk2,' Reacher said.

'Fairly esoteric weapons,' Bannon said. 'And not legally available for sale to the public, because they're silenced. Only government agencies buy them. And only one government agency buys both.'

'Us,' Stuyvesant said, quietly.

'Yes, you,' Bannon said. 'And finally, I looked for Ms Froelich's name in the phone book. And you know what? She's unlisted. So how did these guys know where to deliver the last message?'

'They know me,' Froelich said, quietly.

Bannon nodded. 'I'm sorry, folks, but as of now the FBI is looking for Secret Service people. Not current employees, because current employees would have been aware of the early arrival of the demonstration threat and would have acted a day sooner. So we're focusing on recent ex-employees who still know the ropes. People who knew Ms Froelich. People who knew Nendick, too, and where to find him. Maybe people who left under a cloud and are carrying some kind of grudge. Against the Secret Service, not against Brook Armstrong. Because our theory is that Armstrong is a means, not an end. They'll waste a vice president-elect just to get at you, exactly like they wasted the other two Armstrongs.'

'What about the thumbprint?' Stuyvesant said. 'All our people are printed. Always have been.'

'Our assumption is that we're talking about two guys. Our assessment is that the thumbprint guy is an unknown associate of somebody who used to work here, who is the latex gloves guy. We're not suggesting you've got two renegades.'

'Just one renegade.'

'I'm sorry,' Bannon said. 'Nobody likes to hear their problem is close to home. But it's the only conclusion there is. And it's not good news for days like today. These people are here in town and they know exactly what you're thinking and exactly what you're doing.'

He stood up and left the room.

'Reacher?' Stuyvesant said.

'I'm glad they're pursuing it,' Reacher said. 'Because we need to eliminate all possibilities. If they're right, they'll take care of it for us. So it's one less thing for us to worry about. But I'm pretty sure neither of these guys ever worked here.'

'So who are they?' Froelich asked.

'I think they're both outsiders. I think they're between two and ten years older than Armstrong, both brought up and educated in rural areas where the schools were decent but the taxes were low.'

'What?'

'Think of everything we know, everything we've seen. Then think of the very smallest part of it. The very tiniest component.'

'Tell us,' Froelich said.

Stuyvesant checked his watch. Shook his head. 'Not now,' he said. 'We need to move. You can tell us later. But you're sure?'

'They're both outsiders,' Reacher said. 'Guaranteed.'

TEN

The first Secret Service agents to arrive at the shelter were the line-of-sight team. They had a city surveyor's map and a telescopic sight from a sniper rifle. One agent walked through every step Armstrong was scheduled to take. Every separate pace he would stop and turn around and squint through the scope and call out every window and rooftop he could see. Because if he could see a rooftop or a window, a marksman on that rooftop or in that window could see him. The agent with the map would identify the building concerned and calculate the range. Anything under 700 feet he marked in black.

But it was a good location. The only available sniper nests were on the roofs of the abandoned five-storey warehouses opposite. The guy with the map finished up with a straight line of just five black crosses, nothing more.

Next on scene was a convoy of police vans with five canine units. One unit cleared the shelter. Two more entered the warehouses. The last two were explosives hunters who checked the surrounding streets in all directions on a 400-yard radius. As soon as a building or street was pronounced safe a DC patrolman took up station on foot.

By nine thirty the shelter was the epicentre of a quarter of a square mile of secure territory. DC cops held the perimeter on foot and in cars and there were better than fifty more loose in the interior.

Froelich arrived at ten o'clock, driving a Suburban with Reacher and Neagley riding with her. Stuyvesant was right behind in a second Suburban. Behind him were four more trucks carrying five department sharpshooters and fifteen general-duty agents.

Froelich assembled her people in the shelter's yard and sent the sharpshooters to secure the warehouse roofs. Stuyvesant asked Reacher to go up there with them and check them out.

So Reacher walked across the street with an agent called Crosetti and they ducked past a cop into a damp hallway full of trash and rat droppings. There were stairs winding up through a central shaft. Crosetti was in a Kevlar vest and was carrying a rifle in a hard case.

The stairs came out inside a rooftop hutch. A wooden door opened outwards into the sunlight. The roof was flat, lipped with a low wall. Crosetti walked to the left edge, and then the right. Made visual contact with his colleagues either side. Then he walked to the front to check the view. Reacher was already there.

The shelter's yard was right there underneath them. The back wall where Armstrong would be standing was dead ahead. It was made out of old brick and looked like the execution wall in some foreign prison. Hitting him would be easier than shooting a fish in a barrel.

'What's the range?' Reacher asked. 'Ninety yards?'

Crosetti unsnapped a pocket in his vest and took out a range finder. 'Laser,' he said. He switched it on and lined it up. 'Ninety-two to the wall. Pretty good guess.'

'Practically like standing right next to him,' Reacher said.

'Don't worry,' Crosetti said. 'As long as I'm up here nobody else can be. That's the job today. We're sentries, not shooters.'

'Where are you going to be?' Reacher asked.

Crosetti glanced round and pointed. 'Over there, I guess,' he said. 'Tight in the far corner. I'll face parallel with the front wall. Slight turn to my left and I'm covering the yard. Slight turn to my right, I'm covering the head of the stairwell.'

'Good plan,' Reacher said. 'I'll leave you to it.'

He went back down to the yard. Near the building staff and agents were hauling long trestle tables into place. The idea was to form a barrier with them. The right-hand end would be hard against the shelter's wall. The left-hand end would be three feet from the yard wall opposite. There would be a pen six feet deep behind the line of tables. Armstrong and his wife would be in the pen with four agents.

Froelich walked out of the shelter towards Reacher. 'We're doing fine here,' she said. 'So I want you to take a stroll. Neagley's already out there. You know what to look for.'

He turned and walked back out to the street.

REACHER AND NEAGLEY arrived back at the shelter at noon exactly. Inside the yard everything was ready. The serving tables were lined up. Froelich was detailing positions for the general-duty agents.

'OK, listen up,' Froelich called. 'Remember, it's very easy to look a little like a homeless person, but very hard to look *exactly* like a homeless person. I'm going to be serving behind the tables with the Armstrongs and the personal detail. We're depending on you not to send us anybody you don't like, OK?'

Reacher squeezed through at the left-hand end of the serving tables and stood in the pen. Behind him was a wall. To his right was a wall. To his left was the shelter. Ahead to his right was the approach line. Any individual would pass four agents at the yard entrance and six more as he shuffled along. Ten suspicious pairs of eyes before anybody got face to face with Armstrong himself. Ahead to the left was the exit line. Three agents funnelling people into the hall. He raised his eyes. Dead ahead were the warehouses. Five sentries on five roofs. Crosetti waved. He waved back.

'OK?' Froelich asked. She was standing across the serving table from him. 'I want you and Neagley freelance in the yard.'

'OK,' he said.

WITH FIFTEEN MINUTES to go the cooks passed pans of food out through the kitchen window. Reacher leaned on the shelter wall at the end of the line of serving tables, on the public side. He would be looking at the approach line. A half-turn to his right, he would be looking into the pen. People would have to skirt round him with their loaded plates. He wanted a close-up view. Neagley stood six feet away, in the body of the yard.

Reacher couldn't see because of the brick walls but he heard the motorcade. A Metro cruiser pulled past the entrance, then a Suburban, then a Cadillac limo that stopped square in the gateway. An agent stepped forward and opened the door. Armstrong stepped out and turned back and offered his hand to his wife. Cameramen pressed forward. The Armstrongs stood up straight together and paused a moment by the limo's door and smiled for the lenses. Mrs Armstrong was a tall blonde woman whose genes had come all the way from Scandinavia a couple of hundred years ago. She was wearing pressed jeans and a puffed-up goose-down jacket.

Armstrong was in jeans too, with a red plaid jacket buttoned tight. His personal detail surrounded them and eased them into the yard.

Froelich led them into the pen behind the serving tables. One agent took each end and stood with arms folded. The third agent and Froelich and the Armstrongs took the middle to do the serving, with the third agent on the left, then Armstrong, then Froelich, then Armstrong's wife. Armstrong picked up a spoon. Checked the cameras were on him and raised it high.

'Happy Thanksgiving, everybody,' he called.

The crowd swarmed slowly through the gateway. They were a subdued bunch. Most of them were swaddled in several heavy layers. Each had to pass the six screening agents. The first recipient looped past the last agent and took a plastic plate from the first server and was subjected to the brilliance of Armstrong's smile. Armstrong spooned a turkey leg onto the plate. The guy shuffled along and Froelich gave him vegetables. Armstrong's wife added the stuffing. Then the guy shuffled past Reacher and headed inside for the tables.

It continued like that. Armstrong was smiling. The line of homeless people shuffled forward.

The line was still thirty people long when it happened.

Reacher sensed a dull chalky impact nearby and then something stung him on the right cheek. In the corner of his eye he saw a puff of dust around a small crater on the surface of the back wall. No sound. No sound at all. A split second later his brain told him: *Bullet. Silencer*. He looked at the line. Nobody moving. He snapped his head left and up. *The roof.* Crosetti wasn't there. Crosetti *was* there. He was twenty feet out of position. He was shooting. *It wasn't Crosetti.*

Then he tried to defeat time and move faster than the awful slow motion of panic would allow. He pushed off the wall and turned towards Froelich as slowly as a man running through a swimming pool. His mouth opened and desperate words formed in his throat and he tried to shout them. But she was already well ahead of him.

She was screaming, '*G-u-u-n!*'

She was jumping sideways at Armstrong. She drew her knees up and landed square on his upper chest. Breath punched out of him and his legs buckled and he was going down when the second silenced bullet hit her in the neck. There was no sound. Just a spray of blood in the sunlight, as fine as autumn mist.

She went down. Reacher turned and saw the slope of a shoulder on the roof, moving backwards out of sight.

Then time restarted and a hundred things happened at once, all at high speed, all with shattering noise. Agents hauled Armstrong's wife to the ground. Agents pulled their guns and started firing at the warehouse roof. There was shouting and wailing from the crowd. People were stampeding. Reacher fought his way through the wreckage to Froelich. Agents were dragging Armstrong out from underneath her. Auto engines were revving. Tyres were squealing. Sirens were yelping. Armstrong disappeared off the floor and Reacher fell to his knees in a lake of blood next to Froelich and cradled her head in his arms. She was completely limp and still, but her eyes were wide open. They were moving slowly from side to side.

'Is he OK?' she whispered. Her voice was very quiet.

'Secure,' Reacher said.

He slid a hand under her neck. He could feel blood. It was pulsing out. More than pulsing. It was like a warm hard jet, driven by her blood pressure. It forced its way out between his clamped fingers.

'Medics,' he called.

Nobody heard him. There was too much noise.

'Tell me it wasn't one of us,' Froelich whispered.

He flattened his hand hard against the back of her neck. The flow of blood loosened his grip, like it was hosing his hand away. His hand was slipping and floating on the tide.

'Medics,' he called again, louder.

But he knew it was useless. Her heart was doing its job, thumping away valiantly, pumping her precious blood straight out onto the concrete around his legs.

She looked up at him. 'Remember?' she whispered. 'How we met?'

'I remember,' he said.

She smiled. She was very pale now. The blood was frothing and foaming at her neck. Her lips were white. Turning blue.

'I love you, Joe,' she whispered. Then she smiled, peacefully.

'I love you too,' he said.

He held her for long moments more until she bled out and died in his arms about the same time Stuyvesant gave the cease-firing order. There was sudden silence. The coppery smell of hot blood and the acid stink of gunsmoke hung in the air. Reacher looked up and saw a cameraman shouldering his way towards him with his lens tilting down like a cannon. Saw Neagley stepping into his path. Saw the cameraman pushing her. She didn't seem to move a muscle but suddenly the cameraman was falling. He saw Neagley catch the camera and heave it straight over the execution wall. He heard it crash to the ground. He heard an ambulance siren starting up in the distance. He saw Stuyvesant's pressed grey slacks next to his face.

Stuyvesant stood there until they heard the ambulance in the yard. Reacher waited until the paramedics got very close. Then he laid

Froelich's head gently on the concrete. Stood up, sick and cramped and unsteady. Stuyvesant caught his elbow and walked him away.

'I didn't even know her name,' Reacher said.

'It was Mary Ellen,' Stuyvesant told him.

The paramedics fussed around for a moment. Then they went quiet and covered her with a sheet. Left her there for the medical examiners and the crime scene investigators. Reacher sat down, with his back to the wall. His clothes were soaked with blood. Neagley sat down next to him. Stuyvesant squatted in front of them.

'What's happening?' Reacher asked.

'They're locking the city down,' Stuyvesant said. 'Roads, trains, the airports. Bannon's got all his people out, and Metro cops, US Marshals, cops from Virginia, State troopers. Plus our people.'

'Was Armstrong OK?'

'Completely unharmed. Froelich did her duty.'

There was a long silence. Reacher looked up.

'What happened on the roof?' he asked. 'Where was Crosetti?'

'Crosetti was decoyed somehow,' Stuyvesant said. 'He's in the stairwell. He's dead too. Shot in the head.'

'Where was Crosetti from?' Reacher asked.

'New York, I think. Maybe Jersey. Somewhere up there.'

'That's no good. Where was Froelich from?'

'She was a Wyoming girl,' Stuyvesant said.

Reacher nodded. 'That'll do,' he said. 'Where's Armstrong now?'

'The White House,' Stuyvesant said. 'In a secure room.'

'I need to go talk to him. Right now.'

'You can't.'

Reacher looked away, beyond the fallen tables. 'So try to stop me.'

Stuyvesant was quiet for a long moment. 'Let me call him first,' he said. He stood up awkwardly and walked away.

'You OK?' Neagley asked.

'Did you see the shooter?'

Neagley shook her head. 'I was facing front. Did you?'

'A glimpse,' Reacher said. 'One man.'

'Hell of a thing,' Neagley said. 'So what now?'

He shrugged. 'You should go home to Chicago.'

'You?'

'I held her while she bled to death. I'm not going to walk away.'

'Then I'll stick around, too.'

'I'll be OK on my own.'

'I know you will,' Neagley said. 'But you'll be better with me.'

Reacher nodded. He saw Stuyvesant picking his way back through the yard. Hauled himself upright with both hands against the wall.

'Armstrong will see us,' Stuyvesant said. 'You want to change?'

Reacher looked down at his clothes. They were soaked with Froelich's blood. 'No,' he said. 'I don't want to change.'

ELEVEN

There was a double ring of hasty police roadblocks on every thoroughfare around the White House. Stuyvesant kept his strobes going and was waved through all of them. He showed his ID at the White House vehicle gate and parked outside the West Wing. A marine sentry passed them to a Secret Service escort who led them inside. They went down two flights of stairs to a vaulted basement. There were rooms down there with steel doors. The escort stopped in front of one of them and knocked.

The door was opened from the inside by one of Armstrong's personal detail. Armstrong and his wife were sitting together on chairs at a table in the centre of the room. The other two agents were leaning against the walls.

'What's the situation?' Armstrong asked.

'Two casualties,' Stuyvesant said quietly. 'The sentry on the warehouse roof, and M.E. herself. They both died at the scene.'

'Did you get the people who did it?' Armstrong asked.

'The FBI is leading the hunt. Just a matter of time.'

'I want to help,' Armstrong said.

'You're going to help,' Reacher said.

Armstrong nodded. 'What can I do?'

'You can issue a formal statement,' Reacher said. 'Immediately. In time for the networks to get it on the evening news, saying you're cancelling your holiday weekend in North Dakota out of respect for the two dead agents. Saying you're going absolutely nowhere before you attend a memorial service for your lead agent in her home town in Wyoming on Sunday morning. Find out the name of the town and mention it loud and clear.'

'OK,' Armstrong said. 'I could do that, I guess. But why?'

'Because they won't try again here in DC. Not against the security you're going to have at your house. So they'll go home and wait.

Which gives me until Sunday to find out where they live.'

'You? Won't the FBI find them today?'

'If they do, that's great. I can move on.'

'And if they don't *and* if you fail?'

'Then they'll show up in Wyoming to try again. At Froelich's service. Whereupon I'll be waiting for them.'

'No,' Stuyvesant said. 'We can't secure a situation out west on seventy-two hours' notice. And I can't use a protectee as *bait*.'

'He doesn't have to actually go,' Reacher said. 'There probably won't even *be* a service. He just has to say it.'

Armstrong shook his head. 'I can't say it if there isn't going to be a service. And if there is a service, I can't say it and not show up.'

'If you want to help, that's what you've got to do.'

THEY LEFT THE ARMSTRONGS in the West Wing basement and were escorted back to the Suburban.

'Take us to the motel,' Reacher said. 'I want to get a shower. Then I want to meet with Bannon.'

'Why?' Stuyvesant asked.

'Because I'm a witness,' Reacher said. 'I saw the shooter.'

'You got a description?'

'Not really,' Reacher said. 'It was only a glimpse. But there was something about the way he moved. I've seen him before.'

STUYVESANT DROVE THEM to the Hoover Building. The balance of power had changed. Killing federal agents was a federal crime, so now the FBI was in charge. Bannon met them in the main lobby and took them up in an elevator to their conference room.

'My agency extends its sympathies to your agency,' Bannon said.

'You haven't found them,' Stuyvesant said.

Bannon shook his head. 'No,' he said. 'We didn't find them. We're still looking, of course, but being realistic we would have to say they're out of the District by now.'

'Outstanding,' Stuyvesant said.

Bannon made a face. 'There's nothing to be gained by yelling at us. Because we could yell right back. Somebody got through the screen *you* deployed. Somebody decoyed *your* guy off the roof.'

'How did they get up there at all?' Neagley asked.

'Not through the front,' Bannon said. 'There was a shitload of cops watching the front. They saw nothing. Not down the back alley either. There was a cop on foot and a cop in a car watching, both ends. They all say they saw nobody either. So we think the bad guys got into a building a block over. Walked through it and out a rear door into the alley halfway down. Then they skipped ten feet across the alley and got in the back of the warehouse and walked up the stairs. No doubt they exited the same way.'

'How did they decoy Crosetti?' Stuyvesant said.

Bannon shrugged again. 'There's always a way, isn't there?' He looked back at Reacher. 'You saw the shooter,' he said.

Reacher nodded. 'For a quarter-second, maybe. As he moved away.'

'And you figure you've seen him before.'

'But I don't know where. There was something about the way he moved, that's all. The shape of his body. His clothing, maybe.'

'Was he the guy from the garage video?'

'No,' Reacher said.

'Your theory still standing?' Stuyvesant asked Bannon.

'Yes,' Bannon said. 'We're still looking at your ex-employees. Now more than ever. Because we think that's why Crosetti left his post. We think he saw somebody he knew and trusted.'

THEY DROVE THE HALF-MILE west on Pennsylvania Avenue, parked in the garage and rode up to the Secret Service's own conference room.

'I'm afraid Bannon might be right,' Stuyvesant said. 'That it is somebody inside our community.'

'His theory is like a big pyramid balancing on its point. Very impressive until it falls over,' Reacher said. He's betting everything on the fact that Armstrong hasn't been told. But there's no logic in that. Maybe these guys *are* targeting Armstrong personally. Maybe they just didn't know you wouldn't tell him.'

'The weapons are persuasive,' Neagley said. 'And the way that they knew Froelich's address.'

Reacher nodded. 'But I still don't believe it,' he said.

'Why not?' Stuyvesant asked.

'Get the messages and take a real close look.'

Stuyvesant left the room. Came back with a file folder. He opened it up and laid the six FBI photographs in a line down the table.

You are going to die.

Vice-President-elect Armstrong is going to die.

The day upon which Armstrong will die is fast approaching.

A demonstration of your vulnerability will be staged today.

Did you like the demonstration?

It's going to happen soon.

'So?' Stuyvesant asked.

'Look at the fourth message,' Reacher said. '*Vulnerability* is correctly spelled. And look at the last message. The apostrophe in *it's* is correct. Lots of people get that wrong, *it's* and *its*.'

'So?'

'The messages are reasonably literate.'

'OK.'

'Now look at the third message.'

'What about it?'

'It's a little fancy,' Neagley said. 'A little awkward and old-fashioned. The *upon which* thing. And the *fast approaching*.'

'Exactly,' Reacher said. 'A little archaic.'

'But what does all this prove?' Stuyvesant asked.

'Have you ever read the Constitution?' Reacher said.

'I guess I've read it,' Stuyvesant said. 'A long time ago, probably.'

'Me too,' Reacher said. 'Some school I was at gave us a copy each. It's a legal document. So when somebody prints it up as a book, they can't mess with it. They have to reproduce it word for word. They can't modernise the language, they can't clean it up.'

'Obviously not.'

'The early parts are from 1787. The last amendment in my copy was the twenty-sixth, from 1971, lowering the voting age to eighteen. A span of a hundred and eighty-four years. With everything reproduced exactly like it was written down at the particular time.'

'So?'

'One thing I remember is that, in the first part, *Vice President* is written without a hyphen between the two words. Same in the latest part. But in the stuff written in the middle period, it's *Vice-President* with a hyphen between the words. So clearly from the 1860s up to the 1930s it was considered correct usage to have a hyphen there.'

'These guys use a hyphen,' Stuyvesant said.

'They sure do,' Reacher said. 'Right there in the second message.'

'So what does that mean?'

'Two things,' Reacher said. 'We know they paid attention in class, because they're reasonably literate. So the first thing it means is they went to school someplace they used old textbooks and manuals that were way out of date. Which explains the third message's archaic feel, maybe. And which is why I figure they might be from a poor rural area with low school taxes. Second thing it means is they never worked for the Secret Service. Because you guys are buried in paperwork. Anybody who worked here would have written *Vice President* a million times in their career. All with the modern usage without the hyphen. They would have gotten totally used to it that way.'

'Maybe the other guy wrote it,' Stuyvesant said. 'The one who didn't work here. The one with the thumbprint.'

'Makes no difference,' Reacher said. 'They're a unit. And perfectionists. If one guy had written it wrong, the other guy would have corrected it. But it wasn't corrected, therefore neither of them knew it was wrong. Therefore neither of them worked here.'

'What are the exact implications?' Stuyvesant asked.

'Age is critical,' Reacher said. 'They can't be older than early fifties, to be running around doing all this stuff. They can't be younger than mid forties, because you read the Constitution in junior high, and surely by 1970 every school in America had new books.'

Stuyvesant nodded. 'If neither of them worked for us, how did they know where M. E. lived?'

'Nendick told them.'

Stuyvesant nodded. 'OK. But what would be their motive?'

'Animosity against Armstrong personally. It has to be. Think about the time line here. Armstrong became the running mate during the summer. Before that nobody had ever heard of him.'

Stuyvesant stared down at the table. 'So where do we start?'

'With Armstrong. We figure out who hates him and why.'

STUYVESANT CALLED A GUY from the Office of Protection Research at home and ordered him into the office. Reacher and Neagley waited in reception. There was a TV in there and Reacher wanted to see if Armstrong delivered on the early news. It was a half-hour away.

'Close your eyes,' Neagley said. 'Clear your mind. You need to concentrate on the shooter.'

Reacher shook his head. 'I won't get it if I concentrate.'

'So think about something else. Use peripheral vision. Pretend you're looking somewhere else. The next roof along, maybe.'

He closed his eyes. Recalled the sounds he had been hearing. Nothing much from the crowd. The clatter of serving spoons. Froelich saying *Thanks for stopping by*. Mrs Armstrong saying *Enjoy*. Then he heard the soft *chunk* of the first silenced bullet hitting the wall. It had missed Armstrong by four feet. Probably a rushed shot. The guy comes up the stairs, stands in the rooftop doorway, calls softly to Crosetti. *And Crosetti responds*. The guy waits for Crosetti to come to him. Maybe backs away into the stairwell. Crosetti comes on. Crosetti gets shot. The guy runs to the lip of the roof. Kneels and fires before he's really settled. The miss craters the brick and a small chip flies off and hits Reacher in the cheek. The guy racks the bolt and aims more carefully for the second shot.

Reacher opened his eyes. 'I want you to work on how they lured Crosetti away from his post. I want to know how they did that.'

'I'll work on it,' Neagley said. 'You work on the shooter.'

He closed his eyes again and recalled the spray of blood and his immediate instinctive reaction. *Incoming lethal fire. Point of origin?* He had glanced up and seen the curve of a shoulder. It was moving. The shape and the movement were somehow one and the same thing.

'His coat,' he said. 'The shape of his coat over his body, and the way it draped when he moved.'

'Seen the coat before?'

'Yes. Not on the garage video. Not the same guy, either. This guy was taller and leaner. Some length in his upper body. It gave the coat its drape. I think it was a long coat. It *flowed* like a long coat. Like the guy was moving fast.'

'He would be. Far as he knew he'd just shot Armstrong.'

'No, like he was always energetic, decisive in his movements.'

Reacher gestured for the duty officer to turn the television sound up for the news. The story led the bulletin, obviously. When coverage switched back to the anchorman, he announced that Armstrong's reaction had been immediate and emphatic.

The picture cut to tape of an outdoors location Reacher recognised as the West Wing's parking lot. Armstrong was standing there with his wife. He talked about his sadness that two agents had died. He extolled their qualities, offered sympathy to their families. He went on to say he hoped it would be seen that they had died protecting democracy itself, not just himself in person. He promised swift and certain retribution against the perpetrators of the outrage. But he finished by saying that as a mark of respect, he was remaining in Washington and cancelling all engagements until he had attended a memorial service for his personal friend and protection team leader. He said the service would be held on Sunday morning, in a small country church in a small Wyoming town called Grace.

The bulletin cut to football highlights. The duty officer muted the sound. Reacher closed his eyes. Rehearsed his upward glance once again. The curve of the shooter's shoulder, swinging away, *swooping* away. The coat flowing with him. *The coat.* He ran it all again, like a tape. He froze on the coat. *He knew.* He opened his eyes wide.

'Figured how yet?' he asked.

'Can't get past Bannon's take,' Neagley answered. 'Crosetti saw somebody he knew and trusted.'

'Man or woman?'

'Man, according to you.'

'OK, say it again.'

Neagley shrugged. 'Crosetti saw some man he knew and trusted.'

Reacher shook his head. 'Two words short. Crosetti saw some *type of* man he knew and trusted.'

'Who?' she asked.

'Who can get in and out of anywhere without suspicion?'

Neagley looked at him. 'Law enforcement?'

Reacher nodded. 'The coat was long, kind of reddish-brown, faint pattern to it. Too thin for an overcoat, too thick for a raincoat, flapping open. It swung as he ran.'

'As who ran?'

'That Bismarck cop. He ran over to me after I came out of the church. It was him on the warehouse roof.'

'It was a *cop*?'

'THAT'S A SERIOUS allegation,' Bannon said. 'Based on a quarter-second of observation from ninety yards during extreme mayhem.'

They were back in the FBI conference room, with Stuyvesant.

'It was him,' Reacher said. 'No doubt about it.'

Bannon made a face. 'Description?'

'Tall,' Reacher said. 'Sandy hair going grey. Lean face, lean body. Long coat, some kind of a heavy twill, reddish-brown, open. Tweed jacket, white shirt, tie, grey flannel pants. Big old shoes.'

'Age?'

'Middle or late forties.'

'Rank?'

'He showed me a gold badge, but he stayed twenty feet away. I couldn't read it. He struck me as a senior guy. Maybe a detective lieutenant, maybe even a captain.'

Bannon opened a file. Pulled a sheet of paper. Studied it carefully. 'Our Bismarck field office listed all attending personnel,' he said. 'There were forty-two local cops on the field. Nobody above the rank of sergeant except for two: the senior officer present, a captain, and his second-in-command, a lieutenant.'

'We should get Bismarck PD to send photographs,' Stuyvesant said.

'That would take days,' Bannon said. 'And who would I ask? I might be speaking directly to the bad guy.'

'So speak to your Bismarck field office,' Neagley said. 'Wouldn't surprise me if they had illicit summaries on the whole police department, with photographs.'

Bannon smiled. 'You're not supposed to know about things like that.' Then he stood up and went out to his office.

He came back into the room after fifteen minutes.

'Bad news,' he said. 'Bismarck PD had nobody there in plain clothes. It was a ceremonial occasion. They were in full uniform. All forty-two of them. The captain and the lieutenant were in full dress uniform. White gloves and all. The guy was not a Bismarck cop.'

Reacher said nothing.

'But he was obviously making a pretty good stab at impersonating a Bismarck cop,' Bannon said. 'He convinced you, for instance. Clearly he had the look, and the mannerisms.'

Nobody spoke.

'So nothing's changed,' Bannon said. 'We're still looking at recent Secret Service ex-employees. Because who better to impersonate a cop than some other law-enforcement veteran who worked his whole career alongside cops at events exactly like that one?'

TWELVE

The staffer from the Office of Protection Research was waiting when Reacher and Neagley and Stuyvesant got back to the Treasury Building. He was about Reacher's age and looked like a university professor. His name was Swain. Stuyvesant introduced him and disappeared. Swain led Reacher and Neagley to an area that clearly doubled as a library and a lecture room.

'I heard what the FBI is saying,' Swain said.

'You believe it?' Reacher asked.

Swain just shrugged. 'You're Joe Reacher's brother, aren't you?'

Reacher nodded.

'I worked with him,' Swain said. 'Way back. He used to encourage random observations.'

'So do I,' Reacher said. 'You got any?'

'This situation feels different from anything else I've seen. The hatred is visible. Assassinations fall into two groups, ideological or functional. A functional assassination is where you need to get rid of a guy for some political or economic reason. An ideological assassination is where you murder a guy because you hate him, basically. But usually the hatred is well hidden, down at the conspirator level. All we see is the result. But this time the hatred is right in our face. They've gone to a lot of trouble to make sure we know all about it.'

'So what's your conclusion?'

'The early phase was extraordinary. The messages? Think about the risks. They put unbelievable resources into the early phase. So I have to assume they felt it was worth while.'

'But it wasn't,' Neagley said. 'Armstrong has never even seen any of the messages. They were wasting their time.'

'Simple ignorance,' Swain said. 'These guys thought they were getting right to him. So I'm convinced it's personal. Aimed at him, not us. They wanted to scare him, make him suffer first. And something else,' he continued. 'I think we're miscounting. How many messages have there been?'

'Six,' Reacher said.

'No,' Swain said. 'I think there have been seven. I think Nendick delivered the second message, and *was* the third message. You got here and forty-eight hours later you got to Nendick. But we'd have gotten there sooner or later. And what was waiting for us? Nendick wasn't just a delivery system. He was a message *in himself*. He showed what these people are capable of. Assuming Armstrong was in the loop, he'd have been getting pretty shaky by that point.'

'Then there are nine messages,' Neagley said. 'On that basis, we should add in the Minnesota and the Colorado situations.'

'Absolutely,' Swain said. 'Everything has fear as its purpose.'

Reacher stared at the floor. 'What are the thumbprints about?'

'They're a taunt, a boast, a tease,' Swain said. 'They induce the fear that these guys are too clever to be caught.'

'I think we missed something,' Reacher said. 'We've assumed they knew the thumbprint was untraceable. But I think they expected it *would* be traceable. I think our guys gambled and got unlucky. Suppose you picked a random male aged about sixty or seventy. What are the chances he'd have been fingerprinted at least once?'

'Pretty good, I guess,' Neagley said. 'All immigrants are printed. American born, he'd have been drafted for Korea or Vietnam and printed even if he didn't go.'

'OK,' Reacher said. 'So I don't think the thumbprint comes from one of the guys themselves. I think it comes from some innocent bystander. From somebody they picked at random. And it was supposed to lead us directly *to* that somebody.'

Neagley stared at Reacher. 'What for?' she said.

'So we could find another Nendick,' he said. 'The thumbprint *was* a message, just like Swain says Nendick was. We were supposed to trace the print and find the guy and find a Nendick situation. Some terrified victim, too scared to open his mouth and tell us anything. A message in himself. But by pure accident our guys hit on somebody who had never been printed, so we didn't find him.'

'But there were six paper messages,' Swain said. 'Probably twenty days between the first one going in the mail and the last one being delivered to Froelich's house. So what does that mean? All the messages were prepared in advance?'

'No,' Reacher said. 'I think they printed them as they went along. I think they kept the thumbprint available to them at all times.' Nobody spoke. 'Fire up a computer,' Reacher said. 'Search NCIC for the word *thumb*.'

'WE'VE GOT a big field office in Sacramento,' Bannon said. 'Three agents are already mobile. A doctor, too. We'll know in an hour.'

This time Bannon had come to them. They were in the Secret Service conference room, Stuyvesant at the head of the table, Reacher and Neagley and Swain on one side, Bannon on the other.

'It's a bizarre idea,' Bannon said. 'What would they do? Keep it in the freezer?'

'Probably,' Reacher said. 'Thaw it a bit, print it on the paper.'

'What are the implications?' Stuyvesant said.

Reacher made a face. 'We can change one major assumption. Now I would guess they've both got prints on file, and they've both been wearing the latex gloves.'

'Two renegades,' Bannon said.

'Not necessarily ours,' Stuyvesant said.

'So explain the other factors,' Bannon said. 'Show me these are private citizens gunning for Armstrong personally.'

Stuyvesant glanced at Swain, but Swain said nothing.

'You've got no case,' Bannon said. 'I mean, who cares about a vice president? They're nobodies.'

'Let me start from the beginning,' Swain said. 'The vice president is there to be a candidate. His design life lasts from when he's tapped in the summer until election day. He's there to be the attack dog. He's got to be able to say the stuff the presidential candidate isn't allowed to say. Meanwhile the presidential candidate stands around looking statesmanlike.'

'And you think Armstrong trod on enough toes to get himself assassinated for it?'

'The timing is persuasive,' Stuyvesant said. 'This whole thing was triggered by something recent. He pissed somebody off.'

'Somebody who owns Secret Service weapons,' Bannon said. 'Somebody who knew where Froelich lived.'

Stuyvesant said nothing. Bannon checked his watch. Took his cellphone out of his pocket and laid it on the table in front of him.

'I'm sticking with the theory,' he said. 'Except now I'm listing both of the bad guys as yours. If this phone rings and Reacher turns out to be right, that is.'

The phone rang right then. He picked it up and clicked it on. He said 'Yeah' and then listened. Then he clicked the phone off.

'Sacramento?' Stuyvesant asked.

'No,' Bannon said. 'Local. They found the rifle.'

THEY LEFT SWAIN BEHIND and headed over to the FBI labs inside the Hoover Building. An expert staff was assembling.

'Was it a Vaime Mk2?' Bannon asked.

'Without a doubt,' one of the techs said.

'Serial number on it?'

The guy shook his head. 'Removed with acid.'

'So where is it now?'

'We're fuming it for prints,' the guy said. 'But it's hopeless. We got nothing on the fluoroscope. Nothing on the laser. It's been wiped.'

'Where was it found?'

'In the warehouse. Behind the door of a third-floor room.'

'I guess they waited in there,' Bannon said. 'Maybe five minutes, slipped out at the height of the mayhem. Cool heads. Get the rifle.'

It came out of the laboratory still smelling of the hot superglue fumes that had been blown over it in the hope of finding latent fingerprints. It had a powerful scope fixed to the sight mounts.

'That's the wrong scope,' Reacher said. 'That's a Hensoldt. Vaime uses Bushnell scopes.'

'Yeah, it's been modified,' one of the techs said.

'By the factory?'

The guy shook his head. 'I don't think so,' he said. 'High standard, but it's not factory workmanship.'

'So what does that mean?' Bannon asked. 'Is a Hensoldt better than a Bushnell?'

'Not really,' Reacher said. 'They're both fine scopes. Like BMW and Mercedes.'

'So a person might have a preference?'

'Not a government person,' Reacher said. 'He works with what he's got. I don't see somebody going to their department armourer and asking him to junk a thousand-dollar Bushnell just because he prefers the feel of a thousand-dollar Hensoldt.'

'So why the switch?'

'I'm not sure,' Reacher said again. 'Damage, maybe. But a government repairer would use another Bushnell. They don't just buy the rifles. They buy crateloads of spare parts along with them.'

'Suppose they were short? Suppose the scopes got damaged a lot?'

'Then they might use a Hensoldt, I guess. Hensoldts usually come with SIG rifles. You need to look at your lists again. Find out if there's anybody who buys Vaimes *and* SIGs for their snipers.'

Stuyvesant was staring into the distance. 'We bought SIGs,' he said, quietly. 'We had a batch about five years ago. Unsilenced semi-automatics, as an alternative option. But we don't use them much because they're a little inaccurate for close crowd situations. They're mostly stored. We use the Vaimes everywhere now. So I'm sure the SIG parts bins are still full.'

Bannon's phone rang again. He clicked it on and put it to his ear and said 'Yeah' and listened. 'Two?' he asked. Listened some more. 'OK.' He clicked the phone off. 'Upstairs,' he said.

Stuyvesant and Reacher and Neagley followed him to the conference room.

'His name is Andretti,' Bannon said. 'Age seventy-three, retired carpenter, retired volunteer firefighter. He's got granddaughters. That's where the pressure came from.'

'Is he talking?' Neagley asked.

'Some,' Bannon said. 'Sounds like he's made of slightly sterner stuff than Nendick.'

'So how did it go down?'

'He frequents a cop bar outside of Sacramento, from his fire-fighting days. He met two guys in there.'

'Were they cops?' Reacher asked.

'Cop-like,' Bannon said. 'That was his description. They got to talking, they got to showing each other pictures of the family.'

'And?'

'He clammed up on us for a spell, then our doctor took a look at his hand. The left thumb has been surgically removed. Well, not really *surgically*, but there was an attempt at neatness. Andretti stuck to his carpentry story. Our doctor said, no way was that a saw. Andretti talked some more. He lives alone. Widower. The two cop-like guys had wormed an invitation home with him. They were asking him, what would you do to protect your family? It was all rhetorical at first, and then it got practical fast. They told him he would have to give up his thumb or his granddaughters. His choice. They held him down and did it. They took his photographs and his address book. Told him now they knew what his granddaughters looked like and where they lived. Told him they'd take out their ovaries the same way they'd taken off his thumb. And he was ready to believe them, obviously. He would be, right? They stole a cooler from the kitchen and some ice from the refrigerator to transport the thumb. They left and he made it to the hospital.'

'Descriptions?' Stuyvesant asked.

Bannon shook his head. 'Too scared,' he said. 'My guys talked about Witness Protection for the whole family, but he's not going to bite. My guess is we've got all we're going to get.'

Nobody spoke for a long time.

'I'm going back to see Swain,' Reacher said. 'I'll walk.'

'I'll come with you,' Neagley said.

IT WAS A FAST HALF-MILE west on Pennsylvania Avenue.

'You OK?' Neagley asked.

'Feeling guilty,' Reacher said. 'I should have told Froelich to double the sentries on the roof. Might have saved her.'

'They were masquerading as cops,' Neagley said. 'They'd have walked through a *dozen* sentries.'

'You think Bannon looks like a cop?' Reacher asked.

Neagley smiled, briefly. 'Exactly like a cop,' she said. 'He probably was a cop before he joined the Bureau.'

'What makes him look like a cop?'

'Everything. Every single thing. It's in his pores.'

'Something in Froelich's pep talk,' Reacher said. 'Just before Armstrong showed up. She was warning her people. She said it's very easy to look a little like a homeless person, but very difficult to look exactly like a homeless person. I think it's the same with cops. If I put a tweed sports coat on and grey flannels and plain shoes and held up a gold badge, would I look like a cop?'

'A little. But not exactly.'

'But these guys *do* look exactly like cops. I saw one of them and never thought twice. And they're in and out of everywhere without a single question.'

'It would explain a lot of things,' Neagley said. 'They were right at home in the cop bar with Nendick. And with Andretti. And they knew about DNA on envelopes, and the NCIC computer thing. Cops would know that the FBI networks all that information.'

'And the weapons. They might filter through to second-tier SWAT teams or State Police specialists. Especially refurbished items with nonstandard scopes.'

'But we know they aren't cops.'

'We know they aren't Bismarck cops,' Reacher said. 'Maybe they're cops from somewhere else.'

SWAIN WAS STILL WAITING for them.

'You need to tell us what you know about the campaign,' Reacher said. 'Who got mad at Armstrong?'

There was a short silence. Then Swain looked away.

'Nobody,' he said. 'He upset people, for sure. But nobody signifi-cant. I just wanted to get the FBI off their track. I don't think it was one of us. I don't like to see our agency getting abused that way.'

'So you've got a feeling and we've got a hyphen,' Reacher said.

'What do we do now?'

'We look somewhere else,' Neagley said. 'If it's not political it must be personal.'

'I'm not sure if I can show you that stuff,' Swain said. 'It's sup-posed to be confidential.'

'Is there anything bad in it?'

'No, or you'd have heard about it during the campaign.'

'So how can it hurt to let us take a look?'

'I guess it can't.'

They headed towards the library. When they got there the phone was ringing. Swain picked it up and then handed it to Reacher.

'Stuyvesant, for you,' he said.

Reacher listened for a minute and then put the phone down.

'Armstrong's coming in,' he said. 'He's upset and restless and wants to talk to everybody he can find who was there today.'

THEY LEFT SWAIN and walked back to the conference room.

Stuyvesant came in a minute later. 'We're going to be thin on the ground,' he said. 'I gave most people twenty-four hours and I'm not dragging them back in just because the protectee can't sleep.'

Two more guys came in five minutes later. Reacher recognised one of them as a rooftop sharpshooter and the other as one of the agent screen around the food line.

Armstrong's security preceded him like the edge of an invisible bubble. He nodded sombre greetings all round. 'Thank you,' he said. 'For performing so well today. I feel I owe you now. Like I won't be free of an obligation until I've done something for you. So don't hesitate to ask me. Anything at all, formal or informal.'

Nobody spoke.

'Tell me about Crosetti,' Armstrong said. 'Did he have family?'

The sharpshooter nodded. 'A wife and a son,' he said.'

Armstrong looked away. 'I'm so sorry,' he said. 'Is there anything I can do for them?'

'They'll be looked after,' Stuyvesant said.

'I spoke with Froelich's folks earlier today,' Armstrong said. 'After I saw you at the White House. I felt I ought to offer my condolences personally. And I felt I should clear my statement with them, before I spoke to the television people. I felt I couldn't misrepresent the situation without their permission, just for the sake of a decoy scheme. But they liked the idea of a memorial service on Sunday. So there will be a service, after all. I'm going to attend it.'

'I advise against that,' Stuyvesant said.

'She was killed because of me. I want to attend her service. It's the least I can do. I respect your judgment, of course. But it isn't negotiable. I'll go on my own, if I have to.'

'That isn't possible,' Stuyvesant said.

Armstrong nodded. 'So find three agents, friends of hers who want to be there with me. And only three. No media and no television. Just us. We can't turn it into a circus. We'll get in and out fast.'

Stuyvesant said nothing.

'I spoke with the director of the FBI,' Armstrong said. 'He told me the suspects got away.'

'It's just a matter of time,' Stuyvesant said.

Armstrong nodded again. 'Thank you for today. Thank you all. From both of us. That's really all I came here to say.'

His personal detail picked up the cue and moved him to the door. Three minutes later a radio call came in from his car. He was secure and mobile north and west towards Georgetown.

'Shit,' Stuyvesant said. 'Now Sunday is going to be a damn nightmare on top of everything else.'

Nobody looked at Reacher, except Neagley. They walked out

alone and found Swain in the reception area. He had his coat on.

'I'm going home,' he said.

'First you're going to show us your files,' Reacher said.

THIRTEEN

The files narrated the whole story of Brook Armstrong's life. The story started on page one with his parents. His mother had grown up in Oregon, moved to Washington State for college, returned to Oregon to start work as a pharmacist. The start-up of her own pharmacy business had three pages all to itself. She was now sick with something feared to be terminal.

His father's education was listed. His military service had a start date and a medical discharge date, but there were no details beyond that. He was an Oregon native who married the pharmacist on his return to civilian life. They moved to an isolated village in the south-west corner of the state and he used family money to buy himself a lumber business. The newlyweds had a daughter soon afterwards and Brook Armstrong himself was born two years later.

The sister's biography was a half-inch thick so Reacher skipped it and started on Brook's education. Armstrong was good at sports. He got excellent grades. The father had a stroke and died just after Armstrong left home for college. Armstrong spent seven years in two universities, first Cornell in upstate New York, then Stanford in California. He met a Bismarck girl at Stanford. They got married, made their home in North Dakota and he started his political career with a campaign for a seat in the State legislature.

'I need to get home,' Swain said. 'It's Thanksgiving and I've got kids and my wife is going to kill me.'

Reacher looked at the rest of the file. There were six more inches of paperwork to go. 'Am I going to find anything if I read all night?'

'No.'

'Was all of it used in this summer's campaign?'

Swain nodded. 'Sure. It's a great bio. That's why he was picked in the first place.'

Reacher nodded. 'OK,' he said. 'Go home.'

Swain picked up his coat and left in a hurry and Reacher sampled his way through the remaining years. Neagley leafed through the endless source material. They both gave it up after an hour.

'Conclusions?' Neagley asked.

'Swain has got a very boring job,' Reacher said.

She smiled. 'Agreed,' she said.

'But something kind of jumps out at me. Something that's not here, rather than something that *is* here. Campaigns are cynical, right? These people will use any old thing that puts them in a good light. So for instance, we've got his mother. We've got endless detail about her college degrees and her pharmacy thing. Why?'

'To appeal to independent women and small business people.'

'OK, and then we've got stuff about her getting sick. Why?'

'So Armstrong looks like a caring, dutiful son. It humanises him. And it authenticates his issues about health care.'

'And we've got plenty of stuff about his dad's lumber company.'

'For the business lobby again. And it touches on environmental concerns. Armstrong can say he's got practical knowledge.'

'Exactly,' Reacher said. 'Whatever the issue, whatever the constituency, they find a bone to throw.'

'So?'

'They took a pass on military service. And usually they love all that stuff. Normally if your dad was in the army, you'd shout it from the rooftops to wrap up another bunch of issues. But there's no detail. He joined, he got discharged. That's all.'

'The father died ages ago.'

'Doesn't matter. They'd have been all over it if there was something to be gained. And what was the medical discharge for? I don't like to see unexplained medical discharges. I'd like to know more about it.'

'I can find out, if you really need me to,' Neagley said. 'I can make some calls. We've got plenty of contacts.'

Reacher yawned. 'OK, do it. First thing tomorrow.'

'I'll do it tonight. The military still works twenty-four hours a day.'

Reacher nodded. 'So make the calls if you want to, but don't wake me up to tell me about them. Tell me about them tomorrow.'

THE NIGHT DUTY OFFICER fixed them a ride back to the Georgetown motel and Reacher went straight to his room. He sat in the chair for a moment and the night-time silence pressed in on him. He was overcome by a sense of something *not there*. A sense of absence. Things that should be there and weren't. *What exactly?* Froelich, of course.

Maybe it was just Armstrong's father's service career on his mind. But maybe it was more than that. Was something else missing?

He slipped into the cold bed and stared at the ceiling for an hour, thinking hard. Then he switched off and made himself sleep.

THERE WAS AN ALARM call from the desk at six o'clock and a minute later there was a knock at the door. Reacher rolled out of bed and wrapped a towel round his waist and checked the spy hole. It was Neagley, with coffee for him. She was all dressed and ready to go. He let her in and sat on the bed and started the coffee.

'OK, Armstrong's father?' she said. 'He was drafted at the end of Korea. Never saw active service. But he went through officer training and came out a second lieutenant and was assigned to an infantry company. They were stationed in Alabama, ordered to achieve battle readiness for a fight everybody knew was already over. And you know how that stuff went, right?'

Reacher nodded sleepily. Sipped his coffee. 'Some idiot captain running endless competitions,' he said.

'And Armstrong senior usually won,' Neagley said. 'He ran a tight unit. But he had a temper problem. If somebody screwed up he could fly into a rage. Happened a couple of times. It's described in the records as uncontrolled temper tantrums. The third time, there was some serious physical abuse and they kicked him out for it. And they covered it up. They gave him a psychological discharge, wrote it up as generic battle stress, even though he'd never been in combat.'

Reacher made a face. 'He must have had friends. And so must you, to get that deep into the records. How many individual victims?'

'We can forget them. There were three, one for each incident. One was KIA in Vietnam, one died ten years ago in Palm Springs and the third is more than seventy years old, lives in Florida.'

'Any chance Armstrong himself inherited the temper?'

'It's conceivable,' Neagley said. 'But I assume the broader picture would have come out already, long ago. The guy's been running for office at one level or another his whole life. And all this started with the campaign this summer. We already agreed on that.'

Reacher nodded, vaguely. 'The campaign,' he repeated. He sat still with the coffee cup in his hand, then got up and walked to the window. Pulled back the shades and looked out at DC under the grey dawn sky. 'How many representatives does New Mexico have?' he asked.

'I don't know,' Neagley said.

'I think it's three. Can you name them?'

'No.'

'Would you recognise any of them on the street?'

'No. What's your point?'

Reacher stared out of the window. 'We're not looking at this thing like real people,' he said. 'To almost everybody out there in the country all these politicians are absolute nobodies. Froelich admitted nobody had ever heard of Armstrong before.'

'So?'

'So Armstrong did one absolutely basic, fundamental thing in the campaign. He put himself in the public eye, nationally. For the very first time in his life ordinary people outside of his home state saw his face. Heard his name. I think this all could be as basic as that.'

'In what way?'

'Suppose his face came back at somebody from way in the past. Completely out of the blue. Like a sudden shock.'

'Like who?'

'Like you're some guy somewhere and long ago some young man lost his temper and smacked you around. You never see the guy again, but the incident festers in your mind. Years pass, and suddenly there's the guy all over the papers and the TV. He's a politician, running for vice president. You never heard of him in the years before, because you don't watch CNN. But now, there he is, everywhere, in your face. So what do you do?'

'You think about some kind of revenge,' Neagley said. 'OK. It's a theory. But where can we go with it?'

'Armstrong himself, maybe,' Reacher said.

'Time to get going,' Neagley said. 'We meet with Bannon at seven. Are we going to tell him?'

'No,' Reacher said. 'He wouldn't listen.'

THEY WERE LATE into the conference room. Bannon and Stuyvesant were already there.

'The FBI is not going to have agents in Grace, Wyoming,' Bannon said. 'Special request from Armstrong, via the Director. He doesn't want a circus out there.'

'Suits me,' Reacher said.

'You're wasting your time,' Bannon said. 'The bad guys know how this stuff works. They were in the business. They'll have understood his statement was a trap. So they won't show up.'

Reacher nodded. 'Won't be the first trip I ever wasted.'

'Ballistics tests are in,' Bannon said. 'The rifle we found in the warehouse is definitely the same gun that fired the Minnesota bullet.'

'So how did it get here?' Stuyvesant asked.

'I can tell you how it *didn't* get here. It didn't fly in. We checked all commercial arrivals into eight airports. No firearms manifests. We traced all private planes into the same airports. Nothing suspicious.'

'So they drove it in?' Reacher said.

Bannon nodded. 'But Bismarck to DC is more than thirteen hundred miles. That's more than twenty hours, even driving like a lunatic. Impossible, in the time frame. So the rifle was never in Bismarck. It came in direct from Minnesota. We figure the team was split one and one between Minnesota and Colorado on Tuesday and it stayed split afterwards. The guy pretending to be the Bismarck cop was acting solo at the church. We figure he had the submachine gun only. He knew Armstrong was going to be buried in agents as soon as the decoy rifle was discovered. And a submachine gun is better than a rifle against a cluster of people. Especially an H&K MP5. It's as accurate as a rifle at a hundred yards and a lot more powerful. Thirty-round magazines, he would have chewed through six agents and gotten to Armstrong easy enough.'

'So why was the other guy bothering to drive here at the time?' Stuyvesant asked.

'Because these are your people,' Bannon said. 'They're realistic professionals. They knew they couldn't guarantee a hit in any one particular place. So they went through Armstrong's schedule and planned to leapfrog ahead of each other to cover all the bases.'

'Have you ever hidden out to shoot a man?' Reacher asked.

'No,' Bannon said.

'I have,' Reacher said. 'You need to be comfortable, and relaxed, and alert. And you want somebody you trust watching your back. All your concentration is out there in front of you, and you start to feel an itch in your spine. If these guys are realistic professionals like you say they are, then no way would one of them work that church tower alone.'

Bannon shrugged. 'OK,' he said. 'So there are three of them.'

Reacher shook his head. 'It's two guys,' he said. 'I agree with you, it profiles better. A third guy multiplies the risk by a hundred.'

'So what happened with the rifle?'

'They messengered it, obviously,' Reacher said. 'FedEx or UPS or somebody. Maybe the USPS itself. They probably packaged it up with a bunch of saws and hammers and called it a delivery of tool samples. Some bullshit story like that. Addressed to a motel here, awaiting their arrival. That's what I would have done, anyway.'

Bannon looked embarrassed. Said nothing. Just stood up and left. The door clicked shut behind him. The room went quiet.

'We need to talk,' Stuyvesant said.

'You're firing us,' Neagley said.

He nodded. Put his hand in his inside jacket pocket and came out with two envelopes. He slid them along the tabletop.

'Later,' Reacher said. 'Fire us later. Give us the rest of the day.'

'Why?'

'We need to talk to Armstrong. Just me and Neagley.' He gathered up both envelopes and slid them back along the tabletop.

'I can't let you talk to Armstrong without me,' Stuyvesant said.

'You'll have to,' Reacher said. 'It's the only way he'll talk at all. We need to see him as soon as possible. Then we'll consider ourselves fired and you'll never see us again. You'll never see Bannon again, either. Because your problem will be over a couple of days later.'

Stuyvesant put both envelopes back in his jacket.

WHEN STUYVESANT CALLED Armstrong, Armstrong told him three things: first, his mother's health had taken a sudden turn for the worse, therefore second, he wanted to be flown out to Oregon that afternoon, therefore third, the meeting with Reacher and Neagley would have to be short.

Reacher and Neagley sat in front of Stuyvesant's immaculate desk while he ran through the rules of engagement.

'You are not to reveal anything about the current situation,' he said. 'He doesn't know, and I don't want him to find out from you. Is that understood?'

Reacher nodded.

'Understood,' Neagley said.

'Don't upset him and don't harass him. Remember who he is. And remember he's preoccupied with his mother.'

'OK,' Reacher said.

Stuyvesant looked away. 'I've decided I don't want to know why you want to see him. But I do want to say thanks for everything you've done.' He took the envelopes out of his pocket again and passed them across the desk. 'There's a car waiting downstairs,' he said. 'You get a one-way ride to Georgetown. Then you're on your own.'

THE WHITE TENT was still in place across the sidewalk in front of Armstrong's house. The driver pulled up with the rear door tight against the contour and spoke into his wrist microphone. A second later Armstrong's front door opened and three agents stepped out. One walked forward through the canvas tunnel and opened the car door. Reacher got out and Neagley slid out beside him. They were searched and then the agents led them inside to Armstrong's hallway and through a dogleg in the hallway to a kitchen. Armstrong and his wife were sitting at the table with four different newspapers.

'I'm sorry to hear about your mother,' Neagley said.

Armstrong nodded. 'Mr Stuyvesant told me you want a private conversation,' he said.

'Private would be good,' Reacher said.

Armstrong nodded again. 'Let's go,' he said.

He led them into a side room. Walked round and sat down behind a desk. Reacher and Neagley took a chair each.

'This all feels very confidential,' Armstrong said.

Reacher nodded. 'And in the end I think we'll all agree it should be kept confidential.'

'What's on your mind?'

'Mr Stuyvesant gave us some ground rules,' Reacher said. 'I'm going to start breaking them right now. The Secret Service intercepted six threatening messages against you. The first came in the mail eighteen days ago. Two more came in the mail subsequently and three were hand-delivered.'

Armstrong said nothing.

'You don't seem surprised,' Reacher said.

Armstrong shrugged. 'Politics is a surprising business,' he said.

'I guess it is,' Reacher said. 'All six messages were signed with a thumbprint. We traced the print to a guy in California. His thumb had been amputated and stolen and used like a rubber stamp.'

Armstrong said nothing.

'The second message showed up in Stuyvesant's own office. A technician named Nendick had placed it there. Nendick's wife had been kidnapped to coerce his actions. He was so frightened of the danger to her posed by his inevitable interrogation that he went into a coma.'

Armstrong was silent.

'There's a researcher in the office called Swain who felt that Nendick was a message in himself, making seven messages. We added the guy who'd had his thumb removed. Plus there were two homicides on Tuesday, one in Minnesota, one in Colorado. Two unrelated strangers named Armstrong were killed as a demonstration.'

'Oh no,' Armstrong said.

'So, ten messages,' Reacher said. 'All of them designed to torment you, except you hadn't been told about any of them. But then I started wondering whether we're *still* miscounting. And I'm pretty sure we are. I think there were at least eleven messages.'

'What would be the eleventh?' Armstrong asked.

'Something that slipped through,' Reacher said. 'Something that came in the mail, addressed to you, something that the Secret Service didn't see as a threat. Something that meant nothing at all to them, but something that meant a lot to *you*.'

Armstrong said nothing.

'I think it came first,' Reacher said. 'At the very beginning, before the Secret Service caught on. Like an *announcement*, that only you would understand. So I think you've known about all this all along. I think you know who's doing it, and I think you know *why*.'

'People have died,' Armstrong said. 'That's a hell of an accusation.'

'Do you deny it?'

Armstrong said nothing.

Reacher leaned forward. 'Some crucial words were never spoken,' he said. 'Thing is, if I was standing there serving turkey and somebody started shooting and somebody else was suddenly bleeding to death on top of me, I'd be asking, who the hell *were* they? Why were they *doing* that? Those are fairly basic questions. But you didn't ask them. We saw you twice, afterwards. In the White House basement, and then later at the office. You said all kinds of things. You asked, had they been captured yet? That was your big concern. You never asked who they might be or what their possible motive was. Why didn't you ask? Only one possible explanation. You already *knew*.'

Armstrong was silent.

'So I think you're feeling a little guilty now,' Reacher said. 'I think that's why you agreed to make the television statement for me and that's why you suddenly want to go to the service itself. Some kind of a conscience thing. Because you *knew*, and you didn't tell anybody.'

'I'm a politician,' Armstrong said. 'We have hundreds of enemies. There was no point in speculating.'

'Bullshit,' Reacher said. 'This isn't political. This is personal.'

Armstrong said nothing.

'I think you've got a temper problem,' Reacher said. 'Same as your dad. I think way back before you learned to control it you made people suffer, and some of them forgot about it, but some of them didn't. They repressed it deep down inside until they turned on the TV one day and saw your face for the first time in thirty years.'

'How far along is the FBI with this?' Armstrong asked.

'They're nowhere. They're out beating the bushes for people that don't exist. We're way ahead of them.'

'And what are your intentions?'

'I'm going to help you,' Reacher said. 'Not that you deserve it. It'll be a purely accidental by-product of me standing up for Nendick and his wife, and an old guy called Andretti, and two people called Armstrong, and Crosetti, and especially for Froelich.'

'Will this stay confidential?' Armstrong asked.

Reacher nodded. 'It'll have to. Purely for my sake.'

'Sounds like you're contemplating a very serious course of action.'

'People play with fire, they get burned.'

'So then you'll know my secret and I'll know yours,' Armstrong said.

Reacher nodded. 'And we'll all live happily ever after.'

There was a long silence. Reacher saw Armstrong the politician fade away, and Armstrong the man replace him.

'You're wrong in most ways,' he said. 'But not all of them.'

He leaned down and opened a drawer. Took out a padded mailer and tossed it on the desk.

'I guess this counts as the first message,' he said. 'It arrived on election day. I suppose the Secret Service must have been a little puzzled, but they didn't see anything wrong with it. So they passed it along.'

The mailer was addressed to Armstrong at the Senate. The address was printed on a familiar self-adhesive label in the familiar computer font, Times New Roman, bold. It had been mailed in Utah. Reacher looked inside. Held it so Neagley could see.

There was nothing in the envelope except a miniature baseball bat, the kind sold as a souvenir. It was about an inch wide around the barrel and would have been about fifteen inches long except that it was broken near the handle end. It had been broken deliberately. It had been partially sawn through and then snapped where it was weak. The raw end had been scraped to make it look accidental.

'I don't have a temper problem,' Armstrong said. 'But you're right, my father did. We lived in a small town in Oregon. It was a little lawless, but it wasn't too bad.' He placed his hands palm down on the desk and stared at them. 'I was eighteen. Finished with high school, ready for college, spending my last few weeks at home. We had a mailbox at the gate. My father had made it himself, in the shape of a miniature lumber mill. At Hallowe'en in the previous year it had been smashed up by tough kids out cruising with a baseball bat. My father heard it happening and chased them, but he didn't really see them. We were a little upset, because it was a nice mailbox and destroying it seemed senseless. But he rebuilt it stronger and became obsessed about protecting it. Some nights he hid out and guarded it.'

'And the kids came back,' Neagley said.

Armstrong nodded. 'Late that summer,' he said. 'Two kids, in a truck, with a bat. They were big guys. I didn't really know them, but I'd seen them around. They were brothers, I think. Real hard kids, you know, delinquents, bullies from out of town. They took a swing at the box and my dad jumped out at them and there was an argument. They were sneering at him, threatening him, saying bad things about my mother. They said, bring her out and we'll show her a good time with this bat, better than you can. So then there was a fight, and my dad got lucky. Or maybe it was his military training. The bat had bust in half, maybe against the box. I thought that would be the end of it, but he dragged the kids into the yard and got some chain and pad-locks and got them chained to a tree. They were kneeling down, facing each other round the trunk. My dad's temper had kicked in. He was hitting them with the broken bat. I was trying to stop him, but it was impossible. Then he said he was going to show *them* a good time with the bat, with the broken end, unless they begged him not to. So they begged. I was trying to calm my father down, but these guys were looking at me like I was *participating*. Like I was a witness to their worst moment. There was absolute hatred in their eyes. Like they were saying, you've seen this, so now you have to die.'

'What happened?' Neagley asked.

'My father said he was going to leave them there all night and start up again in the morning. We went inside and he went to bed and I snuck out again an hour later. I was going to let them go. But they were already gone. I never saw them again. I went off to college, never really came home again except for visits.'

'And your father died.'

Armstrong nodded. 'I kind of forgot about the two kids. But I didn't *really* forget. When that package came I wasn't puzzled for a second who had sent it, even though it's been nearly thirty years.'

'Did you know their names?' Reacher asked.

'No,' Armstrong said. 'I didn't know much about them, except I guess they lived in some nearby town. What are you going to do?'

'I know what I'd *like* to do. I'd like to break both your arms and never see you again as long as I live. Because if you'd spoken up on election day Froelich would still be alive.'

Armstrong shook his head. There were tears in his eyes. 'I had no idea it was serious,' he said. 'I just thought it was supposed to unsettle me, just an unpleasant joke. I didn't conceive of any *danger* in it. Maybe I half expected some kind of lame follow-up, but I figured I'd deal with that when it happened. But there *was* no follow-up. It didn't happen. Not as far as I knew. *Because nobody told me*. Until now. I could have given Stuyvesant the whole story if he'd just *asked*.'

'Should I tell Stuyvesant now?' Armstrong asked.

'Your choice,' Reacher said.

There was a long pause. Armstrong the man faded away again, and Armstrong the politician came back to replace him.

'I don't want to tell him,' he said. 'Bad for him, bad for me. People have suffered and died. It'll be seen as a serious misjudgment on both our parts. He should have asked, I should have told.'

Reacher nodded. 'So leave it to us. You'll know our secret and we'll know yours.'

'And we'll all live happily ever after.'

'Well, we'll all live,' Reacher said.

'Descriptions?' Neagley asked.

'Kids, maybe my age,' Armstrong said. 'I only remember their eyes.'

'What's the name of the town?'

'Underwood, Oregon,' Armstrong said. 'Where my mother still lives. And I'm heading right there.'

'Don't worry,' Reacher said. 'I assume they expected you'd remember them, and they didn't anticipate the communication breakdown between yourself and the Secret Service. And they wouldn't want you to be able to lead *them* right to their door. Therefore their door has changed. They don't live in Oregon any more.'

'So how are you going to find them?'

Reacher shook his head. 'We can't find them. Not now. Not in time. They'll have to find us. In Wyoming. At the memorial service.'

'I'm going there too. With minimal cover.'

'So just hope it's all over before you arrive.'

'I can't cancel the appearance. That wouldn't be right.'

'No,' Reacher said. 'I guess it wouldn't.'

FOURTEEN

The protection agents showed them out. They walked the length of the canvas tent and stepped off the kerb into the street. Turned east and got back on the sidewalk and settled in for the trek to the subway. It was late morning and the air was clear and cold.

'We should go shopping,' Neagley said. 'We can't go hunting in Wyoming dressed like this.'

'I don't want you to come with me,' Reacher said.

'Worried about my safety?' Neagley asked. 'Because you shouldn't be. Nothing's going to happen to me. I can look after myself.'

'I'm not worried about your safety,' Reacher said.

'What then? My performance? I'm way better than you.'

'I know you are.'

'So what's your problem?'

'Your licence. You've got a licence, right? To be in the business you're in? And you've got an office and a job and a home and a fixed location. I'm going to disappear after this. You can't do that.'

'Think we're going to get caught?'

Reacher said nothing.

'It's like you told Bannon,' she said. 'I'm lying there lined up on these guys, I need you to watch my back.'

'This isn't your fight.'

'Why is it yours? Because some woman your brother once dumped got herself killed doing her job?'

Reacher said nothing.

'OK, it's your fight,' Neagley said. 'I know that. But whatever thing you've got in your head that *makes* it your fight makes it *my* fight too. Because I've got the same thing in *my* head. And even if we didn't think the same, if I had a problem, wouldn't you help me out?'

'I would if you asked.'

'So we're even.'

'Except I'm not asking.'

'Not right now. But you will be. You're two thousand miles from Wyoming and you don't have a credit card to buy a plane ticket with, and I do. You're armed with a folding knife with a three-inch blade and I know a guy in Denver who will give us any weapons we want, no questions asked, and you don't. I can rent a car in Denver to get us the rest of the way, and you can't.'

They walked on, twenty yards, thirty.

'OK,' Reacher said. 'I'm asking.'

THEY MADE IT to Denver before three in the afternoon mountain time. Neagley signed for a GMC Yukon at the Avis counter. They drove it into the city and parked in a downtown garage. They walked three blocks and Neagley found the store she was looking for.

It was an outdoor equipment place. They bought a birdwatcher's spotting scope and a hiker's map of central Wyoming, then moved to the clothing racks. Neagley went for a walker's heavy-duty outfit in greens and browns. Reacher duplicated his Atlantic City purchases at twice the price and twice the quality. He dressed in the changing cubicle. Left Joe's last surviving suit stuffed in the garbage can.

Neagley found a payphone on the street and made a call. Then they went back to the truck and she drove through the city towards the dubious part of town.

She came off a narrow street into some kind of industrial park. On one corner there was a long, low building with a closed roll-up door and a hand-painted sign that read: EDDIE BROWN ENGINEERING.

Neagley stopped in front of the roll-up door and hit the horn. A guy came out of a personnel entrance and saw who it was. He was tall and heavy through the neck and shoulders. He had an open, amiable face, but he had big hands and thick wrists and wasn't the sort of guy you'd mess with on a whim. He sketched a wave and ducked back inside and a moment later the big door rolled up. Neagley drove in under it and it came back down behind them.

On the inside the building was about half the size it should have been, but apart from that it looked convincing. The floor was grease-stained concrete and there were metalworkers' lathes and drills here and there, and stacks of sheet metal and bundles of steel rods. But the back wall was ten feet closer on the inside than the exterior proportions dictated. Clearly there was a room concealed behind it.

'This is Eddie Brown,' Neagley said.

'Not my real name,' the big guy said.

He accessed the concealed room by pulling on a big pile of scrap metal. It was all welded together and welded in turn to a steel panel hidden behind it. The whole thing swung open on silent oiled hinges like a giant three-dimensional door. The guy calling himself Eddie Brown led them through it into a whole different situation. The room was lined by shelves and racks. On three walls the shelves held handguns. The racks were full of long guns, rifles, shotguns and machine guns. The fourth wall was lined with boxes of ammunition.

'Take what you need,' Eddie said.

'Where do the serial numbers lead to?' Reacher asked.

'The Austrian Army,' Eddie said. 'Kind of fizzle out after that.'

Ten minutes later they were back on the road, with Reacher's new jacket spread out in the Yukon's load space over two nine-millimetre Steyr handguns, a Heckler & Koch MP5 submachine gun, an M16 rifle, and boxes full of 200 rounds for each weapon.

THEY ENTERED WYOMING after dark, driving north on I-25. The town called Grace was still five hours away, well beyond the city of Casper.

'We'll stop in Medicine Bow,' Reacher said. 'Sounds like a cool place. We'll aim to get to Grace at dawn tomorrow.'

Medicine Bow didn't look like much of a cool place in the dark, but it had a motel about two miles out with rooms available. Neagley paid for them. Then they found a steakhouse a mile in the other direction and ate twelve-ounce sirloins. The place closed up around them so they took the hint and headed back to their rooms. Reacher left his coat in the truck, to hide the firepower from curious eyes. They said good night in the lot. Reacher went straight to bed.

He woke up at 4.00am, Saturday. Through the wall he could hear Neagley singing in the shower. He rolled out of bed and showered and dressed. Met her out by the car. It was still pitch dark. Very cold.

An hour north, a roadside diner was opening for breakfast. They sat at a table and ate eggs and bacon and drank strong bitter coffee.

'Maybe they won't show,' Neagley said. 'Bannon figured they'd know it was a trap.'

'They'll show,' Reacher said. 'They've been challenged. And they've got more than enough screws loose to jump right on it.'

They got back on the road.

'I guess Casper will have a police department,' Reacher said.

Neagley nodded at the wheel. 'Could be a hundred strong.'

'And they'll be responsible for Grace,' Reacher said. 'So any other cops we find there are our guys.'

'You're still certain they're cops?'

He nodded. 'It's the only way everything makes sense. And you know what the clincher is? *The two dead Armstrongs.* How the hell do you just *find* two white guys with fair hair and blue eyes and the right age and above all the right first and last names? There's only one practical way of doing it—the national DMV data base. Driving licence information, names, addresses, dates of birth, photographs. And nobody can get into it, except cops, who can dial it right up.'

'OK, they *are* cops,' Neagley said. 'But cops would have heard of Armstrong long ago, wouldn't they?'

'Why? If you worked in some rural police department in Maine or Florida you might know the New York Giants' quarterback but there's no reason you'd have heard of North Dakota's junior senator.'

Neagley drove on. 'So which is it?' she asked. 'Maine or Florida?'

'California's a possibility,' Reacher said. 'Oregon isn't. They wouldn't have revealed their identity to Armstrong if they still lived in Oregon.

Nevada's a possibility. Or Utah or Idaho. Anywhere else is too far.'

'From what?'

'From Sacramento. How long does a stolen cooler of ice last? Nevada or Utah or Idaho. That's my guess. Not California. I think they wanted a state line between them and the place they went for the thumb. Feels better, psychologically. I think they're a long day's drive from Sacramento. Which means they're probably a long day's drive from here, too. So I think they'll be coming in by road.'

'When?'

'Today, if they've got any sense.'

'The bat was mailed in Utah,' Neagley said.

Reacher nodded. 'OK, so scratch Utah.'

'So Idaho or Nevada. We better watch for licence plates.'

THEY STOPPED on the outer edge of Casper for gas and more coffee and a bathroom. Then Reacher took a turn at the wheel. When dawn came, they were in a transition area, where the mountains shaded randomly into the high plains. They drove on, another whole hour.

'Turn here,' Neagley said.

It was just a dirt road, leading south to the middle of nowhere. He made the turn. They drove on, twenty miles, thirty. The road rose and fell. Then it peaked and the land fell away in front of them into a fifty-mile-wide bowl of grass and sage. The road ran through it and crossed a river in the base of the bowl. Two more roads ran in to the bridge from nowhere. There were tiny buildings scattered randomly. The whole thing looked like a capital letter K, lightly peppered with habitation where the strokes of the letter met at the bridge.

'That's Grace, Wyoming,' Neagley said. 'Where this road crosses the south fork of the Cheyenne river.'

Reacher eased the Yukon to a stop. 'How many ways in?'

Neagley traced her finger over the map. 'North or south,' she said. 'On this road. The other two roads peter out in the brush.'

'Which way will the bad guys come?'

'Nevada, they'll come in from the south. Idaho, from the north.'

'So we can't stay right here and block the road.'

One of the buildings was a pinprick of white in a square of green. *Froelich's church*, he thought. He opened his door and got out of the car. Walked round to the tailgate and came back with the bird-watcher's scope. Steadied it against the open door and put it to his eye.

The church stood inside the south angle of the K. It had a stone foundation and the rest of it was clapboard painted white. South of its graveyard was a cluster of two-storey buildings. North of the church were more of the same. Houses, stores, barns. Along the short legs of the K were more buildings. There were cars and pick-ups parked here and there. Some pedestrian activity. It looked like the population might reach a couple of hundred.

Reacher passed Neagley the scope and she stared down through it.

'They'll set up to the south,' she said. 'All the pre-service activity will happen south of the church. They've got some natural cover.'

'How will they aim to get away?'

'They'll expect roadblocks north and south,' she said. 'Local cops. Their badges might get them through, but I wouldn't be counting on it. There might be confusion, but there won't be crowds.'

'So how?'

'I know how I'd do it,' she said. 'I'd ignore the roads altogether. I'd take off across the grass, due west. Forty miles of open country in some big four-wheel-drive, and you hit the highway. I doubt the Casper PD has got a helicopter. Or the Highway Patrol.'

'Armstrong will come in a helicopter,' Reacher said. 'Probably from some air-force base in Nebraska.'

'But they won't use his helicopter to chase the bad guys. They'll be exfiltrating him or taking him to a hospital. Standard protocol.'

'Highway Patrol would set up north and south on the highway. They'll have nearly an hour's warning.'

Neagley lowered the scope and nodded. 'I'd anticipate that. So I'd drive straight *across* the highway and get back off-road. West of the highway is ten thousand square miles of nothing between Casper and the Wind River Reservation, with only one major road through it. They'd be long gone before somebody whistled up a helicopter and started the search.'

Reacher climbed back into the Yukon. 'Let's go to work,' he said.

THERE WAS A GENERAL STORE offering postal services and a break-fast counter. There was a feed supplier's office and a hardware store. There was a one-pump gas station.

'They won't come here,' Reacher said. 'This is the most exposed place I've ever seen.'

Neagley shook her head. 'They won't know that until they've seen it for themselves.'

'Where are we going to stay?'

She pointed. 'Over there.'

It was a cedar building with a sign that read: CLEAN ROOMS.

'Terrific,' Reacher said.

'Go south,' Neagley said. 'Let's see the church.'

The road passed the church and the graveyard, then the cluster of buildings, then a couple of abandoned barns, then maybe twenty or thirty small houses, and then the town finished and there was just grassland ahead. But it wasn't flat. There were crevices and crevasses worn smooth by winds and weather. They undulated calmly, up and down to maximum depths of ten or twelve feet, like slow ocean swells. The grass was a yard high, brown and dead and brittle.

'You could hide an infantry company in there,' Neagley said.

Reacher turned the car and headed back towards the church. Pulled over and parked level with the graveyard. Reacher glanced west to the horizon and saw grey clouds massing over the distant mountains.

'It's going to snow,' he said.

'We can't see anything from here,' Neagley said.

She was right. The church was built right in the river valley bottom. The road to the north was visible for maybe a hundred yards. Same in the south. It ran in both directions and rose over gentle humps and disappeared from sight.

'They could be right on top of us before we know it,' Neagley said. 'We need to be able to see them coming.'

Reacher nodded. Opened his door and climbed out of the car. Neagley joined him. There was a new grave site to the west of the church, marked out with tape. There was flat, empty land opposite the church on the east side of the road. It was a big enough space to land a helicopter. He imagined Armstrong climbing out of it. Approaching the church. The vicar would probably greet him near the door. Reacher walked over and stood where Armstrong might stand. Scanned the land to the south and west. *Bad news*. There was some elevation there, and about 150 yards out there were waves and shadows in the moving grass that must mean dips and crevices in the earth beneath it. There were more beyond that, all the way to infinity.

'How good do you think they are?' he asked.

Neagley shrugged. 'I'd be worried out to about five hundred yards. Stuyvesant needs to bring a surveillance helicopter. This angle is hopeless, but you could see everything from the air.'

'Armstrong won't let him,' Reacher said. 'But we've got the air. We've got the church tower.' He turned and walked back towards it. 'Forget the rooming house,' he said. 'This is where we're going to stay. We'll see them coming, north or south, night or day. It'll all be over before Stuyvesant or Armstrong even get here.'

They were ten feet from the church door when it opened and a clergyman stepped out, closely followed by an old couple. The clergyman was middle-aged and looked very earnest. The old couple were both maybe sixty years old. The man was tall and stooped. The woman was still good-looking, a little above average height, trim and nicely dressed. Reacher knew who she was immediately. And she knew who he was, or thought she did. She stopped walking and just stared at him the same way her daughter had. 'You?' she said. 'Or is it?'

'I'm his brother,' Reacher said. 'I'm very sorry for your loss.'

She nodded and walked off, towards the dirt road. The clergyman followed her, and so did Froelich's father.

There was a notice board near the church door, in a slim cabinet with glass doors. At the top was a hastily typed announcement that this Sunday's eight o'clock service would be dedicated to the memory of Mary Ellen Froelich. Reacher checked his watch.

'Twenty-two hours,' he said. 'Time to lock and load.'

They brought the Yukon nearer to the church and opened the tailgate. Bent over and loaded all four weapons. They took a Steyr each. Neagley took the H&K and Reacher took the M16. They distributed the spare rounds between them. Then they locked the car and left it.

They hauled the oak door open and stepped inside. It was similar to the Bismarck building. It had the same three bell ropes hanging down inside the tower. The same staircase. They went all the way up and found a ladder bolted to the wall, with a trap door above it.

Reacher led the way up the ladder and through the trap door. The bell chamber was not the same as the one in Bismarck. It had a clock added into it. There was a four-foot cube of brass machinery mounted centrally on iron girders just above the bells. The clock had two faces, mounted in the openings where the louvres had been, to the east and the west. The machinery was ticking loudly.

'We've got no view east or west,' Reacher said.

Neagley shrugged. 'North and south is all we need,' she said. 'That's where the road runs.'

'I guess,' he said. 'You take the south.'

He crawled over to the louvre facing north. Knelt up and looked out. He could see the whole town. He could see the dirt road leading north. Maybe ten straight miles of it. It was completely empty.

'You OK?' he called.

'Excellent,' Neagley called back. 'I can almost see Colorado.'

'Shout when you spot something.'

'You too.'

THE AIR WAS COLD and seventy feet above ground the breeze was a wind. It came in through the louvres. They had been there two hours, and had seen nothing and heard nothing except for the clock.

'I got something,' Neagley called. 'SUV, I think, coming in from the south.'

Reacher picked up the birdwatcher's scope. 'Catch,' he called.

He tossed it over the clock shaft. Neagley twisted and caught it and turned back to the louvre panel. Put the scope to her eye.

'Might be a Chevy Tahoe,' she called. 'Light gold metallic.'

Reacher looked north again. The road was still empty. He could see ten miles. It would take ten minutes to cover ten miles even at a fast cruise. He crawled over next to Neagley and stared out south. There was a tiny gold speck on the road, maybe five miles away.

She passed him the scope. He squinted through it. The truck looked dirty and travel-stained. The sun's reflection made it impossible to see who was riding in it.

'Why is it still sunny?' he said. 'I thought it was going to snow.'

'Look to the west,' Neagley said.

He put the scope down and put the left side of his face tight against the louvres. Closed his right eye and looked out sideways with his left. The sky was split in two. In the west it was almost black with clouds. In the east it was pale blue and hazy. Shafts of sunlight blazed down through mist where the two weather systems met.

'Some kind of inversion,' Neagley said. 'I hope it stays where it is or we'll freeze our asses off up here.'

'It's about fifty miles away.'

'And the wind generally blows in from the west.'

'Great.' He picked up the scope again and checked on the golden truck. It was maybe a mile closer, bucking and swaying on the dirt. It must have been doing about sixty.

'What do you think?' Neagley said.

He handed back the scope. 'I should check north,' he said.

He crawled back to his own louvre. There was nothing happening in the north. The road was still empty.

'It's a Chevy Tahoe for sure,' Neagley called. 'It's slowing down.'

'See who's in it?'

'I've got sun and tinted glass. No ID. Half a mile out now. Nevada plates, I think. They're covered in mud. It's right on the edge of town. It's going real slow now. Looks like a reconnaissance cruise. It's not stopping. It's getting real close. I'm looking down at the roof. I'm going to lose them any second. It's right underneath us now.'

Reacher stood up tight against the wall and peered down at the best angle he could get. He heard the sound of an engine over the moan of the wind. A metallic gold hood slid into view. Then a roof. The truck passed all the way underneath him and rolled through the town and crossed the bridge at maybe twenty miles an hour. It stayed slow for a hundred more yards. Then it picked up speed fast.

'Scope,' he called.

Neagley tossed it back to him and he watched the truck drive away to the north. The rear window was tinted black and the rear bumper was chrome. He could see lettering that read CHEVROLET TAHOE. The rear plate was indecipherable. It was caked with road salt.

'It's heading out,' he called.

It took ten whole minutes to drive out of his field of vision. It rose up over the last hump in the road and then disappeared.

'Anything more?' he called.

'Clear to the south,' Neagley called back.

'I'm going down for the map. You can watch both directions while I'm gone. Do some limbo dancing under this damn clock thing.'

He crawled to the trap door and went down out of the church towards the car. Saw Froelich's father standing next to it.

'Mr Stuyvesant is on the phone for you,' he said. 'From the Secret Service office in Washington DC.'

'Now?'

'He's been holding twenty minutes. I've been trying to find you.'

'Where's the phone?'

'At the house.'

The Froelich house was one of the white buildings on the short southeastern leg of the K. The old guy led the way into a front parlour. There was a table under the window with a telephone. Reacher held the phone to his ear. 'Stuyvesant?' he said.

'Reacher? You got any good news for me?'

'Not yet. You coming in by chopper?'

'That's the plan. He's still in Oregon right now. We're going to fly him to an air base in South Dakota and then take a short hop in an air-force helicopter. We'll have eight people altogether, including me.'

'He only wanted three.'

'He can't object. We're all her friends.'

Reacher looked out of the window. 'OK, so you'll see the church easy enough. You'll land across the street to the east. There's a good place right there. Then he's got about fifty yards to the church door. I can guarantee the immediate surroundings. But you're going to hate what you see further out. There's about a hundred-fifty-degree field of fire to the south and west. And there's plenty of concealment.'

'I can't do it,' Stuyvesant said. 'I can't bring him into that. Or any of my people. You're going to have to deliver.'

'We will if we can.'

'How will I know? You don't have radios. Cellphones won't work out there. And it's too cumbersome to keep on using this land line.'

'We've got a black Yukon,' Reacher said. 'Right now it's parked on the road, right next to the church, to the east. If it's still there when you show up, then pull out and go home. Armstrong will just have to swallow it. But if it's gone, then we're gone, and we won't be gone unless we've delivered, you follow?'

'OK, understood,' Stuyvesant said. 'A black Yukon east of the church, we abort. No Yukon, we land. I guess we won't be seeing you either way. So, good luck.'

'You too,' Reacher said. He put the receiver back. Then he turned and saw Mr Froelich watching him from the parlour doorway.

'They're coming here, aren't they?' the old man said. 'The people who killed my daughter? Because Armstrong is coming here.'

'They might be here already,' Reacher said.

Mr Froelich shook his head. 'Everybody would be talking about it.'

'OK,' Reacher said. 'If you hear about anybody new in town, come and tell me.'

The old man nodded again. 'You'll know as soon as I do. And I'll know as soon as anybody new arrives. Word travels fast here.'

'We'll be in the church tower,' Reacher said.

REACHER WALKED BACK to the Yukon and took the hiker's map off the back seat. Then he climbed the church tower and found Neagley shuttling back and forth between the north and south side.

'All clear,' she said, over the tick of the clock.

He unfolded the map and spread it out flat on the bell chamber floor. Put his finger on Grace. It was in the centre of a rough square made by four roads. The square was maybe eighty miles high and eighty wide, split into two more or less equal rectangles by the dirt road that ran north to south through Grace.

'What do you think?' Neagley asked.

'I think that in the whole history of the western United States no person has ever just *passed through* Grace, Wyoming. It just slows you down, because it's a dirt track. And would you even notice the track? Remember what it looked like at the north end?'

'And we've got a hiker's map,' Neagley said. 'Maybe it's not even on a regular road map.'

'So that truck passed through for a reason,' Reacher said.

'Those were the guys,' Neagley said.

THEY WAITED. The sun fell away into afternoon and the temperature dropped like a stone. Neagley went for a walk and came back with a bag from the grocery store. They ate an improvised lunch. Then they developed a new look-out pattern based on the fact that no vehicle could get all the way through either field of view in less than eight minutes. So they sat comfortably and every five minutes they knelt up and shuffled over to their louvres and scanned the length of the road. The regular physical movement helped against the cold.

Reacher watched and waited, and listened to the clock. The sound was loud and precise and tireless. He had had enough just before four o'clock. He used the blade of his knife to cut through the accumulation of old paint and lifted one of the louvres out of the frame. He pushed it into the clock mechanism. The gear wheels jammed on it and the clock stopped. He pulled the wood out again and slotted it back in the frame. The silence was suddenly deafening.

It got colder. They started shivering. But the silence helped. Suddenly, it helped a lot. Reacher crawled over and checked his partial view to the west, then crawled back and picked up the map. Stared at it hard, lost in thought. He used his finger and thumb like callipers and measured distances. *Forty, eighty, a hundred and twenty, a hundred and sixty miles. Average speed maybe forty. That's four hours.*

'Sun sets in the west,' he said. 'Rises in the east.'

'On this planet,' Neagley said.

Then they heard the staircase creak below them. They heard feet on the ladder. The trap door lifted an inch and fell back and then crashed all the way open and the vicar put his head up into the bell chamber and stared at the submachine gun pointing at him from one side and the M16 rifle from the other.

'I understand the need for security,' he said. 'And we're honoured to host the Vice President-elect, but I really can't permit engines of destruction in a hallowed building.'

'What time does the sun set?' Reacher asked.

The vicar looked a little surprised by the change of subject. But he answered very politely. 'Soon,' he said.

'And when does it rise?'

'This time of year? A little before seven o'clock, I suppose.'

'OK,' Reacher said. 'Thanks.'

'Did you stop the clock?'

'It was driving me nuts.'

'That's why I came up. Do you mind if I set it going again?'

Reacher shrugged. 'It's your clock.'

'I know the noise must be bothersome.'

'Doesn't matter,' Reacher said. 'We'll be out of here as soon as the sun sets. Weapons and all.'

The vicar hauled himself up into the chamber and fiddled with the mechanism. He used a lever to force the exterior hands round to the correct time. Then he turned a gear wheel until the mechanism picked up momentum and started again. 'Thank you,' he said.

'An hour at most,' Reacher said. 'Then we'll be gone.'

The vicar nodded and threaded himself down through the trap door. Pulled it closed after him.

'We can't leave here,' Neagley said. 'Are you crazy? They could come in at night easy as anything.'

'They're already here,' Reacher said. 'Or almost here.' He pulled the louvre out of the frame again and handed it to her. Crawled to the bottom of the ladder that led up through the roof to the outside. Climbed up it and eased the roof trap door open. 'Stay low,' he called. He swam out, keeping his stomach flat on the roof.

There was a three-foot wall round the edge of the roof. Reacher turned a circle on his stomach and leaned down and took the louvre from Neagley. Then he got out of her way and let her crawl up next to him. The wind was strong and the air was bitterly cold.

'Now we kind of kneel low,' he said. 'Close together, facing west.'

They knelt together, shoulder to shoulder, hunched down.

'OK, like this,' he said. He held the louvre in front of his face, with his left hand holding the left end. She took the right end in her right hand. They shuffled forward on their knees until they were tight against the low wall. He eased his end of the louvre level with the top of the wall. She did the same.

'More,' he said. 'Until we've got a slit to see through.'

They raised it higher until it was horizontal with an inch of space between its lower edge and the top of the wall. They gazed through the gap. They would be visible if somebody was watching the tower very carefully, but overall it was a pretty unobtrusive tactic.

'Look west,' he said. 'Maybe a little bit south of west.' They squinted into the setting sun. They could see forty miles of waving grass. It was like an ocean, bright and golden in the evening backlight. Beyond it was the darkening snowstorm. 'Watch the grassland,' he said.

They knelt there for minutes. The sun inched lower. The last rays tilted flatter into their eyes. Then they saw it. About a mile out into the sea of grass the dying sun flashed gold once on the roof of the Tahoe. It was crawling east through the grassland, coming directly towards them, bouncing over the rough terrain.

'They were smart,' Reacher said. 'They read the map and had the same idea you did, to exit across open country to the west. But then they looked at the town and knew they had to come in that way too.'

The sun slid into the low clouds and the shadow raced east across the grassland and the golden light died. Twilight came and there was nothing more to be seen. They lowered the louvre and crawled back down into the bell chamber. Neagley picked up the Heckler & Koch.

'Not yet,' Reacher said.

'So when?'

'What will *they* do now?'

'They'll get as close as they dare. Then they'll set up and wait.'

Reacher nodded. 'They'll turn the truck round and park it facing west in the best hollow they can find about a hundred, two hundred yards out. They'll check their sight lines to the east and make sure they can see but can't be seen. Then they'll sit tight and wait for Armstrong to show.'

'That's fourteen hours.'

'Exactly,' Reacher said. 'We're going to leave them out there all night. We'll let them get cold and stiff and tired. Then the sun will rise right in their eyes. We'll be coming at them out of the sun. They won't even see us.'

FIFTEEN

They hid the long guns under the pew nearest the church door and left the Yukon parked where it was. Walked up towards the bridge and took two rooms in the boarding house. Then they headed for the grocery store to get dinner ingredients.

The breakfast counter was all closed down, but the woman in the store offered to microwave something from the freezer cabinet. She seemed to assume Reacher and Neagley were a Secret Service advance detail. Everybody seemed to know Armstrong was expected at the service. She heated up some meat pies and some slushy vegetables. They ate them at the darkened counter.

The rooms in the boarding house were clean, as advertised. They had one single bed in each. Reacher let Neagley take the room nearer to the bathroom. Then she joined him in his room for a spell, because she was restless and wanted to talk. They sat side by side on the bed, because there was no other furniture.

'We'll be going up against a prepared position,' she said.

'The two of us against two bozos,' he replied. 'You worried now?'

'It's gotten harder.'

'Tell me,' he said. 'I'm not making you do this, am I?'

'You can't do it alone.'

'I could do it alone one-handed with my head in a bag.'

'We know nothing about them.'

'But we can make some kind of an assessment. The tall guy in Bismarck is the shooter, and the other guy watches his back and drives. Big brother, little brother. There'll be a lot of loyalty. It's a brother thing. This whole deal is a brother thing.'

Neagley said nothing.

'I'm not asking you to participate,' Reacher said.

Neagley smiled. 'You're an idiot. I'm worried about you, not me.'

'Nothing is going to happen to me,' Reacher said. 'I'm going to die an old man in some lonely motel bed.'

'This all is a brother thing for you too, isn't it?' Neagley said.

'Has to be. I don't really give a damn about Armstrong. I liked Froelich, but I would never have known her except for Joe.'

'Are you lonely?'

'Sometimes. Not usually.'

She moved her hand, very slowly. Her fingers moved imperceptibly over the washed-out counterpane until they were a fraction from his. Then they lifted and moved until they were just a fraction above. Then she brought her hand down and her fingers touched the backs of his fingers, very lightly. He turned his hand over. She laced her fingers through his fingers and squeezed. He squeezed back.

He held her hand for five long minutes. Then she slowly pulled it away. Stood up and stepped to the door. Smiled.

'See you in the morning,' she said.

HE SLEPT BADLY and woke at five. Dressed in the dark and walked down the stairs and out into the night. It was bitter cold and there was snow in the air.

There was no light. The town's windows were dark, there were no streetlights, no moon, no stars. The church tower loomed in the middle distance. He walked along the dirt road. Found the church door and went inside. Crept up the tower stairs by feel. Found the ladder and climbed up into the bell chamber. Found the next ladder. Climbed up onto the roof. Crawled over to the west wall and raised his head. The landscape was infinitely dark. He could see nothing.

He waited in the cold. It set his eyes watering and his nose running. He shivered violently. If *I'm* cold, they're nearly dead, he thought. And sure enough, after thirty minutes he heard the sound he had been listening for. The Tahoe's engine started. It was somewhere out there to the west, maybe a couple of hundred yards distant, but it sounded deafening in the night silence. It idled for ten whole minutes, running the heater. He couldn't fix an exact location by sound alone. But then they flicked the dome light on and off for a second. He saw a brief yellow glow deep in the grass. The truck was in a dip. They would probably use it as the shooting platform. Lie on the roof, aim, fire, jump down, jump in, drive away.

He fixed the memory of the yellow flash in his mind against the location of the tower. It was 150 yards out, maybe thirty yards south of perpendicular. He crawled back into the bell tower, down to the nave. He retrieved the long guns from under the pew and left them on the ground underneath the Yukon. He didn't want to put them inside. Didn't want to answer their flash of light with one of his own.

Then he walked back to the boarding house and found Neagley coming out of her room. It was nearly six o'clock. She was showered and dressed. They went into his room to talk.

'They still there?' she asked.

He nodded. 'But there's a problem. We can't start World War Three out there an hour before Armstrong gets here. And we can't leave two corpses lying around a hundred and fifty yards from town. People here have seen us. We need to drive them off and take them down somewhere deserted.'

'OK, how?'

'They're Edward Fox. They're not John Malkovich. They want to live to fight another day. We can make them run if we do it right.'

THEY WERE BACK at the Yukon before six thirty. Snowflakes were still drifting in the air. But the sky was beginning to lighten in the east.

Neagley slung the Heckler & Koch over her back. 'See you later,' she whispered.

She walked west into the graveyard. He saw her turn a little south and then she disappeared in the darkness. He walked to the base of the tower and stood against the middle of the west wall and recalculated the Tahoe's position. Pointed his arm towards it and walked back, keeping the target locked in. He laid the M16 on the ground with the muzzle pointing a little south of west. He stepped behind the Yukon and leaned on the tailgate and waited for the dawn.

It came slowly. Reacher watched the sun and waited until it climbed high enough to hurt his eyes and then he unlocked the Yukon and started the engine. He blipped it loud and turned the radio on full blast. He found some rock and roll and left the driver's door open. Then he picked up the M16 and knocked the safety off and put it to his shoulder and fired a single burst of three, aiming a little south of west directly over the hidden Tahoe. He heard Neagley answer immediately with a triple of her own. The MP5 had a distinctive chattering sound. She was triangulated in the grass 100 yards due south of the Tahoe, firing directly north over it. He fired again, three more from the east. She fired again, three more from the south. The four bursts of fire crashed and rolled and echoed over the landscape. They said: *we . . . know . . . you're . . . there.*

He waited thirty seconds, as planned. There was no response from the Tahoe's position. He raised the rifle again. Aimed high. Squeezed the trigger. *We.* The Heckler & Koch chattered far away to his left. *Know.* He fired again. *You're.* She fired again. *There.*

No response. He wondered for a second whether they'd slipped through the town to the east. He spun round and saw nothing behind him except lights snapping on in windows. He turned back ready to fire again and saw the Tahoe burst up out of the grass 150 yards in front of him. The dawn sun flashed gold and chrome against its tailgate. It bucked over a rise with all four wheels off the ground and crashed back to earth and accelerated away from him into the west.

He threw the rifle into the Yukon's back seat and slammed the door and killed the radio and accelerated into the grassland. The terrain was murderous. The car crashed and bounced over ruts and pitched wildly over long swells. He steered one-handed and clipped his belt with the other. He saw Neagley racing towards him through the grass. He jammed on the brakes and she wrenched the front passenger door open and threw herself in. He took off again and she slammed the door and belted herself in, then jammed the Heckler & Koch between her knees and braced herself with both hands on the dash like she was fighting a roller-coaster ride.

He curved north until he found the swath the Tahoe had blasted through the grass. He centred himself in it and hit the gas. The car was leaping and shuddering, taking off then crashing back to earth.

He hit the gas harder. He was doing nearly fifty miles an hour. Then sixty. The faster he went, the better it rode.

'I see them,' Neagley called.

They were 200 yards ahead, intermittently visible as they bucked up and down through the sea of grass. Reacher pressed on and pulled a little closer. He had the advantage. They were clearing a path for him. He crept up to about 100 yards back and held steady.

Ten minutes later they were ten miles west of Grace and felt like they had been badly beaten in a fistfight. Reacher's head was hitting the roof over every bump and his arms were aching. His shoulders were wrenched. Neagley was bouncing around at his side.

Over the next ten murderous miles the terrain shaded into something new. They were in the middle of nowhere. Grace was twenty miles behind them and the highway was twenty miles ahead. The grade was rising. There was more rock. And there was snow on the ground. Within another mile the chase had slowed to twenty-miles-an-hour. They were inching down forty-five-degree faces, plunging hood-deep through accumulated snow in the bottoms, clawing up the rises with their transmissions locked in four-wheel-drive.

'We're going to get stuck,' Neagley said.

'They got in this way,' Reacher said. 'Got to be able to get out.'

They lost sight of the Tahoe every time it dropped into a ravine. They glimpsed it only when they laboured up a peak and caught sight of it on a peak of its own three or four dips in front. They had slowed to walking pace. Far to the west the snowstorm was wild. The weather was blowing in fast.

'It's time,' Reacher said. 'Any one of these ravines, the snow will hide them all winter.'

'OK, let's go for it,' Neagley said. She buzzed her window down and a flurry of snow blew in on a gale of freezing air. She picked up the Heckler & Koch and clicked it to full auto.

Reacher accelerated hard and plunged through the next two dips as fast as the truck could take it. Then he jammed on the brakes at the top of the third peak and flicked the wheel left. The truck slewed sideways and slid to a stop with the passenger window facing forward and Neagley leaned all the way out. The gold Tahoe reared up ahead and she loosed a long raking burst of fire aimed low at the rear tyres and the fuel tank. The Tahoe paused fractionally and then rocked over the peak of its rise and disappeared.

Reacher spun the wheel and hit the gas and crawled after it. The stop had cost them maybe 100 yards. He ploughed through three ravines and stopped again on the fourth peak. The land fell away twenty feet into a broad gulch, thick with snow. The Tahoe's tracks turned sharply right and ran away to the north, through a tight curve in the ravine, and then out of sight behind a snow-covered outcrop.

The Tahoe might have U-turned, Reacher thought. It could retrace its path and be back near the church just before Armstrong touched down. But to chase it blind would be suicide. Because it might not be doubling back at all. It might be waiting in ambush round the next corner. Or circling right round and aiming to come up behind them. Reacher glanced at his watch. They had been gone nearly thirty minutes. Therefore it would take nearly thirty to get back. And Armstrong had been due in an hour and five.

'Feel like getting cold?' he said.

'No alternative,' Neagley said. She opened her door and slid out into the snow. Ran clumsily to her right, fighting through the drifts, over the rocks, aiming to connect the legs of the U. He took his foot off the brake and nudged the wheel and eased down the slope. Turned right in the ravine bottom and followed the Tahoe's tracks. If he *was* driving straight into an ambush, he was happy enough to do it with Neagley standing behind his opponents with a submachine gun in her hands.

But there was no ambush. He came round the rocks and turned back east and saw nothing at all except empty wheel tracks in the snow and Neagley standing fifty yards further on. He raced up to her. She fought her way through the drifts and pulled the door.

'Hit it,' she said. 'They must be at least five minutes ahead of us.'

He touched the gas. All four wheels spun uselessly. The truck stayed motionless and all four tyres whined in the snow and the front end dug in deeper.

'Shit,' he said.

He tried again. Same result. He put the transmission in reverse, then drive, then reverse, then drive. The truck rocked back and forth, six inches, a foot. But it didn't climb out of the trench.

Neagley glanced at her watch. 'Armstrong's in the air now. And our car isn't parked next to the church any more. So he's going to go ahead and land.'

'You do it,' Reacher said. 'Keep it rocking back and forward.' He unclipped his belt and opened his door and slid out into the snow.

He floundered round to the rear of the truck. Neagley slid across into the driver's seat. She built up a rhythm, drive and reverse, drive and reverse. Reacher put his back against the tailgate and hooked his hands under the rear bumper. Moved with the truck as it pushed back at him. Straightened his legs and heaved as it moved away. Finally he felt the truck climb out of the trench and he fell back into the snow.

He rolled up through the stink of gasoline exhaust. The truck was twenty yards ahead, Neagley driving as slow as she dared. He chased after it. Caught the door handle and flung the door open and floundered alongside the truck until he had built enough speed. Then he hauled himself into the seat and slammed the door. She stamped hard on the gas and the violent, battering roller-coaster ride came back.

He stared through the windshield. Nothing there. No Tahoe. It was long gone. All that remained were its tracks through the snow, deep twinned ruts that narrowed in the distance ahead. They pointed towards the town of Grace like arrows.

Then they changed. They swooped a tight ninety-degree left and disappeared into a narrow north–south ravine that ran steeply downhill. The Tahoe's tracks were visible for fifty yards then swerved out of sight again, a sharp right behind a rock outcrop the size of a house. Neagley braked hard as the grade fell away. She stopped, and Reacher's mind screamed *An ambush now?* a split second after her foot hit the gas again and her hands turned the wheel. The Yukon locked into the Tahoe's ruts and its two-ton weight slid it helplessly down the icy slope. The Tahoe burst out of hiding, backwards, directly in front of them. It skidded to a stop across their path.

Neagley was out of her door before the Yukon stopped moving. She rolled in the snow and floundered away to the north. The Yukon slewed violently and stalled in a snowdrift. Reacher's door was jammed shut by the depth of the snow. He forced it half open and scraped out through the gap. Saw the driver spilling from the Tahoe, slipping and falling in the snow. Reacher pulled his Steyr from his pocket. Thrashed round to the back of the Yukon and crawled forward through the snow along its other side. The Tahoe driver was holding a rifle, rowing himself through the snow with its muzzle. He was heading for the rock. He was the guy from Bismarck. Lean face, long body. He even had the same coat on. It was flapping open. Reacher raised the Steyr and steadied it against the Yukon's fender and tracked the guy's head. Tightened his finger on the trigger. Then he heard a voice, loud and urgent, right behind him.

'Hold your fire,' the voice called.

He turned and saw a second guy ten yards north and west.

Neagley was stumbling through the snow directly ahead of him. He had her Heckler & Koch held low in his left hand. A handgun in his right, jammed in her back. He was the guy from the garage video. Tweed overcoat, short, wide in the shoulders, a little squat. No hat this time. He had the same face as the Bismarck guy, a little fatter. The same greying sandy hair, a little thicker. *Brothers*.

'Throw the weapon down, sir,' he called.

It was a perfect cop line. Neagley mouthed *I'm sorry*. Reacher reversed the Steyr in his hand. Held it by the barrel.

'Throw down the weapon, sir,' the squat guy called again.

His brother from Bismarck changed direction and ploughed forward through the snow and moved in closer. He raised the rifle. It was pointing straight at Reacher's head. Reacher tossed his pistol high in the air. It arced thirty feet through the falling snow and landed and buried itself in a drift.

The guy from Bismarck fumbled in his pocket with his left hand and pulled out his badge. Held it high in his palm. Fumbled the badge away again and brought the rifle to his shoulder and held it level and steady. 'We're police officers,' he said.

'I know you are,' Reacher said back. He glanced around. The guy from the garage video pushed Neagley nearer.

'But who are you?' the Bismarck guy asked. 'You here to make the world safe for democracy?'

'I'm here because you're a lousy shot,' Reacher said. 'You got the wrong person on Thursday.' Then he moved very cautiously and pulled his cuff and checked his watch. And smiled. 'And you lose again. It's too late now. You're going to miss him.'

The Bismarck guy shook his head. 'Police scanner. In our truck. We're listening to Casper PD. Armstrong is delayed twenty minutes. There was a weather problem in South Dakota. So we decided to hang out and let you catch us up. Because we don't like you. You're poking around where you're not welcome. In a purely private matter. So consider yourselves under arrest. You want to plead guilty?'

Reacher said nothing.

'Or you just want to plead?'

'Like you did? When that baseball bat was getting close?'

The guy went quiet for a second. 'Your attitude isn't helping your cause,' he said.

'Whatever happened, it was thirty years ago.'

'A guy does something like that, he should pay.'

'The guy died.'

The Bismarck cop shrugged. 'You should read your Bible, my friend. The sins of the fathers, you ever heard of that?'

'What sins? You lost a fight, is all.'

'We never lose. Sooner or later, we always win. And Armstrong *watched*. Snot-nosed rich kid. A man doesn't forget a thing like that.'

Keep him talking, Reacher thought. *Keep him moving*. But he looked into the crazed eyes and couldn't think of a thing to say.

'The woman goes in the truck,' the guy said. 'We'll have a little fun with her, after we deal with Armstrong. But I'm going to shoot you right now.'

'Not with that rifle,' Reacher said. *Keep him talking. Keep him moving*. 'The muzzle is full of slush. It'll blow up in your hands.'

There was a long silence. The guy calculated the distance between himself and Reacher, just a glance. Then he lowered the rifle. Reversed it in his hands, in and out fast, long enough to check. The muzzle was packed with icy snow.

'You want to bet your life on a little slush?' the Bismarck guy asked.

'Do you? The breech will blow, take your ugly face off.'

The guy's face darkened. But he didn't pull the trigger. 'Step away from the car,' he said, like the cop he was.

Reacher took a long pace away from the Yukon.

'And another.'

Reacher moved again. He was six feet from the car. Six feet from his M16. He glanced around. The Bismarck brother held the rifle in his left hand and put his right under his coat and came out with a handgun. It was a Glock. *Probably police department issue*. He released the safety and levelled it one-handed at Reacher's face.

'Not that one either,' Reacher said. 'That's your work gun. Chances are you've used it before. So there are records. They find my body, the ballistics will come right back at you.'

The guy stood still for a long moment. Put the Glock away again. Raised the rifle. Shuffled backwards through the snow towards the Tahoe. The rifle stayed level with Reacher's chest. The guy fumbled behind him and opened the Tahoe's rear door, driver's side. Dropped the rifle in the snow and came out with a handgun, all in one move. It was an old M9 Beretta, scratched and stained with dried oil. The guy tracked forward again through the drift. Stopped six feet away from Reacher. Raised his arm. Unlatched the safety with his thumb and levelled the weapon straight at the centre of Reacher's face.

'No records on this one,' he said. 'Say good night now.'

'On the click,' Reacher said.

He stared straight ahead at the gun. Saw Neagley's face in the corner of his eye. Saw that she didn't understand what he meant, but saw her nod anyway. It was just a fractional movement of her eyelids. Like half a blink. The Bismarck guy smiled. Tightened his finger. His knuckle shone white. He squeezed the trigger. There was a dull click.

Reacher came out with his ceramic knife already open and brushed it sideways across the guy's forehead. Then he caught the Beretta's barrel in his left hand and jerked it up and jerked it down full force across his knee and shattered the guy's forearm. Pushed him away and spun round.

Neagley had hardly moved. But the guy from the garage video was inert in the snow by her feet. She was holding her Heckler & Koch in one hand and the guy's handgun in the other. 'Yes?' she said.

He nodded. She stepped a pace away so her clothes wouldn't get splashed and pointed the handgun at the ground and shot the garage guy three times. A double-tap to the head, and then an insurance round in the chest. The Bismarck guy was stumbling around in the snow, completely blind. Blood was pouring out of the wound in his forehead and running down into his eyes. He was cradling his broken arm.

Reacher took the Heckler & Koch from Neagley and set it to fire a single round and waited until the guy had pirouetted round and shot him through the throat. The guy pitched forward on his face and lay still and the snow turned bright red all around him.

'How did you know?' Neagley asked, quietly.

'It was Froelich's gun,' he said. 'They stole it from her kitchen. I recognised the scratches and the oil marks. She'd kept the clips loaded in a drawer for about five years.'

'It still might have fired,' Neagley said.

'The whole of life is a gamble,' Reacher said. 'Wouldn't you say?'

He waded over and retrieved his Steyr from where it had fallen. The snow was already starting to cover the two bodies. He took wallets and badges from the pockets. Wiped his knife clean on the Bismarck guy's twill coat. Neagley wiped the garage guy's pistol on her coat and dropped it. Then they floundered back to the Yukon and climbed inside. Took a last look back. The scene was already rimed with new snow, whitening fast. It would be gone within forty-eight hours. The icy wind would freeze the whole tableau inside a long smooth east–west drift until spring.

Neagley drove, slowly. Reacher piled the wallets on his knees and started with the badges.

'County cops from Idaho,' he said. 'Some place south of Boise.'

He put both badges into his pocket. Opened the Bismarck guy's wallet. There was a milky plastic window on the inside with police ID behind it.

'His name was Richard Wilson,' he said. 'Basic grade detective.'

There was an Idaho driving licence in the wallet. And scraps of paper, and almost $300 in cash. He spilled the paper on his knees and put the cash in his pocket. Opened the garage guy's wallet. It had a driving licence, nearly $200, and ID from the same police department.

'Peter Wilson,' he said. 'A year younger.'

Reacher put the cash in his pocket and glanced ahead. There was a small black dot in the air. The church tower was barely visible, almost twenty miles away. The Yukon bounced its way towards it. The black dot grew larger. There was a blur of rotors above it. The wallets slid off Reacher's knees and the paper scraps scattered.

'Golf clubs,' Reacher said. 'Not tool samples.'

'What?'

He held up a scrap of paper. 'A UPS receipt. Next-day air. From Minneapolis. Addressed to Richard Wilson, arriving guest, at a DC motel. A carton, a foot square, forty-eight inches long. Contents, one bag of golf clubs.' Then he went quiet. Stared at another scrap of paper. 'Something else,' he said. 'For Stuyvesant, maybe.'

THEY WATCHED the distant helicopter land and stopped right there in the middle of the empty grassland. Reacher piled the badges with the police IDs and the driving licences on the passenger seat and then hurled the empty wallets far into the landscape.

'We need to sanitise,' he said. They wiped their prints off all four weapons and threw them into the grass, north and south and east and west. Emptied the spare rounds from their pockets and hurled them away. Followed them with the birdwatcher's scope.

Then they drove the rest of the way to Grace slow and easy and bumped up out of the grassland and parked near the waiting helicopter and got out. They could hear the groan of the organ and the sound of people singing inside the church.

They stood there for fifteen minutes. There was a mournful piece from the organ, and then quiet, and then the muffled sound of feet moving on dusty boards. The big oak door opened and a small crowd filtered out into the sunshine. The vicar stood outside the door with Froelich's parents and spoke to everybody as they left.

Armstrong came out after a couple of minutes with Stuyvesant at his side. They were surrounded by seven agents. Armstrong spoke to the vicar and shook hands with the Froelichs and spoke some more. Then his detail brought him to the helicopter. He saw Reacher and Neagley and detoured near them, a question in his face.

'We all live happily ever after,' Reacher said.

Armstrong nodded once. 'Thank you,' he said, and then turned and walked on towards the chopper.

Stuyvesant came next, on his own. 'Happily?' he repeated.

Reacher gathered the badges and the IDs and the licences from his pockets. Stuyvesant cupped his hands to take them all.

'Maybe more happily than we thought,' Reacher said. 'They were cops, from Idaho, near Boise. You've got the addresses there. I'm sure you'll find what you need. The computer, the paper and the printer, Andretti's thumb in the freezer. Something else, maybe.'

He took a scrap of paper from his pocket.

'I found this too,' he said. 'It was in one of the wallets. It's a register receipt. They went to the grocery store late on Friday and bought six TV dinners and six big bottles of water.'

'So?' Stuyvesant said.

Reacher smiled. 'My guess is they were making sure Mrs Nendick could eat while they came out here. I think she's still alive.'

Stuyvesant snatched the receipt and ran for the helicopter.

REACHER AND NEAGLEY said their goodbyes at Denver Airport the next morning. Reacher signed over his fee cheque to her and she bought him a first-class ticket on United to New York La Guardia. He walked her to the gate for her Chicago flight. She didn't say anything. Just placed her bag on the floor and stood directly in front of him. Then she stretched up and hugged him, fast, like she didn't really know how to do it. She let go after a second and picked up her bag and walked down the jetway. Didn't look back.

He made it into La Guardia late in the evening. Took a bus and a subway to Times Square and walked Forty-second Street until he found B.B. King's new club. A four-piece guitar band was just finishing its first set. He walked back to the ticket taker.

'Was there an old woman here last week?' he asked. 'Sounded a little like Dawn Penn? With an old guy on keyboards?'

The ticket taker shook his head. 'Nobody like that. Not here.'

Reacher nodded once and stepped out into the shiny darkness. It was cold on the street. He headed west for the Port Authority and a bus out of town.

LEE CHILD

'When I'm writing a book, I have an idea of where I want the story to end up but, other than that, I just start somewhere and let the plot work itself out. It helps keep the story as unpredictable as possible,' says Lee Child of the method he has used to produce his six hugely entertaining thrillers starring Jack Reacher.

Without Fail, however, got off the ground in a very different way. 'I went to a fan convention in Denver,' Child explains, 'where they were holding a charity auction, and I offered to include the name of the highest bidder as a minor character in my next book. The bidding quickly became a contest between two women and reached a tremendous figure. I was delighted for the charity but worried the women might later regret what they'd done, so I halted the bidding and said that for that kind of money the winner could be a *major* character. The bidding restarted, but there was still no sign of a winner. I stepped in again and offered to feature *both* women's names in the book. Luckily, one wanted to be the love interest while the other wanted to be Reacher's buddy, with the proviso that the love interest should die a cruel death!'

With his main cast members established—the two winning bidders were immortalised as M. E. Froelich and Frances Neagley, both of whom assist and are attracted to hero Jack Reacher in *Without Fail*—Child then had to set about researching the novel's background. 'This was difficult, as you can imagine, because the secret service is secret, after all! They won't tell a writer anything. But I have a loyal reader (I can't say who on pain of death) who is still being protected by the service and who helped out, so the details, I'm pleased to say, are pretty accurate.'

In the wake of the devastating terrorist attack on New York on September 11, 2001, *Without Fail* seems particularly relevant. One reviewer called it 'The perfect thing for Dick Cheney's bedside reading,' and, as Child himself says, 'Although VIP security is tighter than ever now, the fundamental problem of protecting people who live public lives still remains.'

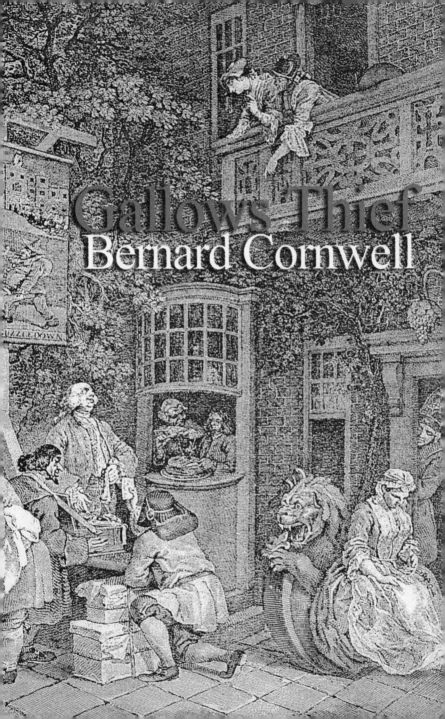

Gallows Thief

Bernard Cornwell

It is 1817, and on Old Bailey, one of London's busiest streets, crowds gather to watch prisoners from Newgate Prison fall victim to the hangman's noose.

Soon it will be the turn of Charles Corday, a society portrait painter, charged with murder. A murder he swears he did not commit.

Is he innocent, as he claims? If so, who *did* kill the Countess of Avebury? Rider Sandman, the Home Secretary's newly appointed Investigator, has just seven days to find out.

1

Sir Henry Forrest, banker and alderman of the City of London, almost gagged when he entered the Press Yard for the smell was terrible, worse than the reek of the sewer outflows where the Fleet Ditch oozed into the Thames. It was a stink from the cesspits of hell, an eye-watering stench that took a man's breath away and made Sir Henry take an involuntary step backwards, clap a handkerchief to his nose and hold his breath for fear that he was about to vomit.

Sir Henry's guide chuckled. 'I don't notice the smell no more, sir,' he said, 'but I suppose it's mortal bad in its way, mortal bad. Mind the steps here, sir, do mind 'em.'

Sir Henry gingerly took the handkerchief away and forced himself to speak. 'Why is it called the Press Yard?'

'In days gone by, sir, this is where the prisoners was pressed. They was squashed, sir. Weighed down by stones, sir, to persuade them to tell the truth. We don't do it any longer, sir, more's the pity, and as a consequence they lies like India rugs, sir.' The guide, one of the prison's turnkeys, was a fat man with leather breeches, a stained coat and a stout billy club. He laughed. 'There ain't a guilty man or woman in here, sir, not if you asks them!'

Sir Henry tried to keep his breathing shallow so he would not have to inhale the noxious miasma of ordure, sweat and rot. 'There is sanitation here?' he asked.

'Very up to date. Proper drains in Newgate, sir. But they're filthy animals, sir. They fouls their own nest, sir.' The turnkey closed and bolted the barred gate by which they had entered the yard. 'The condemned have the freedom of the Press Yard, sir, during daylight,' he said, 'except on high days and holidays like today.' He grinned, letting Sir Henry know this was a jest. 'If you turn to your left, sir, you can join the other gentlemen in the Association Room.'

'The Association Room?' Sir Henry enquired.

'Where the condemned associate, sir, during the daylight hours, sir,' the turnkey explained, 'and those windows to your left, sir, those are the salt boxes.'

Sir Henry saw, at the end of the long yard, fifteen barred windows on three floors. The cells behind were called the salt boxes. He had no idea why they were called that, but knew that the fifteen salt boxes were Newgate's condemned cells. A doomed man, his eyes a mere glitter behind the thick bars, stared back at Sir Henry who turned away as the turnkey hauled open the heavy door of the Association Room. 'Obliged to you, Sir Henry,' the turnkey knuckled his forehead as Sir Henry offered him a shilling in thanks for his guidance through the prison's labyrinthine passages.

Sir Henry was greeted by the Keeper, William Brown, a lugubrious man with a bald head and heavy jowls. A priest wearing a cassock, a surplice, and an old-fashioned wig, stood smiling unctuously beside the Keeper. 'Pray allow me to name the Ordinary,' the Keeper said, 'the Reverend Doctor Horace Cotton. Sir Henry Forrest.'

Sir Henry took off his hat. 'Your servant, Doctor Cotton.'

'At your service, Sir Henry,' the prison chaplain responded fulsomely, after offering Sir Henry a deep bow.

'Sir Henry,' the Keeper confided, 'is here on official duty.'

'Ah!' The Reverend Cotton's eyes opened wide, suggesting Sir Henry was in for a rare treat. 'And is this your first such visit?'

'My first,' Sir Henry admitted.

'Souls have been won for Christ by this experience,' Doctor Cotton said. He smiled, then bowed obsequiously as the Keeper ushered Sir Henry away to meet the other six guests who had come for the traditional Newgate breakfast. The last of the guests, Matthew Logan, needed no introduction, for he and Sir Henry were City aldermen. The Court of Aldermen were the official governors of Newgate Prison. Logan took Sir Henry's arm and led him to the hearth where they could talk privately.

'You're sure you want to see this through?' Logan asked his friend solicitously. 'You look damned pale.'

Sir Henry was a good-looking man, lean, tall and straight-backed

with a clever and fastidious face. He was a banker, rich and successful. His hair, prematurely silver, for he was only a few days past his
fiftieth birthday, gave him a distinguished appearance, yet at that
moment he looked old, frail, emaciated and sickly. 'I'm never at my
shining best this close to dawn, Logan,' he explained.

'Quite,' Logan said, 'but this ain't an experience for everyone,
though I must say the breakfast afterwards is good. The Keeper
serves devilled kidneys on hanging days. How is Lady Forrest?'

'Florence keeps well, thank you for asking.'

'And your daughter?'

'Eleanor will doubtless survive her troubles,' Sir Henry said drily.
'A broken heart has yet to prove fatal.' He held his hands towards the
remnants of the fire that was waiting to be blown back into life.
'Poor Eleanor. If it was up to me, Logan, I'd let her marry, but
Florence won't hear of it.'

'Mothers usually know best about such things,' Logan said airily,
and then the room's murmur of conversation died as the guests
turned towards a barred door that had opened with a harsh squeal.
A man carrying a stout leather bag stumped in. He was burly, red-
faced and dressed in brown gaiters, black breeches and a black coat
that was buttoned too tightly over his protuberant belly. He respectfully pulled off a shabby brown hat when he saw the waiting gentry.

'That,' Logan told Sir Henry under his breath, 'is Mister James
Botting, more familiarly known as Jemmy, the petitioner.'

Sir Henry reminded himself that men should not be judged by their
outward appearance, though it was hard not to disapprove of a being
as ugly as James Botting, whose raw-beef slab of a face was disfig-
ured by warts and scars. Botting slung his leather bag onto a table,
unbuckled it and brought out eight coils of thin white cord. He
arranged them on the table in a row. Next he took out four white
cotton sacks, each about a foot square, that he placed by the coiled
lines, and last of all he produced four heavy ropes. Each rope looked
to be about ten or twelve feet long and each had a noose tied into one
end and an eye spliced in the other. James Botting laid the ropes on
the table and then stepped back. 'Good morning, gentlemen,' he said.

'Oh, Botting!' The Keeper spoke in a tone which suggested he had
only just noticed Botting's presence. 'A very good morning to you.'

'And a nice one it is too, sir,' Botting said. 'There ain't a cloud in
sight, sir. Still just the four customers today, sir?'

'Just the four, Botting.'

'They've drawn a good crowd, sir, they have, a very good crowd.'

'Good, very good,' the Keeper said vaguely, then returned to his conversation with one of the breakfast guests.

Logan looked back to Sir Henry. 'We watch the proceedings up to a point, Sir Henry, but then we retire for devilled kidneys.' Then he held up his hand. 'Hear it?'

Sir Henry could hear a clanking sound. The room had fallen silent again and he felt a kind of chill dread.

Another turnkey came into the room. He knuckled his forehead to the Keeper, then stood beside a slab of timber that squatted on the floor. The turnkey held a stout hammer. Then the Sheriff and Under-Sheriff appeared in the doorway, ushering the prisoners into the Association Room. There were three men and a woman. The last was scarce more than a girl and had a pale and frightened face.

'Brandy, sir?' One of the Keeper's servants appeared beside Matthew Logan and Sir Henry.

'Thank you,' Logan said, and took two of the beakers. He handed one to Sir Henry. 'It settles the stomach,' he said.

The prison bell suddenly began to toll. The girl twitched at the sound, then the turnkey ordered her to put a foot onto the wooden anvil so her leg irons could be struck off. Sir Henry sipped the brandy and feared it would not stay down. His head felt light, unreal. The turnkey hammered the rivets from the first manacle and Sir Henry saw the girl's ankle was a welt of sores.

The bell tolled on and it would not stop now until all four bodies were cut down. Sir Henry was aware that his hand was shaking.

Logan was gazing at the quivering girl. 'She stole her mistress's pearl necklace. She must have sold it, for the necklace was never found. Then the tall fellow next in line is a highwayman. The other two murdered a grocer in Southwark.'

The girl, moving awkwardly because she was unaccustomed to walking without leg irons, shuffled away from the makeshift anvil.

Botting snapped at her to come to him. 'Drink that if you want it.' He pointed to a beaker of brandy that had been placed on the table next to the ropes. The girl spilt some because her hands were shaking, but she gulped the rest down and then dropped the beaker, which clattered on the flagstones. 'Arms by your side, girl,' Botting ordered.

'I didn't steal anything!' she wailed.

'Quiet, my child, quiet.' The Reverend Cotton had moved to her side and put a hand on her shoulder. 'God is our refuge and strength, child, and you must put your faith in him. Do you repent your foul sins, child?' the Ordinary said.

'I stole nothing!'

Sir Henry forced himself to draw long breaths. 'Did you escape those Brazilian loans?' he asked Logan.

'Sold them on to Drummonds,' Logan said, 'so I'm damned grateful to you, Henry, damned grateful.'

'It's Eleanor you must thank. She saw a report in a Paris newspaper and drew the right conclusions. Clever girl, my daughter.'

'Such a pity about the engagement,' Logan said. He was watching the doomed girl who cried aloud as Botting fastened her elbows with a length of cord behind her back, drawing the line so tight that she gasped with pain.

'Hands in front, girl!' Botting snapped and, when she awkwardly lifted her hands, he secured her wrists in front of her body.

The highwayman put a coin on the table beside the brandy beaker. 'Good lad,' the hangman said quietly. The coin would ensure the highwayman's death would be as swift as Botting could make it.

'Eleanor's very unhappy,' Sir Henry said, his back now turned on the prisoners, 'I can tell.'

'Sandman was a very decent young man,' Logan said.

'He is a very decent young man,' Sir Henry agreed, trying to ignore the girl's soft sobbing. 'But quite without prospects now. And Eleanor cannot marry into a disgraced family.'

'Indeed she cannot,' Logan agreed.

Sir Henry shook his head. 'And none of it is Rider Sandman's fault, but he's penniless now. Quite penniless.'

Logan frowned. 'He's on half-pay, surely?'

Sir Henry shook his head. 'He sold his commission, gave the money towards the keep of his mother and sister.'

'But Eleanor, surely, is not without suitors?'

'Far from it,' Sir Henry sounded gloomy. 'They queue up in the street, Logan, but Eleanor finds fault.'

'She's good at that,' Logan said softly, but without malice for he was fond of his friend's daughter, though he thought her over-indulged. 'Still,' he said, 'doubtless she'll marry soon?'

'Doubtless she will,' Sir Henry said, for his daughter was not only attractive but it was also well known that Sir Henry would settle a generous income on her future husband, which was why Sir Henry was sometimes tempted to let her marry Rider Sandman, but Eleanor's mother would not hear of it. Florence wanted Eleanor to have a title, and Rider Sandman had none, and now he had no fortune either. Sir Henry's thoughts about his daughter's prospects were driven away by a shriek from the doomed girl. He turned to see that James Botting had hung one of the heavy noosed ropes about her shoulders and she was shrinking from its touch.

The Reverend Cotton opened his prayer book. The prisoners were all now pinioned.

The Sheriff and Under-Sheriff, both wearing robes and chains of office and carrying silver-tipped staves, went to the Keeper, who bowed to them before presenting the Sheriff with a sheet of paper.

'"I am the resurrection and the life,"' the Reverend Cotton intoned, '"he that believeth in me, though he were dead, yet shall he live."'

The Sheriff nodded and thrust the paper into a pocket of his fur-trimmed robe. Until now the four prisoners had been in the care of the Keeper of Newgate, but now they belonged to the Sheriff of the City of London. The Sheriff hauled a watch from a fob pocket and clicked open its lid. 'Time to go, I think.'

The Sheriff led the procession out of the Association Room. The Reverend Cotton had a hand on the girl's neck, guiding her as he read the burial service aloud. Prisoners in the cells overlooking the Press Yard shouted protests and farewells as they passed. The Sheriff led the procession down a flight of stone stairs into the gloomy passage that ran beneath the main prison.

'I didn't steal anything!' the girl suddenly screamed.

'Quiet, lass,' the Keeper growled. All the men were nervous. They wanted the prisoners to cooperate and the girl was close to hysteria.

'"Lord, let me know mine end,"' the Ordinary prayed.

'Please!' the girl wailed. 'No, no! Please.' A turnkey closed on her in case she collapsed, but she stumbled on.

Sir Henry watched the prisoners climb the steps at the end of the tunnel and wished he had not come.

At the top of the stairs was the lodge, a cavernous entrance chamber that gave access to the street called Old Bailey. The Debtor's Door that led to the street stood open, but no daylight showed for the scaffold had been built directly outside. The noise of the crowd was loud now and the prison bell was muffled, but the bell of St Sepulchre's on the far side of Newgate Street was also tolling for the imminent deaths.

'Gentlemen?' The Sheriff turned to the breakfast guests. 'If you'll climb the steps to the scaffold you'll find chairs to right and left.'

Sir Henry saw in front of him the dark hollow underside of the scaffold supported by raw wooden beams. Black baize shrouded the planks at the front and side of the stage, which meant that the only light came from the chinks between the timbers that formed the scaffold's elevated platform. Wooden stairs climbed to a roofed pavilion at the scaffold's rear. The roof was there to keep the honoured guests dry in inclement weather, but today the sun was bright enough to make Sir Henry blink as he emerged into the pavilion.

A huge cheer greeted the guests' arrival. No one cared who they were, but their appearance presaged the coming of the prisoners. Old Bailey was crowded. Every window that overlooked the street was crammed and there were even folk on the rooftops.

'Ten shillings to rent a window,' Logan explained. He pointed at a tavern opposite the scaffold. 'The Magpie and Stump has the most expensive windows because you can see right down into the pit where they drop.' He chuckled. 'But we, of course, get the best view.'

Sir Henry wanted to sit at the back of the pavilion, but Logan had already taken one of the front chairs and Sir Henry just sat. He was overwhelmed. So many people! Everywhere faces looking up at the black-draped platform. The scaffold was in front of the roofed pavilion, thirty feet long and fifteen feet wide and topped by a great beam that ran from the pavilion's roof to the platform's end. Butchers' hooks were screwed into the beam's underside and a ladder was propped against it.

'It'll be the girl they've come to see,' Logan said. He was evidently enjoying himself. How little we know our friends, Sir Henry thought, then he rather wished that Rider Sandman was here. He had always liked Sandman. He had been a soldier and he suspected he would not approve of death made this easy.

'I should let him marry her,' he said.

'What?' Logan had to raise his voice because the crowd was shouting for the prisoners to be brought on.

'Nothing,' Sir Henry said.

Then the crowd saw the girl as she climbed the stairs behind a turnkey. The roar of the crowd was massive, crushing, and then the people surged forward. His mind swimming, Sir Henry suddenly noticed the four open coffins that lay on the scaffold's edge. The girl's mouth was open and tears ran down her cheeks as Botting led her onto the trap door at the platform's centre. It creaked under their weight. Botting took a cotton bag from his pocket and pulled it over the girl's face. She screamed and tried to twist away from him, but the Reverend Cotton put a hand on her arm as the hangman took the rope from her shoulders and clambered up the ladder. He slotted the small spliced eye over one of the butcher's hooks, then climbed back down. He pulled the noose down around her head, tightened the slip knot under her left ear, then gave the rope a small jerk as if to satisfy himself that it would take her weight. She screamed.

Sir Henry closed his eyes.

'"O teach us to number our days,"' the Ordinary read in a singsong voice, '"that we may apply our hearts unto wisdom."'

'Amen,' Sir Henry said fervently, too fervently.

The four prisoners were all now lined up on the trap door, cotton bags over their faces and nooses about their necks. 'Confess your sins!' the Reverend Cotton urged them.

The crowd shouted for silence, hoping there would be some final words.

'I did nothing!' the girl screamed.

'Now, Botting!' The Sheriff wanted it done quickly and Botting brushed past to go down the stairs at the back of the pavilion.

Only the four condemned and the Ordinary were now out in the sunlight. The girl was swaying and under the thin cotton that hid her face Sir Henry could see her mouth was opening and closing.

Under the platform the hangman jerked the rope that pulled out the baulk of timber supporting the trap door. The timber shifted, but did not slide all the way. Sir Henry, unaware that he was holding his breath, saw the trap door twitch. The crowd uttered a collective yelp that died away when they realised the bodies had not dropped, then Botting gave the rope an almighty heave and the trap door swung down to let the four bodies fall. It was a short drop, only five or six feet, and it killed none of them. 'It was quicker when they used the cart at Tyburn,' Logan said, leaning forward, 'but we get more Morris this way.'

Sir Henry did not need to ask what Logan meant. The four were twitching and jerking. They were doing the Morris dance of the scaffold, the dying capers that came from the stifling, throttling struggles of the doomed. Sir Henry saw none of it, for his eyes were closed. The crowd cheered itself hoarse, because Botting climbed up to squat on the highwayman's shoulders to hasten his dying.

'There's the first one gone,' Logan said, as Botting clambered down, 'and I've got a mortal appetite now, by God!'

Three of the four still danced, but ever more feebly. The dead highwayman swung with canted head as Botting hauled on the girl's ankles. Sir Henry could suddenly take no more of the spectacle and so he stumbled down the scaffold steps into the cool, dark stone shelter of the lodge and vomited.

2

Rider Sandman was up late that Monday morning because he had been paid seven guineas to play for Sir John Hart's eleven against a Sussex team—the winners to share a bonus of a hundred guineas— and Sandman had scored sixty-three runs in the first innings and thirty-two in the second, but Sir John's eleven had still lost. That had been on the Saturday and Sandman, watching the other batsmen, had realised that the game was being thrown. The bookmakers were being fleeced because Sir John's team had been expected to win handily, not least because the famed Rider Sandman was playing for it, but some-one must have bet heavily on the Sussex eleven. Rumour said that Sir John himself had bet against his own side.

So Captain Rider Sandman, late of His Majesty's 52nd Regiment of Foot, walked back to London. He walked because he refused to share a carriage with men who had accepted bribes to lose a match. He loved cricket, he was good at it, but he detested corruption and he possessed a temper. He fell into a furious argument with his treacherous teammates and, when they slept that night in Sir John's comfortable house and rode back to London in comfort next morn-ing, Sandman did neither. He was too proud.

Proud and poor. He could not afford the stagecoach fare because in his anger he had thrown his match fee back into Sir John Hart's face. So he walked home, spending the Saturday night in a hayrick and trudging all Sunday until the right sole was almost clean off his boot. He reached his rented attic room in Drury Lane very late that night and he stripped himself naked and fell into the narrow bed and slept. Just slept. When the trap door dropped in Old Bailey, Sandman was still dreaming, his ears filled with the thump of hoofs and the crash of muskets and cannon. The dream was going to end with the cavalry smashing through the thin, red-coated ranks, but then the rattle of hoofs melded into a rush of feet on the stairs and a sketchy knock on his door. He opened his eyes and then, before he could call out any response, Sally Hood was in the room. Sally laughed. 'I bleeding woke you. Gawd, I'm sorry!'

'It's all right, Miss Hood. What's the time?'

'St Giles's just struck half after eight,' she told him.

'Oh lord!' Sandman sat up in bed and remembered he was naked.

'There's a gown hanging on the door, Miss Hood, would you . . .'

Sally found the dressing gown. 'It's just that I'm late,' she explained, 'and my brother's brushed off and I've got work, and the dress has to be hooked up, see?' She turned her back, showing a length of bare spine. 'I'd have asked Mrs Gunn to do it,' Sally went on, 'only there's a hanging today so she's off watching. It's all right, you can get up now, I've got me peepers shut.'

Sandman climbed out of bed warily, for there was only a limited area in his tiny attic room where he could stand without banging his head on the beams. He was a tall man, with pale gold hair, blue eyes and a long, raw-boned face. He was not conventionally handsome—his face was too rugged for that—but there was a capability and a kindness in his expression that made him memorable. He pulled on the dressing gown. 'A good job, I hope?' he asked Sally.

'Ain't what I wanted,' Sally said, 'because it ain't on stage.' She called herself an actress, though Sandman had seen little evidence that the stage had much use for Sally, who clung to the very edge of respectability. 'But it ain't bad work and it is respectable.'

'I'm sure it is,' Sandman said. He wondered why she sounded so defensive about a respectable job; and Sally wondered why Sandman, who was palpably a gentleman, was renting an attic room in the Wheatsheaf Tavern in Drury Lane. Down on his luck, that was for sure, but the Wheatsheaf was famously a flash tavern, a home for every kind of thief from pickpockets to burglars to shop-breakers, and it seemed to Sally that Captain Rider Sandman was as straight as a ramrod. But he was a nice man, Sally thought. He treated her like a lady, and though she had only spoken to him a couple of times, she had detected a kindness in him. 'And what about you, Captain?' she asked. 'You working?'

'I'm looking for employment, Miss Hood,' Sandman said, and that was true, but he was not finding any. He was too old to be an apprentice clerk, not qualified to work in the law or with money, and too squeamish to accept a job driving slaves in the sugar islands.

'I heard you was a famous cricketer,' Sally said. 'You can earn money at that, can't you?'

'Not as much as I need,' Sandman said, 'and I have a small problem here. Some of the hooks are missing.'

'That's 'cos I never get round to mending them,' said Sally, 'so just do what you can. Thread this through the gaps, Captain,' Sally said, dangling a frayed silk handkerchief over her shoulder. 'And by the by, if you're going down to breakfast then do it quick 'cos you won't get a bite after nine o'clock. The 'sheaf's always crowded when there's a hanging at Newgate,' Sally explained. 'Makes the folk hungry. That's where my brother went. He always goes down Old Bailey when there's a scragging.' Sally's brother was a mysterious young man who worked strange hours. He and Sally rented two large rooms on the Wheatsheaf's first floor. 'They like him to be there. He usually knows one of the poor bastards being twisted, see?'

'Twisted?'

'Hanged, Captain. Twisted, scragged or nubbed. Doing the Newgate Morris, dancing on Jemmy Botting's stage. You'll have to learn the flash language if you live here, Captain.'

'I can see I will,' Sandman said, and had just begun to thread the handkerchief through the dress's gaping back when Dodds, the inn's errand boy, pushed through the half-open door and grinned.

'You'll catch flies if you don't close your bloody gob,' Sally told Dodds. 'He's just hooking me up.'

Dodds ignored this tirade and held a sealed paper towards Sandman. 'Letter for you, Captain.'

'You're very kind,' Sandman said, and stooped to his folded clothes to find a penny to tip the boy.

Sally pushed Sandman's hand away and snatched the letter from Dodds. Then she pushed him out of the room and slammed the door.

Sandman finished threading the silk handkerchief through the fastenings, then he stepped back. 'You look very fetching, Miss Hood.' The pale green dress was printed with cornflowers, and the colours suited Sally's honey-coloured skin and curly hair that was as gold as Sandman's own. She was a pretty girl with clear blue eyes and an infectious smile.

'You think so? Thank you. Close your eyes, turn round three times, then say your loved one's name aloud before you open the letter.'

Sandman smiled. 'And what will that achieve?'

'It will mean good news, Captain.' She smiled and was gone.

Sandman looked at the letter, then paused. He felt like a fool, but he closed his eyes, turned three times then spoke his loved one's name aloud: 'Eleanor Forrest,' he said, then opened his eyes, tore off the letter's red wax seal and unfolded the paper. He read the letter and tried to work out whether or not it really was good news.

The Right Honourable Viscount Sidmouth presented his compliments to Captain Sandman and requested the honour of a call at Captain Sandman's earliest convenience at Lord Sidmouth's office.

Sandman's first instinct was that the letter must be bad news, that his father had dunned Viscount Sidmouth and that his lordship was writing to make a claim on the pathetic shreds of the Sandman estate. Yet his father, so far as Rider Sandman knew, had never encountered Lord Sidmouth and he would surely have boasted if he had, for Sandman's father had liked the company of important men. And there were few men more important than His Majesty's Principal Secretary of State in the Home Department.

So why did the Home Secretary want to see Rider Sandman?

There was only one way to find out.

VISCOUNT SIDMOUTH was a thin man. He was thin-lipped and thin-haired, had a thin nose and a thin jaw that narrowed to a weasel-thin chin and his thin voice was precise, dry and unfriendly. He had made Sandman wait for two hours. Now the Home Secretary frowned across the desk at his visitor. A grandfather clock ticked loudly in the corner of the office. 'You were recommended by Sir John Colborne. You were in Sir John's battalion at Waterloo, is that not so?'

'I was, my lord, yes.'

Sidmouth grunted as though he did not entirely approve of men who had been at Waterloo and that, Sandman reflected, might well have been the case, for the wars against Napoleon were two years in the past now, yet still Britain seemed divided between those who had fought against the French and those who had stayed at home. The latter, Sandman suspected, were jealous and liked to suggest, oh so delicately, that they had sacrificed an opportunity to gallivant abroad because of the need to keep Britain prosperous. 'Sir John tells me you seek employment?' the Home Secretary asked.

'I must, my lord.'

'You have no income?' Sebastian Witherspoon, the Home Secretary's private secretary, a young man with plump cheeks and sharp eyes, asked from his chair beside his master's desk.

'Some,' Sandman said, and decided it was probably best not to say that the small income came from playing cricket. The Viscount Sidmouth did not look like a man who would approve of such a thing. 'Not enough,' Sandman amended his answer, 'and much of what I do earn goes towards settling my father's debts.'

Witherspoon frowned. 'In law, Sandman,' he said, 'you are not responsible for any of your father's debts.'

'I am responsible for my family's good name,' Sandman responded. Sandman's father, faced with the threat of imprisonment or exile because of his massive debts, had taken his own life and thus left his name disgraced and his wife and family ruined.

The Home Secretary gave Sandman a long, sour inspection. 'I need a man to undertake a job,' he said, 'though I should warn you that the position is temporary.'

He gestured towards a basket that stood waist high on the carpeted floor and was crammed with papers. Some were scrolls, some were folded and sealed with wax, while a few showed legal pretensions by being wrapped in scraps of red ribbon. 'Those, Captain, are petitions. A condemned felon may petition the King for clemency or, indeed, for a full pardon. All such petitions come to this office, and if the crime is not too heinous, and if persons of quality are willing to speak for the condemned, then we might show clemency. We might commute a sentence of death to, say, one of transportation.'

'You, my lord?' Sandman asked, struck by Sidmouth's use of the word 'we'.

'The petitions are addressed to the King,' the Home Secretary explained, 'but the responsibility for deciding on the response is left to this office, and my decisions are then ratified by the Privy Council.' Sidmouth tossed a petition to Sandman. 'Once in a while, a petition will persuade us to investigate the facts of the matter. On those very rare occasions, Captain, we appoint an Investigator.' He paused. 'A person condemned to death,' the Home Secretary explained, 'has already been tried and found guilty by a court of law. It is not our policy, Captain, to undermine the judiciary, but, very infrequently, we do investigate. That petition is just such a rare case.'

Sandman unrolled the petition. '"As God is my wittness,"' he read, '"hee is a good boy and could never have killd the Lady Avebury as God knows hee could not hert even a flie."' There was much more in the same manner.

'The matter,' Lord Sidmouth explained, 'concerns Charles Corday. The petition, as you can see, comes from Corday's mother, who subscribes herself as Cruttwell, but the boy seems to have adopted a French name. God knows why. He stands convicted of murdering the Countess of Avebury. The wretched man raped and stabbed the Countess and he thoroughly deserves to hang. He is due on the scaffold when?' He turned to Witherspoon.

'A week from today, my lord,' Witherspoon said.

'Then why investigate the facts?' Sandman said.

'Because the petitioner, Maisie Cruttwell, is a seamstress to Her Majesty, Queen Charlotte, and Her Majesty has graciously taken an interest.' Lord Sidmouth's voice made it plain that he could have gladly strangled King George III's wife for being so gracious. 'It is my loyal duty to reassure Her Majesty that there is not the slightest doubt about the wretched man's guilt. I have therefore written to Her Majesty to inform her that I am appointing an Investigator who will examine the facts and thus offer an assurance that justice is indeed being done.' Sidmouth pointed a bony forefinger at Sandman. 'I am asking whether you will be that Investigator, Captain.'

Sandman hesitated. He doubted he possessed the qualifications to be an investigator of crime. Lord Sidmouth mistook the hesitation for reluctance. 'The job will hardly tax you, Captain,' he said testily, 'the wretch is plainly guilty and one merely wishes to satisfy the Queen's womanly concerns. A month's pay for a day's work.'

Sandman needed a month's pay. 'Of course I shall do it, my lord,' he said. 'I shall be honoured.'

Witherspoon stood, the signal that the audience was over, and the Home Secretary nodded his farewell. 'Witherspoon will provide you with a letter of authorisation,' he said, 'and I shall look forward to receiving your report. Good day to you, sir.'

Sandman followed the secretary into an anteroom where a clerk was busy at a table. 'It will take a moment to seal your letter,' Witherspoon said, 'so, please, sit.'

Sandman read the petition again, but it presented no arguments against the facts of the case. Maisie Cruttwell claimed her son was innocent, but could adduce no proof of that assertion.

'This letter,' Witherspoon was now heating a stick of wax over a candle flame, 'confirms that you are making enquiries on behalf of the Home Office and it requests all persons to offer you their cooperation. Note though, Captain, that we have no legal right to require them to do so,' he said as he dripped the wax onto the letter, then carefully pushed a seal of authentication into the scarlet blob, 'so we can only request it. I suggest your enquiries need not be laborious. There is no doubt of the man's guilt. You will find Corday in Newgate and if you are sufficiently forceful then I have no doubt he will confess to his brutal crime and your work will then be done. What we do not want, Captain, is to complicate matters. Provide us with a succinct report that will allow my master to reassure the Queen and then let us forget the wretched matter.'

'And if he's innocent?' Sandman asked.

Witherspoon looked appalled at the suggestion. 'How can he be? He's already been found guilty!'

'Of course he has,' Sandman said as he took the letter from

Witherspoon. 'His Lordship mentioned an emolument.' He hated talking of money, it was so ungentlemanly. 'Mister Witherspoon I wondered whether I might persuade you to cash? There will be inevitable expenses . . .' His voice tailed away because, for the life of him, he could not think what those expenses might be.

Both Witherspoon and the clerk stared at Sandman as though he had just dropped his breeches. 'Cash?' Witherspoon asked.

Sandman knew he was blushing. 'You want the matter resolved swiftly,' he said, 'and . . .' Again his voice tailed away.

'Prendergast,' Witherspoon spoke to the clerk, 'pray go to Mister Hodge's office and ask him to advance us fifteen guineas,' he paused, looking at Sandman, 'in cash.'

The money was found and Sandman left the Home Office. Damn poverty, he thought, but the rent was due at the Wheatsheaf and it had been three days since he had eaten a proper meal.

He could afford a meal now. A meal, some wine and an afternoon of cricket. It was a tempting vision, but Sandman was not a man to shirk duty. He would forgo the meal and postpone the cricket.

For there was a murderer to see.

IN OLD BAILEY the scaffold was being taken down. Traffic had been allowed back into the street so Sandman had to dodge between wagons, carriages and carts to reach the prison gate, where he found a uniformed porter.

'Your honour is looking for someone?'

'I am looking for Charles Corday. My name is Sandman,' he explained, 'Captain Sandman, and I'm Lord Sidmouth's official Investigator. I should, perhaps, pay my respects to the Governor?'

'The Keeper won't thank you for any respects, sir, on account that they ain't needful. You just goes in, sir, and sees the prisoner. What was your fellow called?'

'Corday.'

'He's condemned, is he? Then you'll find him in the Press Yard, your honour.' The porter took hold of Sandman's lapel to add emphasis to his next words. 'He'll tell you he didn't do it, sir. There ain't a guilty man in here, not one! Not if you ask them. They'll all swear they didn't do it, but they all did.' He grinned and released his grip on Sandman's coat. 'Do you have a watch, sir? You do, sir? Best not take anything in that might be stolen. It'll be in the cupboard here, sir, under lock and key. Round that corner, sir, you'll find some stairs. Go down, sir, follow the tunnel and follow your nose.'

Two turnkeys, both armed with cudgels, guarded the gate that led to the Press Yard. 'Charles Corday?' one responded when Sandman enquired where the prisoner might be found. 'You can't miss him. He looks like a bleeding girl, sir. Pal of his, are you?' The man grinned, then the grin faded as Sandman stared at him. 'I don't see him in the yard, sir,' the turnkey had been a soldier and he instinctively became respectful under Sandman's gaze, 'so he'll be in the Association Room, sir. That door over there, sir.'

The Press Yard was a narrow space compressed between high, dank buildings. What little light came into it arrived over a thicket of spikes that crowned the Newgate Street wall beside which a score of prisoners, identifiable because of their leg irons, sat with their visitors. Sandman crossed the yard and went into the Association Room, a large space filled with tables and benches. A coal fire burned in a big grate where stew pots hung from a crane. The pots were being stirred by two women who were evidently cooking for a dozen folk seated round one of the long tables. The only turnkey in the room, a youngish man armed with a truncheon, was also at the table, sharing a gin bottle and the laughter which died abruptly when Sandman appeared. The other tables fell silent as forty or fifty folk turned to look at the newcomer. Something about Sandman spoke of authority, and this was not a place where authority was welcome.

'I'm looking for Charles Corday!' Sandman called, his voice taking on the familiar officer's tone. No one answered. 'Corday!'

'Sir?' The answering voice was tremulous and came from the room's farthest and darkest corner. Sandman threaded his way through the tables to see a pathetic figure curled against the wall there. Charles Corday looked scarce more than seventeen, and he was thin to the point of frailty, with a deathly pale face framed by long fair hair that did, indeed, look girlish. He had long eyelashes, a trembling lip and a dark bruise on one cheek.

'You're Charles Corday?' Sandman felt an instinctive dislike of the young man, who looked too delicate and self-pitying.

'Yes, sir.' Corday's right arm was shaking.

'Stand up,' Sandman ordered. Corday blinked in surprise but obeyed. 'I've been sent by the Home Secretary,' Sandman said, 'and I need somewhere private where we can talk. We can use the cells, perhaps. Do we reach them from here? Or from the yard?'

'The yard, sir,' Corday said, though he scarcely seemed to have understood the rest of Sandman's words.

Sandman led Corday towards the door. 'Come for a farewell

cuddle, Charlie, has he?' a man in leg shackles enquired. The other prisoners laughed. Sandman just kept walking, but then he heard Corday squeal and turned to see that a greasy-haired and unshaven man was holding Corday's hair like a leash. 'Give us a kiss, Charlie,' the man demanded.

'Let him go,' Sandman said.

'You don't give orders here, culley,' the unshaven man growled. 'There aren't any orders here, so you can—' The man stopped suddenly, then gave a curious scream.

Rider Sandman had ever suffered from a temper. He fought against it, but his soldiers had known Captain Sandman was not a man to cross because he had that temper as sudden and as fierce as a summer thunderstorm. And he was strong enough to lift the unshaven prisoner and slam him hard against the wall. Then the man screamed because Sandman had driven a fist into his belly. 'I said let him go,' Sandman snapped, his voice seething with a promise of terrible violence. His right hand was about the prisoner's throat.

There was utter silence in the Association Room.

The turnkey, as appalled by Sandman's anger as any of the prisoners, nervously crossed the room. 'Sir? You're throttling him, sir.'

Sandman suddenly came to his senses, then let the prisoner go.

'Come, Corday,' Sandman ordered, and stalked out of the room.

Sandman led a terrified Corday across the Press Yard to the steps which led to the salt boxes and climbed the stairs to find an empty cell on the first floor. 'In there,' he told Corday, and the frightened youth scuttled past him. A rope mat lay on the floor, evidently to serve as a mattress; blankets for five or six men were tossed in a pile under the high-barred window, while an unemptied night bucket stank in a corner.

'I'm Captain Rider Sandman,' he introduced himself to Corday, 'and the Home Secretary has asked me to enquire into your case.'

'Why?' Corday, who had sunk onto the pile of blankets, nerved himself to ask.

'Your mother has connections,' Sandman said shortly. 'The Queen has requested an assurance of your guilt.'

'But I'm not guilty,' Corday protested.

'You've already been condemned,' Sandman said, 'so your guilt is not at issue.' He could not imagine this despicable creature resisting his demands for a confession. Corday looked pathetic, effeminate and very close to tears. He was wearing dishevelled but fashionably elegant clothes; black breeches, white stockings, a frilled white shirt and a blue silk waistcoat—all, Sandman suspected, expensive.

'I didn't do it!' Corday protested again. His thin shoulders heaved, his voice grizzled and tears ran down his pale cheeks.

Sandman could not imagine himself beating a confession out of a prisoner. It was not honourable, and could not be done, which meant the wretched boy would have to be persuaded into telling the truth, but the first necessity was to stop him weeping. 'Why do you call yourself Corday,' Sandman asked, hoping to distract him, 'when your mother's name is Cruttwell?'

'I'm a portrait painter,' Corday said petulantly, 'and clients prefer their painters to have French names. Cruttwell doesn't sound distinguished. Would you have your portrait painted by Charlie Cruttwell when you could engage Monsieur Charles Corday?'

'You're a painter?' Sandman could not hide his surprise.

'Yes!' Corday, his eyes reddened from crying, looked belligerently at Sandman. 'I was apprenticed to Sir George Phillips.'

'He's very successful,' Sandman said scornfully, 'despite possessing a prosaically English name.'

'I thought changing my name would help,' Corday said sulkily. 'Does it matter?'

'Your guilt matters,' Sandman said sternly, 'and, if nothing else, you might face the judgment of your Maker with a clear conscience if you were to confess it.'

Corday stared at Sandman as though his visitor were mad. 'I'm guilty of aspiring to be above my station but do I look like a man who has the strength to rape and kill a woman?' He did not. Sandman had to admit it, at least to himself, for Corday was an unimpressive creature, weedy and thin, who now began to weep again.

'Stop crying, for God's sake!' Sandman snarled, and immediately chided himself for giving way to his temper. 'I'm sorry,' he muttered.

Those last two words made Corday stop weeping. He looked at Sandman and frowned in puzzlement. 'I didn't do it,' he said softly.

'So what happened?' Sandman asked.

'I was painting her,' Corday said. 'The Earl of Avebury wanted a portrait of his wife and he asked Sir George to do it.'

'He asked Sir George, yet you were painting her?' Sandman sounded sceptical.

'Sir George drinks,' Corday said scornfully. 'He starts at breakfast and bowzes till night, which means his hand shakes. So he drinks and I paint.'

Sandman wondered if he was being naive, for he found Corday curiously believable. 'You painted in Sir George's studio?' he asked.

'No,' Corday said. 'Her husband wanted the portrait set in her bedroom, so I did it there. It was to be a boudoir portrait. They're very fashionable because these days all the women want to look like Canova's *Pauline Bonaparte*.'

Sandman frowned. 'You confuse me.'

'The sculptor Canova,' Corday explained, 'did a celebrated likeness of the Emperor's sister and every beauty in Europe wishes to be depicted in the same pose. The woman reclines on a chaise longue, an apple in her left hand and her head supported by her right. The salient feature is that the woman is naked.'

'So the Countess was naked when you painted her?'

'No,' Corday hesitated, then shrugged. 'She wasn't to know she was being painted naked, so she was in a morning gown and robe. We would have used a model in the studio to do the tits. I was just doing the preliminary work, the drawing and tints. Charcoal on canvas with a few colours touched in; the colours of the bed covers, the wallpaper, her ladyship's skin and hair. Bitch that she was.'

Sandman felt a surge of hope, for the last four words had been malevolent, just as he expected a murderer would speak of his victim. 'You didn't like her?'

'I despised her!' Corday spat. 'She was a trumped-up whore. But just because I didn't like her doesn't make me a rapist and murderer. Besides, do you really think a woman like the Countess of Avebury would allow a painter's apprentice to be alone with her? She was chaperoned by a maid all the time I was there.'

'There was a maid?' Sandman asked.

'Of course there was. An ugly bitch called Meg.'

'And, presumably, Meg spoke at your trial?'

'Meg has disappeared,' Corday said tiredly. 'When it came to the trial she couldn't be found, which is why I am going to hang. But there was a maid there.' He began to weep again.

Sandman stared down at the flagstones. 'Where was the house?'

'Mount Street,' Corday was hunched and sobbing.

Sandman was embarrassed by Corday's tears, but persevered now from genuine curiosity. 'And you admit to being in the Countess's house on the day she was murdered?'

'I was there just before she was murdered!' Corday said. 'There were back stairs, servants' stairs, and there was a knock on the door there. A deliberate knock, a signal, and the Countess insisted I leave at once. So Meg took me down the front stairs and showed me the door. I had to leave everything, the paints, canvas, everything, and that convinced the constables I was guilty. So within an hour they came and arrested me at Sir George's studio.'

'Which is where?'

'Sackville Street. Above Gray's, the jewellers.' Corday stared red-eyed at Sandman. 'What will you do now?'

Sandman was nonplussed. He had expected to listen to a confession and then go back to the Wheatsheaf to write a respectful report. Instead he was confused.

'I shall make enquiries,' he said gruffly, and suddenly he could not take the stench and the tears and the misery any more and so he turned and ran down the stairs. He came into the fresher air of the Press Yard, then had a moment's panic that the turnkeys would not unbolt the gate into the tunnel, but of course they did.

The porter unlocked his cupboard and took out Sandman's watch, a gold-cased Breguet that had been a gift from Eleanor. Sandman had tried to return the watch with her letters, but she had refused to accept them.

'Find your man, sir?' the porter asked.

'I found him.'

'And he spun you a yarn, I've no doubt,' the porter chuckled. 'But there's an easy way to know when a felon's telling lies, sir.'

'I should be obliged to hear it,' Sandman said.

'They're speaking, sir, that's how you can tell they're telling lies.' The porter thought this a fine joke and wheezed with laughter as Sandman went down the steps into Old Bailey.

He stood on the pavement oblivious to the crowd surging up and down. He felt soiled by the prison. He clicked open the Breguet's case and saw it was just after half past two. *To Rider*, Eleanor's inscription inside the watch case read, *in aeternam*, and that palpably false promise did not improve his mood.

He thrust the watch into his fob pocket and walked northwards. He was torn. Corday had been found guilty and yet his story was believable. Doubtless the porter was right and every man in Newgate was convinced of his own innocence, yet Sandman was not entirely naive. He had led a company of soldiers with consummate skill and he reckoned he could distinguish when a man was telling the truth. And if Corday was innocent then the fifteen guineas that weighed down Sandman's pockets would be neither swiftly nor easily earned.

He decided he needed advice. So he went to watch some cricket.

3

Sandman reached the Artillery Ground just before the City clocks struck three, the jangling of the bells momentarily drowning the applause of the spectators. It sounded like a large crowd and, judging by the shouts, a good match. The gatekeeper waved him through. 'I ain't taking your sixpence, Captain.'

'You should, Joe.'

'Aye, and you should be playing, Captain. Been too long since we seen you bat.'

'I'm past my prime, Joe.'

'Past your prime, boy? Past your prime? You aren't even thirty yet. Now, go on in.'

A raucous jeer rewarded a passage of play as Sandman walked towards the boundary. The Marquess of Canfield's eleven were playing an England eleven and one of the Marquess's fielders had dropped an easy catch. Sandman glanced at the blackboard and saw that England, in their second innings, were only sixty runs ahead and still had four wickets in hand.

He strolled past the carriages parked by the boundary. The white-haired Marquess of Canfield, ensconced with a telescope in a landau, offered Sandman a curt nod, then pointedly looked away. A year ago, before the disgrace of Sandman's father, the Marquess would have called out a greeting, but now the Sandman name was dirt. But then, from another open carriage an eager voice shouted, 'Rider! Here! Rider!'

The voice belonged to a tall, ragged young man who was very bony and lanky, dressed in shabby black and smoking a clay pipe that trickled a drift of ash down his waistcoat and jacket. His red hair was in need of scissors, for it collapsed across his long-nosed face and flared above his collar. 'Drop the carriage steps,' he instructed Sandman, 'come on in. How are you, my dear fellow? You should be playing. You also look pale. Are you eating properly?'

'I eat,' Sandman said, 'and you?'

'God preserves me, in His effable wisdom He preserves me.' The Reverend Lord Alexander Pleydell settled back on his seat. 'I see my father ignored you?'

'He nodded to me.'

'Ah! What graciousness. Is it true you played for Sir John Hart?'

'Played and lost,' Sandman said bitterly. 'They were bribed.'

'Dear Rider! I warned you of Sir John! Man's nothing but greed. He only wanted you to play so that everyone would assume his team was incorruptible and it worked, didn't it? Would you like some tea? Of course you would. Oh, well struck, sir! Go hard, sir, go hard!' He was cheering England on. 'Hughes, my dear fellow, where are you?'

Lord Alexander's manservant approached the carriage. 'My lord?'

'Hughes, I think we might venture a pot of tea and cake from Mrs Hillman's stall, don't you?' His lordship put money into his servant's hand. 'Truly you look pale, Rider, are you sickening?'

'Prison fever.'

'My dear fellow!' Lord Alexander looked horrified. 'Prison fever? And for God's sake sit down.' The carriage swayed as Sandman sat opposite his friend. They had attended the same school, where they had become inseparable friends and where Sandman, who had always excelled at games and was thus one of the school's heroes, had protected Lord Alexander from the bullies who believed his lordship's clubbed foot made him an object of ridicule. Sandman, on leaving school, had purchased a commission in the infantry while Lord Alexander, who was the Marquess of Canfield's second son, had gone to Oxford where, in the first year that such things were awarded, he had taken a double first. 'Don't tell me you've been imprisoned,' Lord Alexander now chided Sandman.

Sandman smiled and described his afternoon, though his tale was constantly interrupted by Lord Alexander's exclamations of praise or scorn for the cricket, many of them uttered through a mouthful of cake. 'I must say,' he said when he had considered Sandman's story, 'I should deem it most unlikely that Corday is guilty.'

'But he's been tried.'

'My dear Rider! My dear, dear Rider! Have you ever been to the Old Bailey sessions? Of course you haven't, you've been far too busy smiting the French. But I dare say that inside of a week those judges get through five cases a day apiece. These folk don't get trials, Rider, they come blinking into the Session House, are knocked down like bullocks and hustled off in manacles! It ain't justice!'

'They are defended, surely?'

'What barrister will defend some penniless youth accused of sheep stealing?'

'Corday isn't penniless.'

'But I'll wager he isn't rich. Oh, well struck, Budd, well struck!

Run, man, run!' His lordship took up his pipe. 'The whole system,' he said between puffs, 'is pernicious. They'll sentence a hundred folk to hang, then only kill ten of them because the rest have commuted sentences. And how do you obtain a commutation? Why, by having the squire or the parson or his lordship sign the petition. You see, Rider, what is happening? Society, that's the respectable folk, you and me, have devised a way to keep the lower orders under our control. We make them depend upon our mercy. We condemn them to the gallows, then spare them and they are supposed to be grateful. Grateful! It is pernicious.' Lord Alexander was thoroughly worked up now. His long hands were wringing together. Then a happy idea struck him. 'You and I, Rider, we shall go to a hanging!'

'No!'

'It's your duty, my dear fellow. Now that you are a functionary of this oppressive state you should understand just what brutality awaits these innocent souls. I shall write to the Keeper of Newgate and demand that you and I are given privileged access to the next execution. Oh, a change of bowler. This fellow's said to twist it very cannily. And by the way, I saw Eleanor last Saturday,' Lord Alexander said with his usual tactlessness.

'I trust she was well?'

'I'm sure she was, but I rather think I forgot to ask. But she looked well. She asked after you, as I recall.'

'She did?'

'And I said I had no doubt you were in fine fettle. She and I met at the Egyptian Hall. Eleanor had a message for you.'

'She did?' Sandman's heart quickened. His engagement to Eleanor might be broken off, but he was still in love with her. 'What?'

'What, indeed?' Lord Alexander frowned. 'Slipped my mind, Rider, slipped it altogether. Dear me, but it can't have been important. And as for the Countess of Avebury!' He shuddered.

'What of her ladyship?' Sandman asked, knowing it would be pointless to pursue Eleanor's forgotten message.

'Ladyship! Ha! That baggage,' Lord Alexander said, then remembered his calling. 'Poor woman. If anyone wanted her dead I should think it would be her husband. The wretched man must be weighted down with horns!'

'You think the Earl killed her?' Sandman asked.

'They're estranged, Rider, is that not an indication?'

'Estranged?' Sandman was surprised because he could have sworn Corday had said the Earl had commissioned his wife's portrait, but why would he do that if they were estranged? 'Are you certain?'

'I have it on the highest authority,' Lord Alexander said, 'I am a friend of the Earl's son and heir, Christopher. He was at Brasenose when I was at Trinity, then went off to study at the Sorbonne. The dead woman, of course, was Christopher's stepmother.'

'He talked to you of her?'

'There was little love lost in that family, I can tell you,' Alexander said. 'Father despising the son, father hating the wife, wife detesting the husband and the son bitterly disposed towards both. I must say the Earl and Countess of Avebury form an object lesson in the perils of family life. Oh, well struck! Good man! Scamper, scamper!'

Sandman sipped his tea. 'Corday claimed that the Earl commissioned the portrait. Why would he do that if they're estranged?'

'You must ask him,' Lord Alexander said, 'though my guess is that Avebury, though jealous, was still enamoured of her. She was a noted beauty and he is a noted fool. Mind you, I doubt her husband would have struck the fatal blow himself. Even Avebury is sensible enough to hire someone else to do his dirty work.'

'Is the son still in Paris?'

'He came back. I see him from time to time.'

'Could you introduce me?'

'To Avebury's son? I suppose so.'

The game ended at shortly past eight when the Marquess's side, needing only ninety-three runs to win, collapsed. Their defeat pleased Lord Alexander, but made Sandman suspect that bribery had once again ruined a game. He could not prove it, and Lord Alexander scoffed at the suspicion. 'Are you still lodging in the Wheatsheaf? You do know it's a flash tavern?'

'I know now,' Sandman admitted.

'Why don't we have supper there? I can learn some demotic flash. Hughes? Summon the carriage horses, and tell Williams we're going to Drury Lane.' Flash was the slang name for London's criminal life and its language. No one stole a purse, they filed a bit or boned the cole or clicked the ready bag. Prison was a sheep walk or the quod, Newgate was the King's Head Inn. A good man was flash scamp and his victim a mum scull.

Lord Alexander was reckoned a mum scull but a genial one. He learned the flash vocabulary and paid for the words by buying ale and gin. He did not leave till well past midnight and it was then that Sally Hood came home on her brother's arm, and they passed Lord Alexander who was standing by his carriage, holding himself upright by gripping a wheel. He stared after Sally open-mouthed. 'I am in love, Rider,' he declared too loudly.

Sally glanced back and gave Sandman a dazzling smile.

Lord Alexander kept staring after Sally until she had vanished through the Wheatsheaf's front door. 'I have been smitten by Cupid's arrow.' He lurched after Sally, but his club foot slipped on the cobbles and he fell full length. 'I wish to marry the lady' he said from the ground. In truth he was so drunk he could not stand, but Sandman, Hughes and the coachman managed to get his lordship into his carriage and then it rattled away.

IT WAS RAINING next morning. Sandman had a headache and made tea over the back-room fire where the tenants were allowed to boil their water. Sally hurried in, ladled herself a cup of water and grinned. 'I hear you was jolly last night?'

'Good morning, Miss Hood,' Sandman groaned.

She laughed. 'Who was that cripple cove you was with?'

'He is my friend,' Sandman said, 'the Reverend Lord Alexander Pleydell, second son of the Marquess of Canfield.'

Sally stared at Sandman. 'He said he was in love with me.'

Sandman had hoped she had not heard. 'And doubtless when he is sober, Miss Hood, he will still be in love with you.'

Sally laughed at Sandman's tact. 'Is he really a reverend? He don't dress like one.'

'He took holy orders when he left Oxford,' Sandman explained, 'but he's never looked for a living. He doesn't need a parish or any other kind of job, because he's rather rich.'

'Is he married?' Sally smiled mischievously.

'No,' Sandman said, and did not add that Alexander regularly fell in love with every pretty shopgirl he saw.

'Well, I could do a hell of a lot worse than a crocked parson, couldn't I?' Sally said, then gasped as a clock struck nine. 'Lord above, I'm late.' She ran.

Sandman pulled on his greatcoat and set off for Mount Street. He had six days to discover the truth, and he decided he would begin with the missing maid, Meg. If she existed, she could confirm or deny the painter's tale. He was soaked to the skin by the time he reached the house where the murder had taken place.

It was easy to tell which was the Earl of Avebury's town house, for even in this weather a broadsheet seller was crouching beneath a tarpaulin in an effort to hawk her wares just outside the murder house.

'Tale of a murder, sir,' she greeted Sandman, 'just a penny.'

'Give me one.' She extricated a sheet from her tarpaulin bag, then Sandman climbed the steps and rapped on the front door. The windows of the house were shuttered .

'There's no one home,' the woman selling the broadsheets said.

'But this is the Earl of Avebury's house?' Sandman asked.

'It is, sir, yes,' she said.

Just then the front door of the next house along opened and a middle-aged woman appeared on the step. She shuddered at the rain, then put up an umbrella. 'Madam!' Sandman called.

'Sir?' The woman's dowdy clothes suggested she was a servant.

Sandman took off his hat. 'Forgive me, madam, but Viscount Sidmouth has charged me with investigating the sad events that occurred here. Is it true there was a maid called Meg in the house?'

The woman nodded. 'There was, sir, there was.'

'Do you know where she is?'

'They've gone, sir. To the country, sir, I think.' She dropped Sandman a curtsy, clearly hoping it would persuade him to go away.

'The country?'

'They went away, sir. And the Earl, sir, he has a house in the country, sir, near Marlborough, sir.'

Sandman pressed her more, but it seemed evident that there was little more to learn in Mount Street, so he walked away.

Though Lord Alexander might scorn British justice, Sandman found it hard to be so dismissive. He had spent most of the last decade fighting for his country. It was unthinkable to Sandman that a freeborn Englishman would not get a fair trial. Yet Meg undoubtedly existed. That confirmed part of Corday's tale, and cast doubt on Sandman's stout belief in British justice.

He was walking east on Burlington Gardens, when he saw that the end of the street was plugged by a stonemason's wagon, so he turned down Sackville Street where a small crowd was standing under the awning of Gray's jewellery shop, sheltering from the rain. The name reminded Sandman of something.

Corday had said that Sir George Phillips's studio was here. Sandman stopped and stared up past the awning but could see nothing in the windows above the shop. He stepped back to the pavement to find a doorway to one side, plainly separate from the jewellery business, furnished with a well-polished brass knocker. He lifted the knocker and rapped it hard.

A black pageboy of thirteen or fourteen opened the door wearing a shabby livery and a wig.

'Is this Sir George Phillips's studio?' Sandman asked.

'If you ain't got an appointment,' the pageboy said, 'then you ain't welcome.'

'I have got an appointment,' Sandman said grandly, 'from Viscount Sidmouth.'

'Who is it, Sammy?' a voice boomed from upstairs.

'He says he's from Viscount Sidmouth.'

'Then let him up! Let him up! We are not too proud to paint politicians. We just charge the bastards more.'

'Take your coat, sir?' Sammy asked, giving a perfunctory bow.

'I'll keep it.' Sandman edged into the tiny hallway, which was decorated in a fashionable striped wallpaper and hung with a small chandelier. But as Sandman climbed the stairs the elegance was tainted by the reek of turpentine. The room at the top was a salon where Sir George could show his finished paintings, but it had become a dumping place for half-finished work, for palettes of crusted paint, old brushes and rags. A second flight of stairs went to the top floor and Sammy indicated that Sandman should go on up. 'You want coffee, sir?' he asked. 'Or tea?'

'Tea would be kind.'

The ceiling had been knocked out of the top floor to open the long room to the rafters, then skylights had been put in the roof. A black stove dominated the studio's centre, serving as a table for a bottle of wine and a glass. Next to the stove an easel supported a massive canvas while a naval officer posed with a sailor and a woman on a platform at the farther end. The woman screamed when Sandman appeared, then snatched up a cloth that covered a tea chest.

It was Sally Hood. She was holding a trident and wearing a brass helmet and nothing else, though her hips and thighs were mostly screened by an oval wooden shield on which a union flag had been hastily drawn. She was, Sandman realised, Britannia. 'You are feasting your eyes,' the man beside the easel said, 'on Miss Hood's tits. And why not? As tits go, they are splendid.'

'Captain,' Sally acknowledged Sandman in a small voice.

'Your servant, Miss Hood,' Sandman said, bowing.

'Good Lord Almighty!' the painter said. 'Have you come to see me or Sally?' He was fat as a hogshead, with great jowls and a belly that distended a paint-smeared shirt decorated with ruffles. His white hair was bound by a tight cap of the kind worn beneath wigs.

'Sir George?' Sandman asked.

'At your service, sir.' Sir George attempted a bow. He was so fat he could only manage a slight bend. 'You are welcome,' he said, 'so long as you seek a commission. Viscount Sidmouth sent you?'

'He doesn't wish to be painted, Sir George.'

'Then you can bugger off!' the painter said.

Sandman ignored the suggestion, instead looking about the studio. Two youths were flanking Sir George, both painting waves on the canvas, and Sandman guessed they were his apprentices. The canvas itself, at least ten feet wide, showed a solitary rock in a sunlit sea on which a half-painted fleet was afloat. An admiral was seated on the rock's summit, flanked by a good-looking young man dressed as a sailor and by Sally Hood undressed as Britannia. Then Sandman noticed that the boy who was posing as the admiral was wearing a gold-encrusted uniform and his empty right sleeve was pinned to his coat's breast. 'The real Nelson is dead,' Sir George had been deducing Sandman's train of thought, 'so we make do with young Master Corbett there. For God's sake, Sally, stop hiding.'

'You ain't painting,' Sally said, 'so I can cover up.' She had dropped the grey cloth and was instead wearing her street coat.

Sir George picked up his brush. 'I'm painting now,' he snarled. 'Too grand suddenly to show us your bubbies, are you?' Sir George looked at Sandman. 'Has she told you about her lord? The one who's sweet on her? We'll soon all be bowing and scraping to her, won't we?'

'She hasn't lied to you,' Sandman said. 'His lordship exists, I know him, he is indeed enamoured of Miss Hood, and he is very rich. Rich enough to commission a dozen portraits from you, Sir George.'

Sally gave him a look of pure gratitude while Sir George, discomfited, dabbed the brush into the paint on his palette. 'So who the devil are you?' he demanded of Sandman.

'My name is Captain Rider Sandman.'

'Navy, army, fencibles, yeomanry or is the captaincy a fiction?'

'I was in the army,' Sandman said.

'You can uncover,' Sir George explained to Sally, 'because the captain was a soldier, which means he's seen more tits than I have.'

'He ain't seen mine,' Sally said, clutching the coat to her bosom.

Sir George stepped back to survey his painting. ' *The Apotheosis of Lord Nelson*, commissioned by their Lordships of the Admiralty. Sammy,' Sir George shouted. 'Where's the tea? Are you growing the bloody tea leaves? Bring me some brandy!' He glared at Sandman. 'So what do you want of me, Captain?'

'To talk about Charles Corday.'

'Oh, Good Christ alive,' Sir George blasphemed. 'Charles Corday?' He said the name very portentously. 'Sally, for God's sake, pose as you're paid to!'

Sandman courteously turned his back as she dropped the coat. 'The Home Secretary has asked me to investigate Corday's case.'

Sir George laughed. 'His mother's been bleating to the Queen. Lucky little Charlie. You want to know whether he did it?'

'He tells me he didn't.'

'He's hardly likely to offer you a confession, is he?' Sir George said. 'But he's probably telling the truth. At least about the rape.'

'He didn't rape her?'

'It would have been against his nature.' Sir George gave Sandman a sly glance. 'Our Monsieur Corday, Captain, is a pixie.'

'A pixie? Never mind. I think I know what you mean.'

Sir George laughed at Sandman's expression. 'Nasty little buggers. They'll hang you for being one of those, so it don't make much difference to Charlie whether he's guilty or innocent of murder, do it?'

Sammy brought up a tray on which were some ill-assorted cups, a pot of tea and a bottle of brandy. The boy poured tea for Sir George and Sandman, but only Sir George received a glass of brandy.

'Are you sure?' Sandman asked him.

'Of course I'm bloody sure. You could unpeel Sally right down to the raw and he wouldn't bother to look, but he was always trying to get his paws on young Sammy here, wasn't he, Sammy?'

'I told him to fake away off,' Sammy said.

'Good for you, Samuel!' Sir George said. He put down his brush and gulped the brandy. 'And you are wondering, Captain, are you not, why I would allow such a person into this temple of art? Because Charlie was good. He drew beautifully, Captain, drew like the young Raphael. He was a joy to watch. He could paint as well as draw. The picture of the Countess is there if you want to see how good he was.' He gestured to some unframed canvasses stacked against a table. 'Find it, Barney,' Sir George ordered one of his apprentices.

'Why did you let him paint the Countess?' Sandman asked.

Sir George laughed. 'Let me guess. He said I was drunk, so he had to paint her ladyship?'

'Yes,' Sandman admitted.

Sir George was amused. 'The lying little bastard.'

'Why?' Sandman persisted.

'Think about it,' Sir George said. 'Because, Captain, once the canvas got back here we were going to make the lady naked. That's what the Earl wanted. But does a man hang such a painting in his morning room for the titillation of his friends? He does not. He hangs it in his dressing room or in his study where none but himself can see it. And what use is that to me? If I paint a picture, Captain, I want all London gaping at it. I want them queueing up those stairs begging me to paint one just like it for themselves. I paint the profitable pictures, Charlie was taking care of the boudoir portraits.'

The apprentice had been turning over the canvasses and Sandman now stopped him. 'Let me see that one,' he said, pointing to a full-length portrait.

The apprentice pulled it from the stack and propped it on a chair so that the light from a skylight fell on the canvas. It showed a young woman sitting at a table with her head cocked in what was almost a belligerent fashion. Her red hair was piled high to reveal a long and slender neck circled by sapphires. She was wearing a dress of silver and blue with white lace at the neck and wrists. Her eyes stared boldly out of the canvas and added to the suggestion of belligerence, softened by the merest suspicion that she was about to smile.

'Now that,' Sir George said reverently, 'is a very clever young lady. You like it, Captain?'

'It's—' Sandman paused. 'It's wonderful,' he said lamely.

'It is indeed,' Sir George said enthusiastically, stepping away from Nelson to admire the young woman whose red hair was brushed away from a forehead that was high and broad, whose nose was straight and long and whose mouth was generous and wide, and who had been painted in a lavish sitting room beneath a wall of ancestral portraits, though in truth her father was the son of an apothecary and her mother a parson's daughter. 'Miss Eleanor Forrest. Her nose is too long, her chin too sharp, her eyes more widely spaced than convention would allow to be beautiful and her mouth is too lavish, yet the effect is extraordinary, is it not?'

'It is,' Sandman said fervently.

'Of all the young woman's attributes,' Sir George had dropped his bantering manner and was speaking with real warmth, 'it is her intelligence I most admire. I fear she is to be wasted in marriage.'

'She is?' Sandman had to struggle to keep his voice from betraying his feelings.

'The last I heard,' Sir George returned to Nelson, 'she was spoken of as the future Lady Eagleton, yet Miss Eleanor is much too clever to be married to a fool like Eagleton.' Sir George snorted. 'Wasted.'

'Eagleton?' Sandman felt as though a cold hand had gripped his heart. Had that been the import of the message Lord Alexander had forgotten? That Eleanor was engaged to Lord Eagleton?

'Lord Eagleton, heir to the Earl of Bridport and a bore. A bore, Captain, a bore and I detest bores. Barney, find the Countess.'

The apprentice hunted on through the canvasses. Sandman stared out of the front windows, looking into Sackville Street. Was Eleanor really to marry? He had not seen her in over six months and it was very possible. Her mother, at least, was in a hurry to have Eleanor walk to an altar, for Eleanor was twenty-five now and would soon be reckoned a shelved spinster. Damn it, Sandman thought.

'This is it, sir.' Barney, the apprentice, propped an unfinished portrait over Eleanor's picture. 'The Countess of Avebury, sir.'

Another beauty, Sandman thought. The painting was hardly begun, yet it was strangely effective. A charcoal drawing had been made of a woman reclining on a bed. Corday had then painted in patches of the wallpaper, the material of the tent surrounding the bed, the bedspread, the carpet, and the woman's face. He had lightly painted the hair, making it seem wild as though the Countess was in a country wind, and though the rest of the canvas was hardly touched somehow it was still breathtaking and full of life.

'Oh, he could paint, our Charlie, he could paint.' Sir George, wiping his hands with a rag, had come to look.

'Is it a good likeness?'

'Oh, yes,' Sir George nodded, 'indeed yes. She was a beauty, Captain. A woman who could make heads turn, but she was out of the gutter. She was an opera dancer and Avebury was a fool. He should have kept her as his mistress, but never married her.'

'You said, did you not,' Sandman asked, 'that the Earl of Avebury commissioned the portrait? Yet I heard he and his wife were estranged?'

'So I understand,' Sir George said airily, then gave a wicked laugh. 'He was certainly cuckolded. Her ladyship had a reputation, Captain, and it didn't involve comforting the afflicted.'

'Why would a man estranged from his wife spend a fortune on her portrait?' Sandman asked.

'The ways of the world, Captain,' Sir George said, 'are a mystery even unto me. You'd have to ask his lordship. I believe he lives near Marlborough, though he's reputed to be a recluse so I suspect you'd be wasting your journey. Maybe he wanted revenge on her? There is none so conscious of their high estate as an ennobled whore, Captain, so why not remind the bitch of what brought her the title? Ah!' He rubbed his hands as his servant climbed the stairs with a heavy tray. 'Dinner! Good day to you, Captain, I trust I have been of service.'

Sandman was not sure Sir George had been of any service, unless increasing Sandman's confusion was of use.

'THAT FAT BASTARD never offers us dinner!' Sally Hood complained. She was sitting opposite Sandman in a tavern on Piccadilly where they shared a jug of ale and a bowl of salmagundi: a cold mixture of cooked meats, anchovies, hard-boiled eggs and onions. Sally tore a piece of bread from the loaf then smiled shyly at Sandman. 'I was so embarrassed when you walked in.'

'No need to be,' Sandman said. On his way out of Sir George's studio he had invited Sally to join him and they had run through the rain and taken shelter in the Three Ships.

Sally shook salt into the bowl, then stirred the mixture vigorously. 'I know it ain't actressing,' she said, 'but it's money, isn't it? And I shouldn't have said anything about your friend. I felt such a fool. But I don't want to be doing this for ever. I'm twenty-two now and I'll have to find something soon. When life's good, it's very good. Two years ago I never seemed not to be working. But these last three months? Nothing! But I've got a private show coming up,' she added.

'Private?' Sandman asked.

'A rich cove wants his girl to be an actress, see? So he hires the theatre and he pays us to sing and dance and he pays an audience to cheer and he pays the scribblers to write her up in the papers. You want to come? It's Thursday night at Covent Garden.'

'If I can I'll come,' Sandman promised.

'It's only the one night so it ain't going to pay any bills. What I need,' Sally said, 'is to join a company, and I could if I was willing to be a frow. You know what that is? Of course you do. But I'm not a frow!'

'I never supposed you were.'

'My brother Jack would kill anyone who said I was a frow.'

'Good for Jack,' Sandman said. 'I rather like your brother.'

Sally's brother, on the few occasions Sandman had encountered him, had seemed a confident, easy-mannered man. He was popular, presiding over a generous table in the Wheatsheaf's taproom, and he was strikingly handsome, attracting a succession of young women. He was also mysterious, for no one in the tavern would say exactly what he did for a living. 'What does your brother do?' Sandman asked Sally now.

'You don't know who he is?' Sally asked.

'Should I?'

'He's Robin Hood,' she said, then laughed when she saw Sandman's face.

'Good Lord,' Sandman said. Robin Hood was the nickname of a highwayman who was wanted by every magistrate in London.

Sally shrugged. 'I keep telling him he'll end up doing Jemmy Botting's hornpipe, but he won't listen. He's good to me, he is, and he wouldn't let no one touch me.' She frowned. 'Everyone in the 'sheaf knows who he is, but none of them would tell on him.'

'Nor would I,' Sandman assured her.

'Of course you wouldn't,' Sally said, then grinned. 'So what about you? What do you want out of life?'

'I suppose I want my old life back.'

'War? Being a soldier?' She sounded disapproving.

'No. Just the luxury of not worrying about where the next shilling comes from.'

Sally laughed. 'We all want that.' She poured some oil and vinegar into the bowl and stirred it. 'So you had money, did you?'

'My father did. He was a very rich man, but then he made some bad investments, he borrowed too much money, he gambled and he failed. He blew his brains out.'

'Gawd,' Sally said, staring at him.

'So my mother lost everything. She now lives in Winchester with my younger sister, and I try to keep them alive. I pay the rent, look after the bills, that sort of thing.' He shrugged. 'This all happened a year ago, and I'd already left the army by then. I was going to get married, but of course she couldn't marry me when I became penniless because her mother wouldn't let her marry a pauper.'

'Because she was poor as well?' Sally asked.

'On the contrary,' Sandman said, 'her father had promised to settle six thousand a year on her. My father had promised me more. But once he went bankrupt, of course . . .' Sandman shrugged.

Sally was staring at him wide-eyed. 'Six thousand pounds? Bloody hell! So now you're working for the Home Secretary.'

'I fear it is very temporary employment.'

'Thieving people off the gallows? That's full bloody time if you ask me.' She stripped the meat from a chicken bone with her teeth. 'But are you going to get Charlie out of the King's Head Inn?'

'Do you know him?'

'Met him once,' she said, 'and fat Sir George is right. He wouldn't know what to do with a woman, let alone rape one! And whoever killed her gave her a right walloping and Charlie ain't got the meat on his bones to do that kind of damage. What does it say there?' She pointed to the penny broadsheet that Sandman had taken from his pocket and smoothed on the table.

'According to this,' Sandman said, 'the Countess was stabbed twelve times. Corday's knife was in her throat.'

'He couldn't have stabbed her with that,' Sally said dismissively, 'it ain't sharp. It's for mixing paint up, it ain't for cutting.'

'So it's a palette knife,' Sandman said.

'He didn't do it, did he?' Sally said after a moment's reflection. She frowned and Sandman sensed she was debating whether to tell him something. Then she shrugged. 'Sir George lied to you,' she said quietly. 'I heard him tell you the Earl wanted the painting, but he didn't.'

'He didn't?'

'They was talking about it yesterday,' Sally said earnestly, 'him and a friend, only he thinks I don't listen. I just stand there catching cold and he talks like I wasn't anything except a pair of tits. It wasn't the Earl who ordered the painting, Sir George told his friend.'

'Did he say who did commission the painting?'

Sally nodded. 'It was a club, only he'd be mad if he knew I'd told you 'cos he's scared to death of the bastards.'

'A club commissioned it?'

'Like a gentlemen's club. It's got a funny name. The Semaphore Club? No, that ain't right. Something to do with angels.'

'Seraphim?'

'That's it! The Seraphim Club.'

'I've never heard of it.'

'It's meant to be real private,' Sally said. 'It's in St James's Square, so they've got to have money. I was asked to go there once, only I wouldn't 'cos I'm not that sort of actress.'

'But why would the Seraphim Club want the Countess's portrait?' Sandman asked.

'God knows,' Sally said.

'I shall have to ask them.'

She looked alarmed. 'Don't tell them I told you! Sir George will kill me! And I need the work, don't I?'

'I won't say you told me,' he promised her, 'and anyway, I don't suppose they killed her.'

'So how do you find out who did?' Sally asked.

'I don't know,' Sandman admitted ruefully. 'I suppose that I ask questions. I talk to everyone and hope I can find the servant girl.' Sandman told her about Meg and how he had gone to Mount Street and been told that all the servants had been discharged. 'Or they might have gone to the Earl's house in the country,' he said.

'Ask the other servants in the street and all the other streets nearby,' Sally said. 'One of them will know. Servants' gossip tells you everything. Oh my gawd, is that the time?' A clock in the tavern had just chimed twice. Sally snatched up her coat and ran.

4

It had stopped raining, and St James's Street glistened. Two smart carriages rattled up the hill past an elegantly dressed woman who sauntered down the pavement with a furled parasol. She took no notice of the obscene suggestions shouted at her from the windows of the gentlemen's clubs. She was no lady, Sandman guessed, for no respectable woman would ever walk in St James's Street.

Nothing marked the Seraphim Club's premises, but a crossing sweeper pointed Sandman to a house with shuttered windows on the eastern side of St James's Square. Sandman walked across the square and went to the door that was painted a glossy blue and bore no brass plate. A gilded chain hung in the shallow porch, and when it was pulled a bell sounded deep within the building. Sandman noticed that a spyhole had been drilled through the blue-painted timber. Someone, he reckoned, was peering at him and so he stared back until he heard a bolt being drawn. Then a lock turned and the door was reluctantly swung open by a servant dressed in a waspish livery of black and yellow.

'This is the Seraphim Club?'

The servant hesitated. He was a tall man, and had a face darkened by the sun, scarred by violence and hardened by experience. A brutal but good-looking man, Sandman thought. 'This is a private house, sir,' the servant said firmly.

'Belonging, I believe, to the Seraphim Club,' Sandman said brusquely, 'with whom I have government business.' He waved the Home Secretary's letter and, without waiting for an answer, stepped past the servant into a hall. The floor was a chessboard of gleaming black and white marble squares, and more marble framed the hearth, above which an overmantel was framed with a gilded riot of cherubs, flower sprays and acanthus leaves.

'The government, sir, has no business here,' the tall servant said. He was pointedly holding the front door open as an invitation for Sandman to leave.

Sandman noticed the man's good looks were marred by tiny black scars on his right cheek. Most people would hardly have noticed the scars, little more than dark flecks under the skin, but Sandman had acquired the habit of looking for the powder burns. 'Which regiment?' he asked the man.

The servant's face twitched in a half-smile. 'First Foot Guards, sir.'

'I fought beside you at Waterloo,' Sandman said. He pushed the letter into his jacket pocket, then stripped off his wet greatcoat which, with his hat, he tossed onto a gilded chair. 'I apologise, but the government is like French dragoons. If you don't beat the hell out of them the first time then they come back twice as strong the next.'

The tall servant was trapped between his duty to the club and his fellow-feeling for another soldier, but his loyalty to the Seraphim won. 'I'm sorry, sir,' he insisted, 'but they'll only tell you to make an appointment.'

'Then I'll wait here till they do tell me that,' Sandman said. 'My name's Sandman and I'm here on behalf of Lord Sidmouth.'

'Sir, they don't permit waiting,' the servant said. 'Time to go.'

'It's all right, Sergeant Berrigan,' a smooth voice cut in from behind Sandman, 'Mister Sandman will be tolerated.'

'Captain Sandman,' Sandman said, turning.

A fop faced him, a tall and extraordinarily handsome young man in a brass-buttoned black coat, white breeches and glistening black top boots. A stiff white cravat billowed from a plain white shirt which was framed by his high coat collar. His hair was black and cut very short, surrounding a pale face. It was an amused and clever face, and the man was carrying a quizzing glass, a slender gold wand supporting a single lens through which he gave Sandman a brief inspection before offering a slight bow. 'Captain Sandman,' he said, 'I should have recognised you. I saw you knock fifty runs off Martingale and Bennett last year. My name, by the way, is Lord Skavadale. Do come into the library, please,' he gestured to the room behind him. 'Would you like a warming collation, Captain? Coffee? Tea? Mulled wine?'

'Coffee,' Sandman said. He smelt lavender water as he went past Lord Skavadale into the library—a large, well-proportioned room where a generous fire burned in a wide hearth between the high bookshelves. A dozen armchairs were scattered across the floor, but Skavadale and Sandman were the only occupants. 'Most of the members are in the country at this time of year,' Skavadale explained the room's emptiness, 'but I had to drive up to town on business. And what is your business, Captain?'

'An odd name,' Sandman ignored the question, 'the Seraphim Club?' He looked about the library. The only painting was a life-size, full-length portrait that hung above the mantelpiece. It showed a thin man with a rakish, good-looking face and lavishly curled hair that hung past his shoulders. He was wearing a tight-waisted coat made of floral silk, with lace at its cuffs and neck, while across his chest was a broad sash from which hung a basket-hilted sword.

'John Wilmot, second Earl of Rochester,' Lord Skavadale identified the man. 'You know his work?'

'I know he was a poet,' Sandman said, 'and a libertine.'

'He was indeed,' Skavadale said, 'a poet of the highest wit and rarest talent, and we think of him, Captain, as our exemplar. The seraphim are higher beings, the highest, indeed, of all the angels. It is a small conceit of ours.'

'Higher than mere mortals like the rest of us?' Sandman asked sourly. Lord Skavadale was so courteous, so perfect and so poised that it annoyed Sandman.

'We merely try to excel,' Skavadale said pleasantly, 'as I am sure you do, Captain, in cricket and whatever else it is that you do, and I am being remiss in not giving you an opportunity to tell me what that might be.'

That opportunity had to wait a few moments, for a servant came with a silver tray on which were porcelain cups and a pot of coffee. Neither Lord Skavadale nor Sandman spoke as the coffee was poured and, in the silence, Sandman detected the sound of the clash of metal from a nearby room and realised that men were fencing.

'Sit, please,' Skavadale said when the servant had gone.

'Charles Corday,' Sandman said, taking a chair.

Lord Skavadale looked bemused. 'The young man convicted of the Countess of Avebury's murder. Why do you raise his name?'

Sandman sipped the coffee. The saucer was blazoned with a badge showing a naked golden angel flying on a red shield. 'The Home Secretary,' Sandman said, 'has charged me with investigating the facts of Corday's conviction. There are doubts about his guilt.'

Skavadale raised an eyebrow. 'Why would that bring you to our door, Captain?'

'Because we know that the portrait of the Countess of Avebury was commissioned by the Seraphim Club,' Sandman said.

'Was it, now?' Skavadale asked mildly. 'I do find that remarkable.' He lowered himself to perch on the leather-topped fender.

'What makes the matter more interesting,' Sandman went on, 'is that the commission for the portrait demanded that the lady be depicted naked, though she was not to know.'

'Well, I never,' Skavadale said, but despite the mockery his dark eyes did not look surprised at all. He sipped his coffee. 'I confess I know nothing of this. It is possible that one of our members commissioned the portrait, but alas, they did not confide in me.'

'Is the Earl of Avebury a member?' Sandman asked.

Skavadale hesitated. 'I really cannot divulge who our members are, Captain. This is a private club. But I think it is safe for me to tell you that we do not have the honour of the Earl's company.'

'Did you know the Countess?' Sandman asked.

Skavadale smiled. 'Indeed I did, Captain. Many of us worshipped at her shrine for she was a lady of divine beauty and we regret her death exceedingly. Exceedingly.' He stood up. 'I fear your visit to us has been wasted, Captain. Can I see you to the front door?'

Sandman stood. Just then a door crashed open behind him and he turned to see that one of the bookcases had a false front of leather spines glued to a door, and a young man in breeches and shirt was standing there with a fencing foil in his hand and an antagonistic expression on his face. 'I thought you'd seen the culley off, Johnny,' he said to Skavadale.

Skavadale, smooth as honey, smiled. 'Allow me to name Captain Sandman, the celebrated cricketer. This is Lord Robin Holloway.'

'Cricketer? I thought he was Sidmouth's lackey.'

Lord Robin Holloway had none of Skavadale's courtesy. He was in his early twenties, Sandman judged, and was as tall and handsome as his friend, but where Skavadale was dark, Holloway was golden. His hair was gold, there was gold on his fingers and a gold chain about his neck.

'I'm that too,' Sandman said. 'I came to ask about the Countess of Avebury.'

'In her grave, culley, in her grave,' Holloway said. A second man appeared behind him, also holding a foil, though Sandman suspected from the man's plain shirt and trousers that he was a club servant, perhaps their master-at-arms. 'Did you say your name was Sandman? Ludovic Sandman's son?'

Sandman inclined his head. 'I am.'

'Bloody man cheated me,' Lord Robin Holloway said. His eyes, slightly protuberant, challenged Sandman. 'Owes me six thousand bloody guineas. So what are you going to do about that, culley?'

'Captain Sandman is leaving,' Lord Skavadale said firmly, and took Sandman's elbow.

Sandman shook him off. 'I've undertaken to pay some of my father's debts,' he told Lord Robin. Sandman's temper was brewing. 'I am paying the debts to the tradesmen who were left embarrassed by my father's suicide. As to your debt?' He paused. 'I plan to do nothing whatsoever about it.'

'Damn you, culley,' Lord Robin said, and he drew back the foil as if to slash it across Sandman's cheek.

Lord Skavadale stepped between them. 'Enough! The Captain is going.'

'He's nothing but a slimy little spy for bloody Sidmouth!' Lord Robin said. 'Use the tradesmen's entrance at the back, Sandman. The front door is for gentlemen.'

Sandman walked past Skavadale and Holloway and snatched the foil from the master-at-arms. He turned to Holloway again. 'I'll use the front door. Or does your lordship have a mind to stop me?'

'Robin,' Lord Skavadale cautioned his friend.

'Damn you,' Holloway said, and he twitched up his foil, swatted Sandman's blade aside and lunged.

Sandman parried to drive Holloway's blade high and wide, then slashed his foil across his lordship's face. The blade's tip was buttoned so it could not pierce, but it still left a red welt on Holloway's right cheek. Sandman's blade came back fast to mark the left cheek, then he lowered the sword.

'To hell with you!' Holloway was in a fury now, but while Sandman's temper was cold and cruel, Holloway's was all heat and foolishness. Holloway slashed the foil like a sabre, hoping to strike Sandman's face, but Sandman swayed back, let the blade pass an inch from his nose and then stepped forward and lunged his weapon into Holloway's belly. The button stopped the blade from piercing cloth or skin, and the weapon bent like a bow. Sandman used the spring of the blade to throw himself backwards as Lord Robin Holloway lunged his blade at Sandman's neck.

'You feeble little puppy,' Sandman said, and he began to fight, his rage now released. He stamped forward, his blade a hissing terror, and the button raked Lord Holloway's face, almost taking an eye, then the blade slashed across Lord Holloway's nose, opening it so that blood ran. Lord Holloway cringed away from the pain and then, suddenly, a pair of very strong arms was wrapped about Sandman's chest. Sergeant Berrigan was holding him while Lord Skavadale wrenched the foil from Lord Robin Holloway's hand.

'Enough!' Skavadale said. 'Enough!' He threw Holloway's foil to the far end of the room, then took Sandman's blade. 'You will leave now, Captain,' he insisted.

Sandman shook Berrigan's arms away. 'I was fighting real men,' he told Lord Robin, 'when you were pissing your childhood breeches.'

'Good day, Captain,' Skavadale said coldly.

'If you discover the person who commissioned the portrait,' Sandman said, 'then I would be grateful if you would inform me.' He had no realistic hope that Lord Skavadale would, but asking the question allowed him to leave with a measure of dignity. 'A message can be left for me at the Wheatsheaf in Drury Lane.'

Lord Robin glared at Sandman, but said nothing. He had been whipped and he knew it.

Sandman's hat and greatcoat were brought to him in the hallway where Sergeant Berrigan opened the front door. Sandman stepped past him, then Berrigan slammed the door.

SANDMAN WALKED slowly northwards. Sally had been right. The best way of finding the servant girl Meg, and so discovering the truth, was to ask other servants, which was why he was walking to Davies Street, a place he had assiduously avoided for the last six months.

Yet when he knocked on the door it all seemed so familiar, and Hammond, the butler, did not even blink an eyelid. 'Captain Rider,' he said, 'what a pleasure, sir, may I take your coat?' Hammond hung Sandman's coat and hat on a rack that was already heavy with other garments. 'Have you an invitation card?' he asked.

'Lady Forrest is giving a musical entertainment? I'm afraid I wasn't invited. I was hoping Sir Henry was at home.'

'He is home, sir, and I am sure he will want to receive you. Why don't you wait in the small parlour?'

The small parlour was twice the size of the drawing room in the house Sandman rented for his mother and sister in Winchester, a fact his mother mentioned frequently but which did not bear thinking of now, and so he listened to a tenor singing beyond the double doors that led to larger rooms. There was a patter of applause and then the door from the hall opened. 'My dear Rider!'

'Sir Henry.'

'A new French tenor,' Sir Henry said dolefully, 'who should have been stopped at Dover.' Sir Henry Forrest had never much appreciated his wife's musical entertainments, and usually took care to avoid them. 'I forgot there was an entertainment this afternoon, otherwise I might have stayed at the bank. How are you, Rider?'

'I'm well, thank you. And you, sir?'

'Keeping busy, Rider, keeping busy. The Court of Aldermen demands time and Europe needs money and we supply it.' Sir Henry opened the drawer of a sideboard and took out two cigars. 'Can't smoke in the conservatory today,' he said, 'so we might as well be hanged for fumigating the parlour, eh?' He paused to light a tinderbox, then the cigar. His height, silver hair and doleful face had always reminded Sandman of Don Quixote, yet the resemblance was misleading as dozens of business rivals had discovered too late. Sir Henry had an instinctive understanding of money; how to make it and how to use it. Those skills had helped to build the ships and feed the armies and cast the guns that had defeated Napoleon and they had brought Henry Forrest his knighthood. He was, in brief, a man of talent. 'It's good to see you, Rider,' he said now and he meant it. 'So what are you doing these days?'

'A rather unusual job, which has persuaded me to seek a favour of Hammond, sir.'

'A favour of Hammond, eh?' Sir Henry peered at Sandman as if unsure whether he had heard correctly. 'My butler?' Sir Henry went back to the sideboard where he poured two brandies. 'You will have a glass with me, won't you? So what is it you want of Hammond?'

But before Sandman could explain, the double doors to the drawing room opened and Eleanor was standing there and the light from the large drawing room was behind her so that it seemed as if her hair was a red halo about her face. She looked at Sandman, then took a very long breath before smiling at her father. 'Mother was concerned that you would miss the duet, Papa.'

'The duet, eh?'

'The Pearman sisters have been practising for weeks,' Eleanor explained, then looked back to Sandman. 'Rider,' she said softly.

'Miss Eleanor,' he said very formally, then bowed.

She gazed at him. Behind her, in the drawing room, a score of guests were perched on gilt chairs. Eleanor glanced at them, then firmly closed the doors. 'I think the Pearman sisters can manage without me. How are you, Rider?'

'I am well, thank you, well.' He had thought that he would not be able to speak for the breath had caught in his throat and he could feel tears in his eyes. Eleanor was wearing a dress of pale green silk with yellow lace at the breast and cuffs. She had a necklace of gold and amber that Sandman had not seen before, and he felt a strange jealousy of the life she had led in the last six months. She was, he remembered, engaged to be married and that cut deep. 'And you?'

'I am distraught that you are well,' Eleanor said with mock severity. 'To think you can be well without me? This is misery, Rider.'

'Eleanor,' her father chided her.

'I tease, Papa, it is permitted, and so few things are.' She turned on Sandman. 'Have you just come to town for the day?'

'I live here,' Sandman said.

'I didn't know.' Her grey eyes, almost smoky, with flecks of green in them, seemed huge. Just by looking at her Sandman felt almost light-headed. He stared at her and she stared back.

'Have you been here long?' Eleanor broke the silence.

'Three weeks,' he admitted, 'a little over.'

She looked, Sandman thought, as though he had struck her in the face. 'And you didn't call?' she protested.

Sandman felt himself reddening. 'I was not sure,' he said, 'to what end I should call. I thought you would appreciate it if I did not.'

'Rider came here to see Hammond, of all people, my dear,' Sir Henry said. 'It's not really a social call at all.'

'What on earth do you want with Hammond?' Eleanor asked, her eyes suddenly bright with inquisitiveness. She took a chair and put on an expectant face.

'My dear,' her father began, and was immediately interrupted.

'Papa,' Eleanor said sternly, 'I am sure that nothing Rider wants with Hammond is unsuitable for a young woman's ears, and that is more than I can say for the effusions of the Pearman girls. Rider?'

Sandman told his tale, and that gave rise to astonishment for neither Eleanor nor her father had connected Charles Corday with Sir George Phillips. It was bad enough that the Countess of Avebury had been murdered in the next street, now it seemed that the convicted murderer had spent time in Eleanor's company.

'Best not to tell your mother,' Sir Henry observed gently.

'I doubt he is a murderer,' Sandman put in, and he explained about the missing girl, Meg, and how he needed servants to retail the local gossip about the fate of the staff from Avebury's house. 'If Hammond can ask the maids what they've heard . . .'

'Then you'll learn nothing,' Eleanor interrupted. 'Hammond is a very good butler, but the maidservants are all quite terrified of him. No, the person to ask is my maid Lizzie.'

'You can't involve Lizzie!' Sir Henry objected.

'Why ever not?'

'Because you can't,' her father said. 'It simply isn't right.'

'It isn't right that Corday should hang! Not if he's innocent. And you, Papa, should know that! I've never seen you so shocked!'

Sandman looked enquiringly at Sir Henry, who shrugged. 'Duty took me to Newgate,' he admitted. 'We City aldermen are the legal employers of the hangman and he has petitioned us for an assistant. One never likes to disburse funds unnecessarily, so two of us undertook to discover the demands of his work. Hanging's not a pretty thing, Rider, have you ever seen one?'

'I've seen men after they've been hanged,' Sandman said, thinking of Badajoz. The British army, breaking into the Spanish city despite a grim French defence, had inflicted a terrible revenge on the inhabitants and Wellington had ordered the hangmen to cool the redcoats' anger. 'We used to hang plunderers,' he explained to Sir Henry.

'I suppose you had to,' Sir Henry said. 'It's a terrible death, terrible. I trust I shall never have to witness another.' He shrugged, then said, 'So you think, Rider, that my servants might have heard of this girl Meg's fate?'

'I was hoping so, sir. Or that they could ask questions of the servants who live in Mount Street. The Avebury house isn't a stone's throw away and I'm sure all the servants in the area know each other.'

'I'm sure Lizzie knows everyone in the area,' Eleanor said. 'Lizzie thrives on gossip.'

'There's no danger, is there?' Sir Henry asked Sandman.

'I can't think so, sir. We only want to know where the girl Meg went, and that's merely gossip.'

'Lizzie can explain her interest by saying one of our coachmen was sweet on her,' Eleanor said enthusiastically.

Her father was unhappy at the thought of involving Eleanor, but he was almost incapable of refusing his daughter. Such was his affection for his only child that he might even have permitted her to marry Sandman despite Sandman's poverty and family disgrace, but Lady Forrest had always seen Rider Sandman as second best. He had no title, and Lady Forrest dreamed that Eleanor would one day be a duchess, a marchioness, a countess or, at the very least, a lady. Sandman's impoverishment had given Lady Forrest the excuse to pounce, and her husband could not prevail against his wife's determination. So though Eleanor might not marry where she wanted, she would be allowed to ask her maidservant to delve the gossip from Mount Street.

'I shall write to you,' Eleanor said to Sandman, 'if you tell me where?'

'Care of the Wheatsheaf,' Sandman told her, 'in Drury Lane.'

Eleanor stood and, rising on tiptoe, kissed her father's cheek. 'Thank you, Papa, for letting me do something useful. And thank you, Rider.' She took his hand. 'I'm proud of you. This is a good thing you're doing.' She held onto his hand as the door opened.

Lady Forrest came in. She had the same red hair and the same beauty and the same force of character as her daughter, though Eleanor's grey eyes and intelligence had come from her father. Lady Forrest's eyes widened when she saw her daughter holding Sandman by the hand, but she forced a smile. 'Captain Sandman,' she greeted him in a voice that could have cut glass, 'this is a surprise.'

'Lady Forrest,' Sandman managed a bow, despite his trapped hand.

'Just what are you doing, Eleanor?' Lady Forrest's voice was now only a few degrees above freezing.

'Reading Rider's palm, Mama.'

'Ah!' Lady Forrest was immediately intrigued. She was thoroughly attracted to the idea of supernatural forces. 'So what do you see?'

Eleanor pretended to scrutinise Sandman's palm. 'I scry,' she said portentously, 'a journey.'

'Somewhere pleasant, I hope?' Lady Forrest said.

'To Scotland,' Eleanor said.

'It can be very pleasant at this time of year,' Lady Forrest remarked.

Sir Henry, wiser than his wife, saw a reference to Gretna Green looming. 'Enough, Eleanor,' he said quietly.

'Yes, Papa,' Eleanor let go of Sandman's hand and dropped her father a curtsy.

'So what brings you here, Rid—' Lady Forrest almost forgot herself, but managed a timely correction. 'Captain?'

'Rider very kindly brought me news of a rumour that the Portuguese might be defaulting on their short-term loans,' Sir Henry answered for Sandman, 'which doesn't surprise me, I must say. We advised against the conversion, as you'll remember, my dear.'

'You did, dear, I'm sure.' Lady Forrest was not sure at all, but she was nevertheless satisfied with the explanation. 'Now, come,

Eleanor, you are ignoring our guests. We have Lord Eagleton here,' she told Sandman proudly.

Lord Eagleton was the man whom Eleanor was supposed to be marrying, and Sandman flinched. 'I'm not acquainted with his lordship,' he said stiffly.

'Hardly surprising,' Lady Forrest said, 'for he only moves in the best of circles. I do hope you enjoy your visit to Scotland, Captain.' Then Lady Forrest led her daughter away.

'It'll be a day or two before you get your answer, I'm sure, but let's hope it helps,' Sir Henry said. 'You must come again, Rider.' He took Sandman through to the hall and helped him with his coat.

'You're being very helpful, Sir Henry, and I'm grateful.' And Sandman walked out and away, not even noticing whether it was raining or not. He was thinking of Lord Eagleton. Eleanor had not behaved as though she were in love with his lordship, indeed she had made a face expressing distaste when his name was mentioned, and that gave him hope. But then, he asked himself, what did love have to do with marriage? Marriage was about money and respectability.

And love? God damn it, Sandman thought, but he was in love.

IT WAS NOT RAINING now, indeed it was a beautiful late afternoon. Open carriages, pulled by matching teams with polished coats and ribboned manes, clipped smartly towards Hyde Park for the daily parade. Street bands vied with each other, drums banging and collectors shaking their money boxes. Sandman was oblivious.

He was thinking of Eleanor, and when he could no longer wring any clue as to Eleanor's intentions from every remembered glance and nuance, he wondered what he had achieved in the day. He had learned that Corday had mostly told him the truth, but he had nothing to report to Viscount Sidmouth. So what to do?

He thought about that when he returned to the Wheatsheaf and took his laundry down to the woman who charged a penny for each shirt. Then he stitched up his boots, using a sailmaker's needle and palm leather which he borrowed from the landlord, and he brushed his coat, trying to get a stain out of the tail. He reflected that of all the inconveniences of poverty, the lack of a servant to keep clothes clean was the most time-consuming.

He should go to Wiltshire, he decided. He had no assurance that he would find the girl Meg, but if he waited to hear from Eleanor then it might be too late. The Earl of Avebury was said to be a recluse and Sandman feared he would be summarily ejected from the estate, but that was a risk he would have to take. Catch the mail coach in the morning and he would be there by early afternoon. The mail coach would cost him at least twice as much as a stagecoach, but the stagecoach would not get him to Wiltshire before the evening. Sandman walked down to the mail office on Charing Cross where he paid two pounds and seven shillings for the last of the four seats on the next morning's mail to Marlborough.

He went back to the Wheatsheaf where, in the inn's back room among the beer barrels, he blacked and polished his newly mended boots. He heard Dodds's tuneless whistle and was about to call out a greeting when he heard a stranger's voice. 'Sandman ain't upstairs. You find anything?'

Sandman quietly pulled on his boots. The stranger's voice had been harsh, one not inviting Sandman to identify himself, but rather persuading him to look for a weapon. The only thing to hand was a barrel stave. He held it like a sword as he edged towards the door.

'This tail and a cricket bat,' another man answered and Sandman, still in the shadows, saw a young man holding his bat and his army sword. The two men must have searched his room.

'I'll look in the taproom,' the first man said.

'Bring him back here,' the second said.

The first man went through the service door. Sandman stepped from the back room and rammed the stave into the second man's kidneys. The man lurched forward, gasping, and Sandman seized the man's hair and pulled him backwards. Sandman tripped him so that he crashed back onto the floor, where Sandman stamped hard on his groin. The man shrieked and curled round his agony.

Sandman retrieved the bat and sword that had fallen in the passageway. He feared the man might be carrying a pistol, so he used the sword scabbard to tweak the man's coat aside. And saw yellow and black livery. 'You're from the Seraphim Club?' Sandman asked, and the man gasped through his pain, but the answer was not informative. Sandman felt in the man's coat pockets and found a pistol which he tugged out. 'So why are you here?'

'They wanted you fetched back to the club.'

'Why?'

'I don't know! They just sent us.'

'Just get out,' Sandman said. 'Collect your friend and get out.' Sandman watched the man climb to his feet and followed him into the taproom where a score of customers were seated at the tables. He raised the gun, pointing the blackened muzzle at the ceiling, and the two men fled. Sandman pushed the weapon into his belt as Sally ran across the room.

'What's happening?' she asked.

'It's all right, Sally,' Sandman said.

'Oh bleeding hell, it's not,' she said. She was looking past him, her eyes huge, and Sandman heard the sound of a gun being cocked.

He turned to see a long-barrelled pistol pointing between his eyes. The Seraphim Club had not sent two men to fetch him, but three. The third was Sergeant Berrigan. He was sitting in a booth, grinning. 'It's like French dragoons, Captain,' Sergeant Berrigan said. 'If you don't see the bastards off properly the first time, then sure as eggs they'll be back to trap you.'

And Sandman was trapped.

5

Sergeant Berrigan kept the pistol pointed at Sandman for a heartbeat, then he lowered the flint, put the weapon on the table and nodded at the bench opposite. 'You just won me a pound, Captain.'

'Who do you bleeding think you are?' Sally spat at Berrigan.

'Sally! Sally!' Sandman calmed her. He eased her onto the bench, then sat beside her. 'Allow me to name Sergeant Berrigan,' he told her, 'once of His Majesty's 1st Foot Guards. This is Miss Sally Hood.'

'Sam Berrigan,' the Sergeant said, plainly amused by Sally's fury, 'and I'm honoured, miss.'

'I'm bleeding not honoured.' She glared at him.

'A pound?' Sandman asked Berrigan.

'I said those two dozy bastards wouldn't take you, sir. Not Captain Sandman of the 52nd,' Berrigan said, then snapped his fingers and one of the serving girls came running. Sandman was not particularly impressed that Berrigan knew his old regiment, but he was very impressed by a stranger who could command such instant service in the Wheatsheaf. There was something very competent about Sam Berrigan. The Sergeant looked at Sally. 'Your pleasure, Miss Hood?'

Sally debated with herself for a second, then decided life was too short to turn down a drink. 'I'll have a gin punch, Molly,' she said.

Berrigan put a coin in Molly's palm and folded her fingers over it. 'A jug of ale, Molly,' he said, 'and make sure the gin punch is as fine as any we'd get at Limmer's.' He looked at Sandman. 'Lord Robin Holloway sent those two to persuade you back to the club, and Skavadale sent me. He didn't want you to come to any harm. Lord Robin planned to challenge you.'

'To a duel?' Sandman was amused.

'Pistols, I imagine,' Berrigan was equally amused. 'I can't see him wanting to take you on with a blade again. But I told the Marquess those two would never force you. You were too good a soldier.'

Sandman smiled. 'How do you know what kind of a soldier I was, Sergeant?'

'I know exactly what sort of swoddy you was,' Berrigan said.

He had a good face, Sandman thought, broad, tough and with confident eyes.

Berrigan looked at Sally. 'It was the end of the day at Waterloo, miss, and we was beaten. We was just standing there and dying. We hadn't given in, don't get me wrong, miss, but the bloody Crapauds had us beat. It was day's end and the last of them was still coming up the hill and there were four times as many of them as there were of us. I watched him,' he jerked his head at Sandman, 'and he was walking up and down in front of the line like he didn't have a care in the world. You'd lost your hat, hadn't you, sir?'

Sandman laughed at that memory. 'I had, you're right.' His bicorne hat had been blasted off by a French musket ball.

'Up and down he walked,' Berrigan explained to Sally, 'and the Crapauds had a swarm of skirmishers not fifty paces off and they was all shooting at him and he didn't blink an eyelid. Just walked like it was Sunday in Hyde Park.'

Sandman was embarrassed. 'I was only doing my duty, Sergeant, like you were, and I was terrified, I can tell you.'

'Then he stopped walking,' Berrigan continued, 'and I watched him take his men round the flank of the bastards and he beat them to hell.'

'That wasn't me,' Sandman said reprovingly. 'It was Johnny Colborne who marched us round the flank. It was his regiment.'

'But you led them,' Berrigan insisted. He poured two pots of ale, then raised his own tankard. 'Your very good health, Captain.'

'I'll drink to that,' Sandman said, 'though I doubt your employers would share the sentiment?'

'Lord Robin don't like you,' Berrigan said, 'on account that you made him look a bloody idiot.'

'Maybe they don't like me,' Sandman observed, 'because they

don't want the Countess's murder investigated? I suspect them.'

Berrigan shrugged. 'They're the Seraphim Club, Captain, so yes, they've done murder, and they've thieved, they've bribed. But killing the Countess? I've heard nothing. We servants know most of what they do because we clean up after them.'

'Why the hell do they want to be flash?' Sally sounded indignant. 'They're rich already, ain't they?' It was one thing for her friends at the Wheatsheaf to be criminals, but they had been born poor.

Berrigan looked at her, evidently liking what he saw. 'That's exactly why they do it, miss. Rich, titled and privileged, and on account of that they reckon they're better than the rest of us. The purpose of the club is for them to do whatever they want. What they want, they take, and what gets in their way, they destroy. They don't care,' his tone suggested he was warning Sandman, 'and they're bastards, Captain.'

'Yet you work for them,' Sandman spoke very gently.

'I'm no saint, Captain,' Berrigan said, 'and they pay me well.'

'Why are you telling me all this?' Sandman asked.

'Lord Robin Holloway,' Berrigan said, 'wants you dead, but I won't stand for it, Captain, not after Waterloo.' He looked at Sally. 'We went to the gates of hell, miss, and I didn't think I'd live through it, and nothing been's the same since.' The Sergeant's voice was hoarse with emotion and Sandman understood. Sam Berrigan looked as hard as a cobblestone, and undoubtedly he was, but he was also a very sentimental man. 'There's been hardly a day that I haven't seen you in my mind,' Berrigan went on, 'out on that ridge in that bloody smoke. I don't want you harmed by some spavined halfwit.'

Sandman smiled. 'I think you're here, Sergeant, because you want to leave the Seraphim Club.'

Berrigan leaned back and contemplated Sandman and then, more appreciatively, Sally. She blushed under his scrutiny, and he took a cigar from his inside pocket and struck a light with a tinderbox. 'I don't intend to be any man's servant for long,' he said when the cigar was drawing, 'but when I leave, Captain, I'll set up in business.'

'Doing what?' Sandman asked.

'These,' Berrigan tapped the cigar. 'A lot of gentlemen acquired a taste for these in the Spanish war, but they're curious hard to come by. I find them for the club members and I make almost as much tin that way as I do from wages. You understand me, Captain?'

'I'm not sure I do.'

'I don't need your advice, I don't need your preaching and I don't need your help. Sam Berrigan can look after himself. I just came to warn you, nothing else. Get out of town, Captain.' He stood up.

Sandman smiled. 'I'm leaving London tomorrow, but I'll be back here on Thursday afternoon.'

'You'd better bloody be,' Sally put in. 'It's that private performance. You're coming to Covent Garden to cheer me, aren't you?'

'Of course I am,' Sandman said, and looked back to Berrigan. 'I could do with some help, Sergeant, so when you decide to leave the club, come and find me.'

Berrigan said nothing, then nodded at Sally and walked away.

Sandman watched him leave. 'A very troubled young man,' he said.

'Don't look troubled to me. Good-looking though, ain't he?'

'But he's still troubled,' Sandman said. 'He wants to be good and finds it easy to be bad.'

'Welcome to life,' Sally said.

'So we're going to have to help to make him good, aren't we?'

'We?' She sounded alarmed.

'I've decided I can't put the world to rights all on my own,' Sandman said. 'I need allies, my dear, and you're elected. So far there's you, someone I saw this afternoon, maybe Sergeant Berrigan and . . .' Sandman turned as a newcomer to the taproom knocked down a chair, apologised profusely and fumbled with his walking stick. The Reverend Lord Alexander Pleydell had arrived. '. . . and your admirer makes four,' Sandman finished.

And maybe five, for Lord Alexander had with him a young man with an open face and a troubled expression. 'You're Captain Sandman?' The young man held out his hand.

'At your service,' Sandman said cautiously.

'Thank God I've found you!' the young man said. 'My name is Christopher Carne. The Countess of Avebury was my stepmother.'

'Ah,' Sandman said. 'I'm pleased to meet you.'

'We must talk,' Carne said. 'Dear God, Sandman, you must prevent a great injustice. Please, we must talk.'

Lord Alexander was bowing to Sally and blushing. Sandman knew his friend would be content for a while, so he led Carne to the back of the taproom where a booth offered some privacy.

LORD CHRISTOPHER CARNE was a nervous, hesitant young man with thick-lensed spectacles. He was short, had thin hair and the faintest suggestion of a stammer. In all he was not a prepossessing man. 'My father,' he told Sandman, 'is a dreadful man, just d-dreadful. It is as though the Ten Commandments, Sandman, were quite d-deliberately compiled as a challenge to him. Especially the seventh!'

'Adultery?'

'Of course. He ignores it, Sandman!' Behind his glasses Lord Christopher's eyes widened as though the very thought of adultery was horrid. He was dressed in a well-cut coat and fine shirt, but the cuffs of both were stained with ink, betraying a bookish disposition. 'My p-point is that like many habitual sinners, my father takes umbrage when he is sinned against. He has sinned with many men's wives, Captain Sandman, but he was furious when his own wife was unfaithful.'

'Your stepmother?'

'Just so. He threatened to kill her! I heard him.'

'To threaten to kill someone,' Sandman observed, 'is not the same as killing them.'

'I am apprised of the difference,' Lord Christopher answered with a surprising asperity, 'but I have talked with Alexander and he tells me you have a duty to the painter, Corday. I cannot believe he did it! What cause did he have? But my father, Sandman, my father had cause.' Lord Christopher spoke with a savage vehemence. 'You will perhaps understand,' he went on more mildly, 'if I tell you a little of my father's story.'

Sandman listened. The Earl's first wife, Lord Christopher's mother, had been the daughter of a noble family and, Lord Christopher averred, a living saint. 'He treated her wretchedly, Sandman,' he said, 'abusing her and insulting her, but she endured it with Christian for-bearance until she died. That was in 'nine. God rest her soul. He hardly mourned her,' he said indignantly, 'just went on taking women to his bed, and among them was Celia Collett. She was a mere third his age! But he was besotted and she was clever, Sandman, she was clever.' The savagery was back in his voice. 'She was an opera dancer at the Sans Pareil. Do you know it?'

'I know of it,' Sandman said mildly. The Sans Pareil on the Strand was one of the new unlicensed theatres that put on entertainments that were lavish with dance and song.

'She kept him from her b-bed till he married her, and then she led him a dance!'

'You obviously didn't like her?' Sandman observed.

Lord Christopher blushed. 'I hardly knew her,' he said uncomfort-ably, 'but what was there to like? The woman had no religion, few manners and scarce any education.'

'Does your father care for such things?'

'My father cares nothing for God, for letters or for courtesy,' Lord Christopher said. 'He hates me, Sandman, because the estate is entailed onto me.' Sandman understood that an entailed estate implied that Lord Christopher's grandfather had so mistrusted the present Earl of Avebury that he had made certain he could not inherit the family fortune. Though the present Earl could live off the estate's income, the capital and the land and investments would all be held in trust until he died, when they would pass to Lord Christopher. 'He hates me,' Lord Christopher went on, 'not only because of the entail, but because I have expressed a wish to take holy orders. And my father knows that when the family fortune passes to me it will be used in God's service. That annoys him.'

The conversation, Sandman thought, had passed a long way from Lord Christopher's assertion that his father had committed the murder. 'Your stepmother,' Sandman said, 'had a considerable household in Mount Street. What happened to those servants? Would they have gone to your father's estate?'

Lord Christopher blinked rapidly. 'They might. Why do you ask?'

Sandman shrugged, as if the questions he was asking were of no importance. The truth was that he disliked Lord Christopher and he had no wish to prolong this conversation, so instead of admitting to Meg's existence he just said that he would like to discover from the servants what had happened on the day of the Countess's murder.

'If they're loyal to my father,' Lord Christopher said, 'they will tell you nothing.'

'Why should that loyalty make them dumb?'

'Because he killed her!' Lord Christopher cried. 'Or at least he c-caused her to be killed. He has men who are loyal to him, who do his bidding. You must tell the Home Secretary that Corday is innocent.'

'I doubt it will make any difference if I do,' Sandman said. 'To change the guilty verdict I need either to produce the true murderer, with a confession, or else adduce proof of Corday's innocence that is incontrovertible. Opinion, alas, does not suffice.'

'Dear God!' Lord Christopher seemed astonished and leaned back, looking faint. 'So you have five days to find the real killer? The boy is doomed, is he not?'

Sandman feared Corday was, but he would not admit it. Not yet.

AT HALF PAST FOUR in the morning a pair of lamps glimmered feebly from the windows of the yard of the George Inn. A caped coachman in the Royal Mail's blue and red livery yawned, then flicked his whip at a snarling terrier that slunk out of the way of the massive coach-house doors that were dragged open to reveal a gleaming, dark blue mail coach. The vehicle was manhandled onto the yard's cobbles where a boy lit its two oil lanterns and half a dozen men heaved the mailbags into its boot. The eight horses, high-stepping and frisky, were led from the stables. The two coachmen, both armed with blunderbusses and pistols, locked the boot and then watched as the team was harnessed. 'One minute!' a voice shouted, and Sandman drank the scalding coffee that the inn had provided for the mail's passengers. The lead coachman clambered up to the box. 'All aboard!'

There were four passengers. Sandman and a middle-aged clergyman took the front seat with their backs to the horses, while an elderly couple sat opposite them. Mail coaches were light and cramped, but twice as fast as the larger stagecoaches. The inn yard's gates were dragged open, then the carriage swayed as the coachmen whipped the team out into Tothill Street. The hoofs echoed and the wheels rumbled as the coach gathered speed, but Sandman was fast asleep by the time it reached Knightsbridge.

He woke at about six o'clock to find the coach lurching through a landscape of small fields and scattered coverts. Sandman gazed fixedly out of the window, revelling in being out of London. The air seemed so remarkably clean. There was no pervading stench of coal smoke and horse dung, just the morning sunlight on summer leaves and the sparkle of a stream twisting beneath willows and alders beside a field of grazing cattle.

Sandman's spirits rose as each mile passed. He was happy, he suddenly realised, but quite why, he was not sure. Perhaps, he thought, it was because his life had purpose again, or perhaps it was because he had seen Eleanor and nothing about her demeanour, he had decided, betrayed an imminent marriage to Lord Eagleton.

Lord Alexander Pleydell had hinted as much the previous evening, most of which he had spent worshipping at Sally Hood's shrine, though Sally herself had seemed distracted by her memories of Sergeant Berrigan. Not that Lord Alexander had noticed. He, like Lord Christopher Carne, was struck dumb by Sally, so for most of the evening the two aristocrats had merely gaped at her, until at last Sandman had taken Lord Alexander into the back parlour. 'I want to talk to you,' he had said.

'I want to continue my conversation with Miss Hood,' Lord Alexander had complained pettishly.

'And so you shall,' Sandman assured him, 'but talk to me first. What do you know about the Marquess of Skavadale?'

'Heir to the Dukedom of Ripon,' Lord Alexander said immediately, 'from one of the old Catholic families of England. Not a clever man, and it's rumoured the family has money troubles. They were once exceedingly rich, with estates in Cumberland, Yorkshire, Cheshire, Kent, Hertfordshire and Sussex, but both father and son are gamblers.'

'Lord Robin Holloway?'

'Youngest son of the Marquess of Bleasby and a thoroughly nasty boy. Has plenty of money, no brains, and he killed a man in a duel last year. Are you going to enquire about the whole aristocracy?'

'Lord Eagleton?'

'A fop and an undistinguished bore.'

'The sort of man who might appeal to Eleanor?'

Alexander stared at Sandman in astonishment. 'Don't be absurd, Rider,' he said, lighting another pipe. 'She wouldn't stand him for two minutes!' He frowned as if trying to remember something, but whatever it was did not come to mind.

'Tell me what you know about the Seraphim Club?'

'I have never heard of it, but it sounds like an association of high-minded clergymen.'

'It isn't, believe me. Is there any significance in the word seraphim?'

'The seraphim, Rider, are the highest order of angels. It is also believed that the seraphim are patrons of love. Now, do you think I might go back to my conversation with Miss Hood?'

Lord Alexander stayed till past midnight, became drunk and verbose, then left with Lord Christopher, who had to support his friend as he staggered from the Wheatsheaf declaring his undying love for Sally. Sandman had gone to bed wondering how he would ever wake in time to catch the mail coach, yet here he was, rattling through as glorious a summer's day as any man could dream of.

AT NOON THE COACH clattered into the wide main street of Marlborough. A small crowd was waiting for the mail and Sandman pushed through it and asked a carrier where he might find the Earl of Avebury's estate. Carne Manor was not far, the man said, just over the river. A half-hour's walk. Sandman, hunger gnawing at his belly, walked south until he came to Carne Manor's great brick wall, which he followed until he reached a lodge and a pair of cast iron gates. A gravel drive, thick with weeds, led from the locked gates.

A bell hung by the lodge, but though Sandman tolled it a dozen times no one answered. The spikes on top of the gates looked formidable, so Sandman went back up the lane until he came to a place where an elm, growing close to the wall, made it easy to climb. He paused a second on the coping, then dropped down into the park. He moved carefully, half expecting a gamekeeper or some other servant to intercept him, until he reached the gravel drive.

He saw no one as he followed the drive through a stand of beeches. From the far side of the stand, he could at last see Carne Manor. It was a fine stone building with a façade of three high gables on which ivy grew about mullioned windows. Stables, coach houses and a brick-walled kitchen garden lay to the west, while behind the house were terraced lawns dropping to a stream.

He crossed the great sweep of gravel where carriages could turn in front of the house and climbed the entrance steps. Two glazed lanterns were mounted either side of the porch, though one had a glass pane missing and a bird's nest was smothering its candle holder. He hauled on the bell chain and waited.

A harsh banging to his right made him step back to see that a man was trying to open a leaded window in the room closest to the porch. The window was evidently jammed, but then it jarred open and the man leaned out. He was in late middle age and had a pale face. 'The house,' he said testily, 'is not open to visitors.'

'I hadn't supposed it was,' Sandman said. 'Are you his lordship?'

'Do I look like him?' the man answered in an irritated tone.

'I have business with his lordship,' Sandman explained.

'Business? Business?' The man spoke as though he had never heard of such a thing.

'It is delicate business,' Sandman said emphatically, suggesting it was none of the servant's, 'and my name is Captain Sandman.'

The man retreated inside. Sandman waited.

A window on the other side of the porch was forced open and the same servant appeared there. 'A captain of what?' he demanded.

'The 52nd Foot,' Sandman answered, and the servant vanished.

'His lordship wishes to know,' the servant reappeared at the first window, 'whether you were with the 52nd at Waterloo.'

'I was,' Sandman said.

The servant went back inside, and Sandman heard bolts being shot on the far side of the door, which eventually creaked open.

The servant offered a sketchy bow. 'Captain Sandman. This way, sir.'

The front door opened onto a hall panelled in a dark wood. The servant led Sandman down a passageway into a long gallery lined with tall velvet-curtained windows on one side and paintings on the other. The paintings, so far as he could see in the curtained gloom, were exceptionally fine.

The servant opened a door and announced Sandman. The room into which he had been ushered was vast and the sun was streaming in to illuminate a huge table, smothered in scraps that he thought at first were flowers or petals. Then he saw that the coloured scraps were thousands of toy soldiers. The table had been draped in green baize so that it resembled the valley in which the battle of Waterloo had been fought. He gaped at the model, at least thirty feet long and twenty deep, astonished. Two girls sat at a side table with brushes and paint, which they applied to lead soldiers. Then a squeaking noise had him look into the dazzle by a south window, where he saw the Earl. His lordship was in a wheeled chair and the squeak had been the sound of the axles turning as a servant pushed the Earl towards his visitor.

The Earl was dressed in the old fashion that had prevailed before men had adopted sober black or dark blue. His coat was of flowered silk, red and blue, with enormously wide cuffs and a lavish collar over which fell a cascade of lace. He wore a full-bottomed wig that framed an ancient, lined face that was incongruously powdered and rouged. 'You are wondering,' he addressed Sandman in a shrill voice, 'how the models are inserted onto the centre of the table, are you not?'

The question had not even occurred to Sandman, but now he did find it puzzling, for the table was far too big for its centre to be reached from the sides. 'How is it done, my lord?'

'Betty, dearest, show him,' the Earl commanded, and one of the two girls dropped her paintbrush and disappeared beneath the table. There was a scuffling sound, then a whole section of the valley rose into the air to become a wide hat for the grinning Betty. 'It is a model of Waterloo,' the Earl said proudly.

'So I see, my lord.'

'Maddox tells me you were in the 52nd. Show me where they were positioned.'

Sandman walked round the table's edge and pointed to one of the red-coated battalions on a ridge. 'We were there, my lord,' he said. The model really was extraordinary. It showed the two armies at the beginning of the fight. Sandman could even make out his own company, and assumed that the little mounted figure just ahead of the painted ranks was meant to be himself.

'Why are you smiling?' the Earl demanded.

'No reason, my lord,' Sandman looked at the model again, 'except that I wasn't on horseback that day.'

'Which company?'

'Grenadier.'

The Earl nodded. 'I shall replace you with a foot soldier,' he said. His chair squealed as he pursued Sandman about the table. 'So tell me, did Bonaparte lose the battle by delaying the start?'

'No,' Sandman said curtly.

The Earl was close to Sandman now and could stare up at him with red-rimmed eyes that were dark and bitter. 'Who the devil are you?' the Earl growled.

'I have come from Viscount Sidmouth, my lord, and . . .'

'Who the devil is Viscount Sidmouth?' the Earl interrupted.

'The Home Secretary, my lord.' He produced the Home Secretary's letter, which was waved away. 'I have heard, my lord,' Sandman went on, 'that the servants from your town house in Mount Street are now here?' He had heard nothing of the sort, but perhaps the bald statement would elicit agreement from the Earl. 'I would like to talk with one of them.'

'Are you suggesting,' the Earl asked in a dangerous voice, 'that Blücher might have come sooner had Bonaparte attacked earlier?'

'No, my lord.'

'Then if he'd attacked earlier he'd have won!' the Earl insisted.

Sandman looked at the model. It was impressive, comprehensive and all wrong. It was too clean for a start. Even in the morning, before the French attacked, everyone was filthy because, on the previous day, most of the army had slogged back from Quatre Bras through quagmires of mud and then they had spent the night in the open under successive cloudbursts. Sandman remembered the thunder and the lightning and the terror when some cavalry horses broke free in the night and galloped among the sodden troops.

'So why did Bonaparte lose?' the Earl demanded querulously.

'Because he allowed his cavalry to fight unsupported by foot or artillery,' Sandman said shortly.

'So why did he commit his cavalry when he did, eh? Tell me that?'

'It was a mistake, my lord, even the best generals make them.'

The Earl petulantly slapped the wicker arms of his chair. 'Bonaparte didn't make futile mistakes! The man might be scum, but he's clever scum. So why?'

Sandman sighed. 'Our line had been thinned, we were on the reverse slope of the hill. I doubt we were even visible. From the

French viewpoint, it must have looked as if we just vanished. The French saw an empty ridge, and they must have thought we were all retreating, so they charged. And might I ask your lordship what happened to your wife's servants from Mount Street?'

'Wife? I don't have a wife. Maddox!'

'My lord?' The servant stepped forward.

'The cold chicken, I think, and some champagne,' the Earl demanded, then scowled at Sandman. 'Were you there when the Imperial Guard attacked?'

'I was there, my lord, from the guns that signalled the first French assault to the very last shot of the day.'

The Earl seemed to shudder. 'I hate the French,' he said suddenly. 'I detest them. We brought glory on ourselves at Waterloo, Captain!'

Sandman had met other men like the Earl, men who were obsessed by Waterloo and wanted to know every remembered minute of that awful day, and all had one thing in common: none had been there.

'Tell me,' the Earl said, 'how many times the French cavalry charged.'

'All I wish to know from you, my lord, is whether a maid called Meg came here from London.'

'How the devil would I know what happened to that bitch's servants, eh? And why would you ask?'

'A man is in prison, my lord, awaiting execution for the murder of your wife, and there is good reason to believe him innocent.'

The Earl began to laugh. The laugh came from deep in his narrow chest and brought tears to his eyes. He fumbled a handkerchief from his lace-frilled sleeve and wiped his eyes. 'She wronged a man at the very end, did she?' he asked in a hoarse voice. 'Oh, she was so very good, my Celia, at being bad.' Then he glowered at Sandman. 'So, how many battalions of Napoleon's Guard climbed the hill?'

'Not enough, my lord. What happened to your wife's servants?'

The Earl ignored Sandman because the cold chicken and champagne had been placed on the edge of the table. He summoned Betty to cut up the chicken and, as she did so, he put an arm round her waist. The Earl turned his rheumy eyes on Sandman. 'I have always liked women young,' he said, 'young and tender. You!' This was to the other girl. 'Pour the champagne, child.' The girl stood on his other side and the Earl put a hand under her skirt while she poured the champagne. Sandman turned to look out of the window.

The Earl gobbled his chicken and slurped his champagne. 'I was told,' he dismissed the two girls by slapping their rumps, 'that the French cavalry charged at least twenty times. Was that so?'

Sandman, still looking out of the window, was seeing his recurring dream, watching the French cavalry surge up the slope on the British-held ridge, their horses labouring in the damp earth. In that heat and smoke the French horsemen had never stopped coming, a succession of cavalrymen thumping about the British squares, the smoke of the muskets and cannon drifting over the British standards. 'All I remember clearly, my lord,' Sandman said, turning, 'was feeling grateful to the French, because so long as their horsemen milled about our squares then their artillery could not fire on us.'

'But how many charges did they make?'

'Ten?' Sandman suggested. 'Twenty? They just kept coming. And they were hard to count because of the smoke. And we were looking backwards, too, because once a charge had gone through the squares, my lord, they had to come back again.'

'So they were attacking from both sides?'

'From every side,' Sandman said, remembering the swirl of horsemen, the mud and the screams of the dying horses.

'How many cavalry?' the Earl wanted to know.

'I didn't count, my lord. How many servants did your wife have?'

The Earl grinned. 'Bring me a horseman, Betty,' he ordered, and the girl dutifully brought him a model French dragoon in his green-coat. 'Very pretty, my dear,' the Earl said, then put the dragoon on the table and hauled Betty onto his lap. 'I am an old man, Captain,' he said, 'and if you want something of me then you must oblige me. Betty knows that, don't you, child?' The Earl leered at Sandman. 'You will tell me all I want to know, Captain, and perhaps, when you are done, I shall tell you a little of what you want to know.'

Outside, in the hall, a clock struck six and Sandman felt the despair of wasted time. He sensed that the Earl would play with him all evening and send him away with his questions unanswered.

'Let us begin at the beginning, Captain,' the Earl said, 'let us begin at dawn, eh? It had been raining, yes?'

Sandman walked round the table until he was behind the Earl, where he stooped so his face was close to the stiff hairs of the wig. 'Why not talk about the battle's end, my lord?' Sandman asked in a low voice. 'Why not talk about the attack of the Imperial Guard? Because I was there when we took the bastards in the flank.' He crouched even lower and lowered his voice to a hoarse whisper. 'They'd won the battle, my lord, it was all over except the pursuit, but we changed history in an eyeblink. We marched out of line and we gave them volley fire, my lord, and then we fixed bayonets and I can tell you exactly how it happened. I can tell you how we won, my lord.' Sandman's temper was rising now. 'But you'll never hear that story, my lord, never, because I'll make damn sure that not one officer of the 52nd will ever talk to you! You understand that? Good day, my lord.' He walked towards the door.

'Captain!' The Earl had tipped the girl off his lap. 'Wait!' His rouged face twitched. He badly wanted to know exactly how Bonaparte's vaunted Guard had been beaten off, so he snarled at the two girls and the servants to leave the room.

It still took time to draw the tale from him. Time and a bottle of smuggled French brandy, but eventually the Earl spewed the bitter tale of his marriage. 'Legs,' the Earl said dreamily, 'such legs, Captain. That was the first thing about her I saw.'

'At the Sans Pareil?' Sandman asked.

The Earl shot Sandman a shrewd glance. 'Who've you been talking to?' he demanded. 'Who?'

'People talk in town,' Sandman said.

'My son?' the Earl guessed, then laughed. 'That pasty little weakling? I should have culled that one when he was an infant. His mother was a prayerful mouse, and the bloody fool thinks he's taken after her, but he hasn't. There's me in him. He might be forever on his knees, Captain, but he's always thinking of tits and bum, legs and tits again. He says he wants to be a priest! But he won't. What he wants, Captain, is for me to be dead!' The Earl spat the word. 'So what did the pallid little halfwit tell you? That I killed Celia? Perhaps I did, Captain, or perhaps Maddox did it for me, but how will you prove it, eh?' The Earl waited for an answer, but Sandman did not speak.

'Lord, but that bitch robbed me blind. Never knew a woman to spend money like it! Then when I came to my senses I tried to cut off her allowance. I told the estate's trustees to turn her out of the house, but the bastards left her there. Maybe she was swiving one of them? That's how she made her money, Captain, by diligent swiving.'

'You're saying she was a whore, my lord?'

'Not a common whore,' the Earl said, 'I'll say that for her. She called herself an actress, a dancer.' He turned his rheumy eyes on Sandman. 'Celia used blackmail, Captain. She'd take a young man as a lover, commit the poor fool to write a letter or two begging her favours, and then when he engaged to marry an heiress she threatened to reveal the letters. Made a pretty penny, she did! She told me as much to my face. Told me she didn't need my cash, had her own.'

'Do you know what men she treated thus, my lord?'

The Earl shook his head. He stared at the model battle, unwilling to meet Sandman's eyes. 'I didn't want to know names,' he said softly.

'And the servants, my lord? What happened to them?'

'They ain't here.' He scowled at Sandman. 'I told the trustees to get rid of them. I don't know what happened to Celia's damned servants,' he said, 'and I don't care. Now, damn you, tell me what happened when the Emperor's Guard attacked.'

So Sandman did.

6

Sandman got back to London late on Thursday afternoon, after sleeping fitfully on a pile of straw in the yard of the King's Head in Marlborough. He was irritated, for he reckoned his journey to Wiltshire had been largely wasted. He doubted the Earl of Avebury had killed or arranged the killing of his wife. The only advantage Sandman had gained was to learn that the dead Countess had kept herself by blackmailing her lovers, but that did not help him to discover who those lovers had been.

He used the side door of the Wheatsheaf that opened into the tavern's stableyard, where he pumped water into the tin cup chained to the handle. He drank it down, then turned as the click of hoofs sounded in the stable entrance. Jack Hood was heaving a saddle onto a handsome horse. Like his horse, Jack Hood was tall and dark. He wore black boots, black breeches and a narrow-waisted black coat, and his long black hair was tied with a ribbon of black silk at the nape of his neck. He gave Sandman a grin. 'You look tired, Captain.'

'Tired, poor, hungry and thirsty,' Sandman said, pumping again.

'That's what the square life does for you,' Hood said cheerfully. He slid two long-barrelled pistols into their saddle holsters.

Sandman drank down the water and let the cup drop. 'And what will you do, Mister Hood,' he asked, 'when they catch you?'

'When I'm caught?' Hood asked. 'I'll come to you for help, Captain. Sally says you're a gallows thief.'

'But I haven't stolen one man from the scaffold yet.'

'And I doubt you ever will,' Hood said grimly, 'because that ain't the way the world works. They don't care how many they hang, Captain, so long as the rest of us take note that they do hang.' Hood put his foot into the stirrup and hauled himself into the saddle. 'As like as not I'll finish my days on Jem Botting's dancing floor and I don't lose sleep nor tears over it. The gallows is there, Captain, and we live with it till we die on it, and we won't change it because the bastards don't want it changed. It's their world, not ours.' He pulled on thin black leather gloves. 'There are some coves to see you in the back slum, Captain,' he said, meaning the back parlour. 'But before you talk with them, you should know I took my dinner at the Dog and Duck and I heard a whisper there. Your life, fifty quid.' He raised an eyebrow. 'You've upset someone, Captain. I've spread word in the 'sheaf that no one's to touch you because you've been kind to my Sal, but I can't control every flash bowzing house in London.'

Sandman felt a lurch of his heart. Fifty guineas for his life? 'You would not know, I suppose,' he asked, 'who has staked the money?'

'I asked, but no one knew. So watch yourself, Captain.'

Sandman cut through the barrel room to the passage where there was a serving hatch to the parlour. Viscount Sidmouth had hinted this job would be easy, a month's pay for a day's work, but it was suddenly a life for a month's pay. He nudged the hatch open, careful not to make a noise, then stooped to peer through the crack.

He heard the footsteps behind him, but before he could turn a pistol barrel was cold by his ear. 'A good soldier always makes a reconnaissance, eh, Captain?' Sergeant Berrigan said. 'I thought you'd come here first.'

Sandman turned. 'What are you going to do, Sergeant? Shoot me?'

'Just making sure you ain't got any sticks on you, Captain,' Berrigan said, then used his pistol barrel to push open the flaps of Sandman's jacket and, satisfied that the Captain was not armed, he jerked his head towards the parlour door. 'After you, Captain.'

'Sergeant—' Sandman began, planning to appeal to Berrigan's better nature, but that nature was nowhere to be seen, for the Sergeant just cocked the pistol and aimed it at Sandman's chest. Sandman turned the knob and went into the back parlour.

The Marquess of Skavadale and Lord Robin Holloway were on the settle at the far side of the long table. Both were dressed in superbly cut black coats, blossoming cravats and skin-tight breeches. Holloway scowled to see Sandman. There were still raw scars across his cheeks and nose where Sandman had whipped him with the fencing foil. But Skavadale courteously stood up. 'My dear Captain Sandman, how very kind of you to join us. Please, sit.'

Sandman sat reluctantly, first glancing at Berrigan who lowered the pistol's flint, though he did not put the weapon away. Instead, he stood beside the door and watched Sandman. The Marquess of Skavadale poured some wine. 'A rather raw claret, Captain, but probably welcome after your journey?'

Skavadale looked pained when Sandman shook his head in refusal. 'Oh come, Captain. We're here to be friendly.'

'And I'm here because I was threatened with a pistol.'

'Put it away, Sergeant,' Skavadale ordered, then he toasted Sandman. 'I've learned a little about you in the last couple of days, Captain. I already knew you were a formidable cricketer, of course, but you have another reputation besides.'

'For what?' Sandman asked bleakly.

'You were a good soldier,' Skavadale said.

'So?' Sandman asked bleakly.

'But unfortunate in your father,' Skavadale said gently. 'Now, I understand you are supporting your mother and sister. Am I right?' Sandman neither spoke nor moved. 'If it were not for you, Captain, your mother would long have been reduced to accepting charity and your sister would be what? A governess? A paid companion?'

Sandman still kept silent, yet Lord Skavadale had spoken the truth. Belle, Sandman's sister, was nineteen years old and had only one hope of escaping poverty, which was to marry well, yet without a dowry she could not hope to find a respectable husband. Before her father's death, Belle might have expected to attract an aristocrat and she still yearned for those prospects and, in some obscure way, she blamed Sandman for their loss.

'You are trying to pay off some of your father's debts,' Skavadale said. 'It's very honourable of you. Yet you've a mother and a sister to keep and no employment other than an occasional game of cricket. What will you do, Captain? As I understand it, the Home Secretary's demands upon you are very temporary.'

'What will you do?' Sandman asked.

'I beg your pardon?'

'As I understand it,' Sandman said, remembering Lord Alexander's description of the Marquess, 'you are not unlike me. Your family once possessed a great fortune, but it also possessed gamblers.'

The Marquess looked irritated, but let the insult pass. 'I shall marry well,' he said lightly, 'meaning I shall marry wealth. And you?'

'Maybe I shall marry well, too,' Sandman retorted.

'Really?' Skavadale raised a sceptical eyebrow. 'I shall succeed to a dukedom, Sandman, and that's a great lure to a girl. What's your attraction? Skill at cricket? Fascinating memories of Waterloo?' His lordship's scorn was obvious. 'Girls who possess money,' Skavadale went on, 'either marry more money or else they seek rank, because money and rank, Captain, are the only two things that matter in this world.' Skavadale gave a ghost of a smile. 'You have been denied your share of wealth, Captain. If you will allow us,' he gestured to include Lord Robin Holloway, who had as yet said nothing, 'and by us I mean the whole membership of the Seraphim Club, we should like to remedy that lack.' He took a piece of paper from his pocket, placed it on the table and slid it towards Sandman.

Sandman picked up the paper and saw it was a money draft, payable to Rider Sandman, drawn on the account of Lord Robin Holloway at Coutts Bank, to the value of twenty thousand guineas.

Twenty thousand. He forced himself to take a deep breath. Twenty thousand guineas could pay off his father's small debts, buy his mother and sister a fine house and keep them in country gentility. Most tempting of all, though, was the knowledge that twenty thousand guineas would be a fortune sufficient to overcome Lady Forrest's objections to his marrying Eleanor. He would be a proper gentleman again. He stared at the money draft. It made all things possible.

He looked up into Lord Robin Holloway's eyes. The fool who had wanted to challenge Sandman to a duel was now giving him a fortune? Lord Robin ignored Sandman's gaze. Lord Skavadale smiled at Sandman. It was the smile of a man enjoying another's good fortune, yet it filled Sandman with shame. Shame because he had been tempted, truly tempted.

'I did not expect such kindness from Lord Robin,' Sandman said drily.

'Every member of the Seraphim contributed,' the Marquess said, 'and my friend Robin collated the funds. It is, of course, a gift.'

'A gift?' Sandman repeated the words bitterly. 'Not a bribe?'

'Of course it's not a bribe,' Skavadale said sternly. 'I am offended, Captain Sandman, when I see a gentleman reduced to penury. And when that gentleman is an officer who has fought gallantly for his country, then the offence is all the greater. I told you that the Seraphim Club is composed of men who attempt to excel. What else are angels but beings that do good? So we should like to see you and your family restored to your proper place in society. That is all.'

Lord Skavadale had sounded so reasonable and calm, as though this transaction was something very ordinary. Yet Sandman knew better. 'And what would you want in return?'

Lord Skavadale looked offended. 'I should only expect, Captain,' he spoke stiffly, 'that you would behave like a gentleman.'

'I trust,' Sandman said frostily, 'that I always behave thus.'

'Then you will know, Captain,' Skavadale said pointedly, 'that gentlemen do not perform paid employment.'

'So I write to the Home Secretary and resign as his Investigator?'

'It would be the gentlemanly thing to do,' Skavadale observed.

'How gentlemanly is it,' Sandman asked, 'to let an innocent man hang?'

'Is he innocent?' Skavadale enquired. 'You told the Sergeant you would bring proof from the countryside, and did you?' He waited, but it was plain from Sandman's face that there was no proof. Skavadale shrugged as if to suggest that Sandman might just as well accept the money. But Sandman nerved himself and tore the draft into shreds. He saw Skavadale blink with surprise when he made the first rip, and then his lordship looked furious and Sandman felt a pulse of fear.

The Marquess of Skavadale and Lord Robin Holloway stood. They looked at Sergeant Berrigan and it seemed that some kind of unspoken message was delivered before, without even glancing at Sandman, they went. Their footsteps receded down the passage as cold metal touched the back of Sandman's neck and he knew it was the pistol. He tensed. 'You had your chance, Captain.' Then the Sergeant leaned close to Sandman's ear. 'Watch yourself, Captain.' It was the exact same advice that Jack Hood had given. Sandman heard the door open and shut, and the Sergeant's footsteps fade.

Twenty thousand guineas, he thought. Gone.

THE REVEREND Lord Alexander Pleydell had secured one of the Covent Garden Theatre's stage boxes for the performance. 'I cannot say I am expecting great artistry,' he declared as he followed Sandman through the crowds, 'except from Miss Hood. I am sure she will be more than dazzling.' His lordship, like Sandman, was clutching his pockets for theatre crowds were famous hunting grounds for pickpockets.

Sandman edged closer to the brightly lit awning of the theatre.

'Do you think,' Lord Alexander shouted over the noise of the crowd, 'that Miss Hood will join us for supper after the performance?'

'I'm sure she'll be more than happy to bask in the admiration of one of her admirers.'

'One of?' Lord Alexander asked anxiously. 'You're not thinking of

Kit Carne, are you?' Lord Alexander looked disapproving. 'Kit is not a serious man, Rider. He is weak. The other night he just stared at Miss Hood with a vacant look on his face! Lord knows what she thought of him. But I mustn't be hard on Kit. He has little experience of women and I fear he has no defences against their charms.'

Just then the throng gave an inexplicable lurch and Sandman was able to make a lunge for the doorway. If it was a paid crowd causing the crush, he thought, then it was costing Mister Spofforth a fortune. Spofforth was the man who had taken the theatre for the evening on behalf of his protégée, a Miss Sacharissa Lasorda, who was billed as the new Vestris. The old Vestris was a dazzling Italian actress who was reputed to add three hundred pounds a night to a theatre's takings merely by baring her legs, and Mister Spofforth was now trying to launch Miss Lasorda on a career of similar profitability.

They took their places above the stage's apron. Lord Alexander had a bag full of clay pipes and lit his first of the evening. The house was full, over three thousand spectators, and it was rowdy because a good number were already drunk, suggesting that Mister Spofforth's servants must have dredged the taverns to find his supporters. A group of newspaper writers was being plied with champagne, brandy and oysters in a box opposite Lord Alexander's plush eyrie. Mister Spofforth, an aloof beau with a collar rising past his ears, was in the neighbouring box from where he kept an anxious eye on the journalists, whose verdict could make or break his lover. A dozen musicians filed into the pit and began tuning their instruments.

'I'm putting together a gentlemen's eleven to play against Hampshire at the end of the month,' Lord Alexander said, 'and I rather hoped you'd want to play.'

'I'd like that, yes. But I'm very out of practice,' Sandman warned his friend.

'Then get into practice,' Lord Alexander said testily, polishing the lens of his opera glasses on the tails of his coat.

A cheer sounded as boys went round the theatre extinguishing the lamps. The drummer gave a portentous roll and a player in a cloak leapt from between the curtains to recite the prologue:

> 'In Africa, so far from home,
> A little lad was wont to roam.
> Aladdin was our hero's name . . .'

He got no further before the audience drowned him in a cacophony of shouting, hissing and whistling. 'Show us the girl's pins!' a man yelled from the box next to Sandman. 'Show us her gams!'

Mister Spofforth was looking anxious, but the musicians began to play and that slightly calmed the audience, who gave a cheer as the prologue was abandoned and the heavy scarlet curtains parted to reveal a glade in Africa. Oak trees and yellow roses framed an idol that guarded the entrance to a cave where a dozen white-skinned natives were sleeping. Sally was one of the natives, who were inexplicably dressed in white stockings, black velvet jackets and very short tartan skirts. Lord Alexander bellowed a cheer as the twelve girls got to their feet and began dancing. Others began to jeer. 'Bring on the girl!' the man in the next box demanded. Some of the crowd had rattles that filled the high gilded hall with a crackling and echoing din. 'Oh, this is splendid!' Lord Alexander said with relish.

The theatre's management must have believed that the sight of Miss Sacharissa Lasorda would calm the tumult, for the girl was pushed prematurely onto the stage. Mister Spofforth stood and began to applaud and his claque took their cue and cheered lustily. Miss Lasorda, who played the Sultan of Africa's daughter, was dark-haired and certainly pretty, but whether her legs deserved to be as famous as Vestris's was still a mystery, for she was wearing a long skirt embroidered with crescent moons, camels and scimitars. She bowed to her supporters before beginning to dance.

'Show us your gams!' the man in the next box shouted.

'Skirt off! Skirt off!' the crowd in the stalls began to chant.

Lord Alexander had tears of joy running down his cheeks. 'I do so like the theatre,' he said, 'dear sweet God, I do so love it. This must have cost that young fool two thousand pounds at the very least.'

Sandman did not hear what his friend had said and so leaned towards him. 'What?' he asked.

He heard something smack into the wall at the back of the box and saw, in the shadows there, a puff of dust. He gaped up to see a patch of smoke in the dim heights of an upper gallery box. It was only then that he realised a shot had been fired at him. He was so shocked that he did not move for a few seconds. The audience was going silent. Some had heard the shot over the raucous din, while others could smell the reeking powder smoke.

Sandman snatched open the door to the box and saw two men running up the stairs with pistols in their hands. He slammed the door. 'Meet me in the Wheatsheaf,' he told Lord Alexander, and he swung his legs over the box's balustrade, paused a second, then jumped. He landed heavily, turning his left ankle.

'Captain!' Sally shouted, and pointed to the wings.

Sandman staggered towards the idol guarding the cave mouth. There was a terrible pain in his ankle.

He turned to see the two men in the box, both pointing their pistols, but neither dared fire onto the crowded stage. Then one of the men threw a leg over the box's gilded lip. Sandman limped into the wings, staggered through a tangle of ropes, then down some stairs and, at the bottom, turned into a passage. Every step was agony. He stopped in the passage and flattened himself against the wall. He heard the screams from the dancers on the stage, then the pounding of feet down wooden stairs, and a second later a man came round the corner and Sandman tripped him, then stamped on the back of his neck. The man grunted and Sandman took the pistol out of his suddenly feeble hand and turned the man over. 'Who are you?' he asked, but the man merely spat up at Sandman, who struck him with the pistol barrel, then limped down the passage to the stage door. More footsteps sounded behind him and he turned, pistol raised, but it was Sally running towards him, carrying her cloak.

'You all right?' she asked him.

'Twisted my ankle. I don't think it's broken.'

'Come on. Lean on me.' She tugged him out into the street. A man whistled at the sight of her long legs in the white stockings and she snarled at him, then draped the cloak about her shoulders. 'Bloody hell. What happened?'

'Someone shot at me. A rifle.'

'Who?'

'I don't know.' Sandman said. The Seraphim Club? That seemed most likely, especially after Sandman had turned down their vast bribe, but that did not explain Jack Hood's assertion that there was a price on Sandman's head. 'I really don't know,' he said.

They now walked or, in Sandman's case, hobbled under the piazza of the Covent Garden market. The summer evening meant it was still light, though the shadows were long across cobbles that were littered with the remnants of vegetables and squashed fruit. Flower sellers were arranging their baskets on the pavement, ready for the crowds to come from the two nearby theatres. Sandman constantly glanced behind, but he could see no obvious enemies. 'They'll be expecting me to go back to the Wheatsheaf,' he told Sally.

'They won't know which bleeding door you're going in, though, will they?' Sally said. 'And once you're inside you're bleeding safe, Captain, because there ain't a man there who won't protect you.'

'Are you sure you shouldn't be at the theatre?'

'They ain't ever going to get that bleeding circus started again.'

They reached Drury Lane and Sally opened the Wheatsheaf's front door.

'Is the back parlour free?' Sandman asked the landlord, Jenks.

Jenks nodded. 'The gentleman said you'd be back, Captain, and he kept it for you. And there's a letter for you as well.'

'It must be Lord Alexander,' Sandman explained, 'because he wanted you and me to have dinner with him.' He took the letter from Mister Jenks and smiled at Sally. 'You don't mind?'

'Mind Lord Alexander? He'll just gawp at me like a Billingsgate cod, won't he?' Sally said, then glanced down at her short tartan skirt. 'I'd better change or else his eyes will pop right out.'

As Sally ran up the stairs, Sandman shouldered open the back parlour door and, with relief, sank into a chair. It was dark in the room because the shutters were closed and the candles extinguished, so he pulled the nearest shutter open and saw it was not Lord Alexander who had reserved the back parlour, but Sergeant Berrigan.

The Sergeant raised his pistol and aimed it at Sandman's forehead. 'They want you dead, Captain,' he said.

7

Sandman knew he should do something fast. But by the time he dragged the pistol from his pocket Berrigan would already have fired, so instead Sandman decided he would just keep the Sergeant talking until Sally arrived and could raise the alarm. He rested his left foot on a chair. 'I sprained it,' he told Berrigan, 'jumping onto the stage at Miss Hood's performance. Someone tried to kill me.'

'They sent me, Captain, only me,' Berrigan said, 'and I wasn't at the theatre. So someone other than the Seraphim Club wants you dead, eh?'

Sandman stared at him, wondering who in God's name had put a price on his head. 'It must be a great relief being dishonest,' he said. 'No one trying to kill you, no scruples about accepting thousands of guineas? My problem, Sergeant, is that I so feared being like my father that I set out to behave in an utterly dissimilar manner, to be consciously virtuous. It was exceedingly tedious of me and it annoyed him hugely. I suppose that's why I did it.'

If Berrigan was surprised by this strange admission, he did not show it. Instead he seemed interested. 'Your father was dishonest?'

Sandman nodded. 'If there was any justice in this world, Sergeant, then he would have been hanged at Newgate. He wasn't a felon, he didn't rob stagecoaches or pick pockets, instead he tied people's money into crooked schemes and he'd still be doing it if he hadn't met an even cleverer man who did it back to him.'

Sergeant Berrigan lowered the pistol's cock, then put the weapon on the table. 'My father was honest.'

'He was? Not is?'

Berrigan lit two candles, then lifted a jug of ale that he had kept hidden on the floor. 'My father died a couple of years ago. He was a blacksmith, and he wanted me to learn the trade, but of course I knew better, didn't I?' He sounded rueful. 'I wanted life to be easier than forever shoeing horses.'

'So you joined the army to escape the smithy?'

Berrigan poured the ale and pushed a tankard towards Sandman. 'I was peter hunting.' Peter hunting was the trade of cutting luggage off the backs of coaches. 'I got caught and the beak said I could stand trial or join the army. And nine years later I was a sergeant.'

'A good one, eh?'

'I could keep order,' Berrigan said bleakly.

'So could I,' Sandman said. Sandman had possessed a natural and easy authority. He had been a good officer and he knew it and, if he was honest with himself, he missed it. He missed the war, the certainties of the army, the excitements of campaigning and the companionship of his company. 'You were in Spain?'

'From 'twelve to 'fourteen,' Berrigan said.

'Those were good times,' Sandman said, 'but I hated Waterloo.'

'It was bad,' Berrigan agreed.

'I've never been so damned frightened in my life,' Sandman said. 'The air was warm, like an oven door had been opened. Remember?'

'Warm,' Berrigan agreed, then frowned. 'A lot of folk want you dead, Captain.'

'It puzzles me,' Sandman admitted. 'When Skavadale offered me that money I was convinced that either he or Lord Robin had murdered the Countess. But now? Now there's someone else out there. Maybe this holds the answer?' He lifted the letter that the landlord had given him. 'Can you push a candle towards me?'

The letter was in a handwriting he knew only too well. Eleanor was asking Sandman to meet her next morning at Gunter's confectionery store in Berkeley Square. There was a postscript. *I think I might have news*, she had written.

He lay the letter down. 'Aren't you supposed to shoot me?'

'I'm trying to decide whether Miss Hood will ever talk to me again if I do.'

'I doubt she will,' Sandman said with a smile.

'And the last time I was on your side,' Berrigan said, 'things looked rough, but we did win.'

'Against the Emperor's own guard, too,' Sandman agreed.

'So I reckon I'm on your side again, Captain,' the Sergeant said.

Sandman smiled and raised his tankard in a mock toast. He was pleased, but he was not surprised, because from the very first he had sensed that Berrigan was looking for an escape from the Seraphim. 'Do you expect wages?' he asked the Sergeant.

'We'll split the reward, Captain.'

'There's a reward?'

'Forty pounds,' Berrigan said, 'is what the magistrates pay to anyone who brings in a proper felon.' He grinned. 'So what are we doing tomorrow?'

'Tomorrow,' Sandman said, 'we begin by going to Newgate.' He twisted in the chair as the door opened behind him.

'Bleeding hell,' Sally frowned when she saw the pistol on the table. Then she glared at Berrigan. 'What the hell are you doing here?'

'Come to have supper with you,' Berrigan said, and Sally blushed.

IT WAS RAINING next morning when Sandman and Berrigan walked to Newgate Prison. Sandman was still limping badly. He had wrapped a bandage tight about his boot, but the ankle felt like jellied fire.

The Sergeant had slept in the Wheatsheaf's back parlour after it became clear he was not to be invited to share Sally's bed, though Sandman, watching the two during the evening, had thought it a damn close-run thing.

Sandman had lain awake half the night trying to work out who beyond the Seraphim Club might want him dead, and it had only been when the bell of St Paul's Cathedral rang two o'clock that the answer had come to him. He shared it with Berrigan as they walked down Holborn towards Newgate Street.

'The Seraphim Club decided to buy me off, but the only member with sufficient funds immediately available was Lord Robin Holloway, and he detests me.'

'He does,' Berrigan agreed, 'but they all contributed.'

'No, they didn't,' Sandman said. 'Most of the members are in the country and there won't have been time to solicit them. Skavadale doesn't have the funds. Maybe one or two members in London donated, but I'll wager the largest part of the twenty thousand came from Lord Robin Holloway, and he only did it because Skavadale persuaded him, and I think he privately arranged to have me killed before I could accept or, God forbid, cash his note.'

Berrigan thought about it, then reluctantly nodded. 'He's capable of that. Nasty piece of work, he is.'

'But maybe he'll call off his dogs,' Sandman said, 'now that he knows I'm not taking his money?'

'Except if he killed the Countess, he might still want you nubbed,' Berrigan suggested, then stopped to gaze at the granite façade of Newgate Prison. 'Is this where they hang them?'

'Right outside the Debtor's Door, whichever one that is.'

Berrigan grinned as he climbed the prison steps. 'I always reckoned I'd end up in here.'

A turnkey accompanied them through the tunnel to the Press Yard. 'If you want to see a hanging,' he confided to Sandman, 'then come on Monday, 'cos we'll be ridding England of two of the bastards. There won't be a big crowd, on account neither is what you'd call notorious. You want a big crowd? Hang someone notorious, sir, or string up a woman. The Magpie and Stump got through a fortnight's supply of ale last Monday, and that was only 'cos we scragged a woman. She was hanged for the theft of a pearl necklace and I do hear how the owner found the necklace last week.' The man chuckled. 'Fallen down the back of a sofa!' He shook his head in wonderment. 'It's a strange business, life, isn't it?'

'Death is,' Sandman said bitterly.

The Association Room was crowded because rain had driven the prisoners indoors, and they stared resentfully as Sandman and his companion threaded their way through the tables to find Corday. The artist was evidently a changed man for, instead of cowering from his persecutors, he was now holding court at the table closest to the fire where, with a thick pile of paper and a stick of charcoal, he was drawing a portrait. A small crowd surrounded him, admiring his skill. Corday gave a start of recognition when he saw his visitors, then quickly looked away. 'I need a word with you,' Sandman said.

'He'll talk to you when he's finished,' a huge man, black-haired, long-bearded and with a massive chest, growled from the bench beside Corday. 'There's not much left of Charlie's time.'

'It's your life, Corday,' Sandman said.

'Don't listen to him, Charlie!' the big man said. 'I know what's—' He stopped abruptly. Sergeant Berrigan had gone to stand behind him and made the big man grunt in pain.

'Sergeant!' Sandman remonstrated with mock concern.

'Just teaching the culley manners,' Berrigan said, and thumped the man a second time. 'When the Captain wants a word, you piece of garbage, you jump to attention, you don't tell him to wait.'

Corday looked anxiously at the bearded man. 'Are you all right?'

'He'll be fine,' Berrigan answered for his victim. 'You just talk to the Captain, boy, because he's trying to save your miserable life.'

Sandman edged a woman aside so he could sit opposite Corday. 'I need to talk to you about the maid,' he said softly, 'about Meg. What did Meg look like?'

Corday set aside the half-finished portrait and, without a word, began to sketch on a clean sheet of paper. 'She's young,' he said, 'maybe twenty-four or twenty-five? She has pockmarked skin and mouse-coloured hair. Her eyes have a greenish tint and she has a mole here.' He flicked a mark on the girl's forehead. 'Her teeth aren't good.' He finished the drawing and handed it to Sandman.

Sandman stared at the picture. The girl was more than ugly. It was not just the pox-scarred skin, the narrow jaw, the scrawny hair and small eyes, but a suggestion of knowing hardness. If the portrait was accurate then Meg was not just repulsive, but evil. 'Why would the Countess employ such a creature?' he asked.

'They worked together in the theatre,' Corday said. 'Meg was a dresser.' Corday looked down at the portrait and seemed embarrassed. 'She was more than a dresser, I think. A procuress.'

'How do you know?'

The painter shrugged. 'People talk when you're making their portrait. They forget you're even there. You become part of the furniture. The Countess and Meg talked, I listened.'

'There is a chance,' Sandman said, 'that we shall find her.'

'How great a chance?' Corday's eyes were glistening.

'I don't know,' Sandman said. He saw the hope fade in Corday's eyes. 'Do you have ink here?' he asked. 'A pen?'

Corday had both, and Sandman dipped the steel nib in the ink and began to write. *Dear Witherspoon*, he began, *the bearer of this letter, Sergeant Samuel Berrigan, is a companion of mine and I trust him absolutely*. He dipped the nib into the ink again, conscious that

Corday was reading the words from across the table. *The regrettable possibility occurs that I might need to communicate with his lordship on Sunday next and, in the presumption that his lordship will not be at the Home Office on that day, I beg you to tell me where he might be found. I may have matters of the gravest urgency to report.* Sandman read the letter over, subscribed it, and blew on the ink to dry it, then folded the letter and stood up.

'Captain!' Corday, his eyes full of tears, appealed to Sandman.

Sandman could not offer him any kind of assurance. 'I am doing my best,' he said, 'but I can promise you nothing.' He thrust the portrait inside his coat and led Berrigan back to the prison entrance.

Sandman opened the prison's outer door and shuddered at the sight of pelting rain. He gave Berrigan the folded letter. 'Home Office. You ask to see a man called Sebastian Witherspoon, give him that, then meet me at Gunter's in Berkeley Square.'

Sandman, limping painfully, walked to Berkeley Square and was soaked by the time he arrived at Gunter's. A footman looked askance, then opened the door reluctantly.

Behind the two wide shop windows were gilded counters, spindly chairs, tall mirrors and spreading chandeliers. A dozen women were shopping for Gunter's famous confections: chocolates, meringue sculptures and delicacies of spun-sugar, marzipan and crystallised fruit. Sandman made his way to the large room at the back where a score of tables were set beneath wide skylights of stained glass. Eleanor was not at any of the half-dozen occupied tables, so Sandman took a chair at the back of the room. He ordered coffee and a copy of the *Morning Chronicle*.

He idly read the newspaper. There had been more rick-burnings in Sussex, and three mills burnt in Derbyshire. The militia had been summoned to keep the peace in Manchester, where flour had been selling at four shillings and ninepence a stone. There was a click of footsteps, a wafting of perfume and a shadow fell across his newspaper. 'You look gloomy, Rider,' Eleanor's voice said.

Standing, he looked at her and felt his heart miss a beat, so that he could scarcely speak. 'There is really no good news anywhere,' he managed to say.

'Then we must make some,' she said, 'you and I.' She handed an umbrella and her damp coat to one of the waitresses, and planted a kiss on his cheek. She then glanced at the other tables. 'I'm causing scandal, Rider, by being seen alone with a damp man.' She kissed him again, then stood back so he could pull out a chair for her. 'So let them have their scandal, and I shall have one of Gunter's vanilla ices with the powdered chocolate and crushed almonds. So will you.'

'I'm content with coffee.'

'Nonsense, you will have what is put in front of you. You look too thin.' She sat and peeled off her gloves. Her red hair was drawn up into a small black hat decorated with tiny jet beads and a modest plume. Her dress was a muted dark brown with a barely distinguishable flower pattern worked in black threads and was high collared, almost plain, yet somehow she looked more alluring than the scantily clad dancing girls who had performed on the stage the night before. 'My maid Lizzie is chaperoning me, but I've bribed her with two shillings and she's gone to the Lyceum. Did I see you limping?'

'I sprained an ankle yesterday,' he said, then had to tell the whole story which, of course, enchanted Eleanor.

'I'm exceedingly jealous,' she said when he had finished. 'My life is so dull! I don't jump onto stages pursued by footpads!'

'But you have news?' Sandman asked.

'I think so. Yes, definitely.' Eleanor turned to the waitress and ordered tea and the vanilla confections. 'They have an ice house out the back,' she told Sandman when the girl had gone. 'I asked to see it a few weeks ago. Every winter they bring the ice down from Scotland packed in sawdust and it stays solid all summer. I tried to persuade father to build an ice house, but he just complained about the expense, so I told him I'd save him the cost of a society wedding.'

Sandman gazed into her grey-green eyes, wondering what message was being sent by her apparent glibness.

'How would you save him the expense? By remaining a spinster?'

'By eloping,' Eleanor said, her gaze very steady.

'With Lord Eagleton?'

Eleanor's laugh filled Gunter's back room, causing a momentary hush at the other tables. 'Eagleton's such a bore!' she said, much too loudly. 'Don't tell me you thought I was betrothed to him?'

'I heard that you were.'

'Lord Eagleton wants to marry me, and Mama and he seem to believe that if they wish it long enough then I will surrender, but I can't abide him. He sniffs before he talks.' She gave a small sniff. 'Dear Eleanor, sniff, how charming you look, sniff. I can see the moon reflected in your eyes, sniff.'

Sandman kept a straight face. 'I never told you I saw the moon reflected in your eyes. I fear that was remiss of me.'

They looked at each other and burst out laughing. They had

always been able to laugh since the day they had met, when Sandman was home after being wounded at Salamanca and Eleanor was just twenty and determined not to be impressed by a soldier. But the soldier had made her laugh and still could, just as she could amuse him.

'I gathered a rumour of our betrothal had been bruited about,' Eleanor said, 'so I deliberately told Alexander to inform you I was not going to marry the noble sniffer. Alexander never told you?'

'I fear not.'

'But I told him distinctly!' Eleanor said indignantly. 'I met him at the Egyptian Hall.'

'He told me that much,' Sandman said, 'but he quite forgot any message. He'd even forgotten why he had gone to the Hall.'

'For a lecture by a man called Professor Popkin on the newly discovered location of the Garden of Eden. He wants us to believe that paradise is to be found at the confluence of the Ohio and the Mississippi Rivers. He once ate a very fine apple there. And,' Eleanor went on, 'he encouraged us to follow him to this new world of milk, honey and apples. Would you like to go there, Rider?'

'With you?'

'We could live naked by the rivers,' Eleanor said, and Sandman saw there were tears in her eyes. 'Innocent as babes and avoiding serpents.' She lowered her face so he could not see the tears trickle down her cheeks. 'I'm so very sorry, Rider,' she said quietly. 'I should never have let Mama persuade me to break off the engagement. She said your family's disgrace was too absolute, but that's nonsense.'

'The disgrace is dire,' Sandman admitted.

'That was your father. Not you!' Eleanor dabbed at her eyes with a handkerchief. The waitress brought their ices and Eleanor waited for the girl to move away. 'I have been weeping like a fountain these six months,' Eleanor said, then looked up at him. 'Last night I told Mama I consider myself betrothed to you.'

'I'm honoured.'

'You're supposed to say it is mutual.'

Sandman half smiled. 'I would like it to be, truly.'

'I don't think Father will mind,' Eleanor said. 'But when I told Mother my feelings last night she insisted I ought to visit Doctor Harriman, an expert in feminine hysteria. But I'm not hysterical, I am merely, inconveniently, in love with you.' She sighed as she tasted the ice. 'That is real paradise,' she said. 'Poor Rider. You shouldn't even think of marrying me. You should tip your hat at Caroline Standish.'

'Caroline Standish? I've not heard of her.'

'Caroline Standish is perhaps the richest heiress in England, Rider, and a very pretty girl she is too, but you should be warned that she is a Methodist. The drawback is that you cannot drink ardent spirits in her presence, neither smoke, nor blaspheme, nor really enjoy yourself in any way. Her father made his money in the potteries, but they now live in London and worship at that vulgar little chapel in Spring Gardens. I'm sure you could attract her eye.'

'I'm sure I could,' Sandman said with a smile.

'And I'm confident she will approve of cricket,' Eleanor said, 'so long as you don't play it on the Sabbath. Mind you, she is already betrothed, but there are rumours that she's not altogether persuaded that the future Duke of Ripon is nearly as godly as he pretends. He goes to the Spring Gardens chapel, but only, one suspects, so that he can pluck her golden feathers once he has married her.'

'The future Duke of Ripon?' Sandman went very still. 'Ripon?'

'A cathedral city in Yorkshire, Rider.'

'The Marquess of Skavadale,' Sandman said, 'is the title carried by the heir to the Dukedom of Ripon.'

'That's him!' Eleanor frowned. 'Have I said something wrong?'

'Skavadale isn't godly at all,' Sandman said, and he remembered the Earl of Avebury describing how his wife had blackmailed young men about town. Had Skavadale been blackmailed by the Countess? He was famously short of money and his father's estates were evidently mortgaged to the hilt, yet he had managed to become betrothed to the wealthiest heiress in England, and if he had been ploughing the Countess of Avebury's furrow she would have found him a ripe target for blackmail. His family might have lost most of its fortune, but there would be some funds left, and porcelain, silver and paintings that could be sold; enough left to keep the Countess content.

'I think the Marquess of Skavadale is my murderer,' Sandman said, 'either him or one of his friends.'

'So you don't need to know what Lizzie discovered?' Eleanor asked, disappointed.

'Your maid? Of course I want to know. I need to know.'

'Lizzie discovered that Meg was carried away from the Countess's town house by a carriage that was either black or dark blue, and with a strange coat of arms—a shield showing a red field decorated with a golden angel. I asked Hammond if he knew of it but he didn't.'

'I doubt the College of Arms issued that device. It's the badge of the Seraphim Club.'

'And the Marquess of Skavadale,' Eleanor said quietly, 'is a member of the Seraphim Club?'

'He is,' Sandman confirmed.

She frowned. 'So he's your murderer? It's that easy?'

'The members of the Seraphim Club,' Sandman said, 'believe their rank, their money and their privilege will keep them safe, beyond the law. And quite possibly they're right, unless I can find Meg.'

Eleanor stared at Sandman and her eyes seemed bright and big. 'I am not willing, Rider,' she said, 'to give you up. I tried.'

He reached for her hand and kissed her fingers. 'I have never given you up,' he said, 'and next week I shall talk to your father again.'

'And if he says no?' She clutched his fingers.

'Then we shall go to Scotland,' Sandman said.

Eleanor held tight to his hand. She smiled. 'Rider? My prudent, well-behaved, honourable Rider? You would elope?'

He returned the smile. 'I remember making a decision at Waterloo. If I survived that day, I promised myself, then I would not die with regrets. I would not die with wishes and desires unfulfilled. So yes, if your father refuses to let us marry, then I shall take you to Scotland.'

'Because I am your wish, dream and desire?' Eleanor asked with tears in her eyes and a smile on her face.

'Because you are all of those things,' Sandman said, 'and I love you besides.'

And Sergeant Berrigan, dripping with rainwater, grinned with delight at discovering Sandman at so delicate a moment.

THE SERGEANT BEGAN to whistle as they climbed Hay Hill towards Old Bond Street. It was a cheerful whistle, one that proclaimed that he was not at all interested in what he had just seen, and a whistle that in the army would have been recognised as insubordinate but quite unpunishable. Sandman laughed. 'I was once engaged to Miss Forrest, Sergeant, and Miss Forrest broke off the engagement because her parents did not want her to marry a pauper.'

'Didn't look much like a broken bloody engagement to me, sir.'

'Yes, well. Life is complicated.'

'Talking of complications,' Berrigan said, 'Mister Sebastian Witherspoon was not a happy man. In fact, if I was to be accurate, he was bloody annoyed. He wanted to know what you were bloody up to, Captain, so I told him I don't know a blessed thing sir, and go to hell, sir, but all of it in a deeply respectful manner.'

'But did he tell you where the Home Secretary will be on Sunday?'

'His lordship will be at his home in Great George Street. Mister Witherspoon said his lordship won't thank you for disturbing him on Sunday and anyway Mister Witherspoon, like his holy lordship, trusts that the bloody pixie is hanged by his bloody neck like what he bloody deserves to be.'

'I'm sure he didn't say the last.'

'Not quite,' Berrigan admitted cheerfully. 'So, where are we going now?'

'We're going to see Sir George Phillips, because I want to know if he can tell me exactly who commissioned the Countess's portrait. Know that man's name, Sergeant, and we have our murderer.'

'You hope,' Berrigan said dubiously.

'Miss Hood is also at Sir George's studio. She models for him.'

'Ah!' Berrigan cheered up.

'And even if Sir George won't tell us, I've learned that my one witness was carried away in the Seraphim Club's carriage. So I assume one of the club's coachmen can tell us where they took her.'

'I imagine they might need some persuading,' Berrigan said.

'A pleasing prospect,' Sandman said, arriving at the door beside the jeweller's shop. He knocked and, as before, the door was answered by Sammy. 'Tell Sir George,' Sandman said imperiously, 'that Captain Rider Sandman and Sergeant Samuel Berrigan have come to talk to him.'

'He don't want to talk to you,' Sammy said.

'Go and tell him, child!' Sandman insisted.

Instead Sammy made an ill-judged attempt to dodge past Sandman into the street, only to be caught by Sergeant Berrigan. 'Where were you going, boy?' Berrigan demanded.

'I wasn't going anywhere!' Berrigan drew back his fist. Sammy yelped. 'He told me if you was to come again,' he said hastily, 'I was to go and fetch help.'

'From the Seraphim Club?' Sandman guessed, and the boy nodded. 'Hold onto him, Sergeant,' Sandman said, then began climbing the stairs. 'Fee, fi, fo, fum! I smell the blood of an Englishman!' He chanted at the top of his voice to warn Sally so that Berrigan would not see her naked.

'No further, Captain,' Sir George growled, and pointed a long-barrelled pistol down the stairs at Sandman.

Sandman kept on climbing. 'Don't be such a bloody fool,' he said tiredly. 'Shoot me, Sir George, and you'll have to shoot Sergeant Berrigan, then you'll have to keep Sally quiet, so then you'll have three corpses on your hands.' He climbed the last few steps and took the pistol from the painter's hand. 'Allow me to introduce Sergeant Berrigan.' Sandman saw, with relief, that Sally had received enough warning to pull on a coat. He took off his hat and bowed to her. 'Miss Hood, my respects.'

Berrigan nodded to Sally. 'Miss Hood,' he said, then he saw the canvas and his eyes widened in admiration and Sally blushed.

'He's bleeding hurting me!' Sammy complained.

'You can put Sammy down,' Sandman said to Berrigan, 'because he won't go for help.'

'He'll do what I tell him!' Sir George said belligerently.

'If you tell Sammy to go for help, Sir George,' Sandman said, 'then I shall spread it abroad that your studio deceives women, that you paint them clothed and, when they are gone, turn them into nudes.'

Sir George seemed to deflate like a pricked bladder. He flapped a paint-stained hand at Sammy. 'You can make some tea, Sammy.'

Berrigan put the boy down.

'I'll help you, Sammy,' Sally said, and followed the boy down the stairs. Sandman suspected she was going to get dressed.

Sandman turned to Sir George. 'You're an old man, Sir George, and you're a drunkard. Your hand shakes. You can still paint, but for how long? You're living off your reputation now, but I can ruin that. I can make quite certain that men like Sir Henry Forrest never hire you again to paint their wives and daughters. I know you lied,' Sandman said, 'so now you will tell me the truth.'

'And if I do?'

'Then I will tell no one and we shall leave you in peace.'

Sir George sank onto a stool. He snarled at the apprentices and the two men portraying Nelson and Neptune to go downstairs. Only when they were gone did he look at Sandman. 'The Seraphim Club commissioned the painting.'

'I know that. What I want to know, Sir George, is who in the club commissioned it.'

'I don't know. Really! I don't know! There were ten or eleven of them, sitting at a table. They said they were having the painting done for their gallery and they promised me there'd be others.'

'Other paintings?'

'Of titled women, Captain, naked. She was their trophy. They explained it to me. If more than three members of the club had swived a woman then she could be hung in their gallery.'

'And the Marquess of Skavadale was one of those men?'

'Yes, Skavadale was one. Lord Pellmore was another, I remember. But I didn't know most of them. They didn't introduce themselves.'

Sandman lifted the frizzen of the pistol he had taken from Sir George and saw that it was not primed. 'You have powder and bullets?' he asked, and then, when he saw the fear on the painter's face, he scowled. 'I'm not going to shoot you, you fool!'

'In that cupboard.' Sir George nodded across the room.

Sandman opened the door and discovered a small arsenal, most of it, he supposed, for use in paintings. He tossed a cavalry pistol to Berrigan, then took a handful of cartridges and pushed them into a pocket before stooping to pick up a knife. 'You've wasted my time,' he told Sir George. 'You've lied to me.' He carried the knife back across the room and saw the terror on Sir George's face. 'Sally!' Sandman shouted. 'How much does Sir George owe you?'

'Two pounds and five shillings!' she called up the stairs.

'Pay her,' Sandman said.

'I only have three guineas on me,' Sir George whined.

'Give the three guineas to the Sergeant,' Sandman said.

Sir George handed over the money as Sandman turned to the painting. Britannia was virtually finished, sitting bare-breasted and proud-eyed on her rock in a sunlit sea. The goddess was unmistakably Sally, though Sir George had changed her usually cheerful expression into one of calm superiority. 'You lied,' Sandman said to Sir George, 'and worse. You suspected that Charles Corday did not commit the murder, yet you did nothing to help him.'

Sir George lurched to his feet and called out a protest. 'No!'

Berrigan held Sir George while Sandman took the knife to *The Apotheosis of Lord Nelson*. Sammy had just brought his tray of tea to the stairhead and watched appalled as Sandman slashed down the canvas, then across. 'A friend of mine,' Sandman said as he mutilated the painting, 'is going to get married soon. He doesn't know it, and nor does his intended bride, but they plainly like each other and I'll want to give them a present when it happens.' He excised from the big picture a portrait of Sally. He tossed the knife onto the floor, rolled up the picture of Britannia and smiled at Sir George. 'Thank you for your help. Sergeant? I believe we're finished here.'

'I'm coming with you!' Sally said from the stairs. 'Only someone has to hook me frock up.'

'Duty summons you,' Sandman said to Berrigan.

Sandman was laughing by the time he reached the street, where he waited for Berrigan and Sally.

They joined him when Sally's dress was fastened. 'Who do you know getting married soon?' Berrigan demanded.

'Just two friends,' Sandman said airily.

'Captain!' Sally chided him.

'Married?' Berrigan sounded shocked.

'I am a staunch believer in Christian morality,' Sandman said.

'Speaking of which,' the Sergeant said, 'why have we got pistols?'

'Because our next call, Sergeant, must be the Seraphim Club to talk to the coachmen and I do not like to go there unarmed. I'd also prefer it if they did not know we were on the premises, so when is the best time to make our visit?'

'Go after dark,' the Sergeant said, 'because it'll be easier for us to sneak in, and at least one jervis will be there.'

'Let us hope it's the right coachman,' Sandman said, and snapped open his watch. 'Not till dark? Which means I have an afternoon to while away.' He thought for a moment. 'Shall we meet at nine o'clock, say? Behind the club?'

8

'Bunny' Barnwell, reckoned to be the best bowler in the Marylebone Cricket Club, despite having a strange loping run that ended with a double hop before he launched the ball sidearm, bowled at Rider Sandman on one of the netted practice wickets at Thomas Lord's new cricket ground in St John's Wood.

Lord Alexander Pleydell stood beside the net, peering anxiously at every ball. 'Is Bunny moving it off the grass?' he asked. 'He's supposed to twist the ball so it moves into your legs.'

'Not at all.' Sandman thumped the ball hard into the net.

Barnwell was taking turns with Hughes, Lord Alexander's servant, to bowl to Sandman. Hughes, frustrated at being unable to get anything past Sandman's bat, tried too hard and launched a ball that did not bounce at all and Sandman cracked it out of the net and over the hill where three men were scything the wicket. Making a cricket field on such a slope made no sense to Sandman, but Alexander had a curious attachment to Thomas Lord's new field.

Barnwell tried bowling underarm and was forced to watch his ball follow Hughes's last delivery up the slope. One of the boys who were fielding tried a fast ball at Sandman's legs and was rewarded with a blow that almost took his head off. Sandman was in a savage mood, wondering how he was to keep his promise to Eleanor. How could he marry a woman when he had no means to support her? And where was the honour in some hole-in-the-wall Scottish wedding?

'I thought Hammond could keep wicket, do you agree?' Lord Alexander said.

'This is your team to play Hampshire?'

'No, Rider, it's my proposal for a new Dean and canons of St Paul's Cathedral. What do you think it is?'

'Hammond would be an excellent choice,' Sandman said.

'Edward Budd said he'll play for us,' Lord Alexander said.

'Wonderful!' Sandman spoke with genuine warmth, for Edward Budd was the one batsman he acknowledged as his superior.

'And Simmons is available.'

'Then I won't be,' Sandman said. 'He took cash to throw a game in Sussex two years ago.'

The next delivery came hurtling at Sandman's ankles and he sent the ball all the way to the tavern by the lower boundary fence.

'Simmons is an excellent batsman,' Lord Alexander insisted. 'Including him will give our side an immense batting force, Rider. You, Budd and him? We shall set new records!'

'I won't play with him,' Sandman said. 'Alexander, I love cricket, but if it's to be bent out of shape by bribery then there will be no sport left. The only way to treat bribery is to punish it absolutely.' He spoke angrily. 'Is it any wonder that the game's dying? The game's in decline, Alexander, because it's being corrupted by money.'

'It's all very well for you to say that,' Lord Alexander said huffily, 'but Simmons has a wife and two children. Don't you understand temptation?'

'I think I do, yes,' Sandman said, 'I was offered twenty thousand guineas yesterday.' He nodded at the bowler.

'Twenty thousand?' Lord Alexander sounded faint. 'To lose a game of cricket?'

'To let an innocent man hang,' Sandman said, playing a demure defensive stroke. 'This intellectual bowling is too easy,' he complained. The sidearm delivery, when the ball was bowled from a straight arm held at shoulder height, was curiously known as the intellectual style. 'It has no accuracy.'

'But it has more force than balls bowled underarm,' Lord Alexander declared.

'We should bowl overarm.'

'Never! Never! Ruin the game! An utterly ridiculous suggestion!'

'I just think that overarm bowling will combine force with accuracy,' Sandman suggested, 'and might even present a challenge to the batsman. You wouldn't like to lend me your carriage, would you?'

Lord Alexander looked puzzled. 'My carriage?'

'The thing with four wheels, Alexander, and the horses up front. It's in a good cause. Rescuing the innocent.'

'Well, of course,' Lord Alexander said with admirable enthusiasm. 'I shall be honoured to help you.'

A young man walked towards the practice wickets from the tavern and Sandman recognised Lord Christopher Carne, Avebury's heir. 'Your friend's coming,' he told Lord Alexander.

'My friend? Oh, Kit!'

Lord Christopher waved in response to Lord Alexander's enthusiastic greeting, then noticed Sandman. He blanched, looked annoyed and strode towards him. 'You never told me,' he said accusingly, 'that you were visiting my father. He wrote to me saying you'd visited.'

'Did I need to tell you?'

'It would have been c-courteous,' Lord Christopher complained.

'If I need lessons in courtesy,' Sandman said sharply, 'then I shall go to those who treat me politely.'

Lord Christopher bridled. Sandman danced down the pitch and drove at a delivery with all his strength. The ball took its first bounce just short of the uphill boundary and vanished in the bushes at the top of the hill. Then Sandman heard it crack against the fence and heard a cow mooing in protest from the neighbouring meadow.

'I spoke hastily,' Lord Christopher said in scant apology, 'but I still don't understand why you should go to Carne Manor.'

'I told you why,' Sandman said. 'To discover whether any of your stepmother's servants had gone there.'

'Of course they wouldn't,' Lord Christopher said.

'Last time you thought it possible.'

'That's because I hadn't thought about it p-properly. Those servants must have known precisely what vile things my stepmother was doing in London and my father would hardly want them spreading such t-tales in Wiltshire.'

'True,' Sandman conceded. 'So I wasted a journey.'

'But the good news, Rider,' Lord Alexander intervened, 'is that the Keeper of Newgate has agreed that you and I should attend on Monday!' Lord Alexander turned to a bemused Lord Christopher.

'It occurred to me, Kit, that as the Home Secretary's official Investigator, Rider should know exactly what awful brutality awaits people like Corday. So I wrote to the Keeper and he has very decently invited Rider and myself to breakfast.' He beamed at Sandman. 'Isn't that splendid?'

'I have no wish to witness a hanging,' Sandman said.

'It doesn't matter what you wish,' Lord Alexander said airily, 'it is a matter of duty. I do not approve of the gallows, but if nothing else, Rider, it will be an educational experience.'

'Educational rubbish! I'm not going, Alexander. I shall happily send the real killer to the gallows, but I'm not witnessing a Newgate circus.'

'Do you know who the real killer is?' Lord Christopher asked.

'I hope to know by this evening,' Sandman said. 'If I send for your carriage, Alexander, then you'll know I've discovered my witness. If I don't? Alas.'

'Witness?' Lord Christopher asked.

'If Rider's going to be obdurate,' Lord Alexander said to Lord Christopher, 'then perhaps you should join me for the Keeper's devilled kidneys on Monday?'

'Witness?' Lord Christopher broke in to ask again.

'I trust you'll send for the carriage!' Lord Alexander boomed. 'I want to see that bloody man Sidmouth confounded. Make him grant a pardon, Rider. I shall await your summons at the Wheatsheaf'. He smiled at Lord Christopher Carne. 'Come and have some tea. Rider? You'll have some tea? Of course you will. And I want you to meet Lord Frederick, our club secretary. You really should join the club here. They do a very acceptable tea.'

So Sandman went for a lordly tea.

IT WAS A CLOUDY EVENING and the sky over London was made even darker because there was no wind and the coal smoke hung thick and still above the roofs and spires. The streets near St James's Square were quiet, for there were no businesses in these houses and many of their owners were in the country. Sandman saw a watchman noting him and so he crossed and said good evening and asked what regiment the man had served in and passed some time exchanging memories of Salamanca. Then a lamplighter came round with his ladder and the new gaslights popped on one after the other, burning blue for a time and then turning whiter.

A hackney turned into the street, its horse's hoofs echoing from the house fronts, and stopped close to Sandman. Sergeant Berrigan stepped down, then held the door open for Sally.

'Sergeant! You can't . . .' Sandman began.

'I told you he'd say that,' Berrigan boasted to Sally, 'didn't I tell you he'd say you shouldn't come?'

'You're going for Meg, right?' Sally intervened. 'And she ain't going to take kindly to two old swoddies doing her up, is she? She needs a woman's touch.'

'Meg isn't in the Seraphim Club,' Sandman said. 'We're only going there to find the coachman so he can tell us where he took her.'

'Maybe he'll tell me what he won't tell you,' Sally said to Sandman with a dazzling smile.

Sergeant Berrigan fished in his coat pocket to bring out a key. 'Back way in, Captain,' he said, then looked at Sally. 'Listen, my love, I know . . .'

'Stow it, Sam! I'm coming with you!'

Berrigan led the way, shaking his head. 'I don't know what it is,' he grumbled, 'but the ladies don't half get their own way. You notice that, Captain?'

'True love,' Sandman murmured, then Berrigan put a finger to his lips as they approached a wide carriage gate set in a white wall.

Berrigan walked up to a small door set to one side of the gates and used his key. He pushed the door open, looked into the yard and evidently saw nothing to alarm him, for he stepped over the threshold and beckoned Sandman and Sally to follow.

The yard was empty except for a coach, its blue paint trimmed with gold, that had evidently just been washed, for it stood gleaming in the dusk with water dripping from its flanks and buckets standing by the wheels. The badge of the golden angel was painted on the door. 'Over here, quick,' Berrigan said, and Sandman and Sally followed the Sergeant to the shadow of the stables. 'The coachmen will be in the back kitchen.' He nodded to a lit window in the carriage house, then turned in alarm as a door in the main house was thrown open. 'In here!' Berrigan hissed, and the three of them filed into an alley beside the stables. Footsteps sounded in the yard.

Sandman heard the footsteps getting closer and knew it was only a matter of seconds before they were discovered. But then Berrigan peered out of the alley's far end and dashed across a smaller yard to a door that opened into the rear of the house. 'This way!' he hissed.

Sandman and Sally ran after him and found themselves on a servant's stairway that ran from the basement to the upper floors. 'We'll hide upstairs,' Berrigan whispered, 'till the coast's clear.'

Halfway up the unlit stairway Berrigan edged open a door which led into a carpeted corridor that had walls covered in a deep scarlet paper. It was too dark to see the pictures that hung between the polished doors. Berrigan chose a door at random, opened it and found an empty room. 'We'll be all right in here,' he said.

It was a bedroom; large, lavish and comfortable. The bed itself was high and huge, plump-mattressed and covered with a thick scarlet covering on which the Seraphim's naked angel took flight. Berrigan crossed to the window and pulled back the curtain so he could gaze down into the yard. Sandman's eyes slowly adjusted to the dim light, then he heard Sally laugh and he turned to see her gazing at a picture above the bedhead. 'Good God,' Sandman said.

'There's a lot of those,' Berrigan commented drily.

The picture showed a happy group of naked men and women in a circular arcade of white marble pillars, coupling under the moon that lit the arcade with an unearthly glow. 'Bloody hell,' Sally said respectfully, 'you wouldn't think a girl could do that with her legs.'

Sandman moved to the window and stared down, but the yard seemed empty again. 'I think they've gone back inside,' Berrigan said.

'D'you think they'll come in here?' Sandman asked.

Berrigan shook his head. 'They only use these rooms in the winter.'

Sally giggled at the painting above the empty fireplace, then turned on Berrigan. 'You worked in an academy, Sam Berrigan.'

'It's a club!'

'Bleeding brothel is what it is,' Sally said scornfully.

'I left it, didn't I?' Berrigan protested. 'Besides, it weren't an academy for us servants. Only for the members.'

'What members?' Sally asked, and laughed at her own jest.

Berrigan hushed her, not because she was being coarse, but because there were footsteps in the corridor outside. They came close to the door, passed on, faded.

'It doesn't really help us being up here,' Sandman said.

'Shall we find our coachman?'

They went back down the servants' stairs and crossed the yard. Berrigan went to the side door of the carriage house. He listened there for a few seconds, then raised two fingers to indicate that he thought there were two men on the door's far side. Sandman pulled the pistol from his coat pocket, checked it was primed then edged Berrigan aside, opened the door and walked inside.

The room was a kitchen, tack room and store. A pair of candles burned on the table where two men, one young and one middle-aged, sat with tankards of ale and plates of bread, cheese and cold beef. They turned and stared when Sandman came in, and the older man opened his mouth in astonishment. Sally followed Sandman into the room, then Berrigan came in and closed the door.

'Introduce me,' Sandman said. He was not pointing the pistol at either man, but the two could not take their eyes from it.

'The youngster's a stable hand,' Berrigan said, 'called Billy, while Mister Michael Mackeson's one of the club's two coachmen.'

Mackeson was a burly man, red-faced, with a fine waxed moustache and a shock of black hair that was turning grey at the temples. He was dressed well and could doubtless afford to be, for good drivers were paid extravagantly. They were considered the possessors of a skill so enviable that every young gentleman wanted to be like them. Mackeson gaped at Berrigan who, like Sandman, had a pistol.

'Some weeks ago,' Sandman said sternly, 'a coachman from this club collected a maid from the Countess of Avebury's house in Mount Street. Was that you?'

Mackeson swallowed, then nodded very slowly.

'Where did you take her?' Sandman asked. Mackeson swallowed again, then jumped as he heard the ratcheting sound of Sandman's pistol being cocked.

'Nether Cross,' Mackeson said hurriedly.

'Where's Nether Cross?'

'Fair old ways,' the coachman said guardedly. 'Seven hours? Eight hours? Down near the coast, sir, down Kent way.'

'So who lives there,' Sandman asked, 'in Nether Cross?'

'Lord John de Sully Pearce-Tarrant,' Berrigan answered for the coachman, 'Viscount Hurstwood, Earl of Keymer, Baron Highbrook, lord of God knows what else, heir to the Dukedom of Ripon and also known, Captain, as the Marquess of Skavadale.'

Sandman had his answer at last.

THE CARRIAGE RATTLED through the streets south of the Thames. Its two lamps were lit, but cast a feeble glow that did nothing to light the way so that, once they reached the summit of Shooters Hill, where the road across Blackheath stretched impenetrably black before them, they stopped. The horses were picketed on the green, the two prisoners were locked inside the carriage with the reins strapped tight around the whole vehicle, and the windows were jammed shut with slivers of wood.

It had been Berrigan's idea to take the Seraphim Club's carriage. Sandman had refused at first, saying he had arranged to borrow Lord Alexander's coach and he doubted he had the legal right to commandeer one of the Seraphim Club's carriages, but Berrigan had scoffed at the thought of such scruples. 'You've got to take Mackeson anyway, as he knows the way to Nether Cross, so you might as well take a vehicle he knows how to handle. And, considering what evils the bastards have done, I don't suppose God or man will worry about you borrowing their coach.' Billy, the stable hand, had to be kept from betraying that Sandman had been asking about Meg, so he too must be taken prisoner.

Now, Sandman and his companions had to wait through the dark hours. Berrigan took Sally to a tavern and paid for a room and he stayed with her while Sandman guarded the coach. It was not till after the clocks had struck two that Berrigan loomed out of the dark.

'You can go to sleep,' Berrigan suggested, 'and I'll stand sentry.'

'In a while,' Sandman said. He was sitting on the grass, his back against a wheel and he tilted his head to look at the stars. 'Remember the Spanish night marches?' he asked. 'The stars were so bright it was as though you could reach up and snuff them out.'

'I remember the campfires,' Berrigan said, 'hills and valleys of fire.' He twisted and looked west. 'A bit like that.'

Sandman turned his head to see London spread beneath them like a quilt of fire that was blurred by the red-touched smoke. He could just smell the coal smoke from the great city that spread its hazed lights to the western horizon. 'I do miss Spain,' he admitted.

'It were strange at first,' Berrigan said, 'but I liked it. Did you speak the language?'

'Yes.'

The Sergeant handed Sandman a stone bottle. 'Brandy,' he explained. 'I was thinking,' he went on, 'that if I go and buy those cigars I'll need someone who speaks the language. You and me? We could go there together, work together.'

'I'd like that,' Sandman said.

'There's got to be money in it,' Berrigan said. 'We paid pennies for those cigars in Spain and here they cost a fortune if you can get them at all.'

'I think you're right,' Sandman said, and smiled at the thought that maybe he did have a job after all. Berrigan and Sandman, Purveyors of Fine Cigars? Eleanor's father liked a good cigar and paid well for them, so well that there might even be enough money in the idea to persuade Sir Henry that his daughter was not marrying a pauper. Lady Forrest might never be convinced that Sandman was a proper husband for Eleanor, but Sandman suspected that Eleanor and her father would prevail. He and Berrigan would need money, and who better than Sir Henry to lend it? They would have to travel around Spain, hire shipping space and rent premises in a fashionable part of London, but it could work. He was sure of it. 'It's a brilliant idea, Sergeant,' he said.

'So shall we do it when this is over?'

'Why not? Yes.' He put out his hand and Berrigan shook it.

'We old soldiers should stick together,' Berrigan said, 'because we were damned good, Captain. We chased the Crapauds halfway across Europe, and then we came home and none of the bastards here cared, did they?' He paused, thinking. 'The Seraphim Club wouldn't even let you in if you'd been a swoddy or a sailor.'

Sandman drank from the bottle. 'Yet they employed you?'

'They liked having a guardsman in the hall. I made them feel safe. And they could order me around. Do this, Berrigan, do that.' The Sergeant grunted thanks when Sandman passed him the bottle. 'Most of the time it weren't nothing bad. But then once in a while they'd want something else.' He fell silent, and Sandman kept quiet. After a time he began talking again. 'Once, there was a fellow who was taking one of the Seraphim to court, so we gave him a lesson. And the girls, of course—we paid them off.'

'What sort of girls?'

'Common girls, Captain, girls that had caught their eye on the street. They were kidnapped, raped and paid off.'

'And all the members did that?'

'Some were worse than others. There's always a handful that are ready for any mischief. And one or two of them are more sensible. That's why I was surprised it was Skavadale that scragged the Countess. He ain't a bad one. He's got a ramrod up his arse and he thinks he smells of violets, but he ain't an unkind man.'

'I rather hoped it would be Lord Robin,' Sandman admitted. 'But Skavadale has more to lose,' he explained. 'He is betrothed to a very rich girl. I suspect he was ploughing the Countess of Avebury and she had a nasty habit of blackmail. Skavadale might be relatively poor, but I'll bet he could still scratch together a thousand pounds if the Countess was not to write a letter to the bride to be.'

'So he killed her?' Berrigan asked.

'So he killed her,' Sandman said. 'Poor Corday was painting away when Skavadale comes to visit. He came up the back stairs, the private way, and Corday was hurried off when the Countess realised one of her lovers had arrived.' Sandman was sure that was how it had happened.

Berrigan drank again, then passed the bottle to Sandman. 'So the girl Meg takes the pixie downstairs,' he said, 'and throws him out, then she goes back upstairs and finds what? The Countess dead?'

'Probably. Or dying, and she finds the Marquess of Skavadale there. Perhaps Skavadale had come to plead with the Countess to withdraw her demands and the Countess, desperate for money, had laughed at him. Somehow she drove him into a black rage. Perhaps there had been a knife in the room, perhaps a paring knife, which Skavadale seized and plunged into her, and afterwards, when she lay dying, he put Corday's palette knife into one of her wounds. And then Meg had returned. Or perhaps Meg had overheard the fight and was waiting outside the room when Skavadale emerged.'

'So why didn't he kill Meg as well?' the Sergeant asked.

'Because Meg isn't a threat to him,' Sandman guessed. 'The Countess threatened his betrothal to a girl who could probably pay off the mortgages on all his family's estates. The Countess could have put Skavadale in the gutter, so he kills her, but he didn't kill the maid because she wasn't a threat.'

'So what are they doing with Meg?'

'Maybe they've given her somewhere to live,' Sandman suggested, 'somewhere comfortable so she doesn't reveal what she knows. Perhaps now she's the blackmailer and if she's sensible she's not asking too much, which is why they're content to let her live.'

'But if she is blackmailing him,' Berrigan suggested, 'then she'll hardly tell us the truth. She's got Skavadale strapped down tight, don't she? Why should she save some bloody pixie's life?'

'Because we shall appeal,' Sandman said, 'to her better nature.'

Berrigan laughed sourly. 'Ah well, then,' he said, 'it's all solved!'

'It worked with you, Sergeant,' Sandman pointed out gently.

'That were Sally, that were,' Berrigan said.

'Well, Sergeant,' Sandman said, 'I think you are a most fortunate man. As am I. But I am also a tired one.' He crawled under the carriage, bumping his head on the forward axle. The grass was dry under the carriage and the wind sighed in a nearby stand of trees. Sandman thought of the hundreds of other nights he had slept under the stars and then, just as he decided that sleep would never come, it did.

9

Early next morning Sally brought them a basket with bacon, hard-boiled eggs, bread and a stone jar of cold tea, a breakfast they shared with the two prisoners.

'Time to get ready,' Sandman said, glancing up at the lightening sky. A small mist drifted over the heath as the four horses were watered at a stone trough. After Mackeson and Billy had finished harnessing the horses, Sandman made the younger man strip off his shoes and belt. Without shoes, and with his breeches falling round his knees, the boy would find it hard to escape. Sandman and Sally sat inside with the embarrassed Billy. Mackeson and Berrigan climbed onto the box and then, with a lurching roll, they bounced over the grass and onto the road.

They went south and east past hop fields, orchards and great estates. By midday Sandman had unwittingly fallen asleep, then woke with a start when the carriage lurched in a rut. He blinked, then saw that Sally had taken the pistol from him and was gazing at a thoroughly cowed Billy. 'You can sleep on, Captain,' she said. 'He didn't dare try nothing. Not once I told him who my brother is.'

'I thought we might meet him last night.'

'He only works the north and west roads.' Sally gave Sandman back his pistol. 'Do you think a man can be on the cross and then go straight?' she asked.

Sandman suspected the question was not about her brother, but about Berrigan. As a servant of the Seraphim Club he had certainly known his share of crime. 'Of course he can,' Sandman said.

'Not many do,' Sally averred. She wanted reassurance.

'Maybe your brother will settle down when he meets the right woman,' Sandman suggested. 'A lot of men do that. I can't tell you how many of my soldiers were utter nuisances, complete damn fools, and then they'd meet some Spanish girl and within a week they'd be model soldiers.' He smiled at her. 'I don't think you've anything to worry about, Sally.'

She returned his smile. 'Are you a good judge of men, Captain?'

'Yes, Sally, I am.'

They could not change horses and so Mackeson was pacing the team, which meant they travelled slowly, and the journey was made even slower because the road was in bad condition and they had to pull over whenever a horn announced that a stage or mail coach was behind them. Sandman envied their speed, and worried about time, then told himself it was only Saturday and, so long as Meg really was hiding at Nether Cross, then they should be back in London by Sunday evening and that left plenty of time to find Lord Sidmouth and secure Corday's reprieve. Sandman did not give a damn about his lordship's prayers. Sandman would keep the whole government from its devotions if that meant justice.

In mid-morning, Sandman changed places with Berrigan, Mackeson taking the carriage down ever narrower roads, beneath trees heavy with summer leaves so that both he and Sandman were constantly ducking beneath boughs. They stopped at a ford to let the horses drink, then Mackeson clicked his tongue and the coach climbed between fields where men and women cut the harvest with sickles. Near midday they stopped close to a tavern and Sandman bought ale, bread and cheese, which they ate and drank as the carriage creaked the last few miles. They passed through a village where men played cricket on the green. Then Mackeson, with a careless skill, wheeled the horses between two brick walls and clicked them on down into a narrow lane that ran steep between thick woods of oak. 'Not far now,' he said.

'You've done well to remember the way,' Sandman said. The route had been tortuous and he had wondered whether Mackeson was trying to get lost, but at the last turn, Sandman had seen a fingerpost pointing to Nether Cross.

'I done this journey a half-dozen times with his lordship,' Mackeson said. He flicked the lead horses' reins and they turned smartly towards a tall pair of gates hung between high flint pillars.

Sandman opened the gates, which were latched but not locked, then closed them after the carriage had passed. He climbed back onto the box and Mackeson walked the horses down the long drive that twisted through a deer park until it crossed a small bridge and there, amid the overgrown box hedges of an untended garden, lay a small and exquisitely beautiful Elizabethan house with black timbers, white plasterwork and red brick chimneys. 'Cross Hall, it's called,' Mackeson said. 'They got this one through a marriage in the old days, that's what I heard.'

'Some marriage portion,' Sandman said jealously, for the house looked so perfect under the afternoon sun.

The carriage stopped and Sandman dropped down from the box,

wincing as his weight went onto his damaged ankle. He told Berrigan to wait and make sure that Mackeson did not simply whip the horses back down the drive.

Sandman hammered on the front door. He had no right to be here, he thought, and felt in his tail pocket for the letter of authorisation from the Home Office. He knocked on the door again and stepped back to see if anyone was peering from a window. Ivy grew round the porch, and under the leaves above the door he could just see a shield carved into the plasterwork. Five scallop shells were set into the shield. No one showed at any of the windows, but hen the door was pulled open and a gaunt old man stared at him, and then looked at the carriage with its badge of the Seraphim Club. 'We weren't expecting any visitors today,' the man said in evident puzzlement.

'We have come to fetch Meg,' Sandman replied on impulse. The man, a servant judging by his clothes, had plainly recognised the carriage. Sandman hoped he would assume it had been sent by the Marquess.

'No one said she was to go anywhere.' The man was suspicious. 'So who be you?' The man was tall and had unkempt white hair.

'I told you. We came to fetch Meg. Sergeant Berrigan and I.'

'Sergeant?' The man sounded alarmed. 'You brought a lawyer?'

'He's from the club,' Sandman said, feeling the conversation slide into mutual incomprehensibility. 'His lordship wants her in London.'

'Then I'll fetch the lass,' the man said and, before Sandman could react, he had slammed the door and shot the bolts. Sandman heard a bell ring inside the house and he knew the urgent sound had to be a signal to Meg. He swore.

'That's a good bloody start,' Berrigan said sarcastically.

'But the woman is here and he says he's fetching her.'

'Is he?'

Sandman shook his head. 'Hiding her, more like it. Which means we've got to look for her.'

They took the carriage round to the stables, where they discovered a brick-built tack room that had a solid door and no windows and Mackeson and the stable boy were imprisoned inside while the horses were left in the yard harnessed to the carriage. 'We'll deal with them later,' Sandman declared.

'Collect some eggs later, too,' Berrigan said with a smile, for the stable yard had been given over to chickens, seemingly hundreds of them, most hunting for grain that had been scattered among the weed-strewn, dropping-white cobbles.

Sandman led Berrigan and Sally to the back of Cross Hall. Every door was locked, but Sandman found a window that was inadequately latched and shook it hard until it came open and he could climb into a small parlour with furniture shrouded in dustsheets. Berrigan followed. 'Stay outside,' Sandman warned Sally. 'There could be a fight.'

She nodded agreement, but a moment later clambered through the window. 'I'm coming in,' she insisted. 'I hate bloody chickens.'

'The girl could have left the house by now,' Berrigan said.

'She could,' Sandman agreed, yet his first instinct had been that she would hide somewhere inside, 'but we'll search for her anyway.' He opened a door that led into a long panelled passage. The house was silent. Sandman threw open doors to see dustsheets draped over the furniture. An elaborately carved newel post stood in the hall at the foot of a fine staircase. Sandman glanced into the upstairs gloom as he passed, then went on towards the back of the house.

'No one lives here,' Sally said as they discovered yet more empty rooms, 'except the chickens!'

Suddenly a door opened at the end of the passage.

The tall, gaunt man with the wild white hair stood in the doorway, a cudgel in his right hand. 'The girl you're looking for,' he said, 'is not here.' He raised the cudgel half-heartedly as Sandman approached him, then let it drop and shuffled aside. Sandman pushed past him into a kitchen. A woman, perhaps the gaunt man's wife, sat mixing pastry in a large china bowl at a long table.

'Who are you?' Sandman asked the man.

'The steward here,' the man said, then nodded at the woman, 'and my wife is the housekeeper.'

'You've no business here,' the woman snapped. 'You're trespassing! So make yourselves scarce before they arrest you.'

'Who'll arrest me?' Sandman asked.

'We've sent for aid,' the woman answered defiantly.

'But I come from the Home Secretary,' Sandman said, forcefully. 'I have authority, and if you want to stay out of trouble I suggest you tell me where the girl is.'

The man looked worriedly at his wife, but she was unmoved by Sandman's words. 'You ain't got no right to be in here, mister,' she said, 'so I suggests you leave.'

Sandman ignored her. 'You finish searching down here, Sergeant,' he told Berrigan, 'and I'll look upstairs.' He sensed that the steward and his wife were being untruthful. The steward should have shared his wife's defiance, but instead he behaved like a man with something to hide, and Sandman hurried up the stairs to find it.

The rooms on the upper floor seemed as empty as those below, but then, right at the end of the corridor, next to a narrow stairway to the attics, Sandman found himself in a large bedroom that was clearly inhabited. A fine four-poster bed had a sheet and rumpled blankets. A woman's clothes were draped over a chair. Meg's room, Sandman thought, and he sensed she had only just left. He went back to the door and looked down the passage, but he saw nothing except dust motes drifting in the shafts of late-afternoon sunlight where he had left doors ajar.

Then, where the sun struck the uneven floorboards, he saw his own footprints in the dust and he walked slowly back down the passage, looking into each room again, and in the biggest bedroom, which lay at the head of the fine staircase and had a wide stone fireplace carved with an escutcheon showing six martlets, he saw scuff marks in the dust. Someone had been in the room recently and their footprints led to the stone hearth, then to the window nearest the fireplace, but did not return to the door. Sandman frowned. He could not open the window because the iron frame had rusted shut. So Meg had not escaped through the window. Damn it, he thought, but she was here!

On a whim he crossed to the fireplace, stooped and stared up the chimney, but the blackened shaft narrowed swiftly and hid no one.

The sounds of footsteps on the stairs made him stand and put a hand on the pistol's hilt, but it was Berrigan and Sally who appeared in the doorway. 'She ain't here,' Berrigan said in disgust.

Sandman stared at the fireplace. Six martlets on a shield, and why would the house display that badge inside and five scallop shells on a shield outside? Then a tune came to him, a tune and some half-remembered words that he had last heard sung by a campfire in Spain. '"I'll give you one O,"' he said.

Sally stared at Sandman as though he had gone quite mad.

'"Seven for the seven stars in the sky,"' Sandman said, '"six for the six proud walkers."'

'"Five for the symbols at your door."' Berrigan supplied the next line.

'And there are five scallop shells carved over the front door here,' Sandman said softly, suddenly aware he could be overheard. The song's words were mostly a mystery, but Sandman did know what five symbols at the door meant. He had learned at school that when five seashells were set above a door or displayed on the gable of a house it was a sign that Catholics lived within. The shells had been placed during the persecutions in Elizabeth's reign, when to be a Catholic priest in England meant risking imprisonment, torture and death, yet some folk could not live without the consolations of their faith, and they had marked their houses so that their co-religionists might know a refuge was to be found within. Yet Elizabeth's men knew the meaning of the five shells as well as any Catholic did, so if a priest was in the house the householder would make a priest's hole where he could be cunningly hidden.

'I want kindling,' Sandman said softly. 'Kindling, firewood, a tinderbox and see if there's a big cauldron in the kitchen.'

Berrigan and Sally went back downstairs. Sandman knocked on the panels that covered the walls on either side of the fireplace, but nothing sounded hollow. The window wall and the wall by the passage looked too thin, so it had to be the fireplace wall or its opposite, where a deep cupboard was, but Sandman could discover nothing. That was the point of priest's holes; they were almost impossible to detect.

'Weighs a bloody ton,' Berrigan complained as he staggered into the bedroom and dropped an enormous cauldron onto the floor.

Sally was a few steps behind with a bundle of firewood. 'So what are you doing?' she asked.

'We're going to burn the damn house down,' Sandman said loudly enough for someone two rooms away to hear him. He shifted the cauldron onto the hearth's apron. 'No one's using the house and the roof needs mending. Cheaper to burn it down than clean it up.' He put the kindling in the bottom of the cauldron, struck a spark in the tinderbox and blew on the charred linen till he had a flame that he transferred to the kindling. He nursed the flame for a few seconds, then it was crackling and he put some smaller pieces of firewood on top.

It took a few minutes before the larger pieces caught the flames, but by then the cauldron was belching smoke and, because the cauldron was on the hearth's apron rather than in the fireplace, almost none of the smoke was being sucked into the chimney. Sandman planned to smoke Meg out. He put Berrigan to stand guard outside the bedroom while he and Sally stayed inside with the door shut. The smoke was choking them, so Sally was crouching by the bed. Sandman's eyes were streaming, and his throat was raw, but he fed another piece of wood onto the flames.

He stooped to where the smoke was thinner and hoped that it was infiltrating Meg's ancient hiding place and frightening her. Sally had a dustsheet over her mouth and Sandman knew they could not last much longer, but just then there was a creaking sound, a scream and a crash, and he saw a whole section of the panelling open like a door—only it was not by the fireplace but between the windows, where he had thought the wall too thin for a priest's hole. Sandman pulled his sleeves over his hands and shoved the cauldron under the chimney as Sally snatched the wrist of the screaming, terrified woman who tried to extricate herself from the narrow, laddered shaft that led down from the dislodged panels.

'It's all right!' Sally was saying as she led Meg over to the door.

Sandman followed the two women onto the wide landing where he gasped cool clean air and stared into Meg's red-rimmed eyes. He thought how good an artist Charles Corday was, for the young woman was truly monstrously ugly, even malevolent looking.

And just then a gun fired from the hallway.

Sally screamed as Sandman pushed her down and out of the way. Meg, sensing escape, ran towards the stairs, but Berrigan tripped her. Sandman stepped over her as he limped to the balustrade, where he saw that the sour-looking housekeeper had fired a fowling piece up the staircase. But, like many raw recruits, she had shut her eyes when she pulled the trigger and fired too high, so the duck shot had whipped over Sandman's hair. Half a dozen men were behind her, probably tenants who had come to protect the Duke of Ripon's property, led by a tall, fair-haired giant armed with a musket. The rest had cudgels and sickles.

'You've no business here!' the housekeeper screamed up at him.

'We have every right to be here,' Sandman lied. 'We have been asked by the Government to investigate a murder.' He kept his voice calm as he drew out the Home Secretary's letter which, in truth, granted him no rights whatsoever. He went slowly down the stairs, always keeping his eyes on the man with the gun. He looked oddly familiar and Sandman wondered if he had been a soldier. His musket was certainly an old army musket, but it was clean, it was cocked, and the tall, well-muscled man held it confidently. 'I have here the Home Secretary's authorisation,' Sandman said, brandishing the letter with its impressive seal. 'Does anyone want to read his lordship's letter?' he asked, holding out the paper and knowing that a mention of 'his lordship' would give them pause.

The man holding the musket frowned at Sandman and lowered the weapon's muzzle. 'Are you Captain Sandman?'

Sandman nodded. 'I am,' he said.

'By God, but I saw you knock seventy-six runs off us at Tunbridge Wells!' the man said. He had now uncocked the musket and was beaming at Sandman. 'Last year, it were, I was playing for Kent.'

And, by the grace of God, the big man's name slithered into Sandman's mind. 'It's Mister Wainwright, isn't it?'

'Ben Wainwright it is, sir.' Wainwright pulled his forelock.

'You hit a ball over the haystack, I recall,' Sandman said. 'You nearly beat us on your own!'

'Nothing like you, sir, nothing like you.'

The men with him were all grinning at him now. It did not matter that Sandman was in the house illegally, he was a cricketer and a famous one.

'Now, I want to have a conversation with this young lady. Maybe there's a tavern where we can talk?' Sandman realised it would be sensible to take Meg off the Duke of Ripon's property before someone with a rudimentary legal knowledge accused them of trespass and explained to Meg that she did not have to talk with them.

The confrontation was over. Wainwright assured them that the Castle and Bell was a fine tavern and Sandman dared to hope that all would be well. One conversation now, a dash to London, and justice would be done.

MEG WAS BITTER, sullen and angry. She resented Sandman's incursion into her life, and for a time, sitting in the back garden of the Castle and Bell, she refused even to talk to him. She stared into the distance, drank a glass of gin, demanded another in a whining voice and then insisted that Sandman take her back to Cross Hall. 'My chooks need looking after,' she snapped.

'Your chickens?' That surprised Sandman.

'He let me look after the chooks,' she said defiantly.

Sally came out of the tavern. 'There's a potman bringing the jugs,' she said. She flapped a hand at an irritating wasp, driving it towards Meg who gave a small scream and, when the insect would not leave her, began to cry with alarm.

'Why are you bleeding crying?' Sally demanded. 'You've got no reason to cry. You've been swanning down here while that poor little pixie's waiting to be scragged.'

The potman brought a tray of tankards, glasses and jugs. Sandman poured ale into a pint tankard. 'Why don't you take that to the Sergeant?' he said to Sally. 'I'll talk to Meg.' Berrigan was watering the horses at a duck pond.

Sally took the ale and Sandman offered Meg another glass of gin, which she snatched from him.

'You were fond of the Countess, weren't you?' Sandman asked her.

'I've got nothing to say to you,' Meg said, 'nothing.' She drained the gin and reached for the jug.

Sandman snatched the jug away. 'What's your name?' he asked. He poured some of the gin onto the grass and Meg immediately went very still and looked wary. 'I'm taking you to London,' Sandman told her, 'and you have two ways of going there. You can behave yourself, in which case it will be comfortable, or you can go on being rude, in which case I'm taking you to prison.'

'You can't do that!' she sneered.

'I can do what I damn well like!' Sandman snapped, with sudden anger. 'You are concealing evidence in a murder case!'

She glowered at him for a moment, then shrugged. 'My name's Hargood,' she said in a surly voice, 'Margaret Hargood.'

Sandman poured her another glass of gin. 'The Home Secretary instructed me to investigate the murder of the Countess of Avebury, Miss Hargood, because he fears that a great injustice is about to be done.' The day that Viscount Sidmouth worried about an injustice to a member of the lower classes, Sandman reflected, was probably the day the sun rose in the west, but he could not admit that. 'I believe,' he went on, 'that Charles Corday never murdered your mistress. And we think you can confirm that.'

'I don't know nothing about it,' she said, 'nothing about any murder.' She looked defiantly at Sandman, her eyes as hard as flint.

Sandman sighed. 'Do you want an innocent man to die?' The girl made no answer. 'Do you think the Marquess will protect you?' Sandman demanded. 'I'm astonished he hasn't murdered you already.' That, at least, got some reaction.

'You don't know a bloody thing, do you?' Meg said scornfully.

'I'll tell you what I know,' Sandman said, his anger very close to violence. 'I know that you can save an innocent man from the gallows, and I know you don't want to, and that makes you an accomplice to murder, Miss, and they can hang you for that.' Sandman waited, but she said nothing and he knew he had failed. If the girl would not talk then Corday could not be saved.

He wanted to get Meg back to London swiftly, but Mackeson insisted the horses were too tired to travel. That meant they would have to stay the night in the village. Meg was put in the coach and its doors were tied and windows jammed. Berrigan, Sandman and Sally slept on the grass, guarding Mackeson and Billy, though there was no fight left in either man.

'So what happens now?' Berrigan asked Sandman in the short summer night.

'We take her to the Home Secretary,' Sandman said bleakly, 'and let him pick over her bones.'

It would do no good, he thought, but what choice did he have?

10

It was just after dawn when the main door of Newgate Prison was eased open and the first pieces of the scaffold were carried out into Old Bailey. Part of the fence that surrounded the finished scaffold was placed halfway across the street to divert what small traffic went between Ludgate Hill and Newgate Street this early on a Sunday. William Brown, the Keeper of Newgate, came to the main door where he yawned, lit a pipe, then stepped aside as the beams that formed the framework of the scaffold's platform were carried out. 'It's going to be a lovely day, Mister Pickering,' he remarked to the foreman.

'Be a hot one, sir.'

'Plenty of ale over the street.'

'God be thanked for that, sir,' Pickering said. 'So it's a busy day tomorrow, is it, sir?'

'Just the two,' the Keeper said, 'but one of them is the fellow who stabbed the Countess of Avebury. Bound to attract a fair crowd.'

'And the weather will encourage them, sir.'

'That it will,' the Keeper agreed, 'if it stays fine.' The Keeper tapped out his pipe, then went inside to change for morning service.

SANDMAN WAS in a vile mood that Sunday morning. He had hardly slept, and Meg's whining about being forced to London only made his bad temper worse. Berrigan and Sally were hardly more cheerful, but had the sense to keep silent.

Billy, the stable hand, was left behind in the village. He could hardly get back ahead of the coach and so he could not warn the Seraphim Club and thus it was safe to abandon him. 'But how do I get home?' he enquired plaintively.

'You walk,' Sandman snapped.

The horses were tired, but they responded briskly enough to Mackeson's whip and by the time the sun had climbed above the eastern trees they were going northwards at a fair clip.

Sandman was sharing the box with Berrigan and Mackeson, leaving the carriage's interior for Sally and Meg. 'Maybe she'll talk to another girl,' Sally had said.

The carriage came to a ford and Mackeson stopped the team. As the horses drank, Sandman folded down the steps to let Sally and Meg stretch their legs. He looked quizzically at Sally, who shook her head. 'Stubborn,' she murmured to Sandman.

Meg glared at Sandman, then she sat on the bank. 'I'll kill you,' she said to Sandman, 'if the foxes have eaten my chooks.'

'You care more about your hens than the life of an innocent man?'

'Let him bloody hang,' Meg said.

'You're going to have to talk to other men in London,' Sandman said, 'and they won't be gentle.'

The girl said nothing.

Sandman sighed. 'I know what happened,' he said. 'You were in the room where Corday was painting the Countess and someone came up the back stairs. You hurried Corday down the front stairs, to the street, because it was one of the Countess's lovers, the Marquess of Skavadale.' Meg frowned, looked as if she was about to say something, then just stared away into the distance. 'And the Countess was blackmailing him. She made money that way, didn't she? You were her procuress, weren't you?'

Meg turned her small, bitter eyes on Sandman. 'I was her protector, culley, and she needed one. Too good for her own good, she was.'

'But you didn't protect her, did you?' Sandman said harshly. 'The Marquess killed her, and you discovered that. Did you find him there? Perhaps you saw the murder! So he hid you away and he promised you money.'

Meg half smiled. 'Why didn't he kill me there and then, eh?' She stared defiantly at Sandman. 'If he killed the Countess, why wouldn't he kill the maid? Tell me that, go on!'

Sandman could not. It was, indeed, the one thing he could not explain, though everything else made sense.

'Captain!' Berrigan, sitting up on the coach's box, was staring north. Sandman stared northwards and up a low, thickly wooded hill and, there on the crest where the London road crossed the skyline and made a gash in the trees, was a group of horsemen.

The horsemen were too far away to be clearly visible, but Sandman had the impression they were gazing towards the coach and that at least one had a telescope. 'Could be anyone,' he said.

'Could be,' Berrigan agreed, 'only Lord Robin Holloway likes to wear a white riding coat and he's got a great black horse.'

The man at the centre of the group had a white coat and was mounted on a big black horse. 'Damn,' Sandman said mildly. Had the Seraphim Club connected him with the missing carriage and then started to worry about Meg in Kent? Even as he thought that he saw the group of horsemen spur forward and disappear into the trees. 'Sergeant! Get Meg into the carriage! Hurry!'

There was no room to turn the coach so Sandman told Mackeson to take the first turning off the road. Any lane or farm track would do, but perversely there was none. And then, just as Sandman was despairing of ever finding an escape route, a narrow lane fell off to the right and he ordered Mackeson to take it. The vehicle swung into the lane and then lurched and swayed alarmingly, for the track was nothing but deep old cart ruts that had solidified in the dry mud. But every yard took them farther from the London road.

Sandman made Mackeson stop after a couple of hundred yards and then stood on the carriage roof and stared back, but he could see no horsemen on the road. Then Meg screamed, and Sandman, scrambling down off the roof, heard a slap. The scream stopped and he jumped down to the road. Berrigan dropped the window. 'Only a bleeding wasp,' he said, flicking the dead insect into the hedge. 'You'd think it was a bleeding crocodile the fuss she bleeding makes!'

'I thought she was murdering you,' Sandman said, then he started to climb back up onto the coach, only to be checked by Berrigan's raised hand. He stopped, listened and heard the sound of hoofbeats.

The sound passed. The group of horsemen was on the main road, but they were not coming down this narrow lane. Sandman hauled himself up to the box and nodded to Mackeson. 'Gently now,' he said, 'just ease her on.'

'Can't do nothing else,' Mackeson said reprovingly, nodding ahead to where the lane bent sharply to the left.

The turn was excruciatingly tight. The carriage lurched as the wheels mounted the verge and the horses, sensing the resistance, slackened their pull. Just then the leading left wheel slid down a bank obscured by grass, and the whole carriage tilted and Mackeson flailed for balance as Sandman gripped the handrail on the roof. Then the spokes of the wheel, taking the weight of the whole carriage in the hidden ditch, snapped one after the other and, inevitably, the wheel rim shattered and the coach lurched hard down. Mackeson had somehow managed to stay on his seat. 'I'm telling you she ain't built for the country,' he said resentfully, 'it's a town vehicle.'

'It ain't any kind of bloody vehicle now,' Berrigan said. He had scrambled out and was helping the two women down to the road.

'So what are you going to do?' Mackeson asked with an undisguised note of triumph. The wreck of the coach gave him a kind of revenge for the humiliations that had been heaped on him over the last day and two nights.

'What I'm going to do,' Sandman retorted, jumping down from the box, 'is none of your damn business. But what you're going to do is stay here with the carriage. Sergeant? Cut the horses out of the traces.' Then Sandman turned to Meg and Sally. 'You two are riding bareback,' he said.

'I can't ride,' Meg protested.

'Then you'll bloody well walk to London!' Sandman said, his temper slipping dangerously. 'And I'll make damn sure you do!' He snatched the whip from Mackeson.

'She'll ride, Captain,' Sally said, and sure enough, when the team was cut from the traces, Meg obediently scrambled up to sit on a horse's broad back with her legs dangling down one flank and with her hands gripping the fillet strap that ran along the mare's spine.

Sandman and Berrigan led all four horses back along the lane. It was a risk using the London road, but the horsemen, if they were indeed looking for the missing carriage, had taken their search southwards. Sandman walked cautiously, but they met no one.

A milestone said that London was forty-two miles away.

They trudged on. They were all tired, all irritable, and the heat and the long road sapped Sandman's strength. His clothes felt sticky and filthy, and he could feel a blister growing on his right heel. He was still limping and Sally encouraged him to ride, but he wanted to keep the spare horses fresh and so he shook his head and then fell into the mindless trudge of the soldier's march.

'WHAT HAPPENS when we get to London?' Berrigan broke the silence after they had passed through yet another village.

Sandman blinked as though he had just woken up. The sun was sinking, he saw, and the church bells were calling for evensong. 'Meg is going to tell the truth,' he answered. She snorted in derision and Sandman held his temper in check. 'Meg,' he said gently, 'you want to go back to the Marquess's house, to your chickens, is that it?'

'You know I do,' she said.

'Then you can, but first you're going to tell part of the truth.'

'Part of?' Sally asked, intrigued.

'Part of the truth,' Sandman insisted. He had, without realising it, been thinking about his dilemma and suddenly the answer seemed clear. He had been hired to determine whether or not Corday was guilty. 'It doesn't matter,' he told Meg, 'who killed the Countess. All that matters is that you know Corday did not. You took him out of her bedroom while she was still alive, and that's all I want you to tell the Home Secretary. You can do whatever you want with the rest of your life, but first you have to tell that one small part of the truth.'

And at long last, she nodded. 'I saw Corday out the street door,' she said softly. 'The Countess told him to come back the next day.'

'And you'll tell that to the Home Secretary?'

'I'll tell him that,' she said, 'and that's all I'll tell him.'

'Thank you,' Sandman said.

A milestone told him that Charing Cross lay eighteen miles ahead. Sandman's tiredness vanished. Part of the truth, he thought, would be enough and his job, thank God, would be done.

IN THE DEATH CELL of Newgate Prison, the two men who would die in the morning were given a meal of pease pottage, pork chops and boiled cabbage. The two men were so utterly dissimilar, the Keeper thought, as he waited for them to finish their meal. Charles Corday was slight, pale and nervous while Reginald Venables was a hulking brute with a grimly hard face, yet it was Corday who had committed murder while Venables was being hanged for the theft of a watch.

Corday merely picked at his food then, his leg irons clanking, went to his cot where he lay down and gazed at the vaulted ceiling.

'Tomorrow,' the Keeper began as Venables finished his meal, 'you will be taken from here to the Association Room where your irons will be struck and your arms pinioned.' He paused. 'You will find that your punishment is not painful and is soon done.'

'Bloody liar,' Venables snarled.

'Silence!' the senior turnkey growled.

'If you struggle,' the Keeper continued, 'you will be hanged painfully. It is best to cooperate.' He moved to the door. 'The turnkeys will stay here all night. If you require spiritual comfort then they can summon the Ordinary. I wish you a good night.'

'I'm innocent,' Corday said, his voice close to breaking.

'Yes,' the Keeper said, embarrassed, 'yes indeed.' He found he had nothing more to say on the subject so he just nodded to the turnkeys. 'Good night, gentlemen.'

In the Birdcage Walk, the underground passage that led from the prison to the courtrooms of the Session House, two felons were working with pickaxes and spades. Lanterns had been hung from the passage ceiling and the flagstones, great slabs of granite, had been prised up and stacked to one side. A stench now filled the passageway; a noxious stink of gas, lime and rotted flesh.

'Christ!' one of the felons said, recoiling from the smell.

'You won't find Him down there,' a turnkey said. 'Just get it over with, Tom, then you get this.' He held up a bottle of brandy.

'God bloody help us,' Tom said gloomily, then took a deep breath and struck down with his spade.

He and his companion were digging the graves for the two men who would be executed in the morning. Some of the bodies were taken for dissection, but the anatomists could not take them all and so most were brought here and put into unmarked graves. Although the prison buried the corpses in quicklime to hasten their decomposition, and though they dug up the floor in a strict rotation so that no part of it was excavated too soon after a burial, still the picks and spades struck down into bones.

Tom, ankle-deep in the hole, brought out a yellow skull that he rolled down the passageway. 'He looks in the pink, don't he?' he said, and the two turnkeys and the second prisoner began to laugh.

On the scaffold, two watchmen stood guard. Just after midnight the skies clouded over and a shower blew chill from Ludgate Hill. A handful of folk, eager for the best positions by the gallows, were sleeping on the cobbles and were woken by the rain. They grumbled, shrugged deeper into their blankets and tried to sleep again.

Dawn came early. The clouds shredded, leaving a pearl-white sky laced with the frayed brown streaks of coal smoke. London stirred.

SALLY'S HORSE, a gelding, had fallen lame just after nightfall on Sunday, then Berrigan's right boot had lost its sole. So they tied the gelding to a tree and Berrigan scrambled onto the back of the third horse. Sandman, whose boots were just holding together, led the two girls' horses, and they abandoned the lame beast. The remaining three horses were so tired that Sandman reckoned they would probably have made faster progress by leaving them behind, but Meg had resigned herself to telling the partial truth and he did not want to disturb her by suggesting she walk.

And so they walked on until, well after midnight, they trailed across London Bridge and on to the Wheatsheaf, where Sally took

Meg to her own room and Sandman let Berrigan use his room while he collapsed in the back parlour.

When the bells of St Giles's were ringing six in the morning he woke Berrigan and told him to stir the girls from their beds. Then he shaved, found his cleanest shirt, brushed his coat and washed the dirt from his disintegrating boots before, at half past six, with Berrigan, Sally and a very reluctant Meg in tow, he set out for Great George Street and, he hoped, the end of his investigation.

'BLESS ME!' The turnkey cocked an ear to the sound of a church bell tolling the quarter hour. 'St Sepulchre's telling us it's a quarter to seven already! If you turn to your left, my lords, you can join Mister Brown and the other gentlemen in the Association Room.'

'The Association Room?' Lord Alexander Pleydell enquired.

'Where the condemned associate, my lord, during the daylight hours,' the turnkey explained, 'and those windows to your left, my lord, those are the salt boxes.'

'The salt b-boxes are what?' Lord Christopher Carne, who was very pallid this morning, asked.

'The devil's waiting rooms, my lord,' the turnkey said, then pulled open the Association Room door and ostentatiously held out his hand, palm upward.

Lord Alexander hurriedly brought out a coin. 'Thank you, my good man,' he said.

'Thank you, your lordship,' the turnkey said, tugging his forelock.

William Brown, the Keeper, hurried to meet his two new guests. He recognised Lord Alexander by his clubbed foot and so took off his hat and bowed respectfully. 'Your lordship is most welcome.'

'Lord Christopher Carne,' Lord Alexander introduced his friend. 'His stepmother's murderer is being hanged today.'

The Keeper bowed to Lord Christopher. 'I do trust your lordship finds the experience both a revenge and a comfort.' He led them to where a man in a cassock, a surplice and an old-fashioned wig was waiting with a smile on his plump face. 'The Reverend Doctor Horace Cotton,' the Keeper said.

'Your lordship is most welcome.' Cotton bowed to Lord Alexander. 'I believe your lordship is, like me, in holy orders?'

'I am,' Lord Alexander said, 'and this is Lord Christopher Carne.'

'Ah!' Cotton clasped his hands prayerfully and turned to Lord Christopher, 'I understand that this morning you will see justice done for your family?'

'I hope to,' Lord Christopher said.

'Oh, really, Kit!' Lord Alexander expostulated. 'The revenge your family seeks will be provided in eternity by the fires of hell . . . and it is neither seemly nor civilised of us to hurry men to that fate.'

The Keeper looked astonished. 'You would surely not abolish the punishment of hanging, my lord?'

'Hang a man,' Lord Alexander said, 'and you deny him the chance of repentance. You deny him the chance of being pricked, day and night, by his conscience. It should be sufficient, I would have thought, to simply transport all felons to Australia. By execution we deny men their chance of salvation.'

'It's a novel argument,' Cotton allowed, though dubiously.

Lord Alexander frowned at his friend. 'Are you quite well, Kit?'

'Oh yes, indeed, yes,' Lord Christopher said hastily, but he looked anything but well. There were beads of sweat on his brow and his skin was paler than usual. He took off his spectacles and polished them with a handkerchief. 'It is just that the apprehension of seeing a man launched into eternity is conducive to reflection,' he explained. 'It is not an experience to be taken lightly.'

'I should think not indeed,' Lord Alexander said, then turned an imperious eye on the other breakfast guests who seemed to be look-ing forward to the morning's events with an unholy glee. Lord Alexander scowled at them. 'Poor Corday,' he said. 'It seems likely he is innocent, but proof of that innocence has not been found.'

'If he were innocent, my lord,' the Ordinary observed, 'then I am confident that the Lord God would reveal that to us.'

'Then God had better get his boots on this morning,' Lord Alexander said, then turned as a barred door at the other end of the room opened with a sudden and harsh squeal. A short and burly man carrying a stout leather bag stumped into sight.

'That's the hangman, Botting,' the Ordinary whispered.

Botting placed four coils of white cord and ropes on the table, added two white cotton bags, then stepped back. 'Good morning, sir,' he said to the Keeper. 'Still just the two clients today, sir?'

'Just the two, Botting.'

'Botting!' Lord Alexander intervened, pacing forward with his crippled foot clumping heavily on the scarred floorboards. 'Tell me, Botting, is it true that you hang members of the aristocracy with a silken rope?' Botting looked astonished at being addressed by one of the Keeper's guests.

'A silken rope, sir?' Botting asked weakly.

'My lord,' the Ordinary corrected him.

'My lord! Ha!' Botting said, amused at the thought that perhaps Lord Alexander was contemplating being executed. 'I hates to disappoint you, my lord,' he said, 'but I wouldn't know where to lay hands on a silken rope. Now this,' Botting caressed one of the nooses on the table, 'is the best Bridport hemp, my lord, fine as you could discover anywhere. But silk? No, my lord. If ever I has the high privilege of hanging a nobleman I'll be doing it with Bridport hemp, same as I would for anyone else.'

'And quite right too, my good man.' Lord Alexander beamed approval at the hangman's levelling instincts. 'Thank you.'

Then the guests hauled off their hats because the Sheriff and Under-Sheriff were ushering in the two prisoners.

'Brandy, sir?' One of the Keeper's servants appeared beside Lord Christopher Carne.

'Thank you.' Lord Christopher, his face even paler than before, could not take his eyes from the young man who had come first through the door with legs weighed down by the heavy irons. 'That,' he said to the servant, 'that is Corday?'

'It is, my lord, yes.'

Lord Christopher gulped down the brandy.

And the two bells, the prison tocsin and the bell of St Sepulchre's, began to toll for those about to die.

11

The door of the Great George Street house was opened by Witherspoon, Viscount Sidmouth's private secretary, who raised his eyebrows in astonishment. 'An unseemly hour, Captain?' he observed, then frowned at Sandman's dishevelled state and the ragged looks of his three companions.

'This woman,' Sandman did not bother with the niceties of a greeting, 'can testify that Charles Corday is not the murderer of the Countess of Avebury.'

Witherspoon glanced at Meg. 'How inconvenient,' he murmured.

'Viscount Sidmouth is here?' Sandman demanded.

'We are at work, Sandman,' Witherspoon said severely. 'His lordship does not brook disturbance.'

'This is work,' Sandman said.

'Must I remind you,' Witherspoon said, 'that the boy has been found guilty and the law is due to take its course in one hour? I really cannot see what can be done at this late juncture.'

Sandman stepped back from the door. 'My compliments to Lord Sidmouth,' he said, 'and tell him we are going to seek an audience with the Queen.' He had no idea whether the Queen would receive him, but he was quite sure the Home Secretary did not want the animosity of the Royal Family. 'Good day, Witherspoon.'

'Captain!' Witherspoon pulled the door wide open. 'Captain! You had better come in.'

They were shown into an empty parlour. The house had a makeshift air. It was plainly let on short leases to politicians like Lord Sidmouth. The only furniture in the parlour was a pair of stuffed armchairs and a heavy desk with a throne-like chair behind.

The door opened and Witherspoon ushered in the Home Secretary. Viscount Sidmouth was wearing a patterned silk dressing gown over his shirt and trousers. His eyes, as ever, were cold and disapproving. 'It seems, Captain Sandman,' he said acidly, 'that you choose to inconvenience us?'

'I choose nothing of the sort, my lord,' Sandman said belligerently.

Sidmouth frowned at the tone, then looked at Berrigan and the two women. 'So,' the Home Secretary said with distaste in his voice, 'who do you bring me?'

'My associates, Sergeant Berrigan and Miss Hood and Miss Margaret Hargood,' Sandman introduced them.

The Home Secretary looked at Meg and almost recoiled from the sight of her mangled teeth and pocked skin.

'Miss Hargood was a maid to the Countess of Avebury and was present in the Countess's bedroom on the day of her murder. She escorted Charles Corday from the bedroom before the murder, she saw him out of the house and can testify he did not return. In short, my lord, she can witness that Corday is innocent.' Sandman spoke with a deal of pride and satisfaction. He was tired, he was hungry, and his ankle hurt, but by God he had discovered the truth.

Sidmouth's lips, already thin, compressed into a bloodless line as he looked at Meg. 'Is it true, woman?'

Meg drew herself up, then sniffed. She was not in the least awed by his lordship. 'I don't know nothing,' she said.

'I beg your pardon?' The Home Secretary blanched at the insolence in her voice.

'He comes and kidnaps me!' Meg shrieked, pointing at Sandman. 'Which he got no bleeding right to do! And what do I care who killed her? Or who dies for her?'

'Meg,' Sandman tried to plead with her.

'Get your bleeding paws off me!'

'Dear God,' Viscount Sidmouth said in a pained voice, and backed towards the door. 'Witherspoon,' he said, 'we are wasting our time.'

'Got ever such big wasps in Australia,' Sally said, 'begging your lordship's pardon.'

Even Viscount Sidmouth with his thin, barren lawyer's mind was not oblivious of Sally's charms. In the dark room she was like a ray of sunlight and he actually smiled at her. 'I beg your pardon?'

'Australia's where this mollisher's going on account that she didn't give her testimony at Charlie's trial. She should have done, but she didn't. Protecting her man, see? And you're going to transport her, aren't you, my lord?' Sally reinforced this rhetorical question with a graceful curtsy.

The Home Secretary frowned. 'It is for the courts, my dear, not me to decide . . .' His voice suddenly tailed away for he was staring with astonishment at Meg, who was shivering with fear.

'Very large wasps in Australia,' Sally said with relish, 'with stingers like hatpins.'

'*Aculeata gigantus*,' Witherspoon contributed rather impressively.

'He didn't do it!' Meg said, 'and I don't want to go to Australia!'

'Are you saying,' Sidmouth asked in a very cold voice, 'that Charles Corday did not commit the murder?'

'The Marquess didn't! He didn't!'

'The Marquess didn't?' Sidmouth asked, utterly mystified now.

'The Marquess of Skavadale, my lord,' Sandman explained, 'in whose house she was given shelter.'

'He came after she was dead,' Meg, terrified of the mythical wasps, was desperate to explain now. 'And he was still there!'

'Who was still there?' Sidmouth enquired. 'Corday?'

'No!' Meg said. 'Her stepson,' she said, 'him what had been ploughing his father's field for half a year.'

'Lord Christopher Carne, my lord,' Sandman explained.

'I saw him with the knife,' Meg snarled, 'and so did the Marquess. Lord Christopher! He hated her, see, but he couldn't keep his paws off her neither. Oh, he killed her! It wasn't that feeble painter!'

There was a second's pause in which a score of questions came to Sandman's mind, but then Lord Sidmouth snapped at Witherspoon.

'My compliments to the police office in Queen Square, and I shall be obliged if they will provide four officers and six saddle horses instantly. But give me a pen and paper first, Witherspoon, and wax and seal.' He turned and looked at a clock on the mantel. 'And let us hurry, man.' His voice was sour as though he resented this extra work, but Sandman could not fault him. He was doing the right thing and doing it quickly.

'FOOT ON THE BLOCK, boy! Don't dally!' the turnkey snapped at Charles Corday, who gave a gulp and then put his right foot on the wooden block. The turnkey put the punch over the first rivet then hammered it out. Corday gasped with each blow, then whimpered when the manacle dropped away.

'Other foot, boy,' the turnkey ordered.

The Keeper's guests were silent, just watching the prisoners' faces.

'Right, lad, go and see the hangman!' the turnkey said, and Charles Corday stumbled as he took his first steps without leg irons.

'I do not know,' Lord Christopher said, then stopped.

'What, Kit?' Lord Alexander asked considerately.

Lord Christopher gave a start, unaware that he had even spoken, but then collected himself. 'You say there are doubts about his guilt?'

'Oh indeed, yes, indeed.' Lord Alexander paused to light a pipe. 'Sandman was quite sure of the boy's innocence, but I suppose it can't be proven. Alas, alas.'

'But if the real k-killer were to be found,' Lord Christopher asked, his eyes fixed on Corday who was quivering as he stood before the hangman, 'could that man then be convicted of the crime if Corday has already been found g-guilty of it and been hanged?'

'A very nice question!' Lord Alexander said enthusiastically. 'I confess I do not know the answer. But I should imagine that if the real killer is apprehended then a posthumous pardon must be granted to Corday and one can only hope that such a pardon will be recognised in heaven.'

'Stand still, boy,' Botting growled at Corday. 'Drink that if you want to.' He pointed to a mug of brandy, but Corday shook his head. 'Your choice, lad,' Botting said, then pinioned Corday's elbows.

The Reverend Cotton stepped forward. 'God is our refuge and strength, young man, and a very present help in times of trouble. Call on the Lord and He will hear you. Do you repent of your foul sins, boy?'

'I did nothing!' Corday wailed.

'Quiet, my son, quiet,' Cotton urged him.

'I did nothing!' Corday screamed.

'But surely,' Lord Christopher said to Lord Alexander, 'the very fact that a man already stands c-convicted and has been p-punished, would make the authorities most reluctant to reopen the case?'

'Justice must be served,' Lord Alexander said vaguely, 'but I suppose the real murderer can feel a good deal safer once Corday is dead. Poor boy. He is a sacrifice to our judicial incompetence.'

IT WAS NOT FAR. A quarter of a mile up Whitehall, right into the Strand and three-quarters of a mile to Temple Bar, and after that it was scarcely a third of a mile down Fleet Street and up Ludgate Hill. No distance at all, really, and certainly not after the police office in Queen Square had brought some patrol officers' horses. Sandman and Berrigan were both mounted, and Witherspoon handed the reprieve up to Sandman, who thrust the precious document into his pocket.

'See you in the 'sheaf, Sal!' Berrigan shouted, then lurched back as his mare followed Sandman's gelding. Three patrolmen rode ahead, one blowing a whistle and the other two with drawn truncheons to clear a path through the carts, wagons and carriages.

They passed the royal stables, then took to the pavement in the Strand. They rode past Kidman's the Apothecary, driving two pedestrians into its deep doorway, then past Carrington's, a cutlery store where Sandman had purchased his first sword. Then they galloped past Sans Pareil, the theatre where Celia Collett, actress, had entranced the Earl of Avebury. When their undying love proved to be no more than unmatched lust, she moved back to London where, to keep herself in the luxury she felt her due, she had snared her men and blackmailed them. Then the fattest fly of all came to her web. Lord Christopher Carne, innocent and naive, fell for his stepmother and she had seduced him, and then she had threatened to tell his father and the whole world if he did not pay her money, and Lord Christopher, knowing that when he inherited the estate his stepmother would demand more and more until there would be nothing left but a husk, had killed her.

All this Sandman had learned as the Viscount Sidmouth scribbled the reprieve in his own handwriting. 'The proper thing,' the Home Secretary had said, 'is for the Privy Council to issue this document.'

'Hardly time, my lord,' Sandman had pointed out.

'I am aware of that, Captain,' Sidmouth said acidly as he scrawled his signature. 'You will present this,' he said, sprinkling sand on the wet ink, 'with my compliments, to the Sheriff of London, who will be upon the scaffold. You will explain that there was no time for the proper procedures to be followed.'

Now Sandman and Berrigan rode, the seal on the reprieve still warm, and Sandman thought how killing his stepmother would have brought Lord Christopher no relief, for the Marquess of Skavadale, whose family was near penury, had discovered him almost in the act of the murder and seen his life's problems solved at a stroke. Meg was the witness who could identify Lord Christopher as the murderer. So long as she lived and was under the Marquess's protection, Lord Christopher would pay to keep her silent. And when Lord Christopher became Earl, and so gained the fortune of his grandfather, he would have been forced to pay Skavadale while Meg would have been bribed with chickens.

The Temple Bar was immediately ahead and the space under the arch was crowded with carts and pedestrians. The constables shouted for the carts to move and yelled at the drivers to use their whips. A wagon loaded with cut flowers was filling most of the archway and one of the constables started beating at it with his truncheon. 'Leave it!' Sandman bellowed. He had seen a gap on the pavement and he drove his horse for it. Berrigan followed him, then they were past the arch, Sandman was standing in the stirrups and his horse was plunging towards the Fleet Ditch, sparks flying where its shoes struck the cobbles.

The first church bells began to strike eight and Sandman slapped the horse's rump and rode like the wind.

LORD ALEXANDER, as he passed through the Debtor's Door, saw in front of him the dark hollow interior of the scaffold and thought how much it resembled the underside of a theatre's stage. From the street, the gallows looked heavy, permanent and sombre with its black baize drapery, but from here Lord Alexander could see it was an illusion sustained by raw wooden beams. It was a stage set for a tragedy ending in death.

Lord Alexander was first up the steps and a huge cheer greeted his appearance. He took off his hat and bowed to the mob who laughed and applauded. The crowd was not large, but it filled the street for a hundred yards southwards and quite blocked the junction with Newgate Street immediately to the north.

'We were asked to take chairs at the back,' Lord Christopher pointed out when Lord Alexander sat himself in the very front row. The other guests pushed past to the rearmost chairs.

'We were requested to leave two front-row places for the Sheriff,' Lord Alexander corrected him, 'and there they are. Sit down, Kit, do. What a delightful day! Do you think the weather will last? Budd on Saturday, eh?'

'Budd on Saturday?'

'Cricket, dear boy! I've persuaded Budd to play a single wicket match against Jack Lambert, and Lambert has agreed to stand down if Rider Sandman will take his place! Now that's a match to dream of, eh? Budd against Sandman. You will come, won't you?'

A cheer drowned conversation on the scaffold as the sheriffs appeared in their breeches, silk stockings, silver-buckled shoes and fur-trimmed robes. Lord Christopher seemed oblivious to their arrival, gazing instead at the beam from which the prisoners would hang. Then he looked down and flinched at the sight of the two coffins waiting for their burdens. 'She was an evil woman,' he said softly.

'What did you say, my dear fellow?' Lord Alexander asked.

'My stepmother. She was evil.' Lord Christopher seemed to shiver, though it was not cold.

'Are you justifying her murder?'

'She said she would make a claim on the estate,' Lord Christopher said more emphatically, apparently not hearing his friend's question. He winced, remembering the long letters in which he had poured out his devotion to his stepmother. He had known no women until he had been taken to her bed and he had become besotted by her. She had encouraged his madness until, one day, mocking him, she had snapped the trap closed. Give her money, she had insisted, or else she would make him a laughing stock. He had paid her money, and she demanded more, and he knew the blackmail would never end.

He had not believed himself capable of murder, but as he begged her a final time to return him the letters, she had mocked him, called him puny, said he was a fumbling and stupid boy. He had pulled the knife from his belt, an old blade he used to slit the pages of uncut books. He had stabbed her, then hacked and slashed at her loathsome and beautiful skin, and afterwards he had rushed onto the landing and seen the Countess's maid and a man staring up at him from the downstairs hall, and he had recoiled back to the bedroom. He expected to hear feet on the stairs, but no one came, and he forced himself to be calm and to think. He had been on the landing for only a split second, hardly time to be recognised! He snatched a knife from the painter's table and thrust it into the red-laced body, then searched the dead woman's bureau to find his letters, which he had carried away down the back stairs and burned at home. He had crouched in his lodgings, fearing arrest, then next day heard that the painter had been taken by the constables.

It was not right, of course, that the painter should die, but nor could Lord Christopher be persuaded that he himself deserved death for his stepmother's murder. He would do good with his inheritance! He would be charitable. He would pay for the murder and for Corday's innocence a thousand times over. Sandman had threatened that exercise of repentance and so Lord Christopher had consulted his manservant and promised a thousand guineas to the man who could rid him of that threat. Lord Christopher had rewarded the men his manservant had hired richly even for the attempt on Sandman's life. Now, it seemed, further payment would be unnecessary for Sandman had evidently failed.

'But your stepmother, surely, had no claim on the estate,' Lord Alexander had been thinking about his friend's words, 'unless the entail specifically provides for your father's widow. Does it?'

Lord Christopher made an effort to concentrate on what his friend had just said. 'No,' he said, 'the whole estate is entailed on the heir.'

'Then you will be a prodigiously rich man, Kit,' Lord Alexander said, 'and I shall wish you well of your great fortune.' He turned as a huge cheer greeted the hangman's arrival on the scaffold.

'"I will keep my mouth as it were with a bridle,"' the Reverend Cotton's voice grew louder as he climbed the stairs behind the first prisoner, '"while the ungodly is in my sight."'

Corday tripped on the top step and stumbled into Lord Alexander who gripped his elbow. 'Steady, there's a good fellow,' Lord Alexander said.

The crowd surged forward to crush against the low wooden rail that surrounded the scaffold. The City Marshal's men, arrayed just behind the rail, raised their staves and spears.

Lord Alexander felt assaulted by the noise. This was England at play, he thought, the mob given its taste of blood in the hope that, given this much, they would not demand more. Corday was weeping openly. The crowd liked a man or woman to go to their deaths bravely and Corday's tears were earning him nothing but scorn.

Then the crowd roared in mocking laughter because Corday had collapsed. Botting was in the process of lifting the rope from the prisoner's shoulders ready to attach it to one of the hooks of the beam, when Corday's legs turned to jelly. The turnkey ran forward, but Corday could not stand. He was shaking and sobbing.

'I need a chair,' Botting growled.

One of the guests volunteered to stand and his chair was placed on the trap door. The crowd, realising this was going to be an unusual execution, applauded. Botting and a turnkey hoisted Corday onto the seat and the hangman bound Corday to the chair. Botting clambered up the ladder, attached the rope, then came down and rammed the noose over Corday's head. 'Snivelling little bastard,' he whispered as he jerked the rope tight, 'die like a man.' He took one of the white cotton bags from his pocket and pulled it over Corday's head.

Lord Alexander, appalled by the last few moments, became dimly aware of some disturbance at the southern end of Old Bailey.

'NO POINT IN HURRYING!' a wagon driver called. 'Not if you're going to the hanging. The culleys will be dangling by now!' All the bells of the City had rung the hour, the ones that always chimed early and even the laggards had struck eight, but the funeral bell of St Sepulchre still tolled and Sandman dared to hope that Corday was still alive as he burst out of the tangled traffic at the junction of Farringdon Street and Ludgate Hill and kicked his horse up towards St Paul's Cathedral.

Halfway up the hill he turned into Old Bailey and for the first few yards, the road was blessedly empty, but then as he passed the big yard of Newgate Prison suddenly the seething crowd stretched across the whole street, blocking him. He could see the beam of the gallows and he saw the men on the black scaffold platform beneath and noticed that one seemed to be sitting, which was strange. He drove the horse at the crowd, standing in the stirrups, shouting.

'Make way!' Sandman bellowed. 'Make way!' The crowd protested at his savagery, resisted him, and he wished he had a weapon to thrash at them, but then the constables drove alongside him and thrust at the press of people with their long truncheons.

Then a sigh seemed to pass through the crowd, and Sandman could see no one but a priest on the scaffold's black stage.

Which meant the trap door had opened.

'IT'S RIDER!' Lord Alexander was standing now pointing towards Ludgate Hill, to the annoyance of the guests seated behind him.

The crowd had at last begun to sense that something untoward was happening. They turned and saw the horsemen who were trying to force their way through the crowd.

'Let them through!' some of the people shouted.

'Sit down, my lord,' the Sheriff said to Lord Alexander, who ignored him.

Botting pulled the rope and the trap fell with a thump and the two bodies fell into the scaffold's pit. Venables was dancing and throttling, while Corday's legs were thrashing against the chair.

'Sheriff! Sheriff!' Sandman was nearing the scaffold. 'Sheriff!'

'Is it a reprieve?' Lord Alexander roared. 'Is it a reprieve?'

'Yes!'

'Kit! Help me!' Lord Alexander limped on his club foot to where Corday hung, twitched and gagged. 'Help me haul him up!'

'Let go of him,' the Sheriff bellowed, as Lord Alexander reached for the rope.

'Let go, my lord!' the Reverend Cotton demanded. 'This is not seemly.'

'Get off me, you damned bloody fool!' Lord Alexander snarled as he pushed Cotton away. He then seized the rope and tried to haul Corday back up to the platform, but he did not possess nearly enough strength and could not raise the dying man by even an inch.

Sandman thrust aside the last few folk and rammed his horse against the barrier. He held the reprieve up towards the scaffold, but the Sheriff would not come to receive it. 'It's a reprieve!' Sandman shouted.

'Kit, help me!' Lord Alexander turned to Lord Christopher. 'Kit! Help me!' Lord Christopher, eyes huge behind his thick spectacles, held both hands to his mouth. He did not move.

'What the bloody hell are you doing?' Jemmy Botting shouted from beneath the scaffold and then, to make sure he was not cheated of a death, he hauled downwards on Corday's legs. 'You'll not have him!' he screamed up at Lord Alexander. 'He's mine!'

'Take it!' Sandman shouted at the Sheriff, who still refused to lean down and accept the reprieve, but just then a black-dressed man pushed his way to Sandman's side.

'Give it to me,' the newcomer said. He snatched the paper, hoisted himself onto the railing that protected the scaffold and then, with one prodigious leap, jumped to catch hold of the scaffold's edge. His black boots scrabbled for a lodgment, then he managed to grip the exposed edge left by the fallen trap door and heaved himself onto the platform. It was Sally's brother, and the regulars in the crowd cheered for they recognised and admired him. He was Jack Hood, Robin Hood – the man that every magistrate and constable in London wanted to see caper on Jem Botting's stage. He thrust Corday's reprieve towards the Sheriff. 'Take it, God damn you!' Hood snarled, and the Sheriff, astonished, at last took the paper.

Hood strode to Lord Alexander's side and took hold of the rope, but Jemmy Botting had scrambled onto Corday's lap. 'He's mine!' he shouted. Corday's wheezing breath was drowned in the morning's din. Hood heaved, but could not raise the combined weight of Corday and Botting.

'You!' Sandman snapped at one of the City Marshal's javelin men. 'Give me your hanger! Now!'

The man, cowed by Sandman's snap of command, nervously drew the short curved sword that was more decorative than useful. Sandman snatched the blade from him, then was assaulted by another of the scaffold guards who thought Sandman planned an assault on the Sheriff. 'Bugger off!' Sandman snarled at the man, then Berrigan thumped his fist on the crown of the man's head.

'Hood!' Sandman shouted as he stood in the stirrups. 'Hood!' Sandman had the highwayman's attention now and he tossed him the hanger. 'Cut him down, Hood! Cut him down!'

Hood deftly caught the blade. The constables who had escorted Sandman and Berrigan pushed away the Marshal's men. Lord Christopher Carne, eyes still wide and mouth agape, was staring in horror at Rider Sandman, who at last noticed his lordship. 'Constable,' Sandman spoke to the horseman nearest him, 'that's the man you arrest. That man there.' Sandman pointed and Lord Christopher turned as if to escape, but the stairs from the pavilion led only down to the prison itself.

Jack Hood was sawing the hanger blade at the rope. 'No!' Botting screamed. 'No!' But the rope, though it was supposed to be the best Bridport hemp, cut like rush string and suddenly Corday and Botting were falling and the legs of the chair splintered on the cobbles as the rope's cut end flicked empty in the London wind.

'We must cut him down,' the Sheriff said, having at last read the reprieve.

The crowd, fickle as ever, now cheered because the victim they had despised had cheated the hangman. He would live, he would go free.

Sandman slid from his horse and gave the reins to a constable. Other constables now took hold of Lord Christopher Carne. Sandman could hear the dying Venables's choking noises and turned away, trying and failing to discover some consolation that even one soul had been stolen from the gallows.

'It's over then,' Berrigan said, dismounting.

'It's over,' Sandman said. 'Thank you, Sergeant.'

'Rider!' Lord Alexander shouted from the scaffold. 'Rider!'

Sandman turned back.

'Rider! Would you play a single wicket match? This Saturday?'

Sandman stared in momentary astonishment at his friend, then looked at Hood. 'Thank you,' he shouted, but the words were lost in the crowd's howling. 'Thank you,' he called again, and bowed.

Hood returned the bow, then held up a single finger. 'Just one, Captain,' he called, 'and they'll hang a thousand before you snatch another back.'

'It's against Budd!' Lord Alexander shouted. 'Rider, can you hear me? Rider! Where are you going?'

Sandman had turned away again and now had his arm round Berrigan's shoulder. 'If you want breakfast at the 'sheaf,' he told the Sergeant, 'then you'd best hurry before the crowd fills the taproom. And thank Sally for me, will you? We would have failed without her.'

'We would, too,' Berrigan said. 'And you? Where are you going?'

Sandman limped away from the gallows. 'Me, Sam?' Sandman answered. 'I'm going to see a man about a loan so that you and I can go to Spain and buy some cigars.'

'You're going to ask for a loan,' Berrigan said, 'in those boots?'

Sandman looked down to see that both boot soles were gaping away from the uppers. 'I'm going to ask for his daughter's hand in marriage as well, and I'll wager you the price of a new pair of boots that he'll say yes to both. He's not getting a rich son-in-law, Sam, he's just getting me.'

'Lucky him,' Berrigan said.

Sandman smiled and they walked on down Old Bailey. Behind them Corday blinked in the new day's sunlight. Sandman looked back once from Ludgate Hill and he saw the gallows black as any devil's heart, and then he turned the corner and was gone.

BERNARD CORNWELL

'Writing,' states Bernard Cornwell with characteristic directness, 'is a lot better than working. You just sit down and tell stories. It's fun. I dreamed of doing this. From the time when I was fourteen it was all I wanted to do.'

This prolific author wrote his first novel, *Sharpe's Eagle*, in the late seventies when he had put his career as a television journalist on hold in order to move to the US with his American wife, Judy. Once in the States, he was refused a work permit and so decided to try to earn a living by writing. He was thrilled when *Sharpe's Eagle* earned him a seven-book contract, and he went on to write eighteen hugely popular novels about Richard Sharpe's experiences during the Napoleonic Wars. Cornwell gained even more fans when the books became a television series starring Sean Bean.

Bernard Cornwell's other works of fiction have included thrillers with a seafaring twist (inspired by his love of sailing); a masterly retelling of the legend of King Arthur; a series about the American Civil War; and *Stonehenge*, a fascinating book about the construction of the ancient stone circle. History, which he studied at Oxford, has always been his greatest source of inspiration, as indeed was the case with *Gallows Thief*. 'I was reading a book about the Newgate gallows and I discovered that occasionally an Investigator was appointed to look into the facts of a case. I immediately thought, That's my hero. Rider Sandman would have been one of the first detectives, long before the police force was even thought of.'

Although he has lived in the US for twenty-two years, Bernard Cornwell admits to missing lots of things about Britain, including cricket, rugby, Flowers Original ale, Radio 4 and steak and kidney pudding. 'I miss England all the time,' he declares, 'but I always think that if the worst thing that happens to me is to be happily married to an American and to live on Cape Cod, then I'm a very lucky man!'

HEAD OVER HEELS
IN THE DALES

Gervase Phinn

Excited by the challenge of a new academic year, and blissfully happy about his forthcoming marriage, Yorkshire school inspector Gervase Phinn sets out for the classrooms of the Dales with a spring in his step.

Then some unexpected news from Dr Gore, head of the inspectors' team, really puts the cat among the pigeons.

ONE

'Could you tell me how to spell "sex", please?' The speaker was a flaxen-haired, angelic-faced girl of about six with wide innocent eyes and a complexion a model would die for.

'I . . . b . . . b . . . b . . . beg your pardon?' I stuttered.

I was sitting in the infant classroom of Staplemoor County Primary School on a bright September morning, there to observe the first lesson of the day. The children had just settled down to write their stories when the little angel approached me, paper in hand, pencil poised. ' "Sex." Could you spell "sex" for me, please?'

I had been a County Inspector of Schools in Yorkshire for a little over two years and during that time I thought I had become accustomed to precocious young children. I had been delighted by their humour, intrigued by their responses to my questions and amused by their sharp observations on life. But on a few rare occasions, like this one, I was completely lost for words. My colleague and immediate superior, Dr Harold Yeats, had told me early on that when faced with a child who asks a tricky question or raises an embarrassing topic, I should smile, nod sagely and be as evasive as possible.

'It's like fishing for trout, Gervase,' he confided in me. 'You need to know when to let out the line and when to reel it in. Give it plenty of space, let it tire itself out and then it will stop thrashing. Don't be too quick to explain things to young children—you could get yourself into hot water. Just listen and take your time.'

I took Harold's advice. 'Why do you want me to spell *that* word for you?' I whispered.

'I need it for my story,' replied the child.

'Could you tell me a little about your story?' I asked gingerly.

The child breathed out heavily. 'If you must know, it's about a little black beetle who lives in a big, big garden and is sad and lonely and nobody loves him. All the other little creatures have friends but he just sits there all day long on the compost heap feeling really, really sad and wishing he had someone to play with. Then, one day, a lady beetle climbs onto the compost heap—'

'A lady beetle?' I said.

'That's right, a lady beetle.'

'I see,' I sighed, frantically thinking of the best way to get out of what was likely to become a very uncomfortable situation.

'And then,' continued the child brightly, 'she sees the lonely little beetle and asks him who he is. He tells her that he is just a sad and boring little bug and he's ugly as well and nobody loves him. She tells him he's the beautifulest beetle she has ever seen in the whole wide world and she asks him if she can stay with him for ever and ever. They love each other and then they have lots of little baby beetles.'

'I thought they might do,' I said under my breath.

'But all I want is "sex"!' she said, rather too loudly for comfort.

'Just keep your voice down a little,' I told her. 'What about "cuddle up" or "snuggle"? Those might be better words to use.'

'I don't want "cuddle up" or "snuggle",' she replied tartly. 'I want "sex".' Her voice was now loud enough to attract the attention of the headteacher who swiftly appeared on the scene.

'My goodness, Mr Phinn,' she said, 'you and Melissa seem to be having a very interesting conversation.'

Before I could explain, the child, giving another great heaving sigh, announced, 'He won't spell "sex" for me, Mrs McCardle. I've asked him but he won't spell it. I don't think Mr Phinn's too good at spelling.' The teacher arched an eyebrow. 'You see,' continued Melissa, holding up her paper for Mrs McCardle to see, 'I want to start my story: "Beetles are insects." I can do the "in" but not the "sects".'

'Perhaps you would like to visit the juniors for a while, Mr Phinn,' suggested Mrs McCardle, a knowing twinkle in her eye, 'and then join us again in the infants after morning break. Would that suit?'

'That would suit very well,' I replied, retreating gratefully to the adjoining classroom.

THE JUNIOR TEACHER, Mr Spencer-Hall, was a lean, weary-looking individual with fluffy outcrops of ginger hair and large spectacles which had the habit of slipping down his nose as he talked.

'I've always had a secret dread of school inspectors,' he informed me morosely, pushing up his glasses and producing an expression a child might pull when faced with a plate of cold cabbage. 'I've only met two in my whole career and they put the very fear of God in me.'

'Well, I hope my visit is going to be less distressing, Mr Spencer-Hall,' I told him cheerily.

'What exactly are you going to be doing, Mr Phinn?' he asked with a woeful look on his face.

'Well, I thought I might observe a bit of your teaching,' I replied, 'and then I would like to hear the children read, look at their written work, test their spellings and talk to them a little.'

'It all sounds terribly daunting,' he groaned, 'but I suppose you have a job to do and I'll just have to grin and bear it.'

'I'm afraid you will, Mr Spencer-Hall,' I said.

'And I suppose there will be a report?'

'Yes,' I replied, 'which, of course, I'd be happy to discuss with you.'

'Oh dear,' he moaned again. 'I don't like the sound of that either.'

'The point behind my observing your lesson, Mr Spencer-Hall, is to give you an objective view of your teaching, help you improve and also offer some advice. I think you will find it quite painless.'

'Well, Mr Phinn,' he said sadly, 'those two school inspectors who visited me before were about as painless as having a boil lanced. Seeing them scribbling away in their little black books put me off my stroke and no mistake. I just went to pieces.'

'Well, I hope you will not find me quite as frightening,' I told him. 'Just imagine that I am not there, Mr Spencer-Hall.'

I prepared myself for what I imagined would be an endlessly dull lesson. As it turned out, as soon as Mr Spencer-Hall faced the children he became confident and animated. The children listened attentively as he explained how they might make their writing more vibrant by strengthening their verbs. The idea was that they should produce alternatives to a chosen word.

'What about "looked"?' the teacher asked.

Back came 'glanced', 'peered', 'watched', 'glimpsed', 'gaped', 'peeped' and many others.

'And what about "walked"?' he asked next.

Again there was a lively response: 'limped', 'staggered', 'swayed', 'reeled', 'tottered' and a host more.

The words were listed neatly on the blackboard in a careful cursive script and then the children were set the task of including some of them in a piece of writing.

When Mr Spencer-Hall glanced nervously in my direction, I gave him a reassuring smile and made sure I was not 'scribbling away in my little black book'. He put on a martyred expression, slid his spectacles up his nose and continued.

The first child I heard read that morning was William, a moon-faced boy of about ten, with apple-red cheeks, a thatch of black hair and a ready smile. He presented himself to me armed with a thick and ancient-looking reading book, a folder of his written work and a bizarre construction made of cardboard, matchboxes, lavatory rolls, lollipop sticks and tissue paper.

'Shall we mek a start, then?' he asked me bluntly, rubbing his hands together like someone about to embark on an adventure. 'What's tha want to talk to me abaat fust, then, Mester Phinn, mi readin', mi writin' or mi design technology?'

'You're a confident lad and no mistake,' I told him.

'Aye, well, mi granddad says not to be backwards in comin' for'ards. "Allus speak tha mind. Say what tha's got to say and then shurrup." That's what he says.'

'Very true. Shall we start with that incredible construction of yours, then, William? Is it a factory of some sort?'

'Nay, nay, Mester Phinn, it's an oil refinery. I like doin' models. I'll show you mi abattoir later on, if tha likes. It's got caging pens, holding area, slaughter chamber—'

'Yes, I'd like that,' I replied, trying to sound enthusiastic.

William then explained to me, in some detail, the workings of an oil refinery, asking me finally if I had understood.

When we got to the reading, the boy opened the heavy tome, sliding his second finger along the top of the page and running it behind like a seasoned reader.

'Who taught you to turn pages like that, William?' I asked.

'Granddad. He's a gret reader is mi granddad. Can't get enough books. When we goes to t'library, he gets reight cross when he oppens a book and sees all them grubby thumb marks on t'bottom o' pages. He reckons you 'ave to 'ave respect for books. That's how yer turn the pages of a book, tha knaas, from t'top.'

'Yes, that's right,' I agreed.

''Old a book in your 'and and you're a pilgrim at t'gates of a new city.'

I was stunned into silence. 'What was that you said?'

'Hebrew proverb,' said the boy, scratching the thick thatch of black hair. 'Learnt it off mi granddad. He's a gret one for proverbs and psalms, is mi granddad. He's a preacher, tha knaas. Methodist. He reads his Bible every neet. He reckons that John Wesley learnt to read upside-down. 'As thy 'eard o' John Wesley?'

'I have indeed,' I told him.

'Amazin' man was John Wesley. He was one o' nineteen children.'

'Really? I didn't know that.'

'They say he travelled near on a quarter of a million miles on his 'orse bringing t'word of God to folks. Spent a lot o' time in Yorkshire did John Wesley.'

'Amazing.'

'Mi granddad reads Bible to me. I know all t'stories: Samson, Daniel in t'lions' den, Moses, Noah, Jacob, Joseph. There's some lively stuff in t'Bible.'

'And which is your favourite Bible story?' I asked.

'Waay, it 'ud 'ave to be David and Goliath. It's a cracking good tale, i'n't it? Old Goliath comes ovver dale, huffin' and puffin' and waving' his reight big sword abaat like there's no tomorra and tellin' t'Israelites to send out their champion. Out comes little David, wi' nowt but a slingshot in 'is 'and. "Waaaaay!" rooars old Goliath. "Tha must be jokin'. Is this t'best thy lot can do? Little squirt like thee! I could tread on thee and squash thee. I could breathe on thee and blow thee into t'next week. I'm not feightin' thee." Anyroad, David says to 'im, "I'm thee man," and he reaches into t'beck and pulls out a pebble t'size of a pullet egg and pops it in 'is slingshot and lets fly. By the 'eck it di'n't 'arf shift and it 'its old Goliath smack between 'is eyes.'

'That must have really hurt him,' I ventured.

''Urt 'im? 'Urt 'im?' the boy cried. 'It ruddy well killed 'im!'

I looked down and tried to suppress my laughter. 'Well, what about this book of yours, then, William? Tell me a little bit about it and then perhaps you would like to read me a page.'

'I can do that wi'out any trouble at all, Mester Phinn,' he told me confidently. 'This book is abaat exploration in t'Arctic.' The boy cleared his throat noisily and began, his body hunched and his face close to the page, '"The gale raged about the tent. Captain Scott decided that they must continue with the march despite the appalling weather. To stay there would have meant certain death. Facing chasms and crevasses, thick-crusted snow and mountains of ice, the explorers plodded on. Their fingers were numb with cold and their feet frozen beyond feeling. Slipping and falling, sliding and stumbling, plunging blindly into yawning ravines and escaping only by a miracle, Captain Scott and his party marched onwards."' The boy paused. 'He's a gret one for t'verbs, this writer, i'n't he?'

'He is,' I agreed, chuckling.

'Not so 'ot on t'adjectives, though.'

'No,' I agreed, thinking that Mr Spencer-Hall's lesson had had some impact.

'He died, Captain Scott. He were found frozzen to deeath.'

'Oh yes, I know. It was a very sad end. But it's a marvellous story, isn't it, William? A story of great courage and determination.'

'It is that,' agreed the boy. 'It is that.'

'And you're a grand reader, William.'

'Aye, I'm not too bad, even if I says so mi'self.'

The boy's folder was impressive. There were stories and vivid descriptions, anecdotes and lively accounts. It was clear that Mr Spencer-Hall had taught his pupils well.

One poem in William's folder appealed to me in particular. 'I guess this is about this remarkable granddad of yours, William.'

'It is that,' said the boy. 'And he were reight chuffed wi'it an' all. It's called "T' Dalesman".'

'I'm sure he was. Would you read it for me?'

William coughed and read:

> 'Old man, sitting on the stile,
> Hands like roots and haystack hair,
> Smoky beard and sunshine smile,
> He doesn't have a single care.
>
> 'Old man, staring at the bield,
> Falcon-nosed and raven's eye,
> Thin as the scarecrow in his field,
> He stands and sees the world go by.'

'What's a "bield", William?' I asked.

'Tha not from around here, then? An "off-comed-un", are you?'

Since starting work in rural Yorkshire, I had been called this more times than I can remember—someone from out of the dale, a foreigner. 'I am indeed an "off-comed-un",' I admitted.

'Sometimes in a field tha'll see a wall,' the boy explained. 'It gus noweer, it dunt divide owt, it just stands theer, just a bit o' dry-stone wall. People passing—"off-comed-uns", visitors and the like—they often wonder what the heck it is.'

'Well, what is it, William?' I asked.

'I'm just abaat to tell thee, Mester Phinn. That bit o' wall is a "bield". It's for t'sheep to get behind for a bit o' shelter when t'wind lashes at 'em and rain soaks 'em through. It's a sort of refuge.'

'I see. Well, that's something I've learned this morning.'

'Mi granddad says you nivver stop learnin'.'

I tested William on his spelling and grammar and was well satisfied.

'It's been a real pleasure talking to you,' I told him, closing the folder of work.

'Likewise, Mester Phinn,' he replied. Then, getting to his feet, he patted me on the back as a grandfather might do to his grandson. 'Tek care,' he said, 'and if tha wants to see mi abattoir, it's in t'corner.' Then he departed, whistling merrily as he went.

I added yet another word—'bield'—to my Yorkshire vocabulary, writing it down in my little black book alongside 'arran' (spider), 'barfin' (horse collar), 'biddy' (louse), 'chippy' (starling), 'fuzzock' (donkey) and other wonderfully rich words of dialect.

AT MORNING PLAYTIME I joined Mrs McCardle in her room.

'Your face was a picture with little Melissa and no mistake,' the headteacher told me, smiling. 'You looked completely stunned. Anyway, how did you find Mr Spencer-Hall and his class?'

'Well, the junior children seem to be doing well,' I replied, 'and standards are pretty good. I'll be sending a report next week and will call in again when you have had a chance to read my recommendations.'

'I'm pleased to hear that,' said the headteacher. 'Mr Spencer-Hall's been like a cat on a hot tin roof since he heard you were coming, whittling and worrying and moaning and groaning. He's a bit long in the tooth and has been here many years, but he works hard, prepares his lessons well and the children produce some very praiseworthy work. Sometimes his Prophet of Doom manner is a bit tiresome but his heart's in the right place.'

IN THE INFANT classroom, to which I returned later that morning, the children were busily engaged writing their stories about insects.

One child, tongue stuck out in concentration, was colouring in a grey spidery-legged creature.

'Daddy longlegs?' I remarked.

'Crane fly,' she corrected, pertly.

'Ah yes.'

I came again upon Melissa who was putting the finishing touches to her story about the lonely beetle and his amorous adventures on the compost heap. I asked her how she was getting on.

'It's going very well, thank you,' she told me.

'I would love to see it when it's finished.'

Next to her was an awkward-looking boy with spectacles and big ears. He was sitting in thoughtful silence, his elbows on the desk, his hands propping his chin. 'I'm just thinking for a minute,' he told me seriously. 'My story's about a bee who's lost his buzz and can't find his way back to the hive but I don't know how to spell "nectar".'

'Well, don't bother asking Mr Phinn,' chipped in Melissa, 'he's not very good at spelling, are you, Mr Phinn?'

TWO

Soon after the schools had broken up for summer the previous July, I had taken a few days off to visit my parents in Rotherham. I returned to face a pyramid of paper which had to be dealt with before I could escape for some holiday. However, as I sat there staring at the daunting pile, I thought about the school year we had just finished. I had arranged courses and conferences, directed workshops, carried out surveys, advised school governors and hosted important visitors from the Ministry of Education—all this in addition to inspecting schools. But I reckoned it would be dull indeed compared to the year that lay ahead, which promised to be the most exciting one in my life so far. For, at the end of the previous term, I had asked the woman I loved to marry me and—bingo!—she had said yes.

On that July morning, I had arrived early at the inspectors' office, in buoyant mood despite the dismal, rain-soaked landscape that had rolled past the car window as I drove the short distance from my flat above the Rumbling Tum Café in Fettlesham High Street to County Hall. The room that I shared with my inspector colleagues was cramped and cluttered. There were four heavy oak desks, four ancient ladder-back swivel chairs, four grey metal filing cabinets and a wall of dark bookcases crammed with books, journals and files.

Just as I was about to tackle the pile of paper, there was a clattering on the stairs signalling the imminent arrival of Julie, the inspectors' secretary, in the ridiculously high-heeled shoes she was fond of wearing. Julie, with her bubbly blonde hair, bright smile and constant chatter, brightened up even the dullest of days. She was wonderfully efficient and her ready wit combined with Yorkshire bluntness helped her to keep the school inspectors in order.

Besides myself, in charge of English and drama, there was Sidney Clamp, the immensely creative but entirely unpredictable and sometimes outrageous inspector in charge of creative and visual arts; David Pritchard, the lively little Welshman responsible for mathematics, PE and games, who fired words at all and sundry like a machine gun, and Dr Geraldine Mullarkey, the newest and quietest member of our team, in charge of science and technology. Down the corridor was our team leader, Dr Harold Yeats, the Senior Inspector, one of the gentlest and kindest of people it has been my pleasure to know.

Julie bustled in loaded down as usual with various bags. She was soaking wet and windswept. 'So what happened to summer, then?' she asked as she dropped the dripping bags on an empty desk. 'July? It's more like the monsoon season.' She shook herself like a dog emerging from the sea. 'Why is it that the only time I forget my umbrella, the heavens open? And why is it that madmen in cars wait until you cross the road before they drive through the puddles? I must look like something the cat brought in.'

'Good morning, Julie,' I said, getting up to help her off with her saturated jacket, then hanging it over a chair to dry.

'Thanks,' she said. 'What are you in so early for? It's only just after nine. Schools have broken up, you know. You don't need to get in here at the crack of dawn.'

'I intended to make a start on all this paperwork,' I said, gesturing at the mountain before me, 'but haven't got very far. Look, you go and dry off and I'll make some coffee.'

'Ta, I will.' She headed for the door but stopped suddenly, turned and gave me a knowing smile. 'Oh, what about *you*, then? Bit of a dark horse, aren't you? I hear wedding bells are in the air.'

'Oh, that. Yes. Christine and I are getting married.'

I had first met Miss Christine Bentley, headteacher of Winnery Nook Nursery and Infant School when, as a newly appointed inspector, I had visited her school some two years before. Christine had the deepest blue eyes, the softest mass of golden hair and the smoothest complexion I had ever seen. It had been love at first sight, and the more I had got to know her, the deeper that love became. I just could not get her out of my mind. Now she was to be my wife.

'Congratulations,' Julie said, interrupting my thoughts. 'It was about time you asked her.'

'How did you know?'

'You really don't imagine that news like that stays a secret for long at County Hall, do you? The jungle telegraph was going the day after you proposed.'

'I don't see how anybody could have known,' I said, puzzled.

'Haven't you forgotten about the Queen of the Jungle?' There was a wild gleam in Julie's eye. 'That dreadful woman was on the tom-toms in no time. It's a wonder she didn't send out one of her mile-long memos letting everyone know.'

'Ah,' I sighed, 'I'd forgotten about Mrs Savage.'

'I wish I could,' remarked Julie wistfully.

Mrs Brenda Savage, personal assistant to Dr Gore, the Chief Education Officer, was humourless, patronising and liked her red-nailed fingers in every pie around. She was also very fond of her own voice and all of us had been on the receiving end of her sharp tongue.

'Anyway,' asked Julie, gathering up the wet bags off the desktop, 'how did the Black Widow find out?'

I explained to Julie that I had proposed to Christine on the last day of term in what I thought would be a secluded restaurant in the little Dales village of Ribsdyke. By sheer coincidence, Dr Gore and Mrs Savage had been having dinner there as well and had witnessed my hysterically happy outburst when Christine had said, 'I will.'

With a thud, Julie dropped the bags back onto the desk, put her hands on her hips and said sharply, 'Well, what was *she* doing having dinner with Dr Gore?'

'You'll have to ask her that,' I teased.

'Ask *her*?' Julie screwed up her face. 'I'd as soon play "Postman's Knock" with a sex-starved crocodile. That woman treats me as if I was something discovered on the sole of her shoe. Anybody would think she was secretary of the United Nations the way she carries on. She forgets that some people remember her before she had that face job and when her voice didn't sound like the Queen being garrotted and when that hair of hers was natural and wasn't out of a bottle. As my mother says, "You can never escape your roots."'

'Well, who knows, she might very well be the future Mrs Gore,' I said mischievously. 'They seemed to be getting on very well.'

'No!' gasped Julie. 'You don't think she's getting her hooks into Dr Gore, do you? She's been through three husbands. That would be awful. She's bad enough now, but if she married the CEO she'd be unbearable. She'd be lording it—'

Julie's monologue was interrupted by the shrill ringing of the telephone on my desk. I picked it up. 'Hello, Gervase Phinn here.'

It was the woman herself. 'Good morning, Mr Phinn, Brenda Savage here,' she said with slow deliberation. I waited but there was no 'How are you?' or 'Congratulations on your forthcoming marriage.' She was her predictably cold, formal self. 'Are you still there?'

'Good morning, Mrs Savage,' I replied cheerfully, grinning in Julie's direction. 'What can I do for you?'

Julie took a blustering breath and left the office. '*I'll* make the coffee,' she said on the way out, 'and I'll put plenty of brandy in it.'

'Mr Phinn,' continued Mrs Savage slowly, 'I don't appear to have the inspectors' programmes for next week.'

'Really?' I said.

'I have mentioned to you all, on numerous occasions, how very important it is to have details of the inspectors' timetables in case Dr Gore or one of the councillors needs to make urgent contact.' I attempted to inform her that since schools were on holiday we would all be in the office and that filling in the forms would be a waste of time, but she carried on regardless. 'I have rung Dr Yeats's number several times but there is no response. Could you inform him, when he does arrive, that it is imperative that I have the programmes on my desk by the end of the day? I do not have the time to be constantly reminding you inspectors about these matters. Now, I have work to attend to,' she said, as if I were deliberately detaining her, and, without waiting for a reply, she ended the call.

'Insufferable woman,' I muttered to myself.

'What did Lady Macbeth want, then?' Julie asked, returning with two mugs of coffee which she set down on the desk in front of me. She wore no shoes and her hair, which had dried out a little, looked wild and wiry.

'The inspectors' programmes.'

'Well, she can wait,' Julie said bluntly, straightening her crumpled skirt. 'Why should you be at her beck and call? She's got legs. Wouldn't do her any harm to come and get them. She's got little else to do all day except sharpen her nails.'

'I must say, I thought Harold would be in by now,' I said.

'He usually is,' replied Julie, cupping her hands round a mug. 'But he hasn't been around for a couple of days. I hope he's all right. I found him in his office one day last week, just staring into space. And I even found a couple of mistakes in his last report, not up to his usual meticulous standard. If you ask me, something's bothering him.'

'We have our inspectors' meeting later today,' I told her, 'so I'll find a minute to have a quiet word with him then.'

As THE CLOCK on the County Hall tower struck ten, Sidney and David arrived. I could hear them squabbling like schoolboys all the way up the stairs. The door burst open and Sidney made his usual dramatic entrance, followed closely by David, clutching a wet umbrella. I might have been invisible for all the notice they took of me.

'You're like a Welsh terrier, David,' Sidney was saying, waving his large hands expansively. 'You *will* persist in your pedestrian views like a snappy little dog worrying a rabbit. You just won't let it lie.'

David hooked his umbrella on a shelf, tucked his briefcase away, sat down, and took a deep breath. 'The trouble is, Sidney,' he said in a measured voice, 'you never like anyone to disagree with you. You are unable to accept that just for once you may not be the fount of all knowledge. As my Welsh grandmother used to say—'

'Oh, save me from Celtic words of wisdom,' interrupted Sidney. 'This Welsh grandmother of yours sounds a pain in the neck. I would have consigned her to an old folks' home years ago.'

'As my dear and very much loved Welsh grandmother used to say,' said David, undeterred by the interruption, '"Just because someone talks with conviction and enthusiasm doesn't mean they know what they're talking about. Fancy words butter no parsnips."'

'Good morning, David. Good morning, Sidney. Now, what's all this arguing about?' I asked.

'We are not arguing, Gervase, we are having a professional disagreement,' explained Sidney. 'David is saying that I don't know what I'm talking about when it comes to art, which is, as you know, my specialist subject.'

'I am merely saying,' said David, 'that I am entitled to have a view.'

'Well, let's ask Gervase,' said Sidney, rattling the change in his pocket and staring out of the window. 'Listen, Gervase, would you accept that I know more about art than David?'

'Well, I suppose so but—' I began.

'Which, of course, is not really surprising since I have a master's degree in the subject.'

David lifted both hands to his face, took off his spectacles and folded them on the desk in front of him and breathed loudly through his nose. 'Yes, but the point is—'

'Do stop making that infernal blowing noise, David,' interrupted Sidney yet again, 'you sound like an asthmatic whale. Now, as you agree that I know more about art than you do . . .'

At which point Julie arrived at the door. ''Morning,' she said.

'Good morning, Julie,' said David.

'Good God, Julie!' exclaimed Sidney rising from his chair. 'Whatever have you done to your hair? It looks as if you've had your head in a spin-dryer.'

Julie ignored Sidney's remark. 'Do you want coffee?' she asked.

'That would be splendid,' said David. 'Then if Mr Clamp will leave me alone, I shall make a start on my in-tray.'

'The thing is, David,' Sidney interrupted, 'I do not profess to possess a deep-seated knowledge about mathematics, therefore I keep my own counsel. I am somewhat tentative about making pronouncements about things of which I know little. You, on the other hand—'

Julie turned to me and said, 'Aren't you going to tell them the news?'

'Well, I would have,' I replied, 'if I had been able to get a word in.'

'Don't give me any bad news,' said Sidney, sitting back down. 'It's the school holidays and I don't want bad news, extra work, contentious issues, problems or difficulties. I have had enough of those this year. I intend clearing my desk and then spending two glorious weeks in Italy. Well, what is this news that is so important?'

'I'm getting married,' I said.

'Dear boy!' exclaimed Sidney, jumping from his chair and thumping me vigorously on the back. 'Why ever didn't you say? What wonderful news! Well done! At last, you are to make delectable Miss Christine Bentley of Winnery Nook, the Aphrodite of the education world, the Venus of Fettlesham, an honest woman.'

'Congratulations, Gervase,' said David, reaching over to shake my hand. 'You are made for each other. And when is the big day?'

'We're thinking of next April,' I replied.

'Not hanging about, are you?' observed Julie.

'You're quite right not to wait,' Sidney remarked, leaning back expansively in his chair. 'I mean, neither of you are spring chickens. If you're thinking of starting a family you need to get cracking.'

'Now he's an expert on marital affairs,' snorted David. 'If I were you, Gervase, I would take his comments with a great pinch of salt.'

'You see,' spluttered Sidney, 'just like a snappy little Welsh terrier.'

'Hush a moment,' commanded David, raising a hand. 'If I am not mistaken, those fairy footsteps on the stairs tell us our esteemed leader is on his way up.'

Harold Yeats, Senior County Inspector, was a bear of a man, well over six foot tall, with a great jutting bulldog jaw. With his broad shoulders, arched chest and hands like spades, he looked more like an underworld enforcer than a school inspector. But Harold was a gentle giant, warm-hearted, generous and courteous to all. He also had encyclopaedic knowledge and an amazing memory.

'Harold!' boomed Sidney as he caught sight of him at the door. 'Gervase is to tie the knot.'

Harold smile warmly, and shook my hand. 'Yes, yes, I heard from Dr Gore this morning. Congratulations, Gervase. She's a lovely young woman, Miss Bentley. You are a very lucky man.'

'Dr Yeats,' said Julie, 'did Brenda the barracuda find you?'

'The *what*?' asked Harold, his brow furrowing.

'Mrs Savage. She wants the inspectors' programmes for next week.'

'Ah, yes, I did see her when I was leaving Dr Gore's office and she mentioned something of the sort. But that can wait. Now, look everyone, would you all sit down for a moment, there's something very important I have to say. I did think of waiting to tell you at a full team meeting but, as you know, Geraldine is at a conference in York this week so won't be able to join us.'

'I was wondering where our pale Irish beauty was,' remarked Sidney. 'She's not the most forthcoming of people. I had no idea she was away this week.'

'Well, she is,' said Harold. 'Anyhow, if you would all give me your attention . . .'

'If it's bad news, Harold,' said Sidney, 'I don't want to know.'

Harold gave a weak smile. 'Well, Sidney, I don't know whether it's good or bad news to be honest.' He paused and touched his brow with his long fingers. 'I'm going to retire.'

'*Retire?*' we all shouted in unison.

'That's right. Dr Gore has asked me to see out the next academic year which is only fair. That gives him the chance of advertising my job, short-listing and interviewing in good time for my replacement to start next September. That's why I was with Dr Gore this morning.'

'Whatever has brought this on?' exclaimed David.

'I've been thinking about it for some time,' said Harold.

'But why, Harold?' I asked. Are you all right, physically, I mean?'

'Oh yes, I'm fine, there's nothing wrong with me—apart from feeling things are getting a bit too much. I've been reviewing things a little lately, my future, what I want to do with the rest of my life and, to be frank, I'm ready to finish.'

Julie arched an eyebrow and gave me a knowing look.

'You can't finish, Harold!' snapped Sidney. 'It's out of the question.'

'Yes, I can, Sidney,' said Harold softly. 'I've had enough. Last term was particularly difficult. The increased number of inspections and the additional demands from the Ministry. I'm tired, Sidney. All those conferences away from home, weekend courses, lengthy reports, inspections and late nights attending this, that and the other. I'm ready to pass the baton to a younger person with more stamina.'

'We all feel tired at the end of a busy term, Harold,' I said. 'You'll feel a whole lot better after a holiday and a good rest.'

'Exactly,' agreed Sidney. 'Now, put further thoughts of retiring from your mind.'

'I'm afraid I can't do that,' said Harold. 'I have made up my mind.'

'Good God, you're serious,' whispered Sidney.

'Well, I'm devastated,' said David. 'I don't mind saying so. I'm completely lost for words.'

'Hasn't that old Welsh grandmother of yours got an apt little saying for the occasion?' asked Sidney.

'I suppose she'd say what she said about Lloyd George,' said David sadly. 'We will never see his like again.'

'That's most kind of you, David,' said Harold, 'but life does go on. None of us is indispensable.'

'This is a shock, Harold,' I said. 'It really is.'

'It's quite dreadful news, dreadful,' continued Sidney. 'I feel physically sick. And I'll probably hate your replacement.'

'You not get on with people?' said David. 'The very idea.'

'I suppose the person taking over could be an internal promotion, someone on the team already,' said Sidney. 'What about Gervase taking over? He could do it.'

'Now hold on,' I said hurriedly.

'That is really not for me to say, Sidney,' said Harold. 'The post will be advertised and Gervase's application, should he wish to apply, will be considered along with the rest.'

'But you could put a good word in with the powers that be, Harold,' persisted Sidney.

'You overestimate my influence, Sidney,' replied Harold.

'Now, the suggestion of Gervase having a go for the job,' said David thoughtfully, 'is certainly something on which we could agree, Sidney. "Better the devil you know", as my grandmother was wont to remark.'

'Do I get a say in all this?' I asked. Before anyone could answer, the telephone on my desk rang and I snatched it up. 'Yes, Mrs Savage, Dr Yeats is here. I'll pass you over to him.'

For the remainder of the day I attempted to knuckle down to the work of clearing my desk, but my thoughts kept wandering back to Harold's shock announcement. 'What about Gervase taking over?' Sidney had said. I would have to think long and hard about that one.

THREE

Connie, the caretaker of the Staff Development Centre, was a down-to-earth Yorkshire woman with an acerbic wit and a habit of using the most inventive malapropisms. She had no conception of rank, and treated everyone the same—with a bluntness bordering on the rude. If the Pope were to pay a visit to the Staff Development Centre and make use of the washroom facilities, Connie would no doubt detain His Holiness as he departed, with the words: 'I hope you've left them Gents as you found them!' It was Connie who was at the controls when people were on her territory.

She could be quite unnerving. During the coffee break, teachers attending courses at the Centre would find an ample woman with a bright copper-coloured perm, dressed in a brilliant pink nylon over-all, surveying them with a malevolent expression. At lunchtime they would sense that small sharp eyes were watching from behind the serving hatch, making certain not a crumb from their sandwiches fell on the spotless carpet. And, at the end of the day, Connie would stride around her empire, feather duster held like a field-marshal's baton, to make sure that everything was left as it had been found.

The Staff Development Centre, where all the courses and confer-ences for teachers took place, was a tribute to Connie's hard work and dedication. Not a speck of dust was to be seen anywhere and the building always smelt of lavender furniture polish and carbolic soap.

Everyone who knew her was prepared to tolerate her abrupt manner and sharp tongue—for everyone knew that deep down she had a heart of gold—everyone, that is, except Sidney. Sidney—noisy, unpredictable, untidy, madly creative—was guaranteed to ruffle the feathers of her duster and wind Connie up to distraction.

I arrived at the SDC one dull Friday afternoon in the third week of the new term to prepare for an English course I was to direct the fol-lowing Monday. In the entrance hall stood Connie, in fierce discus-sion with the man himself. She was dressed, as usual, in her pink nylon overall and was clutching her feather duster magisterially.

'Look here, Connie,' Sidney was explaining to her, 'you have to accept a bit of mess. Art is not like mathematics, you know, it's not orderly, it's not methodical, it's not tidy. We artists use messy materi-als like paints, charcoals, crayons, clay, cardboard, glue, pencils, paper.' He waved his hands about theatrically. 'People have to express themselves, and they are therefore often untidy. It's par for the course.'

Connie pulled one of her many expressions of distaste, the face of someone suffering from acute indigestion. 'Well, it's not part of *my* course, Mr Clamp, and I don't want these artists, as you call them, expressing themselves like that in *my* Centre. They can clear up after themselves. They don't need to leave a trail of debris and destruction behind like what they have this afternoon.'

'Hardly a trail of debris and destruction,' sighed Sidney.

'Oh, yes, they did, Mr Clamp, and I can't be doing with it. Even my little grandson wouldn't leave a mess like that.'

'Einstein said that genius is seldom tidy.'

'I don't care what Einstein or any of your other artificated friends have to say. I am not cleaning up that mess and that's that. It's all very well for you and this Einstein to leave the room as if a bomb has hit it, I'm the one left to pick up the pieces. I'm telling you, it's just not fair to expect me to do it, Mr Clamp. You could have eaten your dinner off of that floor this morning, and look at it now. Anyway,' she said, flourishing her feather duster along a window ledge, 'it's my bingo night and I'm not missing the first house just because I have to stop here to clear up.'

'Good afternoon,' I said loudly, determined to get their attention.

'Hello, Gervase,' moaned Sidney.

'Good afternoon,' said Connie through tight little lips. 'Anyhow, I've said what I had to say, Mr Clamp. It's no skin off my feet if it is just left, but you'd be complaining if you found the room like that at the start of *your* course.'

'Very well, Connie,' Sidney told her, bowing with a flourish. 'I give in. I surrender. I yield. I shall remain behind and return the art room to its pristine splendour and perhaps my kind and obliging colleague here will lend a helpful hand.'

'Oh, no!' I spluttered. 'I'm sorry, Sidney, but I have a course to prepare and then I'm meeting Christine at Mama's Pizza Parlour. You're on your own.'

'What happened to friendship and camaraderie?' asked Sidney to no one in particular. 'Whither the Good Samaritan?'

'He probably didn't have a date and it wasn't his bingo night,' I replied flippantly.

'Very droll,' said Sidney.

'Well, just so long as it gets done,' came Connie's final riposte before she marched off down the corridor, flicking the feather duster at invisible dust and crackling as she went.

'That woman,' said Sidney through clamped teeth, 'will drive me to drink.'

'Don't judge her too harshly,' I said. 'Her heart's in the right place.'

'The right place for Connie's heart, dear boy,' replied Sidney, 'is on the end of a stake.' With that he departed for the art room.

Having checked the equipment in the English room, set out the chairs, displayed a range of materials and put a programme on each table, I headed for the kitchen. By this time Sidney, who had made an attempt to clear up the mess in the art room, had crept away. Connie was wiping the Formica top in front of the serving hatch.

'I don't know how you can share an office with that Mr Clamp,' she snapped. 'I've never met anyone so untidy. Anyway, have you got everything you need for Monday?'

'Yes, all ready and prepared.'

'I put another bulb in the overhead projector, just to be on the safe side. And I've put out some more felt-tip markers and some extra paper on the flip chart. I know how you like to write.'

'Thank you, Connie.'

'Do you want a cup of tea?'

I glanced at my watch. I had a bit of time to kill before meeting Christine. 'Yes, thanks.'

As Connie clanked and clattered in a cupboard, I asked, 'So, was your summer holiday better than last year?' Connie had had a disastrous time in Ireland the previous summer.

'We didn't go nowhere this year,' she said, prising the top off a large tin of biscuits, 'except for a couple of weekends in the caravan at Filey, and then it rained all the time.' She adopted another expression from her extensive repertoire. 'My father went into hospital and I was traipsing back and forth for most of the time.'

'I'm sorry to hear that, Connie,' I said. 'Is it serious?'

'He had a stroke. He was at the Legion playing dominoes when it happened. Next thing he was in casualty and he's been in ever since. He's getting on, you know. Ninety-two next birthday and he still lives on his own. He's very independent is Dad, and been fit as a butcher's dog until now. He smokes like a chimney, eats a full fried breakfast every morning, black pudding included, and he likes a drink. The doctor said it had caught up with him. I said to the doctor, "Well, whatever it is that's caught up with him, it's took its time." "You have to expect these things at his time of life," says he.

"Yes, well, that's as may be," I told him, "but I want my father looking after. I don't want any of this euthenoria business you read about. If he goes into one of them comas," I told him, "don't you dare turn him off. He fought for his king and country. He deserves top treatment, the RIP sort." That's what I told him.'

'So he's still in hospital, you say?' I asked, suppressing a smile.

'Yes. Mind you, he's a lot better than he was when he went in. He was sitting up and entertaining the nurses when I last saw him.'

'Well, that's good news,' I said. 'Perhaps it won't be too long before he's home.'

'Oh yes, well, we'll just have to hope and pray. He was wanting to go to the Cenotaph in London again this year with his British Legion pals. He's a Dunkirk veteran, you know. He always looks forward to his trip to London, all dressed up in his blazer wearing his medals. I'm so proud of him when I see them marching past the Cenotaph. They want to get some of these young hooligans in the army. They have no appreciation or gratitude for what the older generation did for them.' Connie began pouring the tea.

'Well, I hope he'll be home soon,' I said again, accepting the proffered mug. I decided it was time to change the subject. 'I'm getting married, you know.'

'You're not, are you?' she gasped, pausing in her pouring. 'Is it that nice young woman with the blonde hair, Miss Bentley?'

'Well, it's not likely to be anyone else, Connie, is it?' I laughed. 'I'm not exactly your Casanova.'

'Well, I hope you and Miss Bentley will be very happy.'

'Thanks, Connie.'

'You've not known her that long, have you? In my day, we used to walk out together for a few years before we got married. I think the reason for all the divorces these days is that people rush into it.'

'I've been going out with Christine for nearly two years.'

'That doesn't mean a thing. No, gone are the days of long courtships and getting engaged and asking fathers for a daughter's hand. These days, most people don't seem to bother with marriage. They "live over the brush", as my mother would say. They don't have husbands and wives nowadays, they have partners. I ask you! Take my cousin's girl. She's at West Challerton High, supposed to be doing her exams this year. She changes her boyfriends as often as she changes her knickers. I said to my cousin, "It'll end in grief, you mark my words."' Connie took a gulp of tea and grimaced. 'Ted and me have been married for thirty-five years, you know, and hardly a cross word has passed between us.' I had met Ted on a few occasions. He was a small, quiet man with a permanently worried expression. I guessed that Connie's long-suffering husband had thrown in the towel years ago.

Connie picked a biscuit out of the tin. 'I'm glad you've called in today because I wanted to have a quiet word with you about Miss Pilkington.'

Miss Pilkington was the headteacher of Willingforth Primary, the school that Connie's grandchildren, Damien and Lucy, attended. Connie always described her in glowing terms.

'What about Miss Pilkington?' I asked now.

'She's having a bit of trouble at the moment. I'm not one for gossip, but I do think one of you inspectors ought to call in.'

'Well, it's funny that you should mention Willingforth,' I said. 'I've had a request from Miss Pilkington to go and see her next week.'

'Ah well, that's it then. I'll say no more.' She took a gulp of tea. 'But if they don't remove him, there'll be fireworks.'

'Remove him?' I repeated, intrigued.

'As I said, I'm not a hot gossiper, but my Lucy came home at the beginning of this term with tales that would make your hair curl. There's this new boy. Terry they call him. Terry the Terror. He's rude, badly behaved and my Lucy says he spits and swears. Miss Pilkington's at the end of her tether with this lad, so my daughter tells me.' Connie took a gulp of tea. 'There's moves afoot.'

'Moves?'

'To have him sent to another school.'

'Well, I'm going to be there next week, Connie,' I told her. 'Thanks for the tea. I'll see you on Monday.'

HALF AN HOUR LATER, I was sitting at a corner table in Mama's Pizza Parlour, a small, atmospheric restaurant, tucked away down an alleyway just off Fettlesham High Street, waiting for Christine.

As the clock struck six Christine arrived. She made heads turn as she walked towards me.

'Excuse me, young man,' she said, 'may I join you?'

'Of course,' I replied, 'but I must warn you, I find you a devilishly attractive woman and I might just leap over the table and have my wicked way with you.'

'Sssh,' she said, laughing, 'people will hear. Have you been waiting long for me?'

'All my life,' I sighed. 'Let me swim in those limpid pools that are your eyes, hold your lithe body in my arms and smother hot kisses on those yielding lips.'

'Will you be serious! If you won't be sensible I shall pour this jug of water over you. That should cool your burning ardour.'

How lovely she is, I thought to myself as I looked at my wife-to-be across the table. What a lucky man I am.

'So how's Harold?' Christine asked, glancing down the menu.

'Oh, he's fine. I told him at the beginning of the school holidays, when he looked worn out, that the summer break would recharge his batteries. He certainly seems back to his old self.'

I had told her of Harold's intention to retire at the end of the school year and had raised with her the possibility of my applying for his job. She had been less than enthusiastic, suggesting I would have enough on my plate with a new wife and a new house, without taking on additional responsibilities.

'Of course, I'll back you if you really want to go for it,' she had told me. 'But don't you think it's a bit soon for you to start applying for a senior position like that? Think of all the extra work. I would like to see my husband other than just at the weekend.'

I had been thinking about it a great deal since Harold had made the shock announcement a couple of months before, and it was clear that it had also been on Christine's mind.

'Perhaps he'll change his mind about retiring,' she added now.

'No, I don't think so. He's pretty determined.'

'And are you?' asked Christine, looking up from the menu.

'Am I what?'

'Determined—to apply for this job?'

I opened my mouth to answer but the waiter arrived at the table with a bottle of champagne in a silver bucket.

'For you, madam, and you, sir,' he said.

'Oh, how lovely!' cried Christine. 'What a nice thought.' She leaned over the table and squeezed my hand.

'I didn't order any champagne,' I said.

'A gentleman called in earlier,' the waiter informed me. 'It is with his compliments.' He plucked a card from his waistcoat pocket and placed it on the table before me.

Congratulations, it said in a large, unmistakable script, *on capturing the most beautiful woman in Yorkshire. I am sure you will both be idyllically happy. Give Christine a kiss for me. SC.*

'Sidney,' I said, shaking my head and smiling. I passed Christine the card.

'How sweet of him.'

After the waiter had opened the champagne and poured us both a glass, I toasted my future wife. 'To us, and to what lies ahead.'

Her blue eyes shone. 'To us.' And we clinked glasses.

After the first exhilarating sip of bubbly wine, I said, 'Look, Christine, I've not really made up my mind about applying but I am certainly not ruling it out.'

She reached across the table and took my hand again. 'Gervase, I don't see all that much of you now. What is it going to be like if you have Harold's workload? And Sidney and David . . . You get on really well with them as colleagues, but what if you become their boss? I should imagine they can be something of a nightmare to manage. I just want you to give it some serious thought.'

'I will, I promise.' I changed the subject. 'Now, what about tomorrow? Are we still house hunting?'

FOUR

Willingforth Primary School was an imposing grey-stone Georgian building with high leaded windows and a large oak-panelled door. To the front was a small, well-tended lawn with a sun-dial and tubs of bright geraniums. A casual visitor to the village, strolling past, would have no idea that this was a school. There was no playground or notice board, no noise of boisterous children.

The door opened onto one large, bright classroom. In one corner, on a square of carpet, were three fat reading cushions and a small bookcase filled with picture books. On the wall above, in pride of place, was a large coloured sampler decorated with the motto: STRAIGHT WORDS, STRAIGHT DEEDS, STRAIGHT BACKS. The children, sitting on straight-backed wooden chairs, worked at highly polished desks with lids and holes for inkwells. The view of the dale from the window was breathtaking. Acre upon acre of fields, crisscrossed by limestone walls, sloped upwards to a long scar of white rock, wind-scoured and craggy. In the distance clouds oozed over the felltops.

At the request of the headteacher, Miss Pilkington, I was at the school very early that mild autumn day. I had received a blow-by-blow account of Miss Pilkington well before I had met her some two years before. Connie, my informant, had described her as 'one of the old school'. I had rather expected a dragon of a woman, with cold piercing eyes behind steel-rimmed spectacles. But I was wrong. Miss Pilkington had turned out to be a tall, elegant woman, probably in her late forties. Her lessons were well planned, she had extremely good subject knowledge and an excellent relationship with the children.

From my conversation with Connie at the SDC the week before, I knew what this latest visit was likely to be about.

The headteacher was waiting to greet me, dressed in a well-cut suit and cream silk scarf. She looked rather pale and drawn.

'Good morning, Mr Phinn. It's very nice to see you again. I am so grateful that you have come out so early. I really do need your advice.'

'I'm here to listen, Miss Pilkington,' I said.

'Well, shall we sit down? We have about twenty minutes before the children arrive.' She indicated two elegant chairs at the side of the room. 'I really do have something of a problem.' She sat stiffly on one of the chairs and clasped her hands. 'At the beginning of the term, a new boy arrived. Terry Mossup. He is being fostered by a local doctor and her husband and, from what I gather, he is from a very deprived background.' At this point, Miss Pilkington rose from her chair and paced up and down. 'I've been a teacher for twenty-five years and have never ever come across a child like this one. He is just unmanageable. I never thought I would admit this to anyone but he is driving me to distraction. Most of the time he is rude, naughty and destructive, at other times he is totally uncommunicative and just sits there as if in a trance. At one moment he's picking on the other children, refusing to do his work and then a moment later he's taking a spider that he's found and gently putting it outside. He's the only one the cat lets stroke her and he likes nothing better than feeding the birds at playtime. I've had a word with his foster parents, and they have asked me to persevere with him. Oh dear,' she said, swinging round to face me, 'you must think I can't cope.'

'No, not at all,' I hastily reassured her, 'please go on.'

'His foster parents don't want him to go to one of those schools that deals with disruptive pupils. They feel he should feel part of this small community and be treated as a normal little boy. Now, that is all very well, Mr Phinn, but he is not just a normal little boy and I have the other children to think about. I have already had a number of parents complaining and threatening to take their children away from Willingforth unless I . . . well, to be blunt, get rid of him.' Miss Pilkington sat back down on her chair, twisting a handkerchief nervously in her hands. 'The chair of governors, Canon Shepherd, is calling in to see me at lunchtime with one of the parent-governors who has asked for the boy's removal. We have an extraordinary governors' meeting this evening to decide what to do. The canon is all for giving the child a chance but the other governor, who represents the majority view on the governing body, is determined that Terry should go.' She paused to get a breath and when our eyes met, I saw tears. 'I've always believed that children deserve the very best we adults have to give, Mr Phinn, all children, even the very difficult ones. That's why I became a teacher. The boy's file made me weep. It is a catalogue of neglect, mistreatment and deprivation. But Terry is so very, very difficult and, as I said, I do have the other children to think about. Oh dear, I just do not know what to do.'

'Well,' I sighed, 'like you, I don't believe that any child should be put on the scrap heap, written off. But what is certain is that there is no miracle cure, no simple solution. It sounds, however, as though the child does need some specialist help. If he stays here, we could arrange for some classroom support . . . maybe an assistant or additional teacher. Also, I'll have a word with Miss Kinvara, the educational psychologist, and ask her to make a visit. She knows a great deal more than I about children with challenging behaviour.'

'Thank you, that sounds very helpful, but would it be possible, Mr Phinn, for you to stay for the morning so you can see the way Terry behaves, and then attend the meeting at lunchtime with the governors to help us decide what to do?'

'Of course,' I replied.

Miss Pilkington picked up the crumpled handkerchief from her lap, and dabbed her nose. At the noise of excited chatter outside, her back visibly straightened. 'If you'll excuse me a moment, Mr Phinn, I can hear the children arriving. I do like to welcome them each morning.' With that she left the room.

When the children had taken off their coats and changed into their indoor shoes, they sat at their desks ready for the register to be called. All, that is, except one child, a sharp-faced boy of about nine with a scattering of freckles, wavy red hair and a tight little mouth which curved downwards. This, I guessed, was Terry.

'Come along, please, Terry,' said Miss Pilkington, 'take your seat.'

'Who's he, then?' asked the child, pointing in my direction.

'That's Mr Phinn, and please don't point, it's rude.'

'Is he a copper?'

'Just take a seat will you, please, Terry,' said the teacher firmly.

'I can smell coppers a mile off.' The child slumped into a chair.

'He's either a copper or a probation officer.'

'And take what you are chewing out of your mouth, please, Terry,' said Miss Pilkington.

'Haven't finished it yet.'

'Put what you are chewing in here, please, Terry,' said the teacher firmly, holding up a wastepaper basket.

The boy ambled to the front and dropped a bullet of chewing gum in the bin.

What a contrast this morning was compared to my last visit, when I had watched Miss Pilkington outlining to an attentive and interested class the writing task to be undertaken and the children had got on with their work quietly and with genuine enthusiasm. Now the lesson was dominated by Terry who would not sit still, would not do as he was told nor get on with his work. The other children seemed amazingly tolerant of this demanding and disruptive child.

When he had finally been prevailed upon to sit and put something on paper, I approached Terry. He looked up with an aggressive expression on his small face. 'What?' he asked.

'May I look at your work?'

'What for?' He stared coldly at me, like a serpent.

'Because that's what I do for a living.'

'What do you do, then?'

'I'm a school inspector.'

He made a clucking sort of noise and pushed over the paper on which he had been writing. 'It's crap,' he told me.

'Don't use that word,' I told him.

'Why?'

'Because I say so,' I said, looking him straight in the eye. I then began reading what he had written.

'I don't know why you're lookin',' he said. 'It's no good.'

'I'm sure it's not that bad,' I replied, beginning to read.

'It is. I'm rubbish at writing.' He pushed out his lower lip and clenched his eyebrows. 'Anyone can see it's rubbish,' he said.

I tried to decipher the spidery scrawl. 'What's this word?' I asked.

'"Buggered". It says, "I felt buggered."'

'Well, I am sure you can think of a much better word than that.'

'Why?' he asked, defiantly.

'That word is not a very nice word to use.'

'Mi mam uses it. What about "knackered", then?'

'That's as bad,' I said.

'Come on then, what word should I use?'

'Well, you could say that you were very tired or exhausted.'

The boy gave a wry smile. 'Aye, I could I suppose, but it wouldn't sound as good as "buggered", would it?' He read his scrawl in a sing-song sort of voice following each word with grubby finger. '"I got home and flopped onto t'bed. I felt tired and exhausted." That's useless. "Buggered" sounds much better.'

I sighed. 'Perhaps, but it's not a word a child should use.'

'You think I'm daft, don't you?' he said suddenly.

'Not at all,' I assured him. 'I think you are a bright lad, but you need to behave better and not swear or answer back.'

'What you gonna do, then, if I don't? Lock me up? Just 'cos I speaks like this don't mean that I'm daft, you know.'

'I never said you were daft,' I told him. 'What I can't understand is why you don't try and behave yourself?'

'Dunno really. Can't help mi'self.'

'You'd get on a lot better with people if you behaved.'

'S'pose I don't want to get on better wi' people?' he said.

I abandoned the line of questioning and tried another tack. 'Do you like reading?'

'Nope.'

'Music?'

'Nope.'

'What do you like?'

'You asks a bloody lot of questions, don't you?' Before I could respond, he said, mimicking my voice, 'That's another not very nice word for a little boy to use.'

I persevered. 'I hear you like animals.'

'Who told you that?'

'A little bird,' I replied. 'So, you do like animals?' I asked again.

'S'pose so.'

'Why do you like animals?'

He didn't answer immediately but seemed to be lost in thought. 'Because you know where you are wi' animals. They don't mess you around. They like you for what you are. Not like people. And animals don't ask a lot of bloody stupid questions either.'

'And what are you going to do when you leave school?'

'I'm going home. What are you gonna do?'

'Do you miss your last school?'

'Naw, it were crap. I was always in trouble. They all picked on me—teachers, caretaker, lollipop woman, dinner ladies. They sent me to a shrink, bit like you, in a black suit and creaky shoes, who asked a lot of bloody stupid questions. Why this and why that? And would I like to talk about it?' He stared at me with an impudent look on his face. 'Grown-ups allus pretend. They say they're your friends, only trying to help you, they're all nice and kind and then they . . . well . . . Haven't you got owt better to do?'

'No, not really,' I replied. 'And what about here, Terry? Do you think they pick on you here?'

He thought for a moment, twisting his mouth to one side and cocking his head. 'Not as much,' he conceded, 'not as much.' Then as if brought out of a reverie he sat up and screwed up his writing into a tight little ball. 'That's crap.'

AT LUNCHTIME Canon Shepherd, a cheerful little man with tousled hair and flabby cheeks, arrived accompanied by a whey-faced individual with a long nose and a drooping Stalin-like moustache.

'It is very good of you to join our deliberations, Mr Phinn,' said the cleric, offering me a fleshy hand. 'I expect Miss Pilkington has explained our dilemma.'

'Not much of a dilemma as far as I'm concerned,' said his companion. 'The lad's a bad 'un.' This man clearly did not mince his words. 'He should be put where he won't harm himself and others.'

'That's just what we're here to discuss, Mr Gardner,' said the canon sharply. 'I am well aware of your views. But I would like to have the benefit of Mr Phinn's expertise before we make any decisions as to the future of the child.' The canon looked expectantly in my direction.

'Well, Canon, he is without doubt a very difficult boy—' I began.

'We know that,' interposed the parent-governor aggressively. 'It doesn't take a genius to suss that out. We don't need *experts* from County Hall to tell us the blindingly bloody obvious.'

Miss Pilkington raised a hand. 'Please let Mr Phinn finish, Mr Gardner. He saw Terry this morning and I would like his opinion.'

'He's a disturbed child, with low self-esteem, and he tends to react to people with attention-seeking bravado. He's deeply suspicious of adults, probably because he's been let down so many times—'

'Look,' said Mr Gardner, 'we can sit here all afternoon listening to this psychobabble, about how he came from a terrible background, how he's had an awful childhood and that it's not his fault but society's, et cetera et cetera. It's that sort of liberal hogwash—'

'Mr Gardner!' said the canon in a hard and emphatic voice. 'May I remind you that this is a church school. Our vision, our ethos, the very bedrock of our philosophy are the words of Jesus Christ, who talked about compassion, love, understanding and generosity of heart. I don't hear much of that coming from your lips this afternoon. Do you think Jesus would reject this child, turn his back on him? I think not.'

'That's all very well, Canon,' sneered Mr Gardner, his mouth tight, his face white with displeasure, 'but you don't have a child in the school. My Jill has to put up with this little demon and have *her* learning interrupted. I'm not bothered about the boy. I'm bothered about my daughter and *her* education, and I'll tell you this, my telephone has been hot with calls from parents who think as I do. We on the governing body have a responsibility for the education of all the children in this school. If we decide to let this boy disrupt—'

'I don't think Mr Phinn had quite finished, Mr Gardner,' interrupted Canon Shepherd coldly.

'There are two clear alternatives,' I continued quickly. 'One is for the boy to go to a special school. Alternatively, you could see if things get better over the next few weeks. With support, and an environment where there is some stability and consistency of treatment—as he will undoubtedly get here—he may very well improve.'

Miss Pilkington stepped in smartly. 'I think we have to keep trying for the time being,' she said calmly. 'See how things go.'

'You mean let him stay?' demanded Mr Gardner, his moustache bristling with displeasure.

'I mean let him stay,' said Miss Pilkington. 'I am not yet prepared to be defeated.'

'Mr Phinn?' the canon turned his face in my direction.

'It is, of course, a very courageous decision,' I replied quietly, 'but if you want a personal opinion, I think it is the right one.'

THE DAY FOLLOWING my meeting at Willingforth School, I had telephoned Kath Kinvara, one of the county educational psychologists. She was a level-headed, down-to-earth and very amusing woman, whom I had frequently consulted about children with learning difficulties, special educational needs and behavioural problems. I knew that she had since gone to Willingforth Primary to meet Miss Pilkington and the boy.

Now, a couple of weeks later, I was walking along the top corridor of County Hall when I ran into her. 'Hello, Kath, how are you?'

'Hi, Gervase. Oh, underpaid and overworked. I hear congratulations are in order. I'm so pleased for you although I can't imagine what someone as beautiful and talented as Christine would see in you.'

'What about looks, charm, charisma, intelligence and a vibrant personality for starters?'

Kath laughed. 'Oh, and another bit of news I've just heard is that Harold Yeats is finishing.'

'He's fifty-nine this year,' I told her, 'and can draw his pension, so he's decided to retire, and who can blame him.'

'Will you be putting in for the job, then?' she asked.

'I don't know, Kath, I really don't know.'

'You ought to have a go. You can't lose anything by applying and you might regret it in later years, particularly if they appoint some-one nobody likes. The chief psychologist who was my boss before I came to Yorkshire was a megalomaniac. He was hell to work for.'

'Well, I don't know. It's a long way off yet. Harold doesn't finish until next July. I'll just have to see.' My tone of voice must have signalled that I wanted an end to this line of discussion.

'Anyhow, I'm really pleased to have bumped into you,' she said. 'Have you got a minute?'

'Yes, of course,' I replied. I opened a door beside us and looked in. 'Shall we pop in here?' We entered an imposing-looking committee room that was dominated by a huge rectangular mahogany table.

'It's about Terry Mossup, the boy at Willingforth,' explained Kath.

'Oh, yes. How's he getting on?'

'Well, there's not been any massive transformation in his behaviour but I think the situation is improving slowly. Terry is still a handful. He's a very unpredictable and mixed-up little boy. His file would fill a whole shelf. Poor kid, he's been knocked from pillar to post by successive "uncles" who go to live with his mum for a while. His elder brothers are into drugs and crime and he's been caught on numerous occasions wandering the streets at night. Then there's his vandalising and truanting. You name it.'

'So how is Miss Pilkington coping?'

'Well, she's finding it really hard but she's trying her best. She was so grateful that you were able to find a classroom assistant—and this is the good news. Terry has quite taken to the young man. He's a very keen footballer and by all accounts seems to have got the lad interested. Terry is a natural ball-player, I hear. And the thing is, Gervase, he's also really bright. I gave him a mathematics test and he did very well. Of course, his reading and written work are below average but I think long school absences account for that. Let's just hope all this perseverance and patience pays off.'

'Yes,' I said doubtfully, 'let's hope.'

I WAS JUST ABOUT to leave the office one cold morning three or four weeks later when the telephone rang.

'Hello, Mr Phinn, it's Miss Pilkington here from Willingforth School. Could you come over when you have a free moment?'

'Yes, of course.'

'It's not urgent but we've been doing some poetry work and the children have produced some delightful riddles. I know you collect poems for the county anthology and some of these would be ideal.'

'How's Terry?'

'Well, why don't you come out and see for yourself?'

She sounded a whole lot like her old self; in fact, she sounded as if she was pretty pleased with life. I immediately telephoned the school I was intending to visit that morning and put back my appointment. I was due to arrange the short-listing of candidates for the vacant deputy headteacher post but that could wait. I just had to see what the situation was like at Willingforth.

Later that morning I entered the large, bright classroom to find Miss Pilkington positively beaming. She nodded her head in the direction of a boy in the corner scratching away on a large piece of paper with a fair-haired, athletic-looking young man sitting along-side him. It was Terry and the classroom assistant.

'Children,' the headteacher said, 'could we all say "Good morning" to Mr Phinn?' There was an enthusiastic chorus of 'Good morning'. 'And may I introduce you to Mr White, our new teacher-assistant.' I learned later that Roland White was having a gap year before univer-sity and teacher training. The young man smiled in my direction.

'Good morning,' I said.

'Now, children,' continued Miss Pilkington, 'Mr Phinn has called in to look at the lovely poetry work you have been doing.'

Terry looked up from his work and nodded. 'All right?' he shouted.

'Yes, fine. Are you?' I called back.

'Mustn't grumble,' he replied.

This was one of Yorkshire's most prized phrases. When any Yorkshireman or -woman is asked how they are feeling, the speaker is likely to reply with this time-honoured expression. Things were clearly rubbing off on the boy.

I decided to spend a little time with the rest of the children prior to approaching Terry.

'Riddles are sort of word puzzles,' explained a fresh-faced boy of about eleven, pointing to his work. 'Some are over nine hundred years old. We've been writing riddles of our own.' He read out:

'I'm a real square!
Dry as dust, grey as a stone,
Paper thin and perforated.
I may be square and full of holes,
But in hot water my flavour bursts,
For I am the quencher of thirsts.
What am I?'

'A tea bag!' I exclaimed. 'That's brilliant.'

The next pupil was busy embellishing her poem with intricate pencil drawings as I approached. I read:

I'm an icy blossom,
A tiny piece of frozen paper,
A cold white petal,
A winter pattern.

'It's a snowflake,' she told me with a nervous smile.

'Excellent,' I said.

Eventually I found my way to Terry's desk. 'And have you done a riddle, Terry?' I asked.

'Yep.'

I was waiting for him to tell me it was 'crap', but he looked in his folder and produced a sheet of crumpled paper covered in spidery writing. I took it from him, straightened it out and read:

They walk all over me,
They beat me,
They wipe their feet on me,
They nail me to the floor,
They wear me out,
They leave me to fade in the sunlight.

I was lost for words. I looked at the sharp-faced boy. Was this about him? The neglected, mistreated child, whom adults had treated as a doormat, who had been walked over all his young life?

'It's a carpet,' I said quietly.

'Good, i'n't it?'

'It's very good.'

Miss Pilkington appeared at my side. 'Would you like to tell Mr Phinn where you went last week, Terry?'

'I had a trial game for the Fettlesham Juniors. Football, you know. Don't s'pose I'll get in, but it were worth 'aving a go.'

'Go on with you, Terry,' said the young man, Roland White. 'You'll be playing for one of the big clubs one day.'

The face brightened up but he tried to appear casual. 'Yeah, I bet.'

'And we've been to a farm since your last visit,' said Miss Pilkington. 'Tell Mr Phinn what you saw, Terry.'

'Pigs, we saw some pigs, big pink buggers they were—sorry, miss,' he clapped his hand over his mouth. 'And we saw some sheep.'

'And can you guess, Mr Phinn, who the farmer picked to help him get the sheep into the fold?'

'I have no idea,' I said conspiratorially.

'It was Terry.'

'Was it?' I said, sounding very impressed.

'Aye, it were,' said the boy.

'Mr Clough, the farmer, said he'd never had such a good helper before.'

'Mr Clough has a sheepdog called Meg,' said the boy. 'She were great. She wouldn't leave me alone, miss, would she? Kept jumping up and following me.'

'I think animals really know when you like them,' I observed.

Miss Pilkington smiled. I knew what she was thinking. *So do children.* 'Terry had never been to a farm before,' she explained aloud. 'He had never seen such animals close up, had you?'

'No, miss, and I want to work on a farm when I leave school.'

I thought of my first visit and remembered what he had answered when I had asked him what he wanted to do when he left school. There had certainly been some remarkable changes since then.

LATE FRIDAY AFTERNOON was the only time when all the inspectors were likely to be together in the office. On such occasions we could wind down, have a mug of tea, exchange gossip and talk about the trials and tribulations of the week. We were never in a great rush and those who lived outside Fettlesham generally waited until the heavy Friday evening traffic eased before setting off home. The exception was Gerry who was usually keen to get away.

One Friday afternoon in early October I got back to the office just after five o'clock. Sidney was in a particularly provocative frame of mind. He was standing watching Gerry as she attempted to push a set of thick folders into her briefcase. 'Do you have to be so remarkably accomplished at everything, Gerry?' he asked her.

'What do you mean?' she replied, laughing.

'Well, according to the pestilential Mrs Savage, in her latest poison-pen memorandum, you are the only one of us who had all the final reports and guidelines completed by the end of last term and you are the only one of us who has correctly filled in her wretched engagement sheets.'

'I just like to keep on top of things, Sidney,' she told him, giving him one of her disarming Irish smiles. 'You know what I'm like.'

Actually, I thought to myself, I don't know what you are like. None of us did. Dr Geraldine Mullarkey was something of a mystery. She was an extremely pretty, slender young woman with short raven-black hair, a pale, delicately boned face and great blue eyes with long lashes. She had everything: brains, looks, personality, a sense of humour and, during her short time as the county inspector for science and technology, she had made a very big impression. The CEO had received many complimentary letters from headteachers and governors, and her training courses were always vastly oversubscribed. She had been a member of the inspectors' team now for over a term but we still knew very little about her. Gerry kept her life outside work strictly to herself.

'Were you one of those insufferably industrious little girls at school,' Sidney asked, 'who was top in everything, best at sports, brilliant at music, won all the prizes on Speech Day? A rather prissy, precocious little missy with a butter-wouldn't-melt-in-the-mouth expression?'

'No, Sidney,' replied Gerry, cramming yet more papers into her bag. 'Quite the opposite, in fact. I was the bane of my teachers' lives.'

'Geraldine, how many more files are you intending to stuff into your bag?' asked Sidney.

'Oh, do leave the poor woman alone,' said David.

'I just wish to impress upon our fair colleen that by taking home all this extra work and being amazingly industrious, we mere, weak, inadequate mortals appear somewhat less than efficient in comparison.' He gestured to his desk where a heap of dogeared folders balanced dangerously. Geraldine's desk was empty save for a telephone, two small, neatly stacked piles of reports and an empty in-tray.

'I can't hang around tonight, either,' I told no one in particular as I emptied the contents of my briefcase on my desk. 'I have a meeting.'

'On a Friday night?' exclaimed Sidney. 'Another workaholic.'

'I know why Sidney is feeling inadequate,' said David. 'He's worried about Harold's replacement. You are in a state of panic, Sidney, because you think we may get a martinet of a Senior Inspector who will get wise to your little games and ruses, how you wriggle your way out of anything that involves extra work.'

Sidney snorted. 'Utter rubbish! Anyway, Geraldine, I think you are overdoing it. You should slow down a bit. Work is, after all, not the be-all and end-all. In fact, I think what you need is a good man.'

'Give me strength,' sighed David. 'He's into marriage counselling.'

'An attractive young woman like you,' continued Sidney unperturbed, 'could have your pick. I take it there is no one on the scene at the moment? Someone we don't know about, tucked away in a remote cottage in the Dales?'

'Not at the moment,' replied Gerry, now clearly irritated by Sidney's probing. The smile had disappeared. 'I must be off.'

'No secret lover?'

'Sidney,' she said sharply, 'it is none of your business.'

'Well said,' agreed David. 'Now, leave the poor woman alone.'

Sidney merely changed tack, and directed his questions to me. 'By the way, Gervase, are you going to apply for Harold's job?'

I threw the question back at him. 'Why don't you apply, Sidney?'

'No, not me. The more I view those who are at the top of the tree, the more convinced I become that I am much better off on the grass below, gently grazing, rather than being blown hither and thither by the winds of educational change. But you are somewhat younger, Gervase, so what about it?'

'I haven't decided yet,' I replied dismissively.

'You want to get on and apply,' he carried on. 'You will need the extra funds—a newly married man with an expensive wife and mortgage and then, of course, when the children start arriving . . .'

'I agree, you should apply, Gervase,' said Gerry as she put on her coat. 'You'd make a brilliant Senior Inspector.'

'I certainly would not go that far!' exclaimed Sidney. 'But as David's tiresome Welsh grandmother would no doubt remark from her inglenook: "He would make a tidy job of it." Gervase is a reasonably personable young man, good company, has a pleasant enough manner. I'm sure he would be competent enough in the post.'

'Would you mind not talking about me as if I weren't here?' I remarked.

'Yes, I think we could all live with him as Senior Inspector,' continued Sidney, oblivious to my comment. 'He is a good sort at heart, if a little stuffy at times.'

'Stuffy!' I exclaimed. 'Stuffy!'

'I wouldn't say "stuffy" exactly,' David said, joining in. 'Just a trifle on the serious side perhaps, prone to be self-critical—'

'I'm going,' I told them, rising to leave, 'before my whole character is laid out like a body on an operating table.'

'Well, I'm off, too,' Gerry said. She snatched up her bulging brief-case and headed for the door. 'Have a good weekend, everyone.'

'She always rushes off, doesn't she?' said Sidney when Gerry had gone. 'Never stays for a chat or a drink after work. Very mysterious. I reckon it's highly likely she has a man tucked away. And speaking of mystery, Gervase, pray tell us what's this clandestine meeting of yours this evening? It's not another woman, is it? You're not playing fast and loose with the affections of the delectable Miss Bentley?'

'If you must know, Sidney, I'm meeting Sister Brendan at a CAFOD charity event at St Bartholomew's School in Crompton.'

'CAFOD?' cried Sidney. 'CAFOD! That sounds like a prophylactic for constipation. What the devil is CAFOD?'

'Catholic Aid for Overseas Development,' I told him. 'Sister Brendan has asked me to speak to the Yorkshire branch to raise money for the street children of South America.'

Sidney was in his customary pose, leaning back in his chair, staring upwards. 'It's rather a contradiction of terms, isn't it—Yorkshire and charity? The typical Yorkshireman, in my experience, has short arms and long pockets and lives by the Yorkshire motto of *Brasso, Inclutcho, Intacto.*'

It was definitely time I left, I decided. Sidney, in this sort of mood, could keep going all evening.

MUCH LATER, on the way home from the fundraising event at St Bartholomew's, I stopped off at the late-night chemist in Fettlesham High Street. I had a tickly feeling in the back of my throat and thought I might be coming down with a cold. I smiled as I entered the shop, remembering the last time I had called there. It had been after I had visited a school and had left with some 'little lodgers', as Christine had euphemistically described them. I had been extremely embarrassed having to ask for a shampoo to get rid of head lice.

The same young woman who had sold me the head-lice medication was serving now. She obviously recognised me. 'Not more head lice, is it?' she asked, *sotto voce*, as I approached the counter.

'No, thank goodness,' I replied. 'Just something for a cold, please. One of those lemon drinks and a bottle of aspirin should do it.'

As she selected the necessary items from the display in front of her, the pharmacist appeared from behind a glass screen. 'Dr Mullarkey?' he enquired, looking past me. I turned and there, sitting in a small alcove, was Gerry. She gave me a shocked, wide-eyed look.

'Yes, that's me,' she said, rising to take the packet from his hand. 'Hello, Gervase.'

'Hello, Gerry,' I replied.

'Give him two of these, three times a day,' said the pharmacist. 'If the condition worsens, I suggest you get in touch with your doctor, but it sounds as if it's just a bit of flu and he'll be over it in a few days.'

'That will be three pounds fifty, please,' said the shop assistant.

'Thank you,' replied Gerry, fumbling around nervously in her purse for the right amount. Before I could enquire after the health of 'him', she pushed the money into the assistant's hand, gave me an embarrassed smile and said, 'Must be off. Have a lovely weekend.'

Perhaps Sidney was right, I thought to myself. Perhaps she does have a secret lover tucked away somewhere deep in the Dales after all. It was certainly very mysterious, very mysterious indeed.

FIVE

The scenery in the Yorkshire Dales includes some of the most varied in the British Isles. There is a breathtaking beauty to the hay meadows of Wensleydale and Swaledale, where buttercup and clover blaze along the valley bottoms. There is a simple pastoral beauty to the close-cropped sheep pastures of Ribblesdale, smooth and soft as a billiard table, where rock rose and mountain pansy flourish. This is a land of contrasts: of dark, scattered woodland creeping up the steep slopes, soaring fellsides leading to vast empty moors, great rocky wind-scoured crags, bubbling becks leading into curling rivers, great swathes of crimson heather and golden bracken.

With each season this vast, beautiful landscape changes dramatically, but it is in winter that the most spectacular transformation takes place. It is then that the multicoloured canvas of pale green fields and dark fells, twisting roads and endless silvered walls, cluttered farmsteads and stone cottages, squat churches and ancient inns, are enveloped in one endless white covering, and a strange, colourless world stroked by silence emerges.

It was a bright, cold morning, a week before the schools broke up for Christmas, and I was scheduled to visit two small schools. There were flurries of snow in the air as I drove out along Fettlesham High Street, and by the time I had reached the open road great flakes had started to fall thick and fast. Soon the snow began to settle in earnest and in no time it was draping the branches of the skeletal trees, lacing the hedgerows, covering walls and roofs. The rays of a watery winter sun pierced the high feathery clouds making the snow glow a golden pink. The scene was magical.

My car crawled up the narrow road to St Helen's, a tiny Church of England school nestling in a fold of the dale near Kirby Ruston. I had last visited the school on a mild autumn afternoon. Gone were the brilliant colours, the thick carpet of yellow and orange leaves and the rusty bracken slopes. Now it was a patchwork of white, crisscrossed with the dark walls.

The interior of the school was warm and welcoming. A tall Christmas tree stood in one corner of the classroom, festooned with coloured lights and decorations; a large rustic crib was set in the opposite corner. Every wall was covered with children's Christmas paintings in reds, greens and golds.

Mrs Smith, the headteacher, was more than surprised to see me. 'My goodness, Mr Phinn,' she said, brushing flakes of snow off my coat, 'I really didn't think you would venture out here in this weather. I hope you'll get back to Fettlesham.'

'It was not too bad when I started out,' I explained. 'If it doesn't ease off, Mrs Smith, I'll go back and fix another time to visit.'

The snow, however, did soon stop, so I decided to stay and carry out the inspection as planned. It was nearly lunchtime by the time I had heard the children read and looked through their books, examined the teachers' lesson notes, and observed two lessons.

'Well, things are fine, Mrs Smith,' I told the headteacher. 'No major worries that I can see. I'll get the full written report off to you before the end of the week.'

'That's reassuring, Mr Phinn,' she said. 'Now, if you have the time, perhaps you would like to see our Nativity. We're performing it for parents later this afternoon in the village hall and are having one last run-through to iron out any creases, so to speak. An objective view would be very much appreciated.'

'I should love to stay,' I said.

While the children put on their costumes, I helped push the desks and chairs to the back of the classroom, to leave a large space in the front. Then, having ensconced myself on the teacher's chair at the far side of the room, I sat back to see yet another Nativity play. This would be the third I had seen in a fortnight. I wondered if it was going to be as memorable as the others.

THE HIGHLIGHT of the first Nativity play of the season had been the Annunciation. Mary, a pretty little thing of about six or seven, had been bustling about the stage, wiping and dusting, when the Angel of the Lord had appeared stage right. The heavenly spirit had been a tall, self-conscious boy with a plain, pale face and sticking-out ears. He was dressed in a flowing white robe, large paper wings and sported a crooked tinsel halo. He glanced around suspiciously and sidled up to Mary, as a dodgy market trader might.

'Who are you?' Mary asked sharply, putting down her duster and placing her hands on her hips.

'I'm the Angel Gabriel,' the boy replied with a deadpan expression and in a flat voice.

'Well, what do you want?'

'Are you Mary?'

'Yes.'

'I come with tidings of great joy.'

'What?'

'I've got some good news.'

'What is it?'

'You're having a baby.'

'I'm not.'

'You are.'

'Who says?'

'God, and He sent me to tell you.'

'Well, I don't know nothing about this.'

'It will be a boy and He will become great and be called—um—' The boy stalled for a moment. 'Er—called Son of the Most High, the King of Kings.'

'What if it's a girl?'

'It won't be.'

'You don't know, it might be.'

'It won't, 'cos God knows about these things.'

'Oh.'

'And you must call it Jesus.'

'I don't like the name Jesus. Can I call him something else?'

'No.'

'What about Gavin?'

'No,' the angel had snapped. 'You have to call it Jesus. Otherwise you don't get it.'

'All right, then,' Mary had agreed. 'I don't know what I'm going to tell Joseph,' she added, putting on a worried expression.

'Tell him it's God's.'

'OK,' Mary said, smiling for the first time and picking up her duster.

When the Angel of the Lord had departed, Joseph entered. He was a cheeky-faced little boy dressed in a brown woollen dressing gown, thick blue socks and a multicoloured towel over his head, held in place by the inevitable elastic belt with a snake clasp.

'Hello, Mary,' he said cheerfully. 'Have you had a good day?'

'Yes, pretty good,' she told him, nodding theatrically.

'Have you anything to tell me?'

There was a slight pause before she replied. 'I am having a baby— oh, and it's not yours.'

The audience laughed and clapped at this, leaving the two small children rather bewildered.

THE HIGHLIGHT of the second Nativity play I'd seen that year had been the entrance of the Three Kings. Someone had gone to town on the costumes for the little boys who came in clutching their gifts tightly. They were resplendent in gold and silver outfits, topped by large bejewelled crowns that shone brilliantly under the stage lights.

'I am the King of the North,' said one little boy, kneeling before the manger and laying down a brightly wrapped box. 'I bring you gold.'

'I am the King of the South,' said the second, kneeling before the manger and laying down a large coloured jar. 'I bring you myrrh.'

'I am the King of the East,' said the third and smallest child, kneeling before the manger and laying down a silver bowl. 'And Frank sent this.'

NOW, AT ST HELEN'S, the Christmas play was being staged rather differently. Mrs Smith explained that she had asked the children to write the different parts of the Christmas story in their own words. Four of the best readers would read the narrative while the other children mimed the actions.

Mary sat centre stage, staring into space. The first little reader began the story: 'Long, long ago there was a girl called Mary and she lived in a little white house with a flat roof.' Then the angel appeared, a large boy wearing what looked like part of a sheet with a hole cut in it for his head. He stretched out his arms dramatically as the reader continued: 'One day, God sent an angel and he told Mary she was going to have a very special baby boy and His name would be Jesus.'

A beaming little boy with red cheeks strode into the scene and positioned himself behind Mary, who was still gazing serenely into the middle distance. He put a parcel on the floor, then placed his hand on Mary's shoulder and stroked her fair hair.

A second reader took over: 'In a town called Naz'reth, there was an old man called Joseph and he was a carpenter.' The angel appeared again and stretched out his arms. 'God sent an angel to him as well and told him to marry Mary. So Joseph asked Mary to marry him and she said, "Yes, please," and soon expected the baby. Joseph came home from work and he bought Mary some baby clothes and a big box of chocolates.' Joseph bent down, picked up the parcel and dumped it in Mary's lap. At which point she stood up and they both left the stage.

Three children shuffled on, followed by a fourth smaller child carrying a toy sheep. The reader continued: 'In the fields there were these shepherds looking after their sheep.' The angel appeared again and stretched out his arms. 'The angel went to see them as well. When they saw this great shining light, they were really, really scared. "Ooooh-er, ooooh-er," they went. "What's that?" "Don't be frightened," said the angel. "I bring you tidings of great joy. Today, a little baby boy will be born and you have to go and see Him." "Righto," said the shepherds.'

Three more children appeared, staring upwards and pointing, at which stage a rather large girl pushed the second reader out of the way, and started to read: 'The three kings were very rich and they wore beautiful clothes and had these crowns and things. They looked at the stars every night. One night one of the kings said, "Hey up, what's that up there, then?" "What?" said the other kings. "That up there in the sky? I've not seen a star like that one." "You know what?" said another king. "It means there's a new baby king been born. Shall we go and see Him?" "All right."'

Meanwhile, Mary and Joseph reappeared, pulling behind them a cardboard donkey on wheels. 'Mary and Joseph went to Beth'lem on a donkey,' piped a small boy in trousers too big for him, 'but there was no room in the inn so they had to stay in a barn round the back. Mary had her little baby and she wrapped Him up nice and warm and kissed Him and called Him Jesus, just as God had told her to.'

Children began to enter slowly and gather round the baby. 'And from the hills came the shepherds and the three kings following a big star, and they all loved baby Jesus. He was small and cuddly and He laughed. "Why is He laughing?" asked the shepherds. "Because God's tickling Him," said Mary.'

Last of all came the little shepherd boy and he laid the toy sheep before the manger. 'And they sang a lullaby for the baby Jesus, and everyone was happy,' read the small boy. And then all the children sang 'Away in a Manger' in clear, high voices.

I sat and looked around me: the children's faces were glowing with pleasure, Mrs Smith was wiping away a tear, the lights of the fir tree twinkled and the walls were ablaze with the colours of Christmas. Outside the classroom window a pale sun cast a translucent light and the whole world gleamed silver. This was indeed something spiritual.

TWO DAYS LATER I had received a letter written on pale, embossed and scented paper, confirming an invitation I'd accepted to speak at the Totterdale and Clearwell Golf Club's Christmas Ladies' Night. The Honourable Mrs Cleaver-Canning, the club's captain, suggested—and it was clear from the tone of the suggestion that there was little point in arguing—that I should leave my car at 1 Prince Regent Row, the imposing Georgian villa in Fettlesham where she lived, and that her husband would drive us both down in the Mercedes. I was not at all sorry about this, since the morning's snow, which had melted a little during the day, had frozen and the roads were lethally icy.

I arrived at the elegant white-fronted house at the appointed hour, parked my car in the drive and scrunched across the gravel to the impressive porch with its stone pillars. In the middle of the ornately carved door hung a vast wreath of holly, ivy and bright red ribbons.

I was welcomed by an elderly, slightly stooped man with wisps of sandy-grey hair and a handlebar moustache. He looked like an ageing Biggles. I assumed him to be the old family retainer, but it soon became apparent that he was Mr Cleaver-Canning. 'Ah,' he said in a deep, throaty voice, 'Mr Phinn. Come in, come in. Nasty weather, isn't it? The better half is upstairs and will be down in a moment. We'll go into the drawing room, if you'd like to come this way.'

Above the ornate fireplace of the sumptuously furnished room I now entered, hung a huge portrait in oils of a heavily bemedalled and beplumed cavalry officer.

'That's Margot's three or four times great-grandfather General Sir George Sabine Augustus Cleaver-Bolling in his uniform of Colonel of the 12th Royal Lancers. Impressive looking chap, isn't he?'

'Yes, indeed,' I said, staring up at the self-important-looking man mounted on a rearing horse.

'Brought the Cleaver hyphen with her when she married me. Didn't fancy plain old Canning. Anyway, do sit down. I'll just give

Margot a call.' He shuffled off and once in the hall shouted up the stairs. 'Margot! Mr Phinn's here.'

Back came a short and impatient reply, 'I'm coming!' Then came barked instructions: 'Start the car up, Winco, and get it warm.'

'Already warm and waiting,' he called back.

I wandered round the room in wonderment. On a table was a selection of photographs in elaborate silver frames. A plump, curly-headed girl with large eyes and pouting lips posed with a pony. Various severe-looking old men and women, all in black, stared out with disapproving expressions. In pride of place was a black and white picture of a handsome, dashing young RAF officer with a head of wavy hair, a bristling moustache and an infectious grin. It was a younger Mr Cleaver-Canning when he'd been a wing commander. Hence 'Winco'. He wore the ribbon of the Distinguished Flying Cross.

There was the sound of heavy footsteps on the stairs, followed by a whispering outside the door. 'I have asked you, Winco, on so many occasions, not to shout up the stairs.' Then the Honourable Mrs Cleaver-Canning entered the drawing room. She was an ample-bosomed, impeccably groomed woman with pale purple hair and grey eyes so large they made her appear permanently surprised. Her mouth was a shining bow of scarlet lipstick, and she was dressed in an amazing black, low-cut dress that made her great bosom bulge.

'Ah, Mr Phinn, how very nice to see you.' She turned regally to Winco who was hovering at the door. 'Haven't you changed yet?'

'I'm not going, am I?'

'Well, not to the dinner, you're not, but you are driving us there and you can't very well take us looking like the gardener. Put on your blazer and flannels. But get us a sherry first, will you, Winco? Amontillado, Mr Phinn?'

'Yes, thank you.'

'Righto,' Winco said jovially and ambled out of the room, returning a moment later with two glasses of sherry on a small silver salver. He then departed to get changed.

'It's a dreadful night,' remarked Mrs Cleaver-Canning. 'I just hope Winco takes care. Once he gets behind the wheel he thinks he's in a cockpit. The roads are awfully slippery. So dangerous.'

She was speaking of the man who no doubt had faced a wing of Messerschmitts, guns blazing; who had scrambled into the cockpit of his Hurricane or Spitfire four, five, six times a week, risking life and limb; who had flown lonely dawn patrols. I sipped my sherry and stared at the formidable woman in black. Enemy aircraft must have been a bit of a breeze compared to her, I thought to myself.

Shortly, Winco appeared, smart in a blazer, flannels and RAF tie.

'Right,' stated Mrs C-C, 'shall we go, Mr Phinn?'

I did not believe what next came out of my mouth. 'Righto,' I said, following her to the door.

THE TOTTERDALE and Clearwell Golf Club was packed with about a hundred obviously well-heeled women. I let my gaze sweep across them and felt my heart lurch. Why on earth had I agreed to this?

Mrs C-C introduced me to the ladies of her committee and I made small talk with Mrs Daphne Patterson, who had heard me talk at a charitable function and had recommended me to Mrs Cleaver-Canning in the first place. Then the Master of Ceremonies announced: 'Dinner is now served.' I followed Mrs Cleaver-Canning as she made her queenly progress to the middle of the top table where she faced the chattering throng. She stood as though posing for a photograph, her commanding stare flicking over the guests until their voices fell away and she had secured their full attention.

'Please be seated, ladies,' she said authoritatively, 'and gentleman,' she simpered. 'Welcome to our Christmas Ladies' Night and may I wish you all the compliments of this very special season. May I also welcome our principal guest and speaker, Mr Gervase Phinn, who we shall be hearing from later. Mr Phinn has waived a personal fee and will be donating the cheque to a charity close to his heart.' There was a flutter of applause. 'I'm not exactly aware what it is, but it has something to do with child prostitution in South America.'

'To prevent it rather than promote it,' I muttered under my breath.

The dinner was a very convivial affair. Mrs C-C, who sat on my left, proved to be an interesting dinner companion after she had imbibed a good few glasses of wine. Between mouthfuls of melon and prawn cocktail, poached breast of guinea fowl and lemon mousse, she gave an entertaining description of the golf club activities that had taken place during the previous year.

She was halfway through demolishing a mince pie when she said, 'We do like our speaker to present the balls.'

'The balls?'

'Yes, if you wouldn't mind. You can do it before you speak. I, as the lady captain, dispense the cups, shields and medals to the winners of the year's competitions. But a presentation box of golf balls is given to the oldest member, the newest member and the member who has spent most time on the greens.'

'I see,' I replied. 'Well, yes, certainly I'll make the presentation.'

Mrs Hills, the lady captain-elect, sat on my right and also proved to be an interesting companion. I learned that she was a woman of property and she gave me some advice on where to look for houses.

'I have four cottages,' she informed me. 'A couple on the coast at Robin Hood's Bay and two more here in Totterdale, just north of Fangbeck Bridge in the village of Hawthwaite.'

'You don't by chance want to sell one of them, do you?' I asked.

'No, no,' she replied. 'They are a precious source of income and, anyway, I couldn't part with them. They've been in the family for years. But one of the cottages in Hawthwaite might be for rent soon.'

'It may come to that, but we would like to start married life in a house of our own,' I said. 'It's so beautiful here in Totterdale, isn't it? I think it has some of the most magnificent views in the county. My fiancée and I have looked for property here but it is so expensive. I expect we will end up in a modern semi in Fettlesham.'

'Totterdale is in the National Park, you see, so there are strict regulations on the building of anything new, and conversions have to follow very stringent rules. It's a whole lot cheaper to the north of Crompton or at Ribsdyke. You ought to try there.'

My thoughts, however, were still on Totterdale. 'Actually, I have an idea one of my colleagues rents a cottage somewhere in Totterdale. Geraldine Mullarkey. I don't know whether you know her but—'

'Well, well, well!' Mrs Hills interrupted. 'What a coincidence. Of course I know her. She's one of my tenants in Hawthwaite. Delightful young woman. But I didn't know she was in your line of work. I thought she must be a medical doctor. She's never in during the day and keeps herself very much to herself when she is at home. So she's a school inspector, is she?'

'Yes, Geraldine and I actually share an office.'

'Well, I couldn't hope for a better tenant. She's so pleasant and friendly, she's done wonders with the garden, and the inside is like a palace. I've only called a couple of times because, as I said, she is a very private person. Her little boy is a poppet, isn't he?'

I'm sure my mouth fell open. 'I'm sorry, what did you say?'

'Dr Mullarkey's little boy, Jamie. I said he was a poppet.'

'Little boy?'

'Yes. You surely knew she had a little boy?'

'Yes, yes, of course,' I replied, trying to conceal the shock of the revelation. 'I'd just for the moment forgotten his name. Jamie, that's right. How old is Jamie now, then?'

'He must be three, nearly four, because he starts in the nursery next year. He's such a good little boy and as bright as a button. I know this because my sister's girl is the childminder in the village, and she loves him to bits. I don't know anything about Dr Mullarkey's husband except I think he works abroad.'

My head was in a whirl, and I had to escape. 'I wonder if you would excuse me for a moment, Mrs Hills, I need to wash my hands before my speech.' I began to push back my chair.

'Getting a few butterflies, Mr Phinn?' she teased. 'You mustn't worry about your audience. The lady members won't eat you.'

Mrs Cleaver-Canning added, 'Hurry back, Mr Phinn, it's almost time to present your balls.'

'I'll not be long,' I said and dashed for the Gents.

'Ladies!' boomed Mrs Cleaver-Canning behind me. 'There will be the Loyal Toast in five minutes, then a comfort break and after that we will start the proceedings.'

In the Gents, I tried to come to terms with the bombshell. Geraldine had a child! None of us in the office had had an inkling. And what about her husband or partner? Was she divorced? Why was she so secretive? But now I thought about it, things did make more sense. She was always evasive about where she lived. 'Somewhere in the wilds,' she would say. She had never mentioned anything about her life before she had become a school inspector, or her interests outside the office. She never stayed in the office for the usual badinage at the end of the day and only attended speech days or evening functions like school plays and concerts when she had to. It all made sense now. But why had she never said anything? Well, I decided, if she wanted to keep Jamie a secret, so be it. I wouldn't spill the beans.

I was too preoccupied with the news of Gerry's secret life to feel nervous about the rest of the evening. Following the presentation of the balls and the trophies, I stood and spoke and received a very warm reception, probably because a great deal of alcohol had been consumed and my audience were in Christmas good humour. Clutching a generous cheque for CAFOD, I clambered into a beautifully warm car to be chauffeured back to 1 Prince Regent Row by Winco. The lady captain of the golf club slumped in the back, rather the worse for wear. 'I hope you haven't been winking, drinco,' she remarked. 'It'sh very icy and we don't want an accident and all end up in hoshpital. So take your time and go shlowly.'

'Righto!' replied the wing commander, pushing his foot down on the accelerator and skidding out of the car park.

SIX

The following morning the team of inspectors was in the Staff Development Centre, giving Harold feedback on one of the endless Ministry of Education initiatives that were sent to try our patience.

'Colleagues,' said Harold, 'you have worked extremely hard and I am very grateful. I can put all this together in the next couple of days and get it off to the Ministry before Christmas.'

'Since we have done such a sterling job of work, Harold,' I said, 'and as a small token of your gratitude, may we have the remainder of the day off to complete our Christmas shopping?'

'I'm afraid not, Gervase. There is a lot to get through. In addition, I have asked Mrs Savage to join our meeting later this afternoon. There are a number of items on the agenda which involve her.'

'Oh dear,' I groaned, 'that's the Christmas spirit out of the window.'

'It has completely and utterly spoilt the rest of my day,' said David. 'I have avoided that woman assiduously this term, dodged her memos, eluded her telephone calls, evaded her wretched forms and now I am dragooned into spending an afternoon with her.'

'David,' said Gerry laughing, 'this is a time of peace and goodwill.'

'I am happy to dispense peace and goodwill to everyone with the exception of that woman,' replied David, screwing up his face.

'I really do think you are being a little unkind,' said Harold. 'I know Mrs Savage can be rather difficult and sometimes short with people, but she is a colleague and I do hope you will all show her some courtesy when she arrives.' Before any of us could reply, he stood up and headed for the door. 'Let's have some lunch.'

LATER THAT DAY, we were lingering in the staff lounge having a cup of tea, while Harold sorted out his papers and made some urgent telephone calls before the start of the final session, when Sidney asked, 'How is the house hunting going, Gervase?'

'Oh, we've looked at a few places. Christine and I have our heart set on an old country cottage with a view but they are so expensive.'

'You live in an old cottage, don't you, Gerry?' said Sidney, availing himself of the opportunity to do a little probing.

'Yes, I do,' she replied without elaborating.

'In Bartondale, isn't it?'

'Totterdale,' she replied.

'Oh, Totterdale. It's very picturesque up there,' said Sidney, 'and not an arm and leg away from Fettlesham. Are there any cottages for sale in Totterdale, then? You could have the Phinns as neighbours.'

'Well, very few come on the market,' Gerry replied defensively. 'It's rather a pricey area. I rent—' She was interrupted in mid-sentence by Connie making a sudden entrance.

'Good afternoon,' she said, scrutinising the room for any mess.

'Good afternoon, Connie,' we all chorused.

'I thought I'd let you know, my stepladders have materialised.'

'I didn't know they were missing,' I said.

'Yes, they disappeared from the storeroom. At first, I thought Mr Clamp had taken them to do his arty displays.'

'Would I do such a thing, Connie?' said Sidney.

'Yes,' said Connie sharply. 'Then I thought it might be Mr Pritchard using them for his PE classes.'

David raised his hand to his face in mock horror. 'I would never do anything of the sort.'

'Yes, you would, Mr Pritchard. You did last year. Anyway, the steps have materialised. The maintenance men used them when they were pruning the creeper on the fence at the back. Just took them out of the store without a by-your-leave and then left them out. I do wish folks would put things back where they found them.'

'I am sure you impressed this upon them, Connie,' said Sidney, 'in your usual indefatigable way.'

'Do you know, Mr Clamp, I can never make head nor tail of what you are on about half the time. It's all double Dutch to me.'

'Where has plain English gone?' said David. 'Where is the language of Chaucer and Shakespeare and Oscar Wilde?'

'Anyway,' continued Connie, 'they'll not be walking off with my stepladders again. I've put a lock and chain around them.'

'A little drastic, Connie,' observed Sidney. 'Isn't there a law about chaining people up.'

'The ladders!' snapped Connie.

'How's your father?' I asked, deeming it wise to change the subject.

'Not too good, I'm afraid. They're keeping him in hospital for the time being. I don't think we'll see Dad at home for Christmas.'

'If there's anything we can do, Connie,' said Gerry, 'let us know. You might want running in to the hospital, that sort of thing.'

'Thank you for offering, but I've got my Ted and my daughter, Tricia. I really came in to tell Dr Yeats that that Mrs Savage has arrived from County Hall and she's waiting in the meeting room. I had to tell her to park her car away from my entrance again. If looks could kill, I'd be six foot under. People just don't read notices.'

'Dr Yeats is making a few telephone calls,' I said, getting to my feet. 'I'll tell him she's arrived.'

'Colleagues!' cried Sidney, jumping up as if he had sat on something sharp. 'Let us face the enemy. Once more unto the breach, dear friends, once more! Stiffen the sinews, summon up the blood, disguise fair nature with hard-favoured rage. "Cry God for Harold, Yorkshire and Dr Gore!"'

'Double Dutch,' mumbled Connie shaking her head.

MRS SAVAGE WAS STANDING stiffly by the window with an expression of icy imperturbability on her face. She wore an expensive navy-blue blazer with gold buttons over a stone-coloured dress, silk scarf and an assortment of heavy jewellery. She turned slowly to face Harold, with a clash of bracelets and a false smile. 'Ah, Dr Yeats,' she said.

'Mrs Savage,' said Harold, giving her a great toothy grin. 'It is good of you to join us. Do take a seat. Would you like some coffee?'

'No, thank you,' she replied loftily. 'I only drink herbal tea.'

'Well, I don't think Connie runs to that at the Centre. Shall we make a start, then?' We all sat at the large square table, and Harold smoothed his hair, shuffled some papers and took out his pen. 'Right, well, the first item on the agenda is—'

'Before we begin, Dr Yeats,' said Mrs Savage, picking up an envelope on the table in front of her, 'I have brought with me the short list for the post of Senior Inspector. The CEO and the Subcommittee have whittled the large number of applicants down to ten and Dr Gore has asked if you would cast your eye over them and give him your views before he makes the final selection. We will be calling five for interview in the New Year.' She was careful to avoid looking at me.

There had been no need for Mrs Savage to make such a public show of the whole thing. She could have given the applications to Harold much more discreetly. But I knew her little game. She was aware that I had applied for the post and was wanting me to know that it had attracted a wide and high-quality field and that I stood little chance. After a lot of soul-searching and late-night conversations with Christine, I had decided to put in an application.

'Thank you, Mrs Savage,' said Harold, reaching over and plucking the envelope from her hand. I could see he was far from pleased with her little ploy.

'And I don't need to impress upon you, Dr Yeats, that the contents of that envelope are strictly confidential.'

Harold stared at her for a moment before replying. 'No, Mrs Savage, you do not have to impress that upon me. I am fully aware of the procedures regarding the appointment of staff. Now, let us look at the first item on the agenda—secretarial support.' His gaze remained on Mrs Savage. 'As you are aware, Dr Mullarkey swelled our ranks last term and this has resulted in a great deal of additional paperwork for Julie, our secretary, to deal with—'

'May I stop you there one moment, Dr Yeats,' said Mrs Savage, swivelling a large ring round one of her fingers. 'The young woman in your office is not designated as a secretary. She is a clerical assistant.'

'No matter what you call her, we refer to her as our secretary,' said Harold firmly. 'Julie does the work of a secretary—and more. Anyway, we are now in need of someone else to help out.'

Mrs Savage smiled. It was not a pleasant smile. 'I am afraid the ongoing strategic situation in the Education Department, Dr Yeats, is that we have a serious clerical personnel establishment shortfall.'

'A what?' asked Sidney, sitting bolt upright in his chair.

'Not enough staff,' explained David.

'This was the direct result of necessary downsizing some years ago,' Mrs Savage explained.

'Downsizing?' said Sidney.

'Sacking,' explained David.

'We are now looking to enhance our staffing complement.'

'Employ some more people,' said David.

'So, what you are saying, Mrs Savage,' I said, trying not to laugh, 'is that you recognise that we are understaffed and you are going to sort out another secretary for us.'

'Clerical assistant,' corrected Mrs Savage.

'You can call the person whatever you like, Mrs Savage,' said David. 'All we need is someone to help Julie. And it is pretty urgent.'

Mrs Savage eyed him acidly. 'I cannot, at this stage, promise anything, Mr Pritchard. I shall see what I can do.'

'Let's move on,' said Harold. 'The next item on the agenda is the Fettlesham Show.' There was a series of audible sighs and groans from around the table. 'Yes, yes, I know, but it is fast coming round again and we all have to pull our weight.'

'Harold,' said Sidney, 'the Fettlesham Show is an opportunity for farmers, local shopkeepers and craftsmen to mount displays and exhibitions, but why do we, as educationalists, have to be a part of this? It is nothing whatsoever to do with inspecting schools.'

'We go through the reasons every year, Sidney,' began Harold wearily but he was, once more, interrupted by Mrs Savage.

'If I may, Dr Yeats. Dr Gore is very keen that the Education Department is represented at the show, because it gives us an opportunity to tell the general public what we are about, to give information about the schools and colleges in the county. It is an excellent public relations exercise.'

'Do you know, Mrs Savage,' said David, 'you have mentioned the words "us" and "we", but I should point out that it is *this* team which has to do the work. Dr Yeats has to man that wretched Education Tent, and I and my colleagues have all the exhibitions to mount.'

'May I remind you, Mr Pritchard,' said Mrs Savage tartly, 'that there are some of us who work extremely hard behind the scenes dealing with all the administration.'

'And what administration would this be?' enquired Sidney.

'This is getting us nowhere,' broke in Harold. 'You will be pleased to hear, Mrs Savage, that we will be organising exhibitions of children's work. However, I cannot, at this stage, promise much more.'

'Dr Gore is particularly keen,' said Mrs Savage as if she had not heard, 'that this year we have a significant presence. Last year, the art competition was, for some unaccountable reason, cancelled.'

'I can account for that, Mrs Savage, if you have five hours,' remarked Sidney.

'The sports events did not take place,' she continued blithely.

'With good reason,' said David.

'And the poetry competition was judged by some local poet rather than you, Mr Phinn.'

'Which can be fully explained,' I said.

'Now, this year, Dr Gore hopes that all the activities of previous years, and more, will be up and running. I shall, of course, be co-ordinating everything and should be only too happy to join you, Dr Yeats, at the advisory desk in the Education Tent on the day to give what help and support I can.' I smothered a grin as I saw Harold wince. 'I am sure that Dr Gore and I can rely on the inspectors to give this matter their full and immediate attention.'

'We shall have to see what we can do,' muttered Harold.

The remainder of the afternoon seemed to drag interminably. At six o'clock, Connie popped her head round the door. She had abandoned her pink nylon overall in favour of a large grey duffle coat with fur-trimmed hood, thick woollen scarf tied in an enormous knot under her chin and short green boots. She looked like an Eskimo. 'How long are you going to be?' she asked bluntly.

'Nearly finished, Connie,' said Harold.

'I'm locking up in ten minutes,' she told us. 'I'm doing my rounds.'

'We won't be long now,' said Harold.

'It's getting very icy tonight so be careful on the path. I've put some salt and sand down but it's still very slippery. It's cold enough to freeze the flippers off an Arctic penguin. Oh, and whose is that fancy red sports car out the front?' She knew very well who the owner of the sports car was since she had asked the owner to remove it on many occasions.

'It's mine,' said Mrs Savage coldly. 'You may recall that you asked me earlier to park it well away from your entrance, which I did.'

'Well, you've left your lights on,' said Connie.

'I sincerely hope you haven't got a flat battery, Mrs Savage,' said Sidney with mock concern. 'That *would* spoil your evening.'

SEVEN

I t was the first week back after the Christmas break and the office was unusually quiet. Gerry and I found ourselves alone there.

'So what sort of Christmas did you have?' she asked, looking up from her papers.

'Oh, rather more hectic than last year,' I replied. 'I spent a few days with Christine's parents in Shipley before going to my parents for Boxing Day, and then we had a weekend to ourselves in Settle. We went to the same excellent hotel as last Christmas—it is really comfortable and has marvellous food. We walked for miles and spent hours discussing weddings and honeymoons and houses.'

'Of course, it's only a few months now before the big day, isn't it? Have you decided where you're going to live yet?'

'Well, we really want somewhere in easy reach of both Christine's school and County Hall. Ribsdyke is quite nice, Willingforth is lovely but expensive, Mertonbeck is a possibility but a bit out of the way. I really like Totterdale, where you live, but the houses are expensive and hard to come by.'

'What sort of house have you in mind?'

'Ideally, we'd like that small country cottage in honey-coloured stone with roses round the door; the one you see on postcards, with uninterrupted views of open countryside. Everybody else wants it, too, I'm afraid. We've got a mass of brochures from the estate agents and just love one particular cottage in Hawksrill, but it's being sold at auction and one never knows what they will fetch.'

When I saw that Gerry was staring pensively out of the window, I asked, 'What about you, did you have a nice Christmas?'

'Yes, I did, thanks. Pretty quiet, but very pleasant.' As usual, she wasn't giving much away.

'Did you go back to Ireland?'

'No, I stayed here.'

'By yourself?'

'Yes, well, no, I had friends round and . . . I had some family over. Gervase, you haven't seen the note Harold sent round about the Fettlesham Show, have you? I've put it down somewhere and can't lay my hands on it.'

'It's right there under your nose,' I said, pointing to a green memorandum that could not be missed.

'Oh, yes. I'm actually looking forward to taking part in the Fettlesham Show. I thought I'd get a group of students to mount an exhibition of writing and drawings on wildlife, animal conservation, that sort of thing. What do you think?'

Gerry clearly wanted to keep off the subject of what she had done over Christmas so I decided to probe no more. 'Sounds good,' I said, 'but I would go easy on the animal conservation bit. This is a fox-hunting and grouse-shooting county, you know, and there's some wildlife many of the locals are not very keen on preserving—pigeons and rooks, moles and rats, for example. I once made the great mistake of reading a Beatrix Potter story to a group of infants, most of whom lived on farms. "What a pity it would be if Mr McGregor caught poor little Peter Rabbit," I told them. It went down like a lead balloon. "Rabbits!" said one little lad. "We shoot 'em!"'

'I'll remember that,' said Gerry, laughing.

The clattering on the stairs signalled the imminent arrival of Julie. She entered a moment later with a broad smile on her face. 'I could kiss that darling man!' she exclaimed. 'I could squeeze him to death. I don't know what he said to Mrs Savage, but Dr Yeats is a miracle worker. I've got an assistant to help me with all the paperwork and, wait for it—it's a he, a chap! He can type, file, do everything.'

'Wow!' laughed Gerry. 'A man!'

'I've not got him all to myself, mind. He's spending half his time with the psychologists downstairs and half his time with me up here. His name's Frank. You know, of all the people who have dealings with that dreadful woman, Dr Yeats is the best. He has her eating out of his hands.'

'It's called charm and patience,' said Gerry. 'Usually a highly successful formula.'

'I don't care what it's called. He's got me an assistant. Now, who's for a cup of coffee?'

'No, thanks, Julie,' I said, rising to go, 'I have a full day in schools today so must be off. Actually, I only called in to see if there was any news on who's being called for interview. I'll be in tomorrow early. There's that course outline to finish, if you can get round to it today. It is pretty urgent, I'm afraid.'

'No worries,' replied Julie. 'I shall give it to Frank.'

MY FIRST SCHOOL VISIT that day was to St Bartholomew's Roman Catholic Infant School in the dour industrial town of Crompton. Sister Brendan saw my car pull up outside her office window and moments later was at the entrance waiting to greet me.

'Good morning, Mr Phinn,' she said cheerfully, ushering me inside.

'Good morning, Sister.'

'And have you had a restful Christmas?'

'Yes, indeed, and what about you?'

'Lovely. Now, I've put you with Mrs Webb and the juniors first thing. Then after morning playtime, you're with me and the little ones. Is that acceptable to you?'

'That's fine. And how *is* Mrs Webb?'

The last time I had inspected St Bartholomew's Roman Catholic Infant School, Mrs Webb had been on a guided tour of the Holy Land, called 'Walking in the Footsteps of Jesus', when she had fallen down a pothole and broken a leg. Monsignor Leonard, the local parish priest, had remarked to Sister later that had Mrs Webb been sensible and worn sandals, such as Jesus might have worn, she would not have found herself hospitalised in Jerusalem.

'I'm afraid her leg is still not right,' Sister Brendan told me, 'but I have to say that Mrs Webb is a woman of great faith and fortitude.'

Mrs Webb was waiting for me. She was a prim, red-faced woman with small quizzical eyes and she sported a thick brown elastic stocking on one leg. Her classroom was bright and cheerful, the walls covered with glossy travel posters. In pride of place, on a small table at the front of the room, stood two plaster statues with small vases of fresh flowers before them. One statue was of the Virgin Mary, draped in a pale blue cloak and wearing a golden crown. The other was of Jesus who, I noticed, wore very substantial footwear; the sort of sandals that would stand up to the potholes of the Holy Land.

I spent an interesting time with Mrs Webb's junior class, who were busy writing little poems on paper cut-outs of footsteps.

'Later, I shall type out all the poems and make a small anthology, which the children can take home to their parents. I shall mount the original footsteps along the wall and call the display "Walking in the Footsteps of the Poet".'

I was tempted to say, 'Rather safer than "Walking in the Footsteps of Jesus"' but thought better of it.

For the remainder of the morning I joined the infants, who were busy painting with all the confidence and enthusiasm that only very young children have. At such a young age, children depict the world as a bright, bold, happy place full of round, pink, smiling faces, houses like smiling boxes and blue trees. They spatter and daub, smudge and smear, splashing on colours with abandon and making great swirling curves and huge blobs with their brushes.

'Tell me about this,' I said to Mary, a small girl with a round face. Her drawing depicted a brightly coloured, egglike figure with long spidery fingers, kneeling before what looked like an immense coloured lake with tiny rocks, bits of driftwood and floating weed in it.

'It's someone saying a prayer,' explained the child.

'I see,' I said. 'And is this a lake?'

'No, that's the sick,' Mary replied, dipping her brush into a large pot of mustard-coloured paint. 'She's saying a prayer for the sick.'

The next child I encountered, a serious-faced girl with more paint on herself than on the large piece of paper in front of her, had drawn what I thought was a snake. The long, multicoloured creature curled and twisted across the page like a writhing serpent from a fairy story.

'That's a very colourful snake,' I commented.

'It's not a snake,' the child told me, putting down her brush and folding her little arms across her chest. 'It's a road.'

'Ah, yes, I can see now,' I said tactfully. 'Is it a magic road?'

'No. It's an ordinary road.'

'But it's full of greens and reds and blues. It looks like a magic road to me. Perhaps it leads to an ice palace beyond the ragged clouds where the Snow Queen lives.'

The child observed me for a moment. 'It's an ordinary road and doesn't lead to any ice palace.'

'Why all the colours?' I asked, intrigued.

Her finger traced the curve of the road. 'Those are the diamonds and those are the rubies and those are the emeralds.'

'It *is* a magic road!' I teased.

'No, it's not,' the child replied, 'it's a "jewel" carriageway.'

PART OF MY BRIEF was to visit newly qualified teachers in the county a number of times during their first year in the profession to observe them teach, and examine their lesson plans and record keeping.

One afternoon I was on such a visit to Tarncliffe Primary School which, tucked between the village shop and the grey-brick Primitive Methodist chapel, didn't resemble a school at all. From the pavement, the door opened directly onto one large classroom and curious passers-by would often peer through the leaded windows to observe the pupils at work. On one occasion an elderly couple had walked in in search of a pot of tea for two and a toasted tea cake.

The headteacher, Miss Drayton, ran an excellent school. Her former assistant had retired the previous term and a new member of staff, Mr Hornchurch, had been appointed. My visit that afternoon was to assess the new teacher's competency. Prior to meeting Mr Hornchurch and observing his teaching, I sat with Miss Drayton in her small office.

'Well, Mr Phinn,' she said, smiling, 'I've either got someone who will turn out to be brilliant or someone who will be a millstone about my neck. I knew it would be a bit of a risk when we made the appointment but Mr Hornchurch had something about him, something that convinced me he would make an outstanding teacher. He's an enthusiast for a start, and I like enthusiasts because they get children to be enthusiastic. He's also very hard-working and spends hours outside school time organising trips, coaching the football team, getting together a group to go carol singing and much much more. Standards in English and mathematics have soared since he started, and the children are book-mad.'

'He sounds amazing,' I said. 'What's the downside?'

'Well, to be perfectly blunt, he's eccentric. He's unpredictable, untidy and sometimes infuriating. He does the most brilliant thing one minute, like the project on astronomy when he had the whole class and their parents sitting in the playground in the middle of the night identifying all the constellations. Then the following week he took the children on a trip to the Wildlife Centre at Willowbank and failed to notice one child climbing into the pond area. After the child had got home and had his tea, he had been sent upstairs to get ready for bed. His mother discovered him sitting in the bath with a baby penguin paddling away merrily in there with him.'

Something told me that Miss Drayton rather admired Mr Hornchurch's idiosyncrasies, and relished recounting them. 'I shall be very interested in your assessment of him,' she said.

Dividing the one large room was a wooden partition. On one side of it were the infants, in the charge of Miss Drayton, on the other, the juniors with Mr Hornchurch. Walking through into Mr Hornchurch's classroom was like entering a scene from *The Old Curiosity Shop*—a mass of clutter and colour. There were boxes of every conceivable shape and size stacked in a corner, huge abstract art posters and paintings covering the walls, piles of books, a basket of footballs and cricket equipment, a trestle table full of interesting-looking objects. In the centre of this confusion was Mr Hornchurch, a tall, pale-faced man in his early twenties, with an explosion of wild, woolly hair and a permanently startled expression.

'Do come in, Mr Phinn, and find a chair if you can. This is Mr Phinn, children, and he's a school inspector. Here to see if I'm any good as a teacher. That's right, Mr Phinn, isn't it? So, if he asks you what sort of teacher I am, you all have to tell him that I am absolutely brilliant. Now, eyes front, everyone listening, please.'

I climbed over boxes and stacks of books and found a chair tucked away in the corner next to the trestle table. While Mr Hornchurch was settling the children, I had an opportunity to look at the objects on the table. There were birds' skulls, old tins, bits of pottery, coins, little brass figures, curiously shaped pebbles, fossils and shells—a fascinating potpourri of objects.

'I've taught the children something about the qualities of a good story, Mr Phinn,' the teacher explained to me. 'About the need for a gripping opening paragraph, intriguing ending, authentic characterisation, significant detail, figurative language, imagery, etc. We've read and discussed some really interesting and descriptive extracts and I've now asked them to attempt something similar, something really colourful and vibrant and full of atmosphere. OK, let's get on.'

It sounded to me far too advanced for the children in the class, but I was in for a surprise. The lesson I observed was one of the best I had seen. The pupils were encouraged to give their opinions, and the teacher constantly challenged them to justify their points of view.

The children then began writing their own stories and the quality of the writing that I saw as I walked round was remarkably good.

One boy, who frequently consulted his dictionary before scribbling away, passed his paper over for me to see. 'We've all been asked to write a descriptive paragraph in a different genre,' he explained.

'Genre?' I repeated.

'You know, science fiction, mystery, adventure, historical. I've written a ghost story.' Not only was the boy's piece extremely vivid, it was also neat and accurate.

'Are you really a school inspector?' asked the boy when I had finished reading it, and had congratulated him.

'Yes, I am.'

'And are you really here to see if Mr Hornchurch is a good teacher?'

I tried to evade the question. 'Well, I'm really interested in how well you pupils are doing.'

'But you have to do a report on him?'

'I do report on the lesson, yes.'

'Well, he's a really good teacher and I'm not saying that because he told us to. I didn't much enjoy school before this year, and now I do. I can read better, my mum can read my writing, and my arithmetic is miles better. This year, we've been to castles and museums, the fire station and a wildlife centre, all sorts of interesting places. School was all right before Mr Hornchurch came, but now it's brilliant.'

'I'm pleased to hear it,' I said.

Towards the end of the afternoon, Mr Hornchurch instructed the children to put away their folders and to sit up straight. He then climbed onto his desk, crossed his legs and, much to my amazement, proceeded to place a large cardboard box, which had been adapted to resemble a television set, on his head. There was a cutaway square (the screen) and various felt blobs (the knobs).

'Will someone please turn me on?' he asked pleasantly.

One of the boys came to the front and made a clicking sound as he 'turned him on'.

'Hello, children,' began the teacher in the voice of the storyteller. 'Welcome to the world of the story. My story today is about the child who could not cry. Once, many, many years ago . . .'

Along with the entire class, I sat transfixed as Mr Hornchurch related a captivating folk tale, using a range of accents. When the story ended, the same boy came to the front and 'turned him off'.

What was I going to say to this wildly eccentric but obviously very talented young teacher? I thought to myself. His classroom was a mess, the lesson plans were scrappy and his planning virtually non-existent. And yet the quality of the teaching was quite outstanding.

'You see, Mr Phinn,' explained the teacher after the children had filed out of the classroom, 'children these days live in a television culture. The average eleven-year-old watches thirty hours of television a week. We've got to get them to read, haven't we, but more importantly to encourage them to become lifelong readers and enjoy books. I find that if I pretend to be a television set, lift the text from the page so to speak, the children listen better.' I was lost for words. 'So how was my lesson, then, Mr Phinn? he asked. 'Will I do?'

'Before I give you the feedback on the lesson, Mr Hornchurch,' I began, 'perhaps you might remove the box.'

WHEN I ARRIVED BACK in the office that afternoon, Julie popped her head round the door and told me Harold wanted to see me as soon as I got back. I knew it was going to be news about whether I had been short-listed or not, and felt terribly nervous.

Harold looked up as I entered his office. 'Ah, Gervase, yes, do come in. I am glad—er, that we have been able to find a time to talk. Have you had a good day today?'

'Thank you, yes,' I replied. I could see by his expression and tell by his uncharacteristic fumbling for words that he was about to tell me that I had not been put on the short list.

'I'm not on the short list, am I?' I said.

'I'm afraid not,' he replied.

'Oh,' was all I could muster up to say.

'Dr Gore will, no doubt, be having a personal word with you but he wanted me to break the news. The fact is, the calibre of the applicants for this position has been particularly high, and all have considerably more experience than you. You have only been a school inspector a little over two years, and Dr Gore and the Education Subcommittee feel you need more time in the job before you can aspire to a senior position of this kind.' Harold rubbed the side of his nose with a forefinger. 'I expect you are very disappointed with this news, Gervase, but your time will come.'

'Thanks, Harold,' I said quietly. 'I thought it was a bit of a long shot when I sent in the application. I just felt it was worth a try.'

'As I'm sure you know,' continued Harold, 'Dr Gore values your work highly, as I do, so don't be too downhearted.'

'Thanks, Harold,' I said again. Then I asked, 'Do you have a few more minutes? There is another matter I wanted your advice on.'

'Of course. Fire away.'

Harold sat hunched over his desk, his head cupped in his large hands, listening intently as I described my visit to Tarncliffe School and my dilemma over what to do about young Mr Hornchurch. When I had finished, he steepled his fingers and said, 'I've come across this sort of teacher before and they are the devil's own job to deal with, but the bottom line is this: Do the children in his care get a good education? I think it's as simple as that. Are his lessons interesting, challenging, broadly based? Does he thoroughly know the subjects he teaches, and does he develop the children's knowledge and understanding of them? Does he have good discipline, mark children's books carefully and constructively? If he is doing all that, then he is doing more than many. The most important thing, Gervase, as you well know, is the teaching, not the paperwork or the neatness of his classroom. Everything pales into insignificance compared with the quality and effectiveness of the teaching.'

I nodded. Would I ever be as wise an inspector as Harold?

'You see, Gervase, we don't want a profession of clones. Teachers are as different as any other professionals. Look at our office and how different we all are. That is what makes the world so interesting. You might think that I'm a little easy on Sidney, letting him climb on his bandwagons. Well, Sidney is like your Mr Hornchurch. He can be the bane of one's life—unpredictable, full of schemes and projects and mad ideas—but, deep down, I know he is passionate about his subject, about education and about children. You cannot stifle that creativity. We need enthusiasts in education. To confine that sort of personality would destroy so much good. He needs channelling, he requires a light touch on the tiller, not a heavy hand. So I would say to this young man at Tarncliffe, "You are in many ways an exceptional teacher but you have to conform to some extent. Tidy up your room, plan your lessons better so people like us can see what the pupils have been doing, keep records so parents can see what progress their children are making, but, above all, continue to be imaginative, enthusiastic—and different."'

On my way back to the main office, I decided that no new Senior Inspector could ever be quite as understanding and tolerant as Harold. I was so deep in thought that I bumped into a young man carrying a stack of files.

'Hi!' he said. 'I'm Frank.'

'Gervase Phinn,' I said. 'Pleased to meet you.'

'Ah, Mr Phinn—you'll find the course outline you wanted typing on your desk. Anything else just pop in my in-tray. See you later.'

With that, he headed down the stairs, whistling.

WHEN I GOT BACK to the office, my colleagues had returned from their various school visits and were hanging around to hear my news.

'Well?' asked Sidney.

'I'm not on the short list,' I replied, slumping into my chair.

'Oh, that's tough,' said Gerry, and came over and placed a hand on my arm. 'I'm really sorry.'

'Yes, a damn shame,' said David. 'Did Harold give a reason?'

'Not enough experience,' I replied.

'Well, that's true enough,' said Sidney. 'You've not been in the job five minutes.'

'That's right,' said David. 'Put your sensitive counselling skills to good use, and make a man feel better. He wants some sympathy and understanding, not you telling him he shouldn't have applied.'

'In actual fact, it was me who encouraged Gervase to go for the job. Anyway, it's not the end of the world, is it? He might have changed had he become our boss—all serious and demanding and full of his own importance. I'm sure your old Welsh grandmother would say to him, if she were here, that it is probably for the best.'

'She would almost certainly have said,' David riposted, '"If you get knocked to the floor, pick yourself up, dust yourself down and start all over again."'

AS SOON AS the other inspectors had gone home, I telephoned Christine at Winnery Nook School.

'I'm really quite relieved,' she said. 'I think we will both have more than enough on our plates without the extra pressures of a new job.'

'Yes, I know, that's what you said before.'

'You're not too disappointed, are you, darling?'

'Well, I thought I might have got an interview at the very least. It's a bit of a knock to my ego, isn't it? I just hope Harold's successor is as easy to work for and as supportive as he's been.'

'As you know, I'm stuck here this evening for a governors' meeting, but it should be finished by eight thirty. Why don't I take you out then and you can drown your sorrows?'

'Yes, all right.'

'Well, you don't sound all that enthusiastic,' she chided. 'Cheer up! It's not the end of the world. Incidentally, I went round to the estate agent's at lunchtime, and have got some brochures to show you.'

'OK.'

'Our dream cottage might be among them, darling.'

'Yes, of course.'

'With honey-coloured stone walls and a grey slate roof—and roses round the door and a view across the dale.' She was trying so very hard to cheer me up.

'Sorry, Christine,' I said, snapping out of it. 'I must sound a real misery guts. Of course, we'll go out tonight.'

'Fine. See you at the school at about eight thirty, then.'

'Oh, and there was something else,' I told her.

'Oh dear,' sighed Christine. 'This sounds ominous. What is it?'

'I love you,' I said softly, and put down the telephone.

EIGHT

On the day of the interviews for the Senior Inspector post, all of our team were in early and we gathered for a cup of coffee. Harold was looking very smart in a charcoal-grey suit, white shirt and highly polished shoes. He looked as nervous as a candidate for the job, pacing up and down the office like a caged animal.

'Harold,' sighed Sidney, 'I would be most grateful if you would refrain from wandering around. You are putting us all on edge.'

Harold was clearly not taking much notice. He stopped pacing, however, glanced at his watch, and looked abstractedly into the middle distance.

'What time are the candidates arriving, Harold?' I asked.

'I'm sorry,' said Harold, 'did you say something, Gervase?'

'What time are the candidates arriving?' I repeated.

'Oh, not until nine. Interviews begin at nine thirty. I think I'll drive up to the SDC, though, to make sure everything is ready.'

'But it's not eight o'clock yet,' said Sidney. 'Connie will still be buffing her brasses, wiping her surfaces and poking into every conceivable orifice with that fearsome feather duster of hers.'

'Someone might arrive a bit early,' said Harold thoughtfully. 'I'd better go, just to be on the safe side.'

'What are the candidates like, Harold?' asked David. 'Are they personable, pleasant, congenial, easy to get along with? Have they a sense of humour? Are they people people or systems people?'

'I'm not psychic, David,' replied Harold, chuckling. 'I haven't met any of them yet. I'm only going on what was on their application forms which seemed to me to be first-rate.'

'But you must have got a feel for them,' said Sidney.

'Look, I am not on the interview panel, so it is irrelevant what I think or feel. My function today is merely to make sure things go smoothly. Now,' Harold continued, 'I hope that you will all be at the SDC at about five thirty, when we should know who my successor is and you will have the opportunity of meeting him or her.'

As I strolled towards my car across the formal gardens in front of County Hall, I just had a feeling that things would not be quite as happy in the office after Harold retired.

I ARRIVED at the Staff Development Centre a little after five, to find Connie and Mrs Savage outside the kitchen in heated conversation. Connie was attired in her usual bright pink overall, and had her arms folded tightly over her chest. Mrs Savage was wearing a magnificent scarlet dress into which she looked as if she had been poured. The pink and scarlet duo clashed horribly as, obviously, did their opinions.

'Look,' Connie was saying, 'I knock off at five. I've been here since the crack of dawn and I don't get paid for stopping on, pandering to the likes of all these councillors and officials. I've been in and out, up and down like a fiddler's elbow all day, taking them in refreshments and I don't know what. I bought six bottles of gold top and four packets of garibaldi biscuits this morning and now there's nothing, not a crumb to be had. They are like gannets, the lot of them.'

'I am only asking you to provide one further tray of refreshments, not to lay on a running buffet for a hundred people,' said Mrs Savage tartly. 'It sounds a perfectly reasonable request to me.'

'Yes, well, it might do to you, because you're not the one what has to do it,' retorted Connie undeterred.

Mrs Savage caught sight of me approaching. 'Ah, Mr Phinn, perhaps you can persuade the janitor here—'

'Excuse me!' snapped Connie. 'I am the Centre Caretaker.'

Mrs Savage sucked in her breath and screwed up her face as if she had something unpleasant in her mouth. 'I am attempting to get the caretaker here to provide some tea and biscuits for the interview panel but she is most reluctant to do so.'

'And I've just told her that I knock off at five and it's ten past now and there's no biscuits or milk left. I have a bus to catch and a home to go to.'

'Well, perhaps you could pop down to the shops and get some milk and biscuits before you depart,' said Mrs Savage.

'I'm doing no popping down to no shops. Only place I'm popping to is home.' With that Connie took off her pink overall, hung it behind the kitchen door, put on her outdoor coat and marched off down the corridor.

'I shall, of course, be mentioning this altercation to Dr Gore,' shouted Mrs Savage after the departing figure.

'You can tell the Queen of Tonga, for all I care,' yelled back Connie without turning her head. 'I'm off home.'

'The woman is impossible!' Mrs Savage told me with a twist of her mouth. 'I don't intend to be spoken to like that by a cleaner.'

'Actually, Mrs Savage, Connie does a very good job here.'

'That's as may be, Mr Phinn,' said Mrs Savage, bristling like an angry cat, 'but that is no excuse for such ill-mannered behaviour.'

I decided to change the subject. 'I gather that the interviews haven't finished yet,' I said.

'Well, the interviews themselves have,' said Mrs Savage, regaining her composure, 'but the panel is still deliberating. Now, I've got to go back in and tell Dr Gore that there are no more refreshments.' She waited for a reply but when it was not forthcoming, continued in a much sweeter tone of voice, 'I think it will be some time before the panel has made up its mind, so I wonder, Mr Phinn . . .'

I knew what was coming next. 'I'll go and get some milk,' I said.

'Oh, thank you,' she said. 'That is *most* kind of you. I would, of course, go myself but Dr Gore does like me to be on hand at all times. He relies very heavily upon me.' There was an enigmatic smile playing on her lips. 'Oh, and some biscuits, too—chocolate digestive, I think. The ones the caretaker provided tasted like cardboard.'

Connie was waiting at the bus-stop when I drove out of the Centre. I pulled into the kerb. 'Come on, get in, Connie. I'll give you a lift.'

She climbed in next to me. 'Thanks, Mr Phinn, you're a real gentleman. But don't take me home, I'm a fair way out of town.' She put on the seat belt. 'In fact, to tell the truth, I wasn't going home. If you could take me to the High Street, I can walk to my bingo from there.'

'Righto!' I said, in my best Winco-style.

'You weren't long at the Centre. Have they picked somebody, then?'

'No, I'm on a commission to get the milk and biscuits,' I replied.

'Huh!' she snorted. 'Well, I wouldn't do it. It wouldn't hurt Lady High and Mighty to get on her bike and go to the shops. All she's done all day is swan around the Centre on those high heels, looking important. She wants to watch it, walking round like something out of a jeweller's window. Fall over and she'd have difficulty getting up with all that metal on her. She's like a gramophone record which has got the needle stuck. "Oh yes, Dr Gore," "Oh no, Dr Gore." She's about as much use as a pulled tooth, as my father used to say.'

'I forgot to ask you, Connie,' I said, 'how is your father?'

She stared down at her lap. 'He died,' she said quietly.

'Oh, I am sorry, Connie. I thought he was on the mend.'

'Well, he'd come out of hospital, seemed to pick up a bit, then he had another stroke, more serious this time. I think he was losing some of his facilities.' She was silent for a moment, then sniffed and shook her head. 'It was a lovely service and that young vicar, I've got to hand it to him, was wonderful. I've not always seen eye to eye with him, what with his jeans and his motorbike blocking my entrance, but my goodness he was good. Gave a beautiful sermon about Dad and how he had served his king and country and how there ought to be more people in the world like him. Lucy, my little granddaughter, read a poem called "Granddad" which she wrote special and we had his favourite hymns: "Fight the Good Fight" and "Onward, Christian Soldiers". It was lovely.'

'Well, I'm very sorry. He was a remarkable man, by all accounts. Let me know if there's anything I can do, Connie.'

'Thanks, but it's all sorted out now.' We had reached the High Street and Connie asked me to stop. She put her hand on the door handle. 'I hear you put in for Dr Yeats's job, then?'

'Yes,' I replied.

'It'll take a big man to fill his shoes. A real gentleman is Dr Yeats. So, why didn't they interview you, then?' she asked bluntly.

'It's not really a question I can answer, Connie. You would have to ask those who did the short-listing.'

'I think you would have done a good job myself,' she said.

'Thank you, Connie, that's very kind of you.'

'You mustn't get too down. As my old dad said to me when I failed my eleven-plus examination: "When one door closes, another shuts."' She climbed from the car, then bent for a parting piece of advice. 'And you make sure you let Lady Hoity-Toity make the tea. Mind you, she probably doesn't know the difference between a teapot and a bedpan.'

When I arrived back at the SDC with the milk and biscuits, my three colleagues had arrived and were sitting in the staff lounge.

'It's not like you to be late, Gervase,' said Gerry, glancing at the clock on the wall. 'It's nearly six.'

'I've been on an errand,' I explained.

'They're certainly taking their time,' said Sidney. 'They've been prattling on all day. You would think by now they could have arrived at a decision. The trouble is, you see, people who sit on these interview panels have one thing in common: too much time on their hands and verbal diarrhoea.'

'Isn't that two things in common?' asked David: "too much time on their hands" *and* "verbal diarrhoea"?'

Sidney sighed heavily. 'I really do despair of people who like the sound of their own voices.'

'I'm saying nothing,' I remarked.

'Are you going to bid for the house in Hawksrill, then, Gervase?' asked Gerry.

'Yes,' I said, reaching into my briefcase and pulling out the estate agent's brochure. 'So long as we get a positive surveyor's report, we will bid. It will be a complete waste of time, I'm sure, because it is bound to go miles beyond what we can afford. But it will give us some practice at bidding in an auction.'

Sidney plucked it from my hands and read: '"A beautiful listed cottage in a delightful position overlooking a watercolour landscape near the picture-postcard Dales village of Hawksrill. The ground floor is partially and tastefully modernised and decorated. The upper floor would benefit from further attention. Entrance hall, cloakroom, living room, kitchen, two bedrooms. Small mature garden to front, magnificent view across open countryside to rear."'

'Sounds lovely,' said Gerry.

'Sounds full of estate agent's fanciful language,' said Sidney. 'You have to read between the lines, Gervase. When they say "small compact garden to front", they mean a window box. When they say "in need of modernisation", they mean a ruin. This is what they really should have said about this property: "The previous owner of Peewit Cottage, an incontinent hermit, let it go to rack and ruin. The crumbling pile is at the end of a rough muddy track, well trodden by herds of smelly cattle and flocks of lazy sheep. Those looking for a primitive and lonely life will relish the absence of a toilet, mains electricity, gas, central heating and running water, but there are lovely views beyond the power station and grain silos."'

'Very droll,' I remarked. 'But don't worry, Sidney, we're having a thorough survey,' I told him.

'I'm not in the least worried, dear boy. It's you and Christine who need to worry. You never stop shelling out money when you buy an old house. You want a smart apartment or a modern town house in

Fettlesham, within walking distance of the office.'

'Oh, I wish they would hurry up,' sighed David.

'Go and reconnoitre will you, Gerry,' said Sidney, 'and get Connie to rustle us up a cup of tea on the way back.'

'Connie's gone,' I told him. 'She went nearly an hour ago.'

'And you can rustle up your own cup of tea, Sidney,' said Gerry.

'I shall,' said Sidney springing to his feet, 'and, being such a good-natured fellow, I shall bring one back for my slothful colleagues.'

When he had gone David shook his head wearily. 'I really don't know what the new Senior Inspector will make of Sidney. I hope he has a strong constitution, a bizarre sense of humour and the patience of Job.'

Sidney returned five minutes later with the tea. 'It looks as if they're finished,' he said conspiratorially as he set down the tray. 'They are all standing about looking pleased with themselves and shaking hands. And I have just passed Mrs Savage pushing a tea trolley back to the kitchen. I asked her if she had a new job. Her face was a picture, well, not really a picture, more of a gargoyle.'

'Did you see who they appointed?' asked Gerry.

Before Sidney could respond, the door opened and Harold breezed in rubbing his large hands together and with a great toothy smile on his face. 'Colleagues!' he boomed. 'May I introduce you to my successor. This is Mr Simon Carter.'

'WELL, I RATHER took to him,' said Sidney the next morning in the office. We were discussing the Senior Inspector designate. 'He seems an amiable and positive sort of chap and he was most interested in the work I have been doing in art and design. Asked me all about my projects and exhibitions. He was genuinely interested, I could tell.'

'Yes,' added David, nodding. 'I have to agree for once, Sidney. He seems like a good sort. I think he'll be a real asset to the team.'

'Well, it will not be the same without Harold, but life goes on and this fellow seems a pretty good egg.' Sidney looked over in my direction. 'You are very quiet, Gervase. How did you find our Mr Carter?'

'He certainly seemed a very friendly man, as you say, keen to know all about us, and, from what he said, he has plenty of ideas for various initiatives. I think he'll be good.'

'And, of course,' said Sidney mischievously, 'he's relatively young as well, intelligent, quite good-looking and he isn't married. Play your cards right, Geraldine, and you could be in with a chance. Now, that *would* be interesting.'

Gerry grimaced and shook her head. 'And completely out of the question, Sidney,' she replied. 'So don't start getting any ideas. Mr Carter is definitely not my type.'

'And what *is* your type?' asked Sidney.

'Well, let's just say not Mr Simon Carter.'

'Do I take it you are less than impressed with our new SI?' asked David.

'I shall keep an open mind about him,' answered Gerry. 'I am a scientist after all. I shall give you my opinion after he's been in the job for a few weeks.'

'I don't think you liked him, did you?' said Sidney bluntly. 'Come on, be honest. You just didn't like him.'

'Well, if you want me to be honest, Sidney,' Gerry said, turning to face him, 'no, I can't say I did. There was something about Mr Carter which didn't quite ring true. I can't put my finger on it, but I don't think he is all that he seems.'

'Methinks you worry unnecessarily, Geraldine, my dear,' said Sidney, standing to go. 'I think you will find we will get on with Simon Carter like a house on fire.'

Prophetic words as it turned out.

NINE

'**D**o the mandarins at the Ministry of Education, in their sublime wisdom,' began the headteacher, 'appreciate the volume of reports, recommendations, national guidelines, statutory orders, assessment procedures, statistical analyses, comparative data, projects and initiatives and I don't know what else, which appear like the plagues of Egypt on the average headteacher's desk every week? Does anyone down there in London ever consider sitting down and attempting to coordinate this little lot?' She paused to indicate, with a sweep of her hand, the tower of thick files, fat brown envelopes and bulging folders before her on the desk. 'If I had to wade through this each week, I should spend my entire time paper-shuffling to the detriment of my main concern, which is educating young people.'

I was sitting somewhat subdued before Mrs Rose, headteacher of Crompton Secondary School, which was one of the most 'challenging' schools in the county. I felt it politic to listen. 'Now, as you know,

Mr Phinn,' she continued, 'we have in this school some of the most difficult, demanding and disruptive young people of any school and I honestly believe that we are trying our level best to teach them to be good citizens and to achieve their potential. But it is an uphill battle.' She paused for a moment and looked down again at the desk piled high with papers. 'And now we have another major national initiative, which I am sure is well intentioned, but is something which will add to the pressures of an already exhausting and stressful job. I just wish all these administrators, consultants, advisers and inspectors—present company excepted—would let us get on with the teaching.'

After the week I had just had, the last thing I needed was a long diatribe about the pressures and stresses of teaching. I felt like the Egyptian messenger in the production of *Antony and Cleopatra* that Christine and I had seen some months back. As the messenger is beaten viciously about the head by the furious queen, after he informs her of her lover's marriage to Octavia, the poor man attempts to tell her: 'Gracious madam, I, that do bring the news, made not the match.' In other words—don't shoot the messenger. I felt like repeating the lines to Mrs Rose who sat at her desk with all the authority and bearing of the formidable Egyptian queen herself.

Someone in the Ministry of Education undoubtedly had enjoyed dreaming up 'Language and Literacy for Learning' which Dr Gore had dumped at my door. English inspectors from selected authorities were charged with observing a range of lessons to evaluate how effective teachers were in teaching reading and writing skills. When I flicked through the lengthy commentary from the Ministry and read the accompanying letter from Miss de la Mare, HMI, explaining the process, I knew it was going to represent half a term's work. All the information had come in glossy folders. On each cover was a group of smiling students dressed in smart blazers, pristine white shirts, and school ties, all in animated conversation with each other in what appeared to be the best-equipped library in the country. Behind them posed a beaming young teacher who looked as if she were moonlighting from her day job as a fashion model. So while I could readily sympathise with Mrs Rose when she launched into her tirade about this particular initiative, I was in no mood to listen.

'Well, Mrs Rose,' I said irritably, cutting her off and starting to put the folders and the papers in my briefcase, 'perhaps this is not the best time to discuss the initiative.'

'There is never a best time, Mr Phinn,' she told me. 'We are up to our eyes all the time. Look,' she said, her voice softening a little, 'I am the very last person to dismiss something out of hand before I have given it a chance, particularly if it might be to the benefit of the students. You'd better tell me more about this project.'

So I explained how the Ministry had asked that a sample should be taken across the board—high-achieving schools, ones where results were low, large and small, urban and rural, grammar, secondary modern, comprehensive and special schools. The headteacher listened attentively as I stressed the advantages of taking part, especially the extra funding.

'Now, Mr Phinn, let me get this straight. You will spend a day in the school examining the written work of the students in a range of subjects, and a further day looking at the way the teachers use language in their lessons?'

'Yes, and I will also be interested in the kind of language the students use,' I added.

'Well, you will find, Mr Phinn,' replied Mrs Rose, 'that a good number of our students have a very colourful, if somewhat limited command of the English language.'

'Not that kind of language,' I told her, smiling.

'And you are going to focus on just one student, are you?'

'That's right. I would like to join a boy or a girl for the day. It's called pupil pursuit.'

'Pupil pursuit,' repeated the headteacher, shaking her head. 'Why is it, do you think, that the Ministry is so very fond of custodial words, phrases and metaphors? Education is full of such terms, isn't it? We've got governors, inspectors, officers, detention, exclusion, suspension, discipline, terms, authority and, of course, those at the Ministry are very adept at using long sentences. As you can tell, Mr Phinn,' concluded Mrs Rose, smiling for the first time that morning, 'I do still have a sense of humour.' She tapped the folder and thought for a moment. 'All right, then, we'll give it a go.'

THE FOLLOWING FRIDAY I arrived at the school to undertake the pupil pursuit. Crompton Secondary School, a flat-roofed, grey-coloured building built in the 1950s, was in a deeply depressing part of the town. Nearby was a litter-strewn shopping precinct where every premises had a grille on the window.

Mrs Rose had telephoned the previous afternoon to tell me which pupil she had selected to be 'pursued'. 'I couldn't decide between Bianca and Dean,' she had said. 'Their attitude to life is not dissimilar, but Dean can be more disruptive so I've chosen Bianca. In fact, she and Dean are friends, so I expect you will be seeing a fair bit of Dean anyway.'

Mrs Rose had asked me to meet Bianca in the library before the start of school. She was fifteen; a tall, morose-looking girl with lank hair and a pale, unhealthy-looking face, and she was dressed in an exceptionally tight blouse, very short skirt and huge platform shoes. She looked very different from the students on the front of the glossy folder that I held in my hand.

'So whatcha gunna be doin', then?' she asked in a weary, apathetic tone of voice.

'I am going to be joining you for all today's lessons,' I explained.

'Eh?'

'I said, I am going to be joining you for all today's lessons. I shall observe the teaching and also be talking to the students.'

'Wha' for?'

'Because that's my job. I'm a school inspector.'

'A wha'?'

'A school inspector,' I repeated.

'And you just watch teachers?'

'That's right.'

'Don't you have a proper job, then?'

I decided not to answer that. 'I am here to see how well the students are doing in their lessons.'

'Well, it's dead boring,' she told me bluntly, scrutinising a broken nail. 'It's like watching these really really boring television programmes that you can't turn off. I don't understand what t'teachers are on about most of t'time.' She turned her attention to another broken nail. 'So watcha want to watch t'lessons for?'

'As I said, I am here to see how well the students are doing. I'm going to be listening to the language in the classroom.'

'You'll 'ear a lot. Some of t'lads have mouths like sewers.'

At this point, the most aggressive-looking adolescent I had ever seen in my life came into the library. He resembled a younger version of Magwitch, the convict in *Great Expectations*. He had a bullet-shaped, closely shaven head, several large metal studs in his ear and an expression that would stop a clock. When he came closer, I saw that he was decorated with a selection of unusual tattoos. On his knuckles *LOVE* and *HAT* were spelt out in large blue letters, and stretching from ear to ear across his neck, was a series of dots, between small tattooed scissors. In the middle, just above his Adam's apple, were the words *CUT HERE*. I learned later that one of his friends had decided to try and emulate this artistry himself with a needle and some Indian ink, using a mirror. He was now destined to go through life with the word *TUC* emblazoned across his throat.

'Who's 'e then?' the youth asked Bianca threateningly.

'Eh?' she grunted, chewing at the remains of the broken nail.

'Him, who is 'e?'

'Inspector,' said the girl.

'Copper?'

'Naw, school inspector.'

'What's 'e 'ere fer?'

'He's following me around for t'day.'

'Tha wants to tell somebody.'

'Naw, he's watching what gus off in t'lessons.'

'Well, he's not watching me!'

I was being discussed as if I were not there. 'Excuse me,' I said to the boy. 'You can speak to me directly, you know. I'm not invisible.'

'Eh?'

'You can ask me yourself what I am doing today.'

'I know what tha doing. She's just told me and I'm telling thee, tha not watching me!'

'No, I don't intend to,' I replied.

Just what was I in for, I thought to myself, and just how do the teachers cope with the likes of this lad?

'His name's Dean,' Bianca told me, as he shuffled off, hands deep in his pockets, 'and he fancies me.'

Struth! I thought.

The first lesson was mathematics. The teacher, Mr McNab, a bear of a man with a thick red beard, lined the class up outside his door, before explaining that he believed in firm discipline and what a retrograde step it was when the misguided powers that be abolished corporal punishment. 'When I taught in Glasgow, Mr Phinn, we were gi'en a thick leather strap called a tawse and they didna mess aroond after getting a dose o' that across their backsides, I can tell ye.'

On each desk had been placed a pencil, the end of which had been sliced away and a number written on the exposed wood, a square of paper, a rubber (also numbered) and a textbook.

'I keep their noses to the grindstone here, Mr Phinn. Keep 'em busy, I do. Gi' this lot an inch and they'll tek a mile. I don't encourage any talking in my class because once started, they willna stop. This lot live by the code of "If it moves, nick it, if it doesnae, kick it." You see, they come from inadequate homes where they are allowed to get awa' wi' murder. They're left to roam the streets, get up tae all sorts of mischief and mayhem. What a lot of these lads need is security. That's what they want—security.'

'Yes,' I agreed. 'Children tend to prosper from a caring and secure background.'

Mr McNab threw back his head and snorted. 'Waay, not that sort of security, man,' he blustered. 'I mean maximum security. I'd lock the buggers up!'

The students worked their way through the exercise in the textbook with the teacher patrolling the desks, peering over shoulders and fixing, with a rattlesnake glare, anyone who looked up.

At the end of the lesson I accompanied Mr McNab, who was on yard duty, into the playground, where he continued to enlighten me about his educational philosophy. 'Of course, I've tried group work, paired work, discussion, this interactive learning carry-on, but it just doesnae work with this sort of pupil. They know every trick in the book. And they know all their rights as well. Canna lay so much as a little finger on 'em these days.'

When the bell rang for the end of break, Mr McNab lined the pupils up and they filed into school. A large boy continued to sit on the wall, making no attempt to go in; he just sat there, chomping away on a large chocolate bar.

'You boy!' shouted the teacher.

'What?' the boy shouted back, spluttering bits of crumb and chocolate in the process.

Mr McNab clamped his mouth together and his eyes became hard and angry. He strode over to the wall and his loud voice rang over the school yard. 'When ye talk to a teacher, laddie, ya say "sir"!'

'What . . . sir?'

'Are ya deaf?'

'No.'

'Sir!' roared the teacher.

'No . . . sir.'

'Didna you hear the bell?'

'Yeah . . . sir.'

'What's yer name, laddie?'

'Sean.'

'Sean what?'

'Sir.'

'No! No! Your second name, yer great pudding!'

'Smith . . . sir.'

'Well, what are ye doing sitting on the wall when the bell has gone, Smith?'

'Having a rest . . . sir.'

Mr McNab's voice suddenly became low and threatening. He was as tense as an overwound clock. 'I dinna like your attitude at all, Smith. Now, ye get up off that wall, tidy yerself up, and get yerself to yer next lesson. I'll see you after school for a detention.'

'I can't, sir.'

'And why, pray, canna ya?' demanded the teacher, his eyes nearly popping from their sockets and his face as red as his hair.

'I left this school last year. I work at the garage across the road, sir. I only came over to give my brother a message from our ma.'

I avoided meeting Mr McNab's eye as we made our way back into school.

The next lesson was chemistry. 'Equipment?' the teacher repeated with a hollow laugh, when I asked about the resources the students would be using. 'You mean Bunsen burners, bottles of acid, glass beakers? I don't give this lot rulers, Mr Phinn, never mind equipment.'

During the very noisy lesson, while a tired-looking woman in a white coat was attempting to explain osmosis, a topic way beyond the pupils' understanding and of no interest to them whatsoever, Dean, the heavily tattooed individual, leaned back on his seat casually so his face was level with my own and commented in a voice loud enough to carry, 'She's not up to much, is she?'

'I suggest you keep your clever comments to yourself,' I retorted. 'Listen to the teacher and be quiet!'

He scowled and continued to rock on two legs of the chair.

The first lesson of the afternoon was geography. Dean was the centre of attention for the whole hour, talking loudly, poking the boy in front, flicking paper, making fatuous comments and generally being a nuisance. The teacher, a man with a long, wrinkled face of tragic potential, appeared resigned to the poor behaviour of the pupils.

'The lesson was terribly disorganised,' I told him afterwards.

'It was, wasn't it?' he agreed, nodding slowly.

'How do you feel about the criticism?' I asked him.

'How do I feel?' he repeated. 'Now, that's a question and a half. I feel like a lion tamer without a whip, if you want me to be frank.'

I stared at him for a moment. 'Is it always like this?'

'Mostly,' he replied, 'but I don't let it get to me. I've got high blood pressure, you see, so I can't get too excited.' His face suddenly brightened. 'I finish at the end of next term. I'm going to open a health food shop in Fettlesham.' He sighed happily. 'These pupils, as you have no doubt surmised, Mr Phinn, have very limited language skills. So when faced with some of the examination questions they just cannot make head nor tail of them. I mean, on last year's paper one of the questions was about Scottish lochs affording deep-water berthage. Well, I ask you, how many people could understand that?'

My response could not have been more forthright. 'Surely that is your job, to teach them?' I responded.

'Ooooh, easier said than done, Mr Phinn,' he replied amiably, as if the criticism were some sort of commendation.

'Have the students been on any geography field trips?' I asked.

'I did take a group to Whitby once but it was more trouble than it was worth. Getting them on the coach was like rounding up a herd of wild horses.'

At afternoon break Bianca told me that the final lesson of the day would be religious education with Mr Griffith.

When Bianca and I arrived at the classroom, the students were, to my great surprise, lining up in an orderly fashion. The noise level for the first time that day was unusually low. Dean seemed to have undergone a miraculous transformation. He just nodded at Bianca when she slipped in beside him. I joined the end of the line awaiting the arrival of Mr Griffith, and a minute later a diminutive man dressed in a bright and baggy orange track suit, appeared. He looked as if he had survived the electric chair, for his wild hair, which was the colour and texture of wire wool, stuck up fantastically.

'Who is that at the back? Come out!' he roared. I stepped forward. 'Oh! I'm very sorry. It's a school inspector. I thought it was a new boy.' He made a flourish with his hand. 'We are greatly honoured, five set nine, to have with us such an eminent visitor. Mr Flynn, is it?'

'Phinn,' I told him.

'Ah, yes, Phinn, as in the shark. Well, you are in, Mr Phinn, for a rare treat this afternoon. What's he in for, five set nine?'

'A rare treat!' the class chorused.

'Stand up straight there, Dean,' said the teacher, 'nice and smart. Look tidy boy, look tidy.'

Dean immediately did as he was told.

'This is my very favourite class, you know, Mr Phinn,' the teacher told me. 'They are a grand lot. What are you, five set nine?'

'A grand lot,' the pupils chorused.

When the pupils had settled down, the teacher fixed them with a dramatic stare and began. 'Now, we got up to the part last week where Pontius Pilate had washed his hands of Jesus. Do you know what they did then?'

'No, sir,' chorused the class.

'Great big whip!' Mr Griffith estimated the size of the whip by pulling his hands slowly apart to the length of about three feet. 'That big, Francine.'

'Ooooo!' whimpered a large girl on the front desk. Her eyes were wide in amazement.

'And they scourged Him with it!' The teacher provided us all with a most impressive and realistic mime of the whipping. 'Good word that, "scourge". I'll write it on the blackboard.' The teacher looked in my direction. 'Pity we can't do a bit of scourging in schools, Mr Phinn. A touch of the old scourging would do Dean a power of good, wouldn't it, Dean?'

'Yes, sir,' the boy replied with good humour.

'Now, after they had whipped Him and hit Him and kicked Him and called Him names, do you know what they did next?'

'No, sir,' chorused the class a second time.

'They laughed and jeered and called Him "King of the Jews". And do you know what they did next?'

'No, sir,' chorused the class a third time.

'Great big cross!' Mr Griffith estimated the size of the cross by stretching his hands heavenwards. 'That big, Francine!'

'Ooooo!' murmured the girl, her hand to her mouth.

'And they made Him drag it through the streets, all the while mocking and cursing Him. Simon of Cyrene came out of an alleyway to help Him with the cross, but he was pushed back by the Roman soldiers who made Jesus drag the instrument of His death to the Hill of Skulls.' Mr Griffith paused for effect. 'Now, I'm talking here about the Son of God. The Son of God! He could have clicked His fingers and they would have all been dust under His sandals. He had the power to devastate—to *devastate*—the whole world but He didn't, see. He let them hurt Him and humiliate Him and He never raised a finger against them. Now I bet you that if someone did that to you, Dean, and you had the power just by raising a finger to kill the lot of them, you wouldn't just stand there and take it, would you?'

'No, sir,' replied the boy forcefully.

'Then why did Jesus let them do all that to Him? What was the point of all that suffering? Just think about it for a moment.' A silence descended on the class. 'You see,' continued the teacher after a minute, 'not only was Jesus the gentlest, most loving and completely harmless man in the world, He was also the most courageous. They crucified Him. They nailed Him to that cross and He died. And the soldiers gambled over the only things He owned—the few clothes from His back—and His mother watched Him die a slow and painful death and His friends deserted him. His best friend, Peter, denied he even knew Him. Three times he said, "I do not know this man." And there hung the Son of God who had harmed no one.'

I had heard the story of the Crucifixion a thousand times but, on this occasion, when that awesome silence fell on the class, I felt tears pricking my eyes. I glanced across at Dean. He sat, mouth open like a netted fish, totally captivated by the saddest story of all time.

'But do you know what they did before they crucified Him?' roared the teacher, making the whole class, myself included, jump.

'No, sir,' I heard myself saying.

'They took a crown of thorns—a crown of thorns—and they rammed it, yes, they rammed it on His head.'

In the deathly silence which greeted this, Dean turned to me and said with a curl of the top lip, 'The bastards!'

At the end of the lesson, when the pupils had set off home, Mr Griffith walked with me to the staff room.

'How did I get on then, Mr Phinn?' he asked.

I looked down at my notebook. 'I've not written a thing,' I replied.

'My father was a great Baptist preacher in Wales, you know. After chapel, he valued education above all else. Of course, that's a Welsh characteristic, you know. Lloyd George once said: "The Welsh have a passion for education and the English have no particular objection to it." Well, my father brought the Bible to life, see. He lifted the sacred text off the page.' Mr Griffith stopped and gripped my arm. 'Why don't you come back at Christmas—I do a lovely Herod!'

TEN

'Are you getting all nervous, then?' Julie asked, placing a cup of coffee on my desk. I was sorting through my mail in the office prior to setting off for my last official school visit of the spring term.

'I am a bit, Julie,' I admitted. 'It's a big step, marriage.'

'Particularly if you've been living on your own for so long and used to a certain routine.'

'Well, it's a matter of give and take, isn't it?' I replied.

'In my experience, it's the woman who gives and the man who takes.'

'That is a cliché, and not all men are like that. Anyway, when you get married you have to get used to all your partner's little foibles.'

'Little foibles!' exclaimed Julie. 'You mean dirty habits and peculiar obsessions.'

'And what would a young woman like you know about dirty habits and peculiar obsessions?' I asked, laughing.

Julie sat on the corner of my desk. 'My sisters were love's young dreams until their new husbands started dropping dirty underpants all over the place, coming in stinking of beer, watching football on the television into the early hours, wearing socks three days running, and snoring like bronchial hippopotamuses every night.'

'I can't really imagine Christine dropping dirty underwear all over the place, coming in stinking of beer and snoring like a bronchial hippopotamus,' I told her mischievously.

'I'm not talking about Christine,' Julie said. 'I'm talking about you. Men are different from women. For a start they are more untidy and unhygienic. They are more inconsiderate and irritating. Now take Mr Clamp as a prime example. Can you imagine anything worse than being married to him? He'd drive anyone to drink.'

'Not at all, Julie,' I told her. 'Sidney is a happily married man, his wife loves him dearly and I believe he is very attractive to the opposite sex. Women want to mother him.'

At that very moment, the subject of our conversation breezed in through the office door, dressed in a light cotton suit, pale yellow silk tie and wide-brimmed straw hat. He looked every inch the gentleman about town. 'Almost last day of term for us, Julie,' he exclaimed. 'And last week of freedom for you, Gervase.'

'Don't you start as well,' I told him. 'You two should be wishing me well, not trying to put me off.'

'Of course we wish you well, dear boy,' cried Sidney, putting an arm round my shoulder. 'I am certain beyond doubt that the wedding will go beautifully—you might even make a passable speech—the honeymoon blissfully and your life with the drop-dead gorgeous Miss Bentley in your little love nest—' He stopped abruptly. 'By the way, did you get your cottage?'

SIDNEY'S ASSESSMENT of Peewit Cottage had been remarkably accurate. The 'beautiful cottage' needed a great deal of work. The surveyor's report arrived a week before the auction and it made the property sound as though it were on the verge of collapse. There were 'extensive timber infestations throughout, evidence of rising and penetrating damp, significant deflections to the roof pitches, serious weathering to the stonework, defective guttering, lack of lateral bracing between front and rear walls'—whatever that meant—and 'numerous other urgently needed repairs'.

Christine and I were sitting in the front room of my flat above the Rumbling Tum Café with the greasy aroma of fish and chips drifting up the stairs, reading through page after page of problems. Finally I threw the bulky report onto the table and put my arm round Christine who looked devastated. 'I knew it needed work doing to it,' I said. 'I mean, it's old and hasn't been lived in for ages, but I didn't reckon on all that amount.'

'Me neither,' she replied sadly.

We just sat there in our silent disappointment.

'Well,' I said at last, 'I suppose we had better look for something else—and quickly or we will find ourselves living in this dump for months to come.'

'I suppose so,' Christine replied with tears in her eyes. 'Peewit Cottage—it has such a sonorous ring to it.'

'And a beautiful setting. We'll never find a view like that again.'

'Oh, Gervase, you're making it worse. I need you to tell me it's a dump and that the people who buy it will have a millstone round their necks for the rest of their lives. Don't tell me how beautiful it is.' And she began to cry.

'Come on, Chris,' I said, holding her close and wiping away her tears. 'We'll find somewhere else. I promise.'

'Like one of those smart but oh-so-predictable apartments or town houses in Fettlesham that Sidney suggested? I fell in love with that cottage as soon as I saw it.'

'But just think of all the work needed.'

'I know,' she said, snuggling closer. 'I know it's impossible.'

Later that evening, after a subdued supper, Christine said quietly, 'We could go to next Saturday's auction—if only to see what the cottage goes for. We wouldn't bid or anything. Just go out of interest.'

'I suppose we could,' I replied. 'It can't do any harm seeing what it fetches.'

So, at twelve noon the following Saturday, Christine and I sat nervously on hard, stackable chairs in the back row in Hawksrill village hall for the auction of Peewit Cottage.

The estate agent, a round, jovial man with a shock of silver-white hair, banged his gavel on the table. 'We are here for the public auction of the freehold property known as Peewit Cottage, Hawksrill, in the county of Yorkshire. The particulars of the sale are here'—he stabbed a large official-looking folder—'should anyone who has not received a copy wish to view them before the sale commences. Peewit Cottage is sold with vacant possession on completion of the contract. So, is there anyone wishing to view the particulars of sale before we begin?' He glanced around the room. 'Good. So, will anyone start the bidding. Shall we say . . .'

CHRISTINE AND I sat outside the Golden Ball pub in Hawksrill, staring in silence at the wonderful view before us. The auction had finished over an hour before.

'Well,' I said, breathing out heavily.

'Are you worried?' Christine asked.

'Very, and still a bit shell-shocked.'

'I never realised you were so impulsive. I couldn't believe it when you started bidding.'

'I didn't notice your stopping me,' I replied, looking into her beautiful blue eyes. 'I knew you had your heart set on it. I did too. I just couldn't stop myself, once I'd started.'

'Come here,' Christine said and gave me a great hug and a kiss. 'Oh, Gervase, think of the views and the beams and the quarry-tiled floors and the old fireplaces and the little garden. I can't believe it's ours.'

There had only been three people interested in buying: a local builder, an architect from Leeds and myself. The bidding had started low but increased quickly past the guide price. I had only been to a few auctions, and then to buy books, so I was not at all experienced. However, when the builder waved his paper ostentatiously and the architect nodded confidently, I had entered the fray like a bulldog with a bone, and had hung on until the auctioneer had banged his gavel loud enough to wake the dead and shouted: 'Sold to the young gentleman at the back.'

'Young, mad gentleman' would have been more apt, I thought, my heart hammering so loudly that I thought everyone could hear it.

Before going for our celebratory drink at the Golden Ball, we had walked out of the village and into the open country beyond, in order to turn back and look at the property we had just bought. It looked small and rather sad in the early-afternoon sunshine. The roof, covered in cracked orange tiles, sagged in the middle, and the chimney leaned to one side. Tiny windows were set in the old red sandstone walls and the paint was flaking from the wooden shutters.

Christine wrapped her arms round me and hugged me tightly. 'Isn't it just idyllic?' she sighed.

I could have provided a more appropriate adjective but bit my tongue. The thought uppermost in my mind was: thank heavens I had not got the Senior Inspector's post after all because I would be spending every spare moment trying to make Peewit Cottage habitable.

'It frightens me sometimes,' I told her, 'just how lucky I am. To have you for the rest of my life in our dream cottage. It feels just too good to be true.'

'I'm lucky, too,' Christine said, giving me a kiss.

'You are, Chris, simply the best thing that's happened to me. I'm the luckiest man alive.'

ELEVEN

Christine and I were married on April 15 at St Walburga's Church. I wore a charcoal-grey morning coat and Christine a simple white dress and veil. She needed no elaborate silk wedding gown, embellished with intricate embroidery and studded with pearls, she needed no long lace train held by pageboys in velvet, no fancy necklace or diamond tiara to look stunning. She would have looked the same to me in a threadbare army greatcoat. On that bright spring morning with the sun shining through the stained glass and bathing her in a pale golden light, Christine looked a vision as she walked down the aisle on her father's arm. In her hands she held a delicate posy of grape hyacinth and freesia.

For our honeymoon, Christine and I drove to the Lake District in her Morris Traveller, talking nonstop about Peewit Cottage—what we intended to do with the overgrown garden (typical of us to worry about the least important first), the improvements we envisaged to the kitchen, the cold damp bedrooms and the plumbing. We chatted about colour schemes and furniture, curtains and carpets, wallpaper and window boxes all the way to the Salutation Hotel in Ambleside.

We stayed for just a week, walking on some of the Lake District's beautiful fells. Then we spent the other week of the Easter holidays starting work on Peewit Cottage. An ancient great-aunt of Chris's had died at the beginning of the year, and had left her some furniture which had been stored temporarily in her parents' garage. To start with, we just took over a table and some chairs, ostensibly so we could eat in comfort the cold food we brought with us from the flat— but the end of a hard day's work often found us eating the excellent pies produced by the Golden Ball.

There was absolutely no point in bringing any more furniture, nor having carpets laid, until the woodwork was treated, the damp dealt with and the walls replastered. Only then could we make a start on transforming the place into our dream cottage. We didn't want to spend a single night more than necessary in my small flat above the Rumbling Tum Café, and aimed to move in during half-term.

One afternoon, I abandoned the job of rubbing down the bathroom walls and went outside for a breath of fresh air. I was sitting on the dry-stone wall that enclosed the small garden, staring abstractedly at the breathtaking panorama before me, when I suddenly became aware of a figure observing me from the gate. He was a grizzled old man with a pitted face the colour and texture of an unscrubbed potato, and an impressive shock of white hair. 'How do, squire,' he said.

'Oh, good afternoon,' I replied, clambering down from the wall.

'Admirin' t'view, are tha?'

'Yes, and having a bit of a rest.'

'Hard work, then?' he asked, gesturing towards the cottage.

'Yes, and very dirty,' I replied, brushing a cloud of dust from my overalls.

'Tha must be t'new people 'ere then?' he observed. 'T'wife said a young couple 'ad moved in.'

'That's right.'

'I'm Harry Cotton. Live up by t'beck. I'm tha nearest neighbour.'

'I'm pleased to meet you, Mr Cotton,' I replied, shaking a large hand as rough as sandpaper. 'I'm Gervase Phinn.'

He surveyed the cottage and then with slow deliberation announced, 'I reckon there's a fair bit for tha to do theer, Mester Phinn. I wun't like to tek it on, I'll tell thee that. Been empty for a fair owld time, that cottage, tha knaas. Old Mrs Olleranshaw, 'er who 'ad it afore thee and lived theer all 'er life, must 'ave been deead near on two year now. Her nephew, who inherited it, couldna make up his mind whether to live in it 'imself. That's why it's bin empty so long. Aye, I reckon there's a fair bit to do.'

'Oh, I'm sure we'll get there,' I replied, attempting to sound cheerful. My rustic companion rubbed his chin, twisted his mouth and cocked his head in the direction of the cottage. 'Fair bit of damp, is there?' he enquired grimly.

'Yes, there's damp all right.'

'I thowt so. And woodworm, I reckon?'

'Yes, we have woodworm as well.'

'Bit of subsidence at t'front an' all.'

'Well, you have to expect that sort of thing in a cottage this old.'

'Oh, it's old all reight. One o' oldest in t'village, they reckon. Prob'ly a few ghooasts knockin' abaat. At least tha dunt 'ave a reight big garden to keep on t'top of, any rooad.'

'Actually, I wouldn't have minded a bit more land,' I admitted. 'To grow a few vegetables—that sort of thing.'

'Well, tha can allus get thissen an allotment. There's one goin' just down from me. Ted Poskitt give it up a couple o' years back. Too much for 'im what wi' accident an' all. Nice little plot reight in corner, it is, sheltered. I'd tek it on missen but I've got enough on wi' mi own. Mind you, it'd tek a fair bit of graftin' to clear it and dig it ovver. Ted let it go, tha sees, after 'is accident. He was nivver same. Any rooad, go an' talk to George Hemmings on t'parish council, he'll see you reight.'

'I'll do that,' I said, thinking that it would be rather nice to have an allotment to provide endless supplies of fresh vegetables. 'Thank you for mentioning it.'

'Dry rot,' the old man announced suddenly.

'I beg your pardon?'

'I reckon thas got a bit o' dry rot in that cottage, an' all.'

'I should imagine we have,' I sighed.

'Well, I hope tha fettles it,' he said, staring up at the grey clouds oozing over the felltops. 'I reckon we're in for a bit o' rain. My owld dad used to say when t'blackthorn blossoms come out in early March and when t'sheep is behind walls at midday and when you see worms crawlin' on t'rooad, it's a sure sign of a wet month ahead. Aye, we get a fair bit o' rain up 'ere. Thy shall 'ave to get used to a bit o' wet. I reckon yer roof leaks, an' all. Well, I'll be off.' He raised his hand in greeting before going on his way.

The prophet of doom, I thought wryly, and went back into the cottage to do battle with the bathroom walls again.

OVER THE NEXT FEW WEEKENDS, I worked not in the cottage but on my allotment. Chris had discovered that I wasn't particularly handy when it came to painting. 'Go and dig,' she said, giving me a hug.

I had tracked down George Hemmings the day after Harry Cotton had spoken to me, paid the enormous rent of five pounds for the year and was officially given the lease to cultivate Plot 4. Each Saturday morning, I walked to the other side of the little village where the allotments were. I was like a child with a new toy. Here I set to and tackled the jungle. It was a backbreaking business.

All the allotments, save mine and another at the far side, were lovingly tended. Mine was thick with brambles and sharp-stemmed briars, a crop of dandelions to have pleased a thousand rabbits, frothy white cow parsley, clumps of young and very painful stinging nettles and a mass of other unknown weeds. I set to work with a scythe and eventually managed to clear the whole area. I carefully lifted the maverick daffodil and bluebell bulbs to the side; they could be replanted in the cottage's garden. The worst job was clearing the deep-rooted prickly bushes which seemed to cover half the plot.

Then, one memorable Saturday afternoon, I lit a huge bonfire and watched with great satisfaction as the whole mountain of weeds, branches, bushes and briars went up in smoke.

'Tha's made a good job of that, and no mistake.'

I turned to find Mr Cotton watching over the wall.

'Thank you,' I said, feeling pretty proud of my handiwork. 'I'm glad I've finished,' I told him, wiping my brow. 'It was a big job.'

'It would be,' he commented.

'Those prickly bushes were the worst. The roots seemed to go down for ever.'

'Aye, they do an' all,' agreed my companion.

'Anyhow, it's all cleared now and ready for planting.'

'I nivver knew that owld Albert Tattersall had given up his allotment,' my companion observed.

'Who?' I asked.

'Albert Tattersall. He had this plot. He's 'ad it for near on fifteen year. I nivver knew he'd given it up. I was only in t'pub wi' him past week and 'e never mentioned owt abaat givin' his allotment up.'

'Well, I guess he must have done,' I said. 'George Hemmings confirmed that Plot Four was free for me to take on.'

'Plot Four,' he repeated.

'That's right,' I said, 'I've leased Plot Four.'

'Aye, well, that one you've just dug up is Plot Seven.'

'*What?*' I exclaimed.

'Albert Tattersall's, Plot Seven. Plot Four is at t'other side of allotment.' He waved a hand towards the jungle by the far wall. 'It's reight ovver theer. Tha's gone an' dug wrong plot, sithee.'

'It can't be,' I said feebly. I pointed to the neighbouring plots. There were little white squares fixed in the earth with the plot number on. 'Look, that's Plot Three and there's Plot Five so this one in the middle must be Plot Four.'

'It should be by rights, but it's not,' the old man told me. 'This is Yorkshire, lad. Things are a bit different 'ere. Tha sees it goes alternate like. It sort o' runs contrary like a lot o' things around 'ere.'

'You mean, I've gone and cleared the wrong plot?' I asked.

'Aye, that's the truth on it,' replied Mr Cotton, nodding sagely.

'But why did Mr Tattersall keep an allotment that he never cultivated and never intended to cultivate?' I asked.

'Gooseberries.'

'Gooseberries?'

'You see, owld Albert kept it on for t'gooseberries and then, of course, there's the blackcurrants. Them what would have been growin' on them bushes which you dug up and are now burnin' on tha bonfire.'

'I don't believe it,' I whispered. 'I don't believe it.'

'His wife wins prizes with her gooseberry and blackcurrant jams. Then there's the dandelions. Owld Albert makes a powerful dandelion wine—or used to, more like.'

'And I've dug them all up?'

The old man rubbed his chin and chuckled. 'Every one.' He looked up at the sky. 'Aye well, I shall 'ave to be off. Happen tha'll mek it reight wi' owld Albert,' he remarked.

TWELVE

It was the first day back after the Easter holidays and the full team was in the office, awaiting the arrival of the Senior Inspector designate who had asked to meet with us.

'So how does it feel to be a married man?' Gerry asked me.

'Wonderful,' I replied. 'Marvellous.'

'Let's hope it stays that way,' remarked Sidney, placing his hands behind his head and leaning back dangerously in his chair, 'and that you feel the same way after twenty-five years of it. Marriage is not a bed of roses, you know, particularly for those like you, Gervase, who are dragged to the nuptial altar rather late in life.'

'I was not *dragged* to the altar, Sidney,' I replied, 'and I am not yet in my dotage. I'm sure I'll manage,' I said. 'Millions do.'

'And, of course, millions do not,' continued Sidney, unabashed. 'One in three marriages ends in divorce or separation, you know. A sad fact but very true. Marriage is not all it's cracked up to be.'

'You will be getting a crack in a minute,' David told him, 'if you don't shut up.'

'I don't know how his wife puts up with him,' said Julie, having overheard Sidney's doom-laden speech as she brought in the coffee. 'His wife must be a martyr.'

'Martyrs tend to be dead, Julie,' Sidney told her, smiling.

'A saint then.'

'His wife deserves a medal for bravery, having to put up with him.'

'Oh, I wouldn't go that far,' said Sidney. 'Gervase is a decent enough sort of fellow, and I am sure the delectable Mrs Phinn will learn to put up with him in time.'

'I was talking about you!' snapped Julie, placing the tray noisily on the nearest desk.

'My dear wife, Lila,' announced Sidney, putting on an angelic expression, 'far from considering herself a saint and martyr, thanks her lucky stars she is married to such a creative genius as myself and is prepared to take the rough with the smooth. It's all a matter of give and take. Lila knows how to deal with my little foibles and minor peccadilloes.'

'I know how I'd deal with your little foibles and minor peccadilloes,' said Julie, placing a mug of steaming coffee before him. 'Poison!'

'Do you know, Julie,' said Sidney, sitting up and pushing the coffee away from him in a very theatrical manner, 'I think I will forgo the morning libation.'

'If I had wanted to poison you, Mr Clamp,' Julie retorted, heading for the door, 'I could have done it long ago.'

'Where is he, then?' Sidney suddenly asked, glancing at his watch.

'Who?'

'Mr Carter. Simon. I thought we were here to meet our new leader early this morning?'

'He said nine,' I told him. 'It's only ten minutes to.'

The Senior Inspector designate had called a meeting for us to get to know something about his educational philosophy, as he put it, and for him to consult with us well in advance about his plans for the future. We were all looking forward to meeting him again but, understandably, were a little apprehensive.

'Is Harold not coming, then?' asked Gerry.

'No,' I replied. 'I think he felt it might inhibit Mr Carter.'

'Harold didn't want to come,' said Sidney. 'I can see he would have found it rather difficult. Mind you, *Mister* Carter is certainly very keen. After all, he doesn't start until September.'

'I suppose he wants to get to know a bit more about us before he starts,' said David. 'I expect he will want to make some changes and wants to talk to us about them. It seems sensible to me.'

'Well, I hope there won't be too many changes,' said Sidney.

At the very moment the clock on the County Hall tower struck nine, the door opened and the man himself entered. Mr Simon Carter was a lean, middle-aged man, impeccably groomed in an expensive light grey designer suit, pristine white shirt and discreetly patterned silk tie. His pale face was long and angular; his hair, combed back in rippling waves, was coal black and shiny, and his eyes were dark and narrow. He looked at the four of us staring up at him, then gave us the fullest and most charming of smiles. 'Good morning,' he intoned like a vicar about to start the morning service.

As one, we four inspectors got to our feet. 'Good morning, Mr Carter,' we chorused.

Simon Carter wasted no time. 'Let us commence our discussion,' he said, placing a large black briefcase on Sidney's desk and pulling out a chair.

The meeting started well, with the Senior Inspector designate telling us how pleased he was to have the opportunity of meeting us, that he hoped we would all work together as a team, supporting one another and pulling in the same direction. We had had about an hour of what I reckoned to be fairly constructive discussion when he placed his folded hands carefully in front of him, like a priest about to hear confession, and said, 'I have to say, colleagues, that there seems a great deal to be done. I have been appointed, as you are aware, to take the service forward, to breathe some fresh air into the department and thus changes will be necessary. It is often the case, I have found, that in large education authorities, such as this, which have been relatively successful in retaining high standards, that a certain complacency develops. It very often extends from the senior officers right down to the humble cleaner of the Staff Development Centre.' I could not resist a smile and he pounced on it at once. 'Is there something which amuses you, Gervase?'

'Yes, there is actually,' I replied. 'You have obviously not yet met Connie, the cleaner at the Staff Development Centre. Of all the words one could use to describe her, I think "complacent" and "humble" would come near the very bottom of the list.'

'She's like Attila the Hun with a feather duster,' added Sidney.

'Ah, I rather think I have met her,' said Mr Carter without a trace of a smile. 'There was a woman in a pink overall who was quite rude to me at the interviews. I apparently did something which displeased her—ah, yes, I failed to return my cup to the hatch.'

'That's Connie,' said Sidney, nodding.

'Anyway, that is by the by. What I was endeavouring to say,' he continued, 'is that there is a tendency for large institutions which have plodded on in the same easy-going manner for many years to become moribund.'

'I always thought "moribund" meant on the point of death,' observed Sidney.

'Well, I'm certainly not saying that the department is at death's door,' stated Mr Carter, sounding more conciliatory. 'It is just that some people, from what I have seen so far, cannot think outside the box, see the big picture, go that extra mile. Now, to be perfectly honest, I am not the sort of person to carry passengers. I want to empower people. I want a proactive not a reactive team.'

'Don't you think, Mr Carter,' said David, 'that it would be better to wait and see what you find before jumping to conclusions about the department and making changes? The county has outstanding academic results, excellent schools, a teaching force second to none. Now, if that is moribund—'

'Mr Pritchard, David,' interrupted Mr Carter, 'of course I appreciate all the hard work and have been most impressed by the splendid activities which have taken place and I would be the last person to denigrate the inspectors' efforts, but I have read the county documents and school reports emanating from this office, and there is, to be frank, room for improvement . . .'

'What's wrong with the reports?' snapped Sidney.

'To be frank,' said Mr Carter, quietly but firmly, 'I found the inspectors' reports too wordy and largely lacking in focus. I would like to see them sharper, more incisive. That is one of the reasons why I wished to consult with you before the start of the new term, to try and agree on a better system of reporting on schools.'

'And what form will this take, or rather what form do you feel it should take?' asked Gerry.

'Well, let me explain, Geraldine,' he said, becoming genuinely enthusiastic for the first time. 'In addition to your school-visit reports, I would like more reliable, objective data recorded. I would like to set up some bench marks. The work that Mrs Savage does for you—all those questionnaires and surveys—are of little practical use.' Sidney gave David a knowing look. I could tell what he was thinking. 'What I want to introduce is a teacher-effectiveness inventory, a pupil-attitude questionnaire, a classroom-climate assessment and a resources audit. That sort of thing. It will help us to create an extensive database of information and assist the schools in improving their performance. From this information a league table can then be devised—'

'Sounds like the football pools to me,' said David. 'Will we have premier schools, first division schools, second division schools? Will schools be relegated? Will schools be able to buy teachers as a football team buys players?'

'No, no, don't be facile,' said Mr Carter, 'but there will be an educational league table to encourage schools that are failing to try that bit harder, to go that extra mile. If they are placed in competition with more successful schools, the poor schools will strive to improve, don't you think?'

'No, not really,' replied David. 'I think it is more likely to be divisive. It seems to me pretty self-evident that Sir Cosmo's Grammar will always come near the top of the league and Crompton Secondary School will always be lingering near the bottom. The pupils are of very differing abilities. It doesn't mean that one school is better than the other. They are just different.'

'I think you are rather missing the point,' said Mr Carter irritably. 'What I was endeavouring to explain—'

'Mr Carter, Simon,' said Sidney, interrupting, 'don't you think that doing all these objective tests and assessments will take us away from one of our main tasks—that of *helping* and *supporting* teachers? Are we not in danger of spending too much time weighing the pig and not enough time feeding it?'

Mr Carter sighed. 'It is early days, Sidney. I am sure that when I am in a position to explain my vision more clearly, you will become convinced of the value of these changes.' He glanced at his watch. 'Well, I think this has been a most productive meeting, don't you? But I must be on my way. I have a session with Mrs Savage in a moment.' A number of eyebrows were raised at this declaration. 'I'm going to touch base with her and talk through my game plan.'

'That should prove very interesting,' murmured David, undoubtedly still smarting at being told he was 'facile'.

And that was that. Mr Carter wished us goodbye and departed.

When Julie entered the office a moment later she found the four of us sitting at our desks, stunned into silence.

'Is everything all right?' she asked.

'Please don't say anything, Geraldine,' said Sidney as his colleague opened her mouth to speak. 'Just don't say a word.'

THAT EVENING I snuggled up with Christine on an old sofa we had bought from Roper's Saleroom. We had spent an hour stripping faded and peeling wallpaper off the bedroom walls and were relaxing before returning to the flat in Fettlesham for supper. She rested her head on my chest. 'You're in a very pensive mood,' she said.

'Chris, what would you say if I said I wanted to look for another job?'

'I thought you had got over not being short-listed for the Senior Inspector's post.'

'I have.'

'Well, what's brought all this on, then?'

'Oh, I don't know. I just feel with Harold going things will change.'

'Well, of course things will change. There's nothing wrong with change. You've changed into a happily married man—I hope—and we're going to change this cottage. Things need to change. Things can't stay the same for ever.'

'Some things don't need to change, though. You wouldn't want the view from this window to change, for example, would you?'

'That's different.'

'Exactly. Some changes are for the good, but others are not. The thing is, I think work is going to change for the worse when Harold goes. The new SI came in today and none of us really like him.'

'I thought you did?'

'We did at first, but after the meeting today we changed our minds. He's single-minded and it's clear he wants his own way and everyone to agree with him. He's a systems man and, worst of all, he seems completely humourless. All he talks about is appraisal and assessment and tests and audits. He rarely mentions children. He's hell-bent on bringing in these dreadful form-filling procedures. It sounds a nightmare. I want to work with teachers and children, not be pen-pushing morning, noon and night. He is a very different kettle of fish from Harold.'

'Harold's pretty special, though, isn't he? You can't expect his successor to be a carbon copy of Harold.'

'I don't expect that. It's just that I know I'm not going to get on with Simon Carter. None of us will. I don't think he will be a good boss to work for.'

'There wouldn't be a few sour grapes here, would there?' asked Christine.

'Not at all. Hey, Chris, you're supposed to be sympathetic and understanding and—'

'Agree with everything you say? Look, love, I'm sorry you are feeling depressed about this but it's early days yet. If this ogre of a new Senior Inspector does turn out to be difficult and demanding and you begin to hate the job, then you can think about a move. But let's give the man a chance.' She looked up with those great blue eyes. 'OK?'

'I suppose so,' I replied.

'Now, did you remember to do the shopping, Mr Phinn? I think you said you would cook tonight.'

THIRTEEN

A few days before the half-term break, I was due at Pope Pius X Roman Catholic Primary School in the little market town of Ribsdyke. I was looking forward to the visit because I was going to be accompanied by a man I much admired, Valentine Courtnay-Cunninghame, 9th Earl Marrick, Viscount Manston, Baron Brafferton, MC, DL, one of the representatives on the governing body of the school. On our first visit there together he had become apoplectic about the run-down condition of the premises. 'You inspectors are supposed to comment on the poor state of buildings and the effects upon the children's education,' he told me sternly. 'The whole place wants pulling down and rebuilding.' Lord Marrick had then promised the headteacher that he would be contacting Dr Gore when he returned to the Education Department and would ensure that improvements would be put in hand. Lord Marrick had been true to his word.

I collected Lord Marrick now from the Small Committee Room of County Hall and we were soon heading for the rolling hills of the Dales, leaving behind the noise and bustle of Fettlesham. We were going to attend the opening of the new school building, a development which was largely the result of Lord Marrick's strenuous efforts on the school's behalf.

'Have you met the new Senior Inspector, then?' he asked, stroking his walrus moustache. 'He's a very clever man by all accounts.'

'Yes. Very clever.' Too clever by half, I thought to myself.

'Well qualified, too. All these letters after his name, degrees in this, diplomas in that, member of this, fellow of that. I thought I'd met a kindred spirit when I saw one set of letters after his name. Thought he was a member of the Bull Breeders' Association, too. But then realised it was MBA not MBBA.' He chuckled.

I smiled, too, thinking of the intense-looking man with the piercing eyes and designer suit trying to lead a frisky bull in from the field. 'MBA indicates a Master of Business Administration degree,' I informed Lord Marrick. 'It's a top qualification.'

'So I gather. Then he has those other letters—BAA. I told him that it sounded like a degree in sheepshearing but I don't think he was amused.'

No, I thought, it wouldn't amuse our Mr Carter. I wondered what *would* amuse him. 'I think that is yet another qualification in accounts and administration,' I said.

'Well, he seems to be extremely experienced in management and supervision.'

'Yes,' I remarked, hoping we could leave this particular topic of conversation. I was finding it hugely depressing.

'Gave a very impressive presentation and his interview was a tour de force. Never seen Councillor George Peterson stuck for words. He just sat and stared like a Toby jug. Mr Carter was never stumped for an answer and seems to have done just about everything there is to do in the educational field. Been a headmaster, adviser, lecturer, management consultant. One wonders what he wanted to become a school inspector in Yorkshire for. Must like the scenery.'

'Yes, indeed,' I said.

'You're very quiet this morning, Gervase. Cat must have got your tongue. Is it because you were not considered for the position?' Lord Marrick was nothing if not blunt. 'Is that what's getting you down? Dr Gore did mention that you had put in an application.'

Oh no, I thought. I hope he's not going to be another on the long list of people to tell me I hadn't had enough experience for such a senior position, that my time would come. 'I did apply, Lord Marrick, yes, that's true,' I replied. 'I was disappointed, of course, but—'

'You need a few more years under your belt yet, if you don't mind me saying.'

'No, of course not.'

'Takes that much longer in the Dales, you know, than in other parts of the country, for people to get to know you. It takes some time to get used to "off-comed-uns", as they say. My family are just about accepted by the locals and we've been here since the time of the Normans. Give it a few more years.'

'I will,' I replied. 'Thank you for the advice.'

'I hope it doesn't sound like advice. I was merely making an observation. I was told by my father never to give unsolicited advice—the clever man doesn't need it and the foolish man never takes it.'

I continued to drive with my eyes firmly on the road, past grey-stone farmhouses and cottages, long hedgerows in bright new leaf, and fields studded with hawthorn trees in luxuriant blossom. Despite all this beauty, which would normally lift my spirits sky-high, I just felt in the dumps.

'Of course, I never pulled up any roots at school, you know,' Lord Marrick admitted, twisting the ends of his moustache. 'Sent away at nine, I was, mother crying her eyes out at the station, nanny having hysterics, sisters clinging on to me for dear life, father telling me to keep my chin up, stiff upper lip and all that. Pretty bleak those first couple of years, I don't mind telling you. Then I got into sport. Spent most of my time on the rugger or cricket pitch after that, and the hardest work I did was to ensure that I attended the minimum number of lessons. My grandson found one of my old school reports a few weeks ago. A master had written: "Now I have deciphered Courtnay-Cunninghame's spidery scribble, I have discovered that he is unable to spell." Not a lot of laughs when I was at school. I do think it's important to have a sense of humour. There's enough doom and gloom in the world. A good laugh does you good, that's what I always think.' He thought for a moment, then said, 'You know, this new chap, Carter, was a bit of a serious cove. I hope he's going to be all right.'

So do I, I thought to myself. So do I.

WE SOON ARRIVED at the school and its new appearance came as quite a shock. In place of the featureless building that had been erected just after the war and had had the appearance of an army barracks, there now stood a handsome red-brick building with long picture windows and an orange pantile roof. The area round the school had been landscaped, and scrubby lawn and cracked paving had been replaced with a play area with benches and picnic tables, surrounded by flowering shrubs and young newly planted trees.

Lord Marrick clambered from the car, put his hands on his wide hips, surveyed the building with great satisfaction and growled, 'Not bloody bad, eh?'

The entrance hall to the school was very different as well. On my previous visit I had been reminded more of a hospital than a school. Now the area was brightly decorated and an eye-catching mural stretched the full length of the wall. There were modern tables and chairs, tall glass display panels, attractively framed prints and, in pride of place, a large portrait of Pope Pius X with arms outstretched and eyes looking heavenwards.

Mrs Callaghan, the headteacher, was an attractive woman with friendly eyes and light sandy hair tied back. She hurried across the hall to greet us. 'Lord Marrick, Mr Phinn. It's so nice to see you again.'

We followed her into her room and listened as she outlined the programme for the afternoon. First, we would attend assembly, then be given a tour of the school. At the end of the afternoon, when the governors and parents had arrived, everyone would gather in the school hall and Lord Marrick would undertake the official opening of the new building. I was representing Dr Gore and had nothing to do but mingle and be pleasant. I was still not, however, feeling in a very pleasant frame of mind.

Lord Marrick and I chose to sit at the back of the new school hall and watched the children enter—smart, cheerful and well behaved— to the taped strains of some lively martial music. I have spent many an hour observing school assemblies and have heard countless homilies from headteachers. Some have been tedious affairs with rows of wriggling, inattentive children having to endure a rambling headteacher who frequently finishes by launching into a good telling-off about some infringement of the school rules. Other assemblies have been inspirational and thought-provoking, capturing the children's imaginations. The assembly I watched that afternoon was one of the latter.

'Good afternoon, children,' said Mrs Callaghan cheerfully. 'I would like to extend a very special welcome today to our two important visitors, Earl Marrick and Mr Gervase Phinn. Later this afternoon, children, Earl Marrick will be officially opening our new building and unveiling a plaque to celebrate the rebirth of Pope Pius the Tenth School. It is a very important day for us.

'We always dreamed of a new school,' she said, looking round the bright new hall. 'We always dreamed of light, airy classrooms, long colourful corridors, a well-stocked library with a carpet and cushions and easy chairs. We always dreamed of a sports field and a playground, a modern kitchen, sparkling toilets and, most especially, a spacious school hall. Some thought it would remain just a dream, an idea that would never come true. We have had so many disappointments along the way, so many hurdles and detours and standstills, and there have been many times when we have felt like giving up. But we didn't. We believed in our dream and today our dream has come true. In a few hours' time, our new school will be officially opened.' The headteacher paused to compose herself. She was clearly finding this quite an emotional occasion. 'All of you will have your dreams and you must never, never give up on them, for dreams *do* come true. In your own lives, children, there will be times when you have worked so hard for something and all your efforts seem to come to nothing. Times when you have walked a thousand steps towards your goal only to find yourself back in the place from where you started. At times like these, you will feel disappointed, let down, bewildered. You will feel like giving up. Well, you must carry on. You must continue to believe in yourself and follow your dreams.'

Mrs Callaghan then went on to talk about various events which would take place the next week, and this gave me time to think about what she had said. I realised just how selfish and ungrateful it was of me to be so pessimistic and downhearted. I had a beautiful wife, a lovely cottage and a good job. What had I got to be so miserable about? It was as if Mrs Callaghan had chosen her words just for me.

SOME TIME LATER, after having talked to the governors, I rejoined Lord Marrick who was holding sway with a group of teachers. The subject under discussion would have depressed me immensely a short time ago, but now the black cloud had lifted and I was in a much better frame of mind.

'I was just telling the present company, Mr Phinn,' said Lord Marrick, 'that we were talking on the way over here this afternoon about the appointment of the new Senior Inspector and all those letters he has after his name. I was recalling that the headteacher before Mrs Callaghan had a similar string of qualifications.'

'But I was appointed,' said Mrs Callaghan, 'with just a teaching certificate and not a degree to my name.'

'Well, it's not the qualifications that matter in the long run. It's the calibre of the person. I don't mind saying, Mrs Callaghan, and you've heard me say this before, you run a cracking good school.'

'And that was a cracking good assembly earlier on,' I added. It had certainly given me food for thought.

At the end of the school day, Lord Marrick cut a long length of bright blue ribbon fixed across the entrance to the hall, pulled a silk cord to uncover a plaque set in the wall, and made a short but elegant speech. Then, as the children sweetly sang some country songs, I sat blissfully listening and staring beyond them through the large picture window at the sweeping green dale beyond.

ONE BRIGHT EARLY June Saturday morning, Christine and I moved into Peewit Cottage, saying a thankful farewell to the flat over the Rumbling Tum Café and the cooking smells that wafted malodorously up the stairs. The woodworm and damp treatment on the cottage, the repointing, replastering and redecorating had just about cleaned out our bank account but we couldn't have been happier. The sun was shining, the birds were singing and we were so excited at the prospect of starting married life in our very own home. I had hired a van on the previous Saturday and, with David's help, had moved the bits of furniture that Christine had inherited from her great-aunt. My sister had donated some pots and pans, carpets and curtains, my brother Michael had presented us with a sideboard and Sidney had arrived unannounced one evening at my flat with an assortment of cutlery, garden tools, shelves and rugs.

'I've been having a clearout in the garage, dear boy,' he told me, 'and thought some of these might come in handy.'

The only article of furniture we needed to buy was a bed.

The Sunday before we moved into the cottage, Christine and I spent a morning browsing around Roper's Saleroom in Collington.

The main room, where the auctions took place, was crammed with the most wonderful antique furniture: Regency mahogany sideboards, delicate inlaid rosewood tables, satinwood desks, Edwardian wing armchairs, bowfronted cupboards and tall grandfather clocks. All of it was way out of our price range.

And then we saw the bed. It took up an inordinate amount of space at the side of the saleroom and, surrounded by such exquisite furniture, looked amazingly plain and ugly with its dark oak headboard, thick buttoned mattress and heavy square legs.

'What do you think?' I asked.

'It's a bit large,' Christine replied, 'and it's not the most elegant of pieces, is it?'

'Looks aren't everything,' I pointed out.

'I'm not sure. Perhaps we ought to get a new one.'

'It's very comfortable,' I told her, sitting on the thick mattress and bouncing up and down. 'A modern bed wouldn't fit in. A cottage the age of ours needs to have older furniture and this is really well-made. I can tell. It will last for ever, this bed.'

'I have no doubt about that.' Christine gave a wry smile.

'Well, shall we stay for the auction and see what it goes for? I mean, it will probably be well out of our price range anyway.' When had we said that before? We should have learned by now.

So we stayed for the auction and sat through item after item, most of which fetched an exorbitant price.

'Ours is the next lot after this one,' I whispered to Christine.

'I really don't know whether we should bid, Gervase,' she said. 'Are you really sure about this?'

'Lot 368,' the auctioneer intoned. 'A turn-of-the-century solidly constructed, iron-framed and impressively large bed in oak. Shall we start the bidding at one hundred pounds?'

'I am not sure about that bed,' Christine said, later that evening. 'I still think we should have gone for something more modern.'

'Well, it's too late now,' I told her. 'We've bought it and Roper's are delivering it next Saturday. It may not be a Louis the Fourteenth masterpiece but I think we got a real bargain.'

'By the time we've bought a new mattress, it won't be so much of a bargain,' said Christine, who had insisted we throw away the old mattress. 'But, I agree, it's a great bed.'

The bed arrived the day we moved in. I was exchanging pleasantries with our neighbour, Harry Cotton, over the dry-stone wall, when a huge dark green removal van bearing the words 'Roper's Auctioneers of Distinction' printed in gold lettering on the side drew up outside the cottage.

'More furniture, then,' observed Harry, scratching his shock of white hair. 'At this rate, you won't have room to swing a dormouse.'

'Just a bed,' I replied.

'Aahh well,' he chuckled, winking theatrically. 'Tha'll be needing a bed an' no mistake. I reckon you and yer new missus'll be putting that to good use, if tha follows my drift.'

I did not wish to follow his drift and went to greet the three men in green overalls, with the Roper's logo embroidered in yellow, who had just jumped out of the van.

'Mr Phinn?' asked a young man with closely cropped dyed-blond hair and a large gold stud in his ear.

'That's right,' I replied.

'We're here with the bed. Where do you want it?'

'Where do you think he wants it?' bayed Harry Cotton, shouting over the wall. 'In my experience, beds go in t'bedrooms, sithee.'

'OK, granddad,' said the young man. 'Keep you hair on. I was just asking.' Then he asked Harry mischievously, 'Are you going to give us a lift with it, then?'

'Am I 'ell as like,' he said. 'I've had a double hernia, me. T'eaviest thing I lift these days is a pint o' bitter.'

The three men, with my help, struggled and strained to get the bed out of the removal van and we dumped it at the door of the cottage. It looked gigantic.

'Do you think you'll get it through the door?' I asked apprehensively. 'It looks a lot bigger here than it did in the saleroom.'

'We'll get it through the door, no trouble,' said the young man with the short hair and the stud. 'We can upend it. Getting it up the stairs is a different matter altogether.'

'Well, they got it down,' said Harry as he observed proceedings from the wall. 'So they must 'ave got it up.'

'How do you mean?' I asked.

Harry rubbed his chin and cocked his head in the direction of the cottage. 'That theer bed what you 'ave just bought, belonged to old Mrs Olleranshaw. It used to be in her front bedroom.'

'Mrs Olleranshaw!' I exclaimed. 'The old lady who owned the cottage before us?'

'The very same.'

'But I thought you told me she had died two years ago.'

'She did. It were her nephew, young Nigel, 'im what came into her money. He only got around to selling her stuff at t'beginning of this year. Some of it went to Roper's, I believe. Aye, that theer bed used to be in her front bedroom.' He chuckled, a long low chuckle. 'It's a rum do, i'n't it? All that heffort gerrin' it down and then it 'as to go up ageean.'

'Are you sure this is the same bed, Harry?' I asked.

'Oh yes, it's t'same bed, sure as eggs is eggs. She was ill for a long time was Mrs Olleranshaw. Spent a deal of time in that there bed a-moanin' and a-groanin'.' He scratched his chin and nodded sagely. 'Breathed her last in it an' all.'

At this point, Christine emerged from the cottage, looking radiant in the spring sunshine and smiling widely.

'Ah, the bed,' she said. 'It's arrived.'

'I was just saying to your 'usband, Mrs Phinn,' said Harry. 'This is the bed that old Mrs Olleranshaw died in.'

FOURTEEN

We could hear Sidney chortling to himself as he climbed the stairs to the office.

'Someone is in a remarkably good mood,' commented David, looking up morosely and peering over the top of his spectacles. He pushed away from him the report he was attempting to complete and leaned back in his chair.

'It's Friday,' I reminded him, trying to sound cheerful, 'and the prospect of a nice quiet weekend.'

'Huh!' snorted my companion, shaking his head wearily. 'Not if I haven't finished this wretched report.'

A moment later, Sidney strode through the door, threw his brief-case onto his desk with a flourish and flopped heavily into the nearest chair. Then he tossed back his head and laughed so loudly that Julie came bustling in to see what the noise was.

'Whatever is it?' she asked. 'Are you having some sort of a turn?'

'No, Julie,' replied Sidney. 'I am perfectly well, thank you. I am laughing. I am having a hearty laugh which, so the philosophers tell us, is a sign of a healthy soul. "A merry heart doeth good like a medicine." Book of Proverbs,' he continued, unabashed.

'"And a heavy fist doeth great damage to the features of the intolerably jovial." Book of David.'

'Well, this will warm those little Welsh cockles of yours,' smiled Sidney. 'I have just heard the most wonderfully amusing story. It was so absurdly entertaining, I just cannot stop chuckling to myself.'

'Well, you can share it with us,' I told him. 'We're not feeling too happy with the world at the moment, are we, David?'

'That is putting it mildly,' remarked David gloomily, plucking the spectacles from his nose. 'Every blessed report I write, I keep thinking of the new Senior Inspector and what he said. I tell you, I've been put right off my stroke since *Mister* Carter criticised our reports. I'm certain he was looking directly at me when he fired the broadside about flabby writing. I do tend to be a bit wordy, I have to admit, and am a little anecdotal, but I have always found—'

'You are sounding paranoid,' Sidney interrupted. 'He was referring to all of us. You are, if truth be told, rather loquacious, David, but at least you do not use that ceaseless flow of limp metaphors and maxims beloved of management gurus like Simon Carter and our very own Brenda Savage. They use a sort of verbal wallpaper to cover the cracks in their thinking and the gaping holes in their arguments. Anyway, our new Senior Inspector was staring at *me* when he made that particular comment. You are taking it far too personally.'

'I didn't like him,' observed Julie, examining a broken nail. 'He's got cold fishy eyes and warm clammy hands. He asked me if I was the clerical ancillary—I ask you!—and told me he would be reviewing my roles and responsibilities as soon as he's settled in. If he starts interfering, I shall tell him to stick his job.'

'So don't keep this very funny story to yourself, Sidney,' I said. 'We could do with cheering up.'

'Well,' began Sidney, 'have either of you been into West Challerton High recently?'

'Yes, I was there last week to attend Prize-giving and Speech Day,' I told him.

'And met the new headmaster?'

'Yes, of course I did. He would hardly miss Prize-giving, would he?'

'You know, then, how inflated and self-promoting the man is and so full of his own importance, swanning around the place in his academic gown, hands behind his back like Napoleon?'

'Napoleon tucked his hand inside his coat, didn't he?' asked Julie.

'Am I allowed to finish this story,' demanded Sidney, 'without petty interruptions?'

'Go on, go on,' I urged. 'We'll be here all night at this rate.'

'Well, earlier this week, when I was on a two-day visit to the school, inspecting the visual arts department, the headmaster had this final-year pupil in his room when I arrived. He asked me to wait in the outer room—that little glass adjunct that he euphemistically calls his personal assistant's office. As I sat there waiting I could hear the conversation as clearly as if he were sitting next to me. He says, "Well now, Delores—"'

At this point the telephone rang.

I picked up the receiver. 'Hello?'

'Gervase, it's me, Gerry,' came a distressed voice down the phone. 'I'm in a spot of bother.'

'What's happened?' I asked. I cupped my hand over the receiver. '*Will* you be quiet,' I told Sidney, who had decided to continue to regale Julie and David with the account of West Challerton High.

'My car's broken down,' said Gerry. 'It suddenly cut out and I'm stranded here in a lay-by on the wrong side of Fettlesham. I have to get home in a hurry because I have something urgent to do. I really *have* to get back. Could you possibly collect me and take me home? I wouldn't ask, Gervase, if it weren't really important.'

'Of course, no problem. Tell me exactly where you are.'

'Look,' I told my colleagues when I had put down the telephone and interrupted Sidney yet again, 'I've got to go and get Gerry. Her car's broken down.'

'I'm forever telling her about that old car of hers,' said David. 'It's not safe, an attractive young woman driving all over the county in an old jalopy like that.'

'It's not as if she can't afford a better car,' remarked Julie. 'Some of us, of course, have to make do with public transport. And on that subject, I'm off since I'll miss my bus if I don't get my skates on,' and, with a wave of her hand, she left the room.

'But what about my story?' shouted Sidney after her. 'I haven't finished my story.'

'Tell us another time,' called back Julie.

'Well, I shall make a move,' said David, putting the report in his briefcase and rising. 'I've had this week in a big way.'

'I really don't know why I bother,' said Sidney, shaking his head and slumping back in his chair. 'I really don't know why I bother.'

GERRY WAS WAITING at the side of the road, pacing up and down and looking uncharacteristically anxious and impatient. I had never seen her in such an agitated state.

'Oh, thank goodness,' she said breathlessly, as I opened the passenger door for her to jump in. 'It's really good of you to collect me, Gervase. I'm so grateful.'

'No problem at all. Now,' I said, as I eased out into the traffic, 'I take it we are heading for Hawthwaite?'

'Oh, yes, please,' replied Gerry. 'I really am sorry to be such a nuisance. The car just suddenly cut out. I phoned the breakdown people but they said they'd be over an hour and I just didn't know what to do. Did I drag you away from anything important?'

'Just one of Sidney's stories. I was glad to get away, to be honest. It was lucky you caught me because I was about to make tracks when your call came through.' Gerry did not reply but rubbed her hands together uneasily, then glanced at her watch.

'So, what's the emergency?' I asked.

She was silent for a moment. 'Oh, it's . . . I really don't know what to say. I honestly don't know where to start.'

'You don't have to tell me if you don't want to,' I said gently. 'I'll just drop you off home and ask no questions. I can be very discreet, you know, and if you need any more help . . .'

'I do appreciate your coming out. I know you will want to get on home and Christine will be wondering where you've got to. And on Friday night as well.' She glanced at her watch again.

'Oh, she's used to my staying out late. Anyway, it's unlikely she's back from school yet. She stays late most evenings. I often get home before her and—'

Geraldine was clearly not listening. 'Actually, could you drop me off just the other side of Fangbeck Bridge? There's a row of red-brick cottages, just past the Three Feathers pub.'

'Oh yes, I know them. But I thought you said you lived at the other side of the village?'

'I do,' Gerry replied, 'but I have to collect someone.' She took a deep breath, and then said, 'And then if you could run us home . . .'

'Do you want me to collect you in the morning,' I asked her, 'and give you a tow to a garage?'

'No, no, you've been really kind as it is. I'll be able to deal with the car myself.' She glanced at her watch again. 'Gervase, there is some-thing I have to tell you,' she began, 'and I really don't know where to start. The someone I have to collect . . . oh, this is very difficult . . .'

'I think I can save you the embarrassment, Gerry,' I said. 'I assume it is your little boy?'

There was a sharp intake of breath. 'However did you know?'

'I was speaking at the Totterdale and Clearwell Golf Club dinner and I sat next to Mrs Hills, the woman you rent the cottage from. She told me you had a child.'

'When was this?' Gerry asked, still in a shocked whisper.

'Oh, some time before Christmas.'

'You've known for over six months?'

'Yes.'

Gerry released a huge sigh, then threw back her head and gave a little laugh. 'And here I was thinking that it was the world's best-kept secret. Why ever didn't you mention it?'

'I assumed you wanted to keep it a secret.'

'How many other people know?'

'None, so far as I know. I haven't said a word to anyone—and that includes Christine.'

'Thank you, Gervase, a hundred times. Heavens, that's another thing I have to thank you for.'

'I shall continue to remain as silent as the grave. But what I cannot understand, Gerry, is why you have decided to keep it such a secret? I mean, it's not as though we are living in the Dark Ages. Who nowadays is going to bother about someone who's a single parent?'

'It might not be the Dark Ages, Gervase, but this is Yorkshire, not London. People can be very narrow-minded. And do you imagine for one moment that I would have had a hope in hell of getting this job if it were known that I had a three-year-old son to look after and no husband? Just think of some of those who sit on the interview panels—Councillor Peterson, for example, with his ghastly comments about young women not being able to handle the difficult lads and his prehistoric views on a woman's place being at home, cooking and cleaning and looking after the kiddies. It's difficult enough for a woman to get a senior position in such a man's world as it is, without being unmarried and with a young child.'

'Mmm, I see what you mean. But, you know, Yorkshire people are generally very warm and generous and usually don't judge others too hastily. I think you would have been rather surprised at the reaction, had you taken the risk.'

'It will eventually have to come out,' continued Gerry. 'I realise that. Jamie starts nursery school after the summer holidays and you know what the jungle telegraph is like.'

'So no one, except myself, knows then?' I asked.

'Harold knows. I thought it only fair to tell him before they offered me the job, and he said that so long as it did not affect my work, it was nobody's business but my own.'

'That sounds like Harold,' I said.

'He's been a tower of strength and I will really miss him terribly. I am dreading the arrival of Simon Carter, I have to say. He doesn't strike me as the most understanding and tolerant of men. He has already told me he expects lots of late meetings and evening events. I've not stopped worrying since that dreadful encounter with him when he outlined all the changes he intends making.

'Anyway, I'll have to face that when I have to. I always try to collect Jamie from the childminder at six. She'll baby-sit for me as well so long as I give her good notice. It's worked out pretty well.' She glanced at her watch for the umpteenth time. 'Until today, that is. She's arranged to go out this evening.'

'Well, we are nearly there now,' I reassured her. 'And I wouldn't worry about Mr Carter. As Connie would say, "You can burn that bridge when you get to it."'

EARLY THE FOLLOWING Monday morning Sidney, David, Gerry and I were at the Staff Development Centre for an inspectors' meeting.

'Thanks a million for Friday,' said Gerry quietly, placing a bottle of wine before me. 'I was in a real state. I hope you and Christine will enjoy this.'

'Oh, you shouldn't have bothered,' I told her, 'but thanks. It's very thoughtful of you. Has the car been fixed?'

'No, not yet. I'm in a hire car this week, but I should have it back next Monday.' She sounded her usual composed and confident self.

'As I said to Gervase the other night,' said David, peering over the top of his spectacles, 'you ought to get yourself a reliable vehicle, Geraldine. You could have broken down in some dark, deserted place in the middle of nowhere with no sign of life for miles. Then what would you have done?'

'I shudder at the thought,' Gerry said.

'I mean, you read all the time about young women being attacked along lonely country roads, dragged into the bushes and assaulted, left for dead in a ditch, buried—'

'David,' I interrupted, 'must you be such a prophet of doom? You are getting more and more depressing lately.'

At that moment, Sidney entered the room, pursued by Connie wearing her usual bright pink nylon overall. In place of the feather duster, that morning she held aloft a lethal-looking mop.

'I was merely pointing out, Connie,' Sidney was saying in a weary tone of voice, 'that there is little point in putting a notice that says "Wet Floor" right at the end of the corridor where no one can see it. The sign would be better, I would have thought, placed in the entrance, to forewarn those who are foolhardy enough to venture through the door in the first place that the floor is like an ice rink. I very nearly fell full length.'

'Putting the notice in the entrance would be a health and safety hazard,' announced Connie. 'People could fall over it.'

'And people could, and I nearly did, slip on the wet floor,' said Sidney.

'I always do my floors on a Monday morning, Mr Clamp, you know that. Eight o'clock prompt before the teachers arrive at nine for their courses is when I do my floors. I always have done and I always will do. I never deleviate from my routine. It's your fault for being late.' Before Sidney could respond, Connie turned her attention to the rest of us and smiled. 'Now, I called in to say I have had a phone message from Dr Yeats, who said he would be a bit late. He's tied up with that Mrs Savage at the moment.'

'I can't think of anything more unpleasant,' remarked David.

'So, since we have a little time on our hands,' said Sidney, glancing in the direction of Connie, before gently pulling out a chair and making sure it did not leave a mark on the highly polished floor, 'I shall conclude my story of Delores and the headmaster of West Challerton High School.' He looked in the direction of Connie as if to indicate that she could get on with her mopping, but she remained where she was, standing sentinel with her mop, like Britannia.

'If you must,' said David.

'I was telling David and Gervase that I was doing a two-day inspection in West Challerton High School and eavesdropping on a conversation between that dreadfully pompous headmaster and one of the older pupils. This girl was due to have a baby, and he was explaining to her that she could still come in for her examinations, which she would sit in a small room rather than the hall. He was also informing her that the Outward Bound week over the summer holidays was off because she was not in a fit state, being five months pregnant, to go grass-skiing and abseiling. Well, on the following day old Pennington-Smith stands up in assembly, before all the staff and pupils, and announces, "There is a spare place now available on the Outward Bound week because of a late withdrawal." Sidney's face creased with laughter. 'I nearly died when I heard what he said. All the staff had to go out for laughing.'

David gave a weak smile, but I know I must have looked acutely embarrassed because I could not avoid immediately thinking of Gerry's circumstances.

'Well, I thought it was hilarious,' said Sidney, looking crestfallen. 'A spare place due to a late withdrawal!'

'Mr Clamp,' said Connie, who was still listening from the door and shaking her mop like a spear, 'Delores, for your information, happens to be my cousin's girl and I'll tell you this. Those who get into trouble like what she did are the innocent ones, those what men take advantage of. It is no laughing matter bringing up a child without a father. No laughing matter at all.' With that she stomped out.

Sidney hunched his shoulders, pulled the most excruciating expression and whispered across the table, 'Tell me where the hole is so I can crawl into it.'

'It was in rather bad taste,' remarked David. 'Even for you, Sidney.'

'Well how was I to know the girl was Connie's cousin's daughter?' moaned Sidney. 'She'll put toilet bleach in my tea after this.'

'Connie's right,' said Gerry. 'It's no laughing matter bringing up a child without a father. It's a real struggle. I should know.'

'And why should you know, my dear Geraldine?' I opened my mouth to try to head Sidney off but I was too late. 'Don't tell us that you have a love child.'

'Well, yes, Sidney, actually I do.'

Sidney, for once, was completely lost for words.

'It is perhaps not the most brilliant time to tell you, but I have a little boy called Jamie. He's three. Jamie's father is married and has a family. I guess I should have told you.'

There was what seemed like an interminable silence. It was broken by Sidney. 'Well, Gerry, I . . . er . . . congratulations. I really am sorry,' he said, giving her a pathetic hangdog look. 'I didn't know . . . You are quite right. It's . . . it's no laughing matter.'

'Actually, your Delores story was quite amusing,' said Gerry, smiling, 'and you weren't to know.'

'But why didn't you say anything?' asked David. 'You surely didn't think that we wouldn't be supportive?'

'No,' replied Gerry quietly, 'I never thought that. I suppose I was just afraid of the gossip, what other people would say. It was rather silly of me to keep it a secret.'

'We all have skeletons in our cupboards,' announced Sidney, now recovered somewhat from his earlier embarrassment.

'Some more than others, I guess,' remarked David, looking fixedly at Sidney. Then he turned his attention on me. 'You are pretty quiet, Gervase. Aren't you surprised? Ah! Perhaps you already knew.'

'Yes,' I replied. 'I met Jamie on Friday night when I took Gerry home when her car broke down. A smashing kid.'

Gerry threw me a grateful glance. There was no point in letting on that I had known for months.

At that moment Harold breezed in. 'Sorry, sorry I'm late. I was tied up at County Hall with Mrs Savage and just could not get away.' He smiled indulgently at David and Sidney who were chortling like schoolboys. He placed himself at the head of the table and pulled out a wad of papers, which he placed before him, and rubbed his large hands vigorously. 'Well now, colleagues, I've got some rather interesting news.' He took a deep breath, gave a great toothy smile and announced. 'I am staying on for another term, maybe two.'

'You are *what*?' we all exclaimed.

'Staying on,' repeated Harold. 'Dr Gore has asked me to withdraw my resignation for the time being and hold the fort until my successor has been appointed.'

'But your successor has been appointed,' I said. 'Or have I missed something?'

'Mr Simon Carter, as you correctly point out, Gervase,' explained Harold, 'was indeed appointed but has unexpectedly resigned.' There was a distinctly gleeful tone in his voice.

'He's really *resigned*?' cried Sidney.

'Yes, he has decided that the job is not right for him,' continued Harold. 'If truth be told, I think he found the prospect a little too challenging. He has decided to return to management consultancy.'

'Well, he certainly knew all the buzz words,' said David. 'He seemed to have memorised all the catchphrases and clichés there are. I for one am delighted he is not taking over.'

'This is great news indeed, Harold!' exclaimed Sidney.

'But is he allowed to break his contract?' asked Gerry. 'He accepted the position, didn't he?'

'You are right, Geraldine,' Harold told her. 'He would, under normal circumstances, be required to honour the contract he signed, but Dr Gore has spoken to members of the Education Subcommittee and sorted all that out. He certainly would not want a Senior Inspector whose heart was not in the job. I have to say, he was secretly very pleased when Mr Carter requested to be released from his contract. He had become increasingly unsure about the man. He found him very intense and tiring and had also received numerous complaints about his abrasive manner. Evidently Mr Carter has trodden on a great many toes. He has already managed to upset the resource manager, the principal architect, the chief psychologist, the principal school librarian, various councillors and members of the Education Subcommittee and then it came to a head with Mrs Savage.'

'He upset Mrs Savage?' demanded David in mock horror. 'Well, if he upset Mrs Savage then he just has to go.'

'It was quite a dramatic confrontation, I hear,' explained Harold, 'and the corridors of County Hall were echoing with their voices. Evidently Mr Carter got on pretty well with Mrs Savage at their first meeting but, having looked a little bit more thoroughly into her role and responsibilities, he found that there was room for some "organisational realignment". Although it was hardly in his remit, he began to quiz her about her administrative duties, told her she spent far too much time on inessential tasks and then, when he cast his covetous eye on that plush office of hers, she evidently, in colloquial parlance, "lost it". She threatened him with Dr Gore and he threatened her with "downsizing".'

'Downsizing Mrs Savage!' I exclaimed. 'He certainly picked the wrong person to attempt to downsize.'

'Blowing up, yes,' added David, 'but downsizing, oh no. The thought is inconceivable!'

'Evidently he wanted to streamline everything,' chuckled Harold.

'I would have just loved to have been a fly on the wall,' said Sidney, leaning back on his chair. 'I am tempted to feel sorry for Mrs Savage, but I will resist the temptation and just enjoy a small gloat.'

'So he's definitely not coming?' I asked.

'No, Gervase, for the umpteenth time, he's definitely not coming,' replied Harold. Then he added, 'And due to his late withdrawal, you are stuck with me for the time being.'

The whole room erupted into wild laughter.

'Is it something I said?' asked Harold, totally perplexed.

FIFTEEN

My duties at the Fettlesham Show during my first year as a school inspector had sounded as though they would be pretty straightforward: I had been deputed to judge the children's poetry competition. All I was required to do was judge the poems, say a few words, and present the book tokens and rosettes to the five winners.

'It's a job of minimal duties, so you will be able to spend a very pleasant, uneventful day out,' Harold had informed me—and Harold had been wrong. The judging of the poetry competition had been a nightmare. My decision to award the first prize to a child who had written a delightful poem—albeit a non-rhyming one—about her granny had seemingly been greeted with disbelief by everyone save for the winner's parents. The Dales poetess, Philomena Phillpots, a woman of apparently outstanding poetic talent and immense experience, felt that a piece of writing was not a poem unless it rhymed.

At the beginning of the summer term, Harold had called the inspectors together for another meeting to discuss the plans for this year's Fettlesham Show. We had sat there, glumly, waiting to be told what our duties would be.

I had hardly dared ask. 'Am I judging the poetry again?'

'No, no,' Harold had replied. 'Philomena Phillpots has been persuaded to take that on, much, I guess, to your relief.'

'Phew! Yes, that is a great burden lifted.'

'However,' Harold had continued, pausing momentarily to give me a great, wide smile, 'you *have* been nominated to adjudicate the children's verse-speaking competition.'

'The what?' I exclaimed.

'Now, don't get all flustered. It is the competition where youngsters recite their favourite poems. It's pretty straightforward and much easier, I should imagine, than judging the quality of a piece of poetry. Much less contentious. And you'll be fine this time because you will have a couple of other judges to help you reach a decision so it won't all fall on your shoulders. It will be a piece of cake.'

'Who are the other judges?' I had asked warily.

'Well, there's Lord Marrick and Mrs Cleaver-Canning, both of whom I know you get on very well with. It will be like a day out. Like meeting old friends. Take Christine and enjoy yourself.'

One morning, a week after he had given us the welcome news that he would be continuing pro tem as Senior Inspector following the resignation of Simon Carter, Harold came into the main office. I was, in fact, the only inspector present, so he sat himself down at David's desk opposite mine. 'Do you know, Gervase,' he said, 'the Fettlesham Show is imminent and for the first time since I have been involved, I'm rather looking forward to it.'

For the past few days, Harold had been a new man. I believe that he too had been worried by the appointment, but, since he had not been directly involved in it, he was unable to do anything more than try to ensure that he left his job as free from problems as possible.

'Oh, Harold,' I groaned, 'the Fettlesham Show. I can hardly bear to think about it. Do I really have to do that judging?'

'Yes, of course you do. To use the terminology of our late departed Senior Inspector designate, we all have to "run that extra mile, get on board, pull in the same direction, give it our best shot".'

'Don't you dare start on that gobbledegook!' I exclaimed.

'Well, you can't be the only one on the team to take his bat home.'

I aimed a ball of paper at him, which missed by a mile, and he laughed. 'Sorry, it just slipped out. But, to be serious, Gervase, Sidney will be judging the art competition as usual, David is organising the children's sports as he always does and Gerry has kindly agreed to arrange a children's modelling and craft competition. She is really looking forward to it.'

'First-year fervour!' I snorted. 'She'll learn.'

'What about me,' Harold continued, 'stuck in that beastly hot

Education Tent the whole day? At least this year Dr Gore has agreed to join me for part of the day and I shall have Mrs Savage by my side the whole time.'

'Huh, well,' I grumbled, 'perhaps I've got off pretty lightly after all. The thought of a day behind a desk with Mrs Savage is an even more nightmarish scenario than the verse-speaking competition.'

'Splendid!' cried Harold. 'You know, I think you are all rather hard on Mrs Savage. She will be invaluable in deflecting the difficult customers and dealing with contentious issues. Evidently she has become something of a cult figure at County Hall since her clash with Simon Carter. She does have her faults, I will admit, but when the chips are down I would prefer to have Mrs Savage in my corner rather than the opponent's.'

AND SO IT WAS that early on a bright and windless July Saturday, before the gates were opened to the general public, I made my way across the Fettlesham showground in search of the tent where the children's verse-speaking competition was to take place. Under normal circumstances I would have been extremely apprehensive, but that morning I was head over heels. I was walking on clouds. Nothing could possibly ruin the incredibly good mood I was in. The birds were chirping, the sun was shining, there was a spring in my step and all was right with the world—and not just because schools had gone on holiday the day before.

The reason for this elation was that the night before I had heard the most wonderful news. Christine and I had been snuggled on the old sofa in the partially decorated sitting room at Peewit Cottage, when she whispered in my ear, 'I think we will have to get the spare room decorated pretty quickly.'

'Why?' I had asked. 'Are we expecting visitors?'

'Well, yes, we are,' she had said. 'Well, one, anyway.'

'Who?'

She had run the flat of her hand over her stomach and smiled enigmatically at me.

'You don't mean . . . ?' I had stuttered.

'Yes, I'm pregnant.'

Our nearest neighbour, Harry Cotton, must have fallen out of his bed with the noise that I had made. I had run round the cottage like a whirling dervish, whooping and screaming and jumping in the air. It was the best news I had had since—well, since Christine had said she would marry me.

My lovely wife was going to join me around one o'clock when we intended to treat ourselves to a bottle of champagne, a leisurely lunch and then spend the afternoon looking round the exhibitions and stalls. Christine was busy that morning. While Gerry was organising the modelling and craft competition, Christine had offered to look after Jamie since the regular childminder was on holiday.

'We're having a baby! We're having a baby!' I wanted to call out to anyone I met as I made my way across the showground. 'I'm going to be a father! Me! I'm going to be a daddy!' I wanted to run round the showground and yell the news at the top of my voice.

'Don't tell anyone just yet,' Christine had said quietly the evening before. 'Not until I know for sure that the baby is at home here.' She gently stroked her stomach again. So we agreed to wait a couple of weeks before announcing it.

On my way across the showground, I passed the Education Tent and decided to call in briefly to say hello to Harold. I would have loved to have told him our amazing news. To my surprise, I found Mrs Savage seated, as stiff and haughty as ever, behind a large desk in the very centre of the tent, dressed for the occasion in her 'ideal countrywoman's summer ensemble': bright yellow cotton jacket, wheat-coloured roll-top sweater, cream slacks, lime-green silk scarf and expensive pale green boots. Her make-up was faultless, her long nails impeccably manicured, and not a hair was out of place.

'Ah, good morning, Mrs Savage,' I exclaimed, with the exaggerated good humour of a game show host. I was so happy I could have kissed her. 'And how are you on this bright and sunny morning?'

'I'm very well, thank you, Mr Phinn,' she replied formally. 'If you are looking for Dr Yeats, he has gone in search of a cup of tea. We have already been here a good half-hour and no one has seen fit to bring any refreshments round.'

'It's such good news, isn't it, that Dr Yeats will be staying on for the time being?'

'Yes, indeed,' she replied in a noncommittal tone of voice. She was clearly not wanting to prolong this topic of conversation. But I was.

'And so unfortunate that Mr Carter felt unable to join us.'

She looked me straight in the eyes and twitched slightly but merely replied, 'That is a moot point.'

My next comment seemed to wind her up like a clockwork toy. 'He had such great plans for the department,' I remarked casually.

'Huh, he had great plans, all right,' she said malevolently and with a curl of the lip. 'The least said about Mr Carter the better, as far as I am concerned. I have never seen Dr Gore so angry. He's such a calm, rational and even-tempered man but he was apoplectic when Mr Carter went back on his word and informed Dr Gore he wanted something more challenging. More challenging! What a rude and insensitive man he turned out to be!' Her face was flushed with anger and she breathed out heavily. I had clearly touched an extremely raw nerve and I was enjoying the spectacle.

'I thought you rather took to him,' I commented, winding her up again.

'Rather took to him?' she repeated slowly. 'Rather took to him? He was an odious little man and, as you said, it is very good news indeed that Dr Yeats will be remaining with us.' Her voice suddenly softened. 'I have always found Dr Yeats a perfect gentleman and very easy to work with.' Then, a slight smile played on her lips and she looked again into my eyes. 'It will be a big man, or woman, who tries to fill his shoes, Mr Phinn.'

Touché, Mrs Savage, I thought to myself.

At that moment, the subject of our conversation padded heavily into the tent carrying two plastic cups of tea.

'Hello, Gervase. Good to see you,' he said genially. 'Here we are, Brenda, one cup of tea.' He placed the plastic cup down before her. 'I'm sorry I couldn't get that herbal stuff you usually drink but this is warm and wet and better than nothing.'

'It will be most acceptable, Harold,' simpered Mrs Savage, giving him a charming smile. 'And thank you for taking the trouble to fetch me one.' She then reached into a canvas bag beside her chair and produced a china mug into which she poured the contents of the plastic cup. She took a sip and nodded. 'Most acceptable.'

'I can nip back and get you a cup if you would like one, Gervase,' said Harold pleasantly.

'No, thanks. The verse-speaking competition is scheduled for eleven thirty. I'm on my way to check things are organised, and just called in to say hello.'

'Mrs Savage was telling me earlier, Gervase, that the CEO was well pleased with the Literacy and Learning initiative. I'm sure he will have a word with you when he arrives. I'm expecting him to join us later this morning.'

'Really?' I said, smiling as I realised that the pair of them reverted to formal names when it came to business.

'Yes, Dr Gore was very pleased,' said Mrs Savage, looking at me over the rim of her mug as she took another sip of the tea.

'Well, that's good to hear, Mrs Savage,' I said, smiling smugly, and then rather wickedly decided to twist the knife another few turns. 'It's good to know that Dr Gore is back to his calm, rational and even-tempered self after all the trouble with Mr Carter.'

'Mr Phinn,' said Mrs Savage, placing the mug down firmly on the desk, 'I am here to help Dr Yeats deal with enquiries about education, not to discuss Mr Carter, whom you have an unpleasant habit of bringing up.' She was looking hot and flustered again. 'I admit I found Mr Carter a rude and detestable little man and we are well rid of him. And that, Mr Phinn, is my last word on the matter.'

'Yes, of course,' I said meekly, and then returning to the exaggerated good humour of the quiz show host, I bade them both farewell. 'Have a nice day!' I called as I made for the exit.

I had only gone a few more yards in the direction of the bright red and yellow marquee where the verse-speaking competition was to take place when a husky voice boomed behind me, 'Now then, Gervase!' I turned to find Lord Marrick in a striped blazer which had seen better days, a ridiculously large coloured bow tie and battered, wide-brimmed straw hat. 'Good to see you,' he said, holding out a hand. 'How are things?'

'Couldn't be better, Lord Marrick. And what about you?'

'Bloody excellent! Rum do this about Dr Yeats's successor, eh? Fellow upped and went like a fox with the hounds at his heels, I hear.' He fingered the top of his walking stick. 'Didn't take to him myself. Clever man, no doubt about that, but far too much to say. Anyhow, how's married life treating you?'

'Marvellous! Best thing I ever did,' I said.

'Well, let's have a drink in the beer tent later to celebrate the good things of life—but we've got to get this judging over and done with first. Shouldn't be a long job, should it? Come along now, let's get the show on the road, shall we?'

On our way to the tent I was treated to a running commentary. 'Margot Cleaver-Canning is joining us. I know you've met Margot and her long-suffering husband. Mind you, Margot is a splendid woman—feisty, I should say.' He stopped at the entrance to the tent and took my arm. 'My goodness, you should have seen her out hunting. She could hold her own with the best when she was out with the Totterdale. Never seen a more fearless jumper than Margot Cleaver-Canning—although, of course, that was before she carried the extra baggage, if you see what I mean. She'd gallop up to this dry-stone wall and if her mount refused, she'd sort of put her horse in reverse and the beast would kick down the wall to let her through. Trained him to do it, she did. Women like that are the backbone of Britain.'

Mrs Cleaver-Canning was waiting for us in the tent. She was dressed in a shapeless multicoloured cotton tent of a dress, a huge red hat and pristine white gloves.

'Margot, my dear,' boomed Lord Marrick, 'how are you?'

'I'm very well, thank you, Bunny,' she replied, 'and I see you're looking well.'

Bunny? I said to myself. Bunny?! I looked at the rotund, red-cheeked character with his great walrus moustache and his hair shooting up from a square head. It would be difficult to find anyone who looked less like a rabbit than he.

'I'm as fit as a butcher's dog,' growled the peer. 'And look who I've found outside.'

'Good morning, Mr Phinn,' said Mrs Cleaver-Canning, extending a gloved hand regally.

'Good morning,' I replied. 'It's nice to see you again. Is . . . er . . . Winco here too?'

'Good gracious, no! I've sent him off. Winco knows as much about poetry as I do about Messerschmitts. He'll be in the beer tent if I know Winco, regaling anyone who will listen to him about his war exploits. Now, Mr Phinn, Lord Marrick and I are relying on you to help us through this judging how-de-do.'

'I'm sure Gervase here will tell us what to do, Margot. It seems pretty straightforward, as far as I can see,' said Lord Marrick.

'Let's hope so,' I said.

Five square staging blocks had been pushed together to form a makeshift stage at the end of the marquee, facing the judges' table. Behind us were rows of wooden chairs for the audience to sit on.

The organiser of the event was an amiable but completely disorganised man with a soft voice and an absent-minded expression. He had the irritating habit of biting his bottom lip and punctuating all his replies to my questions with, 'Well, what do you think, Mr Phinn?' I checked that there was the requisite number of book tokens and rosettes to award, agreed that I would introduce the event and that Lord Marrick would present the prizes.

I went in search of the showground announcer to ask him to inform the public over his loudspeaker that the verse-speaking competition would be taking place in thirty minutes. When I arrived back in the marquee, I found to my surprise that the place was filling up fast. All the entrants had arrived, been told the order of their appearance and the judges had a list of poems for recitation with the names of all the children. At 11.30 on the dot, I welcomed the audience, told them what a treat was in store and introduced myself and my fellow judges. I then asked for the first child to deliver his piece.

Onto the rostrum clambered a nervous-looking boy who entertained us with a laboured rendering of 'The Highwayman', prompted frequently by a parent who followed his progress in a large book from the side of the stage. After him came a large girl who gave a most original performance of 'Daffodils' by William Wordsworth. Dressed in a bright yellow dress, she took to floating round the stage like a cloud, waving her arms in the air and reciting the verse in a loud sing-song voice. When she got to the lines: 'For oft, when on my couch I lie, In vacant or in pensive mood,' she clapped her hand to her forehead dramatically as though suffering from a particularly painful migraine and put on a face which was neither vacant nor pensive.

The remarkably thin youth who followed her managed to deliver a piece of Shakespeare as if he were recalling a shopping list. Next was an older girl, dressed in a Victorian-style dress with lace-up boots, who accompanied her rendering of 'The Green Eye of the Little Yellow God' with the most elaborate facial expressions. She grimaced as if the boots she was wearing were too tight and belted out the lines with gusto.

And so the performances went on and on until the penultimate entrant strode to the stage like a giraffe. My heart sank. It was Pollyanna Phillpots. When I had judged the ill-fated poetry competition two years before, Pollyanna had been a miniature replica of her mother, Dales poetess, Philomena Phillpots. Thin, gaunt-looking with waist-length sandy hair, dressed in a long, flowered-print dress, the child had produced a trite little verse about gambolling lambs and fluffy white sheep and she and her mother had not been best pleased when it failed to win a prize. Now, here she was again, a great deal taller, and I had an unnerving feeling that in the audience somewhere was the Dales poetess herself, watching me like a hawk. I had heard that Philomena Phillpots would be judging the poetry-writing competition at three o'clock and had made a mental note to give that event a wide birth.

'The poem I am going to recite,' started the girl in the bland tones of an undertaker giving his condolences, 'has been written by my mother, Philomena Phillpots.' There was a favourable murmur from the audience. 'It is called, "In the Country".

'If you are in the country
Well, don't just walk on by
But stay awhile, squat on a stile
And sit beneath the sky.
In this very busy world
A world that's full of care
We never give ourselves
The time to really stop and stare,
To listen to the country sounds
That fill the morning air.
Hear the little beck a-gurgling
See the great dark river burbling
Feel the whispering wind a-teasing
See the winter puddles freezing
Hear the peewit's plaintive calling
See the gentle snow a-falling . . .'

I found myself switching off; the mention of the peewit made me think of our cottage, of Christine, and the news that I was keeping close to my heart.

I came to with a start when, the poem evidently having finally ended, there was a ripple of applause and some exceptionally loud clapping from the back. I didn't need to turn round. I could see in my mind's eye a thin, gaunt-looking woman with waist-length sandy hair and dressed in a long, flowered-print dress. Pollyanna gave a little bow and loped off the stage.

The final entrant, a sharp-faced boy of about ten with a scattering of freckles and wavy red hair, clambered on the rostrum.

'Well, well, well,' I murmured to myself. It was little Terry Mossup of Willingforth School. Miss Pilkington must have worked wonders to have persuaded him to perform.

'This piece of Yorkshire dialect verse was written in 1909 by Ben Turner,' said the boy in a clear and confident voice. Then, looking directly at the audience, he began his poem:

'Whativer task you tackle, lads,
Whativer job you do,
I' all your ways,
I' all your days,
Be honest through and through:
           Play cricket.

'If claads oppress you wi' their gloom,
 An' t'sun seems lost to view,
 Don't fret an' whine,
 Ask t'sun to shine,
 An' don't o' livin' rue:
                                    Play cricket.

'If you're i' debt, don't growl and grunt,
 An' wish at others had
 T'same want o' luck;
 But show more pluck,
 An' ne'er mak others sad:
                                    Play cricket.

'If in your days there's chonce to do
 Good deeds, then reight an' fair,
 Don't hesitate,
 An' wait too late,
 An' say you'n done your share:
                                    Play cricket.

'We've all a row to hoe, that's true,
 Let's do it best we can;
 It's nobbut once
 We have the chonce
 To play on earth the man:
                                    Play cricket.'

The judges retired to the tea tent to deliberate.

'Well, I reckon this is going to be a long business,' said Lord Marrick, stroking his moustache. 'I mean there was a lot of talent there, a lot of talent.'

'And some very interesting, not to say unusual renderings,' added Mrs Cleaver-Canning. 'I thought the girl doing the mime to the "Daffodils" was going to fall off the stage at one point. If I didn't know better I should say she'd been on the cider. And another thing, if I were the mother of the young man reciting that Shakespeare, I would be extremely worried about his health. He looked unnaturally thin to me. Anorexic I should say.'

'Yes, well it's the poems we're here about, Margot, not the state of the entrants' health, so I'm going to put my cards on the table,' announced Lord Marrick. 'I thought one stood out head and shoulders above the rest—the cheeky-faced little lad at the end. Not a line fluffed, good strong voice, bags of confidence and he got the dialect off to a turn. I thought he was best.'

'Well, that's two of us,' said Mrs Cleaver-Canning. 'I loved the poem. My father, God rest his soul, was a stalwart of the Yorkshire Dialect Society for many years and was a great one for encouraging the production of Yorkshire dialect literature. I did think the little boy gave of his best. He was a delight.'

'This is not going to be protracted at all,' I said with a great sense of relief and satisfaction. 'I too think he was the best.'

'Great Scot!' exclaimed Lord Marrick. 'We are unanimous.'

Little Terry Mossup jumped up onto the stage to receive his first prize. He beamed as he took the book token and rosette from Lord Marrick before thanking him. 'Cheers, mate,' he said, giving the peer a wink and a thumbs up. He then faced the audience and, with a tri-umphant look, clenched a fist, punched the air and shouted, 'Yeah!' like a footballer who had just scored the winning goal.

LATER THAT AFTERNOON, I sat with Christine at a table in the sun-shine outside the tea tent. I was so happy. We had had a delicious lunch, and then spent our money rather haphazardly. Christine had bought a stack of saucepans and a patchwork throw for the bed, and I had fallen for a beautifully made bird table which I thought would look great in the garden of Peewit Cottage. With our purchases piled beside us, we were now indulging ourselves with a cream tea.

'Got to eat for two, now,' said Christine, her eyes sparkling. 'But that doesn't mean you have to as well,' and she took the last bit of scone off my plate and popped it into her mouth with a grin.

At that moment, a small boy with ice cream smeared round his mouth and a cone nearly the size of his head walked past.

'Hey, Terry,' I called. 'Well done winning the competition. You did really well.'

The boy came across to where we were sitting. 'Aye,' he agreed. 'I didn't do too bad, did I?'

'This is the winner of the verse-speaking competition,' I told Christine.

'Congratulations,' she said. 'You must have been very good.'

'I was all right,' replied the boy, taking a great lick of his ice cream.

'And are you liking school a bit better now?' I asked.

'Naw, not really,' he replied. 'I wunt go if it was left to me.'

'And are you behaving yourself?' I asked.

'Allus do,' he replied, with a twinkle in the eye.

'And how's the football?'

'Not bad.'

'Did you get into the junior side, then?'

'Naw, they din't want me, but it's not end o' t'world, is it?'

'No,' I agreed. 'And you can always try again next year.'

''Appen I can,' he replied, taking another immense lick of the ice cream. 'Is this your girlfriend, then?' he asked, nodding in the direction of Christine.

'No, this is my wife.'

'Have you got any kids?'

'No, we haven't any children,' I replied, smiling.

'Mi mum—mi real mum—says they're more trouble than they're worth, are kids.' He sniffed and took another lick. ''Appen she's reight.' He thought for a minute. 'It's not been a bad day this, 'as it?'

'No, it's not been a bad day,' I agreed. 'And what have you been learning at school then, Terry?'

'Not much,' he answered. Then after a thoughtful pause, he announced, 'I do know how to mek babies, though.'

Christine choked on the tea she was just at that moment drinking, and coughed and spluttered it all over me, herself and the table. Here we go again, I thought to myself: the inquisitive child who asks a tricky question or regales you with an embarrassingly blunt observation. I prepared myself to smile widely, nod sagely and be as evasive as possible. I tried not to look in the least shocked and replied in a very casual voice, 'Really?'

'Aye, I do. I've just learnt how to mek babies.' He gave his ice-cream cone another elaborate lick. 'Do you know how to mek babies, then?' he asked.

'I do, yes,' I replied and looked over to Christine who was holding a handkerchief to her mouth in an attempt to smother her laughter.

There was another long pause. 'How do you mek babies, then?' the boy asked, looking me straight in the eye.

'You go first,' I told him.

'Well,' he said, looking up at the cloudless blue sky, 'I knock the "y" off and add "i-e-s". Is that how you make babies, then?'

'Exactly,' I replied and, putting my arms round the mother-to-be, I gave Christine a great hug and a kiss.

GERVASE PHINN

Gervase Phinn talks with such infectious enthusiasm about his days as a school inspector in Yorkshire, and the amusing real-life experiences now incorporated into his three best-selling books, that it is no surprise to learn of his increasing popularity as a radio and television interviewee and guest speaker. 'I love it,' he says of the round of charitable functions that he is invited to. 'You meet such incredible, lovely people.' Perhaps, given his talent for performing in front of a crowd, and with a television series of his first two autobiographical novels, *Over Hill and Dale*, and *The Other Side of the Dale*, in the making, Phinn might be tempted to take on a role? 'I'd love to, but I don't think they'd let me. It would be nice just to have a little cameo part, though,' he chuckles.

His latest book is packed with yet more amusing anecdotes and colourful characters, all of which he carefully recorded when he worked full-time in education. 'If you want to be a writer you must become an observer of people and keep a notebook,' he advises. And it isn't just the talented children and dedicated teachers that he writes about. In *Head Over Heels in the Dales*, he also recalls some of the more challenging youngsters from troubled backgrounds. 'It's very sad,' he says, 'but children are influenced, for good or bad, by the adults around them The home environment should be supportive, loving and caring, with no violence, but some children get precious little love. It's terribly difficult to compensate for that.'

Gervase Phinn is convinced that the best schools are those that 'mirror' the best homes. He benefited from a loving family as a boy, and with his wife Christine (the Christine Bentley described in his books), he has provided the same for their four children. Despite his celebrity status, he says that family and teaching remain the best things in his life. 'I still work with children two days a week. It's like going back home really. It's wonderful.'

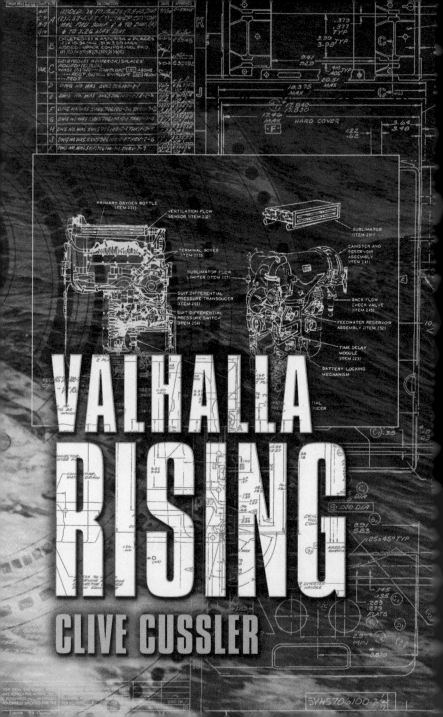

In the course of their investigative work for the National Underwater and Marine Agency, Dirk Pitt and his partner Al Giordino have already encountered far more than their fair share of danger.

Now, as they attempt to prevent the ruthless tycoon Curtis Merlin Zale from seizing control of the world's oil supplies, they find themselves back in deep water, in more ways than one . . .

JUNE 1035
Somewhere in North America

They moved through the morning mist like ghosts, silent and eerie in phantom ships. Tall, serpentine prows arched gracefully on bow and stern, crowned with intricately carved dragons, teeth bared menacingly as if their eyes were piercing the vapour in search of victims.

The little band of immigrants had come across a hostile sea in long, elegantly shaped black hulls. Long oars reached from holes in the hulls and pulled the ships through the waves. Square red-and-white striped sails hung limp in the listless air. Of the paths Norsemen had blazed across the oceans, none was more dangerous than the great voyage across the North Atlantic. Despite the perils of the unknown, they'd boldly sailed through the ice floes and endured vicious storms. Most had survived, but the sea had exacted its cost. Two of the eight ships that had set out from Norway were lost and never seen again.

Finally, the storm-worn colonists reached the west coast of Newfoundland, but they were determined to explore further south, in the hope of finding a warmer climate. They steered a southwesterly course for two days until they encountered a wide bay. Without hesitation, the fleet entered the calmer waters and sailed west.

When first light came, it could be seen that the bay narrowed into a fiord that flowed into the sea. Setting out the oars, the men rowed into the current as their women and children stared quietly at the steep cliffs that emerged from the mist on the west bank of the river. Giant trees forested the rolling land behind the crest. Though they saw no sign of life, they suspected they were being watched by human eyes hidden among the trees. Every time they had come ashore for water, they had been harassed by the Skraelings, their term for any natives that lived in the alien country they hoped to colonise. The Skraelings had not proved friendly, and on more than one occasion had unleashed clouds of arrows against the ships.

The expedition leader, Bjarne Sigvatson, had not allowed his warriors to fight back. He felt that trade with the Skraelings was vital for the survival of the colony.

The incoming tide helped the rowers to make headway into the current. The river's mouth broadened. The land on the sloping shore to the east was green with lush vegetation. Sigvatson pointed to a shadow in the steep rock. 'Pull towards the left bank,' he ordered. 'There looks to be an opening in the cliffs.'

As they drew closer, the forbidding entrance of a flooded cavern grew wide enough for a ship to enter. Sigvatson peered into the gloomy interior and saw that the passage travelled deep under the cliff walls. He ordered the other ships to drift while the mast on his ship was unstepped and laid flat.

As they passed beneath the low arch, the women and children leaned over the bulwarks and stared down at schools of fish in water of startling clarity. They found themselves in a grotto large enough to hold a fleet of ships. Its walls arched upwards into a domed ceiling bare of moss. The chamber was mostly dry. The water level stopped at a ledge that stretched far into the cavern.

Sigvatson shouted through the grotto entrance for the other ships to follow. Then his rowers eased off their strokes and let the ship drift until it bumped lightly against the edge of the cavern's floor.

As the other ships approached the landing, gangplanks were run out and everyone scurried onto dry land, happy to stretch their legs. The foremost matter of business was to serve the first hot meal they'd eaten since an earlier landing hundreds of miles to the north. The children spread out to gather driftwood and soon the women had fires going and were cooking porridge in large iron pots. Some of the men began repairing the wear and tear on the ships from the voyage, while others threw out nets and caught fish.

After the meal, two of Sigvatson's children came running up to him, shouting excitedly. They grabbed his hands and dragged him into the deepest part of the cavern. Lighting torches, they led him into a long tunnel that climbed upwards. Eventually the children stopped and motioned to a small crevice. 'Father, look!' one of them said. 'You can see the stars.' Sigvatson saw that the hole was too narrow to crawl through, but he could clearly see the night sky.

The next day, he put men to work widening the exit hole. When it was big enough for a man to walk through, they found themselves stepping into a large meadow bordered by stout trees. The supply of timber to build houses was limitless. The ground was thick with wild flowers and grass to graze their livestock. It was on this generous land high above the blue fiord bountiful with fish that Sigvatson would build his colony.

IN THE FOLLOWING months the colonists built wooden long houses with massive beams to support a sod roof. They raised a great communal hall with a huge hearth for cooking and socialising and that also served for storage and as a livestock shelter. Hungry for rich land, the Norsemen wasted no time in planting crops. They harvested berries and netted fish in great abundance from the fiord. The Skraelings proved curious yet reasonably friendly. Trinkets, cloth and cows' milk were traded for valuable furs and game. Sigvatson wisely ordered his men to keep their metal swords, axes and spears out of sight. The Skraelings possessed the bow and arrow, but their hand weapons were still crudely made of stone.

When spring came, Sigvatson prepared to send out a large scouting expedition to explore the new land. He chose his younger brother, Magnus, to lead the expedition and selected a hundred men for the journey. After weeks of preparation, sails were raised on six small boats and the little armada set off up the river to find its headwaters. What was to have been a two-month scouting expedition, however, turned into an epic journey of fourteen months. Sailing and rowing, except when they had to haul their boats overland to the next waterway, the men travelled on wide rivers and across enormous lakes. Then they covered and hid their boats and trekked through rolling hills and endless grasslands.

Many months later, they came to a halt when they saw mountain peaks rising in the distance. In awe of the great land that seemed to go on for ever, they decided it was time to turn back. But when the weary travellers finally reached home in midsummer, expecting a joyous welcome, they found tragedy. The entire colony had been burned to the ground and all that was left of their comrades, wives and children were scattered bones.

The anguished warriors might have turned their backs on the carnage and sailed away, but they lusted for revenge. Wild with grief and rage, they collected the remains of their friends and families and carried them down the tunnel to the cavern, where they placed them in the ships. It was part of their traditional ceremony to send the dead to a glorious hereafter in Valhalla. They identified the mutilated remains of Bjarne Sigvatson and laid him in his ship, wrapping him in a cloak and surrounding his body with his treasures from life and buckets of food for the journey.

Traditionally, the ships and their dead would have been buried, but that was not possible. They feared that the Skraelings would dig up and plunder the dead. So the saddened warriors hammered and chiselled at a huge rock above the grotto's entrance until it dropped in a massive spill, tons of boulders jamming together in a chute several feet below the water line, leaving a large unseen opening underwater.

The ceremony completed, the Norsemen prepared themselves for battle, then Magnus Sigvatson led his Vikings towards the village of the Skraelings. Before the sun fell, all hundred of the brave Norsemen found death, along with more than a thousand Skraeling men.

To the Vikings living in Iceland and Norway, the fate of Bjarne Sigvatson's colony became a mystery. No one was left alive to tell their story, and no other immigrant-explorers followed in their path across the truculent seas.

FEBRUARY 2, 1894
The Caribbean Sea

No one on board the old wooden-hulled warship *Kearsarge* could have foreseen the catastrophe that was about to strike. Displaying the flag and protecting United States' interests in the West Indies, she was on a voyage from Haiti to Nicaragua when her lookouts spotted a strange shape in the water a mile off the starboard bow.

'What do you make of it?' Captain Leigh Hunt asked his first officer, Lieutenant James Ellis, as he stared through brass binoculars.

Ellis squinted through a telescope at the object in the distance. 'My first guess is that it's a whale, but I've never seen one move through the water without showing its tail or diving beneath the surface. Also, there's a strange mound protruding forward of its centre.'

'It must be some type of rare sea serpent,' said Hunt.

'No beast I'm aware of,' murmured Ellis in awe.

'I can't believe it's a man-made vessel.'

Ellis put down the telescope. 'Shall we investigate, sir?'

Hunt nodded. 'Order a ten-degree turn to starboard. Increase our speed to full, turn out the crew for gun station two and double the lookouts. I don't want to lose sight of that monster, whatever it is.'

'Aye, sir.' Ellis carried out his orders and soon the ship began to increase her speed, the waves splitting against her bow with sheets of foam as she swung against the wind.

Soon the *Kearsarge* began to close with the strange object, which neither increased nor decreased its speed. A gun crew assembled, rammed a power charge and a projectile down the barrel of a twenty-pound rifled gun and stood back. The gunnery officer stared up at Hunt, who stood next to the helmsman.

'Number two gun loaded and ready to fire, sir.'

'Put a shot fifty yards ahead of the monster's nose, Mr Merryman,' Hunt shouted through his megaphone.

Merryman nodded at the man standing next to the gun with the lanyard in his hand and another man who was aiming the elevation screw on the breech. 'You heard the captain. Lay your shot fifty yards ahead of the beast.'

The adjustment was made, the lanyard was pulled, the big gun roared and leapt back. It was a near-perfect shot, and the shell splashed directly in front of the giant hump that effortlessly slipped through the water. Animal or machine, it ignored the intrusion and maintained its speed and course without the slightest deviation.

'It doesn't appear impressed with our gunnery,' said Ellis.

Hunt peered through his glasses. 'I judge her speed at ten knots against our twelve. We should be alongside in another ten minutes.'

All hands except the engine-room crew were lining the rails now, gazing at the monster, which was closer to the bow of the ship with every passing minute. There was only a ripple on the surface, but white froth could be seen swirling in its wake below. It was near enough now that Captain Hunt and his crew could make out a triangular housing atop the monster, with large round quartz ports.

'She's a man-built vessel,' gasped Hunt in amazement.

'I can't believe it's possible,' Ellis said vaguely. 'Who could have built such an incredible contraption?'

'If not the United States, it has to be of British or German origin.'

'Who can say? She flies no flag.'

As they watched, the strange object slid beneath the waves until it vanished from view. The *Kearsarge* passed directly over the spot where it sank, but the crew could detect no sign of it in the depths.

'She's gone, Captain,' one of the seamen called to Hunt.

'Keep a sharp eye out for her,' Hunt shouted back.

'What do we do if she reappears?' asked Ellis.

'If she won't heave to and identify herself, we'll pour a broadside into her.'

The hours passed and sunset came, as the *Kearsarge* cruised in ever-widening circles in a fading hope of finding the monster again. Captain Hunt was about to break off the pursuit when a lookout in the rigging shouted down to the deck. 'Monster off the port beam about a thousand yards, heading our way.'

The officers and crew rushed to the port railing and stared out over the water. There was still enough light to see it clearly. The long, cigar-shaped vessel appeared to be coming directly towards the *Kearsarge* at a rapid speed.

During the search, the gun crews had stood patiently, their great muzzle-loaders primed and ready to fire. The gunners on the port side quickly ran out their guns and sighted on the approaching apparition. 'Allow for her speed and aim at that projection aft of her bow,' Merryman instructed them.

Adjustments were made and the gun muzzles depressed as the monster loomed in the sights. Then Hunt yelled, 'Fire!'

Six of the *Kearsarge*'s eight guns roared, their explosive blasts shattering the air as fire and smoke spouted from their muzzles. Staring through his binoculars, Hunt could see the shells smash the water on each side of the baffling thing. Then he saw the shell from the twenty-pounder strike the monster's back, bounce into the air and ricochet across the water like a skipping stone.

'She's armoured,' he said, stunned. 'Our shot glanced off her hull without making a dent.'

Unfazed, their nemesis aimed its bow amidships of the *Kearsarge*'s hull, increasing its speed and gathering momentum for the blow.

Hunt and his crew stared in disbelief, gripping the railing to brace themselves for the inescapable collision.

But the expected shock never came. All any of the crew felt was a slight shudder beneath decks. The impact seemed little different from a slight bump against a dock. The only sound was the faint crunch of shredding wood. In that frozen moment, the unearthly thing had slashed cleanly between the *Kearsarge*'s great oak ribs, penetrating deep inside the hull just aft of the engine room.

Hunt gaped in shock. He could see a face through the large transparent view port on the pyramid-shaped housing atop the underwater ram. The bearded face had what seemed to Hunt to be a sad and melancholy expression, as if the man inside felt remorse for the disaster his strange vessel had caused. Then the mysterious craft quickly backed off and fell away into the depths.

Hunt knew the *Kearsarge* was doomed. Down below, sea water poured through the gaping wound into her aft cargo hold. He swung round and stared at a low coral island not two miles away. 'Steer for that reef off the starboard beam,' he shouted to the helmsman.

He just might have time to run his ship aground before she sank.

PART ONE: INFERNO
The South Pacific Ocean

July 15, 2003. The disaster could not have been more catastrophic. Everything that could go wrong did so beyond imagination. The luxurious cruise ship *Emerald Dolphin* was on fire. Flames were slowly devouring the interior of the ship's wedding chapel, located amidships just forward of the sumptuous shopping village. Yet no one on board had the slightest idea of the danger.

On the bridge, the officers went about their watch, oblivious. None of the ship's automatic fire-warning systems hinted at a problem. The console, with its schematic profile of the ship displaying every fire-warning indicator aboard, was a sea of green lights. The one light that should have revealed a fire in the chapel failed to blink red.

At 4.00am, the passengers were all asleep in their staterooms. The bars and lounges, magnificent casino, nightclub and ballroom were empty, as the *Emerald Dolphin* ploughed the South Seas on a cruise from Sydney, Australia, to the islands of Tahiti. Launched only the year before, the *Emerald Dolphin* did not have the flowing, elegant lines of other cruise ships. Her entire superstructure of six decks was round and circled 150 feet beyond and above both sides of the hull, and fifty feet over the bow and stern. There was no funnel.

The pride of Blue Seas Cruise Lines, the new ship sailed on her maiden voyage with every stateroom booked. At 750 feet in length and a gross tonnage of 50,000, she carried 1,600 passengers in opulent style, served by 900 crew.

The marine architects of the *Emerald Dolphin* had gone over the top creating ultramodern glitz in the dining rooms, lounge areas and staterooms. The sports deck featured a four-hole golf course,

Olympic-sized swimming pool and a huge workout gym. A shopping avenue two city blocks long rose three decks high. Escalators, moving ramps and walkways spread throughout the interior of the ship. Sailing on the *Emerald Dolphin* was a unique experience.

The passengers were affluent. Many were doctors, attorneys and entrepreneurs. There was a fair-sized group of senior citizens who looked like they could afford the finest that money could buy.

After dinner, while young couples danced in the ballroom or gambled in the casino, families with children watched the ship's theatre troupe perform the latest Broadway smash success. By 3.00am, the decks and lounges were empty. No passengers who went to bed that night would have thought that the grim reaper was about to swing his scythe at the *Emerald Dolphin*.

At 4.10am, Second Officer Charles McFerrin thought he caught a whiff of smoke as he made a routine tour of the ship. Sniffing the air, he gauged the smell to be strongest at one end of the shopping avenue. Mystified, because no alarm had sounded, he followed the acrid scent until he stood in front of the wedding chapel. Sensing heat on the other side, he pulled the door open.

The interior of the chapel was a raging mass of flames. Stunned, McFerrin stumbled backwards away from the intense heat, tripped and fell to the deck. He quickly recovered and called the bridge on his radio. 'We have a fire in the chapel.'

First Officer Vince Sheffield turned to the fire-systems console. All lights were green. 'McFerrin, are you sure? We've no indication here.'

'It's an inferno,' McFerrin shouted, 'and it's out of control.'

'Are the sprinklers activated?' Sheffield demanded.

'No, and there was no alarm.'

Sheffield was at a loss. The *Emerald Dolphin* had the most advanced fire-alarm and -control system of any ship at sea. Without it, there were no options. He turned to the junior officer on the bridge, Carl Harding. 'McFerrin is reporting a fire in the chapel. Go down and check it out.'

McFerrin fought the conflagration with extinguishers, but he might as well have tried stopping a forest fire with a burlap sack. The flames were unstoppable unless crew members arrived to turn on the water valves and attack the fire with hoses, but only Harding appeared, walking down the shopping avenue at a leisurely pace.

Harding was stunned when he saw the extent of the holocaust. He called up to the bridge. 'Sheffield, for God's sake! Call out the fire crew and engage the fire-control systems!'

Still wallowing in disbelief, Sheffield hesitated before switching on the manual override. 'System is on,' he called.

'Nothing is happening!' McFerrin cried. 'Hurry, man. We can't stop this alone.'

As if in a daze, Sheffield finally reported the blaze to the fire-crew officer and woke Captain Waitkus.

Old by cruise ship standards, Waitkus was five days from his sixty-fifth birthday and was looking forward to retirement. A jolly, popular man, he had been named commander of the *Emerald Dolphin* in honour of his distinguished service to Blue Seas Cruise Lines.

The captain hastened to the bridge and studied the fire-control console. It was awash with green lights. If there was a fire, none of the sophisticated systems was detecting it.

At that moment a crewman rushed up. 'Sir, I smelt smoke when I came round the port promenade deck.'

Waitkus called McFerrin. 'This is Captain Waitkus. You and Harding get out of the chapel. I'm going to close the fire doors and seal off the chapel.'

Waitkus pressed the switch and stood bewildered when the activation light failed to illuminate. 'McFerrin? Have the fire doors closed?'

'No, sir. There is no movement.'

'I can't believe the entire system has shut down,' Waitkus gasped. 'I'm coming down to check out the situation for myself.'

Waitkus entered the bridge elevator, rode down to A Deck and approached the wedding chapel from the side opposite the crew fighting the fire. Unthinkingly, unaware of the enormity of the danger, he jerked open the door behind the altar. A storm of flame burst through the doorway and engulfed him. Almost instantly, his lungs were seared and he was turned into a walking torch. He reeled back in a fireball and was dead before he struck the deck.

KELLY EGAN WOKE and sat up, slowly becoming aware of the faint smell of smoke. She wondered if it was her imagination, but after a few minutes the scent seemed to grow stronger. She set her bare feet on the carpet, which seemed abnormally warm.

Concerned, she pulled a robe over her shoulders and padded across the floor to the adjoining stateroom, which was occupied by her father. Dr Elmore Egan, a Nobel Prize-winning mechanical genius, was travelling on the *Emerald Dolphin* because she carried the revolutionary new engines that he had designed and developed.

Kelly shook him lightly by the shoulder. 'Dad, wake up.'

A light sleeper, her father came instantly awake. 'What is it?'

'I smell smoke,' Kelly answered. 'And the floor feels hot.'

'Are you sure? I don't hear any alarms.'

'See for yourself.'

Egan leaned out of bed and placed both palms on the carpet, then he sniffed the air. He looked up at Kelly and said, 'Get dressed.'

OUTSIDE THE WEDDING CHAPEL, the crew was retreating in its battle against the fire. The portable extinguishers were used up and, to add to their desperation, the fire hoses could not be attached because the valve caps were stuck fast. Two men using their combined strengths could not untwist the caps from their threads with a pipe wrench. It was as if they had been welded shut.

McFerrin hailed the bridge. 'We're losing control down here. Nothing works. Is there any way the engine room can override the systems and close the fire doors?'

'Negative,' answered Sheffield. 'The entire fire-control program is down.'

'Give the alarm and send the passengers to the lifeboat stations.'

Sheffield was aghast. 'Only Captain Waitkus can give such a command. He went down to judge the situation for himself.'

McFerrin had seen no sign of Waitkus. 'For the love of God, man, give the alarm and warn the passengers before the fire breaks onto the stateroom decks.'

Sheffield was swept by indecision. What should he *do*? 'You're absolutely certain the situation warrants such drastic action?'

'Unless you get the fire-control systems operational in the next *five minutes*, this ship is doomed and everybody on it,' McFerrin shouted.

BELLS CLANGED AND SIRENS whooped throughout the ship, the only warning system that functioned on command. Drugged by sleep, 1,600 passengers reacted slowly, mystified by the emergency alarm going off at 4.25 in the morning. Most were calm, pulling on comfortable clothes and their life jackets, as they had been instructed to do during the drills, before moving to their lifeboat stations. Only those few who stepped out on their verandahs to see what the fuss was all about were confronted with reality. They saw billowing clouds of smoke and tongues of flame on the decks below. The sight was terrifying. Only then did panic begin to mushroom.

Dr Egan had led his daughter to the observation deck where they could get an overall view of the ship. His worst fears were confirmed when he saw the conflagration rolling from amidships seven decks below. He could also see the blaze eating along both decks where the lifeboats were mounted in their davits. On the stern, crewmen were feverishly throwing life-raft canisters into the sea, where the rafts were ejected and automatically inflated. The crew did not seem to consider that the ship was still moving at cruise speed, and the empty rafts were soon left floating far in the wake of the ship.

Ashen-faced, Dr Egan spoke sharply to Kelly. 'Go to the café on B Deck and wait there. I must retrieve my papers from my stateroom.'

The elevators were jammed, so Kelly and her father had to fight their way down the stairwells among hordes of frightened passengers. People who lived responsible and disciplined lives had suddenly become a pitiful rabble.

The crew did their best to control the general chaos. But it was a lost cause. Without the haven of the lifeboats, there was no place for anyone to go but over the side into the water. The crew moved about the frightened throng, checking their life jackets and assuring them that rescue ships were on the way.

It was a forlorn hope. Still in paralysis, Sheffield had yet to send out a mayday call. In a few minutes, it would be too late. The flames were less than fifty feet from the radio room.

KELLY EGAN STRUGGLED through the madness to the café on B Deck at the stern of the *Emerald Dolphin*, and found it already crowded. Entire families were there. Children were whining in terror; women in bathrobes stood amid others who had dressed stylishly; several men wore sport jackets over Bermuda shorts. The one thing they all had in common was a fear of death.

Kelly was contemplating going back to look for her father when he appeared, carrying a brown leather case. 'It's bedlam,' he gasped.

'What can we do?' she asked anxiously. 'Where can we go?'

'In the water,' answered Egan. 'It's our only hope.' He looked solemnly into his daughter's eyes. They sparkled like sapphires when the light hit them. He could never help marvelling at how much she looked like her mother at the same age. They were both tall, with model proportions. Kelly's long, straight, maple-sugar brown hair framing a strong face with high cheekbones, sculptured lips and perfect nose were a mirror image, too. His heart felt an indescribable heaviness at realising that Kelly's life was in jeopardy.

'There's no reason to jump until the ship stops,' he said. 'There are bound to be ships coming to rescue us.'

ON THE BRIDGE, First Officer Sheffield gazed unseeing over the darkened sea. He was still standing there when McFerrin burst onto the bridge. The second officer's face was blackened, his uniform scorched. He grabbed Sheffield roughly.

'The ship is cruising directly into the wind. It's like feeding the fire with a giant bellows. Why haven't you given orders for her to stop?'

'That's the captain's prerogative.'

'Where *is* Captain Waitkus?'

'I don't know,' Sheffield said vaguely. 'He never came back.'

'Then he must have died in the fire.' McFerrin saw that it was useless trying to communicate with his superior. He grabbed the phone and called down to the chief engineer. 'Chief, this is McFerrin. Captain Waitkus is dead. The fire is beyond our control. Shut down the engines and get your men topside. You'll have to make your way to either the bow or the stern.'

'Why don't we just head for the lifeboats?' asked Chief Engineer Garcia.

'All the lifeboats have been destroyed. The *Emerald Dolphin* is doomed. Get out while you can. Keep the generators going. We'll need light to abandon the ship.'

Garcia instantly gave the order to shut down.

'Have any ships responded to our mayday call?' McFerrin asked.

Sheffield stared blankly. 'Mayday?'

McFerrin immediately read the incoherence in Sheffield's tone and was horrified. He called the radio room, but heard only static. Exhausted and in pain from his burns, McFerrin sagged despairingly against the ship's control counter. 'More than two thousand people are about to die with no hope of a rescue,' he murmured in solemn frustration. 'And we can do nothing but join them.'

TWELVE MILES TO the south, a pair of opaline green eyes examined the red glow on the northern horizon. The man stepped into the pilothouse of the oceanographic survey vessel, *Deep Encounter*, and picked up a pair of binoculars. He focused the glasses and stared into the distance.

He was a tall man, three inches more than six foot tall, and a lean 185 pounds. The black hair was wavy with a touch of grey at the temples. The face was tanned and craggy. He was obviously someone who spent far more time under sun and sky than under the fluorescent lights of an office. He wore blue denim shorts under a colourfully flowered Hawaiian shirt. It was the uniform of the day for Dirk

Pitt when he was on a deep-water research project within 1,000 miles of the equator. As special projects director for the National Underwater and Marine Agency, he spent nine months out of each year at sea. On this expedition, the NUMA scientists were conducting a deep-water geological survey in the Tonga Trench.

After studying the glow, he leaned into the radio room. The radio operator looked up sleepily and said automatically, 'Latest satellite weather forecast reports heavy squalls headed our way with thirty-mile-an-hour winds.'

'Perfect for flying a kite,' Pitt said, smiling. 'Have you picked up any distress signals in the last hour?'

The operator shook his head.

'A large ship off to the north looks like it's on fire. See if you can make contact.'

Pitt turned to Leo Delgado, the officer on duty. 'I'd like you to turn north at full speed. I believe we have a ship on fire. Wake Captain Burch and ask him to come to the pilothouse.'

Burch came almost immediately, wearing only a pair of polka-dot shorts. 'What's this about a ship on fire?'

Pitt handed him the binoculars. Burch peered at the horizon. 'You're right. She's blazing like a torch. I make her out to be a cruise ship. A big one.'

'I requested Delgado to head towards her at full speed. I hope you don't mind my stepping in your territory. I thought it would save a few minutes.'

Burch grinned. 'You gave the same order I would have given.'

The survey ship came alive, as crew and scientists were assigned special duties. The ship's two thirty-five-foot launches were made ready to drop into the water. Slings were attached to the two deck cranes, so that groups of people could be pulled from the water. Every ladder and rope on the ship was coiled ready to be thrown over the sides, along with cradles to lift children and the elderly on board.

The ship's doctor prepared a casualty station in the mess room. The cook set out bottles of water, pots of coffee and vats of soup. Officers instructed crewmen to channel survivors onto different parts of the ship. With an overall length of 230 feet and a fifty-foot beam, *Deep Encounter* was not designed to support large numbers of passengers. If the expected horde was not placed strategically, the ship could capsize.

Fully dressed, Captain Burch ordered the radio operator to contact other ships in the area. There were only two within 100 miles:

the *Earl of Wattlesfield*, a British container ship thirty-seven miles to the east, and an Australian frigate now charging towards them with sixty-three miles to go.

Every soul who did not have a duty to perform lined the rails, staring at the red glow lighting up the sky. Closer and closer, the survey ship pounded towards the burning cruise liner. Talk trailed off as the extent of the disaster became more shocking with each passing mile. Fifteen minutes later, they all stood as if put in a trance by the incredible drama unfolding before them.

Two-thirds of the ship was a vortex of flames. Her superstructure was a twisted, seething tangle of red-hot steel. What was left of the lifeboats hung in their davits, barely recognisable.

'Good Lord,' mumbled Burch. 'No one got away in the boats.'

'Looks as if they were all burned before they could be launched,' Pitt said grimly.

There came a screeching roar as the interior decks collapsed. It felt as if someone had opened the door of a blast furnace. It was light enough now to observe the charred debris that littered the liner. Burning flakes of paint and shards of Fibreglass filled the air. Pitt and Burch's first impression was that nobody could be alive in such a holocaust, but then a crowd of people became visible on five of the liner's open stern decks. At the sight of *Deep Encounter*, a steady stream of them began to leap into the water and swim towards her.

Burch leaned over the railing and shouted an order. 'Away the boats. Get to those people in the water before they float out of sight.'

'Can you bring *Deep Encounter* under the stern?' asked Pitt.

Burch looked sceptical. 'I won't be able to get close enough for them to jump on board.'

'The nearer the fire gets to them, the more will leap over the side. Hundreds will die before we can pick them all out of the water. If we tie up to the stern, her crew can throw lines for the passengers to slide down to our deck.'

Burch looked at Pitt. 'In this sea, we'll beat hell out of *Deep Encounter* against that monster. We could sink ourselves as well.'

'Better to try and fail than never to try at all,' Pitt said.

'You're right,' Burch agreed. He began orchestrating the controls of the survey ship, gently nudging her starboard hull sideways against the massive stern of the *Emerald Dolphin*.

For the passengers, the sight of the turquoise-painted NUMA survey ship ploughing through the water in the light of the new dawn came like a miracle. The people on the afterdecks cheered madly.

They saw salvation at hand. It was to prove an optimistic assessment. *Deep Encounter*'s officers quickly realised that their ship was too small to take aboard even half the people still clinging to life.

Not yet realising Pitt and Burch's intent, Second Officer McFerrin, who had reached the stern with a loudhailer, called out, 'Do not come any closer. There are people in the water.'

Pitt snatched his own loudhailer and shouted back. 'Understood. Our boats will pick them up as fast as possible. Stand by, we're going to approach and tie next to you. Please have your crew ready to take aboard our lines.'

McFerrin was astonished. He couldn't believe the NUMA captain and crew were willing to risk their own lives and ship in a rescue attempt. 'How many can you take on board?' he enquired.

'How many have you got?' Pitt asked back.

'Over two thousand. Up to twenty-five hundred.'

'Two thousand,' Burch groaned. 'We'll sink like a rock with two thousand people piled on the decks.'

Pitt shouted back. 'Other rescue ships are on the way. We'll take all if we can. Have your crew drop lines so your passengers can descend to our deck.'

Burch moved his ship slowly forward, swinging towards the liner inches at a time. Everyone on board *Deep Encounter* stared in awe at the great stern soaring over them. Then came the scraping sound of steel against steel. Thirty seconds later, the two ships were firmly lashed together. The instant all lines were secure, Pitt shouted for the *Emerald Dolphin*'s crew to begin lowering the passengers.

'Families with children first,' McFerrin shouted through his loudhailer to the crew. The old tradition of women and children first was now commonly ignored by modern seamen in favour of keeping families intact. The younger, single passengers and the senior citizens stood back bravely and watched as crewmen lowered husbands, their wives and young children down to *Deep Encounter*.

The evacuation seemed to be going efficiently, but as the fire came closer, the heat intensified and the fumes made it difficult to breathe, the crowd turned back into a frightened mob. Suddenly, there was a mad rush by those who decided to take their chances in the water. They fell like rain, colliding with those already in the water. Several dropped onto the deck of *Deep Encounter*, sustaining major injuries or dying horribly on impact. Others fell between the ships and were crushed to death when the waves pushed the hulls together.

Before long, a small sea of dead bodies was drifting in the debris.

KELLY WAS SCARED. Dr Egan was determined that he and his daughter would endure the heat and the smoke and climb down to safety when their turn came, but the undisciplined rush by the mob forced Egan against the railing. Suddenly, a heavy man with red hair emerged from the human surge and tried to snatch Egan's leather case from his hands. The engineer refused to release it.

In horror, Kelly watched the struggle between the two men. An officer, a black man with a face of hardened obsidian, stood watching with what seemed total indifference. 'Do something!' Kelly screamed at him. 'Help my father.'

But to Kelly's astonishment, the black officer began to help the red-haired man in his struggle for the leather case.

Pushed by the combined physical force of the two men, Egan lost his balance and stumbled back against the railing. His feet lifted free of the deck and the momentum pitched him overboard headfirst. The black officer and the red-haired man froze, then melted back into the crowd. Kelly screamed and rushed to the railing in time to see her father strike the water. She held her breath, waiting for what seemed like an hour but was less than twenty seconds, before his head rose to the surface. His life jacket was gone, having been torn from his body by the impact. He looked unconscious.

Suddenly, Kelly felt hands around her throat. Dazed and in shock, she frantically kicked backwards and her foot caught the attacker in the groin. There was a sudden intake of breath and the pressure on her throat relaxed. She spun round, and saw that it was the black officer. Then the red-haired man launched himself at Kelly, but she clutched the collar of her life jacket and leapt into the void.

Everything became a blur during the fall, then she splashed into the water, the impact knocking the breath out of her. Down she plunged in an explosion of bubbles, as the sea closed over her. She stroked upwards, helped by her life jacket, before she finally burst into the air. She sucked in several deep breaths as she looked around for her father, and saw him floating about thirty feet away. She swam to him and put one arm round his shoulders. 'Dad!' she cried.

Egan's eyes fluttered open and he stared at her, his face twisted in pain. 'Kelly, save yourself,' he said. 'I can't make it.'

'I'll hold on to you, Dad. We can use your case as a float.'

'Take it,' he muttered. 'Keep it safe until the proper time.'

'I don't understand.'

'You'll know . . .' He barely got the words out. His face contorted in agony and he sagged.

Kelly was shocked at his defeatism until she realised that her father was dying before her eyes. As for Egan, he knew he was dying. But there was no panic, no terror. He accepted his fate. His biggest regret was not the loss of his daughter—he knew she would be all right. It was not knowing if the discovery he had created on paper would work. He looked into Kelly's eyes and smiled faintly.

Kelly looked around desperately for a rescue boat. The nearest was less than 200 feet away. She swam several yards, waved her hands and shouted. 'Over here!' But the rescuers were too engrossed in pulling others from the sea. Kelly backstroked back to where her father had been, but he was not to be seen. Only the leather case floated there.

AT FIRST THE SURVIVORS streamed onto *Deep Encounter*, but the stream soon became a flood of humanity. The crew manning the boats frantically fished people out of the water as more and more of them threw themselves into the sea. The water under the stern became alive with screaming men and women, hands reaching out for the boats, afraid they would be missed. During the first thirty minutes, more than 500 people were pulled out of the water. Another 200 made it to the rafts alongside *Deep Encounter* and were lifted on board by the slings attached to winches. The rescuers concentrated only on the living. Any bodies found to be dead when pulled into the boats were returned to the sea to make room for those who still clung to life.

Retrieving and carrying twice the capacity of passengers allowed under maritime regulations, the boats came round to the stern of *Deep Encounter*, where they were quickly lifted on board by one of the boom cranes. The survivors were then able to step on deck without climbing the side, and those who were injured, were immediately carried to the ship's hospital and medical station. This system, devised by Pitt, was far more efficient and actually emptied the boats and put them back in the water in half the time it would have taken to unload the exhausted survivors from the boats and heave them over the sides one at a time.

Burch could not allow his mind to stray to the rescue operation. He concentrated on keeping *Deep Encounter* from bashing in her hull against the massive stern of the *Emerald Dolphin*. It was a battle that he did not always win. He'd wince, knowing that hull plates were being crushed and buckled, and that water was beginning to spurt through the ruptures. In the pilothouse, Leo Delgado computed weight and list factors as literally tons of survivors poured onto the survey ship. Already, the Plimsoll marks, indicating the maximum load level on the hull, were eighteen inches below the surface.

Pitt both masterminded and directed the rescue operation. It seemed he was everywhere, giving orders, pulling survivors from the water, directing boats and helping to work the boom cranes.

He saw that the ship was becoming dangerously overloaded and ran to check with Delgado. 'How bad is it? We've still another thousand to go.'

'In this sea, the waves will start surging over the gunwales if we take on another five hundred.'

Absorbing the bad news, Pitt gazed up at the multitude of people being lowered on the lines. Then he looked down as a rescue boat unloaded another sixty survivors. There was no way he could condemn hundreds of people to their deaths by refusing to save them aboard the survey ship. A partial solution formed in his mind. He hurried to the work deck and assembled several of the ship's crew.

'We've got to lighten the ship,' he said. 'Cut the anchors and chain. Hoist the submersibles over the side and let them drift in the water. We can pick them up later. Every piece of equipment that weighs over ten pounds, toss it overboard.'

As the crew set to, Pitt was cheered to see that the hull rose out of the water by nearly six inches.

Next he instructed the men in the boats as they came alongside, 'Our load problem is critical. After you pick up your final haul of survivors, remain adrift next to the ship. Do not send anyone aboard.'

The message was acknowledged by a wave of the hand as the helmsmen steered the boats back towards the people in the water.

Pitt looked up as McFerrin hailed him from above. From his vantage point, the second officer could see that the survey ship, despite the equipment that was jettisoned, was still dangerously low in the water. 'How many more can you take on board?'

'How many people are still left up there?'

'Four hundred here on the stern, give or take. Mostly crew now.'

'Send them down,' Pitt instructed him. 'Is that the lot?'

'No,' answered McFerrin. 'Half the crew escaped to the bow.'

'Can you give me a number?'

'Another four hundred and fifty.' McFerrin looked at the big man on *Deep Encounter* who seemed to be running the evacuation with incredible efficiency. 'May I have your name, sir?'

'Dirk Pitt, special projects director for NUMA. And you?'

'Second Officer Charles McFerrin.'

'Where is your captain?'

'Captain Waitkus is missing,' McFerrin replied, 'believed dead.'

Pitt could see that McFerrin had suffered burns. 'Hurry down, Charlie. I've got a bottle of tequila waiting for you.'

'I prefer Scotch.'

'I'll distil a bottle especially for you.'

Pitt turned away as the cry of a child seemed to come from beneath his feet. He ran to the rail and looked down. A young girl, no more than eight years old, was hanging on to a rope that dangled over the side. Pitt reached down and pulled her free of the water.

'Did you have a nice swim?' he asked, trying to diminish her shock.

'It's too rough,' she said as he passed her into the waiting arms of Misty Graham, one of *Deep Encounter*'s three marine biologists.

In that instant, a glimmer of light brown hair caught Pitt's eye. The face could not be seen, but a hand made a paddling gesture. Pitt ran twenty feet down the deck for a closer look, hoping against hope that the woman had not drowned. The head rose slightly above the water, far enough for him to see two large blue eyes.

Without another second's hesitation, Pitt climbed on top of the railing and dived in. Twenty feet and he was there, pulling her head from under the water. Despite her drowned-rat appearance, he could see that she was very attractive. Only then did he notice that she was gripping the handle of a small suitcase that had filled with water and was dragging her down.

'You fool!' he snapped. 'Let go of it!'

'I won't!' she hissed, with a determination that surprised him.

He didn't argue but began towing her to *Deep Encounter*. Willing hands pulled her on board. One of the female scientists threw a blanket round the woman and was about to guide her down a companionway when Pitt stopped her.

'What's so important in that briefcase that you almost died trying to save it?'

'My father's lifework.' She looked forlornly into the ash-coated water and whispered, 'He's down there.' Then she disappeared down the companionway.

ONLY WHEN THE *Emerald Dolphin*'s stern was free of the last passenger did the crew begin to board the crowded survey ship. Pitt sent the ship's officers up to the pilothouse to report to Captain Burch. To a man, they offered their services, which were gracefully accepted.

McFerrin was the last man down. Pitt was waiting for him and caught his arm to keep him from falling. He looked at the seared flesh on McFerrin's fingers and said, 'A pity I can't shake the hand of a brave man.'

McFerrin looked around the survey ship, seeing the waves slosh over the work deck. 'It would seem,' he said calmly, 'that you are in a perilous situation.'

'We do what we can,' Pitt joked with a grim smile.

Pitt sent McFerrin to the hospital, then shouted to Burch. 'That's the last of them on the stern, Skipper. The rest went for the bow.'

Burch nodded. 'The helm is yours,' he said to the helmsman. 'Take us round to her bow nice and easy.'

Burch was relieved to move his ship away from the cruise liner. He sent Delgado to sound the hull for buckled plates and leaks due to the battering. While he waited for the report, he called down to Chief Engineer House. 'How does it look in your neighbourhood?'

Down in the engine room, Chief House stood on the walkway between the engines and eyed the thin stream of water pooling around their mountings. 'My guess is we have major structural damage somewhere up forward. I've ordered my crew to set up auxiliary pumps and hoses to help stem the flood.' He looked around at the cruise ship survivors who were jammed in every inch of his beloved engine room. 'What does it look like topside?' he asked.

'Packed like Times Square on New Year's Eve,' answered Burch.

Delgado returned to the pilothouse. 'Several of the plates are sprung,' he said. 'Water is coming in at an alarming rate. The pumps won't be able to cope if the sea gets much worse.'

'Round up the damage-control crew and go to work on the hull. Shore up and reinforce the plates the best you can.'

'Yes, sir.'

Burch stared apprehensively at the sullen grey clouds building to the southwest.

Pitt followed the captain's gaze. 'What's the latest on the weather?'

'We're in for a blow within the next two hours.'

Pitt wiped his brow. 'Our only salvation is in staying afloat long enough to transport the survivors to another vessel.' He stepped into the radio room. 'Any word from the Aussies and the tanker?'

'According to radar, the *Earl of Wattlesfield* is only ten miles away. The Aussie frigate still has thirty miles to go.'

'Tell them to push hard,' Pitt said gravely. 'If that storm strikes before they get here, they may not find anyone left to rescue.'

THE INTERIOR OF THE *Emerald Dolphin* was disintegrating, bulkhead toppling against bulkhead, deck falling onto deck. No longer a ball of raging flame, she was melting down into a dying furnace.

Pitt was staring at her with deep sadness, when McFerrin came and stood next to him.

'How are your hands?' asked Pitt solicitously.

McFerrin held them up and displayed bandages that looked like white mittens. His face, with burnt and reddened skin, was smeared with antiseptic lotion and looked like an unsightly Halloween mask. 'Not easy going to the bathroom, let me tell you.'

Pitt smiled. 'I can imagine.'

McFerrin, on the verge of tearful rage, gazed entranced at the ghastly sepulchre. 'It should never have happened,' he said, his voice quavering with emotion.

'What do you think caused it?'

McFerrin turned from the glowing, twisted hulk. His face strained in anger. 'It was not an act of God. I can tell you that.'

'You think it was terrorism?' Pitt asked incredulously.

'There is no doubt in my mind. The fire spread too quickly for it to have been accidental. None of the automated fire-warning or fire-control systems went into operation. And when they were manually engaged, they refused to function.'

'What mystifies me is why your captain failed to send off a distress signal. We turned towards you only after we saw the glow of your fire on the horizon.'

'First Officer Sheffield!' McFerrin fairly spat out the name. 'He was incapable of command decisions. When I found that no message had been sent, I immediately contacted the radio room, but it was too late. The fire had already reached it and the operators had fled.'

Pitt gestured up at the bow of the cruise ship. 'I see life up there.'

A large group could be seen waving excitedly on the forepeak of the ship. Fortunately for them, the bow was upwind from the fire and acrid smoke that had streaked towards the stern.

McFerrin peered up at the tiny figures. 'They look like they might be OK for a while. The fire's going the other way.'

'It's better we leave them until another ship arrives or the weather settles down,' said Burch, approaching from the pilothouse.

'It's obvious we can't stay afloat in rough seas with another four hundred people on board,' Pitt agreed.

The wind was rising from ten miles an hour to thirty. The sea was tossing foam, and the swells came marching in like an irresistible force, nearly ten feet high. It was a warning of the fury to come.

Pitt studied the two boats trailing in the wake. He was gravely concerned about their situation. The sea was too chaotic for them to come alongside and unload their passengers. Pitt looked at Burch. 'I suggest, Skipper, that we come around on the lee side of the cruise ship and use her for a shelter from the storm. If we can't get the boat crews and the survivors on board, we've got to move them to calmer water.'

Burch nodded. 'A sound recommendation. We'll keep the boats tied close to our stern in case their situation becomes critical and they have to come on board.' He looked at the dark clouds that were rushing across the water like a swarm of locusts. 'I can only hope God gives us a fighting chance.'

'Do you know if anyone up there has a radio?' Pitt asked McFerrin.

'All officers carry portable radios.'

'Their frequency?'

'Twenty-two.'

Pitt spoke into the radio. '*Emerald Dolphin*, this is *Deep Encounter*. Is there an officer on board who can read me? Over.' He repeated the request three times through heavy static before a voice came back.

'I hear you, *Deep Encounter*,' a woman's voice replied.

'I have a woman,' said Pitt, looking at McFerrin.

'It sounds like Amelia May, our chief purser.'

'Can you estimate the number of passengers and crew left on board?' Pitt asked her.

'My best guess is four hundred and fifty crew, with about sixty passengers. When can we begin to abandon the ship?'

'Our ship is loaded far beyond capacity,' said Pitt. 'We are also in danger of sinking, due to a crushed hull. You must hold out until the weather slackens or a rescue ship arrives. Do you understand?'

'Yes, I understand,' she echoed. 'The wind is blowing the fire aft and the heat is bearable.'

'Not for long,' Pitt warned her. 'The *Dolphin* is swinging round. The fire and smoke will move closer.'

There was a pause, then Amelia said resolutely, 'I guess we'll have to break out the marshmallows.'

THE RAINS CAME in a sudden deluge, covering the *Emerald Dolphin* in a cloud of steam.

'Bring her within two hundred feet,' Burch ordered the helmsman.

Chief Engineer House called the bridge. 'The leaks are getting worse. I can't guarantee how much longer the pumps can keep up.'

'We've come under the hull of the cruise ship,' replied Burch. 'I'm hoping her bulk will protect us from the worst of the storm.' He turned to Pitt, who was peering into the wet gloom with binoculars. 'Any sign of the container ship or the Aussie frigate?'

'The heavy rain has cut visibility to a bare minimum, but radar has the container ship closing within a thousand yards.'

Burch wiped the moisture from his brow. 'I hope the captain is a good seaman, because he's going to need all the experience he's got.'

CAPTAIN MALCOLM NEVINS, master of the container ship *Earl of Wattlesfield*, sat in an elevated swivel chair with his feet propped on the bridge counter and contemplated the radar screen. Just ten minutes earlier, the burning ship was in visual contact, but then the storm closed in, curtaining off all view.

Nevins wondered what kind of hell he was about to find. The radio reports from the American survey vessel described over 2,000 people trying to escape the *Emerald Dolphin*. In all his thirty years at sea, he could not recall a disaster of such magnitude.

The sheets of rain parted for a minute, revealing the blazing ship enshrouded by smoke and steam. 'Engines on slow,' Nevins ordered. 'Are the boat crews standing by?'

'Ready to lower away,' answered First Officer Arthur Thorndyke.

'We'll lay to as close as we can.' Nevins peered at the torched remains of the ship's lifeboats. 'The loss of life must be horrendous.'

'I don't see the American survey vessel.'

Nevins read the situation instantly. 'The Americans must be on her sheltered side.'

The *Earl of Wattlesfield* lumbered steadily through the chaotic waters, daring the elements to throw their best at her. At 68,000 tons, she was more than a city block long. For ten years she had sailed through every kind of sea without losing one container or one life. She was considered a lucky ship.

As the *Earl of Wattlesfield* slowly rounded the *Emerald Dolphin*, Nevins felt despondent. Then, abruptly, he was staring at an entirely unexpected spectacle. *Deep Encounter* was rolling heavily in waters reflecting the orange flames, her hull sunk almost to the gunwales, her decks overflowing with huddled figures. No more than twenty yards behind her stern, two launches bobbed up and down, their interiors also filled with human bodies.

The radio operator leaned from the radio room. 'Sir, I have someone on the American ship.'

'Put them on the speaker.'

A voice boomed through the amplifiers. 'Are we ever glad to see you. I'm Dirk Pitt, special projects director for the National Underwater and Marine Agency.'

'Captain Nevins here. How many survivors do you have on board?'

'About eighteen hundred, with another hundred still in the boats. There are still more than five hundred crew and passengers on the forepeak of the cruise ship.'

'Any danger they may be burned?'

'Their ship's officers report that they're in no immediate peril,' explained Pitt. 'I respectfully suggest, Captain, that we transport as many people as possible from our ship to yours while we're still afloat. We'd be grateful if you took those in our rescue boats first. They're having the worst of it.'

'We will indeed.' Nevins turned to Thorndyke. 'It's a miracle they put all those people on such a small ship.'

'A miracle it is,' murmured Thorndyke. 'To paraphrase Churchill, Never have so many been saved by so few.'

KELLY SAT ON THE deck in one of *Deep Encounter*'s storerooms, her knees pulled up to her chin. Survivors were so crammed into the small storeroom that only the women could sit. No one seemed to pay any attention as she laid her head in her hands and cried. She felt a wave of sorrow over her father's death.

Why had it happened? Who was the red-haired man and why had he struggled with her father? And why hadn't the black officer intervened instead of helping the attacker? They appeared to be attempting to snatch her father's case. She looked down at the salt-stained leather case that she still held tightly against her breasts, wondering why its contents were so important that her father had died for them.

She fought off exhaustion and forced herself to stay awake in case the red-haired man reappeared and made another attempt to take it from her. But the hot, humid closeness of so many bodies made her drowsy, and she finally drifted off in a fitful sleep.

She woke suddenly to find the storeroom empty of people.

A woman who'd introduced herself earlier as a marine biologist gently brushed the damp hair from Kelly's eyes. 'A British container ship has arrived and we're transferring everyone over to her,' she said.

'Can't I stay aboard this ship?' asked Kelly.

'I'm afraid not. We're taking on water and there is doubt whether we can stay afloat through the storm.'

The woman left the storeroom to herd other passengers topside. Kelly stiffly rose to her feet, her back aching from sitting on the floor. She was almost to the doorway when suddenly she found herself staring into the icy features of the red-haired man. He stepped inside the storeroom and closed the door.

'What do you want?' she whispered fearfully.

'Your father's case,' he answered in a deep voice. 'You won't be hurt if you hand it over. Otherwise, I will have to kill you.'

Kelly could see resolve in the cold black eyes. And something else. The man was going to kill her whether she gave him the case or not.

'Are you going to shoot me?' Kelly asked, desperately stalling.

'I don't use guns and I don't use knives.' He held up his huge hands and grinned. 'These are all I need.'

She felt panic stab her as he moved towards her. His eyes had the smug gleam of an animal that has its quarry trapped. Panic turned to terror as he reached out and clutched her. She screamed and crumpled to the deck.

He lifted her up in one effortless motion. The murderous expression had been replaced by a leer of lust. As if in slow motion, he pressed his lips against hers. Her eyes flew wide and she tried to scream again.

'Scream all you wish,' he said. 'I like it.' He pinned her against a bulkhead and his hands began to move roughly over her body.

'Please, you're hurting me.'

His hands moved up to her throat and he began to squeeze.

A black cloud fell over Kelly's eyes. 'No, please,' she whispered

'Sweet dreams, dear heart.'

Then a voice behind him said, 'Your technique for romancing women leaves a lot to be desired.'

The red-haired killer released Kelly's throat and spun round. A shadowy figure was standing in the doorway, one outstretched hand casually resting on the door latch. The killer whipped into a martial-arts position and launched his foot at the intruder.

Unknown to the killer and Kelly, Dirk Pitt had heard the screams and silently opened the door, then stood there appraising the situation. There was no time to go for help. He braced himself for the attack he knew would come. He twisted out of the doorway into the passageway as the killer's foot sliced through the air. The intended blow missed Pitt's head by an inch and impacted on the frame of the door. The ankle bone broke with an audible crack.

Any other man would have writhed in agony. Not this one, not this man trained to ignore pain. The killer glanced down the passageway to make sure Pitt was alone and then he came forward. He leapt towards his prey, hands chopping the air like axes.

Pitt stood as if frozen until the last microsecond. Then he dropped to the deck and rolled towards his assailant, who tripped on his body and crashed in a heap. Pitt was on the red-haired killer like lightning. He pinned the man to the deck and clapped his hands violently against the ears. The man's eardrums burst as though an ice pick had been jabbed from one side of his head to the other. The killer wrenched to one side, hurling Pitt against a closed door. Pitt was stunned at the brutal strength of the man. He lashed out, smashing down on the killer's broken ankle.

The face twisted into a hideous grimace. He was hurt now, but he was still the aggressor, and he continued his advance towards Pitt, dragging his mangled foot behind him. It didn't take a wizard's grey matter for Pitt to realise that he was no match for a highly trained killer. He backed away, looking for an advantage.

Suddenly Kelly appeared in the doorway behind the killer. She was holding the leather case. Pitt saw his opportunity.

'Run!' he shouted. 'Up the stairs and onto the deck!'

The killer whirled round as Kelly ran towards the stairway and he took off after her. It was the move Pitt had hoped for.

He leapt onto the back of the killer in a brutal football tackle, falling with all his weight on the other's body. He heard his attacker's head hit the steel deck with a sickening thump and felt the body go limp. For a moment, Pitt lay on top of the man, breathing heavily. Then he noticed the killer's head was twisted in an unnatural position and the eyes were unseeing. He pressed his fingers against the carotid artery but there was no hint of a pulse. The killer was dead. Pitt assessed the situation. None of it made sense. All he knew was that he had walked in on an attempted murder. Now he was staring at a total stranger he had killed. 'I'm as rotten as you are,' he murmured. Then he thought of the woman.

Pitt came to his feet, stepped over the sprawled body and hurried up the stairs. The work deck was crowded with survivors. The rain lashed their heads and shoulders while they moved in line and climbed into the *Earl of Wattlesfield*'s rescue boats.

Pitt searched for the woman with the leather case, but she was not in the group that was being transported across the water. She must still be on board. He had to find her. How else could he explain the dead body? And how else would he ever find out what was going on?

THINGS WERE FINALLY looking up for *Deep Encounter*. Without the horde of survivors on board, the battered survey ship rose five feet out of the water. The crew went to work to shore up the damaged hull. Then the Australian guided-missile frigate arrived and thankfully the storm passed and the sea settled down to a mild chop.

McFerrin was the last man off the survey vessel. Before he boarded the container ship's lifeboat, he personally thanked the entire crew and scientists. 'Your rescue of so many souls will go down in the annals of sea history,' he told them.

'I regret we couldn't have saved them all,' Burch said quietly.

'What you did was nothing short of miraculous.' Then McFerrin turned and placed his bandaged hands on Pitt's shoulders. 'Dirk, it has been a privilege. Your name will be spoken with honour in the McFerrin home. I sincerely hope we meet again.'

'We must,' said Pitt jovially. 'I owe you a bottle of Scotch.'

'Goodbye, ladies and gentlemen of NUMA. God bless you all.'

'Goodbye, Charles. They don't come better than you.'

McFerrin climbed down into the *Earl of Wattlesfield*'s lifeboat and gave a final salute as it swung away.

'Now what?' Pitt asked Burch.

'First, we pick up the submersibles or Admiral Sandecker will have us beheaded,' he said, referring to the chief director of NUMA. 'Then we set a course for Wellington, the nearest port with a ship-yard and the dry-dock facilities to repair our damage.'

He had to shout to be heard above the sounds coming from the sky. The air above the ships swarmed with aircraft chartered by the international news media, covering what would become known as the most magnificent rescue operation in the history of the seas.

'Have you thought of how you're going to explain that body lying below?' asked Burch. Pitt had told him about the fight.

'I can only tell what I know.'

'Actually, your problem has been solved,' Burch said, with a devious grin. 'I threw your friend over the side. He's joined the other poor souls who died. As far as I'm concerned, the matter is closed.'

'Skipper,' Pitt said, with a twinkle in his eye, 'you're OK. I don't care *what* they say about you.'

'Captain,' the radio operator interrupted, 'Captain Nevins of the *Earl of Wattlesfield* would like a word with you.'

'Put him on the speaker.'

'Go ahead, sir.'

'Captain Birch here.'

'Captain Nevins here. If you chaps are going to try for Wellington, I'll be most happy to shepherd you along the way, since that's the closest major port to disembark the survivors.'

'I accept your kind offer,' replied Burch. 'I hope we don't slow you down too much.'

'Wouldn't do for the heroes of the hour to sink along the way.' Nevins paused. 'If you could pass between my ship and the Aussie frigate, we'd like to give you a send-off. Over and out.'

'Maybe they want to say aloha and throw streamers.' Pitt laughed.

To the ship's crew and the NUMA scientists, it was an ordeal just to stand on their two feet, but stand they did, straight and proud, as Pitt lined them up on the deck. Only the helmsman stood alone in the pilothouse, steering the survey vessel between the *Earl of Wattlesfield* and the Australian frigate. The little survey ship seemed dwarfed.

Pitt and Burch stared up, startled to see the crew of the frigate turn out as if for a formal military review. Then suddenly the silent air was shattered by the whoops of the ships' air horns and the cheers of the more than 2,000 survivors who lined the rails of the container ship and frigate. Pandemonium broke out across the water. Men, women and children all waved wildly and shouted. Shredded newspapers were thrown in the air like confetti. Only at that moment did everyone on board *Deep Encounter* fully realise what their magnificent exploit had achieved. Tears flowed unashamedly.

Then, almost as one, each head turned and gazed for the last time at the lamentable image that only twenty-four hours before had been one of the most beautiful ships ever to sail the seas. Pitt stared, too. He could not help but wonder who had been responsible.

'I bet curiosity is eating you alive,' said Burch. 'What motive would a madman have for murdering twenty-five hundred helpless men, women and children?'

'As soon as she's towed into Sydney Harbour, an army of marine fire-insurance investigators will sift through the ashes,' Pitt said.

'If anyone can ferret out the cause, they can,' said Burch.

'I hope you're right, Skipper. I'm just glad it's not on my shoulders.'

Never would Pitt have predicted that he would be the one called upon to solve the mystery.

THE FIRST TUG to reach the *Emerald Dolphin* was the Quest Marine Offshore Company's *Audacious*, one of the largest tugs in the world. Once Captain Jock McDermott was in sight of the smouldering cruise liner, he opened contact with Blue Seas Cruise Line officials, who, after half an hour of bargaining, named Quest Marine as the principal salvage contractor for what was left of the *Emerald Dolphin*.

Closing on the liner, which still glowed red, McDermott and his crew were stunned at the devastation.

'She ain't worth nothin' more than scrap,' spat the first officer, Herm Brown.

The ship's phone buzzed and McDermott picked up the receiver.

'This is Captain Harlow of the frigate off your port beam. Whom am I speaking to?'

'Captain Jock McDermott of the Quest Marine tug *Audacious*.'

'Now that you've arrived, Captain McDermott, I can leave station.'

'I'm surprised you didn't depart two days ago,' McDermott replied.

'We've been busy picking up the bodies of the cruise liner's victims who died in the water. I was also asked to remain nearby and report on the wreck's position after it became classed as a menace to navigation. I hope she stays afloat until you reach harbour. Good luck.'

McDermott turned to Brown. 'We'd best get to work.'

The tug's motor launch was lowered into the water. Brown and four of the crew motored directly under the great overhanging bow. There were at least thirty ropes hanging from the railings above. Luckily, among them were two Jacob's ladders with wooden rungs. Brown went first. Keeping a wary eye on the sharks circling in the water below, he stepped onto a rung and climbed steadily upwards. After he and three of his crew had ascended to the forepeak, a line was pulled up, slipped round an enormous towing bollard that had been smeared with grease, and passed back down to the launch.

Brown watched the launch return to the tug, where the line was secured to the end of a cable wound round a huge winch. By using the bollard as a pulley, the winch was engaged and began pulling the line running between the two ships. With no power on board the *Emerald Dolphin*, it was no small chore to lift aboard the tug's massive eight-inch-diameter tow cable weighing one ton per 100 feet.

'Cable secured,' Brown notified McDermott over his radio. 'We're coming back aboard.'

'Acknowledged.'

Ordinarily, a small crew would remain on board a derelict under tow, but without knowing to what extent the fire had ravaged the *Emerald Dolphin*'s hull, there was too great a danger. If she should abruptly head for the sea floor, the men might not have time to escape and would be sucked down with her.

As soon as the launch and its crew were back aboard the tug,

McDermott gave the order for dead slow ahead. Brown paid out the cable until the cruise ship was a quarter of a mile astern. Then he set the brake and the winch took up the strain as the *Audacious* began to inch forward. Every man on the tug held his breath to see how the *Emerald Dolphin* would act.

Like an obedient elephant led by a mouse, the immense liner came slowly into the tug's churning wake and stayed there.

Ten hours later, the *Audacious*'s engines were towing the enormous hulk at a respectable two knots. The tug's searchlight illuminated the *Emerald Dolphin*'s gutted forward superstructure. The crew took turns on watch, making sure the tow followed as planned.

After midnight, the ship's cook took his turn. He lit a cigarette and gazed dutifully at the ponderous mass following astern. Two hours later, fighting off drowsiness with his tenth cigarette, he heard what sounded like a deep rumble from within the hulk. He was about to write it off to his imagination when he noticed that something had changed: the ship was sitting lower in the water.

Under the searchlight, a huge billow of smoke issued from the wreckage forward of amidships. The *Emerald Dolphin* was foundering.

The cook ran up onto the bridge, shouting, 'She's sinking. She's going under.'

McDermott heard the commotion and burst from his cabin. One look was enough to tell him that if they didn't cut the tow cable the sinking liner would take the *Audacious* down with her. He was joined by Brown and together they ran to the giant winch.

Frantically, they struggled to release the brake, watching the massive cable unreel ever faster until it became a blur. They could only hope that when the cable finally unwound, its end would rip from its connectors. If not, the *Audacious* would be pulled under by the stern.

The dead cruise ship was plunging deeper with unexpected speed. Already her bow was diving beneath the surface. Her rudder lifted out of the water. The stern hung there and then slowly followed the bow into the black sea until the entire ship plummeted out of sight, leaving a great swelling of air bubbles.

Only one row of cable remained wound round the reel, but suddenly it became taut and the stern of the tug dipped abruptly, jerking the bow out of the water. The drum spun for the last time as the cable's entire length was yanked sharply into the abyss.

Then, with an earsplitting shriek, the end of the cable shot off the drum and whipped out of sight into the sea. Released from the strain, the tug's bow came down hard as she righted herself, rocking on her keel before settling down. The crew stood in stunned silence.

McDermott held up a hand. 'Listen!' he said sharply.

Everyone gazed at the spot where the *Emerald Dolphin* had vanished. Out of the night, a voice was shouting, 'Help me!'

Brown played the searchlight on the water. A man could be seen less than 100 feet off the stern.

'Throw him a line,' Brown ordered a crewman.

A rope was heaved over the side. The man caught it and two crewmen pulled him to the stern and heaved him aboard. He was dark-skinned, and wearing a ship's officer's uniform.

McDermott looked at the man questioningly. 'May I ask where you came from?'

The stranger smiled. 'I am Sherman Nance, the *Emerald Dolphin*'s passenger relations officer. I fell and struck my head. When I woke up, you had the ship under tow.' Except for his soaking-wet uniform he looked none the worse for his experience.

'Seems incredible you weren't burned to death.'

'I fell into a companionway that was spared by the fire.'

'Well, Mr Nance,' said McDermott, 'you'd better get out of that wet uniform. My first officer can lend you dry clothes. I'll see that our cook gives you something to drink and fixes a hearty meal.'

After Nance was escorted below, Brown peered at the captain. 'Uncanny that he survived without a singed eyebrow.'

McDermott sighed. 'It's not our concern. I now have the distasteful duty of notifying the directors that we lost our tow.'

'She shouldn't have sunk so fast,' Brown growled. 'It ain't natural.'

'I agree,' McDermott said with a shrug. 'But it's out of our hands.'

As soon as the *Audacious* reached Wellington, Sherman Nance disappeared. After McDermott gave his report to insurance investigators, he was told that no officer named Sherman Nance was listed on the *Emerald Dolphin*.

WHILE THE *Earl of Wattlesfield* stood by, *Deep Encounter* homed in on the signal beacons of the drifting submersibles. Once they were secured, the two ships resumed their course towards Wellington.

Dead tired after securing the submersibles, Pitt straightened up his cabin from the mess made by the forty people who had managed to pack into the small enclosure during the cruise ship's evacuation. He threw his clothes into a laundry bag and stepped into the small shower. There he soaped and rinsed before towelling dry, stepping out of the shower and staring into the mirror above the brass sink.

The face and body on the other side were not what they were ten years ago. The hair was still thick, black and wavy, but grey was creeping in along the temples. The piercing green eyes beneath dense eyebrows had yet to dim, but deep lines spread from their corners. The face was slowly achieving a weathered look. The nose still seemed reasonably straight, considering that it had been broken on three different occasions. He was not Errol Flynn-handsome, but he still possessed a presence that made people turn and stare in his direction when he entered a room.

He lightly ran the fingers of one hand over the several scars spread across his body, reminders of his many adventures during his two decades of service with the National Underwater and Marine Agency. Though he had attended the Air Force Academy and still held a commission as a major in the air force, he had jumped at the chance to serve under Admiral James Sandecker and the newly formed oceanographic and marine science agency. Never married, he had come close during a long-running relationship with Congresswoman Loren Smith, but his job at NUMA and hers in Congress were just too demanding for marriage.

Two of his former loves had died under tragic circumstances, Summer Moran in a devastating underwater earthquake off Hawaii, and Maeve Fletcher, shot by her sister off the coast of Tasmania.

It was Summer who never ceased to haunt his dreams. He always saw her swimming into the depths to find her father who was trapped in an underwater cavern, her lovely body and flowing red hair vanishing into the green water of the Pacific. When he'd reached the surface for air and found her gone, he'd tried to dive back, but the men in the boat that rescued him knew it was hopeless and physically restrained him from returning.

Since that time, he had lived only for his work on and under the water. The sea became his mistress. Except for his home in an old aircraft hangar on one corner of Washington's Ronald Reagan Airport, which contained his car and aeroplane collection, he was always happiest when on a research ship sailing the oceans of the world.

He sighed, put on a towelling robe and lay down on his bed. He was about to drift off to sleep when the girl with her father's briefcase jumped into his mind. Suddenly it became obvious: she was still hiding on board *Deep Encounter*.

Ignoring the lure of sleep, he dressed quickly and began his search at the stern end of the platform deck, peering into every nook and cranny. It was a slow process because there were so many places amid the stores and equipment where someone could hide.

He checked out the repair parts storeroom and almost missed it, that little something seemingly out of place. He noticed several cans of lubricating oils, neatly stacked on a workbench. He knew they should have been stored in a wooden storage crate. He walked over to the crate and eased open the lid.

Kelly Egan was sleeping a sleep so sound she did not stir. The leather case was propped against the side of the crate, and one of her arms hung over it. He smiled, removed a clipboard from a bulkhead hanger, tore off a page from the pad and wrote a note.

Dear Lady,
When you wake, please come to my cabin on deck level two, number eight. Food and drink will be waiting.
Dirk Pitt.

He laid the note gently on her chest, closed the lid and quietly stepped from the parts storeroom.

AT SEVEN IN THE EVENING, Kelly rapped on Pitt's door. 'I'm Kelly Egan. I'm so sorry to have caused you—'

'No trouble at all,' he interrupted, leading her inside. He motioned to a tray of sandwiches and a pitcher of milk. 'Not exactly a gourmet dinner, but about the best the cook could do.' He held up a woman's blouse and shorts. 'One of our scientists loaned some clothes. Eat and take a shower. I'll come back in half an hour. Then we'll talk.'

When Pitt returned, Kelly had showered and already finished off the sandwiches and milk. She smiled. 'You must be wondering why I didn't leave the ship.'

'The thought crossed my mind.'

'I was afraid.'

'Of the man who attacked you? I'm happy to report that he joined the other victims who drowned.'

'There was another one,' she said hesitantly. 'A ship's officer, an accomplice of the red-haired man who tried to kill me. Together, they attempted to steal my father's case, but all they succeeded in doing was push him into the water—'

'Can you describe this officer?'

'He was a tall black man. African-American, I suppose.'

'What is so important that your father had to die for it?' said Pitt, gesturing at the case at her feet.

'My father is—' she paused, 'was Dr Elmore Egan, a brilliant man. He was both a mechanical and a chemical engineer.'

'Dr Egan was a widely respected inventor, wasn't he?' said Pitt. 'The creator of several different types of water-propulsion engines and a highly efficient diesel fuel.'

'You know that?' Kelly was impressed. 'Well,Dad's latest project was the development of magnetohydrodynamic engines.'

'Like the propulsion units in the *Emerald Dolphin*.'

She nodded. 'Dad created a revolutionary design. He compounded the electricity found in sea water before running it through a magnetic core tube kept at absolute zero by liquid helium. The electrical current produced then sets up an energy force that pumps the water through thrusters for propulsion.'

'Are you saying his engine's only outside fuel source is sea water?'

'Not exactly. Early in his research and development, he reached a roadblock when his experimental engine experienced extreme friction problems. The engines only had a life span of a few hours before grinding to a halt. He and a close associate, Josh Thomas, then formulated a new oil that was a hundred times more efficient than any commercial oil available. Now Dad had a new power source that could run indefinitely without measurable wear for years.'

'So the super oil was the element that advanced your father's magnetohydrodynamics engine from the drawing board to reality. Can the oil formula be duplicated?'

'Formula, yes. Process, no.'

'Dr Egan could have become enormously wealthy by working out royalty agreements on his oil and engine.'

Kelly shrugged. 'Dad wanted the world to benefit from his discovery. Besides, he was working on an even greater project.'

'Did he tell you what it was?'

'He said it was better that I didn't know.'

'He wanted to protect you,' said Pitt.

A sad look came into Kelly's eyes. 'Basically Dad was a good father, but his work came first. I think he invited me on the maiden voyage of the *Emerald Dolphin* as a way of bringing us closer together.'

Pitt sat thoughtfully for nearly a minute. Then he nodded at the leather case. 'Don't you think it's time you opened it?'

'I want to,' she said hesitantly, 'but I'm afraid.' She held the leather case on her lap and giggled. 'For all I know, it's Dad's laundry.'

Slowly, she clicked the latches and lifted the lid. 'Oh, good Lord!' she gasped. 'I don't understand. It's never been out of my hands.'

Pitt leaned down and peered inside the leather case. It was empty.

TWO HUNDRED MILES out of Wellington, the meteorological instruments predicted calm seas and clear skies for the next four days. Now that *Deep Encounter* was no longer in any immediate danger of flooding and sinking, Captain Nevins ordered his container ship to pass ahead and reach Wellington as quickly as possible. With 2,000 unexpected passengers on board the *Earl of Wattlesfield*, food supplies were critically low. As the great ship surged past, the crew and passengers of the *Emerald Dolphin* waved goodbye.

Captain Nevins sailed his ship into Wellington six hours ahead of *Deep Encounter* and met with a joyous, yet solemn, welcome. Thousands of people lined the waterfront, staring silently and talking softly as the container ship slowly eased into a berth. New Zealand's heart went out to those who had miraculously survived the worst ship fire in maritime history.

A spontaneous outpouring of sympathy for the living and the dead swept the country. Homes were thrown open to the survivors. Food and clothing were passed out in abundance. Customs officials cleared them through with only a few questions, since almost all had lost their passports in the fire. Airlines put on extra aircraft to fly them to their home cities. Members of the news media descended in swarms and besieged the survivors, who were eager to get ashore and notify friends and relatives of their rescue. It was the largest news event in the country's recent history, and the lead story was the heroic rescue by the crew and scientists of *Deep Encounter.*

As *Deep Encounter* came through Cook Strait and headed for Wellington, it was met by a small fleet of private yachts that swelled to hundreds of vessels of every description. Fireboats escorted the ship to a dock, their hoses spraying a curtain of water high in the air. The crew and scientists had no idea they had become instant celebrities. They stood on the work deck, amazed at the reception.

Kelly, perched next to Pitt on the bridge wing, turned and looked into his eyes. 'I guess this is goodbye. I'm on the first available flight to New York.'

'I don't get to the city often, but next time I'm in town, I'll call you for dinner.'

'I'd like that.' She scribbled her phone number on a scrap of paper and gave it to him. Then she stood on her toes, abruptly circled her arms round Pitt's head, pulled him down and kissed his lips long and hard. 'Thank you, Dirk Pitt, for saving my life.' She took a few steps, then turned. 'My father's leather case.'

'Yes?' he answered, unsure of her meaning.

'It's yours.'

With that, Kelly stepped down the gangway and was swallowed up by a crowd of reporters.

While Burch and the others were fêted in the city, Pitt remained aboard ship and gave a full report over satellite phone to Admiral Sandecker in the NUMA headquarters building in Washington.

'I owe everybody on board the *Encounter* a sincere vote of thanks on behalf of the agency,' said Sandecker.

'Does that mean we all get a rise?' asked Pitt sarcastically.

'You're lucky I don't take the ship repairs out of your pay.'

Pitt wasn't fooled for a second. He would have bet the admiral was already computing bonus cheques, and he would have been right.

'That's not all you might want to deduct,' said Pitt roguishly. 'We had to jettison almost all our equipment.'

'The submersibles, too?' Sandecker's voice took on a serious tone.

'We set them adrift but picked them up later.'

'Good, you're going to need them to dive on the *Emerald Dolphin*. Your job now is to survey what's left of her for evidence relating to the fire and her unexplained sinking.'

'I'm not a fire investigator. What am I supposed to look for?'

'Don't worry,' said Sandecker. 'I'm sending someone experienced in marine disasters. He's also an expert in deep submergence vehicles.'

'Anybody I know?' asked Pitt.

'You should. He's your assistant special projects director.'

'Al Giordino!' Pitt exclaimed happily. 'You couldn't have sent a better man.'

'Yes,' Sandecker said slyly. 'I thought you'd think so.'

ALBERT GIORDINO TRUDGED across the gangway to the deck of *Deep Encounter*. At five foot four inches and 175 pounds, he was all muscle. His Italian ancestry was apparent in his olive skin, black curly hair and walnut-coloured eyes. Friends since childhood, Pitt and Giordino had played on the same football teams in high school and at the Air Force Academy. Wherever one went, the other was sure to follow. Their adventures together above and under the sea had become legend.

'Ahoy the ship!' Giordino shouted. He waited before shouting again. A figure walked onto the bridge and a familiar face stared down at him.

'Can you restrain yourself?' Pitt asked in mock seriousness. 'We don't take kindly to barbarians coming aboard.'

'In that case, you're in luck,' said Giordino. 'You could use a vulgar rowdy to liven up the place.'

In a minute, they were unashamedly embracing. 'The boat looks like a tomb,' Giordino said. 'Where is everyone?'

'Staying in the city, accepting awards. Not my style.'

Giordino gave him a look of genuine respect. 'It figures.'

After Giordino had unpacked, he entered Pitt's cabin and set down a wooden box. 'I brought you a present.'

'Is it Christmas already?' Pitt said, laughing. He opened the box. 'You're a good man, Albert. A bottle of Don Julio Reserve blue agave anejo tequila.'

Giordino held up two sterling-silver cups. 'Shall we test it?'

Pitt pulled off the cork top and poured the light brown liquid into the cups. He toasted, 'To a successful dive on the *Emerald Dolphin*.'

'Where exactly did she go down?' Giordino asked.

'The Tonga Trench. At about nineteen thousand feet.'

'That's pretty deep. What sub do you plan on using?'

'The *Abyss Navigator*. She's built for the job.'

Giordino paused. 'She has yet to be tested that deep.'

'No better opportunity to see if her designers knew their stuff,' said Pitt offhandedly. 'Captain Burch and I hope to get under way the day after tomorrow.'

Giordino noticed the leather briefcase sitting in the corner of the cabin. 'Is that the case that you mentioned belonged to Dr Egan?' He picked it up. 'Quite old. German made. Egan had good taste.'

'You want it? You can have it.'

Giordino lifted the lid—and nearly two quarts of oil flowed into his lap. He sat there in shock as it soaked his trousers and pooled on the carpet. 'I never knew you had a thing for practical jokes.'

Pitt's face reflected pure astonishment. He peered into the case. 'I don't. I had nothing to do with this. This case was empty when I checked it yesterday. I don't understand why somebody would sneak in here and fill it with oil.'

'Then where did it come from? It obviously didn't just materialise.'

'I haven't the foggiest idea,' said Pitt. 'But I'm betting we'll find out before the voyage is over.'

THE MYSTERY of who put the oil in Egan's leather case was set aside as Pitt and Giordino began checking the equipment and electronic systems of the *Sea Sleuth*, the survey vessel's autonomous underwater vehicle (AUV). During the voyage to the grave of the *Emerald*

Dolphin, they discussed the wreck probe procedure with Captain Burch and the ocean engineers on board. All agreed that for reasons of safety the autonomous vehicle should be sent down first rather than the manned submersible, *Abyss Navigator*.

Seven feet high by six feet wide by seven feet in length, *Sea Sleuth* looked like a huge elongated egg. Unlike earlier robotic vehicles, she was completely autonomous; her propulsion and video cameras were operated from the command room of *Deep Encounter*.

A crewman came up to Pitt and Giordino. 'Captain Burch said to let you know that we're three miles from the target.'

'Thank you,' said Pitt. 'Right, Al, let's head up to the bridge and see how the *Dolphin* looks on the side scan sonar.'

Burch and other NUMA scientists were in the command centre massed around the computer-enhanced screen, watching the seabed 20,000 feet below. The flat, desertlike surface was covered with grey-brown silt. No wasteland came close to being so desolate.

'Something's coming,' announced Burch, who had the best view.

Slowly, the recorder showed a hard image that took on a man-constructed shape.

'That's her,' stated Pitt firmly.

'It's not the right size for the *Emerald Dolphin*,' Giordino observed.

Burch pointed at the screen. 'Al's right. We're only seeing part of her. She probably disintegrated on the way down.'

Giordino stared at the sea ahead. 'The most logical scenario is that she sank intact and shattered when she struck bottom.'

Pitt shook his head. 'If that were the case, the wreckage would be more concentrated.'

'Then what caused her to break up on the way down?' Burch asked.

'With luck,' Pitt said slowly, 'we'll find the answers when *Sea Sleuth* lives up to her name.'

Anticipation reigned as the AUV was swung over the stern. One final check of her electronic systems, and then she was slowly dropped into the blue Pacific. Inside the command centre, Giordino sat in front of a console. He would pilot the *Sea Sleuth* during its journey into the abyss. Few men knew more about the eccentricities of piloting an AUV four and half miles deep under the ocean.

Next to him, Pitt operated the cameras and lighting systems. Behind them, Misty Graham sat at a table studying a copy of the *Emerald Dolphin*'s construction plans.

Giordino reported the depth readings every ten minutes as *Sea Sleuth* descended. Finally, after two and a half hours, the sensors began to transmit a rapidly narrowing gap with the bottom. Soon the drab silt of the sea floor came into view on the monitors. 'Which way?' Giordino asked Burch.

'Move on a heading of eighteen degrees. You should run into her hull in another four hundred feet.'

Ten minutes later, a phantom shape loomed. The dark mass rose beyond view of the monitors. 'Target ahead,' Giordino called out.

Gradually, features of the wreck became distinguishable. They came on slightly off the starboard bow near the anchor. Unlike other shipwreck discoveries, this one was not greeted with cheers. Everyone was silent, as if they were looking at a coffin. Giordino eased *Sea Sleuth* along the hull. His calculated cautiousness paid off. He stopped the AUV ten feet away from a massive opening, the plates contoured into jagged unrecognisable shapes.

'Hold station,' Pitt instructed him. 'This looks interesting.'

'That wasn't caused by the fire,' said one of the ship's crew.

'The wreckage is blown from the inside out,' observed Pitt. 'Take us along the hull until we reach where it broke off from the amid-ships section.'

Giordino moved *Sea Sleuth* on a parallel path with the hull. In another 200 feet, they came on a second, even larger, hole. This one also indicated an interior blast.

Misty examined the deck plans closely. 'I see nothing here that would cause such damage.'

The AUV then passed round the part of the hull that had broken away from the rest of the ship. It looked as though the *Emerald Dolphin* had been wrenched apart by some gargantuan force.

The abhorrent sight was left behind as the AUV passed over the bleak ocean landscape again.

'What course to the stern section?' Giordino asked Burch.

'You should find it three hundred yards on a ninety-degree course west,' said Burch.

Here, the bottom was littered with all kinds of debris. Dishes, bowls and cups, many still in stacks, unfolded in the silt. It seemed macabre that objects so fragile had endured the terrible fire and a drop into the abyss without being shattered.

'Stern coming up,' Giordino alerted them, and the final section of the sunken ship began to materialise. Now the men and women of *Deep Encounter* found themselves staring once again at the decks where survivors had abandoned the ship.

Giordino inched the vehicle round debris and stopped it at a point where the ship's stern section was ripped open. They could all plainly see that the massive steel keel was warped and curled downwards where it had been torn in half.

'Only explosives could have done that,' Pitt commented.

'That would explain her abrupt sinking,' added Burch. 'She went down so fast she almost took the tugboat with her.'

'Someone had a motive for sinking her in the deepest part of the ocean so that her wreckage couldn't be examined.'

'So where does that leave us?' asked Misty.

Pitt stared at the monitors. 'We have to dig deeper and come up with enough proof for an investigation that will lead to the murderous slime responsible for the loss of the ship and more than a hundred lives.'

'Dig deeper?' enquired Giordino, smiling as if knowing the answer. 'How?'

Pitt looked at his friend through Machiavellian eyes. 'You and I go down in the *Abyss Navigator* and bring home the goods.'

THE NERVE CENTRE of the *Abyss Navigator*, a four-man submersible, was a titanium alloy ball that housed the pilot and the technician who controlled the life-support systems, external lights, cameras and the two manipulator arms mounted under the round hull. A metal basket sat under the mechanical fingers to retrieve any artefacts picked off the bottom.

This trip the *Abyss Navigator* was carrying three people. Misty Graham had joined Dirk and Al. After studying the deck plans of the *Emerald Dolphin*, she knew more about specific compartment locations than anyone on the survey ship.

'Bottom coming up,' Giordino announced.

Like land materialising through a fog, the bottom took shape as the submersible's shadow appeared on the silt.

'We need a direction,' Pitt called Burch in the command centre four miles above.

'Follow a course of one hundred and forty degrees.'

Giordino engaged the thruster motors and fourteen minutes later the mangled wreckage came into view.

'Where to?' Giordino enquired.

Misty took several moments to study the deck plans and get her bearings. Finally, she circled an area and passed it to Giordino.

'You want to go inside?' he asked Pitt.

'As far as we can,' Pitt replied. 'If possible, I'd like to penetrate into the chapel where the fire started.'

Giordino stared doubtfully into the blackened wreckage. 'We could easily get trapped in there.' He gripped the control column. 'Tell me when.'

Before Pitt gave the word, he called up *Deep Encounter* to report. But there was no response.

'Odd,' he said, perplexed. 'They're not answering.'

'The communications equipment probably malfunctioned,' Giordino said calmly.

Pitt wasted no more time. They had an hour of bottom time left. 'Go on in,' he ordered.

There was a mild current but not enough to cause Giordino a problem. The dim outline of what was left of the decks came out of the gloom. 'Rise to the fourth deck,' directed Misty. 'It leads through a shopping mall to the chapel.'

Slowly, Giordino manoeuvred the sub upwards. As they reached the deck Misty had indicated, both men stared inside the wreckage, now illuminated by the four forward lights. Melted pipes and electrical wiring hung down like distorted tentacles. Giordino eased the submersible into the maze. They soared through the charred wreckage of the shopping avenue. The stylish boutiques had all burned to nothingness. Giordino cautiously navigated round piles of debris that rose like a range of hills.

'Coming to the site of the chapel,' Misty notified them. 'Halt in another thirty feet.'

Giordino covered the distance then stopped the sub. It hung over the space once occupied by the *Emerald Dolphin*'s nondenominational chapel. The only distinguishing evidence was melted floor mountings in the rows that had held the pews.

Pitt leaned over the console that controlled the manipulator arm. He began probing the charred debris with its mechanical fingers. Finding nothing of interest, he glanced at Giordino. 'Move us five feet forward.'

Giordino complied. Thirty minutes later, Pitt had examined most of the chapel area. He found what he was looking for in the last sweep: a strange-looking object or substance less than six inches in length, smooth and rounded, with a greenish tint.

'Time is up,' Giordino warned. 'We don't have much oxygen.'

'I think we may have found what we came for,' said Pitt.

He slowly worked the fingers of the manipulator under the object and lifted it free of the incinerated debris. Cautiously he set the payload into the artefact basket. 'Let's head for home.'

Giordino aimed the submersible back through the shopping avenue area. Abruptly, there was a clunk and the sub jerked to a stop. For a moment, neither man spoke. Misty's hands came together against her breasts in sudden fear.

'I do believe you struck something,' Pitt said casually.

'It would seem so,' Giordino replied, about as agitated as a three-toed sloth who didn't like the taste of a leaf he was chewing on.

Pitt stared through the overhead viewport. 'The ballast tank is hung up on a beam. It must have fallen after we passed.'

Giordino gently eased the *Abyss Navigator* backwards. There was a horrendous screeching noise, then the sub broke free.

'The tank does not look good,' reported Pitt. 'Luckily, we won't need it for the trip home.'

Outwardly, Giordino looked as serene as a millpond, but down deep he was greatly relieved when he had evaded the maze of debris and piloted the *Abyss Navigator* into open water again.

As soon as they were clear of the wreck, Pitt called the surface again. He received no reply. 'I don't understand why the communications phone is inoperative,' he said slowly. 'There is nothing wrong with the system at this end.'

Three hours later, the water began to turn from deep black to deep blue again. Looking through the overhead port, they could see the sea's surface sparkling above. Less than a minute later, the *Abyss Navigator* broke the surface.

There were still no communications with *Deep Encounter*. They could not see the survey ship because the top port offered no horizontal vision. They waited for the divers but, after ten minutes, there was no sign of them.

'Maybe the ship sank,' Giordino said, jokingly.

'Don't say that,' Misty scolded him.

'Crack the hatch and have a look.'

Pitt turned the wheel that snugged the hatch down, then stood still breathing in the fresh sea air. His eyes made a 360-degree sweep of the horizons. A storm of incredulity swept through him.

The seas were empty. *Deep Encounter* had vanished.

AT ALMOST THE same moment the *Abyss Navigator* reached the seabed, Leo Delgado noticed a fast-moving blip on the radar screen. 'We have a visitor.'

Burch walked out onto the bridge wing. A bright orange-and-white boat cut the water towards *Deep Encounter*.

'What do you make of her?' asked Delgado.

'An oil company work boat,' replied Burch. 'I wonder where she came from. There are no oil rigs within a thousand miles.'

The radio operator joined them. 'I have their skipper on the ship's phone.'

The captain switched on the bridge wing speaker. 'This is Captain Burch of the NUMA ship *Deep Encounter*. Go ahead.'

'Captain Wheeler of the Mistral Oil Company boat *Pegasus*. Do you have a doctor on board? We have a badly injured man.'

'Come alongside and I'll send over our ship's doctor.'

'Better we bring him aboard your ship. We have no medical facilities.'

'I'll have a crew standing by to hoist a stretcher on board.'

The work boat came to a stop about fifty yards away and a launch was lowered. A man covered with blankets on a litter was laid across the seats accompanied by four others. The launch was soon next to *Deep Encounter* and the injured man carried on board.

Suddenly, the visitors threw back the blankets and snatched up automatic weapons. The man on the stretcher leapt to his feet, took a gun and ran towards the bridge.

Under international law, survey ships were not allowed to carry arms. Burch and Delgado could do nothing but stand helpless until the intruder stepped onto the bridge deck.

The hijacker had an executive air about him. The hair was prematurely grey, the face dark. 'Captain Burch, I presume. I hope you will offer no resistance.'

'What in hell are you doing on my ship?' Burch demanded.

'Confiscating it,' replied the intruder. 'No one will be harmed.'

As he spoke, the launch soon returned with more armed men.

'This is madness,' snarled Burch indignantly.

An armed hijacker approached. 'Sir, the ship is secure.'

'Then prepare to get under way. I want full speed.'

'Where are you taking us?' demanded Delgado.

'It's not your concern,' the man rasped carelessly.

'We cannot leave!' Burch said sharply. 'We have a submersible down on the seabed with two men and a woman inside.'

The pirate shrugged. 'They will have to make land on their own.'

'They'll have no hope of rescue this far off the shipping lanes,' pleaded Burch. 'You'll be signing their death warrants.'

'Not my problem.'

Burch stared at the black man as if he was mad. 'God help you if those men die,' he said.

Rudi Gunn, NUMA's chief of operations, entered Sandecker's office. 'Sorry to interrupt, Admiral, but we have a serious problem. *Deep Encounter* and all on board have vanished.'

Sandecker sat with icy calm. 'How long has it been since they last responded?'

'Ten hours.'

'My instructions are that all ships report every two hours.'

'Someone claiming to be Captain Burch did make contact every two hours. We now know it was not the captain. The voice system recording all our communications did not accept the voice pattern.'

'I can't believe the ship and all on board vanished into thin air.'

'A friend at the National Oceanic Atmospheric Agency analysed satellite weather photos of the area. No sign of her.'

'A phoney voice giving up-to-date reports.' The admiral stared at Gunn. 'You're suggesting that *Deep Encounter* was hijacked.'

'It's beginning to look that way. She must have been sailed out of range before the satellite passed over.'

Sandecker stiffened. 'Pitt and Giordino were on the project,' he said.

'The last report by Captain Burch stated that they were preparing to lower into the water for their descent.'

'Have you contacted the Australian and New Zealand governments and requested an extensive search?'

Gunn nodded. 'They assured me of their full cooperation.'

'Obtain satellite photos for a one-thousand-square-mile grid of the area. *Deep Encounter* has to be out there somewhere.'

Gunn headed for the door. 'I'll see to it.'

Sandecker sat staring at a photo gallery that covered one wall. His eyes settled on a picture of Pitt and Giordino standing next to a submersible. They were like the sons he'd never had.

'What mischief,' he muttered softly to himself under his breath, 'have you two guys got yourself into this time?'

After accepting the disappearance of *Deep Encounter*, Pitt, Giordino and Misty concentrated on staying alive. They found no trace of flotsam or an oil slick, so they assumed that for whatever reason the survey ship had sailed away and would soon return.

But night passed. The sun rose and set twice more and still no sign of the mother ship. Hope of a rescue dwindled. A passing ship would have to be almost on top of them to spot the *Abyss Navigator*. Their homing beacon reached out for twenty miles, but its signal was only programmed to be received by *Deep Encounter*. Their only hope was if a rescue craft came within a two-mile range of their radio.

Water was the first priority. Fortunately, rainsqualls were frequent. A vinyl mat caught the rain and sent it down a crease into their water bottles. Using tools for emergency repairs, Pitt fashioned a series of hooks. For fishing lines, Giordino disassembled electronic wiring. Within ten hours, they had a small stock of raw fish, expertly scaled and gutted by Misty. It had little taste, but no one complained.

'I wonder if Admiral Sandecker is aware of our situation,' said Misty softly.

'I'll bet he's moving heaven and hell to launch a search-and-rescue operation,' said Pitt confidently.

The fourth day broke under gloomy skies. The routine never varied. Catch water if possible, catch fish if possible, and search the horizon. Each person stood a two-hour watch. During Misty's watch, an aircraft flew within a mile of the drifting submersible. Despite her frantic waving, the aircraft continued on. 'It was a rescue plane,' she cried. 'He flew right over and didn't see us.'

'Our hatch tower is too tiny,' said Giordino. 'From the air we're as obvious as a flyspeck on a barn door.'

'Then how will they ever find us?' Misty asked.

In the next two days, three more planes flew over and failed to spot them. Knowing that rescuers were coming so close without discovering them was disheartening.

The grey skies cleared at sunset. Giordino was on watch, leaning over the rim of the hatch tower, dozing off.

He woke up to music. He splashed his face with sea water but the music was still there. A Strauss waltz. Then he saw a light, no more than 400 yards away.

He groped for a flashlight. Now he could see the outline of a small vessel. He switched the flashlight on and off. 'Over here! Over here!'

'What is it?' Pitt called out below.

'Some kind of boat!' Giordino shouted back.

Pitt picked up the portable radio and began calling on five different frequencies.

'They haven't seen us,' Giordino groaned.

'Hello, hello, please respond,' Pitt implored.

His only reply was static. Disappointment settled over the submersible as Giordino watched the lights fade into the darkness.

Suddenly a voice cracked over the submersible's speaker. 'Who am I talking to?'

'Castaways!' Pitt snapped back. 'You sailed right past us.'

'Hold tight. I'm coming round.'

A spotlight swept the surface of the water before finally stopping on Giordino.

'Do not be alarmed,' came the voice again. 'I will pass over you and stop above your tower when it is aligned with my stern.'

Giordino stared aghast at the brightly lit vessel bearing down on him. It looked like no oceangoing yacht he'd ever seen. His state of mind quickly turned from apprehension to relief as twin catamaran hulls slipped past the submersible with five feet of clearance to spare. He gazed in awe as the superstructure moved overhead.

Only then did he think to report to Pitt and Misty. 'It's a catamaran. We're directly under his stern.' Then he disappeared.

Misty came out of the hatch like a champagne cork, astounded at her first view of the incredible vessel above. She stood on the luxurious rear deck with its table and conches without remembering scrambling up the stairway.

Pitt reset the beacon on the submersible, then closed and secured the hatch before climbing onto the catamaran. For a few moments, the three stood there alone. They watched as a figure stepped down from the wheelhouse. He was the same height as Pitt but fifteen pounds heavier and thirty years older. His grey hair and beard gave him the appearance of an old waterfront wharf rat.

'Three of you in that little life raft,' he said in amazement.

'Not a life raft,' said Pitt. 'A deep ocean submersible.' He offered their rescuer a brief summary of how they came to be lost at sea. 'It is imperative that we call our headquarters in Washington and advise the director of NUMA that we've been found.'

The old man nodded. 'Come up to the wheelhouse. The *Periwinkle* has the finest communications systems of any yacht on the water.'

Pitt studied the old man. 'We've met before.'

'Yes, I suspect we have.'

'My name is Dirk Pitt.' He turned to the others. 'My shipmates, Misty Graham and Al Giordino.'

The old man warmly shook hands with all. Then he grinned. 'I'm Clive Cussler.'

'We were certainly lucky you happened past,' said Misty.

'I'm on a round-the-world cruise,' Cussler elaborated. 'My last port was Hobart in Tasmania. I'm bound for Papeete, Tahiti.'

He led the way up to the wheelhouse. Tinted windows ran in a 360-degree circle. There were no conventional instruments, no wheel or throttle levers. The helm station was a large executive chair in front of seven liquid crystal display screens encased in walnut cabinets.

Cussler motioned Pitt to sit in the chair. 'The satellite phone is in the panel to your right. Just press the blue button and you can all speak and listen to the other party.'

Pitt thanked him and dialled up Sandecker's private line. The admiral, as always, answered on the first ring. 'Sandecker.'

'Admiral, this is Dirk.'

There was a pregnant pause. 'You're alive and well?'

'Hungry but otherwise healthy. Al and Misty are here beside me.'

Pitt could hear the admiral's sigh of pleasure through the earpiece. 'I've got Rudi here in my office. I'll switch to the speaker.'

'Dirk!' boomed Rudi Gunn's voice. 'We've had every rescue unit from Australia and New Zealand searching for you.'

'We were picked up by a passing yacht. We spent several hours on the sea bottom investigating the wreck but when we ascended to the surface the ship had vanished.'

'It's beginning to look like *Deep Encounter* was hijacked.'

'What?'

'They must have boarded the ship while you were on the bottom.'

'But why?' questioned Giordino. 'What earthly good is an oceanographic survey ship to pirates? Where's the motive?'

'Motive . . .' Pitt let the word hang in the air. 'The same people who torched and then sank the cruise ship wanted to prevent us from discovering evidence of arson.'

'Were you able to survey the wreck?' asked Gunn.

'Yes,' said Pitt. 'There's no doubt about it, the bottom was blown out of the *Emerald Dolphin* in at least six places.'

'The murderous scum never figured on a survey ship with submersibles that could go down twenty thousand feet,' Gunn said.

Misty looked stricken. 'Which brings us to the possibility that everyone on *Deep Encounter* has been killed in the cover-up.'

There was silence.

Pitt began to focus. 'We saw no sign of debris after we broke the surface. My guess is that they took the ship and everyone on board and hid them as bargaining chips should their plans go wrong.'

'But when it begins to look like they're in the clear,' Gunn continued, 'will they dispose of the proof of their crimes?'

'We can't let that happen,' said Misty, distressed. 'If what Dirk suggests is accurate, we only have a little time to save our friends.'

'The problem is where to look,' said Sandecker. 'There's no trace of it anywhere, nor of the hijacker's vessel.'

'I'll bet I know how to find both ships,' said Pitt confidently. 'We need to expand our search grids.'

'The top speed of *Deep Encounter* is no more than fifteen knots,' said Gunn. 'There is no way she could have sailed out of the original satellite camera range.'

'Chief Engineer House got twenty knots out of her during our dash towards the burning cruise ship,' Pitt informed him. 'The hijackers might have taken our vessel in tow and increased her speed by another four to six knots.'

Sandecker was sceptical. 'Makes no difference. We increased the range of the satellite cameras and there was still no sign.'

'True,' Pitt said, 'but you were looking on the water.'

'We didn't consider land,' admitted Gunn thoughtfully.

Giordino spoke up. 'The nearest landmass from where the cruise liner sank is the northern tip of New Zealand.'

'No,' said Pitt quietly, 'there are the Kermadec Islands no more than two hundred nautical miles to the south.' He looked at Cussler. 'Are you familiar with the Kermadec Islands?'

'I've cruised around them. Raoul Island is the largest, but it's just thirteen miles square. The only residents are goats and rats.'

'Is there a harbour large enough to anchor a small ship?'

'More like a lagoon,' replied Cussler, 'but it's a safe anchorage.'

'How about foliage for camouflage?'

'Raoul is lush and heavily wooded. They could cover a pair of small ships well enough.'

'I'll ask that the next satellite that passes over that part of the Pacific aim its cameras on the Kermadecs,' said Sandecker.

Pitt punched off the connection and turned to Cussler. 'Any possibility you could make a detour by the Kermadecs?' he asked.

THE GREEN SEA merged with the water flowing through the channel of the large lagoon that nestled between the lava cliffs of Raoul Island. Inside the narrow channel, the lagoon widened into a small but respectable anchorage. From the sea, only a tiny section of the lagoon could be seen through the slit between the cliffs. High atop the west side of the entrance, more than 300 feet above the surf, a small shack built of palm fronds perched dangerously close to the edge. The native look was a façade. Beneath the palm fronds were walls built of concrete blocks. The interior was air-conditioned and the windows were tinted. A security guard sat inside, studying the vast expanse of ocean with a large pair of binoculars. Stacked against one wall were four missile launchers and two automatic rifles. With this arsenal, he could have held off a small navy trying to force its way into the lagoon.

He yawned and changed the discs in his CD player. He had just pushed the play button when his eye caught a movement. He swung the binoculars and focused on the strangest-looking yacht he had ever seen; not a sailing boat but a twin-hulled catamaran power cruiser, cutting through the water at close to forty knots.

He turned to the radio and switched on the transmitter. 'I have a yacht approaching from the northeast.'

'Any sign of weapons or armed personnel?' replied a voice like sandpaper.

'None.'

'She doesn't look threatening?' asked the rough voice.

'Not unless you consider two naked people in a Jacuzzi threatening.'

'Stay on the air and report any suspicious movement. If she turns into the channel, you know what you have to do.'

The guard glanced at the missile launchers. 'A pity to destroy such a handsome boat.' He watched until it became a tiny speck in the distance. Then he called over the radio again. 'The yacht is gone. It appears as if she dropped anchor in the open lagoon on the south end of Macauley Island.'

'Then she's harmless,' said the rough voice.

'It would seem so.'

'Watch her lights after dark and make sure she stays put.'

'I suspect she settled in for the night. Her passengers are probably going to barbecue steaks on the beach.'

'I'll fly a reconnaissance in the helicopter and see if you're right.'

MISTY AND GIORDINO were not naked in the hot tub. They were wearing swimsuits provided by Cussler. They were, however, sipping rum collinses as the boat cruised under the steep cliffs of Raoul Island. Cussler and Pitt were not as lucky. The old man sat at the helm station, eyeing the depth sounder and examining the coral reefs that could have sliced the *Periwinkle*'s twin hulls like razor blades through cardboard. Pitt lay sweating under a pile of towels on the lounge deck, videotaping the guardhouse at the top of the cliffs.

Once the yacht was anchored, they all settled into the main salon and gazed at the monitor while Pitt played the tape on the VCR. The telephoto lens revealed the guard peering at them through binoculars. Added to the video was the soundtrack of the conversation between the guard and his colleague, as recorded by Cussler's high-tech communications systems.

'They don't take kindly to strangers,' Pitt said as a helicopter flew over the yacht. 'What say we go out and wave to them?'

A red and yellow helicopter was hovering off the *Periwinkle*'s stern. Pitt sprawled on a couch while Giordino stood partially under the deck overhang, videotaping the aircraft. Misty and Cussler stood beside the Jacuzzi and waved. The pilot of the helicopter waved back and returned to Raoul Island.

As soon as the craft was a speck in the sky, they headed back to the salon. Giordino pulled a tape from the camera and slid it into the VCR. The zoom focus clearly showed a sandy-haired man with a grizzled beard at the controls and a black man flying as copilot.

Cussler clicked off the remote. 'What happens now?'

'As soon as it's dark, we build a small raft and attach lights on it so it looks like a boat lit up from a distance. Then we sail back under cover of the cliffs, out of sight of the guard. After that, Al and I swim up the channel to the lagoon to have a look round. If we're right, and *Deep Encounter* is hidden under camouflage, we sneak aboard, overpower the hijackers, free our friends and sail off into the blue.'

'That's the plan?' asked Giordino, his eyes squinting as if seeing a mirage in the desert.

'That's the plan,' Pitt echoed.

Misty looked dumbstruck. 'Two of you up against fifty or more armed hijackers? That's the craziest scheme I've ever heard.'

'The Aussies can be here in twenty-four hours,' said Cussler.

'Twenty-four hours from now may be too late.'

'You'll have a long swim,' said Cussler. 'From where I'll moor the boat, the inside of the lagoon is over a mile.'

'We'll be lucky to get in by midnight,' muttered Giordino.

'I can cut your time by two hours,' said Cussler. 'I have a dive thruster that will pull you through the water. You can use it to propel you both in tandem.'

'Is there nothing I can say to talk you out of it?' Misty pleaded.

'No,' said Pitt, his lips spread in a comforting smile. 'This thing has to be done. There wouldn't be security at the entrance to the channel if there wasn't something inside someone wanted to hide. We have to find out if it's *Deep Encounter*.'

'And if you're wrong?'

The smile was gone and Pitt's face became tense. 'If we're wrong, then our friends will die because we failed to save them.'

IT TOOK THE THREE men two hours to tie several palm tree trunks together into a raft and then construct a rough outline of the *Periwinkle* from driftwood. A small battery was connected to a string of lights on the framework.

'It ain't pretty,' said Giordino. 'But it should fool the security guard sitting five miles away.'

Cussler engaged the *Periwinkle*'s big engines. Then he shifted the lights to the raft and threw the yacht into darkness. He steered towards Raoul Island by radar, keeping the speed down to ten knots.

Cussler aimed the twin bows towards the tiny light high on the cliffs. 'I'll bring us inside the rocks just in front of the channel,' he explained. 'From there you'll have to rely on the thruster. Keep well clear of the surf pounding on the cliffs until you reach calm water.'

As soon as the boat was moored, he said, 'This is as far as I go.'

Pitt and Giordino pulled on fins and masks. Cussler patted both of them on the shoulder. 'Good luck. I'll wait as long as I can.'

They dropped into the warm black water and swam for several minutes, then paused and looked back. The *Periwinkle* was invisible. Giordino wrapped his arms round Pitt's legs as the thruster was switched on; the motor hummed and the jets began pulling them through the water at nearly three knots.

Pitt could only navigate by compass and by the sound of the surf. Then his ears distinguished two separate booms, suggesting that the waves were striking opposite sides of the channel. He let the thruster pull them towards the island until the surf was heard thundering on his right and left, but not ahead. Then he switched off the thruster and allowed the waves to carry them through the channel entrance.

From the glimpse he'd had of the lagoon when the *Periwinkle* had passed the entrance, Pitt estimated that it stretched in a straight line approximately a third of a mile from the sea. Feeling the impetus of the waves slacken, he engaged the thruster again. In less than fifteen minutes, they passed under the high cliffs into the open lagoon. Pitt angled the thruster off to the side of the beach until he could feel sand beneath his feet.

Two vessels were moored side by side in the lagoon, made formless by camouflage netting that was draped over both ships. They swam towards the larger of the two. Without hesitation, Pitt pulled off his fins, handed them to Giordino, and began climbing the anchor chain. He pulled himself up until he was even with the hawsepipe.

From the light from an open port, he could just make out the welded letters on the bow. They read: *Deep Encounter*.

Pitt lowered himself back down the anchor chain. 'She's *Deep Encounter*,' he informed Giordino quietly.

'How do we get aboard without a gangplank or a ladder?'

'The hijacker's ship is smaller. We can go over the stern, then work our way on board *Deep Encounter*.'

Pitt guessed right. The pirates' vessel was low enough for them to struggle aboard. Pitt was in the act of climbing over the stern railing when Giordino's fingers dug into his arm.

'Someone's standing in the shadows by the aft deckhouse.' Giordino spoke softly in Pitt's ear.

Pitt slowly raised his head. A figure was outlined in the darkness, puffing on a cigarette. Quiet as a wraith, Giordino climbed over the stern railing, stepped across the deck and hooked his big hands round the man's neck. There was a brief struggle, and then the body went limp. Pitt searched the man's clothing, discovering a folding knife and a snub-nosed revolver. 'We're in business,' he proclaimed.

Giordino nodded. 'Let's hope he stays in slumberland for the next hour,' he said, hiding the body.

Pitt passed the knife to Giordino, who studied it morosely. 'Why can't I have the gun?'

'You're the one who always watches old Errol Flynn movies.'

'He used a sword, not a cheap switchblade.'

'Just pretend.'

Without another word of complaint from Giordino, they crossed the work deck. They halted at the gangplank between the two ships and sneaked a look inside one of the ports. Pitt counted twenty-two hijackers sitting in a large mess room. There were enough guns stacked around to start a revolution.

He and Giordino flattened themselves against the port superstructure. Pitt pointed to the wide patch of painted cardboard that was crudely taped on the side. 'Let's see what they're hiding.'

He peeled off the duct tape and stared at the markings beneath. He could just discern the image of a three-headed dog with a serpent for its tail. Directly beneath was the word CERBERUS. He retaped it.

'See anything?' Giordino asked.

'Enough.'

They crossed the gangplank between the two ships, half expecting hijackers to blast away at them with automatic weapons. Now Pitt was on home ground. He knew every inch of *Deep Encounter*.

They slipped through a hatch and moved up a companionway to the pilothouse. It was empty. Pitt went into the communications room. While Giordino stood guard outside, he picked up the satellite phone and dialled Sandecker's cellphone. The admiral answered. Pitt gave a brief report on finding *Deep Encounter*.

'My crew and scientific team?' asked the admiral.

'The issue is still in doubt,' answered Pitt. 'I will contact you when I have a positive answer.' Then he closed the connection.

They left the pilothouse and dropped down to the next deck. Pitt entered his stateroom and was surprised to find his faithful old Colt automatic right where he'd left it. He shoved it under the waistband of his shorts and handed the revolver to Giordino. Next, Pitt retrieved a penlight and aimed it into the passageway. 'Let's move on.'

They dropped down to the engine room, and as they approached they could hear the murmur of voices. Pitt put his ear to the steel door and listened. The voices seemed to be heavy with scorn.

Pitt pushed the door a fraction of an inch. It moved noiselessly. They clearly heard the voices now. Two came from strangers, but the others were as familiar as his own. The two unknowns seemed to be taunting their prisoners.

'Won't be long now and you'll see what it's like to drown.'

'Yeah. Your ears burst like they were punctured with ice picks,' said his partner nastily. 'You'll have a blast, won't they, Sam?'

'You kill us,' said Captain Burch angrily, 'and every investigative force in the world will hang your butts higher than a kite.'

'Not without evidence of the crime,' said the hijacker called Sam.

'Our crew should be coming aboard in another half-hour,' his partner said. 'After that, you NUMA people will get to study all them denizens of the deep first-hand.'

Through the crack in the hatch, Pitt could see the hijackers were holding automatic weapons. Pitt nodded at Giordino. They opened the door and walked in shoulder to shoulder.

The hijackers sensed movement behind them but didn't turn, thinking it was their friends. Sam said, 'You guys are early. You people better start praying. It's almost time to meet your maker—'

That was as far as he got. Giordino picked him up off the deck and smashed his head against a bulkhead, as Pitt swung his .45 against the other guard's jaw, crumpling him in a heap on the deck.

Sitting on the floor with their legs chained together was the entire company of *Deep Encounter*. They stared in shock at seeing the two men they'd thought were lost for ever. Then they began coming to their feet and were on the verge of cheering when Pitt hissed, 'Quiet! We'll have an army of guards rushing in.'

Giordino looked at Chief Engineer House. 'What have you got to cut the chains?'

'You'll find a pair of cable cutters in the toolroom.'

Giordino returned in thirty seconds and began feverishly cutting. Pitt rushed up to the outer deck to see if the rescue had been discovered but the decks of the pirate ship were still empty. When he returned, Chief House and his crew were already preparing to get the survey ship under way.

'This is where I leave you,' Pitt said to Burch. 'There is a guard on the cliffs above the entrance to the channel. I'm guessing he has enough firepower to stop any ship leaving the lagoon.'

'It's a black night. We might be able to sneak out to sea without the guard spotting us,' said Burch.

'No good,' said Pitt. 'The minute you get under way, the hijackers will know about it. They'll alert the guard. I've got to get there first.'

'I'll come with you,' Giordino said firmly.

Pitt shook his head. 'You're the best man to repel boarders before the ship slips away.'

Giordino shook Pitt's hand. 'Good luck, pal.'

'Same to you.' Then Pitt was gone.

As THE CREW HURRIED about their duties, Giordino took the two hijackers' automatic rifles and stationed himself a few feet away from the gangplank leading to the pirate ship. He didn't think he could win a firefight, but he could easily keep boarders off the survey vessel once it got under way. He could have pushed the gangplank into the water, but thought better of making any unnecessary sound. It would fall of its own accord after *Deep Encounter* began to move.

Two of the survey ship's crewmen crawled along the deck and cast off the mooring lines. Now comes the fun part, Giordino thought to himself, as he heard the clatter from the anchor chain.

On the bridge, Captain Burch was holding the ship's portable phone to his mouth. 'OK, Chief. Take us the hell out of here.'

The ship lurched forward.

True to expectations, three of the hijackers rushed out of the mess room. One yelled, 'Stop! You can't leave ahead of schedule.'

It was not in Giordino's nature to lie quiet. He called out. 'Sam sez you're a drooling imbecile who can't be trusted to raise a toilet seat.'

A crowd of hijackers made a run for the gangplank. Two were halfway across when Giordino shot them in the knees. At that moment, the end of the gangplank fell away.

The hijackers rallied in the blink of an eye. Before *Deep Encounter* had covered 100 yards, the work boat leapt to the pursuit. A volley of shots rang out, answered by Giordino.

They were pounding through the channel now. Behind them, the work boat was coming on at twice the speed of *Deep Encounter.*

All eyes looked up towards the tiny light that shone from the security guard's watch house. Could Pitt get there before they reached the channel entrance?

THE PATH TWISTED tortuously up the cliffs. Pitt's feet ached from pounding on the lava rock and had begun to bleed, as he had worn only socks under his dive fins. He ran hard, never once reducing his pace to a trot. He threw a quick glance over his shoulder at hearing the sound of gunfire. The movement of lights flickering on the lagoon told him that *Deep Encounter* was under way.

Ten yards from the guardhouse he froze. The guard was standing on the edge of the cliff, staring at the survey ship surging through the channel. He was holding some kind of weapon in his hands. Pitt tensed as he recognised it as a missile launcher. A wooden crate on the ground held a supply of missiles. He watched as the guard raised the missile launcher to his shoulder.

All thought of stealth was forgotten. If the guard fired a missile into *Deep Encounter*, fifty innocent people would die. Recklessly, Pitt hurled himself across the final ten yards.

The blast from the launcher flashed over Pitt's head as he smashed his shoulder into the guard's chest. They crashed to the ground as the missile, its aim altered by the impact, struck the side of a cliff fifty feet above *Deep Encounter.* The explosion sent rock bursting across the channel, fragments raining down on the survey ship.

The guard struggled to his feet and swung his hands in a vicious judo chop, pounding into the top of Pitt's skull. Pitt came within a hair of blacking out but recovered in an instant, came to his knees and swung his right fist into the guard's stomach.

As the guard doubled over, Pitt grabbed the missile launcher and swung it like a club, knocking the man sideways. Despite his injuries, the guard straightened and lunged at Pitt like a wounded boar.

Pitt jumped deftly to his feet and stepped aside. The guard reeled past and fell over the edge of the cliff. His unexpected defeat came so quickly, he failed to cry out. The only sound came from a distant splash far below. With cold efficiency, Pitt quickly pulled a missile from the crate, shoved it into the launcher and aimed it at the pirate ship plunging through the channel behind *Deep Encounter*. He aimed through the simple sights and pulled the trigger.

The missile screeched away into the night and struck the work boat square amidships. The entire channel was suddenly illuminated, as a brilliant orange-and-red ball painted the cliffs. The detonation had ruptured the fuel tanks, turning the boat into a raging inferno.

Pitt felt few feelings of remorse. The men on board had been killers. *Deep Encounter* and everyone on her were free from harm now. That was all that mattered.

He hurled the missile launcher over the cliff and limped into the guardhouse, where he found a first-aid kit. Minutes later, his throbbing feet were swabbed with antiseptic and encased in bandages. Then he emptied a can half filled with gasoline for the generator and picked up a box of matches. Pitt stepped from the guardhouse, fired the matchbox and threw it through the doorway. As the interior erupted in flames, he hobbled down the path to the lagoon.

When he arrived, he found Giordino and Misty waiting for him. Resting on the beach was a launch from the survey ship.

Giordino embraced him. 'For a while there, I thought you'd been sidetracked by a luscious native girl.'

Pitt hugged his friend in return. 'I guess I *did* cut it a mite close.'

Misty threw her arms round him. 'I can't believe you're still alive.'

Pitt gave her a gentlemanly kiss. 'You came in the ship's launch?'

'The old man transferred me on board *Deep Encounter*. Then he sailed off to continue his round-the-world cruise.'

'I never got a chance to thank him,' said Pitt regretfully.

PART TWO: GUARD OF HADES
Washington, DC

July 25, 2003. Despite the lengthy plane trip, Pitt postponed the comforts of home and headed straight for NUMA headquarters in an agency Jeep. He parked and took the elevator up to the tenth floor, the domain of Hiram Yaeger, the agency's computer genius.

With his greying hair tied in a ponytail, Yaeger looked like an old hippie. His library contained every known fact about the oceans since recorded history. He'd also created a technically advanced computer named Max that was nearly human. He'd programmed photos of his wife into its holographic image.

Yaeger was taken aback at Pitt's appearance. The special projects director seemed like a lost soul. Despite several hours of sleep on the aeroplane, his eyes looked tired and washed out. His face had over a week's growth of scraggly beard. 'For the man of the hour, you look like second-class roadkill,' Yaeger said.

Pitt shook Yaeger's hand. 'I came directly from the airport just to harass you.'

'I don't doubt it for a moment.' Yaeger knew well Pitt's aversion to compliments. He skipped talk of recent events and motioned Pitt to sit down. 'What brings you to my world of electronic manipulation?'

Pitt laid Egan's leather case on Yaeger's desk and opened it. He unwrapped the greenish object taken from the chapel floor of the *Emerald Dolphin*. It was rounded and smooth and twisted in a spiral. 'I'd like to have this analysed and identified.'

Yaeger examined the odd-shaped thing for a moment. 'I'll have the chemistry lab do a number on it. Anything else?'

Pitt passed over the video cassettes from the *Abyss Navigator*. 'Computer-enhance and digitise these into three-dimensional images. And one final thing.' He laid a drawing on the desk. 'Have you ever seen a company logo like this?'

Yaeger looked at Pitt's crude drawing of the three-headed dog with a snake for a tail and the word CERBERUS beneath. 'Where did you see it?'

'It was covered up on the side of the pirates' work boat.'

'An oil-rig work boat?'

'Yes, the same type,' Pitt replied. 'You're familiar with it?'

'I am,' replied Yaeger. 'You're opening a can of worms if you connect the Cerberus Corporation with the hijacking.'

'The Cerberus Corporation,' Pitt said slowly. 'How stupid of me. I should have known. The conglomerate owns most of the US domestic oil fields, copper and iron mines, and its chemical division makes a thousand different products. It was the three-headed dog that threw me. I failed to make the connection.'

Yaeger sat at his computer and typed. In a chamber just opposite his console, the face and figure of an attractive woman appeared in three dimensions.

'Hello, Max. You know Dirk Pitt.'

The hazy brown eyes flicked from Pitt's feet to his face. 'Yes, I am familiar with him.'

'What can you tell me about Cerberus, the three-headed dog?'

'From Greek mythology,' Max came back instantly. 'Cerberus

guarded the gates of Hades and prevented dead souls from escaping from the underworld. The three heads represented the past, present and future. What the serpent tail signified is not known to me.'

'What can you tell me about Cerberus, the oil, mining and chemical corporation?'

'Have you got about ten hours?' said Max.

'You have that much data on Cerberus?' Pitt asked.

'Not yet. But I will after I've entered their network and those of the companies who do business with them.'

Pitt rose from his chair. 'I'll leave it to you. So long for now, Max. You look stunning.'

'Thank you, Mr Pitt. I like you. A pity our circuits can't integrate.'

THE OLD AIRCRAFT hangar, built in the 1930s for a long-since defunct airline, stood off in one corner of Ronald Reagan International Airport. The corrugated metal walls and roof were coated with orange-brown rust. Its few windows were boarded over, and the door to what once had been the office was weather-worn, with fading and peeling paint.

Pitt parked the NUMA Jeep in the weeds outside the hangar and paused at the entrance door. He glanced at the security camera atop a wooden pole on the other side of the road to see that it had stopped its swivel and was aimed directly at him. Then he punched a sequence of numbers, waited for a series of clicks inside the hangar and turned the brass latch. The ancient door swung open noiselessly. The interior was dark except for a few skylights above an upstairs apartment. He switched on the lights.

The sudden effect was dazzling. Set off in their most elegant magnificence by the bright overhead lights, white walls and epoxy floor, were three rows of beautifully restored classic cars. Sitting incongruously at the end of one row, but just as dazzling as the others, was a 1936 Ford hot rod. On one side of the hangar sat a World War II German jet fighter and a 1929 trimotor transport. Beyond was a turn-of-the-century railroad Pullman car, an odd-looking sailing boat mounted on a rubber raft and a bathtub with an outboard motor attached on one end. The collection of automotive mechanical masterpieces of art were cherished and maintained by Pitt and seen by only his closest friends.

Pitt closed and locked the door. He took a brief tour, as he always did after returning home from an expedition. Tomorrow, he told himself, he would run a soft cloth over the gleaming paint and remove the light coating of dust that had seeped inside the hangar while he was gone. Finishing his inspection, he climbed the antique iron spiral staircase to his apartment, which was perched above the main floor against the hangar's far wall.

In his apartment were all sorts of nautical antiques. The 1,100 square feet of living space, which included a living room, bathroom, kitchen and bedroom, were crowded with objects from old ships sunk or scrapped. There was a large wooden-spoked helm from an ancient clipper, a compass binnacle from an Orient tramp steamer, ships' bells and divers' helmets. The furniture came from ships that had sailed the seas in the nineteenth century. Ship models in glass cases sat on low shelves, while marine paintings hung on the walls.

After a good night's sleep in his large goosedown-mattress bed, Pitt got up early the next morning, shaved and put on a dark business suit. He ate a light breakfast and drove across the river to the NUMA headquarters. He took the elevator from the underground parking area straight up to the fourth floor. When the doors opened, he stepped out onto an ornate mosaic tile floor with scenes of ships at sea that stretched down the corridor. The entire floor was empty. At seven o'clock, he was the first to arrive.

He stepped into his corner office, removed his coat and hung it on an old-fashioned clothes stand. Pitt seldom spent more than three months out of the year at his desk; he preferred working in the field. For the next two hours he sorted through his mail and studied the logistics of future NUMA scientific expeditions around the world.

At nine o'clock sharp his secretary, Zerri Pochinsky, entered the outer office. Seeing Pitt at his desk, she rushed in and gave him a kiss on the cheek. 'Welcome back. I hear you're to be congratulated.'

'Don't you start in,' Pitt grumbled, happy to see Zerri.

Her tone became official. 'Admiral Sandecker wants you in the conference room at eleven o'clock sharp.'

'Giordino, too?'

'Giordino, too.'

For the next few hours, Pitt worked on his detailed report of the crazy events of the past two weeks, from his sighting of the burning cruise liner to *Deep Encounter*'s escape from the hijackers. He left out the possible Cerberus connection, because at this point he didn't have the slightest notion where the corporation entered the picture. He left it to Hiram Yaeger to continue tracing the thread.

At eleven, Pitt entered the conference room and closed the door behind him. Sandecker and Rudi Gunn were already seated at the long conference table. Two other men rose from their chairs to greet him. They were Wilbur Hill, a director of the CIA, and Charles Davis, special assistant to the director of the FBI.

While they chatted, Hiram Yaeger and Al Giordino walked into the room. 'Well,' said Sandecker. 'Shall we get to it?'

A huge three-sided monitor dropped from the ceiling and the images of the *Emerald Dolphin* taken by the *Sea Sleuth*'s video cameras began to sweep across the screens.

Pitt gave a narration as the submersible moved along the hull of the sunken cruise liner. 'The wreck is broken into three pieces. If you study the way the gaps in the hull are torn outwards, it appears obvious that a series of explosions blew out the hull beneath the water line while the fire-destroyed derelict was under tow.'

'Couldn't the hull have been blown apart when fire reached the ship's fuel tanks?' asked Davis.

'I've had a fair amount of experience investigating terrorist bomb explosions, and I believe Dirk is correct,' said Wilbur Hill. 'The bottom of the hull was not blown out by a concentrated explosion. It burst in several places. It looks as if the explosive devices were spaced equidistant from one another.'

'Who could do it?' asked Davis. 'No one alive was left aboard when it was taken in tow.'

'Not so,' said Gunn. 'The tug's captain, Jock McDermott, reported pulling one of the cruise ship's officers from the sea immediately after it went down.'

'How could the man have survived the fire?'

'McDermott was at a loss to explain. He stated that the man acted as if he was in shock until the tug reached Wellington. Then he slipped ashore and disappeared before he could be questioned.'

'Did McDermott give a description?' Davis probed.

'Only that he was a black man.'

Sandecker spoke slowly. 'The prime issue here is that the *Emerald Dolphin* was deliberately sunk to block any investigation to find the cause of the fire. The sinking was a cover-up.'

Davis stared at Sandecker. 'If your theory is correct, Admiral, that leads to the possibility that the fire was an act of arson. I can't conceive of any motive to destroy a cruise ship and twenty-five hundred crew and passengers. Certainly not without a terrorist group claiming responsibility, and none has come forward.'

'I agree it's incomprehensible,' said Sandecker. 'But if that's where the facts lead us, that's where we'll go.'

'What facts?' Davis persisted. 'It would be impossible to find evidence that the fire was caused by man and not by an accident.'

'I believe Dirk and Al have given us the evidence to prove the fire was deliberate,' said Yaeger.

Everyone at the table looked at him expectantly, waiting for him to continue, but Pitt spoke first. 'Our lab identified the material?'

'What are we talking about?' asked Hill.

'A substance we found in the chapel area, where the fire started,' answered Giordino.

'Our NUMA scientists identified it as a highly incendiary material known as Pyrotorch 610,' Yaeger continued. 'Once it has been ignited, it's almost impossible to extinguish.'

Pitt reached over and shook Giordino's hand. 'Good work, partner.'

Sandecker looked across the table at Hill and Davis. 'Gentlemen, it seems we have a grievous crime on our hands. I hope you will launch an immediate investigation.'

'Now that we definitely know a crime was committed,' said Davis, 'I believe we can all work together to find the answers.'

'You can begin with the hijacking of *Deep Encounter*,' said Pitt. 'I don't doubt there is a connection.'

Hill wasn't sold. 'What possible grounds could they have had for stealing a NUMA ship?'

'It was hardly a simple theft,' Pitt said acidly. 'They meant to sink the ship and kill every man and woman on board. You want a motive? They were out to stop us from making a deep-water survey of the wreck. They were afraid of what we might discover.'

'Who could be responsible for such evil?' said Gunn.

'You might start with the Cerberus Corporation,' said Yaeger.

'Nonsense,' snorted Davis. 'One of the nation's largest and most respected companies involved with attempting to murder more than two thousand people on the other side of the world? Can you imagine General Motors, Exxon or Microsoft committing crimes of mass murder? I certainly can't.'

'I couldn't agree with you more,' said Sandecker. 'But Cerberus hardly has lily-white hands. They've been involved with some pretty shady business deals.'

'They've been investigated by congressional committees on several occasions,' added Gunn.

'None of which amounted to more than political wool-gathering,' retorted Davis.

Sandecker grinned. 'It's pretty tough for Congress to reprimand an outfit that gives both political parties enough funding every election to launch ten Third World countries.'

Davis shook his head. 'I'd have to see hard proof before you sold me on investigating Cerberus.'

'Would it help if I told you the scientists at Cerberus's chemical division created Pyrotorch 610?' Yaeger asked.

Davis quickly came back. 'The material was probably stolen.'

'At least the FBI has a place to start,' said Sandecker to the FBI agent. He turned to Hill. 'And what of the CIA?'

'The first thing is to mount a salvage expedition on the remains of the pirate ship and see what turns up.'

'Can NUMA help you with that project?' asked Pitt.

'No, thank you,' said Hill. 'We have a private company we work with on underwater investigations.'

'So be it,' said Sandecker.

'Just one other question. Who owned the *Emerald Dolphin*?'

'The Blue Seas Cruise Lines,' replied Gunn. 'A British-based company owned primarily by American stockholders.'

Hill smiled at Davis. 'A domestic as well as an international act of terror. Looks like our two agencies *will* have to work together.'

After Davis and Hill left, Sandecker's eyes narrowed. 'There's no way they're leaving NUMA out of the investigation. We'll go our own way without rocking the CIA and the FBI's boat.' He looked at Pitt and Giordino. 'You two take three days off and rest up. Then come back and get to work.'

Pitt looked candidly back at Sandecker. 'Where do we start?'

'I'll have a plan when you return.'

WHEN PITT GOT BACK to his old aircraft hangar, he took the slip of paper with Kelly's phone number on it and dialled.

She answered after five rings. 'Hello.'

'Hello, Kelly Egan.'

He could hear the intake of breath over the line. 'Dirk! You're back.'

'I'm due for a few days' vacation. I'd like to meet up and talk some more about your father. Did he ever talk to you about his work?'

'The only time was on board the *Emerald Dolphin*. He was proud of the ship's engines, and he explained them to me one night.'

'That's all he ever told you?'

'After a few martinis, he did say he had created the breakthrough of the ages. I thought it was the gin talking.'

'Was nobody aware of all his activities?'

'His associate, Dr Josh Thomas, might have been.'

'Do you know where you can get in touch with him?'

'Yes,' she answered.

'Where is your father's laboratory?' Pitt asked.

'At his home just across the Hudson River in New Jersey, near a town called Englewood Cliffs.'

'Can you call Dr Thomas? I would like to meet him.'

'Any particular reason?'

'To find out what the breakthrough of the ages is all about.'

HIRAM YAEGER was waiting in Sandecker's office when the admiral returned from a press conference. Dr Egan's leather case was on the floor beside his chair. He liked the old case and had begun using it.

'I thought you might want an update on the CIA's dive project on the hijackers' ship,' he said, opening the case and removing a folder.

Sandecker stared at Yaeger. 'Where did you get your information? If they find out Max is hacking CIA files, we'll catch hell.'

Yaeger grinned. 'Believe me, Admiral, they'll never know.' He opened the file. 'The hijackers' boat was built by the Hogan and Lashere Boat Yard of San Diego. She was registered to Barak Oil Company, a subsidiary of Colexico.'

'Colexico,' Sandecker echoed. 'I thought they'd ceased to exist.'

'Colexico was taken over by the Cerberus Corporation.'

Sandecker leaned back in his chair, a smug expression on his face. 'I'd like to see Charlie Davis's face when he hears this.'

'There won't be a direct tie-in,' said Yaeger. 'Ownership of the boat was never transferred.'

'Have the CIA salvage people identified any of the hijackers yet?'

'There's not much left of the bodies to ID. Dental records and fingerprints will probably reveal they were former Special Forces warriors who went to work as mercenaries.'

'Has Max come up with any theories on what possible motives the directors of Cerberus could have for committing mass murder?'

'She can't create a scenario that makes sense.'

'Perhaps Dr Egan is the key,' Sandecker said pensively.

'I'll put Max to work on researching the good doctor's life.'

YAEGER RETURNED to his department and set Max on an in-depth biography of Dr Elmore Egan. He then decided to go home. He put the leather case on the console and opened it to deposit some files and papers inside.

Yaeger was not a man who startled easily. But what he saw stunned him. Cautiously, he dipped his hand inside the case. He rubbed the substance he encountered between his thumb and forefinger.

'Oil,' he muttered to himself, staring blankly at the liquid that half filled the leather case. It's not possible, he thought. The case had not been out of his hands since he'd left Sandecker's office.

KELLY DROVE UP Highway 9 on the west bank of the Hudson River. The wind threw sheets of rain against the car but she handled the Jaguar XK-R hardtop sports car easily. Pitt relaxed in the passenger's seat and enjoyed the drive, watching the countryside roll by.

Kelly turned right onto a narrow asphalt road, which curved like a snake and finally ended at a steel-barred gate that would have stopped a speeding truck. Two television cameras sat atop high poles opposite the road twenty yards behind the gate.

Kelly punched a code in a box embedded in a rock pillar beside the road. Then she took a remote from the glove compartment and punched in another code. Only then did the gates slowly swing open. Once the car was through, they closed quickly so another vehicle could not have followed them inside.

'Your father was certainly security conscious.'

'We're not through yet. There are four guards.'

The road meandered through fields of corn and alfalfa. They were passing a vineyard when a barricade suddenly popped up in front of the car. The minute Kelly stopped, a man stepped out of a large tree trunk with an automatic rifle.

'Hello, Gus. How's the baby girl?'

'We threw her out with the bath water.'

'How wise.' She motioned ahead towards a house that was barely visible through a copse of trees. 'Is Josh here?'

'Yes, ma'am,' answered the guard. 'Dr Thomas hasn't left the premises since your father died. I'm real sorry. He was a fine man.' Then the guard melted back into the tree trunk again.

Pitt looked at her questioningly. 'What was all that about throwing the baby out with the bathwater?'

'A code,' Kelly explained with a smile. 'Had I asked about his baby boy instead of girl, he'd have known I was being held hostage and shot you dead before alerting the other guards.'

Kelly stopped the Jaguar in front of a large two-storey Colonial house with columns on either side of the front porch. Pitt followed her up the steps to a double door carved with the images of Vikings.

'What's the significance?'

'Nothing enigmatic. Dad loved to study Viking history. It was only one of his many passions besides his work.'

She held up a key but punched the doorbell. 'I could let myself in, but I'd rather alert Josh.'

A bald-headed man in his sixties opened the door. He wore a striped shirt and bow tie. At seeing Kelly, he broke into a wide smile and swept her into his arms. Then his face clouded with sorrow. 'I'm so sorry about Elmore.'

'Thank you, Josh.' Kelly introduced Pitt.

'Kelly has told me you were very close to her father,' said Pitt, shaking hands.

'Elmore and I worked together for more than forty years. He was the smartest man I've ever known.'

Thomas led them into the comfortable living room. He returned in a few minutes holding a bottle of chardonnay and three glasses.

Pitt stared at the wine inside his glass as he spoke. 'Tell me, Mr Thomas, what was Dr Egan working on when he died?'

Thomas looked at Kelly, who nodded. 'His big project was the development of a reliable magnetohydrodynamic engine.'

'But magnetohydrodynamic engines have been in the experimental state for twenty years,' said Pitt.

'The first engines would burn out from the extremely high rate of friction build-up. I went to work with Elmore to solve the problem and we came up with a new formula for oil that would not break down under extreme heat and friction.'

'So the two of you developed a super oil,' said Pitt.

'You could call it that.'

'What would its advantages be if used in internal combustion engines.'

'Theoretically, you could run an automobile engine two million miles or more before the internal workings required any repair,' replied Thomas matter-of-factly. 'Aircraft jet engines would especially benefit with longer life and less maintenance. The same for every industrial vehicle from fork lifts to earth movers.'

'Not to mention boat- and ship-propulsion units,' added Pitt.

'Until new technology for energy is perfected that does not rely on moving parts, our formula, which Elmore and I called Slick 66, will have enormous consequences for every mechanical power source that depends on oil for lubrication.'

'How expensive is it to refine and produce?'

'Three cents a gallon more than normal motor oil.'

'I don't imagine the oil companies will be particularly happy about your discovery. They could lose billions of dollars. Unless, of course, they buy your formula and market it themselves.'

Thomas shook his head slowly. 'Elmore never intended to make a dime. He was going to give the formula to the world free of charge.'

'From what you've said, the formula was half yours. Did you also agree to contribute it to the common good?'

Thomas uttered a quiet laugh. 'I'm sixty-five years old, Mr Pitt. I have diabetes, acute arthritis and cancer of both the pancreas and liver. What would I do with a billion dollars?'

'Oh, Josh,' Kelly said despondently. 'You never said . . .'

He reached over and patted her hand. 'Even your father had no inkling. I kept it from everyone until now, when it no longer matters.'

'I see you have heavy security,' said Pitt.

'Yes,' acknowledged Thomas. 'Elmore and I have had our lives threatened many times. I was wounded in the leg after a thief attempted to break into the laboratory.'

'Someone tried to steal your formula?'

'Not just someone, but an entire industrial conglomerate.'

'Do you know who?'

'The same corporation that threw Elmore and me out the door after twenty-five years of dedicated work.'

'You were both fired?'

'At the time, Dad and Josh were still working to perfect the oil formula,' replied Kelly. 'The company's directors began making plans to produce Slick 66 and sell it at enormous profit.'

'Elmore and I wouldn't hear of it,' said Thomas. 'Foolishly, the directors thought they had enough data to produce it on their own, and gave us our walking papers, threatening to sue us if we completed the experiment on our own. Bodily harm and death were also veiled threats. But we went ahead anyway.'

'Do you believe it was your old company who tried to steal the formula?' asked Pitt.

'Who else was aware of our work?' Thomas said. 'When they failed to find the key to our formula, they came after us.'

'Who are *they*?'

'The Cerberus Corporation.'

Pitt felt as if he had been hit over the head with a mallet. 'The Cerberus Corporation,' he echoed.

'Are you familiar with it?'

'Our evidence links them with the burning of the *Emerald Dolphin*.'

Thomas did not appear shocked. 'Curtis Merlin Zale, the man who owns the company, will stop at nothing to protect his interests.'

'He doesn't sound like somebody you'd want as an enemy. What about stockholders?'

'Why should they care, when they're pocketing enormous returns on their investments? Besides, Zale owns eighty per cent of the stock.'

'Strange the government hasn't investigated their operations.'

'Cerberus has its claws into every agency in the state and federal government. Any politician who toes the line will find himself very wealthy.' Thomas paused to pour himself another glass of wine. 'And don't kid yourself that someone might turn informer. The informer's family might be threatened by bodily harm, and if that didn't keep them silent, he or she would simply become a suicide. Believe me, Mr Pitt. These are not nice men.'

'Who does their dirty work?'

'A covert organisation called the Vipers who only take orders from Zale. I know this because Elmore was secretly told by an old friend in the Vipers who warned him that he and I were on the murder list.'

'What happened to the old friend?'

'He disappeared.'

'How is it you and Dr Egan survived for so long?'

'Because the man who directs corporate operations left us alone, planning to steal the formula for the oil and the designs for Elmore's magnetohydrodynamic engine at his convenience.'

'Why wait until the engines were installed in the *Emerald Dolphin*?'

'So they could destroy the ship and blame the cause on the engines,' replied Thomas. 'If they ruined the engines' reputation for reliability, it'd discourage buyers and they could snatch up the patents for a song.'

'But the fire did not start in the engine room.'

'Then my guess is that the operation didn't go as planned.'

Pitt nodded in agreement. 'We found incendiary devices in the ship's chapel where the crew said the fire started. A string of them was probably timed to go off in sequence, beginning in the engine room and travelling to the upper decks until the last one ignited in the ship's chapel. But as you suggest, something went wrong.'

Pitt did not say it, but he realised that failing to condemn the magnetohydrodynamic engines for the disaster was another reason for the ship to be sunk before an official investigation.

Thomas dropped his voice so that Pitt could barely hear him. 'I only pray they don't attempt the same criminal act on the *Golden Marlin*.'

'The new luxury submarine that's designed like an underwater cruise ship?'

'Yes, it begins its maiden voyage two days from now.'

'Why should you be concerned?' enquired Kelly.

Thomas looked at her. 'The *Golden Marlin* is owned by Blue Seas Cruise Lines. The engines were mounted in her, too.'

PITT IMMEDIATELY alerted Admiral Sandecker, who dispatched a NUMA jet to pick him up at Gene Taylor Airfield. Kelly drove even faster on the return trip down the river, arriving only minutes before the jet landed. She insisted that she could be useful, and no argument from Pitt held enough water to keep her from boarding the plane and accompanying him to Washington.

Al Giordino and Rudi Gunn were waiting on the tarmac when the plane taxied to a stop at Langley Field. They were no sooner on the plane than it was airborne again, flying south to Fort Lauderdale, Florida, and the corporate headquarters of Blue Seas Cruise Lines. Gunn had arranged for a Lincoln Town Car as transportation, and within minutes of the jet landing, they were heading towards the harbour with Giordino at the wheel.

The Blue Seas building towered 900 feet above the waterfront on an island where Blue Seas cruise ships docked. The exterior was shaped like a gargantuan sailing boat. The outside elevators were housed in one huge shaft, which rose into the sky like a mast. The lower forty floors of the building housed the offices of the cruise line, while the upper fifty floors housed a hotel for the passengers to stay in before boarding the fleet of cruise ships.

Giordino turned into a tunnel that ran under the water to the island. A valet took the car, and they entered one of the outer elevators and rode three levels up to the main lobby. The secretary to the CEO of Blue Seas Cruise Lines was waiting for them and escorted them up a private executive elevator to the head office on the fortieth floor. Warren Lasch, the president of Blue Seas Cruise Lines, came from behind his desk to greet them.

Rudi Gunn made the introductions, and everyone took a chair.

'Now, then.' Lasch, a tall man with greying hair, peered through dark, coffee-brown eyes that moved from Pitt to Kelly to Giordino to Gunn and back again like a panoramic camera recording a scenic vista. 'What is this all about? Admiral Sandecker seemed adamant over the phone that we postpone the sailing of the *Golden Marlin*.'

'There is fear the ship may suffer the same fate as the *Emerald Dolphin*,' Gunn replied.

'That was an accident,' Lasch said.

Pitt leaned forward. 'I can assure you, sir, that NUMA has found irrefutable proof that the fire was started intentionally and explosives were used to sink the ship while she was under tow.'

'This is the first I've heard about it.' The anger in Lasch's voice was distinct. 'What possible motive could anyone have for destroying the *Emerald Dolphin* and murdering thousands of passengers?'

'We believe the motive was the destruction of Dr Elmore Egan's new magnetohydrodynamic engines,' explained Giordino.

'Why would anyone want to destroy the greatest propulsion technology of the new century?' asked Lasch, baffled. 'I hope you're not going public with such outlandish speculation.'

'Admiral Sandecker agreed that no official report should be released until the investigation is concluded,' said Gunn. 'He believed it would harm the cruise ship industry if the news media began sensationalising the incident.'

'I couldn't agree more,' Lasch conceded. 'But you cannot convince me to delay the sailing of the *Golden Marlin*. I cannot disappoint four hundred passengers.'

'Since we cannot persuade you,' said Pitt, 'can we make a case for increased security on board the ship during the voyage?'

'Boat,' Lasch interrupted, grinning. 'Submarines are called boats. But yes, I agree to extra security.'

Pitt was not finished with his requests. 'I would also like to have a dive team inspect the hull below the water line.'

Lasch nodded curtly. 'I can arrange for divers and extra security. I don't want a repeat of the *Emerald Dolphin* tragedy.'

'Giordino and I would like to go along, if you have no objection,' said Pitt.

'And me,' Kelly said. 'I have a vested interest in my father's work.'

Lasch rose from his chair. 'I see no problem. I'll be happy to arrange for accommodation.'

Gunn shook Lasch's hand. 'Thank you, Mr Lasch. I hope we haven't unduly alarmed you.'

'Please tell Admiral Sandecker I'm grateful, but I foresee no serious problems. The *Golden Marlin* has undergone extensive trials. Dr Egan's engines *and* the emergency systems performed beautifully.'

Riding down in the elevator, Giordino sighed. 'We tried.'

'I'm not surprised,' said Gunn. 'The *Emerald Dolphin* disaster has left the company hanging on the ropes. Postponing the sailing of the *Golden Marlin* would have closed the cruise line for certain.'

After Gunn returned to the airport for the flight back to Washington, Pitt, Giordino and Kelly booked hotel rooms for the night. As soon as he was settled in, Pitt called Sandecker.

'We failed to talk Lasch into postponing the sailing,' Pitt explained. 'But Al and I, along with Kelly, are sailing on the boat.'

Sandecker said, 'I have news for you. The FBI have identified the man behind the fire on the *Emerald Dolphin*.' He handed Pitt a printout of a photograph. 'His name is Omo Kanai. Born in Los Angeles. Enlisted in the army to escape an assault charge. I'll have his photograph sent to your hotel. He worked up through the ranks before transferring into a secret military organisation called CEASE.'

'Never heard of it.'

'CEASE stands for Covert Elite Action for Select Elimination, originally formed to combat terrorism by assassinating terrorist leaders before their actions could threaten American citizens. A decade ago, the President ordered them disbanded. Trained in political and covert murder, Omo Kanai, now a captain, resigned with twelve of his men and formed a commercial assassination company.'

'A Murder Incorporated.'

'Along the same lines. They hire out for killings.'

'Aren't they under investigation?' asked Pitt.

'These guys leave no evidence of their involvement. There is growing fear that future economic wars will lead to death squads. There are a few corporate CEOs here and there who will stop at nothing to achieve power and monopoly.'

'Which brings us to Cerberus.'

'Correct,' Sandecker answered. 'It's evident that not only was Kanai behind the fire on the *Emerald Dolphin* and the explosions that blew out the hull of the liner while under tow, but it was he, impersonating a ship's officer, who sabotaged the fire-control systems.'

'One man could not have done all that alone,' Pitt said dubiously.

'Kanai doesn't always work alone. That's why I'm warning you and Al to be alert every second you're on the *Golden Marlin*.'

THE *GOLDEN MARLIN* looked like no other cruise liner ever built. There were no promenade decks, no stateroom balconies, no smoke or exhaust funnels. Her rounded superstructure was covered with rows of circular viewing ports. A domelike structure above her bow housed the bridge and control room, while on the stern a high fin enclosed an opulent lounge and casino, which revolved around stationary viewing ports.

The *Golden Marlin* was about to change the history of cruising. With her self-sustaining engines, designed by Dr Egan, she could travel throughout the Caribbean Sea for two weeks, in depths up to 1,000 feet, before coming into port for supplies.

'She's beautiful,' exclaimed Kelly, as she stood on the dock in the early morning, staring up at the unique vessel.

Pitt was silent as he studied the seamless titanium hull. He was admiring the workmanship when a ship's officer approached.

'I beg your pardon, but are you the people from NUMA?'

'We are,' answered Giordino.

'I'm Paul Conrad, the boat's first officer. Mr Lasch advised Captain Baldwin of your joining us for the maiden voyage. You'll have a stateroom, Miss Egan. Mr Pitt and Mr Giordino will have to share a cabin in the crew's quarters. Please follow me.'

'One moment,' said Pitt. He walked along the dock to a man and a woman in wet suits who were checking their dive gear. 'Are you the team who is going to inspect the bottom of the hull?'

A slim, handsome man looked at him and smiled. 'Yes, that's right.'

'My name is Dirk Pitt. I requested your services.'

'Frank Martin. This is my wife, Caroline.'

'Pleased to meet you,' said a blonde who nicely filled out her wet suit. 'Can you tell us exactly what we're looking for?'

'Any object attached to the hull, specifically an explosive device.'

Martin looked unfazed. 'And if we find one?'

'If you find one, you'll find others. Don't touch them. A demolition team will be sent in to remove them.'

'A pleasure meeting you, Mr Pitt,' said Martin.

'Good luck,' Pitt said warmly. By the time he reached the gangway, the Martins were in the water. Conrad showed Pitt and Giordino to a small cabin below the passenger decks in the crew's quarters.

'I'd like to meet Captain Baldwin,' said Pitt.

'The captain is expecting you in the officers' dining room in half an hour. An inspection team from the boatbuilder will also be present.'

CAPTAIN MORRIS BALDWIN ran a tight ship and did not intend to have outsiders come on board and disrupt his routine. His face was a stern mask, red and ruddy and never cheerful. Only the magnificent silver mane gave him an air of authority.

He stared around the table in irritation at Pitt, Giordino and the four-man inspection team. 'I warn all of you not to interfere with the operation of this boat, or I will put you ashore in the next port.'

Rand O'Malley, head of the inspection team, smiled sardonically. 'We will not get in your way, Captain. But I expect you to cooperate if we should find a problem.'

'Search all you want,' muttered Baldwin. 'You'll find nothing.'

'I suggest you wait until you receive a report from the divers,' said Pitt. 'They may find foreign objects attached to the hull.'

'This is real life, Mr Pitt,' Baldwin said indifferently, 'not some fantasy tale on television.'

For nearly half a minute, there was silence. Then Pitt was on his feet, leaning on the table with both hands, his eyes boring into Baldwin's.

'I witnessed the terrible havoc on the *Emerald Dolphin*,' Pitt said solemnly. 'The sea bottom is littered with ships whose captains thought they were immune to catastrophe. When it comes, Captain Baldwin, to this boat, it will come with lightning speed before you and your crew can react. And then it will be too late.'

Pitt stood up. 'The people who are determined to destroy your boat are doubtless already on board, posing as one of your officers, your crew or passengers. Do you get the picture, Captain Baldwin?'

Baldwin's expression was without any show of emotion. He said, 'Thank you for your opinion, Mr Pitt. I shall take your words into consideration.' Then he came to his feet and walked towards the door. 'Thank you, gentlemen. We sail in exactly thirty-seven minutes.'

As the room cleared, except for Pitt, Giordino and O'Malley, Giordino irreverently crossed his feet on the conference table. 'Exacting old bird, isn't he?'

'Made out of concrete, that one,' observed O'Malley.

Pitt took an instant liking to the man, as did Giordino. 'I hope you take us more seriously than Captain Baldwin.'

O'Malley grinned with every tooth. 'If you're right, and I'm not saying you ain't, I'm not about to die on this extravagant folly.'

'I take it you're not fond of her,' said Pitt, amused.

'She's overbuilt,' snorted O'Malley. 'More expense and planning went into the decor than into the guts of the engineering systems.'

'My concern is that the disaster will be caused by human hands.'

O'Malley looked at Pitt. 'Do you know how many places a madman could set an explosive that would cause this tub to sink?'

'If the boat is deep underwater, a rupture almost anywhere on the hull would do the trick.'

'That and a puncture in the ballast tanks.'

'There must be an underwater system for evacuation,' said Pitt.

'There is,' answered O'Malley. 'Instead of lifeboats, the passengers enter their assigned pods; they can hold fifty people. Then the entry door is sealed. At the same time, the outer doors open, a stream of air is sent into the ejection system and the pods shoot free and float to the surface. The system is efficient.'

'If you wanted to make the evacuation system inoperable, how would you go about it?'

O'Malley scratched his head. 'Causing a failure in the air-ejection system would be the way I'd go.'

'I'd be grateful if you and your team would check out any tampering with the system very carefully,' said Pitt.

O'Malley looked at him. 'You can depend on it.'

OVER A THOUSAND PEOPLE had come to watch the maiden voyage of the first underwater cruise boat. As the *Golden Marlin* began to edge from the dock, streamers and confetti were thrown as the onlookers waved and shouted a rousing *bon voyage*.

Pitt saw no sign of the divers. His calls to Captain Baldwin on the bridge were not returned. He felt extremely restive, but there was no way he could stop the ship from sailing.

The boat was still in the channel, heading towards the open blue-green sea off Florida, when all passengers were asked to be seated in the theatre, where First Officer Paul Conrad lectured on the operation of the submarine cruise boat and explained the evacuation system. Kelly sat on one side of the theatre in the front while Pitt sat on the other side near the rear. There were six black families on board, but none of the men remotely resembled Omo Kanai. As soon as the lecture was over, a series of gongs rang and the passengers were directed to their evacuation pod stations.

Giordino worked with the team of inspectors, searching for explosives or signs of damaged equipment, while Pitt and Kelly matched up the passengers and staterooms. The search went slowly.

'I'm beginning to doubt Omo Kanai's on board,' said Kelly.

'Unless he's stowed away,' Pitt said, as they studied the pictures of the passengers that had been taken by the ship's photographer when they'd come on board. Kelly seized one. 'He looks familiar. The only problem is that Mr Jonathan Ford is white.'

Pitt shrugged. 'Back to the drawing board.'

At four in the afternoon, chimes sounded over the speakers, the signal that the boat was about to submerge. The passengers hurried to find chairs in front of the viewing ports, then the boat slipped slowly beneath the surface into a deep blue void.

Brilliantly coloured tropical fish in fluorescent purples, yellows and reds swam past the view ports. A school of barracuda, their long sleek bodies radiating as if coated with silver glitter, swam lazily alongside, effortlessly keeping pace with the boat.

The passengers on the port side of the boat were treated to the sight of an ocean sunfish. There was a white-and-orange metallic lustre to its huge oval body, which was ten feet long and nearly as high and probably weighed in the neighbourhood of two tons. A friendly giant of the depths, the sunfish soon fell behind the boat.

Marine biologists brought on board by the cruise line described the fish and explained their characteristics, behaviour and migration patterns in the sea. Curious hammerhead sharks peered through the portholes at the strange creatures on the other side.

First Officer Conrad announced over the speaker system that they were at 600 feet and approaching the bottom. The passengers watched the underwater scenery in wonder as Captain Baldwin carefully guided the *Golden Marlin* fifty feet above the ocean floor.

Suddenly the seabed fell away as the boat soared out over a deep trench that dropped 3,000 feet—2,000 feet deeper than the limits set by the boat's architects for the hull.

Baldwin gave the helm to his third officer as the communications officer handed him a message. 'Find Mr Pitt,' he ordered.

Pitt had no sooner stepped through the door than Baldwin thrust the message at him.

Pitt read aloud. '"Please be advised that the bodies of the divers engaged to inspect the bottom of your ship have been found tied to the dock pilings. Initial investigation shows they were stabbed from the back."' It was signed Detective Lieutenant Del Carter, Fort Lauderdale Police Department.

'What's our depth?' Pitt demanded sharply.

Baldwin pointed at a depth gauge. 'See for yourself. The bottom is two thousand four hundred feet below our keel.'

'Turn round immediately!' Pitt ordered curtly. 'Get into shallow water before it is too late.'

Baldwin's face hardened. 'What are you talking about?'

'The divers were murdered because they found explosives attached to the hull. For the sake of everybody on board, Captain, turn back into shallow water.'

'And if I don't?' Baldwin challenged him.

Pitt's green eyes turned cold as the Arctic. 'I swear I will kill you and take command of the ship.'

Baldwin jerked backwards. Slowly his lips spread in a taut smile. He turned to the helmsman, who was standing stunned, his eyes wide. 'Reverse course and come to full speed,' the captain said. 'Does that satisfy you, Mr Pitt?'

'I suggest you sound the warning signal and send the passengers to the stations at the evacuation pods.'

Baldwin nodded. 'Consider it done.'

'Let's pray we make it in time,' Pitt said.

KELLY WAS SITTING in the purser's office, sifting through the crew's personnel records, when she became aware of a presence. A man had walked into the room without making a sound. Kelly immediately recognised him as the passenger she and Pitt had discussed earlier. A feeling of horror crept over her. 'Your name is Jonathan Ford.'

'We met briefly on the *Emerald Dolphin*.'

Kelly was confused. There was a close resemblance to the black ship's officer who had tried to kill her and her father, but the man standing in front of her was white. 'You can't be . . .'

'Ah, but I am.' He took a handkerchief, dabbed a corner on his tongue and rubbed it on his left hand. The white make-up came off, revealing brown skin underneath.

Kelly tried to run, but the man grabbed her.

'My name is Omo Kanai. My orders are to take you with me.'

'Take me where?' she cried in terror.

'Why, home, of course.'

The answer made no sense to her. She was only aware of the evil in his eyes as he pressed a damp cloth against her face. Then a black chasm opened beneath her feet.

IT WAS A RACE against death now that Pitt was certain explosives had been placed on the hull. He called Giordino over the radio. 'You can knock off the search. The explosives are not inside the ship.'

Giordino hurried to the bridge, followed by Rand O'Malley.

'We just got word that the divers were killed,' Pitt said. 'It looks like the explosives are set to detonate over deep water.'

'Which is where we are now,' said Giordino quietly.

'How soon before we pass into shallow water?' Pitt asked Baldwin.

'Twenty minutes will put us over the edge of the trench and onto the Continental Slope,' Baldwin answered, his face beginning to show signs of stress. 'In ten more minutes, we'll reach the surface and increase our speed.'

Abruptly, the seaman standing at the ship's main console called out. 'Captain, something is happening with the evacuation pods.'

Baldwin stared at the console in shock. All sixteen lights representing the evacuation pods were showing red except for one that still read green. 'They've been activated,' Baldwin gasped.

'And before anyone could board,' added O'Malley grimly. 'We'll never get the crew and passengers off the boat now.'

Pitt knew that whoever had activated the evacuation pods had probably abandoned the boat in one of them, which meant that the explosives could detonate at any moment. Only another 100 feet remained before the boat broke the surface. A collective sigh of relief was heard in the control room as the *Golden Marlin* passed the edge of the Continental Slope.

'Depth under hull five hundred and fifty and rising,' called out Conrad.

The words had barely left his mouth when the boat shuddered and twisted out of control. The great engines wound to a stop as the sea poured into the two wounds caused by the underwater explosives.

Baldwin was under no illusions. His boat was going down. 'Call the engine room and ask the chief engineer to close the watertight doors below and keep the generators going as long as he can,' he snapped. He looked at Pitt. 'I guess now is the time for you to tell me "I told you so".'

Pitt shook his head slowly. 'I take no satisfaction in being right.'

'Bottom coming up.' First Officer Conrad had no sooner spoken than the *Golden Marlin* struck the sea floor and settled in the silt, throwing up a vast brown cloud that blotted out all vision beyond the view ports.

It didn't take a motion picture of the event for the passengers to know something very tragic was in the making. Yet as long as the passenger decks remained water-free and none of the crew looked frightened, no one panicked. Captain Baldwin came on the speaker system and assured everyone that, although the *Golden Marlin* had lost power, things would be back to normal shortly. The story, however, did not fly with the passengers and crew who'd noticed that almost all the evacuation pod chambers were empty. Some milled around in confusion. Some remained at the view ports and gazed at the fish who appeared after the silt settled. Some retired to the lounge and ordered drinks that were now on the house.

Captain Baldwin and his officers began studying emergency procedures, while the engineering crew set the pumps in operation. Fortunately, all the systems apart from propulsion appeared unaffected by damage from the explosions.

Like a man in a daze, Baldwin opened up communications with Lasch at the company headquarters, the coastguard and any ships that were within fifty miles, in that order. He issued a mayday and gave the *Golden Marlin*'s position. That done, he walked first to the engine room for a full report and then roamed the ship, reassuring passengers. He told them that there was a problem with the ballast tanks, and repairs were under way.

Pitt, Giordino and O'Malley went down to the evacuation pod deck. O'Malley checked the system. Less than five minutes after he began, he sighed. 'Whoever activated the pods knew his business. Luckily, it looks like one failed to release.'

'We still have one pod to put the children in,' said Giordino.

'The question is,' said Pitt. 'How many can we put in it?'

AN HOUR LATER, a coastguard cutter arrived and opened communications to the boat. Only then did Baldwin gather the passengers and explain the situation. He stated that it was in keeping with company regulations to send the youngest to the surface in an emergency.

Pitt and O'Malley sat at a computer in the purser's office and estimated the number of bodies the pod could safely carry. While they were absorbed in their work, Giordino left them to look for Kelly.

'How many children on board?' asked O'Malley.

'Fifty-four under the age of eighteen. They should average around eighty pounds.'

'The pods are constructed to carry a total weight of eight thousand pounds. That leaves room for some of the mothers.'

'Take an average weight of one-forty and we have room for nearly twenty-nine mothers.'

O'Malley punched up the families. 'There are twenty-seven on board,' he said with a hint of optimism. 'We still have room for one or two more bodies.'

'We have to send one of us to give a detailed report on the situation down here,' said Pitt.

'I'm more important here,' O'Malley said firmly.

Giordino returned at that moment. 'Kelly has disappeared,' he said.

'Bloody hell,' Pitt swore. He did not doubt for a moment that Kelly had indeed vanished. Suddenly, the photo of a passenger filled his mind. He programmed the passenger list onto the computer and typed in the name Jonathan Ford.

The picture of Ford filled the monitor and Pitt hit the print key. He took a pencil and began shading in the man's face on the print-out. When he was finished, he felt as if a fist had struck him in the stomach—the face matched the FBI photograph of Omo Kamai.

'The man behind the fire on the *Emerald Dolphin* was on board. I'm afraid he escaped in one of the pods and took Kelly with him.'

Followed by Giordino and O'Malley, Pitt hurried to Ford's state-room and kicked the door open. There was no sign of luggage. Giordino pulled a thick roll of paper from the closet and spread it out on the bed.

'The blueprints of the boat,' muttered O'Malley. 'That's how he knew where to place the explosives and activate the evacuation pods.'

Pitt sagged dejectedly into a chair. He saw little hope of saving the other 600-plus souls on board. He looked at O'Malley. 'You know every corner of the boat. Did the boatbuilder install a back-up air-lock system for a chamber rescue?'

'There's a specially configured hatch on the top of the hull, but there is no way all six hundred of us can be rescued before we run out of air.'

'How so?' asked Giordino.

'The *Golden Marlin* was never really intended to remain under water more than four days. After that, the air becomes increasingly unbreathable.'

Pitt turned to Giordino. 'Al, you've got to go topside with the mothers and children.'

Giordino looked incredulous. 'Mrs Giordino's boy is no coward,' he said indignantly. 'I won't jump ship hiding behind women's skirts.'

'Believe me, old friend,' Pitt entreated, 'you can do far more to save everyone by working with me from the surface. It's essential we get an open line down here to purify the air.'

'And just where am I supposed to scare up five hundred feet of hose, a pump capable of pumping enough air to keep six hundred people alive and a method of attaching it.'

Pitt looked at his old pal of almost forty years and grinned. 'You'll think of something.'

WITHIN HOURS the navy's deep submergence rescue vehicle, *Mercury*, and mother ship, *Alfred Aultman*, were pounding towards the disaster scene. Down below on the *Golden Marlin*, children and mothers were loaded on board the evacuation pod. There were tearful farewells with fathers and other relatives.

Giordino looked more forlorn than ever to be the only man. 'I feel like the guy who entered a *Titanic* lifeboat wearing a woman's dress.'

Pitt put his arm round Giordino's shoulder. 'You'll be more crucial to the rescue operation topside.'

'I'll never be able to live this down,' Giordino groaned. 'You'd better come through this, you hear? If it all goes wrong and you don't make it—'

'I'll make it,' Pitt assured him, 'but only with you leading the rescue where it counts.'

They shook hands one final time as Pitt nudged him into the only vacant seat in the evacuation pod. Pitt did his best to keep from grinning as a harried mother thrust one of her crying children into a cringing Giordino's arms. Pitt could not recall seeing a more mournful look, as the door hissed closed. Sixty seconds later, the pod was on its way to the surface.

Pitt turned to O'Malley. 'Is the hatch on the air-lock escape chamber compatible with the one on the navy submersible rescue vehicle?'

O'Malley nodded. 'It was designed to the navy's specifications.'

Pitt was already at the door. 'Show me.'

O'Malley led him to the upper deck, through the galley, and into a tunnel that rose up to a hatch three feet in diameter. O'Malley studied the hatch. Finally, he looked at Pitt. 'Your friend was a thorough character. The frame is buckled and jammed solid around the hatch. It would take a ten-pound plastic charge to blow it free.'

Pitt gazed at the bent and distorted escape hatch in horror. 'Then there is no escape into the rescue vehicle.'

'Not through here,' O'Malley said, knowing all hope of saving 617 souls was gone. He stared at the deck and repeated, 'Not through here. Not through anywhere.'

They carried the disastrous news to Captain Baldwin on the bridge. His face was not pleasant to see. 'We have no hope of rescue?'

'There is always hope,' Pitt said gamely.

First Officer Conrad handed Pitt a phone. 'I'm here on the coast-guard cutter,' a familiar voice crackled down the line.

'How was the ride to the surface, Al?'

'I'm not used to screaming infants. My eardrums are blasted.'

'When will the deep submergence rescue vehicle arrive?'

'Thirty-six hours. How are things down where you are?'

'Not good. Our friend Kanai jammed the escape hatch shut before he left. O'Malley says there is no way of forcing it open without flooding half the ship.'

'We won't throw in the towel at this end,' Giordino promised. 'I'll call Yaeger and have him put Max on the problem. There has to be a way to get you up.'

THE CREW AND PASSENGERS on board the *Golden Marlin* had no knowledge of the hurricane brewing over their heads. Less than two days after the submarine cruise liner had slipped onto the sea bottom, close to a hundred boats drifted over the site carrying hordes of journalists and cameramen. By the third day, the media circus went into high gear in readiness for the final chapter.

Reporters tried to reach Giordino, but he'd gone on board a NUMA survey ship dispatched by Sandecker. He immediately worked with the crew to send down a remotely operated vehicle named *Sea Scout* to inspect the *Golden Marlin* from the exterior. The images on the video monitor only confirmed that the hatch was irreparably jammed. Nothing short of explosives could tear it off, and then only to allow the sea to pour through the opening before any survivors could pass through it. There was no way for those on the other side of the hull to escape.

The next morning the naval support ship carrying the deep submergence rescue vehicle arrived. The captain, Lieutenant Commander Mike Turner, greeted Giordino in a friendly manner.

'I'll have one of my officers show you to your quarters. We won't be launching the *Mercury* for another hour.'

'I hope you'll let me go along if I don't take up needed space.'

Turner smiled. 'You won't be crowding us one bit.'

CAPTAIN TURNER BOARDED a ladder to the Mercury's main hatch, followed by Giordino. Turner introduced his copilot, Chief Warrant Officer Mack McKirdy, a grey-haired sea dog, who acknowledged Giordino with a curt nod.

'Word's out that you probed the wreck of the *Emerald Dolphin* at twenty thousand feet,' said McKirdy. 'This dive's only five hundred and fifty. Should be a piece of cake.'

'Not unless we can hook up with the rescue hatch.'

McKirdy read the gravity in Giordino's eyes. 'If anyone can open a jammed hatch, it's me and the *Mercury*.'

'I hope so,' Giordino murmured. 'Oh, how I hope so.'

The *Mercury* reached the sunken boat in less than fifteen minutes.

The three men felt an eerie sensation at seeing faces inside the Golden Marlin gazing back through the ports. Giordino thought he saw Pitt waving at him, but he couldn't be sure.

They spent three hours making a thorough inspection of the boat, McKirdy steering the submersible close to the damaged areas.

'Were the ballast tanks ruptured?' asked Turner.

'No,' answered Giordino. 'They maintained their integrity. The boat was dragged down by the flow of water entering through the breaks in the hull. What saved the boat was the closing of the water-tight doors, keeping the flooding in the cargo compartment and engine room.'

McKirdy guided the rescue vehicle above the escape hatch. Both he and Turner studied the damage.

Turner didn't look hopeful. 'The sealing flange round the bottom of the hatch is ripped to shreds.'

They all looked at the shattered area around the escape hatch.

'We'll have to lower a pressure chamber down on the hull, form a seal and then cut a hole through the plates large enough to evacuate everyone.' Turner described the process in simple terms. 'We should be able to do the job in forty-eight hours.'

'Too late,' Giordino said bluntly. 'They don't have more than thirty hours of air left in there.'

'You're right,' Turner conceded. 'But there's an outside air connector mounted just forward of the fin on the stern. We have the hose and a pump that puts out more than a thousand pounds per square inch. We can have it ready to supply air in three hours max.'

Ever the pessimist, Giordino said, 'Yes, but you'd better check the exterior connector before you bet your hand.'

McKirdy headed for the forward part of the fin.

'The housing for the air connector looks intact,' said Turner.

'To be on the safe side,' said Giordino, 'why not make certain your hose fitting will match the connector?'

Turner began operating a manipulator arm. Very carefully, he unlatched the four locks.

The sight was not what they expected. The female fitting for the male fitting attached to the air hose was missing. It looked as if it had been removed with a sledgehammer and chisel.

'Who in the world would have done that?' Turner asked.

'A very shrewd fiend,' Giordino muttered, with murder in his heart.

'It's impossible to get a replacement and make repairs before their air runs out,' said McKirdy, studying the damaged connector.

'Are you telling me that over six hundred men and women are going to die while we stand around and watch?' Giordino said.

Turner and McKirdy stared at each other. There was nothing to say.

Giordino had a feeling of unreality. Losing a best friend in an accident was abhorrent enough, but waiting for a perfectly healthy person to die because no one could help him was unacceptable.

THE MOOD INSIDE the *Golden Marlin* was macabre. The passengers ate as scheduled, gambled in the casino, drank cocktails in the lounge and went to bed, as though the cruise had never ended. There was nothing else they could do. The service crew went about their usual duties, waiting on tables and cooking in the galley. It was almost as if they were in denial.

After Giordino had told him the bad news, Pitt sat at the chart table and studied the plans of the ship, searching for some tiny clue to survival. 'There has to be a key,' he said in a low voice. 'There must be a way to attach a hose and pump purified air into the boat.'

Baldwin wiped his brow. 'Not with the hatch and air connector destroyed.'

John Ringer, the ship's doctor, stepped into the control room and dropped heavily into a chair. He was swamped by passengers complaining of headaches, light-headedness and nausea. He was obviously exhausted and on the verge of collapse.

'What we're faced with is asphyxia caused by an insufficient intake of oxygen and insufficient exhalation of carbon dioxide,' he said.

'How much longer do we have?' Baldwin asked Ringer.

'You can feel the lack of oxygen the same as me,' said Ringer quietly. 'Two hours, maybe two hours and thirty minutes, no more.'

'Thank you for your candid opinion, Doctor,' Baldwin said.

Ringer got to his feet. 'I'd better get back to the hospital.'

Pitt went back to scrutinising the plans. 'For every complex problem, there is a simple solution,' he said.

Baldwin started for the door. 'Time for me to put in an appearance in the dining room. Good luck.'

Pitt said nothing. Slowly, a numbing fear seeped into his mind, not a fear for his life, but a fear that he might fail with so many people's lives hanging on his finding a solution. But for a few moments, it also sharpened his senses and flooded him with extraordinary clarity. This was followed by a revelation that struck him with such force it stunned him momentarily. The solution *was* simple. He could only wonder why he hadn't seen it earlier.

He knocked over the stool in his rush to get to the phone. 'Al! Are you there? I have the answer.'

Giordino was taken aback by Pitt's eagerness. 'I'll put you on the speaker.' A moment's pause, and then, 'OK, go ahead.'

'How long will it take you to set up the air hose?'

'You know we can't make a connection,' said Captain Turner.

'I know that. How soon can you be pumping air?'

'We can have it ready to go in three hours.'

'Make it two or you can forget it.'

'What good will it do? We can't make a connection.'

'Will your pump overcome the water pressure at this depth?'

'She puts out five hundred pounds per square inch,' answered McKirdy. 'Twice the pressure of the water at your depth.'

'Get the air hose down here fast,' rasped Pitt. He was beginning to feel light-headed from lack of oxygen. 'Call me when you arrive for further instructions.'

O'Malley had stumbled into the control room in time to hear Pitt's conversation.

'What's your idea?'

'Wait and see,' said Pitt mysteriously. 'It's the most elementary high-school physics class experiment in the book.'

THE *GOLDEN MARLIN* was on the verge of becoming an underwater crypt. The passengers and crew were only minutes from unconsciousness as the carbon dioxide level rapidly reached limits that could no longer support life. Their minds numbed by the lack of oxygen, they were no longer capable of rational thought. No one panicked in the final moments, because no one fully realised their end was near. Baldwin talked to those still sitting in the dining room, encouraging them with words that he knew were meaningless. He was on his way back to the bridge when he sagged to his knees in a corridor and crumpled to the carpet. An elderly couple walked past, looking at the fallen captain through vacant eyes.

In the control room, Pitt was sucking in what little oxygen was left. 'Where are you?' he gasped over the phone. 'We're about done in.'

'We're approaching the control room dome.' Giordino's voice sounded desperate.

Pitt staggered to the main port and saw the *Mercury* descending from above. 'Do you have the hose?'

'Ready to pump when and wherever you say,' answered Chief Warrant Officer McKirdy. Captain Turner had remained on board the *Alfred Aultman* to command the operation from the surface.

'Move towards the break in the hull opposite the engine room.'

'On our way,' Giordino acknowledged.

Five minutes later, McKirdy reported, 'We are level with the gash caused by the explosion.'

Fighting to breathe, Pitt gasped out, 'Insert the end of the air hose as far into the engine room as possible.'

Giordino went to work moving the hose inside the gash with the manipulators. It took him nearly ten minutes before he felt the hose reach the far bulkhead. 'She's in.'

Pitt spoke, inhaling one word, exhaling the next. 'Start . . . pumping.'

The men inside the rescue vehicle complied and a surge of air burst into the engine room.

'What are we doing?' asked Giordino, mystified and grief-stricken as he listened to what he thought were his friend's final words.

Pitt answered in a voice barely above a whisper. 'The air from your hose is blasting out at twice the pressure of the water, forcing it back out into the sea.'

The explanation drained what little fortitude he had left and he slumped to the deck.

Giordino saw the water gush out of the engine room, driven back into the sea by the overwhelming pressure from the air pump on the surface. 'The air is forming a bubble inside,' he shouted to McKirdy.

'Yes, but it's not reaching other parts of the boat.'

But Giordino saw the method to Pitt's madness. 'He's not trying to purify the air inside. He's trying to raise the boat to the surface.'

McKirdy looked at the hull of the boat embedded in the silt, and had grave doubts that it could rise.

'Dirk!' Giordino roared into the phone. 'Talk to me.'

But there was no answer.

THERE WERE EIGHT MEN on the bridge of the *Alfred Aultman*, where fear and defeat hung like a wet blanket. They found it impossible to believe that 617 people were taking their final breaths less than a quarter of a mile below their feet. They gathered round the speaker, conversing as softly as if they were in a church.

'She's coming up. She's coming up.' Six words from the side-scan sonar operator who had never taken his eyes off the recorder.

Turner stared open-mouthed at the recorder. The image of the *Golden Marlin* had moved. 'She's coming up all right,' he confirmed.

Then McKirdy's voice roared out of the speaker. 'She's on her way to the surface. Pumping air into the engine room did the trick.'

Turner began issuing orders to his crew to climb aboard the boat the minute she hit the surface and cut a hole in the top of her hull to pump air inside to revive the passengers and crew. Then he put out a call to every boat within twenty miles to come quickly with any piece of resuscitating equipment they had on board. He also requested every doctor to stand by to board the *Golden Marlin* as soon as his crew gained entry. Time was priceless. They had to get inside quickly if they were to revive the passengers and crew.

The atmosphere among the fleet of ships over the *Golden Marlin* was transformed from one of gloom to jubilation. A thousand eyes were straining at the open water, when a cauldron of bubbles rose to the surface. Then came the *Golden Marlin*. She erupted from the water like an immense cork.

Cheers shattered the air. People shouted themselves hoarse. An armada of rescuers rushed towards the submarine. Turner ordered his rescue crew to gain entry through the hatches, which could be broached now that there was no danger of water pouring in.

The *Mercury* surfaced beside the big boat. Giordino dived into the water and swam towards the rescue crew unlatching the starboard boarding hatch. They heaved it open and peered inside as a stale smell flowed into their nostrils. It was air that they knew was unbreathable. In the same moment, the crew on the other side opened the port hatch, allowing a cross-ventilation of air to blow in and suck out the bad air. Stepping inside, both crews found bodies lying on the deck and went to work resuscitating them.

Giordino had his own priority and rushed to the control room with a growing dread that he was too late to save his dearest friend.

He knelt beside Pitt, who was lying outstretched, eyes closed, seemingly not breathing. Wasting no time feeling for a pulse, Giordino bent down to apply mouth-to-mouth resuscitation. But suddenly, to his astonishment, those mesmeric green eyes fluttered open and a voice whispered, 'I hope this concludes the entertainment part of the programme.'

It was a near thing. All of the passengers and crew of the *Golden Marlin* were brought back from the brink of death. Most, miraculously, revived as fresh air was recirculated throughout the boat.

Captain Baldwin was fêted as a hero who'd helped prevent a major tragedy. Captain Turner and his crew also received acclaim for their part. Only a very few knew of the role Pitt and Giordino had played in saving the ship and all its passengers and crew.

July 31, 2003. Members of the Viper team, led by Omo Kanai, had gained entry to the Egan farm by dressing as sheriff's deputies and driving a car painted like a county patrol vehicle. After killing the road guard, they'd entered the house, seized Josh Thomas and then called in the rest of the guards for a meeting. Once the guards arrived, they were shot and their bodies thrown in a storm cellar.

Omo Kanai threw a sedated Kelly on the floor in front of Josh Thomas, who was bound and gagged in a chair.

He smiled at the scientist before viciously kicking Kelly in her stomach. 'Wake up, Miss Egan. It's time for you to persuade Mr Thomas to reveal your father's oil formula.'

Kelly clutched her stomach, gasping for breath. She gazed at Thomas. 'Don't tell this scum, Josh—'

She spoke no further. Her breath was cut off as Kanai shoved his boot against her neck. 'You are an obstinate young lady,' he said coldly. 'Do you enjoy pain?'

One of Kanai's men entered the room, holding a portable radio. 'A car is approaching the front gate.'

Kanai thought a moment. 'Better to let them enter than turn them away and arouse suspicion.'

'OK, MASTERMIND,' said Giordino. 'How do you open the gate.'

'I punch in the code.'

'Do you know it?'

'No.'

'You drag me up here under the cockamamie notion that Kanai took Kelly to her father's laboratory, and you don't know the security code?'

'What better place to force information out of her and Josh Thomas? The formula has to be hidden in the lab somewhere.'

Pitt leaned out of the window and punched a series of buttons.

'What makes you think Kanai, if he's here, is going to open the gate for us?'

'Because I punched in the name Cerberus for the code.'

Giordino rolled his eyes. 'If I had an ounce of common sense, this is where I'd get out.'

They were on the verge of leaving when the huge gate began to swing open.

'I do believe we struck a chord,' Pitt said, vindicated.

'You know, of course, they'll be waiting to ambush us.'

Pitt drove through the gate. 'We're armed, too.'

'Oh, sure. You've got your antique Colt .45, and all I've got is a screwdriver I found in the glove compartment. The guys we're going up against are loaded down with assault weapons.'

'Maybe we can pick up something along the way.'

Pitt drove past the farmland and slowed as he came to the vineyard, waiting for the barricade. One of Kanai's men in a security guard uniform came to the car and leaned in the window, clutching an assault rifle. 'Can I help you, gentlemen?'

'Where's Gus?' asked Pitt innocently.

'He called in sick,' answered the guard.

'How's his baby girl?'

'Healthy, the last I heard—'

He was cut off as Pitt swung his Colt across the guard's forehead.

Almost before the bogus guard hit the ground, Pitt and Giordino were pulling him into a large tree trunk and down to a security surveillance room underground. Twenty monitors were mounted against one wall, their cameras sweeping the fields and interior of the house. Pitt stood transfixed at the sight of Thomas trussed up and Kelly writhing on the floor. The five Vipers in the room seemed to have no indication they were being observed by cameras.

Giordino sat at the console as Pitt donned the guard's black clothing. He pulled a ski mask over his head, which completed the outfit.

'These guys have no inhibitions when it comes to murder,' said Giordino, as one of the monitors revealed the bodies of Egan's security guards. He switched from one camera to the next, searching for Kanai's men. 'Besides the five in the house, I count two more. One guarding the back door and the other by the barn.'

Pitt nodded at the phones. 'Notify the sheriff's department, report the situation and ask them to send in a SWAT team.'

'And you? What's your gig?'

'In this outfit they'll think I'm one of them,' said Pitt. 'You stay here, monitor the situation and direct the SWAT team.'

'And when Kanai asks where the occupants in the car went?'

'Say they were fertiliser salesmen and you took care of them.'

'How are you going to get from here to the house?'

'The vineyard runs close to the front of the house. I'll make my way through the grapevines, and move onto the front porch from behind the columns. Crossing the grass will be the tricky part.'

'Don't you get us into another fine mess, Stanley,' said Giordino, with the trace of a grin.

'I promise to be good, Ollie.'

Pitt ran more than a hundred yards before the rows of grapevines ended near the front of the house, separated by a narrow strip of lawn. A sudden dash might catch the eye of someone inside the house, so he moved very slowly. Five wooden steps led up to the columned porch, and Pitt trod quietly until he reached the front door. He slowly turned the knob and slipped inside like a shadow.

The living room was entered through an archway. Pitt used a clay pot with a small tropical plant as cover to peer into the room.

Josh Thomas sat slumped in a chair in the centre of the room. Kanai sat on a large leather sofa calmly smoking a cigar. Two of the Vipers stood on opposite sides of the fireplace, weapons at the ready. Another stood beside Thomas, a knife in one hand. The fifth was a giant who gripped Kelly by her long hair with one hand and held her in the air, her feet inches above the carpet. No screams came through her mouth, only agonised moans.

Surprise was on Pitt's side and he considered shooting through the tropical plant. He quickly rejected the idea. He might get two or three of them, but he would surely be peppered with bullets before he could finish the job. Then there was the possibility that a stray bullet could catch Kelly or Thomas. He decided the only hope was to stall for time until the SWAT team showed up. He laid his Colt on the table behind a flower vase and stepped into the room.

At first, Pitt wasn't noticed. Everyone in the room was focused on Kelly, who was struggling with the giant. It was hard for Pitt to stand rigid without attempting to stop the torture. He figured another five minutes would pass before the SWAT team arrived, but he could not stand by and watch Kelly suffer.

He said calmly to Kanai, 'Tell your fat flunky to take his hands off the girl.' And he pulled off the ski mask.

Every Viper in the room immediately recognised Pitt as an impostor, and guns were aimed at his chest.

'Wait!' Kanai shouted. 'Do not kill him yet.'

Kelly momentarily dismissed her suffering and stared in stunned surprise. 'You shouldn't have come!' she gasped.

'You'll be next to die, Kanai,' said Pitt, 'if he doesn't release her.'

Kanai looked bemused. 'And who's going to kill me? You?'

'A SWAT team will be arriving any second. You're trapped.'

Kanai gave a brief tilt of his head towards the giant. 'Set the lady on her feet, Darfur.' He turned his attention back to Pitt. 'Your death will be slow and painful.'

Pitt had to stall as long as he could. 'Did I interrupt something when I crashed the party?' he asked innocently.

Kanai gave him a calculated look. 'I was having a friendly discussion with Miss Egan and Mr Thomas regarding Dr Egan's work.'

'The old find-the-oil-formula routine,' Pitt said dismissively. 'How uncreative of you, Kanai. It seems everybody in the state knows the formula but you and your pals at Cerberus.'

Kanai's eyes widened marginally. 'You are well informed.'

Pitt shrugged. 'It's all in how you interpret the drums.'

Kelly had moved over to Thomas. She removed his gag and was wiping away the blood from his face with her sweater. Thomas looked up through dull eyes at her, murmuring his thanks. The huge Darfur stood behind Pitt, looking like a coyote who had a rabbit trapped in a gulch.

'You may prove to be a blessing in disguise,' Kanai said to him. He turned to Kelly. 'You will give me the oil formula or I will shoot this man in the knees, then the elbows, then I'll blast off his ears.'

Kelly looked at Pitt in anguish. It was the final blow. With Kanai threatening both Pitt and Thomas, she knew she didn't have the fortitude to hold out, and abruptly crumbled.

'The formula is hidden in my father's laboratory.'

'Where?' Kanai demanded.

She started to answer, but Pitt interrupted. 'Don't tell him.'

Darfur stood in front of Pitt. 'Sir, I would consider it an honour if you'd allow me to work on this dog.'

Kanai smiled. 'He's all yours.'

As Darfur turned to lay his rifle against a chair, Pitt lashed out, catching the monstrous man in the groin. Darfur doubled over with a hoarse gasp of pain, but only for a moment. He recovered and struck Pitt in the chest with a sledgehammer punch that sent him crashing to the carpet. Pitt came to his feet, heaving to put air in his lungs. He picked up a coffee table and brought it down on Darfur's head, shattering the wooden surface. The monster shook off the blow and launched himself across the room but Pitt was agile enough to step aside and let the express train crash into a piano. Pitt picked up the piano stool, preparing to smash it into Darfur's face.

The blow never fell. Kanai brought the butt of his gun down on the back of Pitt's head, unleashing a sea of pain that dropped Pitt to his knees, briefly causing him to black out. Through darkness, he became aware of Kelly screaming. As his vision cleared, he saw Kanai twisting her arm until it was a millimetre away from breaking—she had attempted to wrest the gun away from him.

Pitt was jerked to his feet by Darfur, who circled his arms round Pitt's chest and began to squeeze, like a boa constrictor. His mouth was open, but he could not even utter a gasp. The blackness was returning. He was within two seconds of letting death relieve his agony, when abruptly the pressure was released.

As if in a dream, he saw Giordino walk into the room and kidney-punch Kanai from the rear. Kanai dropped the gun and released his grip on Kelly. The other Vipers froze, their guns now aimed at Giordino, waiting for the word from Kanai to shoot.

Darfur gazed apprehensively at the intruder for a moment, but when he saw that Giordino was not carrying a firearm and was a good foot shorter than he, the look on his face reflected an air of disdain. 'Leave him to me,' said Darfur.

He released Pitt, who fell in a heap onto the carpet, and swept Giordino up off the floor in a great bear hug. They stared face to face, inches apart. Darfur's lips were drawn back in an evil leer while Giordino's face was expressionless, with a complete absence of fear.

When Darfur had grasped him round the back above the waist and locked his arms like a vice, Giordino had lifted his arms so that they were free and stretched in the air above the giant's head. Darfur ignored Giordino's raised arms and used every ounce of his enormous strength to constrict the life out of the short Italian.

Pitt, still dazed and in extreme pain, crawled across the room, gasping in agony from his bruised chest and head. Kelly leapt onto Darfur's back with her hands round his face, covering his eyes and wrestling with him, twisting his head back and forth. Darfur easily broke her hold with one hand and tossed her away as if she were a shop window mannequin, sending her sprawling onto the sofa before he resumed his constricting grip round Giordino.

But Giordino didn't need saving. He lowered his arms and tightened his fingers round Darfur's throat, the leer on the giant's face turning to fear as the air was cut off from his lungs. Giordino hung on like a relentless bulldog as Darfur thrashed around the room.

There was a horrible gasping wail as Darfur suddenly went limp and crashed to the floor like a timbered oak tree, with Giordino on top of him. At that instant, a fleet of sheriff's patrol cars and SWAT vans slid to a stop on the gravel driveway. Uniformed men with heavy weapons began dispersing around the house. The sound of approaching helicopters also came through the windows.

'Out the back!' Kanai shouted to his men.

Pitt tried to follow, but he was in no condition for a race and he stumbled to a stop, leaning on a credenza, waiting for the pain to subside. After a minute, he returned to the living room and found Giordino cutting away the ropes that bound Thomas. Pitt helped the scientist to his feet. 'How are you doing?'

Thomas smiled bravely. 'I'll be good as new after a few stitches.'

Pitt put his arm round Kelly. 'You're one tough lady.'

'Did Kanai get away?'

'I'm afraid so, unless the sheriff's deputies can chase him down.'

'Not him,' she said uneasily. 'They won't find him. He'll come back with a vengeance. His bosses at Cerberus won't rest until they have Dad's formula.'

Pitt stared out of the window. Finally he spoke in a quiet voice. 'I have a feeling that the oil formula is not the only thing they're after.'

IT WAS LATE in the afternoon. Darfur and the Vipers that Pitt and Giordino had subdued were handcuffed and driven away in patrol cars to the sheriff's department and booked for the murder of Egan's security guards. Kelly and Thomas gave their statements to the sheriff's homicide investigators, followed by Pitt and Giordino. Kelly was correct in saying the deputies would never catch Omo Kanai. Pitt traced the killer's tracks to the high cliffs above the Hudson River, where he found a rope leading down to the water.

'They must have escaped in a boat,' observed Giordino.

Pitt stared down at the water. 'Amazing how Kanai covers every bet, every contingency.'

'Do you think the Vipers will talk under interrogation?'

'It really wouldn't make much difference if they did,' said Pitt. 'The Viper organisation probably works in cells, each ignorant of the other, under the command of Kanai. I'll bet none of them are aware their true bosses sit in the corporate offices of Cerberus.'

'It stands to reason they're too smart to leave a trail leading to their doorstep.'

Pitt nodded. 'Government prosecutors will never find enough hard evidence to convict them. If they're ever punished for their hideous crimes, it won't be under the law.'

Kelly walked towards them across the lawn. 'You two hungry?'

'I'm always hungry,' Giordino said, smiling.

'I fixed a light dinner while Josh mixed the drinks. He makes mean margaritas.'

'Dear heart'—Pitt put his arm round her waist—'you just said the magic word.'

While Pitt, Giordino and Thomas savoured margaritas that could have jumped from their glasses, Kelly dished up a tuna casserole. Afterwards, they retired to the living room and Thomas poured everyone a glass of forty-year-old port.

Giordino raised his glass. 'Josh is a brave man,' he said respectfully. 'Despite a nasty beating, he told Kanai nothing.'

Thomas shook his head. 'If Dirk had not walked in, I would have spilled the secret of the formula to save Kelly further torture. They could come back. She must go into hiding.'

'I agree,' said Pitt. 'Kanai will no doubt assume that you'll secrete the formula some place other than the farm, which still leaves the two of you as their only key to finding it.' He set down his glass. 'Could you show us Dr Egan's laboratory?'

'There's not much to see,' said Thomas. He led them from the house to the barn. Inside were three counters upon which sat the usual apparatus seen in most chemistry laboratories.

Pitt walked round the room. 'This can't be where Dr Egan designed his engines. I see no drafting tables, no computers, no machinery to construct working models.'

'We do not know where Elmore conducted his research,' said Thomas. 'He was a fine man and a good friend, but he had a secretive streak that was nothing short of fanatical. Elmore would disappear for days, to a laboratory whose location was known only to him.'

'Do you think the secret lab is here on the farm?' asked Pitt.

'We don't know,' replied Kelly. 'When we were certain Dad had left the farm on business or research trips, Josh and I looked everywhere, but never found a clue to its location.'

'What was Dr Egan researching when he died?'

Thomas shrugged helplessly. 'I have no idea. He only said it would revolutionise science and technology.'

'Did he ever take time for pleasure?' enquired Pitt.

'He was passionate about researching the Vikings,' said Thomas.

'He was also a dedicated fan of Jules Verne,' added Kelly. 'His library's in a separate building beside the house, overlooking the river. It was his sanctuary.'

The building was made of stone, and ivy rose on the walls.

Thomas used an old-fashioned key to unlock the thick oak door.

The interior of the library oozed finesse and refinement. The big overstuffed chairs and couch were leather, and the desk, still littered with research papers, was a huge rosewood roll top. Pitt walked beside the bookshelves that ran from floor to ceiling. Paintings of Viking ships hung on the only open wall. On a table sat a model of a submarine nearly four feet in length. The boat was rounded at the ends, with portholes along the sides and a small tower that sat towards the bow. The propeller's blades were shaped like paddles. The brass plaque on the base read, *Nautilus. Launched 1863.*

'Beautiful,' said Pitt. 'Captain Nemo's submarine, isn't it? From *Twenty Thousand Leagues under the Sea*?'

'Dad designed it from an etching in the original book.'

Pitt examined the titles of the books on the shelves. They covered the Viking era. One entire section was devoted to runic alphabets.

Kelly watched Pitt. 'Dad became expert at translating the characters found on rune stones throughout the country.'

'He believed the Vikings came this far south?'

She nodded. 'He was convinced. He found over thirty-five stones with ancient runic alphabets.'

'Did he ever intend to publish his findings?' asked Giordino.

'Not as far as I know. Then, about ten years ago, he lost interest.'

'After the Vikings, Elmore immersed himself in Jules Verne,' Thomas said. 'He collected everything Verne wrote.'

Giordino took one of Egan's Viking notebooks from the shelf. He thumbed through the pages, his face registering bafflement. He flipped through the pages of a second, then looked up, mystified. All the pages in all the notebooks were blank.

'I don't understand,' said Kelly. 'I vividly remember trips into the backwoods searching for rune stones. When he found one, he would translate the messages. I saw him scribble in his notebooks with my own eyes.'

'Your father must have hidden the original notebooks elsewhere,' said Pitt. 'It's getting late. We're not going to solve anything tonight. I suggest we sleep on it.'

No one gave him an argument. They were all dead tired. Pitt was the last to leave the library. He pretended to lock the door before he handed the key to Thomas. Later, when everyone was asleep, he returned. Then he began searching through Egan's research material. A trail and a story began to emerge.

By four in the morning, he had found what he was looking for.

GIORDINO SURPRISED everyone by making breakfast. Afterwards, Pitt and Kelly returned to the library. Kelly noticed the books and papers stacked on the roll-top desk.

'Looks like a little fairy was burning the midnight oil.'

Pitt looked at her. 'Believe you me, it was no fairy.'

She studied the Viking books on the desk. 'What were you after?'

'You said your dad translated thirty-five rune stones. Do you recall the locations?' asked Pitt.

'About five or six come to mind, but they were so far off the beaten track I couldn't tell you how to get anywhere near them.'

'You won't have to.'

'What are you driving at?' she challenged.

'Your father didn't chase round the country looking for Viking inscriptions and then hide his translations for laughs. He set out to accomplish something. I believe it ties in with his experiments.'

Her lips were set in doubt. 'How are you going to find them?'

He picked up a book, *Messages from the Ancient Vikings*, by Dr Marlys Kaiser. 'This lady has compiled a comprehensive record of more than eighty rune stones throughout North America. I think it might pay to visit Dr Kaiser. She lives in a town called Monticello, near Minneapolis. It stands to reason your father would have consulted her,' said Pitt. 'We'll know some answers by this time Sunday.'

'That's four days away. What gives?'

'We're flying to Washington. I want to gather all the data possible before we beat the bushes for old rune stones.'

WHEN PITT'S NUMA jet landed at Langley Field, Congresswoman Loren Smith was waiting to greet him. As he stepped onto the tarmac, she embraced him, snaking her fingers through his wavy black hair and pulling his head down so she could kiss him.

'My wandering one is home,' she said in a sultry tone after she released him.

Kelly hesitated in the doorway of the aircraft, watching Pitt and Loren looking into each other's eyes. She could easily see this was no casual friendship, and she felt a pang of jealousy. Loren was a very beautiful woman, looking stunning in tan shorts, gold sandals and a yellow blouse. Over the course of ten years, her relationship with Pitt had gone from intimate to platonic and back again several times.

Kelly came over, and the two women sized each other up as Pitt introduced them.

'Kelly Egan, may I present Congresswoman Loren Smith.'

'An honour to meet you, Congresswoman,' said Kelly, with a tight little smile.

'Call me Loren,' she replied. 'The honour is mine. I knew your father. Please accept my condolences. He appeared before my committee investigating price-fixing among the oil companies.'

Giordino stepped down from the plane at that moment and hugged Loren. 'Still gorgeous, I see,' he said, gazing from his five foot four inches up at her height of five foot eight.

'How's my favourite Roman?' she asked him.

'Still fighting the barbarians. And you?'

'Still battling the Philistines in the nation's capital.'

'We should change places some time.'

Loren laughed. 'I believe I'd be getting the better of the bargain.'

'What car did you bring?' asked Pitt, knowing she always showed up in one of his collector cars.

She nodded towards an elegant dark green 1938 Packard with long sweeping fenders and two covered spare tyres set deep into wells.

Kelly walked over to the car and ran her fingers over the chrome cormorant mascot on the radiator, her eyes glinting with reverence.

'Would you like to drive it?' asked Loren, giving Pitt an imperious look as they came to a stop by the car. 'I'm sure Dirk wouldn't mind.'

Pitt could see he had little choice in the matter and climbed in the back seat with Loren. Giordino sat in the open front seat next to Kelly, who was in seventh heaven behind the big steering wheel.

The divider window between the front seat and the rear passenger compartment was rolled up. Loren looked at Pitt provocatively. 'Is she staying with you?'

'What an evil mind you have,' Pitt answered with a laugh. 'Actually, I was hoping she could stay with you at your town house.'

'This isn't the old Dirk Pitt I once knew.'

'Sorry to disappoint you, but her life is in danger and she's safer at your place. The Cerberus Corporation won't hesitate to kill her in order to lay their hands on her father's formula for a super oil. I think it wise that she does not stay too close to me.'

Loren smiled. 'I could use some feminine company.' Then the smile faded. 'I had no idea you were mixed up with Cerberus. What do you know that I don't?'

'We're certain that Cerberus and their covert Viper operation are behind the disasters of the *Emerald Dolphin* and the *Golden Marlin*.'

She looked at Pitt steadily. 'I happen to head up the committee that's looking into unfair practices by the Cerberus Corporation. We believe they are trying to build a monopoly by purchasing most of the oil- and gas-producing wells in North America.'

Following Giordino's directions, Kelly drove the old Packard down the dirt road that stopped at Pitt's aircraft hangar apartment. Pitt rolled down the divider window and spoke to Giordino.

'Why don't you drop the ladies off at Loren's house and go to your place to clean up. Then pick us all up around seven. I'll make reservations for dinner.'

'Sounds wonderful,' said Kelly. She turned in her seat and smiled at Loren. 'I hope I'm not causing you any trouble.'

'Not at all,' said Loren graciously.

Kelly gazed at Pitt, her eyes aglow. 'I love driving this car.'

'Just don't become too attached,' he said, grinning at her.

As the Packard town car moved silently down the road, Pitt punched the security code on his remote, entered the hangar and made a call on its cellphone. 'St Julien.'

'Dirk!' roared St Julien Perlmutter, raconteur, gourmand and renowned maritime historian. 'Good to hear your voice.'

'I wonder if you have time for a little research job?'

'I always have time for my favourite godson.'

'May I come over?'

'Yes, indeed. I want to try out a new sixty-year-old port. I hope you'll join me.'

PITT RELAXED in the chair, enjoying a glass of exquisite port in the kitchen of his godfather's Georgetown house, and related what had been happening to him, beginning with the fire on board the *Emerald Dolphin* and ending with the fight in Egan's home above the Hudson River.

'So where do I fit in?' asked Perlmutter, a huge man with a rosy-red nose and sky-blue eyes.

'Dr Egan was a devotee of Jules Verne, especially his book *Twenty Thousand Leagues under the Sea.* I thought that if anybody knew about Captain Nemo's submarine, the *Nautilus*, it had to be you.'

Perlmutter leaned back and stared at the ornate ceiling. 'Verne was either way ahead of his time, or he could see into the future, because the *Nautilus* was extremely technically advanced for 1870.'

'Could someone or some country have built a submarine that might have been half as efficient as the *Nautilus*?' asked Pitt.

'Who's to say?' said Perlmutter. He was about to reach for the port bottle again when a look of revelation swept over his face. 'I just thought of something,' he said, raising his great bulk out of his chair with ease. He disappeared down the hall for several minutes before reappearing with a book in one hand. 'A copy of the board of inquiry minutes concerning the sinking of the US Navy frigate *Kearsarge*. I'd forgotten the strange circumstances behind her grounding on Roncador Reef off Venezuela in 1894.'

'Strange?' asked Pitt.

'Yes, according to her commander, Captain Leigh Hunt, he was attacked by a man-made underwater vessel that resembled a whale. The vessel was chased, then sank into the water before surfacing again and ramming the *Kearsarge*, putting a large hole in her hull. She barely made it to Roncador Reef before she grounded. The crew then made camp on the reef until they were rescued.'

'Sounds like the good captain was heavily into the rum locker,' Pitt said, jokingly.

'No, he was dead serious,' replied Perlmutter, 'and what's important is that his entire crew backed him up. Not one of them who witnessed the spectacle varied his story. Their testimony described a large steel monster that was impenetrable to a series of cannon shots the *Kearsarge* poured into it—they simply bounced off. They also mentioned some sort of pyramid-shaped tower on its back that appeared to have viewing ports. Captain Hunt swore that he saw a face staring back at him through one of the ports, a man with a beard.'

'Did they comment on the monster's size?'

'The crew agreed that it was cigar-shaped, cylindrical with conical ends. As would be expected, they estimated the size anywhere from one to three hundred feet, with a beam of twenty to forty feet.'

'Probably somewhere in between,' Pitt said thoughtfully.

'Come to think of it, the *Kearsarge* was not the only vessel reported sunk by an undersea monster,' Perlmutter went on. 'The US Navy ship, the *Abraham Lincoln*, reported an encounter with an undersea craft that rammed and shattered her rudder.'

'When did that occur?'

'Eighteen sixty-six.'

'Twenty-eight years earlier.'

'Over that time, many ships disappeared under mysterious circumstances,' Perlmutter said. 'Most of them were British warships.'

Pitt set his glass on the table. 'I can't believe a supernatural vessel decades ahead of its time was built by private individuals.'

'Perhaps Jules Verne heard of such a vessel and created Captain Nemo and his *Nautilus* around it.'

'What about Verne?' Pitt enquired. 'There must be a museum that collected all his papers, research records and letters.'

'Dr Paul Hereoux, president of the Society of Jules Verne in Amiens, France, is considered the most knowledgeable man on the author's life.'

'Can we contact him?'

'Better yet,' said Perlmutter, 'in a few days, I plan to travel to Paris. I'll run up to Amiens and talk with Dr Hereoux.'

'I couldn't ask for more,' said Pitt.

AFTER HE RETURNED to his apartment, Pitt made a call to Admiral Sandecker. Then he took a shower and changed. At the sound of the Packard's horn, he exited the hangar and slid into the passenger seat.

'All set?' Giordino asked.

Pitt nodded. 'The admiral has arranged a little party, should we have a problem.'

'You armed?'

Pitt pulled aside his jacket to reveal his old Colt in a shoulder holster.

Giordino twisted in the seat to expose a Ruger double-action P94, 40-calibre automatic slung under one arm. 'Let's hope we're being overcautious.'

A few minutes later, Giordino eased the car to a stop in front of Loren's town house. Two minutes later, the women arrived at the entrance. Loren, stunning in a cotton mock turtleneck and skirt, looked radiant. Kelly wore an embroidered jacket dress.

Giordino turned to Pitt. 'Where to?'

'Rose Hill. The Knox Inn serves home-cooked dishes that send your taste buds to heaven.'

Giordino turned into the parking lot of the Knox Inn. He and Pitt gazed around the lot but saw no sign of suspicious activity. They stepped into the inn, which had been a stagecoach stop as far back as 1772, and Pitt's party were immediately shown by the maître d' to a nice table in the courtyard beneath a large oak tree.

Pitt and Giordino finally began to relax and the time went swiftly, as Giordino ran through his repertoire of crazy jokes that soon had the women clutching their sides in laughter. Pitt merely grinned politely, having heard them all at least fifty times. He scanned the walls of the courtyard and examined the other diners like a TV security camera, but he saw nothing that aroused his interest.

They ordered an assortment of barbecued pork and chicken, grits with shrimp and crab, a southern coleslaw salad and corn on the cob.

It was only after they'd finished dinner and were having key lime pie for dessert that Pitt tensed.

A tall man with reddish-brown hair and a tanned face, flanked by two characters who might as well have worn signs saying 'armed killers', were approaching their table. The intruder walked across the courtyard with an arrogance that suggested he owned half the world.

His eyes lingered on Pitt. 'We have never met, Mr Pitt, but my name is Curtis Merlin Zale.'

Pitt gazed at Zale with studied indifference. He made no effort to rise to his feet.

Zale addressed the ladies. 'Miss Egan, Congresswoman Smith, it is a pleasure to finally meet you.' Then he turned to Pitt and Giordino. 'Gentlemen, your meddling has caused my company a great deal of frustration.'

This guy is smooth, Pitt thought to himself. 'Al and I are just your common, law-abiding citizens who became swept up in your crackpot scheme to create a domestic oil monopoly.'

'It will never happen,' said Loren.

If Zale was dismayed that Pitt and Loren were aware of his grand design, he didn't show it. 'You realise, of course, that my resources far exceed yours.'

'You're delusional if you think you're bigger than the US government,' argued Loren. 'Congress will stop you.'

Zale gave her a patronising smile. 'Do not think you can depend on your fellow legislators, Congresswoman. I have more friends in the Capitol than you.'

'No doubt bribed and blackmailed into submission,' injected Pitt.

Loren's eyes blazed. 'When it's revealed whom you paid off and how much, you will be indicted on more criminal charges than the Mafia Don, John Gotti.'

Zale gave an imperious shake of his head. 'I do not think so.'

'I couldn't agree with you more,' said Pitt. 'You will never be convicted of your crimes because you will most certainly die first.'

Zale decided to fight fire with fire. 'Now that I know where I stand, I shall leave you to your dessert. But my friends here will remain.'

'What does he mean?' asked Kelly fearfully.

'He means that as soon as he is on his way, his flunkies intend to shoot us.'

There was a malignant look in Zale's eyes. He nodded at his two bodyguards and turned to leave. 'Goodbye, ladies and gentlemen. A pity your futures are so short.'

'Before you run off,' said Pitt, 'it might be wise to take your pals with you or they'll follow in an ambulance.'

Zale turned back and stared at Pitt, as his men stepped forward and reached inside their suit jackets. As if rehearsed, Pitt and Giordino lifted their weapons from beneath the table.

'Goodbye, Mr Zale,' Giordino murmured, with a tight smile. 'Next time . . .' And his voice trailed off.

'It seems you came to dinner fully equipped,' said Zale, spreading his hands harmlessly.

'We like to be prepared,' said Pitt nonchalantly.

'You have been warned,' said Zale, his facial expression under control but the skin flushed with rage. Then he strode from the courtyard and into the parking lot. His two hired guns followed behind and entered a Lincoln Navigator, where they sat and waited.

Loren reached over and touched Pitt's hand. 'How can you be so calm? He made my skin crawl.'

'Zale showed his hand when he didn't have to,' said Pitt. 'I can't help but wonder why.'

'Curiosity,' suggested Giordino. 'He had to see with his own eyes the faces of the people who were fouling up his plans.'

After coffee and espresso, Pitt paid the bill. Then Giordino peered into the parking lot. 'Hekyll and Jekyll are sitting in a big SUV under a tree.'

'We should call the police,' said Loren.

Pitt grinned. 'Plans have already been made.' He pulled a cellphone from his jacket pocket, punched a number, spoke no more than four words and turned it off. He smiled at Loren and Kelly. 'You girls wait in the entrance while Al gets the car.'

Loren snatched the keys of the Packard from Pitt's fingers. 'Better I get the car. They won't shoot a helpless female.'

Pitt was about to refuse, but knew deep down that she was right. Zale's men wanted all four of them in their sights.

Loren was fast. She took off like a wraith in the night, reaching the Packard in less than a minute. No stranger to the car's controls, she had the key in the ignition in almost the same motion as she pushed the starter button. The big V-12 engine fired instantly and the accelerator bit hard. Sliding to a stop in front of the restaurant, she glided over to the passenger side of the bench seat as Pitt, Giordino and Kelly piled inside.

Pitt floored the accelerator and the big car surged quietly up the road, gathering speed smoothly. The road was straight, and he took a long look in the rearview mirror at the big Navigator swinging out of the inn's parking lot.

'They're coming after us,' he said, in the monotone of a bus driver telling his passengers to move back from the door.

The Navigator was gaining rapidly on the old Packard. Five miles from the restaurant, the driver had crept up to within 100 yards.

'Everybody down on the floor,' said Pitt.

The ladies did as they were told. Giordino crouched and aimed his Ruger out of the window. A curve was coming up, and the Navigator was approaching on the outside. Pitt swung the Packard round the turn, her big tyres protesting as they skidded sideways across the road.

The instant Pitt had the car heading up a straight section of the road, he peered into the mirror in time to see two big Chevy Avalanches, with machine guns mounted in their cargo boxes, charge out of the woods directly in front of the speeding Navigator.

The driver of the Navigator was caught completely off guard and whipped the wheel to one side, sending the big SUV into an uncontrollable skid onto the grassy shoulder, where it rolled over three times. Armed men burst from the Avalanches and quickly surrounded the upside-down Navigator.

Pitt eased off on the accelerator. 'The chase is over,' he said. 'Sandecker arranged a little entertainment for Zale's hired guns.'

'I have to admit you had me scared for a minute,' said Loren.

'I'll take everyone home,' said Pitt. 'Tomorrow, we take our act on the road again.'

'Where are you going?' asked Loren.

'While you're forming your committee to investigate Cerberus, Al, Kelly and I are heading for Minnesota to look at old rune stones.'

'What do you hope to find?'

'The answer to an enigma,' Pitt said slowly.

MARLYS KAISER gave Kelly a motherly hug. 'Elmore Egan's daughter. I'm so happy to meet you. Your father and I were great friends.'

'I know,' said Kelly. 'He often talked about you.'

'As I told you over the phone,' said Pitt, 'we are investigating Dr Egan's study of rune stones he discovered many years ago.'

Marlys thought for a moment. 'It concerned inscriptions by a group of Norsemen who explored the Midwest in AD 1035. I recall he hoped they would lead him to a cave.'

'Do you have records of them?'

Marlys clapped her hands. 'This is your lucky day. Come out to my office in the barn where I have them filed away.'

Marlys's barn had been converted into a giant office. Rows of bookshelves took up half the space. A huge square table with a computer was piled with photographs, folders and bound reports.

One side of the room was filled with artefacts—ceramic bowls shaped into pots, human heads and figures, and animals. Smaller objects were preserved in a great glass case.

'These were all found in the United States?' asked Pitt.

'Discovered from Colorado to Oklahoma to Georgia.'

'Remarkable that so many ancient people came this way,' said Kelly in awe.

'Our ancestors were just as curious as we are about what's over the horizon.' Marlys swept her arm at chairs and a sofa as she searched the bookcases. 'Make yourselves comfortable while I look for the records of the inscriptions that interested your father.' After a minute, she pulled out two thick reports in metal binders. One held over a hundred photographs, the other was bulky with papers.

She laid down a photograph of a large inscribed rock. 'This is the Bertram Stone, found in 1933.'

Pitt stared at the twiglike markings. 'A few of the letters are the same as our current alphabet.'

'What does the stone say?' Giordino asked.

Marlys inserted a compact disc in her terminal. In a moment the letters were revealed in great detail on the monitor.

'We may never have a totally accurate translation,' she said, 'but runologists agree that the inscription reads: "Magnus Sigvatson passed this way in year 1035 and claimed the lands this side of the river for his brother, Bjarne Sigvatson, leader of our tribe."'

'What do the other stones reveal?' asked Pitt.

'Most of them seem to be boundary markers. Magnus claimed a quarter of what became the United States for his brother, Bjarne, and his tribe. The first and last stone was discovered at the southern end of Lake Champlain in upstate New York.'

Kelly looked puzzled. 'The first and last stone?'

'The Lake Champlain stone was the first inscribed at the beginning of the expedition. When they returned nearly a year later, they made a second inscription on the stone below the first.'

'May we see them?' Pitt asked.

Marlys typed on her keyboard, and a large stone appeared on the monitor. She began to translate the lengthy inscription. '"After six days' travel up the fiord from our settlement, Magnus Sigvatson and his comrades rest here and claim all the land within sight of the water for my kinsman, Bjarne Sigvatson."'

She went on, 'The second inscription carved on the return reads: "Fourteen months after leaving our families, we are but a few days' sail down the fiord to the cave below the high cliffs to our homes. Bless Odin for protecting us. We have discovered paradise. Magnus Sigvatson."'

'Six days' sail down the fiord,' Pitt repeated pensively. 'That would suggest the Norsemen had a settlement in the United States.'

'Has a site ever been discovered?' asked Giordino.

Marlys shook her head. 'Archaeologists have yet to find one.'

'You have to wonder why it disappeared so completely.'

'There are ancient Indian legends that tell of a great battle with strange wild men with long chin hair and shiny heads.'

'They must be referring to the helmets the Vikings wore.'

'Strange that no archaeological evidence of a site has ever been discovered,' said Kelly.

'My guess is that your father was searching for the cave mentioned in the final inscription,' said Pitt. 'The reason he suddenly dropped his research is because he must have found it.'

'Without his papers,' said Giordino, 'we're floundering in the dark.'

Pitt focused on Kelly. 'You and Josh said you searched the farm for your father's hidden laboratory and turned up nothing.'

Kelly nodded. 'Every square inch.'

'How about the cliffs facing the river?'

'One of the first places we looked. We found no sign of caves or a path leading across the face of the cliffs.'

'It's a question of looking in the right place. If we find it, too, it will open the door to your father's secret project.'

'You might take a new direction in your search,' said Marlys. 'Dr Jerry Wednesday at Marymount College in Tarrytown is an expert on the Hudson River Valley Indian tribes. He might be able to throw some light on contact with the Norsemen.'

Pitt looked at Giordino. 'What do you think?'

'When searching for treasure, you can never do enough research.'

'That's what I always say.'

IT WAS VITAL to the interests of the Cerberus empire that the planning session in the company-owned lodge beside Tohono Lake be held in the strictest secrecy. The six men and two women at the table were CEOs of the largest oil companies in the Northern Hemisphere and had congregated to map strategy for the coming months. The ninth person, Curtis Merlin Zale, passed out leather-bound folders and waited for the others to study the contents.

'You all know the predictions,' said Zale, as he began the meeting. 'By 2010, the world's total oil production will peak. That's less than seven years from now. From then until 2050, production will drop to a small fraction of what it is today.'

'If production looks gloomy, the resulting drop in the world economy looks absolutely pitch-dark,' said Jesus Morales, the CEO of the CalTex Oil Company. 'Prices will skyrocket, accompanied by hyperinflation and even rationing. I shudder to think what level transportation costs will hit.'

'I agree.' Sally Morse studied Zale's report. The chief of Yukon Oil, Canada's largest oil producer, she'd joined the secret cabal reluctantly five years earlier, and was beginning to have second thoughts. 'Despite geologists' forecasts, few new fields have been found. The known major oil-producing fields contain ninety-four per cent of the world's oil. As they diminish, prices will rise on an unending curve.'

'It's as though the entire situation were falling into our hands,' said Zale confidently. 'By pooling our resources, our fields and refineries in North America, we can dictate our own terms and price. We can also double production by drilling where the government has not allowed us to go before. Our newly built pipeline systems will carry the oil overland without the expensive use of tankers. If our strategy works according to plan, the only oil and gas sold north of Mexico will be American and Canadian, which will enhance the profits of our respective organisations.'

'The OPEC nations won't roll over and play dead,' said Gunnar Machowsky of Gunnar Oil. 'Tthey'll undercut us at every turn.'

Zale grinned. 'I don't doubt it, but the plan is to make foreign oil so unpopular with American citizens that our elected officials will have to place an embargo on its use.'

'How many legislators do we have in our pockets?' asked Guy Kruse, the director of Eureka Offshore Oil Ventures.

Zale turned to Sandra Delage, the cartel's chief administrator. Delage's lightning mind and razor-sharp organisational skills were admired and respected by everyone at the table. She studied a notebook for a moment. 'As of yesterday, we can safely count on thirty-nine senators and one hundred and ten representatives. I think it's safe to say the White House will also accommodate your counsel.'

'That leaves the environmentalist lobbies,' said Machowsky.

Zale leaned across the table. 'Their protests will be swept aside by the public's outcry when the oil shortage and high prices hits home. We already have enough votes to open new oil fields from Alaska to Florida over the protests of the environmentalists. The American and Canadian governments have no choice but to allow access for drilling in areas where geologists have found rich reserves.'

Jesus Morales leaned back in his chair. 'Now all that is left before we can begin our operation is the completion of the pipeline system.'

Sandra Delage pressed a button on a remote control that lowered a large screen. Almost instantly, a large map of North America filled the screen. A series of black lines travelled across national and state borders from oil fields to refineries to major cities. 'Ladies and gentlemen, our oil transportation system. Thirty-seven thousand miles of underground pipeline will be ready to send oil by the end of the month.'

'Circumventing the environmentalists by laying pipe underground was a brilliant stroke,' said Sam Riley, the chairman of Pioneer Oil.

'An ingenious concept,' said Morales, 'leasing the right-of-way from the railroads and laying pipe along the track.'

'It saved untold billions,' acknowledged Zale. 'It also allows us to pump oil directly into every major city without having to worry about governmental regulations.'

'It's a miracle we've come this far without interference from the Justice Department,' said Sally Morse.

'We've covered our trail well,' said Zale.

Kruse looked at Zale. 'I understand Congresswoman Loren Smith is launching an investigation into Cerberus.'

'Loren Smith is one member of Congress who definitely is not on our side,' said Sally Morse.

Zale looked at her, his eyes cold. 'The matter will be handled.'

'Like the *Emerald Dolphin* and the *Golden Marlin*?' Machowsky murmured sarcastically.

'The end justified the means,' retorted Zale. 'The ultimate goal was accomplished by blaming the disasters on malfunctions by Elmore Egan's engines. All contracts by shipbuilders to install his magnetohydrodynamic engines have been cancelled. And with Egan dead, it's only a matter of days before we have the formula for his super oil. Once we go into production, we will control and share in the profits of the manufacture and sales of his engines. As you can see, we're covering every side of the fuel oil market.'

'Can you assure us that there will be no more interference from NUMA?' asked Riley.

'That is history. No trails lead to Cerberus.'

Dan Goodman of Diversified Oil Resources raised his hand. 'I, for one, applaud your campaign to enrage the general public against foreign oil. With the supertanker disasters your Viper group caused in Fort Lauderdale, Newport Beach and Vancouver, where oil spills invaded highly populated and affluent areas, public outcry to become self-sufficient in oil has soared.'

'The country is on the verge of mass demonstrations over foreign oil,' said Kruse. 'We need only one more incident to push them over the edge.'

A foxlike grin cut Zale's features. 'Such an incident will take place three days from now. A tanker spill magnified by an explosion inside one of the world's busiest harbours.'

Silence fell while the conspirators grasped the consequences. Sandra Delage looked at Zale and then spoke quietly. 'On Saturday at approximately four thirty pm, the *Pacific Chimera*, the largest oil tanker in the world, will enter San Francisco Bay. She will make for the Point San Pedro Mooring, where she would normally tie her bow and discharge her cargo. Only she will not stop. Estimates are that she will plough nearly two blocks into the city before coming to rest. Then charges will be detonated and the tanker and six hundred and twenty thousand tons of oil will go up in an explosion that will devastate the entire San Francisco waterfront area.'

'Oh my God,' muttered Sally Morse. 'How many people will die?'

'What does it matter?' asked Zale coldly. 'More have died in wars that accomplished nothing.' He rose from his chair. 'That will be enough discussion for today.'

Then the most powerful oil moguls of two nations followed Zale to the dining room, where cocktails were waiting.

Only Sally Morse of Yukon Oil remained, visualising the suffering that was about to fall on thousands of innocent men, women and children in San Francisco. As she sat alone, she came to a decision that could very well end her life.

DR JERRY WEDNESDAY of Marymount College smiled as Pitt, Giordino and Kelly introduced themselves. 'I met your father, you know,' he said to Kelly. 'He was researching a Viking expedition he thought had passed through New York in . . . 1035, I believe.'

'Yes, Dad was very interested in the rune stones they left behind.'

'We've just come from Marlys Kaiser in Minnesota,' said Pitt. 'It was she who suggested we meet with you.'

'A grand lady.' Wednesday sat down behind his cluttered desk. 'I suppose Marlys mentioned that Dr Egan thought the Vikings who settled in this area were massacred by the Indians in the valley?'

Kelly nodded. 'She touched on the subject.'

Wednesday retrieved a sheaf of wrinkled papers. 'Very little is known about the early American Indians who lived along the Hudson River. It wasn't until the Dutch began to settle the valley in 1613, and learned the tribal languages, that the legends of the past began to emerge.'

'What did the legends reveal?'

'It's difficult to separate myth from fact,' replied Wednesday. 'One tale that surfaced told of bearded men with white skin and hard heads that gleamed in the sun who built a settlement in the valley. When some went away for a long time—'

'Magnus Sigvatson's men explored the west,' Kelly interrupted.

'The story goes that when the Indians began stealing livestock there was retaliation. The men with hair on the face, as they were called, retrieved the livestock and cut off the hands of the thieves. Unfortunately, one of them was a local chief's son. The chief gathered other tribes and destroyed the foreigners' settlement, slaughtering them all.'

'It must have been a shock for Magnus and his men to return and find their friends and families dead.'

Wednesday nodded. 'The legend describes a great battle with the bearded men with shiny heads, who killed more than a thousand Indians before dying to the last man.'

'Seems odd that no trace of the settlement has been discovered,' observed Pitt.

'The legend says the Indians destroyed the newcomers' settlement, leaving nothing standing for archaeologists to study.'

'Was there ever a reference to a cave?'

'Only on one of the rune stones Dr Egan found.'

Pitt rose, leaned across the desk and shook Dr Wednesday's hand. 'Thank you, Doctor. We're grateful for your time.'

They offered their farewells and headed for the parking lot. The mood was sombre.

'Dad found the settlement,' Kelly said intently. 'I know it.'

'Though any trace of the settlement was destroyed, I'm betting there was a cave and that it still exists,' said Pitt.

'Josh and I never found it,' Kelly said wistfully.

'The Indians could have sealed off the entrance,' advised Giordino.

'I suggest that we make a search from the river below the cliffs,' said Pitt confidently. 'Finding a cavity in the rock under the surface is very possible with the use of side-scan sonar.'

Giordino's cellphone buzzed. 'One moment, Admiral.' He passed the phone to Pitt. 'It's Sandecker.'

Pitt listened without replying. Finally, he handed the phone to Giordino. 'He wants us back in Washington. It seems Curtis Merlin Zale and his pals at Cerberus are about to cause a catastrophe even worse than the *Emerald Dolphin.*'

PART FOUR: DECEPTION
Washington, DC

August 8, 2003. After Kelly left the aircraft in Washington, she was escorted to an unmarked van that transported her to a safe house in Arlington. Pitt and Giordino saw her off, entered a NUMA Lincoln Navigator and relaxed as the driver steered the car towards Landover, Maryland. Twenty minutes later, they drove into the underground VIP parking area of FedEx Field, home of the Washington Redskins football team, and stopped next to a doorway guarded by two security men in combat gear, holding automatic rifles. They studied Pitt and Giordino, comparing their faces to photographs provided by NUMA's security department, before allowing them to pass into a corridor beneath the stadium. Another armed guard studied them, then swung open a door and stepped aside.

'I thought the Cold War was over years ago,' Giordino muttered.

They were mildly surprised to find themselves in the locker room for the visiting football teams. Several people were already seated in the team management office. Loren was there, with a woman they did not recognise. Admiral Sandecker, Rudi Gunn and Hiram Yaeger represented NUMA. Pitt noted Admiral Amos Dover of the coastguard, Captain Warren Garnet of the marines and Commander Miles Jacobs, who was a veteran of navy SEAL operations. He and Giordino had worked with all of them in the past.

He was not familiar with a tall, distinguished-looking man, who wore a black patch over the left eye.

'Dirk,' said Sandecker, 'may I introduce Wes Rader, an old naval friend. Wes is a senior deputy director at the Justice Department and will coordinate all activities from the legal end.'

The admiral turned to the woman beside Loren.

'As some of you are already aware, Ms Sally Morse is the CEO of the Yukon Oil Company. She will describe a grave threat to our national security.' He turned to Sally. 'The stage is yours.'

For the next two hours, Sally gave a detailed narrative of Curtis Merlin Zale's grand scheme to create an oil monopoly and gain enormous wealth while dictating terms to the United States government.

When she finished, Wes Rader turned to Sandecker. 'This threat goes far beyond the people in this room. We've got to notify others immediately. The President, the leaders of Congress, the Joint Chiefs of Staff, my boss at the Justice Department—that's just for starters.'

'We can't,' Sally said. 'Zale has paid out five billion dollars to buy everyone in Washington he can profit from. More than a hundred senators and representatives are in his pocket, along with officials in every government department, including the Justice Department.'

Sandecker passed out a list of names. 'This is the reason for the secrecy,' he said. 'These people have all been bought by Cerberus.'

'Impossible,' said Rader, scanning the names in utter disbelief. 'There would have to be a vast paper trail.'

'All payoff monies are in offshore accounts that would take Justice Department investigators years to track down,' answered Sally.

Rader shook his head. 'I can't believe one man is responsible.'

'Zale had the backing of the most powerful oil barons in the United States and Canada,' Sally replied. 'Yukon Oil, too. I'm as guilty as the others.'

'You've more than atoned by coming to us,' said Loren.

'Why me?' asked Rader. 'I'm only the number-three man at the Justice Department.'

'Your name is not on the list, and your direct superiors' are,' answered Sandecker. 'I know you to be an honourable man who can't be bought. It is up to you to get the ball rolling. Zale and his cronies in the Cerberus cartel must be brought to justice.'

'Where do we begin?' asked Rader. 'I can't simply walk into the attorney general's office and announce that I'm arresting him for taking bribes.'

Sandecker nodded at Hiram Yaeger, who began passing round a bound set of documents several inches thick. 'Utilising Ms Morse's account and our own investigations into Zale's criminal empire, through our NUMA computer facilities, we put together a complete indictment with more than enough solid evidence to convince honest officials.' He looked at Rader. 'Wes, you have to put together a team at Justice whose loyalty you can depend on to build an airtight case.'

Roder stared apprehensively at the thick report on the table in front of him. 'I hope I'm not biting off more than I can chew.'

'I'll give you every assistance from the congressional end,' Loren promised him.

'Our first priority,' said Sandecker, lowering a monitor with a display of San Francisco Bay, 'is to stop that oil tanker.' He looked at Dover, Garnet and Jacobs. 'This is where you gentlemen come into the picture.'

'The coastguard will stop the *Pacific Chimera* from entering the bay,' Dover stated flatly.

Sandecker nodded. 'Sounds simple, Amos. But stopping one of the world's largest supertankers will take more than firing a shot across its bow.'

Dover smiled at Garnet and Jacobs. 'Is this why we have the navy SEALs and Marine Reconnaissance at the table?'

'If the captain of the tanker ignores your commands and continues into the bay, we don't have a lot of avenues open to us,' said Sandecker. 'As a last resort, a combat team will have to be airdropped by helicopter onto the vessel itself and neutralise the crew.'

'Where is the *Pacific Chimera* now?' asked Dover.

Sandecker pressed a button and the chart showed a small image of a ship heading towards the coast of California. 'Approximately nine hundred miles out.'

'That gives us less than forty-eight hours,' said Dover. 'I'll have coastguard cutters waiting to intercept fifty miles out.'

'I'll have a boarding team in the air as back-up,' Garnet assured him.

'My SEALs will be ready to board from the sea,' Jacobs added.

'Well, ladies and gentlemen,' Sandecker said quietly, 'this is as far as NUMA can go in this project. We'll help in any way we're asked, but we are a scientific oceanographic agency and not authorised to act as an investigative agency.'

Dover stood and looked down at Sandecker. 'I'll keep you informed every hour on the status of the operation.'

One by one, they filed out of the locker room. Pitt and Giordino, along with Rudi Gunn, were asked by Sandecker to remain. As he left, Yaeger put his hand on Pitt's shoulder and asked him to drop by NUMA headquarters and come to the computer floor.

The admiral lit a big cigar. 'It looks as if you boys are sidelined for the rest of the game.'

'I'm sure you won't let us sit on the bench for long,' said Pitt.

Gunn adjusted his glasses. 'We'd like Al to head an investigation into the widespread death of coral northwest of the Hawaiian Islands.'

'And me?' asked Pitt.

'You'll be going to Antarctica,' said Sandecker wryly.

A shadow of dissent crossed Pitt's face. 'I will, of course, follow your directives, Admiral. But I respectfully request five days for Al and me to clear up a mystery concerning Dr Egan.'

'The search for his secret laboratory?'

'I believe it is a matter of national security to find out what Dr Egan was working on when he died, before Zale gets there first.'

Sandecker exhaled a cloud of blue smoke. 'That's it, then. Rudi will inform you where and when to report on board your survey ships.' Then he dropped his gruff edge and said, 'I wish you luck on your quest. I'm also curious as to what Egan was conjuring up.'

YAEGER WAS CONVERSING with Max when Pitt arrived. He pulled Egan's case from a cabinet. 'You're just in time for the next act.'

'I don't follow.'

'Every twenty-eight hours, this case turns to magic. So at precisely one fifteen this afternoon—'

'It fills with oil,' Pitt said hesitantly.

'Exactly.' Yaeger opened the case, waved his hand over the empty case like a magician, then closed it. He studied the second hand on his watch and said, 'To reverse the old cliché: now, you don't see it—and now you do.' He lifted the lid. The interior was filled with oil.

'The same thing happened to Al and me on *Deep Encounter*,' said Pitt. He dipped his finger in the oil and rubbed it between his thumb and fingers. 'Feels frictionless. My guess is it's Dr Egan's super oil.'

'The million-dollar question is: where's it coming from?'

'Does Max have a read on it?' Pitt asked, staring at the holograph.

'I'm as mystified as you,' said Max. 'I have a few ideas I'd like to pursue if Hiram doesn't shut me down when he leaves tonight.'

'Only if you promise not to enter confidential or private sites.'

'I will try to be a good girl.'

Pitt could not help laughing. 'Have you ever regretted not making Max a male?'

'Not only do I have to contend with Max,' Yaeger said wearily, 'but I have a wife and two teenage daughters at home.'

'You're a man to be envied, Hiram.'

'That's easy for you to say. You never let a woman into your life.'

'No,' said Pitt wistfully. 'That, I never did.'

UNKNOWN TO PITT, his days of lonely bachelorhood would be temporarily interrupted. He returned to his hangar and observed that wily old Sandecker had sent a security team to patrol the area around him at the deserted end of the airport. The reason did not become apparent until he climbed to his apartment and found Sally Morse stirring the contents of a pot on the stove.

Who said you could invade my personal domain as if you owned it? Who let you in through the security systems? These questions ripened in his mind, but, mild-mannered marine engineer that he was, Pitt simply said, 'Hello, what's for dinner?'

'Beef stroganoff,' answered Sally, turning and smiling sweetly. 'Do you like it?'

'One of my favourites.'

She could tell by the confused expression on his face that he hadn't expected her. 'Congresswoman Smith thought I'd be safer staying here. Especially since Admiral Sandecker has placed a security ring round your hangar,' she explained.

Questions answered, Pitt went to his bedroom to take a shower and change into comfortable shorts and T-shirt.

His bedroom looked as if a bomb had gone off in it. He couldn't believe only one female could have created such chaos until he heard a voice humming in his bathroom.

Kelly was standing in front of a half-steamed mirror wearing a towel. She saw Pitt and smiled.

'Welcome home. I hope Sally and I haven't upset your routine.'

'It was suggested you stay here, too?' he asked.

'Loren thought it safer than her place,' said Kelly. Then as an afterthought, 'I'm sorry, would you like to use the bathroom?'

'Don't mind me,' Pitt said wryly. 'I'll shower downstairs.'

Sally had stepped in. 'I fear we have inconvenienced you.'

'I'll survive,' Pitt said, as he began throwing some things in an overnight bag. 'You ladies make yourselves at home.'

Then he walked from the bedroom and down to the floor below.

Pitt set up house in the Pullman railroad car that sat on rails along one wall of the hangar. A relic from a Hudson River search operation several years ago, he used it as guest quarters when visitors and friends stayed with him.

He took a shower, and had just finished shaving when Sally Morse called from the balcony above that dinner was ready. He shouted an acknowledgement but did not immediately leave the Pullman car and walk up the spiral staircase.

Now that he was removed from any role in the operation to stop Curtis Merlin Zale, the murderous Viper organisation and the Cerberus cartel, Pitt felt lost, without direction. It was not his nature to sit powerless on the outside looking in.

AT ONE IN THE MORNING, Curtis Merlin Zale was seated in a leather executive chair in the Cerberus offices in Washington. He looked up into the dark, sinister eyes of Omo Kanai and smiled. 'The fish took the bait. Sally Morse is here in Washington.'

'A loose cannon in the capital could be dangerous.'

Zale shook his head. 'If you handle your end, she'll have an accident before she can be interrogated.'

'Any idea where she can be found?'

'I have a hundred people looking for her. It's a question of hours.'

Kanai appeared satisfied.

'I assume all is in readiness,' Zale said.

'The operation is planned down to the tiniest detail.'

'Your Viper team is on board?'

'All except me.' Kanai glanced at his watch. 'If I am to direct the final preparations, I must be leaving.'

Zale stood and they shook hands. 'Good luck, Omo. Next time we meet, the US government will have its strings pulled by new hands.'

'And where will you be tomorrow?'

Zale grinned. 'I will be testifying before Congresswoman Smith.'

WHEN LOREN WALKED into the Congressional Office Building hearing room, she was stunned as she stared at the table reserved for those subpoenaed to appear before her committee. There was no army of Cerberus corporate attorneys, no platoon of company directors or officials. Curtis Merlin Zale sat alone.

Loren said a few preliminary words to open the investigation and then thanked Zale for appearing. 'You realise, of course, that you have the privilege of appearing with counsel,' she advised him.

'Yes,' he said in a calm voice, 'but in the spirit of cooperation, I sit here before you ready to answer any and all questions.'

Loren glanced up at the clock on the far wall. It read 9.10am. 'The proceedings may run most of the day,' she informed Zale.

'I am at your disposal for as long as it takes,' he said.

Congresswoman Hope of Texas launched the proceedings. Loren knew that Hope's name was not on the list of those bought off by Cerberus, but she couldn't be positive of her views.

'Mr Zale, is it your position that the United States would be better off if we became self-sufficient in domestic oil and did not require foreign crude from the Middle East and Latin America?'

'Our reliance on foreign oil,' began Zale, 'is draining the economy.'

Oh God, thought Loren, she's playing right into his hands. The questions were given out and the answers returned. Zale, Loren could see, was not daunted. He knew he controlled three of the five members on the Unfair Practices Committee, and he felt in total control. Except for occasionally sneaking a look at his wristwatch, he was completely unfazed.

Loren lifted her eyes to the clock just as often. She found it impossible to keep her mind from wandering to the disaster approaching San Francisco.

AN HOUR BEFORE dawn the coastguard cutter *Huron* intercepted the supertanker *Pacific Chimera* twenty miles west of the Golden Gate. Two coastguard helicopters circled the big ship, accompanied by a Goshawk copter carrying Captain Garnet and his thirty-man Marine Reconnaissance team. An army patrol boat followed at the stern. On board were Commander Miles Jacobs and his navy SEAL team, prepared to shoot grappling hooks onto the deck of the vast tanker.

Admiral Amos Dover, who was in charge of the boarding operation, stood with binoculars pressed against his eyes. 'She's a big one. As long as five football fields end to end, and then some.'

'An ultra, ultra large crude carrier,' observed the cutter's commander, Captain Buck Compton. 'According to her specs, she can carry over six hundred thousand tons of oil.'

'Her captain has got every light from bow to stern turned on.' Dover lowered his glasses. 'Strange that he would advertise his presence so conspicuously.'

'She's British registry,' said Compton, studying the computer data on the tanker. 'That means all hell will break loose if we board a ship flying a foreign flag without proper permission.'

'That's Washington's problem. We're under strict orders.'

Compton took the transmitter from the radio operator. 'To the captain of *Pacific Chimera*. This is the captain of coastguard cutter *Huron*. Where are you bound?'

The supertanker's captain answered almost immediately. 'This is Captain Don Walsh. We are bound for the offshore oil-pumping facilities at Point San Pedro.'

'Tell him to heave to,' muttered Dover.

Compton nodded. 'Captain Walsh, this is Captain Compton. Please heave to for a boarding inspection.'

'Is this necessary?' asked Walsh. 'It will cost the company time and money to stop and it'll throw us off our schedule.'

'Please comply,' answered Compton, in an authoritative tone.

There was no answer of compliance from Captain Walsh, but after a minute Dover and Compton could see that the wake caused by the tanker's churning screws was falling off. It would take nearly a mile to bring her huge mass to a complete stop.

'Order Commander Jacobs and Captain Garnet to board the ship with their assault teams. They're equipped to deal with resistance.'

Compton gave the order and they watched as the pilot dipped the Goshawk helicopter round the stern of the supertanker. It hovered for a minute while Garnet studied the deck for any indication of hostility. Satisfied that the upper deck was clear, he motioned for the pilot to descend.

Jacobs's patrol boat closed along the hull. Grappling hooks shot out and gripped onto the bulwarks. The SEALs quickly scaled the rope ladders and spread across the deck, arms at the ready.

Garnet split his men, sending one team down to the engine room and the other through the stern superstructure, rounding up the crew. As he stepped onto the bridge, Captain Walsh stormed up to him, indignation written across his face.

'What is the meaning of this?' he demanded. 'You people aren't coastguard.'

Garnet ignored him and spoke over his portable radio. 'This is Team One. The crew quarters and wheelhouse are secure.'

'Commander Jacobs?' enquired Dover. 'Report on Team Two.'

'No sign of explosives in the tank areas so far.'

Dover turned to Compton. 'I'm going over.'

On board the *Pacific Chimera* Admiral Dover found an angry Walsh. 'I demand to know what is going on.'

'This ship has been reported to be carrying explosives,' said Dover.

'Explosives!' burst Walsh. 'Are you crazy? This is an oil tanker.'

'Team One reporting,' came Garnet's voice over Dover's radio. 'We can't find explosives in the engine room or stern.'

An hour passed, while Walsh fumed, knowing that each passing minute cost his company many thousands of dollars.

Captain Compton came over from the *Huron*. 'I hope you don't mind my dropping in to see how it's going.'

'Not well,' said Dover in exasperation. 'So far there is no sign of explosives and the crew are not acting like men on a suicide mission. I'm beginning to fear we've been conned.'

Twenty minutes later, Jacobs reported in. 'She's clean, Admiral.'

'You can bet my government will launch a protest,' said Walsh angrily. 'You had no legal cause to stop my vessel.'

'My apologies for any inconvenience,' Dover said, with honest regret. He spoke in a low tone to Compton. 'I'd hate to see the looks on everyone's faces in Washington when I notify them that they've been hoaxed.'

PITT WAS CLEARING his desk of NUMA business before flying to Elmore Egan's farm when Sandecker entered his office. It was obvious the admiral was deeply disturbed.

'Zale threw us a red herring,' Sandecker snarled. 'The *Pacific Chimera* was clean.'

Pitt looked thoughtful. 'The chances are that Zale fed Sally Morse a fake story, knowing she was about to defect.' He looked directly at Sandecker. 'I think he has another disaster up his sleeve.'

'All right,' said Sandecker. 'I'll go along with your thinking, but where does it lead?'

'I'm counting on Hiram Yaeger and Max to come up with the answer,' Pitt said as he got to his feet.

With Sandecker two steps behind, Pitt rushed into Yaeger's office. 'Hiram, the admiral and I need you to launch a new probe.'

Yaeger looked up. 'Max and I are at your disposal.'

'Check all maritime ship arrivals at major US ports for the next ten hours, with emphasis on super oil tankers.'

Max smiled bewitchingly. 'I'll be back to you in sixty seconds.'

Sandecker informed Yaeger of the recent events. 'What bothered me from the beginning was the extraordinary draught of a tanker the size of the *Pacific Chimera*,' he said. 'The bay surrounding the city of San Francisco is too shallow for a ship that size to cross. It would have been grounded long before it could have come ashore.'

'So you're considering the prospect that Zale is sending another tanker into a different port city,' Yaeger suggested.

Max's feminine form materialised on her little stage. 'I believe I have what you gentlemen were after. Of the ultra, ultra large crude carriers, one is bound for Louisiana, but her mooring terminal is a hundred miles from a major city. Another is headed for New Jersey, but she isn't due until tomorrow, and finally, a UULCC bound for Long Beach, California, is still two days out to sea. That's the lot.'

'So the whole exercise was a waste,' murmured Sandecker.

'Looks that way,' said Pitt, dejectedly. 'But why the subterfuge?'

'Did you ever consider a different type of vessel?' asked Max. 'An LNG ship could do far more damage than a UULCC.'

The revelation struck Pitt like a hammer blow. 'A liquefied natural gas tanker!'

'One blew up in Japan back in the forties with nearly the explosive power of the Hiroshima atomic bomb,' Max enlightened them.

'Did you check if any are bound for stateside ports?' asked Yaeger.

'The *Mongol Invader* from Kuwait is scheduled to dock in New York at ten thirty this morning.'

The admiral checked his watch. 'We can eliminate her. She would have docked twenty minutes ago.'

'She's running five hours late,' said Max.

Pitt and Sandecker exchanged stricken expressions.

'That has to be Zale's plan,' said Pitt. 'Feint with the *Pacific Chimera* in the west and strike from the east with the *Mongol Invader*.'

'There's not much time to stop her before she reaches Lower New York Bay and heads into the Narrows,' Max remarked.

Yaeger asked, 'Who owns her?'

'I traced her through paper companies to Cerberus.'

Yaeger grinned. 'Now, why did I think that's who you'd find?'

'LNG tankers have a much shallower draught than oil tankers,' said Sandecker. 'She could make it up the Hudson River before turning and running towards Lower Manhattan.'

'What gas volume is she carrying?' Pitt asked Max.

'Seven million five hundred and seventy thousand three hundred and thirty-three cubic feet of propane. It could conceivably produce a fireball almost two miles wide.'

'What about structural damage?' Sandecker queried Max.

'Heavy,' answered Max. 'Skyscrapers would still stand, but their interiors would be gutted. Other buildings close to the centre of the blast would be destroyed. I won't speculate on the loss of life.'

'All because Zale and the Cerberus cartel want to inflame the American public against foreign oil,' Pitt murmured angrily.

'We've got to stop that ship!' said Sandecker in a cold tone.

Pitt said slowly, 'I'll bet a month's pay Omo Kanai has his Viper group on board.'

Sandecker checked his watch again. 'We have four and a half hours before she enters the Hudson River. I'll report to Admiral Dover and have him alert his coastguard units to launch an intercept.'

'You should also call the New York State Antiterrorist Division,' suggested Max. 'They practise for just such a possibility.'

'Thank you, Max,' said Sandecker. He'd always thought Max was a strain on NUMA's budget, but he had come to realise she was worth every nickel. 'I'll see to it.'

'I'll round up Al,' said Pitt. 'Using NUMA's new tilt-wing *Aquarius* jet, we should be in New York inside an hour.'

'What do you plan to do after you get there?' enquired Max.

'Stop the *Mongol Invader* from destroying half of Manhattan. What else?' Pitt replied.

THE *MONGOL INVADER*, eight bulbous tanks rising from her hull, burrowed through choppy seas at twenty-five knots on course for New York Harbor. Her tanks were full of liquid propane that should have been refrigerated to –265°F. But on this trip the temperature had been raised until it was only twenty degrees below danger level. She was a floating bomb, with the potential to devastate the lower half of Manhattan Island.

Leaning over the railing of the starboard bridge wing, Omo Kanai stared at an overcast sky, secure in the knowledge that his Viper team could easily repel any attempt to board by Special Forces. Any force arrayed against him would find it unlikely that fifteen men who were not fanatical terrorists, but simply well-paid mercenaries, would even think of committing suicide for their employer. This was not a James Bond movie. He smiled to himself. Only those on board the ship knew about the submarine attached to the hull. Once the ship was turned towards the Manhattan shoreline, Kanai and his Viper crew would escape into deep water to avoid the ensuing fireball.

He walked back to the bridge and noted on the instrument console that twenty-knot winds were blowing from the southeast. All the better to expand the fireball, he thought.

His second-in-command, Harmon Kerry, a tough-looking customer with tattoos running up and down his arms, stepped onto the bridge. 'It won't be long now,' he said with more than a hint of pleasure. 'The Americans are in for a nasty surprise.'

'No surprise,' Kanai muttered. 'Not if they realise by now that the *Pacific Chimera* was a decoy. The five hours we were delayed cost us. We may have to face everything they can throw at us.'

The helmsman reported, 'Forty minutes until we reach the bridge.'

Kanai stared at the slowly approaching span. 'If they don't try and stop us soon, they'll never have another chance.'

ADMIRAL DOVER had flown in within fifteen minutes of Sandecker's alert. He stepped into the conference room of the coastguard station, nodding to the men and women at the table. He wasted no time on niceties. 'Have the police patrols flown over the ship?'

A police captain said, 'We have a copter on station. He reports that the tanker is running at full speed towards the harbour.'

Dover sighed. The ship had to be stopped. 'Gentlemen, you've all been briefed. If we can't turn it away, it must be sunk.'

A coastguard commander spoke. 'Sir, if we fire into the tanks, we could turn her into one immense explosion. The intercepting boats, as well as the police helicopters, could be caught in the fireball.'

'If the crew refuses to heave to, then I will have no choice but to call in navy fighters to destroy the ship with air-to-surface missiles. In that event, everyone will be warned in ample time.'

'What are our chances of boarding her, overpowering the crew and cutting off any detonation devices?' asked one of the police.

'Not good if she won't stop, and continues at full speed inside the harbour. I realise New York's Antiterrorist Response Teams are trained for just such emergencies, but I don't want to commit them yet. Any more questions?' There was no response. 'Then I suggest we launch the operation. Time is running out.'

'IT DOESN'T LOOK like any submarine I've ever seen,' Giordino remarked, staring at a sleek vessel that looked more like a luxury yacht than an undersea boat.

Pitt stood beside him on the dock at Sheepshead Bay, south of Brooklyn, admiring the *Coral Wanderer*. She was designed to operate at a depth of 1,200 feet with a range of 200 nautical miles.

A short, burly man approached Pitt with an outstretched hand.

Pitt turned to Giordino. 'Al, may I present Jimmy Flett. A good friend from times past.'

'Glad to meet you,' said Giordino. 'Dirk has often spoken of you.'

'Nothing good, I hope.' Jimmy laughed as he crushed Giordino's hand and got crushed in return.

Flett stared into Pitt's green eyes. 'What do you want with the *Coral Wanderer*? All you said over the phone was that it was a NUMA charter.'

'We intend to use her as a torpedo boat.'

'And what ship do you plan on sending to the bottom?'

'A liquefied natural gas tanker. A team of criminals are intending to run the ship aground in Manhattan, before igniting the gas.'

There were no protests. Flett said simply, 'Since the *Wanderer* doesn't carry torpedo tubes, what have you got in mind?'

Twenty minutes later, the three men had mounted a long pipe that acted as a spar and protruded thirty feet in front of the boat's bow. Two more pipes were secured along the deck. Flett fired up the engines as Giordino attached magnetic explosive canisters to the ends of the two extra spars. The one already mounted had a 100-pound plastic underwater charge bound on the end to a detonator.

The *Coral Wanderer* shot across Sheepshead Bay towards the Verrazano Bridge, cutting a course that would send her on an angle towards the LNG's midships.

'What's her top speed?' Pitt asked Flett.

'Forty-five knots on the surface. Twenty-five beneath.'

'We'll need every knot you can coax out of her when we submerge. Once the *Mongol Invader* gets into the Narrows, it'll be too difficult to blast her from the air without taking out half of Brooklyn and Staten Island.'

'Your plan had better work if the coastguard and New York's finest fail.'

NOW ON BOARD the *William Shea*, Admiral Dover opened contact with the LNG tanker. 'This is the United States Coast Guard. Please heave to immediately and prepare for boarding.'

Dover hailed again, and a third time, but there was no reply. Then abruptly a calm voice spoke. 'This is the master of the *Mongol Invader*. I have no intention of bringing this ship to a stop. You will be advised that any attempt to damage my vessel will bring dire consequences.'

There was no doubt now. The horror was real. Dover gave the order for the helicopters to land their antiterrorist teams on the open deck. At the same time, he directed the *William Shea* and her sister cutter, the *Timothy Firme*, to come alongside with their guns manned.

The first Jayhawk police copter came in low. The pilot matched the speed of the massive vessel and hovered, studying the deck. Satisfied that he had enough room for an unobstructed landing, the pilot flared out the helicopter twenty feet above the bow.

That was as far as he got.

Dover stood shocked, staring through his binoculars, as a missile tore into the helicopter, bursting it open like a firecracker in a tuna can. It hung blazing for a moment before dropping into the water, taking the police antiterrorist team with it. In seconds, it had sunk from sight.

KANAI FELT NO guilt about erasing twelve men from the earth in less than ten seconds. Nor did the flotilla of coastguard cutters and the fireboats that surrounded his ship dispirit Kanai. He felt secure, knowing they would never dare assault him with guns blazing.

With satisfaction, he observed the other helicopters pulling away, their pilots realising that they were defenceless against rocket fire. Kanai turned his attention to the two coastguard cutters approaching the tanker on opposite sides of her hull. Their intention was clear. Both opened fire simultaneously. Their 25mm Bushmaster guns seemed too minuscule to cause damage to such a monster ship.

The starboard cutter concentrated its rounds on the bulkhead of the bridge, while the cutter on the port side blasted away at the lower hull of the stern. The men manning both guns were careful not to aim anywhere close to the giant tanks of propane.

Kanai threw himself to the deck as the 25mm rounds slashed through the bridge, taking out the windows and ripping into the control console. The Viper at the helm was killed instantly. Another fell mortally wounded. Scorning the storm of shells, Kanai shouted, 'Launch surface-to-surface missiles now!'

The *Invader* was less than a mile from the Verrazano Bridge but the bow was swinging to starboard. Kanai noticed that the navigation console was a mass of jagged holes. He called down to the engine room. 'The bridge controls are shot away. Helm the ship from down there. Bring her back on course three-five-five to port.'

He crawled out on the bridge wing and saw a Viper fire a missile point-blank onto the bow of the *Timothy Firme*. It exploded against a bulwark and sent shredded steel cascading across the deck, cutting down the men manning the Bushmaster. Pieces of the gun flew in the sky like burning leaves.

On the opposite side of the *Mongol Invader* another missile bored into the funnel of the *William Shea*, heeling the ship ten degrees and sending out a huge spray of debris. A second missile slammed into the *Timothy Firme*. The explosion scattered steel splinters throughout the forward part of the ship. She lost headway and began to fall away. More savage crashes and explosions rocked both cutters until they drifted helplessly. There would be no further worry from surface ships. Kanai had achieved the tactical advantage.

DOVER CHECKED his body for wounds. He was bleeding from shrapnel cuts on his left shoulder and the side of his head. He picked his way across the shattered wheelhouse. Dead and wounded men spread across the deck of the *William Shea*. He could feel the ship slowing down. The damage below her water line was severe, and she was beginning to sink. The cutters had been sitting ducks.

Clutching the radio, Dover called in the three Air National Guard F-16C fighters that were circling a few miles out to sea.

'Blue Flight, this is Red Fleet. Attack the LNG tanker. But for God's sake, don't strike the tanks containing the propane.'

'Understood, Red Fleet,' replied the flight leader. 'Launching attack *now*.'

The Blue Flight leader sent his two wingmen in while he circled to observe the results of the strike.

Aiming his fighter arrow-straight for the machinery room beneath the big funnel of the *Invader*, the first pilot locked in his missile guidance systems. But a split second before he could fire, a surface-to-air missile blasted into his F-16 from the LNG tanker. The fighter jet burst into a thousand pieces and fell into the sea.

'Break off!' shouted the flight leader to the second aircraft.

'Too late!' broke in the pilot. 'I'm locked on—'

He spoke no more. There was no time to pull out. Another missile belched from its launcher and his plane exploded into a second fireball.

The flight leader froze. He had witnessed two of his closest friends incinerated within seconds of each other. He was too paralysed with shock to launch another attack.

Dover watched the destruction of the two aircraft in horror. The loss of the pilots was appalling, but their failure to stop the LNG tanker before she passed into the upper harbour spelled disaster.

'God help us,' Dover muttered.

'THAT TANKER LOOKS like a line of pregnant women lying on their backs in a spa,' said Jimmy Flett, as he stood at the console helm of the *Coral Wanderer* and closed on the *Mongol Invader*.

'She's even deadlier than she is ugly,' Giordino muttered, eyeing the wreckage.

'She's about a thousand yards from the bridge,' judged Flett. 'Just time for us to submerge and go for her screws and rudders.'

'We'll only get one pass,' said Giordino.

Pitt grinned. 'Then we'll just have to get it right first time.'

He was determined to prevent the *Mongol Invader* from entering the upper harbour, even if it meant putting their lives on the line. He knew with calculated certainty that Omo Kanai was on board. There was a score to settle and he felt a growing wave of rage.

Two hundred yards off the tanker, Flett switched on the ballast tank pumps and the luxury submarine slipped beneath the water as smoothly as if guided by a giant hand. Once it was submerged, Flett picked up speed. From now on there could be no room for error.

Pitt made his way forward to the bow and its viewing port. He picked up a phone. 'Are we connected?'

'We have you on the speaker,' answered Giordino.

Flett read off the numbers. 'A hundred and fifty yards and closing.'

Three agonising minutes dragged by. 'One hundred yards,' Flett notified Pitt.

Pitt could hear the throb of the *Mongol Invader*'s engines and then her plates materialised out of the green gloom. It was an eerie sight to watch the great hull sweep over the submarine.

'We've got her!' Pitt said sharply. He was an extension of Flett's eyes. Only he could make the split-second judgment call when the great bronze screws came into sight. He lay down on the deck with his face less than an inch from the viewing port, eyes straining to see the magnetic explosive charge on the end of the spar protruding from the bow of the *Wanderer*.

'Ready, Jimmy?'

'Say the word,' Flett replied, his voice solid as a stone.

'Now!' Pitt yelled.

Flett reacted with the speed of lightning, shoving the throttles forward until he felt a jar from the front of the boat and then whipping them into reverse. Pitt could only watch as the magnetic charge gripped the steel plates of the tanker's hull an instant before Flett went into reverse.

The massive propellers came like an out-of-control windmill, beating the water of the bay into sparkling foam. On the control bridge, Giordino and Flett were certain that the mighty blades would beat the luxury boat into splinters and their bodies along with it. But in the final seconds, the *Coral Wanderer*'s diesels roared and she leapt astern as the tanker's propellers flailed past no more than two feet from the bow.

Thirty seconds later, the yacht came back on a smoother keel and the throb of the *Mongol Invader* began to fade.

'Now is as good a time as any, Al,' said Pitt.

Giordino pressed a small remote control. A loud thud sounded, followed by a pressure wave that struck the *Coral Wanderer* with the force of a twenty-foot swell.

'Bring her up, Jimmy,' said Pitt. 'Let's see if we did any good.'

Omo Kanai was stunned as the *Mongol Invader* began its unscheduled turn. He shouted down to the engine room, 'Get back on course! Can't you see we've come around!'

'We've lost our starboard screw,' replied the chief engineer. 'We ain't going nowhere.'

Kanai refused to accept defeat. 'We're too close to give up. Once under the bridge, no one can stop us.'

'And I'm telling you, the sooner we get off this gas can, the better.'

Kanai stared up at the great bridge. Less than a few hundred feet had separated success and failure. His eyes swept the water and saw what looked like a private yacht. Then he stared with sudden understanding and anger as the yacht slipped beneath the waves.

'OK, Jimmy,' Pitt said to the submarine yacht's skipper. 'We turned her. Now let's put those big balls of gas on the bottom.'

The instant the water closed over the *Coral Wanderer*, Flett dived at full speed and hung a sharp turn to starboard. An audible thump rocked the luxury submarine as a missile exploded where they would have been if not for Flett's quick manoeuvre.

Pitt returned to the observation view port in the bow. The Viper crew must be preparing to escape, he thought. But where? Then the mammoth hull burst across the view port. 'We're on her, Jimmy.'

Flett expertly turned parallel to the tanker. Then he increased speed as they moved towards the section of the stern that contained the engine room. Using the reverse thrusters he turned until the charge on the end of the second spar was pointing directly against the *Invader*'s plates. The magnetic charge clunked against the hull, and the luxury sub quickly backed away.

When they reached a safe zone, Giordino pushed the detonator switch. Another dull boom raced through the water as the *Wanderer* shook off the pressure wave.

Pitt entered the control cabin. 'Nice work, Jimmy.'

Flett smiled. 'Dare we risk surfacing to see our handiwork?'

'Not yet. There's something I'd like to explore first.'

The wheelhouse gave a lurch as the second charge blew a second gaping void in the tanker's hull. The blast sealed the ship's fate. The *Mongol Invader* was going to the bottom of the bay.

Kanai glanced around the bridge, which looked as if it had been ransacked by a frenzied mob. Holding a towel to his bleeding forehead, he walked over to a cabinet, opened the door and stared at a panel of switches. He set the timer for twenty minutes, then engaged the detonation switch to the ON position.

Harmon Kerry stepped off the ship's outside stairway. Blood oozed from half a dozen wounds, but he seemed not to notice.

'Are the men clear?' Kanai asked.

'As far as I know, they've all left their posts for the escape sub.'

'There is nothing more to be accomplished here.'

Kanai took one last look at the panel with the timer. The numbers on the digital clock were ticking down towards detonation. At least the mission wasn't a total failure. Some death and damage was better than none at all, he thought perversely.

By the time they reached the hatch of the escape sub, they were wading in water. Kanai was the last man to drop through the hatch. Six men, three of them wounded, sat in the cabin—all that remained of the entire Viper team.

Above them they could hear the *Mongol Invader* groaning as her bow lifted into the air. She was only minutes away from sliding onto the bottom.

Kanai was about to engage the motors when, through the forward view port, he saw a strange craft approaching out of the murky water. He realised it was the vessel he'd noticed earlier slipping beneath the waves. He could see a long metal spar sticking out from the bow. Too late he discovered the mysterious boat's purpose.

It surged forward until its spar rammed into the mechanism holding the sub to the bottom of the tanker's hull, jamming the release pins. Kanai's face turned as rigid as a plaster death mask. Frantically, he worked the handle of the release mechanism. It failed to respond.

'Good God, man, hurry!' shouted the chief engineer.

While yanking on the handle with every ounce of his strength, Kanai stared out at the other sub. To his horror, he recognised the man sitting inside the viewing port. 'Pitt!' he gasped.

PITT STARED BACK at Kanai with morbid curiosity. There was a rumble from the sinking tanker as her stern struck the bottom. Slowly, the rest of her hull began to settle.

The expression of horror on Kanai's face switched to one of black fury. He shook his fist at Pitt as the great hull above began to press the sub into the bottom silt. Pitt spread his lips into a wide smile and waved bye-bye. The escape sub vanished in a swirl of muddy water, interred for eternity under the wreck of the *Mongol Invader*.

Kanai died, never knowing that the explosive charges had failed to erupt under the monstrous propane tanks. He died not knowing that a shell fired from the bow guns of the *Timothy Firme* had sliced through the wire leading to the detonators.

The heroic fight by the coastguards had not been in vain.

PART FIVE: FULL CIRCLE
Amiens, France

August 12, 2003. 'Dr Hereoux,' said St Julien Perlmutter, enveloping the Frenchman's slim hand with his great fleshy paw. 'It is an honour to finally meet the esteemed president of the Society of Jules Verne.'

'The honour is mine, to have such a distinguished historian in Mr Verne's home.'

Hereoux showed Perlmutter into a large library containing more than 10,000 books. 'Here is everything Jules Verne ever wrote.'

Perlmutter walked over to a section of manuscripts. 'His unpublished material?'

'You're quite astute. Yes, those are manuscripts he either did not finish or did not believe worthy of publishing.' Hereoux motioned to a couch. 'Please sit down. Tell me, how can I help you?'

Perlmutter lowered his great bulk onto the couch. 'I would like to dig into Verne's research on Captain Nemo and the *Nautilus*.'

'Nemo and his submarine were Verne's greatest creations.'

'Suppose they were not merely creations?' said Perlmutter. 'I have a friend who thinks that Verne used a real-life model.'

A hint of displeasure crossed Hereoux's face. 'You're not the only one who has come here with such a ridiculous proposal.'

'Ridiculous? Yes, but intriguing nonetheless.'

'How can I help you?'

'Allow me to search through these archives.'

Hereoux relaxed. 'Please, consider the library yours.'

'One more request. May I have my chauffeur assist me? I can't climb ladders any more to reach books on the higher shelves.'

'Of course. I will leave you to it. If you have any questions, I'll be in my office upstairs.'

'There is one question. Who categorised the books on the shelves?'

Hereoux smiled. 'Why, Mr Verne. Every book and manuscript and file is set exactly where he left it when he died.'

PERLMUTTER'S CHAUFFEUR, Hugo Mulholland, was a dour fellow, who gazed from sad eyes under a bald head. 'Have you figured out yet where to start?' he asked. 'You've been staring at the books for the past hour.'

'Patience, Hugo,' Perlmutter replied. 'What we're searching for does not lie in an obvious spot, or other researchers would have discovered it long ago.'

Hugo gazed at the thousands of books. 'So which needle in the haystack holds the key?'

'We can eliminate the books and the manuscripts. They will have already been studied by anyone who collects Verne lore. The notebooks, too, have all been pored over by Verne researchers.'

'Sounds to me like you've eliminated every piece of paper.'

'Exactly!' Perlmutter boomed. 'We're looking for a hiding place that is not part of the books and bookshelves.'

'A secret compartment in a piece of furniture or a picture?'

'Furniture and pictures are not permanent. They can be moved or replaced. Think of something that remains constant.'

Mulholland's face brightened. 'The floor!'

'Pull up the rugs,' instructed Perlmutter. 'Examine the seams between the boards. Look for notches where they have been prised up before.'

Mulholland was on his knees for nearly half an hour, scrutinising every board. Suddenly he pulled a dime from his pocket, slipped it between two boards and prised one up. 'Eureka!' he exclaimed.

Perlmutter lay down on the floor and looked beneath the board. There was a leather pouch inside. He gently lifted it out and, with Mulholland's assistance, rose to his feet and sank into the sofa again.

Almost reverently, he untied a small velvet cord from around the pouch and removed a small notebook. He read aloud, translating the French wording engraved on the leather jacket. '"Investigation of the ingenious Captain Amherst."'

Perlmutter began reading the handwritten words less than an eighth of an inch high. A master of six languages, he had no problem in comprehending Verne's narrative about a British scientific mastermind by the name of Cameron Amherst. Though his eyes read the words, his mind conjured up the images of this extraordinary man whom Verne had known and whose life he chronicled.

Two hours later, he leaned back with the expression of a man who has just proposed to the woman he loves and been accepted.

'Find anything of interest?' asked Mulholland.

'Did you notice the ribbon around the pouch?'

Mulholland nodded. 'Couldn't be more than ten years old. If Verne was the last to handle the pouch, the ribbon would have rotted away long ago.'

'Which leads to the conclusion that Dr Hereoux learned Verne's secret a long time ago.'

'What secret is that?'

Perlmutter's voice was soft. 'Pitt was right.'

EIGHT HOURS INTO the congressional hearing, Curtis Merlin Zale was fidgeting nervously, no longer the supremely confident man who had faced Congresswoman Smith and her committee members earlier. Word from Omo Kanai and reports of a disaster in New York should have reached him hours earlier.

Loren was tired. Her aides had informed her that no demolition charges had been found on the *Pacific Chimera*. Two hours later she was alerted to the mission to stop the *Mongol Invader*. She had heard nothing since two o'clock.

Loren knew Zale was tiring, too, and she forced patience on herself. She was waiting, like a lioness in ambush, for the right moment to strike with the information given by Sally Morse. She pulled the papers containing the questions she had prepared from her briefcase.

At that moment, she noticed the faces in the audience suddenly stare behind her. Then a hand touched her shoulder. She turned and found herself gazing up into the face of Dirk Pitt. He looked exhausted, as if he had just climbed a mountain.

'Dirk!' she whispered. 'What are you doing here?'

He didn't look at her as he answered, but stared at Zale and spoke in a voice that carried across the room through her microphone. 'We stopped the liquefied natural gas tanker from blowing up New York Harbor. The ship now rests on the bottom of the sea. Please inform Mr Zale that his entire Viper team went down with the ship and it is now safe for Ms Sally Morse, the CEO of Yukon Oil, to testify before your committee without fear of reprisal.'

Then Pitt exited the chamber.

A vast load was suddenly lifted from Loren's shoulders. 'Ladies and gentlemen, it is getting late and I would like to adjourn this hearing until nine o'clock tomorrow, when Ms Morse will supply the names of everyone who has accepted bribes from Mr Zale. I promise you, the trail of corruption will stun the government and shock the public as no scandal ever has in the past.'

The gallery went mad. Reporters from the major news media surged around Zale and rushed after Loren, but Pitt was waiting at the door and hustled her away.

Zale sat at the table, inundated by a sea of journalists and flashing cameras, like a man in a nightmare. Finally, he rose unsteadily and fought his way through the turmoil. His chauffeur drove him to the Cerberus headquarters and then watched as Zale walked like an elderly senior citizen through the lobby and entered the elevator to his luxurious office.

No man was more isolated from reality. He had no close friends, no family. Omo Kanai was dead. Zale was alone. As he sat behind his desk, he weighed his future and found it ominously dark. It was inevitable that he would end up in prison. His wealth would be taken away by an avalanche of lawsuits. His loyal team of Vipers no longer stood ready to eliminate those who would testify against him. He could never escape. A man of his stature was too easy to track down.

He poured himself a shot of fifty-year-old whisky and sipped it as he opened a side drawer of his desk. From inside an antique snuff-box he took two pills. He downed a final drink, placed the pills under his tongue and relaxed in the big leather chair.

They found Curtis Merlin Zale dead the next morning, his desk clean of papers. There was no note.

SANDECKER WAS IN ONE of his good moods, puffing contentedly on a big cigar. He shook Pitt's hand vigorously. 'Great job. You blew half the stern off the ship without endangering the propane tanks.'

'We were lucky it worked,' said Pitt modestly.

Rudi Gunn also shook Pitt's hand. 'You left us with quite a mess to clean up, but we're already working out contracts with salvage companies.'

'You'd better go on home,' said Sandecker charitably. 'Then take a few days off for your research project on Elmore Egan.'

'Which reminds me,' Gunn said, 'Hiram Yaeger wants to see you.'

Pitt went to the computer floor of NUMA and found Yaeger sitting in a small storeroom, staring at Egan's leather briefcase. As Pitt entered he pointed to it.

'Good timing. It should begin filling in another thirty seconds.'

'Remind me of the timetable?' said Pitt.

'Every inflow takes place twenty-eight hours after the last.'

'Any idea why it's always twenty-eight hours?'

'Max is working on it,' answered Yaeger, closing a heavy steel door. 'This is a secure area. Radio waves, microwaves, sound, light—nothing can penetrate these walls.' Yaeger began to count down with his index finger. 'Now!' he exclaimed.

Before Pitt's eyes, the interior of Egan's case began filling with oil as if poured by an unseen hand. 'It has to be some kind of trick.'

'No trick,' said Yaeger. 'Egan's case is a receiver.'

'I'm drawing a blank,' said Pitt, confused.

Yaeger opened the heavy steel door and led the way back to his sophisticated computer system. 'Max,' he said, 'tell Dirk what we've discovered.'

'Quantum teleportation,' Max said.

Pitt stared at Max. 'That's not possible. Teleportation is beyond the realm of current physics.'

'That's what I thought when I began my analysis. But it's a fact. The oil that appears in the case is originally placed in a chamber somewhere that measures every atom and molecule. The oil is then altered to a quantum state that is sent and reconstructed in the receiver, according to the measurements from the sending chamber.'

'Do you know what you're saying?' said Pitt, totally incredulous.

'Indeed we do,' said Max confidently. 'Though it presents an incredible scientific breakthrough, don't get your hopes up. There is no way a human could be teleported any time in the future. Compared with a human, the molecular make-up of oil is far less complicated.'

Pitt sat down. 'It seems fantastic that Dr Egan created a revolutionary engine in the same time span that he designed a working teleporter. And he did it alone in a hidden lab . . . the location of which we've yet to ferret out.'

'I hope you find it,' said Yaeger. 'The significance of Egan's discovery has mind-boggling possibilities. Substances with basic molecular structures, such as oil, coal, iron or copper ore, could be transported without the use of ships, trains and trucks. His teleportation system can rewrite the entire world of product transportation.'

Pitt said, 'Max, do you have enough data from Dr Egan's case to re-create a teleporter device?'

Max shook her head. 'No, I'm sorry to say. Though I have Dr Egan's receiving chamber as a model, the primary part of the system lies with the sending unit.'

Yaeger laid a hand on Pitt's shoulder. 'I wish Max and I could have given you a more detailed picture.'

'You both did a remarkable job, and I'm grateful,' said Pitt sincerely. 'Now it's my turn to supply the answers.'

PITT STOPPED BY his office to clear his desk, read his mail and answer phone messages, After half an hour he decided to call it a day. At that moment, his phone rang.

'Dirk!' thundered St Julien Perlmutter's voice.

'St Julien. Where are you?'

'In Amiens, France, studying a notebook hidden by Jules Verne almost a hundred years ago.'

'Did it supply you with answers?' asked Pitt, his curiosity kindled.

'You were on the right track. Captain Nemo truly existed, except his real name was Cameron Amherst. Verne met Amherst on a voyage across the Atlantic. It was Amherst who regaled Verne with stories of an underwater vessel capable of going anywhere beneath the oceans. He described in detail the revolutionary propulsion system he had devised to power his submarine.

'Verne loved the sea and owned several yachts. On a voyage off Denmark a great whalelike vessel rose out of the sea and drifted alongside Verne's sailing boat. Captain Amherst hailed him from a forward hatch tower, inviting the writer to come aboard.'

'So the *Nautilus* did exist.'

'Verne stayed on board for nearly two weeks. Ample time for him to study every inch of the vessel, which he exactingly recorded in his book. A few years later, he produced *Twenty Thousand Leagues under the Sea.*'

'What happened to Amherst?'

'According to Verne's notebook, a messenger came to his house in 1895 and gave him a letter from Amherst saying that he had found an underwater cavern on the Hudson River in New York, which would serve as a tomb for him and the *Nautilus.*'

Pitt stiffened, unable to suppress a shout of euphoria. 'The Hudson River?'

'That's what was written in the notebook.'

'St Julien.'

'Yes.'

'I love you to death.'

Perlmutter gave out a chuckle. 'My dear boy, with my colossal body, you could never get near enough to do that.'

THE EARLY-MORNING mist hung over the blue water of the river just as it had nearly 1,000 years ago when the Norsemen arrived. It curled around the NUMA work boat that cruised along the shore beneath the rocky cliffs. The speed was kept to four knots as it dragged the submerged sensor in its wake. Signals from the sensor were sent into the recording unit of the side-scan sonar, and Giordino stared intently at the display of the bottom of the river.

Kelly stood at the helm, steering cautiously, while Pitt peered at the cliffs through wide-angle binoculars.

'Another two hundred yards before we pass beneath Dad's farm,' announced Kelly.

'Any readings, Al?' Pitt asked through the windshield.

'Rocks and silt,' Giordino answered briefly. 'Silt and rocks.'

'Keep an eye out for any indication of a rock slide.'

'If Cameron took his sub inside the cliffs, there must have been an underwater cavity.'

'The question is whether it still exists,' said Pitt.

'One hundred yards,' warned Kelly.

Pitt saw the roofs of Egan's house above. He carefully studied the cliff. 'I see signs of a fall,' he said, pointing at a scattered mass of rock.

Kelly looked at the fathometer. 'The bottom drops off steeply before sloping towards the middle of the river.'

'I have something,' said Pitt casually. 'Looks like man-made markings in the rock.'

'No cave or tunnel from the sonar,' Giordino droned.

Pitt jumped down onto the work deck. 'Let's pull in the sensor and anchor the boat just offshore.'

'You think we should dive before finding a target?' asked Giordino.

'We're directly below Dr Egan's study. If there's a hidden cavern, it has to be around here.'

Kelly expertly turned the boat in a tight circle and shut down the throttle. 'May I come, too?'

'Let us go first. If we find something, I'll surface and wave you in. We'll dive first and check out the landscape.'

The water was as transparent as glass for thirty feet before it faded into a gloom turned green with clouds of minuscule algae. The current pulled at Pitt and Giordino, and they clutched the rocks, pulling their bodies over the moss-coated surfaces.

They came up for air and decided to split the search. Pitt would head upriver and Giordino down. Suddenly, Pitt swam over an open stretch free of the rocks. The bottom was smooth and flat with a channel cut through the rubble, leading towards the shore where the rock slide had fallen into the water. He dived down to look for an opening and found a ledge free of growth that had strange chiselled markings in the hard surface. He surfaced for air, then dived again.

A dark tunnel beckoned him. The skin on the nape of his neck tingled. Another breath on the surface and he entered the opening cautiously. Once inside, he could see that the burrow flared out ten feet ahead. That was as far as he decided to go. He returned to the surface and yelled, 'I found a way inside!'

In less than three minutes, Kelly and Giordino were stroking against the current beside him. Pitt motioned for them to follow him through the narrow tunnel. Finally, just when Kelly feared she only had a few seconds left before opening her mouth and taking in a mouthful of water, the cavity fanned out and she gripped Pitt's ankle, using his momentum to propel her to the surface.

Their heads came free of the water and they found themselves in an immense cavern, its roof towering 200 feet above their heads. Pitt gazed up in wonder at the head of a serpent with bared fangs.

THE GRACEFULLY carved serpent head stared sightlessly at the water flowing into the cavern, as if searching for a distant shore. On an enormous ledge four feet above the water, six wooden boats sat side by side. The serpent rose on the bow post of the largest boat, nearest the rim of the ledge.

The boats were built entirely of oak, the longest stretching more than sixty feet. From the water, the divers could look up at the keels and the broad, symmetrically arched hulls. Oars still protruded through small ports as if waiting for a command to row.

'They're Viking,' Kelly murmured in awe. 'They've been here all the time and nobody knew.'

'Your father knew,' said Pitt. 'He knew from the Viking inscriptions that they had settled on the cliffs above the Hudson River, which led him to the discovery of the tunnel leading down to the cavern from above.'

'They're well preserved,' Giordino observed.

'Let's take a closer look,' Pitt said.

After removing their fins, face masks and weight belts, they climbed a rock-chiselled stairway to the top of the ledge and mounted boarding ramps that ran from the rock to the largest ship. The ramps were sound and obviously put there by Dr Egan.

The light was dim, but they recognised the objects scattered on the floorboards. What looked like a body was wrapped in a burial shroud. Around it, a treasure trove of artefacts had been dumped in disarray. Amber necklaces, gold and silver brooches, silver-and-bronze bracelets lay in piles inside elaborately carved wooden boxes.

Bronze dishes and Oriental incense burners were also lying about.

'My guess is this is Bjarne Sigvatson,' said Pitt.

'He must have been quite a warrior to have accumulated this much wealth,' Giordino muttered, gazing raptly at the treasures.

'From reading Dad's research notebooks,' said Kelly, 'I had the impression important chieftains were sent to Valhalla after a glorious death, along with all their worldly goods and chattels, which included their horses, other animals and their servants. He should also have his battle-axe, sword and shield. I see none of these.'

'The burial was a rush job,' agreed Giordino.

Pitt motioned towards the boarding ramp. 'Let's have a look at the other boats.'

To Kelly's horror, the adjacent boats were strewn with bones. Few skeletons were intact. Most looked as though they had been hacked to pieces. Pitt knelt and studied a skull with a jagged gash in the top of the cranium. 'There must have been a terrible massacre.'

Giordino removed an arrow from a pile of bones and held it up. 'This says Indians.'

'It lends credibility to the legend Dr Wednesday told of the Indians slaughtering all the Vikings in the settlement.'

Kelly looked at Pitt. 'Then the Norse settlement . . .'

'Was located on your father's farm,' Pitt finished. 'He must have found artefacts and was influenced to launch his research project.'

'But why did he keep it a secret?'

'He must have had a good reason,' said Giordino. 'He didn't want an army of archaeologists and reporters invading his privacy during his experiments.'

Pitt spotted a stairway hacked into the rock that led up into a tunnel. He climbed the first four steps with his hand trailing along one wall for support, when his fingers met something that felt like an electrical switch. Suddenly, the entire cavern was illuminated by bright fluorescent lights set into the rock walls.

'Now we can see what we're doing,' said Kelly.

'I know another reason why your father kept this place a secret,' Pitt said deliberately.

Giordino saw the direction in which Pitt's eyes were aimed.

A long, cylindrical iron vessel was moored to a dock along the far side of the cavern. The hull was covered with a thin coating of rust. A small hatch tower was set aft of the forward bow. The vessel had not been visible in the darkened cavern interior until Pitt had turned on the lights.

'That,' said Pitt, with triumph in his voice, 'is the *Nautilus*.'

At the foot of the dock was a pile of stones stacked in the shape of a sarcophagus. Letters carved on a wooden plaque read:

Here lie the mortal remains of Captain Cameron Amherst.
Made famous by the writings of Jules Verne
as the immortal Captain Nemo.

Giordino, who'd gone to explore a side cave, approached. 'I found the source of Dr Egan's electrical energy. There are three portable generating units in there, connected to enough batteries to power a small town.' He pointed down at the dock and the series of electrical cables running through the hatch of the submarine. 'Ten to one he used the interior for his laboratory.'

Giordino walked over to an electrical panel mounted above the dock and pressed a pair of switches. The interior of the vessel was instantly bathed in light that beamed through a series of ports along the roof.

Pitt turned to Kelly. 'Ladies first.'

She found it difficult to take the first step. It seemed to her that she was entering a house of ghosts. Finally, with a great force of will, she entered the hatch and climbed down the ladder.

Pitt and Giordino joined her. In front of them was a door. Pitt opened it and they walked through an ornately furnished dining hall. At the far end another door led into a library, whose shelves Pitt guessed contained more than 5,000 books. He studied the titles on the spines. One side held books on engineering and science. The opposite shelves were stacked with the classics.

The next compartment stretched more than thirty feet. This area, Pitt was certain, was the grand saloon that Verne had described as filled with art treasures. But Elmore Egan had transformed it into a workshop and a chemistry laboratory. The room was filled with counters holding a maze of chemical apparatus, machinery, including a lathe and a drill press, and computer stations with an array of printers and scanners.

Kelly lingered in the laboratory, soaking up her father's presence while Pitt and Giordino entered the next compartment. This section of the *Nautilus* had once served as Captain Amherst's private cabin. Egan had converted it into his think tank. Blueprints and drawings were stacked around a large drafting table.

'Keep going,' said Pitt. 'I want to see his teleportation chamber.'

They walked through a watertight bulkhead into a compartment that had once held the submarine's air tanks. Pitt smiled when he saw a fifty-five-gallon drum marked Slick 66. It was connected to a timing device and a series of tubes, which were themselves connected to a round receptacle on the floor. 'Now we know where the oil comes from that keeps filling up Egan's case.'

'It's amazing that it actually works,' said Giordino.

'As crude as it appears, you're looking at a scientific achievement that will for ever alter the transportation of the future.'

Pitt and Giordino retraced their steps and Kelly followed the two men as they made their way aft in search of the engine room. They passed through a galley into the crew's quarters, where Elmore had stored the treasures that had once adorned the main saloon. Canvases by Leonardo da Vinci, Titian, Raphael and others were stacked in rows. Sculptures in bronze and marble stood in closets. Then there were the treasures that Amherst had salvaged from ancient shipwrecks: gold and silver bars, boxes filled with coins and gemstones. The value of the collection was beyond comprehension.

Giordino took a handful of gold coins. 'If there was ever a question as to how Dr Elmore financed his experiments, what we see here tells it all.'

After walking through another bulkhead, they found themselves in the *Nautilus*'s engine room. The maze of pipes, tanks and strange-looking mechanisms was a plumber's nightmare. A huge gear system with meshing steel teeth dominated the aft end of the room.

Pitt inspected the great engine from every angle. 'I've researched hundreds of marine engines but I've never seen anything that matches this. My best guess is that it's a combination of massive electrical energy and a rudimentary form of magnetohydrodynamics.'

'So Egan used Amherst's engine as a base for his own designs.'

'It must have proved an inspiration for him.'

Kelly approached. 'I'd like to find the passage Dad must have discovered to get back and forth between here and the house.'

Pitt nodded and glanced at Giordino. 'We should contact the admiral and report what we've found here.'

Five minutes, no more, was all it took to climb through the passage leading up to the top of the cliffs. Pitt felt a strange sensation, knowing the Vikings had passed this same way 1,000 years earlier.

Josh Thomas was sitting in Egan's study when he froze in fright. The rug in the centre of the room suddenly rose from the floor. A trap door beneath swung open and Pitt's head popped up.

'Sorry to intrude,' said Pitt. 'But I just happened to be passing.'

PART SIX: GHOST FROM THE PAST
Washington, DC

August 16, 2003. Pitt helped himself to a cup of coffee brewed by Sally Morse. He wanted to remain in bed for the morning, but Sally and Kelly were leaving. After testifying before Loren's congressional committee, Sally was released to resume her duties as chairwoman of Yukon Oil.

Kelly breezed into the kitchen, zipping up her travel bag. 'Sally was kind enough to offer me a lift in her private jet to the airfield near Dad's farm.'

'What are your plans?' Pitt asked.

'I'm setting up a philanthropic foundation in Dad's name. Then I shall donate the art treasures to museums.'

'And the hoard of silver and gold?'

'Some of it goes to finance the Elmore Egan Science Laboratory, which will be set up by Josh Thomas, who plans to recruit the finest young minds in the country. The rest will go to charities.'

Pitt carried their luggage down to the waiting limo.

Sally hugged him. 'It was a privilege knowing you, Dirk Pitt.'

'Goodbye, Sally.'

Kelly kissed him full on the mouth. 'When will I see you again?'

'Not for a while. Admiral Sandecker intends to keep me busy.'

Pitt stood there waving until the limo turned towards the entry gate, then he closed the hangar door and went back to bed.

WHEN LOREN STOPPED by to spend the weekend with Pitt, she found him leaning under the hood of the 1938 green Packard town car. She looked tired after another long day of hearings into the Zale scandal, which had brought the entire government to a screeching halt. 'Hi, big man. What are you up to?'

'These old carburettors were built to use leaded gas. The new unleaded variety has all sorts of weird chemicals that eat hell out of the guts inside. Whenever I drive the old cars, I have to overhaul the carburettors or they gum up.'

'What would you like for dinner?'

'Sure you don't want to dine out?'

'The news media is in a feeding frenzy over the scandal. I'm still considered fair game. The woman who does my hair drove me here in her husband's pick-up truck, with me sitting on the floor.'

'How lucky you are to be so popular.'

Loren made a sour face. 'How about pasta with spinach and prosciutto?'

'It's a date.'

She called down to him an hour later that dinner was ready. After he cleaned up, he entered the kitchen and peered into the pot of boiling pasta.

'It has a nice aroma for pure pasta.'

'It should. I poured half a bottle of chardonnay into it.'

'Then we don't require predinner cocktails.'

They enjoyed the casual dinner, trading sarcasms. It was a regular routine.

'Are your hearings about over?' he asked.

'Tuesday is the final day. From then on, my job is done.'

'You were lucky Sally walked through the door.'

Loren nodded. 'If not for her, Zale would still be causing mayhem. His suicide solved a multitude of problems.'

'What does Justice have in store for his cronies in crime?'

'The Cerberus cartel members will be indicted. The Justice Department is working overtime to build cases against the bureaucrats and politicians who were known to have taken bribes. The consequences of this scandal will be felt for a long time.'

Pitt stared into his wine. 'So where do *we* go from here?'

She touched his hand lightly with her fingers. 'We go on as before.'

'You in Congress and me under the sea,' he said slowly. 'So much for my illusion of becoming a grandfather.'

'It hasn't been easy competing with a ghost.'

'Summer?' He said the name as if he were seeing something far in the distance.

'You've never quite got over her.'

'I thought I did, once.'

'Maeve.'

'When Summer was lost in the sea and Maeve died in my arms, it left an emptiness inside me.' He shook away the memories like a dog shaking away water. 'I'm too sentimental for my own good. I have a wonderful woman and I don't appreciate her the way I should.'

At that moment, Pitt's door buzzer sounded. He peered into the monitor of the security camera. The image of a young man and young woman filled the screen. They were standing at the door beside a pile of luggage.

'Looks like they've come to stay,' Loren said sardonically. 'I'll run down and get rid of them.'

Pitt was taking a sip of wine when Loren's voice came over the intercom. 'Dirk, I think you should come down.'

There was something in the tone of her voice that struck him as peculiar, almost as if she was hesitant to speak. He dropped down the spiral staircase and walked past his collector cars to the entrance door of the hangar.

He found Loren talking to the young couple. The man was a good inch taller than Pitt. Their build and weight seemed nearly identical. The eyes were also a mesmeric opaline green. Pitt gazed at the man's face and stiffened. It was as if he was looking into a mirror that reflected himself when he was twenty-five years younger.

He forced his attention to the woman and his heart increased its beat. She was beautiful, tall and lithe with flaming red hair. She stared back at Pitt through pearl-grey eyes. Memories flooded back.

'Mr Pitt.' The young man spoke in a deep voice. 'My sister and I have waited twenty-three years to meet you.'

'Now that you've found me, how can I help you?' Pitt asked.

'Mother was right. We do look alike.'

'Your mother?'

'Her name was Summer Moran. Our grandfather was Frederick Moran.'

Pitt felt as if a vice were crushing his heart. 'She and her father died in an underwater earthquake off Hawaii many years ago.'

The young woman shook her head. 'Mother survived, but she was critically injured. She was confined to bed for the rest of her life.'

'I can't believe it. I lost her in the sea when she swam back to save her father.'

'Believe me, sir,' said the young lady. 'Mother was saved by my grandfather's men and rushed to hospital in Honolulu. Over a year later, she returned to her family home on the island of Kauai. Fortunately, Grandfather left her a substantial estate.'

'Were you and your brother born before her injuries?' asked Loren.

The woman shook her head. 'She gave birth to us in the hospital a week shy of nine months later.'

'You're twins?' Loren gasped.

'My brother looks like my father. I took after my mother.'

'She never tried to contact me?' Pitt asked grievously.

'She wanted you to remember her as she was.'

Confusion swept over Pitt. 'God, if I had only known.' Summer still haunted his dreams. 'If she's still alive, where is she?'

'Mother died last month,' answered the young man. 'She willed herself to live until my sister and I graduated from college. Only then did she tell us about you. Her last wish was that we meet.'

'And why was that?' Pitt asked, though he was sure of the answer.

'I was named after Mother,' said the young woman. 'My name is Summer, too.'

The man smiled. 'She named me after my father—Dirk Pitt.'

Discovering that Summer had borne him a son and daughter, and then raised them without his knowledge all these years, tore at Pitt's heart. He embraced them. 'You must forgive me. Suddenly discovering that I have two lovely grown children comes as no small surprise.'

'You don't know how happy we are to find you, Father,' said Summer.

Tears came to everyone's eyes. Then Pitt smiled broadly. 'I prefer you call me Dad.'

'You don't mind if we stay here?' asked Summer innocently.

'Is there a dome on the Capitol?' He pointed at the big Pullman car. 'You have your choice of four staterooms. As soon as you settle in, come upstairs. We have a lot of catching up to do.'

The young people stared in astonishment at the collection of classic vehicles. Dirk gazed at a big orange-and-brown car. 'I've loved old automobiles since I was a little boy.'

'A chip off the old block,' said Loren.

Pitt was touched. 'Ever drive a Duesenberg?'

'Oh, no, never.'

Pitt put his arm round his son and said proudly. 'You will, my boy. You will.'

CLIVE CUSSLER

Author, adventurer and classic car collector Clive Cussler has much in common with his fictional hero, Dirk Pitt. He is an authority on underwater exploration, and in 1979 he founded the National Underwater and Marine Agency (NUMA), a non-profit organisation dedicated to preserving maritime and naval history. NUMA, named after the organisation in Cussler's novels, has so far discovered more than sixty significant underwater wreck sites, including that of the *Hunley*, a Confederate submarine that disappeared in 1865, and whose eventual discovery in 1995 has been described as 'the historical find of the century'.

Further blurring the line between author and character, Cussler has made a cameo appearance in all his Dirk Pitt novels since *Dragon*. 'When Pitt and I meet, it's always like the name is familiar, but I can't place the face. I did it originally as a joke, now it's like Hitchcock—I appear in every book! It's fun to do things other authors don't do.'

Like Dirk, who was named after the first of Cussler's three children, the author has a keen interest in classic cars, and owns a collection of more than eighty-five of them. 'But my warehouse is almost full, so I'm not really actively searching like I used to'. He also shares his hero's sense of adventure, cycling to LA in celebration of his fiftieth birthday and bungee jumping on his sixtieth. His plans for his seventieth? 'I'm skydiving. First time'.

Sales of Clive Cussler's books have now exceeded 120 million copies worldwide. He is a fellow of both the Explorers Club of New York and the Royal Geographic Society in London, and has been awarded a doctorate by the State University of New York in recognition of his nonfiction work, *The Sea Hunters,* which explores the world of undersea adventure. He has been married to Barbara Knight for more than forty-five years, and they divide their time between the mountains of Colorado and the deserts of Arizona.

WITHOUT FAIL. Original full-length edition © 2002 by Lee Child. US condensed edition © The Reader's Digest Association Inc, 2002. British condensed edition © The Reader's Digest Association Limited, 2002.

GALLOWS THIEF. Original full-length edition © 2001 by Bernard Cornwell. British condensed edition © The Reader's Digest Association Limited, 2002.

HEAD OVER HEELS IN THE DALES. Original full-length edition © 2002 by Gervase Phinn. British condensed edition © The Reader's Digest Association Limited, 2002.

VALHALLA RISING. Original full-length edition © 2001 by Sandecker, RLLLP. British condensed edition © The Reader's Digest Association Limited, 2002.

The right to be identified as authors has been asserted by the following in accordance with sections 77 and 78 of the Copyright, Designs and Patents Act, 1988: Lee Child, Bernard Cornwell, Gervase Phinn and Clive Cussler.

ACKNOWLEDGMENTS AND PICTURE CREDITS: *Without Fail:* pages 6–7: car: Gettyone Stone; man: Images Colour Library; man firing gun: Telegraph Colour Library; page 8: Gettyone Stone; page 149: Roth Child. *Gallows Thief:* pages 150–152: The Ancient Art & Architecture Collection. *Head Over Heels in the Dales:* pages 274–276: illustration: Warwick Johnson-Cadwell/Eastwing. *Valhalla Rising:* pages 396–398: Getty Photodisc; page 539: Lawrence Ratzkin/Granger Collection, New York; photomontage: Rick Lecoat @ Shark Attack.

DUSTJACKET CREDITS: Spine from top: car: Gettyone Stone; man: Images Colour Library; The Ancient Art & Architecture Collection; Warwick Johnson-Cadwell/Eastwing; Getty Photodisc; photomontage: Rick Lecoat @ Shark Attack. Back jacket: photograph of Lee Child: Ruth Grant.

Printed by Maury Imprimeur SA, Malesherbes, France
Bound by Reliures Brun SA, Malesherbes, France